Science-Fiction Classics

Science-Fiction Classics
The Stories that Morphed into Movies

compiled by
Forrest J. Ackerman

New York

This collection was first published in 1998 by The Orion Publishing Group Ltd.,
London, as *Film Futures: Classic Science Fiction Stories That Morphed Into
Movies*.

Publishers Cataloging-in-Publication Data
Science-fiction classics : the stories that morphed into
 movies / compiled by Forrest J. Ackerman.
  p. cm.
  Reprint of British ed.
  ISBN: 1-57500-040-7
  1. Science fiction, American. 2. Short stories,
American. I. Ackerman, Forrest J.
PS 648.S3A28 1999   813'.0876208
                              QBI99-719.

TV Books, L.L.C.
Publishers serving the television industry.
1619 Broadway, Ninth Floor
New York, NY 10019
www.tvbooks.com

Interior designed by Rachel Reiss
Printed in Canada

Dedication

Wendayne Ackerman
Al Adamson
Aelita
Jack Arnold
J. R. Ayco
John Barrymore
Charles Beaumont
Ford Beebe
Paul Blaisdell
Chesley Bonestell
Leigh Brackett
David Bradley
Tod Browning
David Butler
Mark Carducci
Ted Carnell
Lon Chaney Jr.
Lon Chaney Sr.
Carlos Clarens
Merian C. Cooper
Buster Crabbe
William Crawford
Marcel Delgado
Morris Scott Dollens
Thomas Edison
Maurice Elvey
Willy Fritsch
Karl Freund
Mike Frisby

Georges Gallet
Abel Gance
Hugo Gernsback
Walter Gillings
Herbert Haeussler
Howard Hawks
Robert Heinlein
Ray Heinz
Brigitte Helm
Antonio Hélu
Linus Hogenmiller
Inoshiro Honda
Lucien Hubbard
Otto Hunte
Erich Kettelhut
Rodulf Klein-Rogge
James Koblick
Joe Kučera
Carl Laemmie Jr.
Carl Laemmie Sr.
Fritz Lang
Andrew Lenard
Willy Ley
Celia Lovsky
Rouben Mamoulian
Ned Mann
Fredric March
Raymond Massey
Gerda Maurus

George Méliès
William Cameron Menzies
A. Merritt
Catherine L. Moore
Sam Moskowitz
Kurt Neumann
Joseph Newman
James H. Nicholson
Albert Nuetzell
Herman Oberth
Arch Oboler
Willis O'Brien
Charles Ogle
George Pal
Jack Pearce
Irving Pichel
Erich Pommer
Marlo Racic Jr.
Claude Rains
Michael Rennie
Ralph Richardson
Gunther Rittau

Gene Roddenberry
Charles Schneer
Ernest B. Schoedsack
Walter Schulze-Mittendorf
Jack Seaman
Rod Serling
Eugen Shuften
Kenneth Strickfaden
James V. Taurasi
Ivan Tors
Dorothy Tree
Julius Unger
Karl Vollbrecht
Thea von Harbou
Oskar Wahrmann
Paul Wegener
Mort Weisinger
Manny Weltman
Richard Wilson
H. G. Wells
James Whale
Anne Willkomm

AND THOSE STILL WITH US

Ron Adams
John Agar
David Allen
Kirk Alyn
Pete Atkins
Rick Atkins
Gene Autry
Rick Baker
Jerome Bixby
Ron Borst
Rob Bottin
Ray Bradbury
Anthony Brzezinski
Wiktor Bukato
Bob Burns
Kevin J. Burns

Juan Camacho
John Carpenter
Robert Clarke
Frank Coe
John L. Coker III
Trevor Colby
Chris Collier
Roger Corman
Luigi Cozzi
Wes Craven
Jim Danforth
Joe Dante
Shel Dorf
Bob E. Flick
Stuart Gallbraith IV
Stuart Gardner

Luis Gasca
Rolf Giesen
Denis Gifford
Basil Gogos
Alex Gordon
Bert I. Gordon
Richard Gordon
Boris Grabnar
Val Guest
James Gunn
Kristina Hallind
Mark Hamill
Peter Hamilton
Curtis Harrington
Ray Harryhausen
Reg Hartt
W. Quay Hays
Ion Hobana
Eric Hoffman
Tim Holm
Charles D. Hornig
Hajime Ishida
Greg Jein
George Clayton Johnson
John Johnson
Alex Kill
Stephen King
Peter Kuczka
David Ackerman Kyle
John Landis
Verne Langdon
Walt Lee
Harris M. Lentz III
George Lucas
Bill Malone
Gregory W. Mank
Richard Matheson
Kevin McCarthy
Gloria McMillan
Tony Meadows
Ib J. Melchior

Giorgio Moroder
Josef Nesvadba
William F. Nolan
Charles Osborne
Maureen O'Sullivan
Debbie Painter
Star Trek Players
Caroline Potter
Phil Riley
Jean-Claude Romer
Julius Schwartz
Giovanni Scognamillo
Dr Thomas Seng
Bryan Senn
Wes Shank
Sam Sherman
Robert Short
Hans Sidén
Kurt Siodmak
Dick Smith
John S. Spencer
Steven Spielberg
Joseph Stefano
Gloria Stuart
Gary & Mrs Svehla
Bjo Trimble
Bob Tucker
Bill Tuttle
Peter H. Vollmann
Bill Warren
James Warren
Raven White
Donald C. Willis
Walter Willis
Robert Wise
Dell Wolfensparger
Fay Wray
Weaver Wright
Jim Wynorski
Tetsu Yano

Contents

Welcome to 'Tomoro'

Forrest J. Ackerman

Yes, the filmic futures of next week, next month, next year, next decade, next century! As early as 1919 there was a Brit-made version of H.G. Wells' legendary *First Men in the Moon* and around the same time the Danes cinematically space-voyaged audiences to a (for a change) *peace-loving* Mars in *The Sky Ship*. About a lustrum later the Russians cine-madapted Alexei Tolstoi's *Aelita: The Decline of Mars* to the screen as the variously known *Aelita, the Revolt of the Robots* and *Aelita, Queen of Mars*. Incidentally, in case you're wondering, that's pronounced Ah-eh-*lee*-tah.

By 1932, when I published the first known list of scientifilms (although frankly *Dracula, The Golem, The Cabinet of Dr Caligari* were not in the same category as *Metropolis, Woman in the Moon, The Lost World*, even *Frankenstein*) there were just 32 'imagi-movies' known. Today, as we approach the twenty-first century, there are tens of thousands.

And many of them based on fiction first, simultaneously or afterward. *TransAtlantic Tunnel, From the Earth to the Moon, Destination Moon, Once in a New Moon, 20,000 Leagues Under the Sea, The Mysterious Island, 2001: A Space Odyssey, 2010, 1984, Fahrenheit 451, Village of the Damned, King Kong, Contact*—these and scores more may all be read in fiction form, in fact, if the expected response to this volume warrants it, I am prepared to present volumes featuring trios or quartets or quintuples of the foregoing books in a whole library of genre titles.

In the meantime, I have assembled here some of the most fascinating works ever to reach the screen. The tale that became *The 4-Sided Triangle* has the dramatic elements of a cloning classic before the current popularity of cloning themes.

This Island Earth was born in three parts in the pages fifty years ago of *Thrilling Wonder Stories*, a pulp periodical most difficult to come by today.

The legendary *The Day the Earth Stood Still*, which has been voted the best science fiction film of all time by readers of one of the imagi-movie magazines I edited for two hundred issues, this fascinating tale has a surprise ending in the telling which was not incorporated into the film.

No less fascinating in fiction form is John W. Campbell's 'The Thing from Another World', which has been made as a movie twice. It makes a breathtaking addition to this book.

The 'Lewis Padgett' responsible for the amusing 'scientale' which morphed onto the screen as *The Twonky*, can now be revealed to be a collaboration between the late husband and wife team, Henry Kuttner and Catherine L. Moore.

'John Jessel' is another pen name that might have been lost to the world were it not for the publcation of 'The Adaptive Ultimate' (*She–Devil*) with the byline of its to–this–day–mourned author who died much too young in the mid-30s, Stanley Grauman Weinbaum, but not before he gave the world the sci-fi classic voted the second best of all time by the membership of the prestigious Science Fiction Writers of America, *A Martian Odyssey*.

No compilation of science fiction films could be complete without a Bradbury contribution and 'The Veldt', which served as one-third of *The Illustrated Man* film starring Rod Steiger, serves the purpose memorably.

I am happy to include a second female writer in the volume, the late Amelia Reynolds Long, whose *Weird Tales* story from thirteen lustrums ago, 'The Thought-Monster' (*Fiend without a Face*), still packs a punch.

Ib J. Melchior is best known in modern times for a series of best-selling World War II spy novels but is now being recognized at last as the inspirator of television's *Lost In Space* series.

There are several more stories making up this collection of tales morphed–into–movies which I'll let you discover on your own, but I want to point out that *two* novels are featured, and when you come to *FP 1 Does Not Reply* you can sit down, relax with a bottle of your favorite beverage and some snacks, shrug off your shoes and let Kurt Siodmak—a modern Jules Verne—entertain you with his prophetic tale that took place in an alternate world.

So…turn the pages and enjoy some of the Things that Might Have Come—or Might Yet!

Forrest J. Ackerman
19 February 2098

The Adaptive Ultimate

Stanley G. Weinbaum

Dr Daniel Scott, his dark and brilliant eyes alight with the fire of enthusiasm, paused at last and stared out over the city, or that portion of it visible from the office windows of Herman Bach—the Dr Herman Bach of Grand Mercy Hospital. There was a moment of silence; the old man smiled a little indulgently, a little wistfully, at the face of the youthful biochemist.

'Go on, Dan,' he said. 'So it occurred to you that getting well of a disease or injury is merely a form of adaptation—then what?'

'Then,' flashed the other, 'I began to look for the most adaptive of living organisms. And what are they? Insects! Insects, of course. Cut off a wing, and it grows back. Cut off a head, stick it to the headless body of another of the same species, and that grows back on. And what's the secret of their great adaptability?'

Dr Bach shrugged. 'What is?'

Scott was suddenly gloomy. 'I'm not sure,' he muttered. 'It's glandular, of course—a matter of hormones.' He brightened again. 'But I'm off the track. So then I look around for the most adaptive insect. And which is that?'

'Ants?' suggested Dr Bach. 'Bees? Termites?'

'Bah! They're the most highly evolved, not the most adaptable. No; there's one insect that is known to produce a higher percentage of mutants than any other, more freaks, more biological sports. The one Morgan used in his experiments on the effect of hard X-rays on heredity—the fruit fly, the ordinary fruit fly. Remember? They have reddish eyes, but under X-rays they produced white-eyed offspring—and that was a true mutation, because the white eyes bred true! Acquired characteristics can't be inherited, but these were. Therefore—'

'I know,' interrupted Dr Bach.

13

Scott caught his breath. 'So I used fruit flies,' he resumed. 'I putrefied their bodies, injected a cow, and got a serum at last, after weeks of clarifying with albumen,—evaporating *in vacuo*, rectifying with—But you're not interested in the technique. I got a serum. I tried it on tubercular guinea pigs, and'—he paused dramatically—'it cured! They adapted themselves to the tubercle bacillus. I tried it on a rabid dog. He adapted. I tried it on a cat with a broken spine. That knit. And now, I'm asking you for the chance to try it on a human being!'

Dr Bach frowned. 'You're not ready,' he grunted. 'You're not ready by two years. Try it on an anthropoid. Then try it on yourself. I can't risk a human life in an experiment that's as raw as this.'

'Yes, but I haven't got anything that needs curing; and as for an anthropoid, you get the board to allow funds to buy an ape—if you can. I've tried.'

'Take it up with the Stoneman Foundation, then.'

'And have Grand Mercy lose the credit? Listen, Dr Bach, I'm asking for just one chance—a charity case—anything.'

'Charity cases are human beings.' The old man scowled down at his hands. 'See here, Dan. I shouldn't even offer this much, because it's against all medical ethics, but if I find a hopeless case—utterly hopeless, you understand—where the patient himself consents, I'll do it. And that's the final word.'

Scott groaned. 'And try to find a case like that. If the patient's conscious, you think there's hope, and if he isn't how can he consent? That settles it!'

But it didn't. Less than a week later Scott looked suddenly up at the annunciator in the corner of his tiny laboratory. 'Dr Scott,' it rasped. 'Dr Scott. Dr Scott. To Dr Bach's office.'

He finished his titration, noted the figures, and hurried out. The old man was pacing the floor nervously as Scott entered.

'I've got your case, Dan,' he muttered. 'It's against all ethics—yet I'll be damned if I can see how you can do this one any harm. But you'd better hurry. Come on—isolation ward.'

They hurried. In the tiny cubical room Scott stared appalled. 'A girl!' he muttered.

She could never have been other than drab and plain, but lying there with the pallor of death already on her cheeks, she had an appearance of somber sweetness. Yet that was all the charm she could ever have possessed; her dark, cropped, oily hair was unkempt and stringy, her features flat and unattractive. She breathed with an almost inaudible rasp, and her eyes were closed.

'Do you,' asked Scott, 'consider this a test? She's all but dead now.'

Dr Bach nodded. 'Tuberculosis,' he said, 'final stage. Her lungs are hemorrhaging—a matter of hours.'

The girl coughed; flecks of blood appeared on her pallid lips. She opened dull, watery blue eyes.

'So!' said Bach, 'conscious, eh? This is Dr Scott. Dan, this is—uh'—he peered at the card at the foot of the bed—'Miss—uh—Kyra Zelas. Dr Scott has an injection, Miss Zelas. As I warned you, it probably won't help, but I can't see how it can hurt. Are you willing?'

She spoke in faint, gurgling tones. 'Sure, I'm through anyway. What's the odds?'

'All right. Got the hypo, Dan?' Bach took the tube of water-clear serum. 'Any particular point of injection? No? Give me the cubital, then.'

He thrust the needle into the girl's arm. Dan noted that she did not even wince at the bite of the steel point, but lay stoical and passive as thirty c.c. of liquid flowed into her veins. She coughed again, then closed her eyes.

'Come out of here,' ordered Bach gruffly, as they moved into the hall. 'I'm damned if I like this. I feel like a dirty dog.'

He seemed to feel less canine, however, the following day. 'That Zelas case is still alive,' he reported to Scott. 'If I dared trust my eyes, I'd say she's improved a little. A very little. I'd still call it hopeless.'

But the following day Scott found him seated in his office with a puzzled expression in his old gray eyes. 'Zelas is better,' he muttered. 'No question of it. But you keep your head, Dan. Such miracles have happened before, and without serums. You wait until we've had her under long observation.'

By the end of the week it became evident that the observation was not to be long. Kyra Zelas flourished under their gaze like some swift-blooming tropical weed. Queerly, she lost none of her pallor, but flesh softened the angular features, and a trace of light grew in her eyes.

'The spots on her lungs are going,' muttered Bach. 'She's stopped coughing, and there's no sign of bugs in her culture. But the queerest thing, Dan—and I can't figure it out, either—is the way she reacts to abrasions and skin punctures. Yesterday I took a blood specimen for a Wasserman, and—this sounds utterly mad—the puncture closed almost before I had a c.c.! Closed and healed!'

And in another week, 'Dan, I can't see any reason for keeping Kyra here. She's well. Yet I want her where we can keep her under observation. There's a queer mystery about this serum of yours. And besides, I hate to turn her out to the sort of life that brought her here.'

'What did she do?'

'Sewed. Piece-work in some sweatshop, when she could work at all. Drab, ugly, uneducated girl, but there's something appealing about her. She adapts quickly.'

Scott gave him a strange look. 'Yes,' he said, 'she adapts quickly.'

'So,' resumed Bach, 'it occurred to me that she could stay at my place. We could keep her under observation, you see, and she could help the housekeeper. I'm interested—damn interested. I think I'll offer her the chance.'

Scott was present when Dr Bach made his suggestion. The girl Kyra smiled. 'Sure,' she said. Her pallid, plain face lighted up. 'Thanks.'

Bach gave her the address. 'Mrs Getz will let you in. Don't do anything this afternoon. In fact, it might not hurt you simply to walk in the park for a few hours.'

Scott watched the girl as she walked down the hall toward the elevator. She had filled out, but she was still spare to the point of emaciation, and her worn black suit hung on her as if it were on a frame of sticks. As she disappeared, he moved thoughtfully about his duties, and a quarter-hour later descended to his laboratory.

On the first floor, turmoil met him. Two officers were carrying in the body of a nondescript old man whose head was a bloody ruin. There was a babble of excited voices, and he saw a crowd on the steps outside.

'What's up?' he called. 'Accident?'

'Accident!' snapped an officer. 'Murder, you mean. Woman steps up to this old guy, picks a hefty stone from the park border, slugs him, and takes his wallet. Just like that!'

Scott peered out of the window. The Black Maria was backing toward a crowd on the park side of the street. A pair of hulking policemen flanked a thin figure in black, thrusting it toward the doors of the vehicle.

Scott gasped. It was Kyra Zelas!

A week later Dr Bach stared into the dark fireplace of his living room. 'It's not our business,' he repeated.

'My God!' blazed Scott. 'Not our business! How do we know we're not responsible? How do we know that our injection didn't unsettle her mind? Glands can do that; look at Mongoloid idiots and cretins. Our stuff was glandular. Maybe we drove her crazy!'

'All right,' said Bach. 'Listen. We'll attend the trial tomorrow, and if it looks bad for her, we'll get hold of her lawyer and let him put us on the stand. We'll testify that she's just been released after a long and dangerous illness, and may not be fully responsible. That's entirely true.'

Mid-morning of the next day found them hunched tensely on benches in the crowded courtroom. The prosecution was opening; three witnesses testified to the event.

'This old guy buys peanuts for the pigeons. Yeah, I sell 'em to him every day—or did. So this time he hasn't any change, and he pulls out his wallet, and I see it's stuffed with bills. And one minute later I see the dame pick up the rock and conk him. Then she grabs the dough—'

'Describe her, please.'

'She's skinny, and dressed in black. She ain't no beauty, neither. Brownish hair, dark eyes, I don't know whether dark blue or brown.'

'Your witness!' snapped the prosecutor.

A young and nervous individual—appointed by the court, the paper said—rose. 'You say,' he squeaked, 'that the assailant had brown hair and dark eyes?'

'Yeah.'

'Will the defendant please rise?'

Her back was toward Scott and Bach as Kyra Zelas arose, but Scott stiffened. Something strangely different about her appearance; surely her worn black suit no longer hung so loosely about her. What he could see of her figure seemed—well, magnificent.

'Take off your hat, Miss Zelas,' squeaked the attorney.

Scott gasped. Radiant as aluminum glowed the mass of hair she revealed! 'I submit, your honor, that this defendant does not possess dark hair, nor, if you will observe, dark eyes. It is, I suppose, conceivable that she could somehow have bleached her hair while in custody, and I therefore'—he brandished a pair of scissors—'submit a lock to be tested by any chemist the court appoints. The pigmentation is entirely natural. And as for her eyes—does my esteemed opponent suggest that they too are bleached?'

He swung on the gaping witness. 'Is this lady the one you claim to have seen committing the crime?'

The man goggled. 'Uh—I can't—say.'

'Is she?'

'N-no!'

The speaker smiled. 'That's all. Will you take the stand, Miss Zelas?'

The girl moved lithe as a panther. Slowly she turned, facing the court. Scott's brain whirled, and his fingers dug into Bach's arm. Silver-eyed, aluminum-haired, alabaster-pale, the girl on the stand was beyond doubt the most beautiful woman he had ever seen!

The attorney was speaking again. 'Tell the court in your own words what happened, Miss Zelas.'

Quite casually the girl crossed her trim ankles and began to speak. Her voice was low, resonant, and thrilling; Scott had to fight to keep his attention on the sense of her words rather than the sound.

'I had just left Grand Mercy Hospital,' she said, 'where I had been ill for some months. I had crossed the park when suddenly a woman in black rushed at me, thrust an empty wallet into my hands, and vanished. A moment later I was surrounded by a screaming crowd, and—well, that's all.'

'An empty wallet, you say?' asked the defense lawyer. 'What of the money found in your own bag, which my eminent colleague believes stolen?'

'It was mine,' said the girl, 'about seven hundred dollars.'

Bach hissed, 'That's a lie! She had two dollars and thirty-three cents on her when we took her in.'

'Do you mean you think she's the same Kyra Zelas we had at the hospital?' gasped Scott.

'I don't know. I don't know anything, but if I ever touch that damned serum of yours—Look! Look, Dan!' This last was a tense whisper.

'What?'

'Her hair! When the sun strikes it!'

Scott peered more closely. A vagrant ray of noon sunlight filtered through a high window, and now and again the swaying of a shade permitted it to touch the metallic radiance of the girl's hair. Scott stared and saw; slightly but unmistakably, whenever the light touched that glowing aureole, her hair darkened from bright aluminum to golden blond!

Something clicked in his brain. There was a clue somewhere—if he could but find it. The pieces of the puzzle were there, but they were woefully hard to fit together. The girl in the hospital and her reaction to incisions; this girl and her reaction to light.

'I've got to see her,' he whispered. 'There's something I have to find—Listen!'

The speaker was orating. 'And we ask the dismissal of the whole case, your honor, on the grounds that the prosecution has utterly failed even to identify the defendant.'

The judge's gavel crashed. For a moment his aging eyes rested on the girl with the silver eyes and incredible hair, then: 'Case dismissed!' he snapped. 'Jury discharged!'

There was a tumult of voices. Flashlights shot instantaneous sheets of lightning. The girl on the witness stand rose with perfect poise, smiled with lovely, innocent lips, and moved away. Scott waited until she passed close at hand.

'Miss Zelas!' he called.

She paused. Her strange silver eyes lighted with unmistakable recognition. 'Dr Scott!' said the voice of tinkling metal. 'And Dr Bach!'

She was, then. She was the same girl. This was the drab sloven of the isolation ward, this weirdly beautiful creature of exotic coloring. Staring, Scott could trace now the very identity of her features, but changed as by a miracle.

He pushed through the mob of photographers, press men, and curiosity seekers. 'Have you a place to stay?' he asked. 'Dr Bach's offer still stands.'

She smiled. 'I am very grateful,' she murmured, and then, to the crowd of reporters: 'The doctor is an old friend of mine.' She was completely at ease, unruffled, poised.

Something caught Scott's eye, and he purchased a paper, glancing quickly at the photograph, the one taken at the moment the girl had removed her hat. He started; her hair showed raven black! There was a comment below the picture, too, to the effect that 'her striking hair photographs much darker than it appears to the eye.'

He frowned. 'This way,' he said to he girl, then goggled in surprise again. For in the broad light of noon her complexion was no longer the white of alabaster; it was creamy tan, the skin of one exposed to long hours of sunlight; her eyes were deep violet, and her hair—that tiny wisp unconcealed by her hat—was as black as the basalt columns of hell!

Kyra had insisted on stopping to purchase a substitute for the worn black suit, and had ended by acquiring an entire outfit. She sat now curled in the deep davenport before the fireplace in Dr Bach's library, sheathed in silken black from her white throat to the tiny black pumps on her feet. She was almost unearthly in her weird beauty, with her aluminum hair, silver eyes, and marble-pale skin against the jet silk covering.

She gazed innocently at Scott. 'But why shouldn't I?' she asked. 'The court returned my money; I can buy what I please with it.'

'Your money?' he muttered. 'You had less than three dollars when you left the hospital.'

'But this is mine now.'

'Kyra,' he said abruptly, 'where did you get that money?'

Her face was saintlike in its purity. 'From the old man.'

'You—you did murder him!'

'Why, of course I did.'

He choked. 'My Lord!' he gasped. 'Don't you realize we'll have to tell?'

She shook her head, smiling gently from one to the other of them. 'No, Dan. You won't tell, for it wouldn't do any good. I can't be tried twice for the same crime. Not in America.'

'But why, Kyra? Why did you—'

'Would you have me resume the life that sent me into your hands? I needed money; money was there; I took it.'

'But murder!'

'It was the most direct way.'

'Not if you happened to be punished for it,' he returned grimly.

'But I wasn't,' she reminded him gently.

He groaned. 'Kyra,' he said, shifting the subject suddenly, 'why do your eyes and skin and hair darken in sunlight or when exposed to flashlight?'

She smiled. 'Do they?' she asked. 'I hadn't noticed.' She yawned, stretched her arms above her head and her slim legs before her. 'I think I shall sleep now,' she announced. She swept her magnificent eyes over them, rose, and disappeared into the room Dr Bach had given her—his own.

Scott faced the older man, his features working in emotion. 'Do you see?' he hissed. 'Good Lord, do you see?'

'Do you, Dan?'

'Part of it. Part of it, anyway.'

'And I see part as well.'

'Well,' said Scott, 'here it is as I see it. That serum—that accursed serum of mine—has somehow accentuated this girl's adaptability to an impossible degree. What is it that differentiates life from non-living matter? Two things, irritation and adaptation. Life adapts itself to its environment, and the greater the adaptability, the more successful the organism.

'Now,' he proceeded, 'all human beings show a very considerable adaptivity. When we expose ourselves to sunlight, our skin shows pigmentation—we tan. That's adaptation to an environment containing sunlight. When a man loses his right hand, he learns to use his left. That's another adaptation. When a person's skin is punctured, it heals and rebuilds, and that's another angle of the same thing. Sunny regions produce dark-skinned, dark-haired people; northern lands produce blonds—and that's adaptation again.

'So what's happened to Kyra Zelas, by some mad twist I don't understand, is that her adaptive powers have been increased to an extreme. She adapts instantly to her environment; when sun strikes her, she tans at once, and in shade she fades immediately. In sunlight her hair and eyes are those of a tropical race; in shadow, those of a Northerner. And—good Lord, I see it now—when she was faced with danger there in the courtroom, faced by a jury and judge who were men, she adapted to that! She met that danger, not only by changed appearance, but by a beauty so great that she couldn't have been convicted!' He paused. 'But how? How?'

'Perhaps medicine can tell how,' said Bach. 'Undoubtedly man is the creature of his glands. The differences between races—white, red, black, yellow—is doubtless glandular. And perhaps the most effective agent of adaptation is the human brain and neural system, which in itself is controlled partly by a little greasy mass on the floor of the brain's third ventricle, before the cerebellum, and supposed by the ancients to be the seat of the soul.

'I mean, of course, the pineal gland. I suspect that what your serum contains is the long-sought hormone *pinealin*, and that it has caused hypertrophy of Kyra's pineal gland. And Dan, do you realize that if her adaptability is perfect, she's not only invincible, but invulnerable?'

'That's true!' gulped Scott. 'Why, she couldn't be electrocuted, because she'd adapt instantly to an environment containing an electric current, and she couldn't be killed by a shot, because she'd adapt to that as quickly as to your needle pricks. And poison—but there must be a limit somewhere!'

'There doubtless is,' observed Bach. 'I hardly believe she could adapt herself to an environment containing a fifty-ton locomotive passing over her body. And yet there's an important point we haven't considered. Adaptation itself is of two kinds.'

'Two kinds?'

'Yes. One kind is biological; the other, human. Naturally a biochemist like you would deal only with the first, and equally naturally a brain surgeon like me has to consider the second as well. Biological adaptation is what all life—plant, animal, and human—possess, and it is merely conforming to one's environment. A chameleon, for instance, shows much the same ability as Kyra herself, and so, in lesser degree, does the arctic fox, white in winter, brown in summer; or the snowshoe rabbit, for that matter, or the weasel. All life conforms to its environment to a great extent, because if it doesn't, it dies. But human life does more.'

'More?'

'Much more. Human adaptation is not only conformity to environment, but also the actual changing of environment to fit human needs! The first cave man who left his cave to build a grass hut changed his environment, and so, in exactly the same sense, did Steinmetz, Edison, and as far as that goes, Julius Caesar and Napoleon. In fact, Dan, all human invention, genius, and military leadership boils down to that one fact—changing the environment instead of conforming to it.'

He paused, then continued, 'Now we know that Kyra possesses the biological adaptivity. Her hair and eyes prove that. But what if she possesses the other to the same degree? If she does, God knows what the result will be. We can only watch to see what direction she takes—watch and hope.'

'But I don't see,' muttered Scott, 'how that could be glandular.'

'Anything can be glandular. In a mutant—and Kyra's as much a mutant as your white-eyed fruit flies—anything is possible.' He frowned reflectively. 'If I dared phrase a philosophical interpretation, I'd say that Kyra—perhaps—represents a stage in human evolution. A mutation. If one ventured to believe that, then de Vries and Weissman are justified.'

'The mutation theory of evolution, you mean?'

'Exactly. You see, Dan, while it is very obvious from fossil remains that evolution occurred, yet it is very easy to prove it couldn't possibly have occurred!'

'How?'

'Well, it couldn't have occurred slowly, as Darwin believed, for many reasons. Take the eye, for instance. He thought that very gradually, over thousands of generations, some sea creature developed a spot on its skin that was sensitive to light, and that this gave it an advantage over its blind fellows. Therefore its kind survived and others perished. But see here. If this eye developed slowly, why did the very first ones, the ones that couldn't yet see, have any better chance than the others? And take a wing. What good is a wing until you can fly with it? Just because a jumping lizard had a tiny fold of skin between foreleg and breast wouldn't mean that that lizard could survive where others died. What kept the wing developing to a point where it could actually have value?'

'What did?'

'De Vries and Weissman say nothing did. They answer that evolution must have progressed in jumps, so that when the eye appeared, it was already efficient enough to have survival value, and likewise the wing. Those jumps they named mutations. And in that sense, Dan, Kyra's a mutation, a jump from the human to—something else. Perhaps the superhuman.'

Scott shook his head in perplexity. He was thoroughly puzzled, completely baffled, and more than a little unnerved. In a few moments more he bade Bach good night, wandered home, and lay for hours in sleepless thought.

The next day Bach managed a leave of absence for both of them from Grand Mercy, and Scott moved in. This was in part simply out of his fascinated interest in the case of Kyra Zelas, but in part it was altruistic. She had confessedly murdered one man; it occurred to Scott that she might with no more compunction murder Dr Bach, and he meant to be at hand to prevent it.

He had been in her company no more than a few hours before Bach's words on evolution and mutations took on new meaning. It was not only Kyra's chameleonlike coloring, nor her strangely pure and saintlike features, nor even her incredible beauty. There was something more; he could not at once identify it, but decidedly the girl Kyra was not quite human.

The event that impressed this on him occurred in the late afternoon. Bach was away somewhere on personal business, and Scott had been questioning the girl about her own impressions of her experience.

'But don't you know you've changed?' he asked. 'Can't you see the difference in yourself?'

'Not I. It is the world that has changed.'

'But your hair was black. Now it's light as ashes.'

'Was it?' she asked. 'Is it?'

He groaned in exasperation. 'Kyra,' he said, 'you must know something about yourself.'

Her exquisite eyes turned their silver on him. 'I do,' she said. 'I know that what I want is mine, and'—her pure lips smiled—'I think I want you, Dan.'

It seemed to him that she changed at that moment. Her beauty was not quite as it had been, but somehow more wildly intoxicating than before. He realized what it meant; her environment now contained a man she loved, or thought she loved, and she was adapting to that, too. She was becoming—he shivered slightly—irresistible!

Bach must have realized the situation, but he said nothing. As for Scott, it was sheer torture, for he realized only too well that the girl he loved was a freak, a biological sport, and worse than that, a cold murderess and a creature not exactly human. Yet for the next several days things went smoothly. Kyra slipped easily into the routine; she was ever a willing subject for their inquiries and investigations.

Then Scott had an idea. He produced one of the guinea pigs that he had injected, and they found that the creature evinced the same reaction as Kyra to cuts. They killed the thing by literally cutting it in half with an ax, and Bach examined its brain.

'Right!' he said at last. 'It's hypertrophy of the pineal.' He stared intently at Scott. 'Suppose,' he said, 'that we could reach Kyra's pineal and correct the hypertrophy. Do you suppose that might return her to normal?'

Scott suppressed a pang of fear. 'But why? She can't do any harm as long as we guard her here. Why do we have to gamble with her life like that?'

Bach laughed shortly. 'For the first time in my life I'm glad I'm an old man,' he said. 'Don't you see we have to do something? She's a menace. She's dangerous. Heaven only knows how dangerous. We'll have to try.'

Scott groaned and assented. An hour later, under the pretext of experiment, he watched the old man inject five grains of morphia into the girl's arm, watched her frown and blink—and adjust. The drug was powerless.

It was at night that Bach got his next idea. 'Ethyl chloride!' he whispered. 'The instantaneous anaesthetic. Perhaps she can't adjust to lack of oxygen. We'll try.'

Kyra was asleep. Silently, carefully, the two crept in, and Scott stared down in utter fascination at the weird beauty of her features, paler than ever in the faint light of midnight. Carefully, so carefully, Bach held the cone above her sleeping face, drop by drop he poured the volatile, sweet-scented liquid into it. Minutes passed.

'That should anaesthetize an elephant,' he whispered at last, and jammed the cone full upon her face.

She awoke. Fingers like slim steel rods closed on his wrist, forcing his hand away. Scott seized the cone, and her hand clutched his wrist as well, and he felt the strength of her grasp.

'Stupid,' she said quietly, sitting erect. 'This is quite useless—look!'

She snatched a paper knife from the table beside the bed. She bared her pale throat to the moonlight, and then, suddenly, drove the knife to its hilt into her bosom!

Scott gulped in horror as she withdrew it. A single spot of blood showed on her flesh, she wiped it away, and displayed her skin, pale, un-scarred, beautiful.

'Go away,' she said softly, and they departed.

The next day she made no reference to the incident. Scott and Bach spent a worried morning in the laboratory, doing no work, but simply talking. It was a mistake, for when they returned to the library, she was gone, having, according to Mrs Getz, simply strolled out of the door and away. A hectic and hasty search of the adjacent blocks brought no sign of her.

At dusk she was back, pausing hatless in the doorway to permit Scott, who was there alone, to watch the miraculous change as she passed from sunset to chamber, and her hair faded from mahogany to aluminum.

'Hello,' she said smiling. 'I killed a child.'

'What? My Lord, Kyra!'

'It was an accident. Surely you don't feel that I should be punished for an accident, Dan, do you?'

He was staring in utter horror. 'How—'

'Oh, I decided to walk a bit. After a block or two, it occurred to me that I should like to ride. There was a car parked there with the keys in it, and the driver was talking on the sidewalk, so I slipped in, started it, and drove away. Naturally I drove rather fast, since he was shouting, and at the second corner I hit a little boy.'

'And—you didn't stop?'

'Of course not. I drove around the corner, turned another corner or two, and then parked the car and walked back. The boy was gone, but the crowd was still there. Not one of them noticed me.' She smiled her saint-like smile. 'We're quite safe. They can't possibly trace me.'

Scott dropped his head on his hands and groaned. 'I don't know what to do!' he muttered. 'Kyra, you're going to have to report this to the police.'

'But it was an accident,' she said gently, her luminous silver eyes pityingly on Scott.

'No matter. You'll have to.'

She placed her white hand on his head. 'Perhaps tomorrow,' she said. 'Dan, I have learned something. What one needs in this world is power. As long as there are people in the world with more power than I, I run afoul of them. They keep trying to punish me with their laws—and why? Their laws are not for me. They cannot punish me.'

He did not answer.

'Therefore,' she said softly, 'tomorrow I go out of here to seek power. I will be more powerful than any laws.'

That shocked him to action. 'Kyra!' he cried. 'You're not to try to leave here again.' He gripped her shoulders. 'Promise me! Swear that you'll not step beyond that door without me!'

'Why, if you wish,' she said quietly.

'But swear it! Swear it by everything sacred!'

Her silver eyes looked steadily into his from a face like that of a marble angel. 'I swear it,' she murmured. 'By anything you name, I swear it, Dan.'

And in the morning she was gone, taking what cash and bills had been in Scott's wallet, and in Bach's as well. And, they discovered later, in Mrs Getz's also.

'But if you could have seen her!' muttered Scott. 'She looked straight into my eyes and promised, and her face was pure as a madonna's. I can't believe she was lying.'

'The lie as an adaptive mechanism,' said Bach, 'deserves more attention than it has received. Probably the original liars are those plants and animals that use protective mimicry—harmless snakes imitating poisonous ones, stingless flies that look like bees. Those are living lies.'

'But she couldn't—'

'She has, however. What you've told me about her desire for power is proof enough. She's entered the second adaptive phase—that of adapting her environment to herself instead of herself to her environment. How far will her madness—or her genius—carry her? There is very little difference between the two, Dan. And what is left now for us to do but watch?'

'Watch? How? Where is she?'

'Unless I'm badly mistaken, watching her will be easy once she begins to achieve. Wherever she is, I think we—and the rest of the world—will know of it soon enough.'

But weeks dropped away without sign of Kyra Zelas. Scott and Bach returned to their duties at Grand Mercy, and down in his laboratory the biochemist disposed grimly of the remains of three guinea pigs, a cat, and a dog, whose killing had been an exhausting and sickening task. In the crematory as well went a tube of water-clear serum.

Then one day the annunciator summoned him to Bach's office, where he found the old man hunched over a copy of the *Post Record*.

'Look here!' he said, indicating a political gossip column called 'Whirls of Washington.'

Scott read, 'And the surprise of the evening was the *soi-disant* confirmed bachelor of the cabinet, upright John Callan, who fluttered none other than the gorgeous Kyra Zelas, the lady who affects a dark wig by day and a white by night. Some of us remember her as the acquittee of a murder trial.'

Scott looked up. 'Callan, eh? Secretary of the Treasury, no less! When she said power she meant power, apparently.'

'But will she stop there?' mused Bach gloomily. 'I have a premonition that she's just beginning.'

'Well, actually, how far can a woman go?'

The old man looked at him. 'A woman? This is Kyra Zelas, Dan. Don't set your limits yet. There will be more of her.'

Bach was right. Her name began to appear with increasing frequency, first in social connections, then with veiled references to secret intrigues and influences.

Thus: 'Whom do the press boys mean by the tenth cabineteer?' Or later: 'Why not a secretary of personal relations? She has the powers; give her the name.' And still later: 'One has to go back to Egypt for another instance of a country whose exchequer was run by a woman. And Cleopatra busted that one.'

Scott grinned a little ruefully to himself as he realized that the thrusts were becoming more indirect, as if the press itself were beginning to grow cautious. It was a sign of increasing power, for nowhere are people as sensitive to such trends as among the Washington correspondents. Kyra's appearance in the public prints began to be more largely restrained to purely social affairs, and usually in connection with John Callan, the forty-five-year-old bachelor Secretary of the Treasury.

Waking or sleeping, Scott never for a moment quite forgot her, for there was something mystical about her, whether she were mad or a woman of genius, whether freak or superwoman. The only thing he did forget was a thin girl with drab features and greasy black hair who had lain on a pallet in the isolation ward and coughed up flecks of blood.

It was no surprise to either Scott or Dr Bach to return one evening to Bach's residence for a few hours' conversation, and find there, seated as comfortably as if she had never left it, Kyra Zelas. Outwardly she had changed but little; Scott gazed once more in fascination on her incredible hair and wide, innocent silver eyes. She was smoking a cigarette, and she exhaled a long, blue plume of smoke and smiled up at him.

He hardened himself. 'Nice of you to honor us,' he said coldly. 'What's the reason for this visit? Did you run out of money?'

'Money? Of course not. How could I run out of money?'

'You couldn't, not as long as you replenished your funds the way you did when you left.'

'Oh that!' she said contemptuously. She opened her handbag; indicating a green mass of bills. 'I'll give that back, Dan. How much was it?'

'To hell with the money!' he blazed. 'What hurts me is the way you lied. Staring into my eyes as innocent as a baby, and lying all the time!'

'Was I?' she asked. 'I won't lie to you again, Dan. I promise.'

'I don't believe you,' he said bitterly. 'Tell us what you're doing here, then.'

'I wanted to see you. I haven't forgotten what I said to you, Dan.' With the words she seemed to grow more beautiful than ever, and this time poignantly wistful as well.

'And have you,' asked Bach suddenly, 'abandoned your idea of power?'

'Why should I want power?' she rejoined innocently, flashing her magnificent eyes to him.

'But you said,' began Scott impatiently, 'that you—'

'Did I?' There was a ghost of a smile on her perfect lips. 'I won't lie to you, Dan,' she went on, laughing a little. 'If I want power, it is mine for the taking—more power than you dream.'

'Through John Callan?' he rasped.

'He offers a simple way,' she said impassively. 'Suppose, for instance, that in a day or so he were to issue a statement—a supremely insulting statement—about the war debts. The administration couldn't afford to reprimand him openly, because most of the voters feel that a supremely insulting statement is called for. And if it were insulting enough—and I assure you it would be—you would see the animosity of Europe directed westward.

'Now, if the statement were one that no national government could ignore and yet keep its dignity in the eyes of its people, it would provoke counter-insults. And there are three nations—you know their names as well as I—who await only such a diversion of interest. Don't you see?' She frowned.

'How stupid you both are!' she murmured, and then, stretching her glorious figure and yawning, 'I wonder what sort of empress I would make. A good one, doubtless.'

But Scott was aghast. 'Kyra, do you mean you'd urge Callan into such a colossal blunder as that?'

'Urge him!' she echoed contemptuously. 'I'd force him.'

'Do you mean you'd do it?'

'I haven't said so,' she smiled. She yawned again, and snapped her cigarette into the dark fireplace. 'I'll stay here a day or two,' she added pleasantly, rising. 'Good night.'

Scott faced Dr Bach as she vanished into the old man's chamber. 'Damn her!' he grated, his lips white. 'If I believed she meant all of that.'

'You'd better believe it,' said Bach.

'Empress, eh! Empress of what?'

'Of the world, perhaps. You can't set limits to madness or genius.'

'We've got to stop her!'

'How? We can't keep her locked up here. In the first place, she'd doubtless develop strength enough in her wrists to break the locks on the doors, and if she didn't, all she'd need to do is shout for help from a window.'

'We can have her adjudged insane!' flared Scott. 'We can have her locked up where she can't break out or call for help.'

'Yes, we could. We could if we could get her committed by the Sanity Commission. And if we got her before them, what chance do you think we'd have?'

'All right, then,' said Scott grimly, 'we're going to have to find her weakness. Her adaptability can't be infinite. She's immune to drugs and immune to wounds, but she can't be above the fundamental laws of biology. What we have to do is find the law we need.'

'You find it then,' said Bach gloomily.

'But we've got to do something. At least we can warn people—' He broke off, realizing the utter absurdity of the idea.

'Warn people!' scoffed Bach. 'Against what? We'd be the ones to go before the Sanity Commission then. Callan would ignore us with dignity, and Kyra would laugh her pretty little laugh of contempt, and that would be that.'

Scott shrugged helplessly. 'I'm staying here tonight,' he said. 'At least we can talk to her again tomorrow.'

'If she's still here,' remarked Bach ironically.

But she was. She came out as Scott was reading the morning papers alone in the library, and sat silently opposite him, garbed in black silk lounging pajamas against which her alabaster skin and incredible hair glowed in startling contrast. He watched skin and hair turn faintly golden as the morning sun lightened the chamber. Somehow it angered him that she should be so beautiful and at the same time deadly with an inhuman deadliness.

He spoke first. 'You haven't committed any murders since our last meeting, I hope.' He said it spitefully, viciously.

She was quite indifferent. 'Why should I? It has not been necessary.'

'You know, Kyra,' he said evenly, 'that you ought to be killed.'

'But not by you, Dan. You love me.'

He said nothing. The fact was too obvious to deny.

'Dan,' she said softly, 'if you only had my courage, there is no height we might not reach together. No height—if you had the courage to try. That is why I came back here, but—' She shrugged. 'I go back to Washington tomorrow.'

Later in the day Scott got Bach alone. 'She's going tomorrow!' he said tensely. 'Whatever we can do has to be done tonight.'

The old man gestured helplessly. 'What can we do? Can you think of any law that limits adaptability?'

'No, but—' He paused suddenly. 'By Heaven!' he cried. 'I can! I've got it!'

'What?'

'The law! A fundamental biological law that must be Kyra's weakness!'

'But what?'

'This! No organism can live in its own waste products! Its own waste is poison to any living thing!'

'But—'

'Listen. Carbon dioxide is a human waste product. Kyra can't adapt to an atmosphere of carbon dioxide!'

Bach stared. 'By Heaven!' he cried. 'But even if you're right, how—'

'Wait a minute. You can get a couple of cylinders of carbonic acid gas from Grand Mercy. Can you think of any way of getting the gas into her room?'

'Why—this is an old house. There's a hole from her room to the one I'm using, where the radiator connection goes through. It's not tight; we could get a rubber tube past the pipe.'

'Good!'

'But the windows! She'll have the windows open.'

'Never mind that,' said Scott. 'See that they're soaped so they'll close easily, that's all.'

'But even if it works, what good—Dan! You don't mean to kill her?'

He shook his head. 'I—couldn't,' he whispered. 'But once she's help-less, once she's overcome—if she is—you'll operate. That operation on the pineal you suggested before. And may Heaven forgive me!'

Scott suffered the tortures of the damned that evening. Kyra was, if pos-sible, lovelier than ever, and for the first time she seemed to exert herself to be charming. Her conversation was literally brilliant; she sparkled, and over and over Scott found himself so fascinated that the thought of the treachery he planned was an excruciating pain. It seemed almost a blas-phemy to attempt violence against one whose outward appearance was so pure, so innocent, so saintlike.

'But she isn't quite—human!' he told himself. 'She's not an angel but a female demon, a—what were they called?—an incubus!'

Despite himself, when at last Kyra yawned luxuriously and dropped her dainty feet to the floor to depart, he pleaded for a few moments more.

'But it's early,' he said, 'and tomorrow you leave.'

'I will return, Dan. This is not the end for us.'

'I hope not,' he muttered miserably, watching the door of her room as it clicked shut.

He gazed at Bach. The older man, after a moment's silence, whispered, 'It is likely that she sleeps almost at once. That's also a matter of adaptability.'

In tense silence they watched the thin line of light below the closed door. Scott started violently when, after a brief interval, her shadow crossed it and it disappeared with a faint click.

'Now, then,' he said grimly. 'Let's get it over.'

He followed Bach into the adjacent room. There, cold and metallic, stood the gray cylinders of compressed gas. He watched as the old man attached a length of tubing, ran it to the opening around the steam pipe, and began to pack the remaining space with wet cotton.

Scott turned to his own task. He moved quietly into the library. With utmost stealth he tried the door of Kyra's room; it was unlocked as he had known it would be, for the girl was supremely confident of her own invulnerability.

For a long moment he gazed across at the mass of radiant silver hair on her pillow, then, very cautiously, he placed a tiny candle on the chair by the window, so that it should be at about the level of the bed, lighted it with a snap of his cigarette lighter, withdrew the door key, and departed.

He locked the door on the outside, and set about stuffing the crack below it with cotton. It was far from air-tight, but that mattered little, he mused, since one had to allow for the escape of the replaced atmosphere.

He returned to Bach's room. 'Give me a minute,' he whispered. 'Then turn it on.'

He stepped to a window. Outside was a two-foot ledge of stone, and he crept to this precarious perch. He was visible from the street below, but not markedly noticeable, for he was directly above an areaway between Bach's house and its neighbor. He prayed fervently that he might escape attention.

He crept along the ledge. The two windows of Kyra's chamber were wide, but Bach had done his work. They slid downward without a creak, and he pressed close against the glass to peer in.

Across the room glowed the faint and steady flame of his little taper. Close beside him, within a short arm's length had no pane intervened, lay Kyra, quite visible in the dusk. She lay on her back, with one arm thrown above her unbelievable hair, and she had drawn only a single sheet over her. He could watch her breathing, quiet, calm, peaceful.

It seemed as if a long time passed. He fancied at last that he could hear the gentle hiss of gas from Bach's window, but he knew that that must be fancy. In the chamber he watched there was no sign of anything unusual; the glorious Kyra slept as she did everything else—easily, quietly, and confidently.

Then there was a sign. The little candle flame, burning steadily in the draughtless air, flickered suddenly. He watched it, certain now that its color was changing. Again it flickered, flared for a moment, then died. A red spark glowed on the wick for a bare instant, then that was gone.

The candle flame was smothered. That meant a concentration of eight or ten per cent of carbon dioxide in the room's temperature—far too high to support ordinary life. Yet Kyra was living. Except that her quiet breathing seemed to have deepened, she gave not even a sign of inconvenience. She had adapted to the decreased oxygen supply.

But there must be limits to her powers. He blinked into the darkness. Surely—surely her breathing was quickening. He was positive now; her breast rose and fell in convulsive gasps, and somewhere in his turbulent mind the scientist in him recorded the fact.

'Cheyne-Stokes breathing,' he muttered. In a moment the violence of it would waken her.

It did. Suddenly the silver eyes started open. She brushed her hand across her mouth, then clutched at her throat. Aware instantly of danger, she thrust herself erect, and her bare legs flashed as she pushed herself from the bed. But she must have been dazed, for she turned first to the door.

He saw the unsteadiness in her movements. She twisted the doorknob, tugged frantically, then whirled toward the window. He could see her swaying as she staggered through the vitiated air, but she reached it. Her face was close to his, but he doubted if she saw him, for her eyes were wide and frightened, and her mouth and throat were straining violently for breath. She raised her hand to smash the pane; the blow landed, but weakly, and the window shook but did not shatter.

Again her arm rose, but that blow was never delivered. For a moment she stood poised, swaying slowly, then her magnificent eyes misted and closed, she dropped to her knees, and at last collapsed limply on the floor.

Scott waited a long, torturing moment, then thrust up the window. The rush of lifeless air sent him whirling dizzily on his dangerous perch, and he clutched the casement. Then a slow breeze moved between the buildings, and his head cleared.

He stepped gingerly into the chamber. It was stifling, but near the open window he could breathe. He kicked thrice against Bach's wall.

The hiss of gas ceased. He gathered Kyra's form in his arms, waited until he heard the key turn, then dashed across the room and into the library.

Bach stared as if fascinated at the pure features of the girl. 'A goddess overcome,' he said. 'There is something sinful about our part in this.'

'Be quick!' snapped Scott. 'She's unconscious, not anaesthetized. God knows how quickly she'll readjust.'

But she had not yet recovered when Scott laid her on the operating table in Bach's office, and drew the straps about her arms and body and slim bare legs. He looked down on her still, white face and bright hair, and he felt his heart contract with pain to see them darken ever so faintly and beautifully under the brilliant operating light, rich in actinic rays.

'You were right,' he whispered to the unhearing girl. 'Had I your courage there is nothing we might not have attained, together.'

Bach spoke brusquely. 'Nasal?' he asked. 'Or shall I trephine her?'

'Nasal.'

'But I should like a chance to observe the pineal gland. This case is unique, and—'

'Nasal!' blazed Scott. 'I won't have her scarred!'

Bach sighed and began. Scott, despite his long hospital experience, found himself quite unable to watch this operation; he passed the old man his instruments as needed, but kept his eyes averted from the girl's passive and lovely face.

'So!' said Bach at last. 'It is done.' For the first time he himself had a moment's leisure to survey Kyra's features.

Bach started violently. Gone was the exquisite aluminum hair, replaced by the stringy, dark, and oily locks of the girl in the hospital! He pried open her eye, silver no longer, but pallid blue. Of all her loveliness, there remained—what? A trace, perhaps; a trace in the saintlike purity of her pale face, and in the molding of her features. But a flame had died; she was a goddess no longer, but a mortal—a human being. The superwoman had become no more than a suffering girl.

An ejaculation had almost burst from his lips when Scott's voice stopped him.

'How beautiful she is!' he whispered.

Bach stared. He realized suddenly that Scott was not seeing her as she was, but as she once had been. To his eyes, colored by love, she was still Kyra the magnificent.

The Alien Machine

Raymond F. Jones

Chapter One: Unit 16

The offices of Joe Wilson, purchasing agent for Ryberg Instrument Corporation, looked out over the company's private landing field. He stood there by the window now, wishing that they didn't, because it was an eternal reminder that he'd once had hopes of becoming an engineer instead of an office flunky.

Through the window he saw the silver test ship of the radio lab level off at bullet speed, circle once and land. That would be Cal Meacham at the controls, Joe thought. Even the company pilots didn't dare bring a ship in that way. But Cal Meacham was the best man in the radio instrument business and getting canned was a meaningless penalty for him. He could get the same or higher salary from a dozen other places for the asking.

Joe chomped irritably on his cigar and turned away from the window. Then he picked up a letter from his desk. It was in answer to an order he had placed for condensers for Cal's hot transmitter job—Cal's stuff was always hot, Joe thought. He'd already read the letter three times but he started on it for the fourth.

Dear Mr Wilson:

We were pleased to receive your order of the 8th for samples of our XC-109 condenser. However, we find that our present catalogue lists no such item nor did we ever carry it.

We are, therefore, substituting the AB-619 model, a high-voltage oil-filled transmitting-type condenser. As you specified, it is rated at 10,000 volts with 100% safety factor and has 4 mf. capacity.

We trust these will meet with your approval and that we may look forward to receiving your production order for these items. It is needless, of course, to remind you that we manufacture a complete line of electronic components. We would be glad to furnish samples of any items from our stock which might interest you.

> Respectfully yours,
> A.G. Archmanter
> Electronic Service—Unit 16.

Joe Wilson put the letter down slowly and picked up the box of beads which had come with it. Complete and resigned disgust occupied his face.

He picked up a bead by one of the leads that stuck out of it. The bead was about a quarter of an inch in diameter and there seemed to be a smaller concentric shell inside it. Between the two appeared to be some reddish liquid. Another wire connected to the inner shell but for the life of him Joe couldn't see how that inner wire came through the outer shell.

There was something funny about it, as if it came directly from the inner without passing through the outer. He knew that was silly but it made him dizzy to try to concentrate on the spot where it came through. The spot seemed to shift and move.

'Ten thousand volts!' he muttered. 'Four mikes!'

He tossed the bead back into the box with disgust. Cal would be hotter than the transmitter job when he saw these.

Joe heard the door of his secretary's office open and glanced through the glass panel. Cal Meacham was coming in. He burst open the door with a breeze that ruffled the letters on Joe's desk.

'See that landing I made, Joe? Markus says I ought to be able to get my license to fly that crate in another week.'

'I'll bet he added "if you live that long."'

'Just because you don't recognize a hot pilot when you see one—What are you so glum about, anyway? And what's happened to those condensers we ordered three days ago? This job's *hot.*'

Joe held out the letter silently. Cal scanned the page swiftly and flipped it back onto the desk.

'Swell. We'll try them out. They're down in receiving, I suppose? Give me an order and I'll pick them up on my way to the lab.'

'They aren't in receiving. They came in the envelope with the letter.'

'What are you talking about? How could they send sixteen mikes of ten kw condensers in an envelope?'

Joe held up one of the beads by a wire—the one that passed through the outer shell without passing through it.

'This is what they sent. Guaranteed one hundred percent voltage safety factor.'

Cal glanced at it. 'Whose leg are you trying to pull?'

'I'm not kidding. That's what they sent.'

'Well, what screwball's idea of a joke is this, then? Four mikes! Did you call receiving?'

Joe nodded. 'I checked *good*. These beads are all that came.'

Muttering, Cal grasped one by the lead wire and held it up to the light. He saw the faintly appearing internal structure that Joe had puzzled over.

'It *would* be funny if that's what these things actually were, wouldn't it?' he said. 'Aw—it's crazy!'

'You could just about build a fifty kw transmitter in a suitcase, provided you had other corresponding components to go along.'

Cal picked up the rest of the beads and dropped them in his shirt pocket. 'Get another letter off right away. Better call them on the teletype instead. Tell them this job is plenty hot and we've got to have those condensers right away.'

'Okay. What are you going to do with the beads?'

'I might put ten thousand volts across them and see how long it takes to melt them down. See if you can find out who pulled this gag.'

Cal Meacham left for the transmitter lab. For the rest of the morning he checked over the antenna on his new set, which wasn't getting the soup out the way it should. He forgot about the glass beads completely until late in the afternoon.

As he bent his head down into the framework of the ground transmitter, one of the sharp leads of the alleged condensers struck him through his shirt.

He jerked sharply and bumped his head on the iron framework. Cursing the refractory transmitter, the missing condensers and the practical joker who had sent the beads, he grabbed the things out of his shirt pocket and was about to hurl them across the room.

But a quirk of curiosity halted his hand in midair. Slowly he lowered it and looked again at the beads that seemed to glare at him like eyes in the palm of his hand.

He called across the lab to a junior engineer. 'Hey, Max, come here. Put these things on voltage breakdown and see what happens.'

'Sure.' The junior engineer rolled them over in his palm. 'What are they?'

'Just some gadgets we got for test. I forgot about them until now.'

He resumed checking the transmitter. Crazy notion, that—as if the beads actually were anything but glass beads. There was only one thing that kept him from forgetting the whole matter. It was the way that one wire seemed to slide around on the bead when you looked at it—

In about five minutes Max was back. 'I shot one of your gadgets all to heck. It held up until thirty-three thousand volts—and not a microamp of leakage. Whatever they are they're *good*. Want to blow the rest?'

Cal turned slowly. He wondered if Max were in on the gag too. 'A few hundred volts would jump right around the glass from wire to wire without bothering to go through. Those things are supposed to be condensers but they're not that good.'

'That's what the meter read. Too bad they aren't big enough to have some capacity with a voltage breakdown like that.'

'Come on,' said Cal. 'Let's check the capacity.'

First he tried another on voltage test. He watched it behind the glass shield as he advanced the voltage in steps of five kv. The bead held at thirty—and vanished at thirty-five.

His lips compressed tightly, Cal took the third bead to a standard capacity bridge. He adjusted the plugs until it balanced—at just four microfarads.

Max's eyes were slightly popped. 'Four mikes—they *can't* be!'

'No, they can't possibly be, can they?'

Back in the purchasing office he found Joe Wilson sitting morosely at the desk, staring at a yellow strip of teletype paper.

'Just the man I'm looking for,' said Joe: 'I called the Continental Electric and they said—'

'I don't care what they said.' Cal laid the remaining beads on the desk in front of Joe. 'Those little dingwhizzits are four-mike condensers that don't break down until more than thirty thousand volts. They're everything Continental said they were and more. Where did they get them? Last time I was over there Simon Foreman was in charge of the condenser department. He never—'

'Will you let me tell you?' Joe interrupted. 'They didn't come from Continental—so Continental says. They said no order for condensers has been received from here in the last six weeks. I sent a reorder by TWX.'

'I don't want their order then. I want more of these!' Cal held up the bead. 'But where did they come from if not from Continental?'

'That's what I want to know.'

'What do you mean, you want to know? What letterhead came with these? Let's see that letter again.'

'Here it is. It just says, "Electronic Service—Unit Sixteen." I thought that was some subsection of Continental. There's no address on it.'

Cal looked intently at the sheet of paper. What Joe said was true. There was no address at all. 'You're sure this came back in answer to an order you sent Continental?'

Wearily, Joe flipped over a file. 'There's the duplicate of the order I sent.'

'Continental always was a screwball outfit,' said Cal, 'but they must be trying to top themselves. Write them again. Refer to the reference on this letter. Order a gross of these condensers. While you're at it ask them for a new catalogue if ours is obsolete. I'd like to see what else they list besides these condensers.'

'Okay,' said Joe. 'But I tell you Continental says they didn't even get our order.'

'I suppose Santa Claus sent these condensers!'

Three days later Cal was still ironing the bugs out of his transmitter when Joe Wilson called again.

'Cal? Remember the Continental business? I just got the condensers— and the catalogue! For the love of Pete, get up here and take a look at it!'

'A whole gross of condensers? That's what I'm interested in.'

'Yes—and billed to us for thirty cents apiece.'

Cal hung up and walked out towards the Purchasing Office. Thirty cents apiece, he thought. If that outfit should go into the business of radio instruments they could probably sell a radio compass for five bucks at that rate.

He found Joe alone, an inch-thick manufacturer's catalogue open on the desk in front of him.

'Did this come from Continental?' said Cal.

Joe shook his head and turned over the front cover. It merely said, *Electronic Service—Unit 16*. No indication of address.

'We send letters to Continental and stuff comes back,' said Cal. 'Somebody over there must know about this! What did you want? What's so exciting about the catalogue?'

Joe arched his eyebrows. 'Ever hear of a catherimine tube? One with an endiom complex of plus four, which guarantees it to be the best of its kind on the market?'

'What kind of gibberish is that?'

'I dunno but this outfit sells them for sixteen dollars each.' Joe tossed the catalogue across the desk. 'This is absolutely the cock-eyedest thing I ever saw. If you hadn't told me those beads were condensers I'd say somebody had gone to a lot of work to pull a pretty elaborate gag. But the condensers were real—and here's a hundred and forty-four more of them.'

He picked up a little card with the beads neatly mounted in small holes. 'Somebody made these. A pretty doggoned smart somebody, I'd say—but I don't think it was Continental.'

Cal was slowly thumbing through the book. Besides the gibberish describing unfamiliar pieces of electronic equipment there was something else gnawing at his mind. Then be grasped it. He rubbed a page of the catalogue between his fingers and thumb.

'Joe, this stuff isn't even paper.'

'I know. Try to tear it.'

Cal did. His fingers merely slipped away. 'That's as tough as sheet iron!'

'That's what I found out. Whoever this Electronic Service outfit is, they've got some pretty bright engineers.'

'Bright engineers! This thing reflects a whole electronic culture completely foreign to ours. If it had come from Mars it couldn't be any more foreign.'

Cal thumbed over the pages, paused to read a description of a *volterator incorporating an electron sorter based on entirely new principles*. The picture of the thing looked like a cross between a miniature hot air furnace and a backyard incinerator and it sold for six hundred dollars.

And then he came to the back of the book, which seemed to have a unity not possessed by the first half. He discovered this to be true when he came to an inner dividing cover in the center of the catalogue.

For the first time, the center cover announced, *Electronic Service— Unit 16 offers a complete line of interocitor components. In the following pages you will find complete descriptions of components which reflect the most modern engineering advances known to interocitor engineers.*

'Ever hear of an interocitor?' said Cal.

'Sounds like something a surgeon would use to remove gallstones.'

'Maybe we should order a kit of parts and build one up,' said Cal whimsically.

'That would be like a power engineer trying to build a high-power communications receiver from the ARRL *Amateur's Handbook* catalogue section.'

'Maybe it could be done,' said Cal thoughtfully. He stopped abruptly and stared down at the pages before him. 'But good heavens, do you realize what this means—the extent of the knowledge and electronic culture behind this? It exists right here around us somewhere.'

'Maybe some little group of engineers in a small outfit that doesn't believe in mixing and exchanging information through the IRE and so on? But are they over at Continental? If so why all the beating about the bush telling us they didn't get our order and so on?'

'It looks bigger than that,' said Cal doubtfully. 'Regardless, we know their mail goes through Continental.'

'What are you going to do about it?'

'Do? Why, I'm going to find out who they are, of course. If this is all it seems to be I'll hit them up for a job. Mind if I take this catalogue along? I'd like to use it at home tonight. I'll see you get it back in the morning. I'll probably want to order some more of this stuff just to see what happens.'

'It's all right with me,' said Joe. 'I don't know what it's all about. I'm no engineer—just a dumb purchasing agent around this joint.'

'For some things you can be thankful,' said Cal.

Chapter Two: The Tumbling Barrel

The suburb of Mason was a small outlying place, a moderately concentrated industrial center. Besides Ryberg Instrument there were Eastern Tool and Machine Company, the Metalcrafters, a small die-making plant and a stapling-machine factory.

This concentration of small industry in the suburb made for an equally concentrated social order of engineers and their families. Most of them did have families but Cal Meacham was not yet among these.

He had been a bachelor for all of his thirty-five years and it looked as if he were going to stay that way. He admitted that he got lonesome sometimes but considered it well worth it when he heard Frank Staley up at two A.M. in the apartment above his, coaxing the new baby into something resembling silence.

Cal enjoyed his engineering work with an intensity that more than compensated for any of the joys of family life he might be missing.

He ate at the company cafeteria and went home to ponder the incredible catalogue that Joe Wilson had obtained. The more he thought about the things listed and described there, the more inflamed his imagination became.

He couldn't understand how such engineering developments could have been kept quiet. And now, why were they being so prosaically announced in an ordinary manufacturer's catalogue? It made absolutely no sense whatever.

He settled down in his easy chair with the catalogue propped on his lap. The section on interocitor components held the greatest fascination for him. All the rest of the catalogue listed merely isolated components and nowhere was any other device besides the interocitor mentioned.

But there was not a single clue as to what the interocitor was, its function or its purpose. To judge from the list of components, however, and some of the sub-assemblies that were shown, it was a terrifically complex piece of equipment.

He wondered momentarily if it were some war-born apparatus that hadn't come out until now.

He picked up the latest copy of the *Amateur's Handbook* and thumbed through the catalogue section. Joe had been about right in comparing the job assembling an interocitor to that of a power engineer trying to build a radio from the ARRL catalogue. How much indication would there be to a power engineer as to the purposes of the radio components in the catalogue?

Practically none. He couldn't hope to figure out the interocitor with no more clues than a components catalogue. He gave up the speculation. He had already made up his mind to go to Continental and find out what this was all about—and maybe put in his application for a job there. He *had* to know more about this stuff.

At seven there was a knock on his door. He found Frank Staley and two other engineers from upstairs standing in the hall.

'The wives are having a gabfest,' said Frank. 'How about a little poker?'

'Sure, I could use a little spending money this week. But are you guys sure you can stand the loss?'

'Ha, loss, he says,' said Frank. He turned to the others. 'Shall we tell him how hot we are tonight, boys?'

'Let him find out the hard way,' said Edmunds, one of Eastern's top mechanical engineers.

By nine-thirty Cal had found out the hard way. Even at the diminutive stakes they allowed themselves he was forty-five dollars in the hole.

He threw in his final hand. 'That's all for me for tonight. You can afford to lose your lunch money for a couple of months but nobody will make mine up at home if I can't buy it at the plant.'

Edmunds leaned back in his chair and laughed. 'I told you we were hot tonight. You look about as glum as Peters, our purchasing agent, did today. I had him order some special gears from some outfit for me a while back and they sent him two perfectly smooth wheels.

'He was about ready to hit the ceiling and then he discovered that one wheel rolled against the other would drive it. He couldn't figure it out. Neither could I when I saw it. So I mounted them on shafts and put a motor on one and a pony brake on the other.

'Believe it or not those things would transfer any horsepower I could use and I had up to three hundred and fifty. There was perfect transfer without measurable slippage or backlash, yet you could remove the keys and take the wheels off the shafts just as if there was nothing holding them together. The craziest thing you ever saw.'

Like some familiar song in another language Edmunds' story sent a wave of almost frightening recognition through Cal. While Staley and Larsen, the third engineer, listened with polite disbelief, Cal sat in utter stillness, knowing it was all true. He thought of the strange catalogue over in his bookcase.

'Did you ever find out where the gears came from?' he asked.

'No, but we sure intend to. Believe me, if we can find out the secret of those wheels it's going to revolutionize the entire science of mechanical engineering. They didn't come from the place we ordered them from. We know that much. They came from some place called merely "Mechanical Service—Unit Eight." No address. Whoever they are they must be geniuses besides screwball business people.'

Electronic Service—Unit 16, Mechanical Service—Unit 8—they must be bigger than he had supposed, Cal thought.

He went out to the little kitchenette to mix up some drinks. From the other room he heard Larsen calling Edmunds a triple-dyed liar. Two perfectly smooth wheels couldn't transmit power of that order merely by friction.

'I didn't say it was friction,' Edmunds was saying. 'It was something *else*—we don't know what.'

Something *else*, Cal thought. Couldn't Edmunds see the significance of such wheels? They were as evident of a foreign kind of mechanical culture as the condensers were evidence of a foreign electronic culture.

He went up to the Continental plant the next day, his hopes of finding the solution there considerably dimmed. His old friend, Simon Foreman, was still in charge of the condenser development.

He showed Simon the bead and Simon said, 'What kind of a gadget is that?'

'A four-mike condenser. You sent it to us. I want to know more about it.' Cal watched the engineer's face closely.

Simon shook his head as he took the bead. 'You're crazy! A four-mike condenser—we never sent you anything like this!'

He knew Simon was telling the truth.

It was Edmunds' story of the toothless gears that made it easier for Cal to accept the fact that the condensers and catalogue had not come from Continental. This he decided during the train ride home.

But *where* were the engineers responsible for this stuff? Why was it impossible to locate them? Mail reached Electronic Service through Continental. He wondered about Mechanical Service. Had Eastern received a catalogue of foreign mechanical components?

But his visit to Continental had thrown him up against a blank wall. No one admitted receiving the condenser orders and Cal knew none of Simon Foreman's men were capable of such development.

And that catalogue! It wasn't enough that it should list scores of unfamiliar components. It had to be printed on some unknown substance that resembled paper only superficially.

That was one more item that spoke not merely of isolated engineering advances but of a whole culture unfamiliar to him. And *that* was utterly impossible. Where could such a culture exist?

Regardless of the fantastic nature of the task, he had made up his mind to do what he had suggested only as a joke at first. He was going to attempt the construction of an interocitor. Somehow he felt that there would be clues to the origin of this fantastic engineering.

But *could* it be done? He'd previously dismissed it as impossible but now that it was a determined course the problem had to be analyzed further. In the catalogue were one hundred and six separate components but he knew it was not simply a matter of ordering one of each and putting them together.

That would be like ordering one tuning condenser, one coil, one tube and so on and expecting to build a super-het from them. In the interocitor there would be multiples of some parts, and different electrical values.

And, finally, if he ever got the thing working how would he know if it were performing properly or not?

He quit debating the pros and cons. He had known from the moment he first looked through the catalogue that he was going to try.

He went directly to the Purchasing Office instead of his lab the next morning. Through the glass panels of the outer room he could see Joe Wilson sitting at his desk with his face over a shoe box, staring with an intent and agonized frown.

Cal grinned to himself. It was hard to tell when Joe's mugging was real or not but he couldn't imagine him sitting there doing it without an audience.

Cal opened the door quietly, and then he caught a glimpse of the contents of the box. It was *wriggling*. He scowled, too.

'What have you got now? An earthworm farm?'

Joe looked up, his face still wearing a bewildered and distant expression. 'Oh, hello, Cal. This is a tumbling barrel.'

Cal stared at the contents of the box. It looked like a mass of tiny black worms in perpetual erratic motion. 'What's the gag this time? That box of worms doesn't look much like a tumbling barrel.'

'It would—if they were metallic worms and just walked around the metal parts that needed tumbling.'

'This isn't another Electronic Service—Unit 16 product, is it?'

'No. Metalcrafters sent over this sample. Wanted to know if they could sell us any for our mechanical department. The idea is that you just dump whatever needs tumbling into a box of this compound, strain it out in a few minutes and your polishing job is done.'

'What makes the stuff wiggle?'

'That's the secret that Metalcrafters won't tell.'

'Order five hundred pounds of it,' said Cal suddenly. 'Call them on the phone and tell them we can use it this afternoon.'

'What's the big idea? *You* can't use it.'

'Try it.'

Dubiously, Joe lifted the phone and contacted the order department of Metalcrafters. He placed the order. After a moment he hung up. 'They say that due to unexpected technological difficulties in production they are not accepting orders for earlier than thirty-day delivery.'

'The crazy dopes! They won't get it in thirty days or thirty months.'

'What are you talking about?'

'Where do you think they got this stuff? They didn't discover it. They got it the same way we got these condensers and they're hoping to cash in on it before they even know what it is. As if they could figure it out in thirty days!'

Then he told Joe about the gears of Edmunds.

'This begins to look like more than accident,' said Joe.

Cal nodded slowly. 'Sample of products of an incredible technology were apparently missent to three of the industrial plants here in Mason. But I wonder how many times it has happened in other places. It almost looks like a deliberate pattern of some sort.'

'But who's sending it all and how and why? Who developed this stuff? It couldn't be done on a shoestring, you know. That stuff smells of big money spent in development labs. Those condensers must have cost a half million, I'll bet.'

'Make out an order for me,' said Cal. 'Charge it to my project. There's enough surplus to stand it. I'll take the rap if anybody snoops.'

'What do you want?'

'Send it to Continental as before. Just say you want one complete set of components as required for the construction of a single interocitor model. That may get me the right number of duplicate parts unless I get crossed up by something I'm not thinking of.'

Joe's eyebrows shot up. 'You're going to try to build one by the Chinese method?'

'The Chinese method would be simple,' Cal grunted. 'They take a finished cake and reconstruct it. If I had a finished interocitor I'd gladly tackle *that*. This is going to be built by the Cal Meacham original catalogue method.'

He worked overtime for the next couple of days to beat out the bugs in the airline ground transmitter and finally turned it over to the production department for processing. There'd still be a lot of work on it because production wouldn't like some of the complex sub-assemblies he'd been forced to design—but he'd have time for the interocitor stuff if and when it showed up.

After two weeks he was almost certain that something had gone wrong and they had lost contact with the mysterious supplier. His disappointment vanished when the receiving clerk called him and said that fourteen crates had just been received for him.

Fourteen crates seemed a reasonable number but he hadn't been prepared for the size of them. They stood seven feet high and were no smaller than four by five feet in cross section.

Cal groaned as he saw them standing on the receiving platform. He visioned cost sheets with astronomical figures on them. What had he got himself into?

He cleared out one of his screen rooms and ordered the stuff brought in. Then he began the job of unpacking the crates as they were slowly dollied in. He noted with some degree of relief that approximately one half the volume of the crates was taken up by packing materials—but that still left an enormous volume of components.

In some attempt to classify them he laid the like units together upon the benches around the room. There were plumbing units of seemingly senseless configuration, glass envelopes with innards that looked like nothing he had ever seen in a vacuum tube before. There were boxes containing hundreds of small parts which he supposed must be resistances or condensers—though his memory concerning the glass beads made him cautious about jumping to conclusions regarding anything.

After three hours, the last of the crates had been unpacked and the rubbish carted away. Cal Meacham was left alone in the midst of four thousand, eight hundred and ninety-six—he'd kept a tally of them—unfamiliar gadgets of unknown purposes and characteristics. And he hoped to assemble them into a complete whole—of equally unknown purposes.

He sat down on a lab stool and regarded the stacks of components glumly. In his lap rested the single guide through this impossible maze—the catalogue.

CHAPTER THREE: Assembly Problem

At quitting time he went out for dinner at the plant cafeteria, then returned to the now empty lab and walked around the piles, sizing up the job he'd let himself in for. It would take all his nights for months to come.

He hoped there wouldn't be too much curiosity about his project but he could see little chance of keeping it entirely under cover. Most of all he was concerned with keeping Billingsworth, the chief engineer, from complaining about it. Not that he and Billingsworth weren't on good terms but his was *big* for a sideline project.

It was obvious that certain parts of the miscellaneous collection constituted a framework for the assembly to be mounted on. He gathered these together and set them up tentatively to see if he could get some idea of the size and shape of the finished assembly.

One thing stood out at once. On the bench was a cube of glass, sixteen inches on a side, filled with a complex mass of elements. Twenty-three terminals led from the elements to the outside of the cube. One side of it was coated as if it were some kind of screen. And within one of the framework panels there was an opening exactly the right size to accommodate the face of the cube.

That narrowed the utility of the device, Cal thought. It provided an observer with some kind of intelligence which was viewed in graphic or pictorial form as with a cathode-ray tube.

But the complexity of the cube's elements and the multiple leads indicated another necessity. He would have to order duplicates of many parts because these would have to be dissected to destruction in order to determine some possible electrical function.

Nearly all the tubes fell into this classification and he began listing these parts so that Joe could reorder.

He then turned to familiarizing himself with the catalogue name of each part and establishing possible functions from the descriptions and specifications given.

Slowly through the early morning hours the clues increased. Pieces were fitted together as if the whole thing were a majestic jigsaw puzzle designed by some super-brain.

At three A.M. Cal locked the screen room and went home for a few hours' sleep. He felt elated by the slight success he'd had, the few clues that he seemed to have discovered.

He was in at eight again and went to Joe's office. As always Joe was there. Cal sometimes wondered if he slept in the place.

'I see your stuff came,' said Joe. 'I wanted to come down, but I thought you'd like to work it out alone for a while.'

'I wish you had,' Cal said. He understood Joe's frustrations. 'Come on down anytime. There's something I'd like you to do. On the crates the stuff came in there was an address of a warehouse in Philadelphia. I wrote it down here. Could you get one of the salesmen to see what kind of a place it is when he's through there? I'd rather not have him know I'm interested. This may be a lead.'

'Sure. I think the Sales Office has a regular trip through there next week. I'll see who's on it. What have you found out?'

'Not too much. The thing has a screen for viewing but no clue as to what might be viewed. There's a piece of equipment referred to as a *planetary generator* that seems to be a sort of central unit, something like the oscillator of a transmitter, perhaps. It was mounted in a support that seems to call for mounting on the main frame members.

'This gives me an important dimension so I can finish the framework. But there's about four hundred and ninety terminals—more or less—on that planetary generator. That's what's got me buffaloed but good. These parts seem to be interchangeable in different circuits, otherwise they might be marked for wiring.

'The catalogue refers to various elements, which are named, and gives electrical values for them—but I can't find out which elements are which without tearing into sealed units. So here's a reorder on all the parts I may have to open up.'

Joe glanced at it. 'Know what that first shipment cost?'

'Don't tell me it cleaned my project out?'

'They billed us this morning for twenty-eight hundred dollars.'

Cal whistled, softly. 'If that stuff had been produced by any of the technological methods I know anything about they would have sent a bill nearer twenty-eight thousand.'

'Say, Cal, why can't we track this outfit down through the patent office. There must be patents on the stuff.'

'There's not a patent number on anything. I've already looked.'

'Then let's ask them to send us either the number or copies of the patents on some of these things. They wouldn't distribute unpatented items like this, surely. They'd be worth a fortune.'

'All right. Put it in the letter with your reorder. I don't think it will do much good.'

Cal returned to the lab and worked impatiently through the morning on consultations with the production department regarding his transmitter. After lunch he returned to the interocitor. He decided against opening any of the tubes. If anything should happen to their precarious contact with the supplier before they located him—

He began work on identification of the tube elements. Fortunately the catalogue writers had put in all voltage and current data. But there were new units that made no sense to Cal—*albion factors, inverse reduction index, scattering efficiency.*

Slowly he went ahead. Filaments were easy but some of the tubes had nothing resembling filaments or cathodes. When he applied test voltages he didn't know whether anything was happening or not.

Gradually he found out. There was one casual sketch showing a catherimine tube inside a field-generating coil. That gave him a clue to a whole new principle of operation.

After six days he was able to connect proper voltages to more than half his tubes and get the correct responses as indicated by catalogue specifications. With that much information available he was able to go ahead and construct the entire power supply of the interocitor.

Then Joe called him one afternoon. 'Hey, Cal! Have you busted any of those tubes yet?'

'No. Why?'

'Don't! They're getting mad or something. They aren't going to send the reorder we asked for and they say there are no patents on the stuff. Besides, that address in Philadelphia turned out to be a dud.

'Cramer, the salesman who looked it up, says there's nothing there but an old warehouse that hasn't been used for years. Cal, who can these guys be? I'm beginning to not like the smell of this business.'

'Read me their letter.'

'"Dear Mr Wilson," they say, "We cannot understand the necessity of the large amount of reorder which you have submitted to us. We trust that the equipment was not broken or damaged in transit. However, if this is the case please return the damaged parts and we will gladly order replacements for you. Otherwise we fear that, due to the present shortage of interocitor equipment, it will be necessary to return your order unfilled.

'"We do not understand your reference to patents. There is nothing of such a nature in connection with the equipment. Please feel free to call upon us at any time. If you find it possible to function under present circumstances will you please contact us by interocitor at your earliest convenience and we will discuss the matter further."'

'What was that last line?' Cal asked.

'—"contact us by interocitor—"'

'That's the one! That shows us what the apparatus is—a communication device.'

'But from where to where and from whom to whom?'

'That's what I intend to find out. Believe me I do—now as never before!'

They weren't going to let him open up the tubes or other sealed parts, that was obvious. Cal arranged for an X-ray and fluoroscope equipment and began to obtain some notion of the interior construction of the tubes he could not otherwise analyze. He could trace the terminals back to their

internal connections and be fairly sure of not burning things up with im-
proper voltages to the elements.

Besides the power supply the entire framework with the planetary
generator was erected and a bank of eighteen catherimine tubes was fed
by it. The output of these went to a nightmare arrangement of plumbing
that included unbelievable flares and spirals. Again he found prealigned
mounting holes that enabled him to fit most of the plumbing together
with only casual reference to the catalogue.

Growing within him was the feeling that the whole thing was some incredible intricately designed puzzle and that clues were deliberately
placed there for anyone who would look.

Then one of the catherimine tubes rolled off a table and shattered on
the floor. Cal thought afterwards that he must have stood staring at the
shards of glass for a full five minutes before he moved. He wondered if the
whole project were lying there in that shattered heap.

Gently, with tweezers, he picked out the complex tube elements and
laid them gently on a bed of dustless packing material. Then he called Joe.

'Get off another letter to Continental—airmail,' he said. 'Ask if we can
get a catherimine replacement. I just dropped one.'

'Aren't you going to send the pieces along as they asked?'

'No. I'm not taking any chances with what I've got. Tell them the remains will be forwarded immediately if they can send a replacement.'

'OK. Mind if I come down tonight and look things over?'

'Not at all. Come on down.'

It was a little before five when Joe Wilson finally entered the screen
room. He looked around and whistled softly. 'Looks like you're making
something out of this after all.'

A neat row of panels nearly fifteen feet long stretched along the center
of the room. In the framework behind was a nightmarish assemblage of
gadgets and leads. Joe took in the significance of the hundreds of leads
that were in place.

'You're really figuring it out!'

'I think so,' said Cal casually. 'It's pretty tricky.'

Joe scanned the mass of equipment once more. 'You know, manufac-
turers' catalogues are my line,' he said. 'I see hundreds of them every year.
I get so I can almost tell the inside layout just by the cover.

'Catalogue writers aren't very smart, you know. They're mostly
forty—fifty-dollar-a-week kids that come out of college with a smatter-
ing of journalism but are too dumb to do much about it. So they end up
writing catalogues.

'And no catalogue I ever saw would enable you to do this!'

Cal shrugged. 'You never saw a catalogue like this before.'

'I don't think it's a catalogue.'

'What do you think it is?'

'An instruction book. Somebody wanted you to put this together.'

Cal laughed heartily. 'You must read too much science fiction on your days off. Why would anyone deliberately plant this stuff so that I would assemble it?'

'Do *you* think it's just a catalogue?'

Cal stopped laughing. 'All right, you win. I'll admit it but I still think it's crazy. There are things in it that wouldn't be quite necessary if it were only a catalogue. For instance, look at this catherimine tube listing.

'It says that with the deflector grid in a four-thousand-gauss field the accelerator plate current will be forty mils. Well, it doesn't matter whether it's in a field or not. That's normal for the element under any conditions.

'But that's the only place in the whole book that indicates the normal operation of the tube is in this particular field. There were a bunch of coils with no designation except that they are static field coils.

'On the basis of that one clue I put the tubes and coils together and found an explanation of the unknown "albion factor" that I've been looking for. It's that way all along. It can't be merely accidental. You're right about catalogue and technical writers in general but the guy that cooked this one up was a genius.

'Yet I still can't quite force myself to the conclusion that I was *supposed* to put this thing together, that I was deliberately led into it.'

'Couldn't it be some sort of Trojan Horse gadget?'

'I don't see how it could be. What could it do? As a radiation weapon it wouldn't have a very wide range—I hope.'

Joe turned toward the door. 'Maybe it's just as well that you broke that tube.'

The pile of components whose places in the assembly still were to be determined was astonishingly small, Cal thought, as he left the lab shortly after midnight.

Many of the circuits were complete and had been tested, with a response that might or might not be adequate for their design. At least nothing blew up.

The following afternoon, Joe called again. 'We've lost our connection. I just got a TWX from Continental. They want to know what the devil we're talking about in our letter of yesterday—the one asking for a replacement.'

There was only a long silence.

'Cal—you still there?'

'Yes, I'm here. Get hold of Oceanic Tube Company for me. Ask them to send one of their best engineers down here—Jerry Lanier if he's in the plant now. We'll see if they can rebuild the tube for us.'

'That *is* going to cost money.'

'I'll pay it out of my own pocket if I have to. This thing is almost finished.'

Why had they cut their connection, Cal wondered? Had they discovered that their contact had been a mistake? And what would happen if he did finish the interocitor? He wondered if there would be anyone to communicate with even if he did complete it.

It was so close to completion now that he was beginning to suffer from the customary engineer's jitters that come when a harebrained scheme is finally about to be tested. Only this was about a thousand times worse because he didn't even know that he would recognize the correct operation of the interocitor if he saw it.

It was ninety-eight-percent complete and he still could detect no coherency in the thing. It seemed to turn completely in upon itself. True, there was a massive source of radiation but it seemed to be entirely dissipated within the instrument. There was no part that could conceivably act as an antenna to radiate or collect radiation and so provide means of communication.

Cal went over his circuit deductions again and again but the more he tracked down the available clues, the more certain it seemed that he had built correctly. There was no ambiguity whatever in the cleverly buried clues.

Jerry Lanier finally showed up. Cal gave him only the broken catherimine tube and allowed him to see none of the rest of the equipment.

Jerry scowled at the tube. 'Since when did they put squirrel cages in glass envelopes? What is this thing?'

'Top hush-hush,' said Cal. 'All I want to know is can you duplicate it?'

'Sure. Where did you get it?'

'Military secret.'

'It looks simple enough. We could probably duplicate it in three weeks or so.'

'Look, Jerry, I want that bottle in three days.'

'Cal, you know we can't—'

'Oceanic isn't the only tube maker in the business. This might turn out to be pretty hot stuff.'

'All right, you horse trader. Guarantee it by air express in five days.'

'Good enough.'

❖ ❖ ❖

For two straight nights Cal didn't go home. He grabbed a half hour's snooze on a lab bench in the early morning. And on the second day he was almost caught by the first lab technician who arrived.

But the interocitor was finished.

The realization seemed more like a dream than reality but every one of the nearly five thousand parts had at last been incorporated into the assembly behind the panels—except the broken tube.

He knew it was right. With a nearly obsessive conviction he felt sure that he had constructed the interocitor just as the unknown engineers had designed it.

He locked the screen room and left word with Joe to call him if Jerry sent the tube, then went home to sleep the clock around.

When he finally went back to the lab a dozen production problems on the airline transmitter had turned up and for once he was thankful for them. They helped reduce the tension of waiting to find out what the assembly of alien parts would do when he finally turned on the power to the whole unit.

He was still working on the job of breaking down one of the transmitter sub-assemblies when quitting time came. It was only because Nell Joy, the receptionist in the front hall, was waiting for her boy friend that he received the package at all.

She called him at twenty after five.

'Mr Meacham? I didn't know whether you'd still be here or not. There's a special-delivery boy here with a package for you. It looks important. Do you want it tonight?'

'I'll say I do!'

He was out by her desk, signing for the package, almost before she had hung up. He tore off the wrappings on the way back to the lab.

Chapter Four: Contact!

There it was!

As beautiful a job of duplication as he could have wished for. Cal could have sworn there was no visual difference between it and the original. But the electrical test would tell the story.

In the lab he put the duplicate tube in the tester he'd devised and checked the albion. That was the critical factor.

He frowned as the meter indicated ten percent deviation, but two of the originals had tolerances that great. It would do.

His hand didn't seem quite steady as he put the tube in its socket. He stood back a moment, viewing the completed instrument.

Then he plunged the master switch on the power panel.

He watched anxiously the flickering hands of two-score meters as he advanced along the panels, energizing the circuits one by one.

Intricate adjustments on the panel controls brought the meter readings into line with the catalogue specifications which he had practically memorized by now—but which were written by the meters for safety.

Then, slowly, the grayish screen of the cubical viewing tube brightened. Waves of polychrome hue washed over it. It seemed as if an image were trying to form but it remained out of focus, only a wash of color.

'Turn up the intensifier knob,' a masculine voice said suddenly. 'That will clear your screen.'

To Cal it was like words coming suddenly at midnight in a ghost-ridden house. The sound had come out of the utter unknown into which the interocitor reached—but it was human.

He stepped back to the panel and adjusted the knob. The shapeless color flowed to solid lines, congealed to an image. And Cal stared.

He didn't know what he had expected. But the prosaic color-image of the man who watched him from the plate was too ordinary after the weeks-long effort expended on the interocitor.

Yet there was something of the unknown in the man's eyes too—something akin to the unknown of the interocitor. Cal drew slowly nearer the plate, his eyes unable to leave that face, his breath hard and fast.

'Who are you?' he said almost inaudibly. 'What have I built?'

For a moment the man made no answer as if he hadn't heard. His image was stately and he appeared of uncertain late middle age. He was of large proportions and ruggedly attractive of feature. But it was his eyes that held Cal with such intense force — eyes which seemed to hold an awareness of responsibility to all the people in the world.

'Who are you?' Cal repeated softly.

'We'd about given you up,' the man said at last. 'But you've passed. And rather well too.'

'Who are you? What is this—this interocitor I've constructed?'

'The interocitor is simply an instrument of communication. Constructing it was a good deal more. You'll follow my meaning in a moment. Your first question is more difficult to answer but that is my purpose.

'I am the employment representative of a group—a certain group who are urgently in need of men, expert technologists. We have a good many stringent requirements for prospective employees. So we require them to take an aptitude test to measure some of those qualifications we desire.

'You have passed that test!'

For a moment Cal stared uncomprehendingly. 'What do you mean?

This makes no sense. I have made no application to work with your—your employers.'

A faint trace of a smile crossed the man's face. 'No. No one does that. We pick our own applicants and test them, quite without their awareness they are being tested. You are to be congratulated on your showing.'

'What makes you think I'd be interested in working for your employers? I don't even know who they are, let alone what work they require done.'

'You would not have come this far unless you were interested in the job we have to offer.'

'I don't understand.'

'You have seen the type of technology in our possession. No matter who or what we are, having come this far you would pursue us to the ends of the Earth to find out how we came by that technology and to learn its mastery for yourself. Is it not so?'

The arrogant truth of the man's statement was like a physical blow that rocked Cal back on his heels. There was no uncertainty in the man's voice. He *knew* what Cal was going to do more surely than Cal had known himself up to this moment.

'You seem pretty certain of that.' Cal found it hard to keep an impulsive hostility out of his voice.

'I am. We pick our applicants quite carefully. We make offers only to those we are certain will accept. Now, since you are about to join us, I will relieve your mind of some unnecessary tensions.

'It has undoubtedly occurred to you, as to all thinking people of your day, that the scientists have done a particularly abominable job of dispensing the tools they have devised. Like careless and indifferent workmen they have tossed the products of their craft to gibbering apes and baboons. The results have been disastrous to say the least.

'Not all scientists, however, have been quite so indifferent. There are a group of us who have formed an organization for the purpose of obtaining better and more conservative distribution of these tools. We call ourselves, somewhat dramatically perhaps, but none the less truthfully, *Peace Engineers*. Our motives are sure to encompass whatever implications you can honestly make of the term.

'But we need men—technicians, men of imagination, men of good will, men of superb engineering abilities—and our method has to be somewhat less than direct. Hence, our approach to you. It involved simply an interception of mail in a manner you would not yet understand.

'You passed your aptitude test and so were more successful than some of your fellow engineers in this community.'

Cal thought instantly of Edmunds and the toothless gears and the tumbling barrel compound.

'Those other things—' he said. 'They would have led to the same solution?'

'Yes. In a somewhat different way, of course. But that is all the information I can give you at this time. The next consideration is your coming here.'

'Where? Where are you? How do I come?'

The readiness with which his mind accepted the fact of his going shocked and chilled him. Was there no other alternative that he should consider? For what reasons should he ally himself with this unknown band who called themselves Peace Engineers? He fought for rational reasons why he should not.

There were few that he could muster up. None, actually. He was alone, without family or obligations. He had no particular professional ties to prevent him from leaving.

As for any potential personal threat that might lie in alliance with the Peace Engineers—well, he wasn't much afraid of anything that could happen to him personally.

But in reality none of these factors had any influence. There was only one thing that concerned him. He had to know more about that fantastic technology they possessed.

And they had known that was the one factor capable of drawing him.

The interviewer paused as if sensing what was in Cal's mind. 'You will learn the answers to all your questions in proper order,' he said. 'Can you be ready tomorrow?'

'I'm ready now,' Cal said.

'Tomorrow will be soon enough. Our plane will land on your airfield exactly at noon. It will remain fifteen minutes. It will take off without you if you are not in it by that time. You will know it by its color. A black ship with a single horizontal orange stripe, an Army BT-13 type.

'That is all for now. Congratulations and good luck to you. I'll be looking forward to seeing you personally.

'Stand back now. When I cut off, the interocitor will be destroyed. Stand back!'

Cal backed sharply to the far side of the room. He saw the man's head nod, his face smiling a pleasant good-by, then the image vanished from the screen.

Almost instantly there came the hiss of burning insulation, the crack of heat-shattered glass. From the framework of the interocitor rose a blooming bubble of smoke that slowly filled the room as wires melted and insulation became molten and ran.

Cal burst from the screen room and grasped a nearby fire extinguisher, which he played into the blinding smoke pouring from the room. He emptied that one and ran for another.

Slowly the heat and smoke dispelled. He moved back into the room and knew then that the interocitor could never be analyzed or duplicated from that ruin. Its destruction had been thorough.

It was useless trying to sleep that night. He sat in the park until after midnight when a suspicious cop chased him off. After that he simply walked the streets until dawn, trying to fathom the implications of what he'd seen and heard.

Peace Engineers—

What did the term mean? It could imply a thousand things, a secret group with dictatorial ambitions in possession of a powerful technology—a bunch of crackpots with strange access to genius—or it could be what the term literally implied.

But there was no guarantee that their purposes were altruistic. With his past knowledge of human nature he was more inclined to credit the possibility that he was being led into some Sax Rohmer melodrama.

At dawn he turned toward his apartment. There he cleaned up and had breakfast and left the rent and a note instructing the landlord to dispose of his belongings as he wished. He went to the plant in midmorning and resigned amidst a storm of protests from Billingsworth and a forty-percent salary increase offer.

That done, it was nearly noon and he went up to see Joe Wilson.

'I wondered what happened to you this morning,' said Joe. 'I tried to call you for a couple of hours.'

'I slept late,' said Cal. 'I just came in to resign.'

'Resign?' Joe Wilson stared incredulously. 'What for? What about the interocitor?'

'It blew up in my face. The whole thing's gone.'

'I hoped you would make it,' Joe said a little sadly. 'I wonder if we will ever find out where that stuff came from.'

'Sure,' said Cal carelessly. 'It was just some shipping mixup. We'll find out about it someday.'

'Cal—' Joe Wilson was looking directly into his face. 'You found out, didn't you?'

Cal hesitated a moment. He had been put under no bond of secrecy. What could it matter? He understood something of the fascination the problem held for a frustrated engineer turned into a technical purchasing agent.

'Yes,' he said. 'I found out.'

Joe smiled wryly. 'I was hoping you would. Can you tell me about it?'

'There's nothing to tell. I don't know where they are. All I know is that I talked to someone. They offered me a job.'

There it was. He saw it coming in low and fast, a black and orange ship. Wing flaps down, it slowed and touched the runway. Already it was like the symbol of a vast and important future that had swept him up. Already the familiar surroundings of Ryberg's were something out of a dim and unimportant past.

'I wish we could have learned more about the interocitor,' said Joe.

Cal's eyes were still straining toward the ship as it taxied around on the field. Then he shook hands solemnly with Joe. 'You and me both,' he said. 'Believe me—'

Joe Wilson stood by the window and as Cal went out toward the ship he knew he'd been correct in that glimpse he'd got of the cockpit canopy silhouetted against the sky.

The ship was pilotless.

Another whispering clue to a mighty, alien technology.

He knew Cal must have seen it too but Cal's steps were steady as he walked toward it.

The Cosmic Frame

Paul W. Fairman

The blue light flashed out beyond Pelham Woods. It was seen by several of the boys lounging in front of the barber shop on the main street of Kensington Corners. 'Now what in the nation was that?' one of them asked.

'Low lightning. What else?'

'Didn't look like lightning. Held too long. Besides, there's no clouds over there.'

'Might be some low ones you can't see for the trees.'

Sam Carter, fresh from a late-afternoon shave, came out of the barber shop and said, 'What are you fellows arguing about?'

'Just saw a flying saucer.'

Sam grinned. 'Only one? Nobody's got a right to brag these days unless they see at least six. And they've all got to spout at least five colors.'

'This one was blue.'

'Always preferred the yellow ones myself.' The boys grinned lazily and Sam looked across the street and called, 'Lee! Hold up. I'm walking your way.'

Lee Hayden, a big, sour-faced man, stopped and waited and when Sam Carter came abreast, asked, 'What are those no-good loafers jabbering about today?'

'Flying saucers. A blue one this time.'

'Uh-huh. Good a way as any to kill valuable time.'

'Oh, they're all right, Lee. Say—it looks as though things might be getting serious between our kids.'

Lee Hayden snorted. 'Darn fool kids. Don't know their own minds. It's a sign of the times.'

'Oh, I wouldn't say that. My Johnny's pretty serious about life. I've got a hunch Joan will be good for him.'

Lee scowled. 'Kids these days never have a thought about tomorrow—where the next dollar's coming from. All they think about is getting hitched—making more trouble for themselves—going into debt.'

'It always seems to work out, though. Nothing wrong with either of them that marriage won't cure.' Sam Carter was one of the few men in Kensington Corners who liked Lee Hayden. Most people resented his sour outlook on life and his money-grubbing instincts. Sam understood the man, however, and this was fortunate for the sake of Johnny and Joan. Sam said, 'Looks like their date tonight's a pretty important one. Johnny asked me for the Packard. Doesn't want to propose to his girl, I guess, in that stripped-down hot rod of his.'

'They're too young to get married.'

'Well, maybe it won't happen for a while,' Sam said, easily.

'See you later, Lee.' Sam turned in at his gate and Lee Hayden went on down the street, scowling as usual.

While, out beyond Pelham Woods, the space ship with the blue exhaust settled on the surface of Nelson's Pond and sank from sight.

Sam Carter's phone rang sharply. He awoke and shook the sleep from his eyes. He snapped on the light and noted that it was one-thirty as he picked up the phone. 'Hello?'

'Hello—Dad! Are you awake? Listen to me. Please—'

'Johnny! What in the devil's wrong? You in trouble?'

'Bad trouble, Dad!'

Sam's feet were on the floor. 'An accident? Anybody hurt? Damn it, boy! You should have been home a long time ago.'

'Don't lecture me, Dad. Just listen!'

'Where are you? Tell me about it.'

'I took Joan to the dance at Storm Lake and we were on the way home when—'

'When *what*? Talk, boy!'

'We hit—'

'You killed somebody?'

'Yes—well, no—we—'

'For heaven's sake, Johnny! Calm down and tell me. Either you did or you didn't. Don't tell me you ran away from an accident!'

'No—listen, Dad, will you just hang up and get out here as fast as you can? I need help. I need help bad. Just get out here!'

'Okay, son, I'll try and make that hot rod of yours go—'

'It's shot, Dad—it won't run. Call Mr Hayden. Use his car.'

'All right. Where are you?'

'I'm calling from a farmhouse on Garner Road—Frank Williams' place. He's a farmer. You know that back road where—?'

'I know. Where did you have the trouble? Where's the car?'

'At the bend about two miles from Storm Lake. That's where it—it happened. Joan and I'll go back there and wait.'

'Stay where you are—we'll pick you up.'

'No Dad! I didn't tell these people what happened. We'll wait near the car.'

'All right, anything you say. I'll make it as fast as I can.'

Ten minutes later, Sam Carter was sitting beside Lee Hayden as the latter pointed his Chevrolet toward Storm Lake. 'Damn fool kids!' Lee muttered. 'Why didn't you find out what happened? They may have killed somebody. Probably did. The least he could have done was tell you.'

'Let's just get there and find out,' Sam said with tightness in his voice.

They went into Garner Road from the south end and Lee drove slowly along the ruts and chuckholes. 'Why in tarnation did they pick a road like this?'

'It probably looked pretty good to them.'

'I wonder how good it looks now?'

'Can't you drive a little faster?'

'And break a spring? I'm doing the best I can.'

Sam held his impatience in check until the headlights picked out the rear end of the Packard. It stood squarely in the middle of the road.

'Doesn't look as though there's any damage,' Lee said.

'We can't see the front end yet.'

Lee pulled up fifty feet back and the two men got out. There was a flash of white and the two young people appeared from some bushes by the roadside. Joan, a pretty little brunette, looked ethereal in her white party dress—out of place in spike-heel pumps on this lonely country road. Johnny Carter's handsome young face was drawn and pale.

'What were you two hiding from?' Lee demanded.

Sam asked, 'What's wrong here? There's no other car.'

'It wasn't a crackup, Dad. It's around in front. Come on. Joany—you stay here.'

'I—I feel a little weak. I'll get into the Chevy.'

Johnny helped her in and closed the door. Then he turned and said, 'Come on.' As they walked around the Packard, he added, 'Now brace yourselves. You're going to see something you never saw before in your lives.'

They rounded the car and stood for a moment. Then Johnny snapped on the Packard's headlights and Lee Hayden croaked, 'Great God in heaven! Is it real?'

Sam Carter felt a chill run both ways from the center of his spine, freezing his legs and rendering him mute.

Johnny said, 'We were driving along and I wasn't negligent—I swear it. Maybe not too alert, but who'd expect anyone—anything—to appear on this road without lights? Anyhow, I saw a flash of it and hit the brakes, but it was too late. I thought it was a man at first and I got out and—and actually picked it up before I realized—' He took an unconscious step backward and rubbed the sleeves of his coat as though they were covered with filth.

Still frozen, Sam Carter tried to find thoughts to describe the horrible thing. It was not more than four feet long and had a head far too large for the thin body. Its skin was green, the shades varying from deep to very pale. It had thin legs and two spiderlike arms ending in hands with thin delicate fingers and a thumb on either side. Its eyes were lidless and sunk into bony pockets in the round, pale green skull. There was a network of dark veins all over the body and the feet were shapeless pads with neither toes nor heels.

There was a full minute of complete silence. Then Lee Hayden got out a few words. 'Is—is it dead?'

'It's dead all right,' Johnny said. 'When I first came around the car—after I hit it—the big veins were pulsing—you could see its blood—or whatever's in there, moving through. Then they got slower and stopped altogether.'

'That blue light the boys saw,' Sam muttered. 'It *was* a space ship this time.'

Lee Hayden, though his face was still filled with loathing, seemed to have recovered somewhat. 'This one must have wandered away. Never saw a car before. Didn't know there was any danger.'

'Probably attracted by the headlights—held like a moth.'

Johnny said, 'It's ugly right enough, but it looks kind of pathetic, too— lying there dead. Never knew what hit it.'

Sam came out of his shock. 'One of us had better go for the sheriff. You go, Johnny. Take the Chevy and drop Joan off at home.'

'Okay.' The boy turned away.

Lee Hayden had been staring at the hideous thing and a calculating light was now dawning in his eyes. 'Wait a minute, Johnny.' Lee raised his eyes to Sam Carter. 'You realize what this means?'

'I realize that—'

'This is something from outer space, man! An—an extraterrestrial, they call it, that came down to earth in a ship and—and here it is.'

Sam was puzzled. 'I can see it.'

'Right. And you and I—the four of us—are the only ones on earth who know about it.'

'Joany doesn't,' Johnny said. 'I don't think she saw it when we hit it, and after I looked I wouldn't let her go near the front end. I was afraid it would make her sick.'

Lee Hayden's eyes glowed. 'Good. Smart boy! Then there's just the three of us who know.'

Sam Carter frowned at his friend. 'What are you driving at, Lee?'

'Just this—there's money in this thing, Sam! Loads of money! If it's handled right. But we can't go off half-cocked.'

'I'm afraid I don't get you—'

'Use your head! If we call the sheriff and everybody finds out, then we've lost it. There'll be photographers and reporters and the knowledge will be public property.'

'You mean keep it quiet?' Johnny asked. 'Unless we bury it somewhere and forget about it, the public's bound to find out.'

'Of course—we want them to. But in the right way. Not until we've thought it over and figured the best way to exploit it. Get what I mean? How would a showman handle this? How would Barnum have done it? Call in the police and give it to the public in exchange for a lot of publicity and no money? Use your heads—both of you!'

Sam said, 'No, Lee! We've got no right! This is serious. This may be an invasion of some kind. We've got to be public-spirited and the hell with the money.'

Johnny said, 'If we knew Russia was going to attack us tomorrow would we have any right to sell the information to Washington?'

'The boy's right, Lee. We can't fool around with a thing as big as this.'

'The hell we can't. This is no invasion and you both know it. It's a chance to make more money than any of us ever saw.'

'It's not right, Lee.'

'Why not? We aren't going to withhold anything. I say, just take it easy and don't rush into anything with our mouths wide open and spouting information. Twenty-four hours is all we'll need. I'll go to Sioux City and get the thing lined up right. Get a contract with the people who know how to exploit a thing like this if we can't figure out how to do it ourselves.'

'But in the meantime, what if—?'

'Twenty-four hours won't make any difference, I tell you! And in that length of time we can arrange a setup to make fortunes. Sam—don't you want the kids to start out life with a real bankroll? Do you want them to struggle along the way you and I had to? In one day, we can set them up for life—and ourselves too—and without hurting a soul. It's your obligation, Sam. Can't you see it?'

Lee Hayden argued on. After a while, Johnny Carter stopped voicing objections and watched his father, evidently ready to go in either direction Sam decided. The father looked at the son and misinterpreted his manner and expression. He thought, will the boy hold it against me if I deprive him of this opportunity? Do I have a right to deprive him? Possibly Lee is right. Either way, the country will know—the government will be alerted. He turned to Lee Hayden and asked, 'How do you think we should go about it?'

Hayden's eyes brightened. 'I knew you'd see it my way. Now, I'll tell you what we'll do. You and Johnny take the thing home and hide it in your basement. Yours is best because there are only the two of you. I couldn't hide a fly speck in my place that my wife wouldn't find.'

'What about Joan?' Johnny asked. 'She didn't see this thing but she knows something happened. She'll ask questions.'

'You leave my daughter to me. Joan will do as I say—for a while at least. Now, let's get going.'

Johnny went back to Hayden's Chevrolet, turned it laboriously around and headed for home with Joan beside him. Gripping the wheel, he grimly staved off her questions, stopping them finally, with, 'Ask your father when he gets home. He'll tell you about it.'

Joan Hayden crouched miserably in her seat. A fine end, this was, to a romantic date.

After the Chevrolet disappeared, Lee Hayden said, 'Well, we might as well get it over with. You take the arms—I'll grab the feet here, and we'll drop it in the back seat.'

Sam Carter shuddered. 'I'll open the trunk. I wouldn't want to drive back with this thing in the seat behind me—even if it is dead.' He went back and opened the trunk and returned to lift his share of the burden. There was a loathsome, cold, damp softness to the skin that made him shudder as he gripped the arms. There was little weight, however, and they soon had the monstrosity locked in the trunk.

As Sam drove, quiet and sober, Lee Hayden sat staring ahead, leaning tensely forward, as though already reaching for the money that would soon be his. He said, 'Look, Sam—this thing is big—real big.'

'You said that before.'

'But now I get to thinking and I realize the potential. The hell with stopping at Sioux City. I'll head straight to Chicago. And we don't have to ring anyone else in on it.'

'Better be careful. We don't know anything about exploitation.'

'The newspaper men take care of that after they see the thing. They'll give us all the publicity we need. We'll rent a theater in Chicago and do some advertising—'

'They'll laugh at us. They'll think it's a racket.'

'Of course they will—until they see it. Until the newspaper men see it. Then we'll have to rent the stadium.'

'I hope we don't get into any trouble with the government over this thing.'

'How can we? We aren't violating any law. And who can blame us for trying to make a dollar? When they ask us about it we'll tell them.'

'They'll nail us for not reporting an accident,' Sam said, smiling weakly.

Lee Hayden laughed and slapped his friend on the shoulder. 'Good man! I knew you'd be smart and see it my way. What right have we got to turn down money?'

Johnny was home and waiting when they got there. Sam drove straight into the garage. Johnny said, 'I was trying to figure what we'd do with the thing, Dad, so I emptied the deep freeze in the basement. I put everything I could into the refrigerator in the kitchen and just left the rest of the stuff out.'

'Good boy,' Lee said heartily. 'That's using your head. What's a little spoiled food when we're on the cash end of a deal like this?'

They carried the feather-light, green body to the basement under cover of the darkness and laid it to rest in the freezer. Then they went into the kitchen where Sam made coffee and they sat planning their strategy.

'Don't think we ought to rush into this thing,' Lee Hayden said. 'We've got to be kind of careful.'

This surprised Sam Carter. 'How come? You were in such an all-fired hurry—'

'But there's angles. It's practically morning, and if I go kiting off to Chicago after being out all night, the wife's going to start wondering. There'll be rumors all over town. I've got to talk to that girl of mine, too. Keep her quiet until we get this thing rolling.'

Lee Hayden had changed. With something to get his teeth into, he'd assumed leadership in an impressive manner. Sam said, 'All right. Whatever you say, but I'm still a little nervous about—'

'Now take it easy! I tell you everything's going to be all right. You two get some sleep and I'll give you a ring.'

Sam Carter went to bed, but sleep would not come. He lay staring at the ceiling, thinking of the horror that rested in the deep freeze in the basement. The fact that the thing was dead brought little comfort. He had been lying wide-eyed for perhaps an hour, when he heard the noise. He stiffened, strained his ears. The sound came again. No doubt now. From the basement. He got up and clawed for the lamp at his bedside when the door opened. The light snapped on to reveal Johnny's pale, frightened face.

They stared at each other for a long moment. Then Johnny whispered, 'Did you hear it, Dad? From downstairs. It—'

'Lee, I'll bet. He couldn't sleep and came back for another look. Let's go see.'

'He wouldn't do that. You know what I think? It wasn't dead! The thing was still alive and now it's come to and it's prowling the basement. What are we going to do, Dad? We don't know anything about it. Maybe it's dangerous—deadly—'

'Now don't get excited. I'm sure it's Lee.' Sam picked up the phone and dialed. They waited tensely as another of the rattling sounds came from the basement. Then Lee Hayden's voice. 'Hello.'

'Lee—Lee, for God's sake. Get over here! There's trouble. The thing's come alive.'

Lee Hayden didn't even bother to answer. Sam heard the phone slammed down. He pulled on his pants and had just finished with his shoes when the front gate slammed and there were running footsteps on the walk. They met Lee as he came in the front door. 'What's wrong?' he snapped. 'What's happened?'

'There's someone down there,' Johnny said. 'We thought maybe it was you—'

'What would I be doing down there? Why didn't you go find out?'

'Then maybe—maybe the thing came alive.'

'And you didn't check? Do you realize what it would cost us if it got away?'

'But it may be dangerous.'

'Nonsense, but if it did come to, it's ten times more valuable.' Lee was already at the basement door. He went fearlessly down the steps, Sam and Johnny Carter following behind with more caution.

At the foot of the stairs, Lee stopped dead. He pointed. The freezer cover was lifted back. Lee rushed across and looked in. 'It's empty,' he moaned. 'It got away.'

He turned toward the open door leading into the backyard. 'Come on—we've got to catch it—got to get it back!' He dived out into the darkness. Sam, following, snatched a flashlight off its hook by the door.

In the yard, he bumped hard into Lee Hayden, who had stopped suddenly. 'The garage,' Lee whispered hoarsely. 'The side door. It's open!'

Sam flashed the light and the three of them walked softly forward. 'Maybe somebody's just trying to steal it,' Johnny whispered.

Then Sam snapped on the garage light and no one did any more talking.

There were six of the things present. Two of them were carrying the body from the freezer. The other four carried peculiar tubes in their hands, somewhat smaller than Sam's flashlight. And if the creatures were repulsive when dead, they were bone-chilling when alive and functioning. Their cold, lidless eyes bored into the three men and Sam muttered, 'We're done for!'

The creatures regarded them with no fear whatever. There appeared to be contempt in the leering faces, and the tone of the odd, birdlike chirping with which they apparently communicated with each other, heightened Sam's feeling that they were voicing this same contempt. But something told him they were deadly. Sam breathed, 'Don't move! For God's sake, stand where you are! Don't antagonize them!' He had the same feeling he'd have had at facing a den of rattle-snakes; the feeling that one false move would bring out striking fangs.

The creatures seemed to discuss the three among themselves, and Sam was sure the weird squeaking that punctuated the chirpings was their form of laughter. But they made no move to kill, and Sam began to hope they were harmless.

Then he was speedily disabused of the idea. In a concerted move, they turned their small tubes on the front of the Packard. There was no sound, no heat as from a high-frequency ray, only the soft sound of metal being bent and twisted by a hand gloved in velvet. And the three men stared as the front end of the Packard twisted and writhed itself into the same disorder that would have resulted from smashing headlong into a brick wall. Then the truth dawned on Sam—or what appeared to be the truth. 'They aren't mad at us. They think the Packard did it; they're punishing the car for killing their comrade. Don't you get it?'

The creature paid no attention to the words. That emboldened Lee. He said, 'I think you're right. It's incredible! How can they be smart enough to invent and use space ships, and yet not know the car isn't responsible for the killing?'

'I don't know. Shall we back out of here? Make a break for it?'

'I think we'd better stay just as we are,' Lee said promptly.

This last proved good advice because, after demolishing the front end of the car to their satisfaction, the creatures squealed and chirped for a while, evidently voicing their satisfaction, and then trooped out into the darkness. As they moved past, each of them leered at the frozen three, squeaked a nerve-wracking farewell, and the troop was gone, carrying its dead with it.

An explosive sigh from Lee Hayden broke the silence. 'I've got a hunch we were damn lucky,' he said. 'Damn lucky to still be alive.'

'How do you think they found the house?' Johnny asked.

Sam said, 'I don't know and I don't care. I'm just glad they're gone.'

'We've got to do something about this,' Lee Hayden said with virtuous indignation. 'Alert the police. The village—the whole nation may be in danger. It's up to us to do something about it!'

Sam didn't bother to call Lee's attention to his sudden reversal. It didn't seem important now. The only important thing was to spread the word.

They left the garage and headed for the house. But, halfway up the walk, the sound of an approaching car stopped them. The car pulled up in front of the house and two uniformed men got out.

'It's the State Troopers,' Johnny shouted. 'They must have got wind of it already!'

The troopers approached swiftly. Lee began, 'Officers—' but one of them cut him off.

'We're looking for a Mr Sam Carter. We got this address and—'

'I'm Mr Carter,' Sam said. 'There's something—'

'I'll do the talking. You have a son?'

'Of course. This is my son—John Carter—'

'You have a Packard roadster?'

'Yes.'

'Was your son driving it on Garner Road last night? Near the farm of Frank Williams?'

'Why, yes. He took his girl to a dance at Storm Lake and—'

'We know all about that. How do you suppose we traced you down?'

'But why—?'

The trooper scowled. 'Did you think the body would not be found?'

'But you couldn't have—what body—?'

The second trooper snorted in disgust. 'Frank Williams' body. Where a car smashed him into a tree and killed him. From what we can find out, no one used that road last night except your son.'

Johnny stepped forward. 'You mean Frank Williams was found killed on the road?'

'That's right. Now we may be wrong of course. But the car that hit him will be pretty well smashed up. If you'd let us take a thorough look at your car—'

Sam Carter said, 'But this is absurd, officer. There was—there was—'

'Look, all we have to do is check your car. If it's not damaged—'

It dawned on Sam, now, what the green intruders had been up to— what they'd accomplished. They'd killed William—set the scene—

arranged the colossal frameup. He looked at Lee Hayden and said, 'We thought they were mad at the car! We thought—'

The trooper said, 'What are you talking about, mister?'

'Well, there was this little green man from Mars or somewhere, and Johnny hit him when—' Sam stopped talking when he saw the look on the trooper's face. Then he knew how foolish it would sound—how utterly unbelievable. He looked back at Lee Hayden and began to laugh. But there was no mirth in the sound. Only fear—and hopelessness.

Deadly City

Ivar Jorgenson

You're all alone in a deserted city. You walk down an empty street, yearning for the sight of one living face—one moving figure. Then you see a man on a corner and you know your terror has only begun.

He awoke slowly, like a man plodding knee-deep through the thick stuff of nightmares. There was no definite line between the dream-state and wakefulness. Only a dawning knowledge that he was finally conscious and would have to do something about it.

He opened his eyes, but this made no difference. The blackness remained. The pain in his head brightened and he reached up and found the big lump they'd evidently put on his head for good measure—a margin of safety.

They must have been prudent people, because the bang on the head had hardly been necessary. The spiked drink which they had given him would have felled an ox. He remembered going down into the darkness after drinking it, and of knowing what it was. He remembered the helpless feeling.

It did not worry him now. He was a philosophical person, and the fact he was still alive cancelled out the drink and its result. He thought, with savor, of the chestnut-haired girl who had watched him take the drink. She had worn a very low bodice, and that was where his eyes had been at the last moment—on the beautiful, tanned breasts—until they'd wavered and puddled into a blur and then into nothing.

The chestnut-haired girl had been nice, but now she was gone and there were more pressing problems.

He sat up, his hands behind him at the ends of stiff arms clawing into

71

long-undisturbed dust and filth. His movement stirred the dust and it rose into his nostrils.

He straightened and banged his head against a low ceiling. The pain made him sick for a minute and he sat down to regain his senses. He cursed the ceiling, as a matter of course, in an agonized whisper.

Ready to move again, he got onto his hands and knees and crawled cautiously forward, exploring as he went. His hand pushed through cobwebs and found a rough, cement wall. He went around and around. It was all cement—all solid.

Hell! They hadn't sealed him up in this place! There had been a way in so there had to be a way out. He went around again.

Then he tried the ceiling and found the opening—a wooden trap covering a four-by-four hole—covering it snugly. He pushed the trap away and daylight streamed in. He raised himself up until he was eye-level with a discarded shaving cream jar lying on the bricks of an alley. He could read the trade mark on the jar, and the slogan: 'For the Meticulous Man'.

He pulled himself up into the alley. As a result of an orderly childhood, he replaced the wooden trap and kicked the shaving cream jar against a garbage can. He rubbed his chin and looked up and down the alley.

It was high noon. An uncovered sun blazed down to tell him this.

And there was no one in sight.

He started walking toward the nearer mouth of the alley. He had been in that hole a long time, he decided. This conviction came from his hunger and the heavy growth of beard he'd sprouted. Twenty-four hours— maybe longer. That mickey must have been a lulu.

He walked out into the cross street. It was empty. No people—no cars parked at the curbs—only a cat washing its dirty face on a tenement stoop across the street. He looked up at the tenement windows. They stared back. There was an empty, deserted look about them.

The cat flowed down the front steps of the tenement and away toward the rear and he was truly alone. He rubbed his harsh chin. Must be Sunday, he thought. Then he knew it could not be Sunday. He'd gone into the tavern on a Tuesday night. That would make it five days. Too long.

He had been walking and now he was at an intersection where he could look up and down a new street. There were no cars—no people. Not even a cat.

A sign overhanging the sidewalk said: Restaurant. He went in under the sign and tried the door. It was locked. There were no lights inside. He turned away—grinning to reassure himself. Everything was all right. Just some kind of a holiday. In a big city like Chicago the people go

away on hot summer holidays. They go to the beaches and the parks
and sometimes you can't see a living soul on the streets. And of course
you can't find any cars because the people use them to drive to the
beaches and the parks and out into the country. He breathed a little easier and started walking again.

Sure—that was it. Now what the hell holiday was it? He tried to remember. He couldn't think of what holiday it could be. Maybe they'd dreamed
up a new one. He grinned at that, but the grin was a little tight and he had
to force it. He forced it carefully until his teeth showed white.

Pretty soon he would come to a section where everybody hadn't
gone to the beaches and the parks and a restaurant would be open and
he'd get a good meal.

A meal? He fumbled toward his pockets. He dug into them and found a
handkerchief and a button from his cuff. He remembered that the button
had hung loose so he'd pulled it off to keep from losing it. He hadn't lost
the button, but everything else was gone. He scowled. The least they
could have done was to leave a man eating money.

He turned another corner—into another street—and it was like the one
before. No cars—no people—not even any cats.

Panic welled up. He stopped and whirled around to look behind him.
No one was there. He walked in a tight circle, looking in all directions.
Windows stared back at him—eyes that didn't care where everybody had
gone or when they would come back. The windows could wait. The windows were not hungry. Their heads didn't ache. They weren't scared.

He began walking and his path veered outward from the sidewalk until
he was in the exact center of the silent street. He walked down the worn
white line. When he got to the next corner he noticed that the traffic signals were not working. Black, empty eyes.

His pace quickened. He walked faster—ever faster until he was trot-
ting on the brittle pavement, his sharp steps echoing against the buildings. Faster. Another corner. And he was running, filled with panic,
down the empty street.

The girl opened her eyes and stared at the ceiling. The ceiling was a
blur but it began to clear as her mind cleared. The ceiling became a surface of dirty, cracked plaster and there was a feeling of dirt and squalor
in her mind.

It was always like that at these times of awakening, but doubly bitter
now, because she had never expected to awaken again. She reached
down and pulled the wadded sheet from beneath her legs and spread it
over them. She looked at the bottle on the shabby bed-table. There were

three sleeping pills left in it. The girl's eyes clouded with resentment. You'd think seven pills would have done it. She reached down and took the sheet in both hands and drew it taut over her stomach. This was a gesture of frustration. Seven hadn't been enough, and here she was again—awake in the world she'd wanted to leave. Awake with the necessary edge of determination gone.

She pulled the sheet into a wad and threw it at the wall. She got up and walked to the window and looked out. Bright daylight. She wondered how long she had slept. A long time, no doubt.

Her naked thigh pressed against the windowsill and her bare stomach touched the dirty pane. Naked in the window, but it didn't matter, because it gave onto an airshaft and other windows so caked with grime as to be of no value as windows.

But even aside from that, it didn't matter. It didn't matter in the least.

She went to the washstand, her bare feet making no sound on the worn rug. She turned on the faucets, but no water came. No water, and she had a terrible thirst. She went to the door and had thrown the bolt before she remembered again that she was naked. She turned back and saw the half-empty Pepsi-Cola bottle on the floor beside the bed table. Someone else had left it there—how many nights ago?—but she drank it anyhow, and even though it was flat and warm it soothed her throat.

She bent over to pick up garments from the floor and dizziness came, forcing her to the edge of the bed. After a while it passed and she got her legs into one of the garments and pulled it on.

Taking cosmetics from her bag, she went again to the washstand and tried the taps. Still no water. She combed her hair, jerking the comb through the mats and gnarls with a satisfying viciousness. When the hair fell into its natural, blond curls, she applied powder and lipstick. She went back to the bed, picked up her brassiere and began putting it on as she walked to the cracked, full-length mirror in the closet door. With the brassiere in place, she stood looking at her slim image. She assayed herself with complete impersonality.

She shouldn't look as good as she did—not after the beating she'd taken. Not after the long nights and the days and the years, even though the years did not add up to very many.

I could be someone's wife, she thought, with wry humor. I could be sending kids to school and going out to argue with the grocer about the tomatoes being too soft. I don't look bad at all.

She raised her eyes until they were staring into their own images in the glass and she spoke aloud in a low, wondering voice. She said, 'Who the hell am I, anyway? Who am I? A body named Linda—that's who I am. No—

that's *what* I am. A body's not a *who*—it's a *what*. One hundred and four-teen pounds of well-built blond body called Linda—model 1931—no fender dents—nice paint job. Come in and drive me away. Price tag—'

She bit into the lower lip she'd just finished reddening and turned quickly to walk to the bed and wriggle into her dress—a gray and green cotton—the only one she had. She picked up her bag and went to the door. There she stopped to turn and thumb her nose at the three sleeping pills in the bottle before she went out and closed the door after herself.

The desk clerk was away from the cubbyhole from which he presided over the lobby, and there were no loungers to undress her as she walked toward the door.

Nor was there anyone out in the street. The girl looked north and south. No cars in sight either. No buses waddling up to the curb to spew out passengers.

The girl went five doors north and tried to enter a place called Tim's Hamburger House. As the lock held and the door refused to open, she saw that there were no lights on inside—no one behind the counter. The place was closed.

She walked on down the street followed only by the lonesome sound of her own clicking heels. All the stores were closed. All the lights were out.

All the people were gone.

He was a huge man, and the place of concealment of the Chicago Avenue police station was very small—merely an indentation low in the cement wall behind two steam pipes. The big man had lain in this niche for forty-eight hours. He had slugged a man over the turn of a card in a poolroom pinochle game, had been arrested in due course, and was awaiting the disposal of his case.

He was sorry he had slugged the man. He had not had any deep hatred for him, but rather a rage of the moment that demanded violence as its outlet. Although he did not consider it a matter of any great importance, he did not look forward to the six months' jail sentence he would doubtless be given.

His opportunity to hide in the niche had come as accidentally and as suddenly as his opportunity to slug his card partner. It had come after the prisoners had been advised of the crisis and were being herded into vans for transportation elsewhere. He had snatched the opportunity without giving any consideration whatever to the crisis. Probably because he did not have enough imagination to fear anything—however terrible—which might occur in the future. And because he treasured his freedom above all else. Freedom for today, tomorrow could take care of itself.

Now, after forty-eight hours, he writhed and twisted his huge body out of the niche and onto the floor of the furnace room. His legs were numb and he found that he could not stand. He managed to sit up and was able to bend his back enough so his great hands could reach his legs and begin to massage life back into them.

So elementally brutal was this man that he pounded his legs until they were black and blue, before feeling returned to them. In a few minutes he was walking out of the furnace room through a jail house which should now be utterly deserted. But was it? He went slowly, gliding along close to the walls to reach the front door unchallenged.

He walked out into the street. It was daylight and the street was completely deserted. The man took a deep breath and grinned. 'I'll be damned,' he muttered. 'I'll be double and triple damned. They're all gone. Every damn one of them run off like rats and I'm the only one left. I'll be damned!'

A tremendous sense of exultation seized him. He clenched his fists and laughed loud, his laugh echoing up the street. He was happier than he had ever been in his quick, violent life. And his joy was that of a child locked in a pantry with a huge chocolate cake.

He rubbed a hand across his mouth, looked up the street, began walking. 'I wonder if they took all the whisky with them,' he said. Then he grinned; he was sure they had not.

He began walking in long strides toward Clark Street. In toward the still heart of the empty city.

He was a slim, pale-skinned little man, and very dangerous. He was also very clever. Eventually they would have found out, but he had been clever enough to deceive them and now they would never know. There was great wealth in his family, and with the rest of them occupied with leaving the city and taking what valuables they could on such short notice, he had been put in charge of one of the chauffeurs.

The chauffeur had been given the responsibility of getting the pale-skinned young man out of the city. But the young man had caused several delays until all the rest were gone. Then, meekly enough, he had accompanied the chauffeur to the garage. The chauffeur got behind the wheel of the last remaining car—a Cadillac sedan—and the young man had gotten into the rear seat.

But before the chauffeur could start the motor, the young man hit him on the head with a tire bar he had taken from a shelf as they had entered the garage.

The bar went deep into the chauffeur's skull with a solid sound, and thus the chauffeur found the death he was in the very act of fleeing.

The young man pulled the dead chauffeur from the car and laid him on the cement floor. He laid him down very carefully, so that he was in the exact center of a large square of outlined cement with his feet pointing straight north and his outstretched arms pointing south.

The young man placed the chauffeur's cap very carefully upon his chest, because neatness pleased him. Then he got into the car, started it, and headed east toward Lake Michigan and the downtown section.

After traveling three or four miles, he turned the car off the road and drove it into a telephone post. Then he walked until he came to some high weeds. He lay down in the weeds and waited.

He knew there would probably be a last vanguard of militia hunting for stragglers. If they saw a moving car they would investigate. They would take him into custody and force him to leave the city.

This, he felt, they had no right to do. All his life he had been ordered about—told to do this and that and the other thing. Stupid orders from stupid people. Idiots who went so far as to claim the whole city would be destroyed, just to make people do as they said. God! The ends to which stupid people would go in order to assert their wills over brilliant people.

The young man lay in the weeds and dozed off, his mind occupied with the pleasant memory of the tire iron settling into the skull of the chauffeur.

After a while he awoke and heard the cars of the last vanguard passing down the road. They stopped, inspected the Cadillac and found it serviceable. They took it with them, but they did not search the weeds along the road.

When they had disappeared toward the west, the young man came back to the road and began walking east, in toward the city.

Complete destruction in two days?

Preposterous.

The young man smiled.

The girl was afraid. For hours she had walked the streets of the empty city and the fear, strengthened by weariness, was now mounting toward terror. 'One face,' she whispered. 'Just one person coming out of a house or walking across the street. That's all I ask. Somebody to tell me what this is all about. If I can find one person, I won't be afraid any more.'

And the irony of it struck her. A few hours previously she had attempted suicide. Sick of herself and of all people, she had tried to end her own life. Therefore, by acknowledging death as the answer, she should now have no fear whatever of anything. Reconciled to crossing the bridge into death, no facet of life should have held terror for her.

But the empty city did hold terror. One face—one moving form was all she asked for.

Then, a second irony. When she saw the man at the corner of Washington and Wells, her terror increased. They saw each other at almost the same moment. Both stopped and stared. Fingers of panic ran up the girl's spine. The man raised a hand and the spell was broken. The girl turned and ran, and there was more terror in her than there had been before.

She knew how absurd this was, but still she ran blindly. What had she to fear? She knew all about men; all the things men could do they had already done to her. Murder was the ultimate, but she was fresh from a suicide attempt. Death should hold no terrors for her.

She thought of these things as the man's footsteps sounded behind her and she turned into a narrow alley seeking a hiding place. She found none and the man turned in after her.

She found a passageway, entered with the same blindness which had brought her into the alley. There was a steel door at the end and a brick lying by the sill. The door was locked. She picked up the brick and turned. The man skidded on the filthy alley surface as he turned into the areaway.

The girl raised the brick over her head. 'Keep away! Stay away from me!'

'Wait a minute! Take it easy. I'm not going to hurt you!'

'Get away!'

Her arm moved downward. The man rushed in and caught her wrist. The brick went over his shoulder and the nails of her other hand raked his face. He seized her without regard for niceties and they went to the ground. She fought with everything she had and he methodically neutralized all her weapons—her hands, her legs, her teeth—until she could not move.

'Leave me alone. Please!'

'What's wrong with you? I'm not going to hurt you. But I'm not going to let you hit me with a brick, either!'

'What do you want? Why did you chase me?'

'Look—I'm a peaceful guy, but I'm not going to let you get away. I spent all afternoon looking for somebody. I found you and you ran away. I came after you.'

'I haven't done anything to you.'

'That's silly talk. Come on—grow up! I said I'm not going to hurt you.'

'Let me up.'

'So you can run away again? Not for a while. I want to talk to you.'

'I—I won't run. I was scared. I don't know why. You're hurting me.'

He got up—gingerly—and lifted her to her feet. He smiled, still holding both her hands. 'I'm sorry. I guess it's natural for you to be scared. My name's Frank Brooks. I just want to find out what the hell happened to this town.'

He let her withdraw her hands, but he still blocked her escape. She moved a pace backward and straightened her clothing. 'I don't know what happened. I was looking for someone too.'

He smiled again. 'And then you ran.'

'I don't know why. I guess—'

'What's your name?'

'Nora—Nora Spade.'

'You slept through it too?'

'Yes ... yes. I slept through it and came out and they were all gone.'

'Let's get out of this alley.' He preceded her out, but he waited for her when there was room for them to walk side by side, and she did not try to run away. That phase was evidently over.

'I got slipped a mickey in a tavern,' Frank Brooks said. 'Then they slugged me and put me in a hole.'

His eyes questioned. She felt their demand and said, 'I was—asleep in my hotel room.'

'They overlooked you?'

'I guess so.'

'Then you don't know anything about it?'

'Nothing. Something terrible must have happened.'

'Let's go down this way,' Frank said, and they moved toward Madison Street. He had taken her arm and she did not pull away. Rather, she walked invitingly close to him.

She said, 'It's so spooky. So ... empty. I guess that's what scared me.'

'It would scare anybody. There must have been an evacuation of some kind.'

'Maybe the Russians are going to drop a bomb.'

Frank shook his head. 'That wouldn't explain it. I mean, the Russians wouldn't let us know ahead of time. Besides, the army would be here. Everybody wouldn't be gone.'

'There's been a lot of talk about germ warfare. Do you suppose the water, maybe, has been poisoned?'

He shook his head. 'The same thing holds true. Even if they moved the people out, the army would be here.'

'I don't know. It just doesn't make sense.'

'It happened, so it has to make sense. It was something that came up all of a sudden. They didn't have much more than twenty-four hours.' He stopped suddenly and looked at her. 'We've got to get out of here!'

Nora Spade smiled for the first time, but without humor. 'How? I haven't seen one car. The buses aren't running.'

His mind was elsewhere. They had started walking again. 'Funny I didn't think of that before.'

'Think of what?'

'That anybody left in this town is a dead pigeon. The only reason they'd clear out a city would be to get away from certain death. That would mean death is here for anybody that stays. Funny. I was so busy looking for somebody to talk to that I never thought of that.'

'I did.'

'Is that what you were scared of?'

'Not particularly. I'm not afraid to die. It was something else that scared me. The aloneness, I guess.'

'We'd better start walking west—out of the city. Maybe we'll find a car or something.'

'I don't think we'll find any cars.'

He drew her to a halt and looked into her face. 'You aren't afraid at all, are you?'

She thought for a moment. 'No, I guess I'm not. Not of dying, that is. Dying is a normal thing. But I was afraid of the empty streets—nobody around. That was weird.'

'It isn't weird now?'

'Not—not as much.'

'I wonder how much time we've got?'

Nora shrugged. 'I don't know, but I'm hungry.'

'We can fix that. I broke into a restaurant a few blocks back and got myself a sandwich. I think there's still food around. They couldn't take it all with them.'

They were on Madison Street and they turned east on the south side of the street. Nora said, 'I wonder if there are any other people still here—like us?'

'I think there must be. Not very many, but a few. They would have had to clean four million people out overnight. It stands to reason they must have missed a few. Did you ever try to empty a sack of sugar? Really empty it? It's impossible. Some of the grains always stick to the sack.'

A few minutes later the wisdom of this observation was proven when they came to a restaurant with the front window broken out and saw a man and a woman sitting at one of the tables.

He was a huge man with a shock of black hair and a mouth slightly open showing a set of incredibly white teeth. He waved an arm and shouted, 'Come on in! Come on in for crissake and sit down! We got beer and roast beef and the beer's still cold. Come on in and meet Minna.'

This was different, Nora thought. Not eerie. Not weird, like seeing a man standing on a deserted street corner with no one else around. This seemed normal, natural, and even the smashed window didn't detract too much from the naturalness.

They went inside. There were chairs at the table and they sat down. The big man did not get up. He waved a hand toward his companion and said, 'This is Minna. Ain't she something? I found her sitting at an empty bar scared to death. We came to an understanding and I brought her along.' He grinned at the woman and winked. 'We came to a real understanding, didn't we, Minna?'

Minna was a completely colorless woman of perhaps thirty-five. Her skin was smooth and pale and she wore no makeup of any kind. Her hair was drawn straight back into a bun. The hair had no predominating color. It was somewhere between light brown and blond.

She smiled a little sadly, but the laugh did not cover her worn, tired look. It seemed more like a gesture of obedience than anything else. 'Yes. We came to an understanding.'

'I'm Jim Wilson,' the big man boomed. 'I was in the Chicago Avenue jug for slugging a guy in a card game. They kind of overlooked me when they cleaned the joint out.' He winked again. 'I kind of helped them overlook me. Then I found Minna.' There was tremendous relish in his words.

Frank started introductions which Nora Spade cut in on. 'Maybe you know what happened?' she asked.

Wilson shook his head. 'I was in the jug and they didn't tell us. They just started cleaning out the joint. There was talk in the bullpen—invasion or something. Nobody knew for sure. Have some beer and meat.'

Nora turned to the quiet Minna. 'Did you hear anything?'

'Naw,' Wilson said with a kind of affectionate contempt. 'She don't know anything about it. She lived in some attic dump and was down with a sore throat. She took some pills or something and when she woke up they were gone.'

'I went to work and—' Minna began, but Wilson cut her off.

'She swabs out some joints on Chicago Avenue for a living and that was how she happened to be sitting in that tavern. It's payday, and Minna was waiting for her dough!' He exploded into laughter and slapped the table with a huge hand. 'Can you beat that? Waiting for her pay at a time like this.'

Frank Brooks set down his beer bottle. The beer was cold and it tasted good. 'Have you met anybody else? There must be some other people around.'

'Uh-uh. Haven't met anybody but Minna.' He turned his eyes on the woman again, then got to his feet. 'Come on, Minna. You and I got to have a little conference. We got things to talk about.' Grinning, he walked toward the rear of the restaurant. Minna got up more slowly. She followed him behind the counter and into the rear of the place.

Alone with Nora, Frank said, 'You aren't eating. Want me to look for something else?'

'No—I'm not very hungry. I was just wondering—'

'Wondering about what?'

'When it will happen. When whatever is going to happen—you know what I mean.'

'I'd rather know *what's* going to happen. I hate puzzles. It's hell to have to get killed and not know what killed you.'

'We aren't being very sensible, are we?'

'How do you mean?'

'We should at least act normal.'

'I don't get it.'

Nora frowned in slight annoyance. 'Normal people would be trying to reach safety. They wouldn't be sitting in a restaurant drinking beer. We should be trying to get away. Even if it does mean walking. Normal people would be trying to get away.'

Frank stared at his bottle for a moment. 'We should be scared stiff, shouldn't we?'

It was Nora's turn to ponder. 'I'm not sure. Maybe not. I know I'm not fighting anything inside—fear, I mean. I just don't seem to care one way or another.'

'I care,' Frank replied. 'I care. I don't want to die. But we're faced with a situation, and either way it's a gamble. We might be dead before I finish this bottle of beer. If that's true, why not sit here and be comfortable? Or we might have time to walk far enough to get out of range of whatever it is that chased everybody.'

'Which way do you think it is?'

'I don't think we have time to get out of town. They cleaned it out too fast. We'd need at least four or five hours to get away. If we had that much time the army, or whoever did it, would still be around.'

'Maybe they didn't know themselves when it's going to happen.'

He made an impatient gesture. 'What difference does it make? We're in a situation we didn't ask to get in. Our luck put us here and I'm damned if I'm going to kick a hole in the ceiling and yell for help.'

Nora was going to reply, but at that moment Jim Wilson came striding out front. He wore his big grin and he carried another half-dozen bottles of beer. 'Minna'll be out in a minute,' he said. 'Women are always slower than hell.'

He dropped into a chair and snapped the cap off a beer bottle with his thumb. He held the bottle up and squinted through it, sighing gustily. 'Man! I ain't never had it so good.' He tilted the bottle in salute, and drank.

The sun was lowering in the west now, and when Minna reappeared it seemed that she materialized from the shadows, so quietly did she move. Jim Wilson opened another bottle and put it before her. 'Here—have a drink, baby.'

Obediently, she tilted the bottle and drank.

'What do you plan to do?' Frank asked.

'It'll be dark soon,' Wilson said. 'We ought to go out and try to scrounge some flashlights. I bet the power plants are dead. Probably aren't any flashlights either.'

'Are you going to stay here?' Nora asked. 'Here in the Loop?'

He seemed surprised. 'Why not? A man'd be a fool to walk out on all this. All he wants to eat and drink. No goddam cops around. The life of Reilly and I should walk out?'

'Aren't you afraid of what's going to happen?'

'I don't give a good goddam what's going to happen. What the hell! Something's always going to happen.'

'They didn't evacuate the city for nothing,' Frank said.

'You mean we can all get killed?' Jim Wilson laughed. 'Sure we can. We could have got killed last week too. We could of got batted in the can by a truck anytime we crossed the street.' He emptied his bottle, threw it accurately at a mirror over the cash register. The crash was thunderous. 'Trouble with you people, you're worry warts,' he said with an expansive grin. 'Let's go get us some flashlights so we can find our way to bed in one of those fancy hotels.'

He got to his feet and Minna arose also, a little tired, a little apprehensive, but entirely submissive. Jim Wilson said, 'Come on, baby. I sure won't want to lose *you*.' He grinned at the others. 'You guys coming?'

Frank's eyes met Nora's. He shrugged. 'Why not?' he said. 'Unless you want to start walking.'

'I'm too tired,' Nora said.

As they stepped out through the smashed window, both Nora and Frank half-expected to see other forms moving up and down Madison Street. But there was no one. Only the unreal desolation of the lonely pavement and the dark-windowed buildings.

'The biggest ghost town on earth,' Frank muttered.

Nora's hand had slipped into Frank's. He squeezed it and neither of them seemed conscious of the contact.

'I wonder,' Nora said. 'Maybe this is only one of them. Maybe all the other big cities are evacuated too.'

Jim Wilson and Minna were walking ahead. He turned. 'If you two can't sleep without finding out what's up, it's plenty easy to do.'

'You think we could find a battery radio in some store?' Frank asked.

'Hell no! They'll all be gone. But all you'd have to do is snoop around in some newspaper office. If you can read you can find out what happened.'

It seemed strange to Frank that he had not thought of this. Then he realized he hadn't tried very hard to think of anything at all. He was surprised, also, at his lack of fear. He's gone through life pretty much taking things as they came—as big a sucker as the next man—making more than his quota of mistakes and blunders. Finding himself completely alone in a deserted city for the first time in his life, he had naturally fallen prey to sudden fright. But that had gradually passed, and now he was able to accept the new reality fairly passively. He wondered if that wasn't pretty much the way of all people. New situations brought a surge of whatever emotion fitted the picture. Then the emotion subsided and the new thing became the ordinary.

This, he decided, was the manner in which humanity survived. Humanity took things as they came. Pile on enough of anything and it becomes the ordinary.

Jim Wilson had picked up a garbage box and hurled it through the window of an electric shop. The glass came down with a crash that shuddered up the empty darkening street and grumbled off into silence. Jim Wilson went inside. 'I'll see what I can find. You stay out here and watch for cops.' His laughter echoed out as he disappeared.

Minna stood waiting silently, unmoving, and somehow she reminded Frank of a dumb animal; an unreasoning creature with no mind of her own, waiting for a signal from her master. Strangely, he resented this, but at the same time could find no reason for his resentment, except the feeling that no one should appear as much a slave as Minna.

Jim Wilson reappeared in the window. He motioned to Minna. 'Come on in, baby. You and me's got to have a little conference.' His exaggerated wink was barely perceptible in the gloom as Minna stepped over the low sill into the store. 'Won't be long, folks,' Wilson said in high good humor, and the two of them vanished into the darkness beyond.

Frank Brooks glanced at Nora, but her face was turned away. He cursed softly under his breath. He said, 'Wait a minute,' and went into the store through the huge, jagged opening.

Inside, he could barely make out the counters. The place was larger than it had appeared from the outside. Wilson and Minna were nowhere about.

Frank found the counter he was looking for and pawed out several flashlights. They were only empty tubes, but he found a case of batteries in a panel compartment against the wall.

'Who's there?'

'Me. I came in for some flashlights.'

'Couldn't you wait?'

'It's getting dark.'

'You don't have to be so damn impatient.' Jim Wilson's voice was hostile and surly.

Frank stifled his quick anger. 'We'll be outside,' he said. He found Nora waiting where he'd left her. He loaded batteries into four flashlights before Jim Wilson and Minna reappeared.

Wilson's good humor was back. 'How about the Morrison or the Sherman,' he said. 'Or do you want to get real ritzy and walk up to the Drake?'

'My feet hurt,' Minna said. The woman spoke so rarely, Frank Brooks was startled by her words.

'Morrison's the closest,' Jim Wilson said. 'Let's go.' He took Minna by the arm and swung off up the street. Frank and Nora fell in behind.

Nora shivered. Frank, holding her arm, asked, 'Cold?'

'No. It's just all—unreal again.'

'I see what you mean.'

'I never expected to see the Loop dark. I can't get used to it.'

A vagrant, whispering wind picked up a scrap of paper and whirled it along the street. It caught against Nora's ankle. She jerked perceptibly and kicked the scrap away. The wind caught it again and spiralled it away into the darkness.

'I want to tell you something,' she said.

'Tell away.'

'I told you before that I slept through the—the evacuation, or whatever it was. That wasn't exactly true. I did sleep through it, but it was my fault. I put myself to sleep.'

'I don't get it.'

'I tried to kill myself. Sleeping tablets. Seven of them. They weren't enough.'

Frank said nothing while they paced off ten steps through the dark canyon that was Madison Street. Nora wondered if he had heard.

'I tried to commit suicide.'

'Why?'

'I was tired of life, I guess.'

'What do you want—sympathy?'

The sudden harshness in his voice brought her eyes around, but his face was a white blur.

'No—no, I don't think so.'

'Well, you won't get it from me. Suicide is silly. You can have troubles and all that—everybody has them—but suicide—why did you try it?'

A high, thin whine—a wordless vibration of eloquence—needled out of the darkness into their ears. The shock was like a sudden shower of ice water dashed over their bodies. Nora's fingers dug into Frank's arm, but he did not feel the cutting nails. 'We're—there's someone out there in the street!'

Twenty-Five feet ahead of where Frank and Nora stood frozen there burst the booming voice of Jim Wilson. 'What the hell was that?' And the shock was dispelled. The white circle from Wilson's flash bit out across the blackness to outline movement on the far side of the street. Then Frank Brook's light, and Nora's, went exploring.

'There's somebody over there,' Wilson bellowed. 'Hey, you! Show your face! Quit sneaking around!'

Frank's light swept an arc that clearly outlined the buildings across the street and then weakened as it swung westward. There was something or someone back there, but obscured by the dimness. He was swept by a sense of unreality again.

'Did you see them?'

Nora's light beam had dropped to her feet as though she feared to point it out into the darkness. 'I thought I saw something.'

Jim Wilson was swearing industriously. 'There was a guy over there. He ducked around the corner. Some damn fool out scrounging. Wish I had a gun.'

Frank and Nora moved ahead and the four stood in a group. 'Put out your lights,' Wilson said. 'They make good targets if the jerk's got any weapons.'

They stood in the darkness, Nora holding tightly to Frank's arm. Frank said, 'That was the damndest noise I ever heard.'

'Like a siren?' Frank thought Jim Wilson spoke hopefully, as though wanting somebody to agree with him.

'Not like any I ever heard. Not like a whistle, either. More of a moan.'

'Let's get into that goddam hotel and—'

Jim Wilson's words were cut off by a new welling-up of the melancholy howling. It had a new pattern this time. It sounded from many places; not nearer, Frank thought, than Lake Street on the north, but spreading outward and backward and growing fainter until it died on the wind.

Nora was shivering, clinging to Frank without reserve.

Jim Wilson said, 'I'll be damned if it doesn't sound like a signal of some kind.'

'Maybe it's a language—a way of communication.'

'But who the hell's communicating?'

'How would I know?'

'We best get to that hotel and bar a few doors. A man can't fight in the dark—and nothing to fight with.'

They hurried up the street, but it was all different now. Gone was the illusion of being alone; gone the sense of solitude. Around them the ghost town had come suddenly alive. Sinister forces more frightening than the previous solitude had now to be reckoned with.

'Something's happened—something in the last few minutes,' Nora whispered.

Frank leaned close as they crossed the street to the dark silent pile that was the Morrison hotel. 'I think I know what you mean.'

'It's as though there was no one around and then, suddenly, they came.'

'I think they came and went away again.'

'Did you actually *see* anyone when you flashed your light?'

'No—I can't say positively that I did. But I got the impression there were figures out there—at least dozens of them—and that they moved back away from the light. Always just on the edge of it.'

'I'm scared, Frank.'

'So am I.'

'Do you think it could all be imagination?'

'Those moans? Maybe the first one—I've heard of people imagining sounds. But not the last ones. And besides, we all heard them.'

Jim Wilson, utterly oblivious of any subtle emanations in the air, boomed out in satisfaction: 'We don't have to bust the joint open. The revolving door works.'

'Then maybe we ought to be careful,' Frank said. 'Maybe somebody else is around here.'

'Could be. We'll find out.'

'Why are we afraid?' Nora whispered.

'It's natural, isn't it?' Frank melted the beam of his light with that of Jim Wilson. The white finger pierced the darkness inside. Nothing moved.

'I don't see why it should be. If there are people in there they must be as scared as we are.'

Nora was very close to him as they entered.

The lobby seemed deserted. The flashlight beams scanned the empty chairs and couches. The glass of the deserted cages threw back reflections.

'The keys are in there,' Frank said. He vaulted the desk and scanned the numbers under the pigeon holes.

'We'd better stay down low,' Jim Wilson said. 'Damned if I'm going to climb to the penthouse.'

'How about the fourth floor?'

'That's plenty high enough.'

Frank came out with a handful of keys. 'Odd numbers,' he said. 'Four in a row.'

'Well I'll be damned,' Jim Wilson muttered. But he said no more and they climbed the stairs in silence. They passed the quiet dining rooms and banquet halls, and by the time they reached the fourth floor the doors giving off the corridors had assumed a uniformity.

'Here they are.' He handed a key to Wilson. 'That's the end one.' He said nothing as he gave Minna her key, but Wilson grunted, 'For crissake!' in a disgusted voice, took Minna's key and threw it on the floor.

Frank and Nora watched as Wilson unlocked his door. Wilson turned. 'Well, goodnight all. If you get goosed by any spooks, just yell.'

Minna followed him without a word and the door closed.

Frank handed Nora her key. 'Lock your door and you'll be safe. I'll check the room first.' He unlocked the door and flashed his light inside. Nora was close behind him as he entered. He checked the bathroom. 'Everything clear. Lock your door and you'll be safe.'

'Frank.'

'Yes?'

'I'm afraid to stay alone.'

'You mean you want me to—'

'There are two beds here.'

His reply was slow in coming. Nora didn't wait for it. Her voice rose to the edge of hysteria. 'Quit being so damned righteous. Things have changed! Can't you realize that? What does it matter how or where we sleep? Does the world care? Will it make a damn bit of difference to the world whether I strip stark naked in front of you?' A sob choked in her throat. 'Or would that outrage your morality.'

He moved toward her, stopped six inches away. 'It isn't that. For God's sake! I'm no saint. It's just that I thought you—'

'I'm plain scared, and I don't want to be alone. To me that's all that's important.'

Her face was against his chest and his arms went around her. But her own hands were fists held together against him until he could feel her knuckles, hard, against his chest. She was crying.

'Sure,' Frank said. 'I'll stay with you. Now take it easy. Everything's going to be all right.'

Nora sniffled without bothering to reach for her handkerchief. 'Stop lying. You know it isn't going to be all right.'

Frank was at somewhat of a loss. This flareup of Nora's was entirely unexpected. He eased toward the place the flashlight had shown the bed to be. Her legs hit its edge and she sat down.

'You—you want me to sleep in the other one?' he asked.

'Of course,' Nora replied with marked bitterness. 'I'm afraid you wouldn't be very comfortable in with me.'

There was a time of silence. Frank took off his jacket, shirt and trousers. It was funny, he thought. He'd spent his money, been drugged, beaten and robbed as a result of one objective—to get into a room alone with a girl. And a girl not nearly as nice as Nora at that. Now, here he was alone with a real dream, and he was tongue-tied. It didn't make sense. He shrugged. Life was crazy sometimes.

He heard the rustle of garments and wondered how much Nora was taking off. Then he dropped his trousers, forgotten, to the floor. 'Did you hear that?'

'Yes. It's that—'

Frank went to the window, raised the sash. The moaning sound came in louder, but it was from the distance. 'I think that's out around Evanston.'

Frank felt a warmth on his cheek and he realized Nora was by his side, leaning forward. He put an arm around her and they stood unmoving in complete silence. Although their ears were straining for the sound coming down from the north, Frank could not be oblivious of the warm flesh under his hand.

Nora's breathing was soft against his cheek. She said, 'Listen to how it rises and falls. It's almost as though they were using it to talk with. The inflection changes.'

'I think that's what it is. It's coming from a lot of different places. It stops in some places and starts in others.'

'It's so—weird.'

'Spooky,' Frank said, 'but in a way it makes me feel better.'

'I don't see how it could.' Nora pressed closer to him.

'It does though, because of what I was afraid of. I had it figured out that the city was going to blow up—that a bomb had been planted that they couldn't find, or something like that. Now, I'm pretty sure it's something else. I'm willing to bet we'll be alive in the morning.'

Nora thought that over in silence. 'If that's the way it is—if some kind of invaders are coming down from the north—isn't it stupid to stay here? Even if we are tired we ought to be trying to get away from them.'

'I was thinking the same thing. I'll go and talk to Wilson.'

They crossed the room together and he left her by the bed and went on to the door. Then he remembered he was in his shorts and went back and got his trousers. After he'd put them on, he wondered why he'd bothered. He opened the door.

Something warned him—some instinct—or possibly his natural fear and caution coincided with the presence of danger. He heard the footsteps on the carpeting down the hall—soft, but unmistakably footsteps. He called, 'Wilson—Wilson—that you?'

The creature outside threw caution to the winds. Frank sensed rather than heard a body hurtling toward the door. A shrill, mad laughter raked his ears and the weight of a body hit the door.

Frank drew strength from pure panic as he threw his weight against the panel, but perhaps an inch or two from the latch the door wavered from opposing strength. Through the narrow opening he could feel the hoarse breath of exertion in his face. Insane giggles and curses sounded through the black stillness.

Frank had the wild conviction he was losing the battle, and added strength came from somewhere. He heaved and there was a scream and he knew he had at least one finger caught between the door and the jamb. He threw his weight against the door with frenzied effort and heard the squash of the finger. The voice kited up to a shriek of agony, like that of a wounded animal.

Even with his life at stake, and the life of Nora, Frank could not deliberately slice the man's fingers off. Even as he fought the urge, and called himself a fool, he allowed the door to give slightly inward. The hand was jerked to safety.

At that moment another door opened close by and Jim Wilson's voice boomed: 'What the hell's going on out here?'

Simultaneous with this, racing footsteps receded down the hall and from the well of the stairway came a whining cry of pain.

'Jumping jees!' Wilson bellowed. 'We got company. We ain't alone!'

'He tried to get into my room.'

'You shouldn't have opened the door. Nora okay?'

'Yeah. She's all right.'

'Tell her to stay in her room. And you do the same. We'd be crazy to go after that coot in the dark. He'll keep 'til morning.'

Frank closed the door, double-locked it and went back to Nora's bed. He could hear a soft sobbing.

He reached down and pulled back the covers and the sobbing came louder. Then he was down on the bed and she was in his arms.

She cried until the panic subsided, while he held her and said nothing. After a while she got control of herself. 'Don't leave me, Frank,' she begged. 'Please don't leave me.'

He stroked her shoulder. 'I won't,' he whispered.

They lay for a long time in utter silence, each seeking strength in the other's closeness. The silence was finally broken by Nora.

'Frank?'

'Yes.'

'Do you want me?'

He did not answer.

'If you want me you can have me, Frank.'

Frank said nothing.

'I told you today that I tried to commit suicide. Remember?'

'I remember.'

'That was the truth. I did it because I was tired of everything. Because I've made a terrible mess of things. I didn't want to go on living.'

He remained silent, holding her.

As she spoke again, her voice sharpened. 'Can't you understand what I'm telling you? I'm no good! I'm just a bum! Other men have had me! Why shouldn't you? Why should you be cheated out of what other men have had?'

He remained silent. After a few moments, Nora said, 'For God's sake, talk! Say something!'

'How do you feel about it now? Will you try again to kill yourself the next chance you get?'

'No—no, I don't think I'll ever try it again.'

'Then things must look better.'

'I don't know anything about that. I just don't want to do it now.'

She did not urge him this time and he was slow in speaking. 'It's kind of funny. It really is. Don't get the idea I've got morals. I haven't. I've had my share of women. I was working on one the night they slipped me the mickey—the night before I woke up to this tomb of a city. But now—tonight—it's kind of different. I feel like I want to protect you. Is that strange?'

'No,' she said quietly. 'I guess not.'

They lay there silently, their thoughts going off into the blackness of the sepulchral night. After a long while, Nora's even breathing told him she was asleep. He got up quietly, covered her, and went to the other bed.

But before he slept, the weird wailings from out Evanston way came again—rose and fell in that strange conversational cadence—then died away into nothing.

Frank awoke to the first fingers of daylight. Nora still slept. He dressed and stood for some moments with his hand on the door knob. Then he threw the bolt and cautiously opened the door.

The hallway was deserted. At this point it came to him forcibly that he was not a brave man. All his life, he realized, he had avoided physical danger and had refused to recognize the true reason for so doing. He had classified himself as a man who dodged trouble through good sense; that the truly civilized person went out of his way to keep the peace.

He realized now that that attitude was merely salve for his ego. He faced the empty corridor and did not wish to proceed further. But stripped of the life-long alibi, he forced himself to walk through the doorway, close the door softly, and move toward the stairs.

He paused in front of the door behind which Jim Wilson and Minna were no doubt sleeping. He stared at it wistfully. It certainly would not be a mark of cowardice to get Jim Wilson up under circumstances such as these. In fact, he would be a fool not to do so.

Stubbornness forbade such a move, however. He walked softly toward the place where the hallway dead-ended and became a cross-corridor. He made the turn carefully, pressed against one wall. There was no one in sight. He got to the stairway and started down.

His muscles and nerves tightened with each step. When he reached the lobby he was ready to jump sky-high at the drop of a pin.

But no one dropped any pins, and he reached the modernistic glass doorway to the drugstore with only silence screaming in his ears. The door was unlocked. One hinge squeaked slightly as he pushed the door inward.

It was in the drugstore that Frank found signs of the fourth-floor intruder. An inside counter near the prescription department was red with blood. Bandages and first-aid supplies had been unboxed and thrown around with abandon. Here the man had no doubt administered to his smashed hand.

But where had he gone? Asleep, probably, in one of the rooms upstairs. Frank wished fervently for a a weapon. Beyond doubt there was not a gun left in the Loop.

A gun was not the only weapon ever created, though, and Frank searched the store and found a line of pocket knives still in neat boxes near the perfume counter.

He picked four of the largest and found, also, a wooden-handled, lead-tipped bludgeon, used evidently for cracking ice.

Thus armed, he went out through the revolving door. He walked through streets that were like death under the climbing sun. Through streets and canyons of dead buildings upon which the new daylight had failed to shed life or diminish the terror of the night past.

At Dearborn he found the door to the Tribune Public Service Building locked. He used the ice breaker to smash a glass door panel. The crash of the glass on the cement was an explosion in the screaming silence. He went inside. Here the sense of desolation was complete; brought sharply to focus, probably, by the pigeon holes filled with letters behind the want-ad counter. Answers to a thousand and one queries, waiting patiently for someone to come after them.

Before going to the basement and the back files of the Chicago Tribune, Frank climbed to the second floor and found what he thought might be there—a row of teletype machines with a file-board hooked to the side of each machine.

Swiftly, he stripped the copy sheets off each board, made a bundle of them and went back downstairs. He covered the block back to the hotel at a dog-trot, filled with a sudden urge to get back to the fourth floor as soon as possible.

He stopped in the drugstore and filled his pockets with soap, a razor, shaving cream and face lotion. As an afterthought, he picked up a lavish cosmetic kit that retailed, according to the price tag, for thirty-eight dollars plus tax.

He let himself back into the room and closed the door softly. Nora rolled over, exposing a shoulder and one breast. The breast held his gaze for a full minute. Then a feeling of guilt swept him and he went into the bathroom and closed the door.

Luckily, a supply tank on the roof still contained water and Frank was able to shower and shave. Dressed again, he felt like a new man. But he regretted not hunting up a haberdashery shop and getting himself a clean shirt.

Nora had still not awakened when he came out of the bathroom. He went to the bed and stood looking down at her for some time. Then he touched her shoulder.

'Wake up. It's morning.'

Nora stirred. Her eyes opened, but Frank got the impression she did not really awaken for several seconds. Her eyes went to his face, to the window, back to his face.

'What time is it?'

'I don't know. I think it's around eight o'clock.'

Nora stretched both arms luxuriously. As she sat up, her slip fell back into place and Frank got the impression she hadn't even been aware of her partial nudity.

She stared up at him, clarity dawning in her eyes. 'You're all cleaned up.'

'I went downstairs and got some things.'

'You went out—alone?'

'Why not. We can't stay in here all day. We've got to hit the road and get out of here. We've overshot our luck already.'

'But that—that man in the hall last night! You shouldn't have taken a chance.'

'I didn't bump into him. I found the place he fixed his hand, down in the drugstore.'

Frank went to the table and came back with the cosmetic set. He put it in Nora's lap. 'I brought this up for you.'

Surprise and true pleasure were mixed in her expression. 'That was very nice. I think I'd better get dressed.'

Frank turned toward the window where he had left the bundle of tele-type clips. 'I've got a little reading to do.'

As he sat down, he saw, from the corner of his eye, a flash of slim brown legs moving toward the bathroom. Just inside the door, Nora turned. 'Are Jim Wilson and Minna up yet?'

'I don't think so.'

Nora's eyes remained on him. 'I think you were very brave to go down-stairs alone. But it was a foolish thing to do. You should have waited for Jim Wilson.'

'You're right about it being foolish. But I had to go.'

'Why?'

'Because I'm not brave at all. Maybe that was the reason.'

Nora left the bathroom door open about six inches and Frank heard the sound of the shower. He sat with the papers in his hand wondering about the water. When he had gone to the bathroom the thought had never oc-curred to him. It was natural that it should. Now he wondered about it. Why was it still running? After a while he considered the possibility of the supply tank on the roof.

Then he wondered about Nora. It was strange how he could think about her personally and impersonally at the same time. He remembered her words of the previous night. They made her—he shied from the term. What was the old cliche? A woman of easy virtue.

What made a woman of that type, he wondered. Was it something inherent in their makeup? That partially opened door was symbolic some-how. He was sure that many wives closed the bathroom door upon their husbands; did it without thinking, instinctively. He was sure Nora had left it partially open without thinking. Could a behavior pattern be traced from such an insignificant thing?

He wondered about his own attitude toward Nora. He had drawn away from what she'd offered him during the night. And yet from no sense of disgust. There was certainly far more about Nora to attract than to repel.

Morals, he realized dimly, were imposed—or at least functioned—for the protection of society. With society gone—vanished overnight—did the moral code still hold?

If and when they got back among masses of people, would his feelings toward Nora change? He thought not. He would marry her, he told him-self firmly, as quick as he'd marry any other girl. He would not hold what she was against her. I guess I'm just fundamentally unmoral myself, he thought, and began reading the news clips.

There was a knock on the door accompanied by the booming voice of Jim Wilson. 'You in there! Ready for breakfast?'

Frank got up and walked toward the door. As he did so, the door to the bathroom closed.

Jim Wilson wore a two-day growth of beard and it didn't seem to bother him at all. As he entered the room he rubbed his hands together in great gusto. 'Well, where'll we eat, folks? Let's pick the classiest restaurant in town. Nothing but the best for Minna here.'

He winked broadly as Minna, expressionless and silent, followed him in exactly as a shadow would have followed him and sat primly down in a straight-backed chair by the wall.

'We'd better start moving south,' Frank said, 'and not bother about breakfast.'

'Getting scared?' Jim Wilson asked.

'You're damn right I'm scared—now. We're right in the middle of a big no-man's-land.'

'I don't get you.'

At that moment the bathroom door opened and Nora came out. Jim Wilson forgot about the question he'd asked. He let forth a loud whistle of appreciation. Then he turned his eyes on Frank and his thought was crys-tal clear. He was envying Frank the night just passed.

A sudden irritation welled up in Frank Brooks, a distinct feeling of dis-gust. 'Let's start worrying about important things—our lives. Or don't you consider your life very important?'

Jim Wilson seemed puzzled. 'What the hell's got into you? Didn't you sleep good?'

'I went down the block this morning and found some teletype machines. I've just been reading the reports.'

'What about that guy that tried to get into your room last night?'

'I didn't see him. I didn't see anybody. But I know why the city's been cleaned out.' Frank went back to the window and picked up the sheaf on clips he had gone through. Jim Wilson sat down on the edge of the bed, frowning. Nora followed Frank and perched on the edge of the chair he dropped into.

'The city going to blow up?' Wilson asked.

'No. We've been invaded by some form of alien life.'

'Is that what the papers said?'

'It was the biggest and fastest mass evacuation ever attempted. I pieced the reports together. There was hell popping around here during the two days we—we waited it out.'

'Where did they all go?' Nora asked.

'South. They've evacuated a forty-mile strip from the lake west. The first Terran defense line is set up in northern Indiana.'

'What do you mean—Terra.'

'It's a word that means Earth—this planet. The invaders came from some other planet, they think—at least from no place on Earth.'

'That's the silliest damn thing I ever heard of,' Wilson said.

'A lot of people probably thought the same thing,' Frank replied. 'Flying saucers were pretty common. Nobody thought they were anything and nobody paid much attention. Then they hit—three days ago—and wiped out every living soul in three little southern Michigan towns. From there they began spreading out. They—'

Each of them heard the sound at the same time. A faint rumble, increasing swiftly into high thunder. They moved as one to the window and saw four jet planes, in formation, moving across the sky from the south.

'There they come,' Frank said. 'The fight's started. Up to now the army has been trying to get set, I suppose.

Nora said, 'Is there any way we can hail them? Let them know—'

Her words were cut off by the horror of what happened. As they watched, the plane skimmed low across the Loop. At a point, approximately over Lake Street, Frank estimated, the planes were annihilated. There was a flash of blue fire coming in like jagged lightning to form four balls of fire around the planes. The fire balls turned, almost instantly, into globes of white smoke that drifted lazily away.

And that was all. But the planes vanished completely.

'What happened?' Wilson muttered. 'Where'd they go?'

'It was as if they hit a wall,' Nora said, her voice hushed with awe.

'I think that *was* what happened,' Frank said. 'The invaders have some kind of a weapon that holds us helpless. Otherwise the army wouldn't have established this no-man's-land and pulled out. The reports said we have them surrounded on all sides with the help of the lake. We're trying to keep them isolated.'

Jim Wilson snorted. 'It looks like we've got them right where they want us.'

'Anyhow, we're damn fools to stick around here. We'd better head south.'

Wilson looked wistfully about the room. 'I guess so, but it's a shame—walking away from all this.'

Nora was staring out the window, a small frown on her face. 'I wonder who they are and where they came from?'

'The teletype releases were pretty vague on that.'

She turned quickly. 'There's something peculiar about them. Something really strange.'

'What do you mean?'

'Last night when we were walking up the street. It must have been these invaders we heard. They must have been across the street. But they didn't act like invaders. They seemed—well, scared. I got the feeling they ran from us in panic. And they haven't been back.'

Wilson said, 'They may not have been there at all. Probably our imaginations.'

'I don't think so,' Frank cut in. 'They were there and then they were gone. I'm sure of it.'

'Those wailing noises. They were certainly signalling to each other. Do you suppose that's the only language they have?' Nora walked over and offered the silent Minna a cigarette. Minna refused with a shake of her head.

'I wish we knew what they looked like,' Frank said. 'But let's not sit here talking. Let's get going.'

Jim Wilson was scowling. There was a marked sullenness in his manner. 'Not Minna and me. I've changed my mind. I'm sticking here.'

Frank blinked in surprise. 'Are you crazy? We've run our luck out already. Did you see what happened to those planes?'

'The hell with the planes. We've got it good here. This I like. I like it a lot. We'll stay.'

'Okay,' Frank replied hotly, 'but talk for yourself. You're not making Minna stay!'

Wilson's eyes narrowed. 'I'm not? Look, buster—how about minding your own goddam business?'

The vague feelings of disgust Frank had had now crystallized into words. 'I won't let you get away with it! You think I'm blind? Hauling her into the back room every ten minutes! Don't you think I know why? You're nothing but a damn sex maniac! You've got her terrorized until she's afraid to open her mouth. She goes with us!'

Jim Wilson was on his feet. His face blazed with rage. The urge to kill was written in the crouch of his body and the twist of his mouth. 'You goddam nosey little squirt. I'll—'

Wilson charged across the short, intervening distance. His arms went out in a clutching motion.

But Frank Brooks wasn't full of knockout drops this time, and with a clear head he was no pushover. Blinded with rage, Jim Wilson *was* a pushover. Frank stepped in between his outstretched arms and slugged him squarely on top of the head with the telephone. Wilson went down like a felled steer.

The scream came from Minna as she sprang across the room. She had turned from a colorless rag doll into a tigress. She hit Frank square in the belly with small fists at the end of stiff, outstretched arms. The full force of her charge was behind the fists, and Frank went backward over the bed.

Minna did not follow up her attack. She dropped to the floor beside Jim Wilson and took his huge head in her lap. 'You killed him,' she sobbed. 'You—you murderer! You killed him! You had no right!'

Frank sat wide-eyed. 'Minna! For God's sake! I was helping you. I did it for you!'

'Why don't you mind your business? I didn't ask you to protect me. I don't need any protection—not from Jim.'

'You mean you didn't mind the way he's treated you—'

'You've killed him—killed him—' Minna raised her head slowly. She looked at Frank as though she saw him for the first time. 'You're a fool,' she said dully. 'A big fool. What right have you got to meddle with other people's affairs? Are you God or something, to run people's lives?'

'Minna—I—'

It was as though he hadn't spoken. 'Do you know what it's like to have nobody? All your life to go on and grow older without anybody? I didn't have no one and then Jim came along and wanted me.'

Frank walked close to her and bent down. She reacted like a tiger. 'Leave him alone! Leave him alone! You've done enough!'

Nonplused, Frank backed away.

'People with big noses—always sticking them in. That's you. Was that any of your business what he wanted of me? Did I complain?'

'I'm sorry, Minna. I didn't know.'

'I'd rather go into back rooms with him than stay in front rooms without nobody.'

She began to cry now. Wordlessly—soundlessly, rocking back and forth with the huge man's bloody head in her lap. 'Anytime,' she crooned. 'Anytime I would—'

The body in her arms stirred. She looked down through her tears and saw the small black eyes open. They were slightly crossed, unfocused as they were by the force of the blow. They straightened and Jim mumbled, 'What the hell—what the hell—'

Minna's time for talking seemed over. She smiled—a smile hardly perceptible, as though it was for herself alone. 'You're all right,' she said. 'That's good. You're all right.'

Jim pushed her roughly away and staggered to his feet. He stood swaying for a moment, his head turning; for all the world like a bull blinded and tormented. Then his eyes focused on Frank.

'You hit me with the goddam phone.'

'Yeah—I hit you.'

'I'm gonna kill you.'

'Look—I made a mistake.' Frank picked up the phone and backed against the wall. 'I hit you, but you were coming at me. I made a mistake and I'm sorry.'

'I'll smash your goddam skull.'

'Maybe you will,' Frank said grimly. 'But you'll work for it. It won't come easy.'

A new voice bit across the room. 'Cut it out. I'll do the killing. That's what I like best. Everybody quiet down.'

They turned and saw a slim, pale-skinned young man in the open doorway. The door had opened quietly and no one had heard it. Now the pale young man was standing in the room with a small, nickle-plated revolver in his right hand.

The left hand was close down at his side. It was swathed generously in white bandage.

The young man chuckled. 'The last four people in the world were in a room,' he said, 'and there was a knock on the door.'

His chuckle deepened to one of pure merriment. 'Only there wasn't a knock. A man just walked in with a gun that made him boss.'

No one moved. No one spoke. The man waited, then went on: 'My name is Leroy Davis. I lived out west and I always had a keeper because they said I wasn't quite right. They wanted me to pull out with the rest of them, but I slugged my keeper and here I am.'

'Put down the gun and we'll talk it over,' Frank said. 'We're all in this together.'

'No, we aren't. I've got a gun, so that makes me top man. You're all in it together, but I'm not. I'm the boss, and which one of you tried to cut my hand off last night.'

'You tried to break in here yelling and screaming like a madman. I held the door. What else could I do?'

'It's all right. I'm not mad. My type—we may be nuts, but we never hold a grudge. I can't remember much about last night. I found some whisky in a place down the street and whisky drives me nuts. I don't know what I'm doing when I drink whisky. They say once about five years ago I got drunk and killed a little kid, but I don't remember.'

Nobody spoke.

'I got out of it. They got me out some way. High priced lawyers got me out. Cost my dad a pile.'

Hysteria had been piling up inside of Nora. She had held it back, but now a little of it spurted out from between her set teeth. 'Do something, somebody. *Isn't anybody going to do anything?*'

Leroy Davis blinked at her. 'There's nothing they can do, honey,' he said in a kindly voice. 'I've got the gun. They'd be crazy to try anything.'

Nora's laugh was like the rattle of dry peas. She sat down on the bed and looked up at the ceiling and laughed. 'It's crazy. It's all so crazy! We're sitting here in a doomed city with some kind of alien invaders all around us and we don't know what they look like. They haven't hurt us at all. We don't even know what they look like. We don't worry a bit about them because we're too busy trying to kill each other.'

Frank Brooks took Nora by the arm. 'Stop it! Quit laughing like that!'

Nora shook him off. 'Maybe we need someone to take us over. It's all pretty crazy!'

'Stop it.'

Nora's eyes dulled down as she looked at Frank. She dropped her head and seemed a little ashamed of herself. 'I'm sorry. I'll be quiet.'

Jim Wilson had been standing by the wall looking first at the newcomer, then back at Frank Brooks. Wilson seemed confused as to who his true enemy really was. Finally he took a step toward Leroy Davis.

Frank Brooks stopped him with a motion, but kept his eyes on Davis. 'Have you seen anybody else?'

Davis regarded Frank with long, careful consideration. His eyes were bright and birdlike. They reminded Frank of a squirrel's eyes. Davis said,

'I bumped into an old man out on Halstead Street. He wanted to know where everybody had gone. He asked me, but I didn't know.'

'What happened to the old man?' Nora asked. She asked the question as though dreading to do it; but as though some compulsion forced her to speak.

'I shot him,' Davis said cheerfully. 'It was a favor, really. Here was this old man staggering down the street with nothing but a lot of wasted years to show for his efforts. He was no good alive, and he didn't have the courage to die.' Davis stopped and cocked his head brightly. 'You know— I think that's what's been wrong with the world. Too many people without the guts to die, and a law against killing them.'

It had now dawned upon Jim Wilson that they were faced by a maniac. His eyes met those of Frank Brooks and they were—on this point at least—in complete agreement. A working procedure sprang up, unworded, between them. Jim Wilson took a slow, casual step toward the homicidal maniac.

'You didn't see anyone else?' Frank asked.

Davis ignored the question. 'Look at it this way,' he said. 'In the old days they had Texas long horns. Thin stringy cattle that gave up meat as tough as leather. Do we have cattle like that today? No. Because we bred out the weak line.'

Frank said, 'There are some cigarettes on that table if you want one.'

Jim Wilson took another slow step toward Davis.

Davis said, 'We bred with intelligence, with a thought to what a steer was for and we produced a walking chunk of meat as wide as it is long.

'Uh-huh,' Frank said.

'Get the point? See what I'm driving at? Humans are more important than cattle, but can we make them breed intelligently? Oh, no! That interferes with damn silly human liberties. You can't tell a man he can only have two kids. It's his God-given right to have twelve when the damn moron can't support three. Get what I mean?'

'Sure—sure, I get it.'

'You better think it over, mister—and tell that fat bastard to quit sneaking up on me or I'll blow his brains all over the carpet!'

If the situation hadn't been so grim it would have appeared ludicrous. Jim Wilson, feeling success almost in his grasp, was balanced on tiptoe for a lunge. He teetered, almost lost his balance and fell back against the wall.

'Take it easy,' Frank said.

'I'll take it easy,' Davis replied. 'I'll kill every goddam one of you—' he pointed the gun at Jim Wilson, '—starting with him.'

'Now wait a minute,' Frank said. 'You're unreasonable. What right have you got to do that? What about the law of survival? You're standing there with a gun on us. You're going to kill us. Isn't it natural to try anything we can to save our own lives?'

A look of admiration brightened Davis' eyes. 'Say! I like you. You're all right. You're logical. A man can talk to you. If there's anything I like it's talking to a logical man.'

'Thanks.'

'Too bad I'm going to have to kill you. We could sit down and have some nice long talks together.'

'Why do you want to kill us?' Minna asked. She had not spoken before. In fact, she had spoken so seldom during the entire time they'd been together that her voice was a novelty to Frank. He was inclined to discount her tirade on the floor with Wilson's head in her lap. She had been a different person then. Now she had lapsed back into her old shell.

Davis regarded her thoughtfully. 'Must you have a reason?'

'You should have a reason to kill people.'

Davis said, 'All right, if it will make you any happier. I told you about killing my keeper when they tried to make me leave town. He got in the car, behind the wheel. I got into the back seat and split his skull with a tire iron.'

'What's that got to do with us?'

'Just this. Tommy was a better person than anyone of you or all of you put together. If he had to die, what right have you got to live? Is that enough of a reason for you?'

'This is all too damn crazy,' Jim Wilson roared. He was on the point of leaping at Davis and his gun.

At that moment, from the north, came a sudden crescendo of the weird invader wailings. It was louder than it had previously been but did not seem nearer.

The group froze, all ears trained upon the sound. 'They're talking again,' Nora whispered.

'Uh-huh,' Frank replied. 'But it's different this time. As if—'

'—as if they were getting ready for something,' Nora said. 'Do you suppose they're going to move south?'

Davis said, 'I'm not going to kill you here. We're going down stairs.'

The pivotal moment, hinged in Jim Wilson's mind, that could have changed the situation, had come and gone. The fine edge of additional madness that would make a man hurl himself at a loaded gun, was dulled. Leroy Davis motioned preemptorily toward Minna.

'You first—then the other babe. You walk side by side down the hall with the men behind you. Straight down to the lobby.'

They complied without resistance. There was only Jim Wilson's scowl, Frank Brooks' clouded eyes, and the white, taut look of Nora.

Nora's mind was not on the gun. It was filled with thoughts of the pale maniac who held it. He was in command. Instinctively, she felt that maniacs in command have one of but two motivations—sex and murder. Her reaction to possible murder was secondary. But what if this man insisted upon laying his hands upon her. What if he forced her into the age old thing she had done so often? Nora shuddered. But it was also in her mind to question, and be surprised at the reason for her revulsion. She visualized the hands upon her body—the old familiar things, and the taste in her mouth was one of horror.

She had never experienced such shrinkings before. Why now? Had she herself changed? Had something happened during the night that made the past a time of shame? Or was it the madman himself? She did not know.

Nora returned from her musings to find herself standing in the empty lobby. Leroy Davis, speaking to Frank, was saying. 'You look kind of tricky to me. Put your hands on your head. Lock your fingers together over your head and keep your hands there.'

Jim Wilson was standing close to the mute Minna. She had followed all the orders without any show of anger, with no outward expression. Always she had kept her eyes on Jim Wilson. Obviously, whatever Jim ordered, she would have done without question.

Wilson leaned his head down toward her. He said, 'Listen, baby, there's something I keep meaning to ask but I always forget it. What's your last name?'

'Trumble—Minna Trumble. I thought I told you.'

'Maybe you did. Maybe I didn't get it.'

Nora felt the hysteria welling again. 'How long are you going to keep doing this?' she asked.

Leroy Davis cocked his head as he looked at her. 'Doing what?'

'Play cat and mouse like this. Holding us on a pin like flies in an exhibit.'

Leroy Davis smiled brightly. 'Like a butterfly in your case, honey. A big, beautiful butterfly.'

'What are you going to do,' Frank Brooks snapped. 'Whatever it is, let's get it over with?'

'Can't you see what I'm doing?' Davis asked with genuine wonder. 'Are you that stupid? I'm being the boss. I'm in command and I like it. I hold life and death over four people and I'm savoring the thrill of it. You're pretty stupid, mister, and if you use that "can't get away with it" line, I'll put a bullet into your left ear and watch it come out your right one.'

Jim Wilson's fists were doubled. He was again approaching the reckless point. And again it was dulled by the gradually increasing sound of a motor—not in the air, but from the street level to the south.

It was a sane, cheerful sound and was resented instantly by the insane mind of Leroy Davis.

He tightened even to the point that his face grew more pale from the tension. He backed to a window, looked out quickly, and turned back. 'It's a jeep,' he said. 'They're going by the hotel. If anybody makes a move, or yells, they'll find four bodies in here and me gone. That's what I'm telling you and you know I'll do it.'

They knew he *would* do it and they stood silent, trying to dredge up the nerve to make a move. The jeep's motor backfired a couple of times as it approached Madison Street. Each time, Leroy Davis' nerves reacted sharply and the four people kept their eyes trained on the gun in his hand.

The jeep came to the intersection and slowed down. There was a conference between its two occupants—helmeted soldiers in dark brown battle dress. Then the jeep moved on up Clark Street toward Lake.

A choked sigh escaped from Nora's throat. Frank Brooks turned toward her. 'Take it easy,' he said. 'We're not dead yet. I don't think he wants to kill us.'

The reply came from Minna. She spoke quietly. 'I don't care. I can't stand any more of this. After all, we aren't animals. We're human beings and we have a right to live and die as we please.'

Minna walked toward Leroy Davis. 'I'm not afraid of your gun any more. All you can do with it is kill me. Go ahead and do it.'

Minna walked up to Leroy Davis. He gaped at her and said, 'You're crazy! Get back there. You're a crazy dame!'

He fired the gun twice and Minna died appreciating the incongruity of his words. She went out on a note of laughter and as she fell, Jim Wilson, with an echoing animal roar, lunged at Leroy Davis. His great hand closed completely over that of Davis, hiding the gun. There was a muffled explosion and the bullet cut unnoticed through Wilson's palm. Wilson jerked the gun from Davis' weak grasp and hurled it away. Then he killed Davis.

He did it slowly, a surprising thing for Wilson. He lifted Davis by his neck and held him with his feet off the floor. He squeezed Davis' neck, seeming to do it with great leisure as Davis made horrible noises and kicked his legs.

Nora turned her eyes away, buried them in Frank Brooks' shoulder, but she could not keep the sounds from reaching her ears. Frank held her close. 'Take it easy,' he said. 'Take it easy.' And he was probably not conscious of saying it.

'Tell him to hurry,' Nora whispered. 'Tell him to get it over with. It's like killing—killing an animal.'

'That's what he is—an animal.'

Frank Brooks stared in fascination at Leroy Davis' distorted, darkening face. It was beyond semblance of anything human now. The eyes bulged and the tongue came from his mouth as though frantically seeking relief.

The animal sounds quieted and died away. Nora heard the sound of the body falling to the floor—a limp, soft sound of finality. She turned and saw Jim Wilson with his hands still extended and cupped. The terrible hands from which the stench of a terrible life was drifting away into empty air.

Wilson looked down at his handiwork. 'He's dead,' Wilson said slowly. He turned to face Frank and Nora. There was a great disappointment in his face. 'That's all there is to it,' he said, dully. 'He's just—dead.' Without knowing it for what it was, Jim Wilson was full of the futile aftertaste of revenge.

He bent down to pick up Minna's body. There was a small blue hole in the right cheek and another one over the left eye. With a glance at Frank and Nora, Jim Wilson covered the wounds with his hand as though they were not decent. He picked her up in his arms and walked across the lobby and up the stairs with the slow, quiet tread of a weary man.

The sound of the jeep welled up again, but it was further away now. Frank Brooks took Nora's hand and they hurried out into the street. As they crossed the sidewalk, the sound of the jeep was drowned by a sudden swelling of the wailings to the northward.

On still a new note, they rose and fell on the still air. A note of panic, of new knowledge, it seemed, but Frank and Nora were not paying close attention. The sounds of the jeep motor had come from the west and they got within sight of the Madison-Well intersection in time to see the jeep hurtle southward at its maximum speed.

Frank yelled and waved his arms, but he knew he had been neither seen nor heard. They were given little time for disappointment however, because a new center of interest appeared to the northward. From around the corner of Washington Street, into Clark, moved three strange figures.

There was a mixture of belligerence and distress in their actions. They carried odd looking weapons and seemed interested in using them upon something or someone, but they apparently lacked the energy to raise them although they appeared to be rather light.

The creatures themselves were humanoid, Frank thought. He tightened his grip on Nora's hand. 'They've seen us.'

'Let's not run,' Nora said. 'I'm tired of running. All it's gotten us is trouble. Let's just stand here.'

'Don't be foolish.'

'I'm not running. You can if you want to.'

Frank turned his attention back to the three strange creatures. He allowed natural curiosity full reign. Thoughts of flight vanished from his mind.

'They're so thin—so fragile,' Nora said.

'But their weapons aren't.'

'It's hard to believe, even seeing them, that they're from another planet.'

'How so? They certainly don't look much like us.'

'I mean with the talk, for so long, about flying saucers and space flight and things like that. Here they are, but it doesn't seem possible.'

'There's something wrong with them.'

This was true. Two of the strange beings had fallen to the sidewalk. The third came doggedly on, dragging one foot after the other until he went to his hands and knees. He remained motionless for a long time, his head hanging limply. Then he too, sank to the cement and lay still.

The wailings from the north now took on a tone of intense agony—great desperation. After that came a yawning silence.

They defeated themselves,' the military man said. 'Or rather, natural forces defeated them. We certainly had little to do with it.'

Nora, Frank, and Jim Wilson stood at the curb beside a motorcycle. The man on the cycle supported it with a leg propped against the curb as he talked.

'We saw three of them die up the street,' Frank said.

'Our scouting party saw the same thing happen. That's why we moved in. It's about over now. We'll know a lot more about them and where they came from in twenty-four hours.'

They had nothing further to say. The military man regarded them thoughtfully. 'I don't know about you three. If you ignored the evacuation through no fault of your own and can prove it—'

'There were four of us,' Jim Wilson said. 'Then we met another man. He's inside on the floor. I killed him.'

'Murder?' the military man said sharply.

'He killed a woman who was with us,' Frank said. 'He was a maniac. When he's identified I'm pretty sure he'll have a past record.'

'Where is the woman's body?'

'On a bed upstairs,' Wilson said.

'I'll have to hold all of you. Martial law exists in this area. You're in the hands of the army.'

✧ ✧ ✧

The streets were full of people now, going about their business, pushing and jostling, eating in the restaurants, making electricity for the lights, generating power for the telephones.

Nora, Frank, and Jim Wilson sat in a restaurant on Clark Street. 'We're all different people now,' Nora said. 'No one could go through what we've been through and be the same.'

Jim Wilson took her statement listlessly. 'Did they find out what it was about our atmosphere that killed them?'

'They're still working on that, I think.' Frank Brooks stirred his coffee, raised a spoonful and let it drip back into the cup.

'I'm going up to the Chicago Avenue police station,' Wilson said.

Frank and Nora looked up in surprise. Frank asked, 'Why? The military court missed it—the fact you escaped from jail.'

'They didn't miss it I don't think. I don't think they cared much. I'm going back anyway.'

'It won't be much of a rap.'

'No, a pretty small one. I want to get it over with.'

He got up from his chair. 'So long. Maybe I'll see you around.'

'So long.'

'Goodbye.'

Frank said, 'I think I'll beat it too. I've got a job in a factory up north. Maybe they're operating again.' He got to his feet and stood awkwardly by the table. 'Besides—I've got some pay coming.'

Nora didn't say anything.

Frank said, 'Well—so long. Maybe I'll see you around.'

'Maybe. Goodbye.'

Frank Brooks walked north on Clark Street. He was glad to get away from the restaurant. Nora was a good kid but hell—you didn't take up with a hooker. A guy played around, but you didn't stick with them.

But it made a guy think. He was past the kid stage. It was time for him to find a girl and settle down. A guy didn't want to knock around all his life.

Nora walked west on Madison Street. Then she remembered the Halstead Street slums were in that direction and turned south on Wells. She had nine dollars in her bag and that worried her. You couldn't get along on nine dollars in Chicago very long.

There was a tavern on Jackson near Wells. Nora went inside. The barkeep didn't frown at her. That was good. She went to the bar and ordered a beer and was served.

After a while a man came in. A middle aged man who might have just come into Chicago—whose bags might still be at the LaSalle Street Station down the block. The man looked at Nora, then away. After a while he looked at her again.

Nora smiled.

Dr Cyclops

Henry Kuttner

Chapter One: Camp in the Jungle

Bill Stockton stood in the compound gate, watching Pedro driving the mules down to the river pasture. The swarthy half-breed's face was split by a broad grin; he twirled his black mustache and sang loudly of a *cantina* in Buenos Aires, thousands of miles to the east.

'How the devil does he do it?' Stockton moaned, shaking the perspiration out of his eyes. 'I can hardly drag myself around in this heat. And that guy actually sings—'

Yet it wasn't only the heat, Stockton knew. There was more to it than that. A feeling of sombre menace—hung heavy above this wilderness encampment. During the weeks of jungle travel from the Andes, through tropical swamp and pest-infested jungle, the feeling had grown stronger. It was in the humid, sticky air. It was in the sickly-sweet, choking perfume of the great orchids that grew outside the stockade. Most of all, it was in the actions of Dr Thorkel.

'He's supposed to be the greatest scientific wizard of the age,' Stockton thought skeptically. 'But for my money he's nuts. Sends a message to the Royal Academy demanding the services of a biologist and a mineralogist, and then asks us to look into a microscope. That's all. Won't even let us get inside that mud house of his!'

There was reason for Stockton's bitterness. He had been literally forced into this adventure. Hardy, the mineralogist, had been taken ill at Lima, and Dr Bulfinch, his colleague, had sought vainly for a substitute. None was available. None, that is, save for a certain beachcomber who was going rapidly to hell with the aid of a native girl, bad gin, and rubber checks.

Bulfinch's assistant, Dr Mary Phillips, had solved the problem. She had bought up the bad checks, threatened Stockton with jail if he refused to come along. Under the circumstances, the one-time mineralogist had shrugged and acceded. Now he was wondering if he had made a mistake.

There was menace here. Stockton sensed it, with the psychic keenness of a professional adventurer. Secrecy was all around him. Why was the mine yard generally kept locked, if the mine actually was worthless, as Thorkel contended? Why had Thorkel seemed so excited when Stockton had mentioned the iron crystals, crystals Thorkel had been unable to see because of his weak vision?

Then, too, there was the matter of the Dicotylinae—certain bones Mary Phillips had found. They were the bones of a native wild pig, but the molar surfaces had proved it a species of midget swine entirely unknown to science—four inches long at maturity. That was odd.

Finally, only an hour ago, Thorkel had blandly said good-bye, only twenty-three hours after the arrival of his guests. Bulfinch had, Stockton mused with a chuckle, thrown a fit. The goatish face had gone gray; the unkempt Vandyke had bristled.

'Are you attempting to intimate that you summoned me—Dr Rupert Bulfinch—ten thousand miles just to look into a microscope?' he had roared.

'Correct,' Thorkel had answered, and went back to his mud house.

So far, so good. But there was trouble ahead. Neither Bulfinch nor Mary would think of leaving, even though that meant defiance of Thorkel. And Thorkel, Stockton felt, was a dangerous customer, cold-blooded and un-scrupulous. His round face, with its bristling mustache and bald dome, could settle into grim, deadly lines.

Moreover, from the first a quiet, unspoken sort of conflict had arisen between Thorkel and Baker, the guide who had accompanied the party from the Andes. Stockton shrugged and gave it up.

Dr Bulfinch came up behind Stockton and touched his arm. There was repressed excitement in the biologist's goatish face.

'Come along,' he said softly. 'I've found something.'

Stockton followed Bulfinch into a nearby tent. Mary Phillips was there, mounting the bones of the midget pig. She was, Stockton thought, much too pretty to be a biologist. A wealth of red-gold hair cascaded over her shoulders, and she had a face that belonged on the silver screen rather than in the lab. She also had a hell of a temper.

'Hello, beautiful,' said Stockton.

'Oh, shut up,' the girl murmured. 'What's the matter, Dr Bulfinch?'

The biologist thrust a rock sample at Stockton.

'Test this.'

The younger man's eyes widened.

'This isn't—hell, it can't be!'

'You've seen pitchblende before,' Bulfinch said with heavy sarcasm.

'Where'd you get it?' Stockton asked, excited.

'Baker found it near the mine shaft. It's uranium ore,' he said quietly, 'and it's a hundred times richer than any deposit ever discovered. No wonder Thorkel wants to get rid of us!' Mentally Stockton added, 'And I'll bet he wouldn't stop at murder to shut us up!'

'Good God!' Bulfinch whispered. 'Radium! Think of the medical benefits of such a find—the help it can give to science!'

There was an interruption. A black streak shot into the tent, followed by a gaunt, disreputable dog, barking wildly. The two circled a table and fled outside again. There was the sound of a scuffle.

Hastily Stockton raised the tent-flap. Pedro, Thorkel's man-of-all-work, was holding the dog, while a cat retreated hastily into the distance.

The half-breed looked up with a flash of white teeth. 'I am sorry. This foolish Paco—' He pulled the dog's tail. 'He does not know he can never catch Satanas. He just wants to play, though. Since Pinto went away, he is lonesome.'

'Yeah?' Stockton asked, eyeing the man. 'Who was Pinto?'

'My little mule. Ah, Pinto was smart. But not smart enough, I suppose.' Pedro shrugged expressively. 'Poor mule.'

A man came out of the gathering twilight—a tall, rangy figure, with a hard-bitten, harsh face—a Puritan gone to seed.

'Hello, Baker,' Stockton grunted.

'Bulfinch told you about the radium?' Baker said, without preamble. 'It's valuable, eh?'

'Yeah. Plenty valuable.' Stockton's eyes narrowed. 'I've been wondering about that. Wondering why you were so anxious to come along when you could have sent a native. Maybe you'd heard about this radium mine, eh?'

Baker's harsh face did not change, but he sent a glance of sheer black hatred toward the house.

'I don't blame you,' he said under his breath. 'It does look screwy. But—listen, Bill, I had a good reason for wanting to come here. If I'd come alone, Thorkel would have been suspicious—shot me on sight, maybe. I'd have had no chance at all to investigate—'

'Investigate what?' Stockton asked impatiently.

'I used to know a little native girl. Nice kid. Mira, her name was. I—well, I thought a lot of her. One day she went off to act as Thorkel's housekeeper. And that was the last I ever heard of the girl.'

'She isn't here now,' Stockton said. 'Unless she's in the house.'

Baker shook his head. 'I've been talking to Pedro. He says Mira was here—and disappeared. Like Pinto, his albino mule.'

The swift tropic night had fallen. A bright moon silvered the compound. And suddenly the two men heard the faint, shrill neigh of a horse, from the direction of Thorkel's house.

Simultaneously the figure of Pedro appeared, running from behind a tent. He cried, 'Pinto! My mule Pinto is in the house. He has come back!'

Before the half-breed could reach the door of the house, it opened abruptly. Thorkel appeared. In the moonlight his bald head and gleaming, thick-lensed spectacles looked oddly inhuman.

'Well, Pedro?' he asked quietly, in a sneering voice.

The other jerked to a halt. He moistened his lips.

'It is Pinto, *señor*—' he whispered.

'You are imagining things,' Thorkel said, with cold emphasis. 'Go back to your work. Do you think I'd keep a mule in the house?'

A new voice broke in.

'Just what do you keep in there, Doctor?'

It was Bulfinch. The biologist emerged from the tent and approached, a lean, gaunt figure in the moonlight. Mary was behind him. Baker and Stockton joined the group. Thorkel held the door closed behind him.

'That is nothing to you,' he said, icily.

'On the contrary,' Bulfinch snapped, 'as I told you, I intend to remain here until I have received an explanation.'

'And as I told *you*,' Thorkel said, almost whispering, 'you do so at your own peril. I will not tolerate interference or prying. My secrets are my own. I warn you: I shall protect those secrets!'

'Are you threatening us?' the biologist growled.

Thorkel suddenly smiled.

'If I showed you what I have in my house, I think you would—regret it,' he observed, a suggestion of subtle menace in his silky tones. 'I wish to be left alone. If I find you still here tomorrow morning, I shall take . . . protective measures.'

His eyes, behind the thick-lensed spectacles, included the group in one ominous glance. Then, without another word, he reentered the house, locking the door behind him.

'Still staying, Doc?' Stockton asked. Bulfinch growled.

'I certainly am!'

There was a brief pause. Then Pedro, who had been listening intently, made a commanding gesture.

'Come with me. I will show you something—'

He hurried around the corner of the house, trailed by the dog Paco. Bulfinch, his thin lips working, followed, and so did the others.

A tall bamboo fence blocked their way. Pedro pointed, and applied his eye to a crack. Stockton tested the gate, which had previously been open. It was barred now, so he joined Pedro and the others.

'Wait,' the half-breed whispered. 'I have seen this before.'

They could see the mine-shaft, with a crude windlass surmounting it. And then a gross, strange figure entered their range of vision. It resembled, at first glance, a man in a diving suit. Every inch of the stocky body was covered with the rubberlike fabric. A cylindrical helmet shielded the head. Through two round eye-plates could be seen the heavy spectacles of Dr Thorkel.

'Uh-huh,' Stockton whispered. 'Protective suit. Radium's dangerous stuff.'

Thorkel went to the mine and began to turn the windlass. Abruptly Stockton felt a hand touch his arm. He turned.

It was Baker.

'Come along,' the other said softly. 'I've opened the door. Cheap lock— and Mary uses hairpins. Now we'll be able to see what he's got hidden in that house.'

'*Sí!* The doctor will be busy in the yard for a long time—' Pedro said, nodding.

Silently the group retraced their steps. The door of the mud house was ajar.

From within came the sound of a shrill neigh, incredibly high and thin . . .

Chapter Two: The Little People

The room was disappointingly bare. Across from the front door was another, apparently leading to the mine yard. Another door was in the right-hand wall, and a small mica window was let into it.

There were heavy wooden chairs, a work-bench, and a table bearing microscope and notebooks. On the bench were several small wicker baskets. Littered carelessly about the floor were a rack of test-tubes, books, a beaker, two or three small boxes, and a dirty shirt or two.

Pedro pointed to the floor.

'Hoof prints—Pinto was here, yes!'

Mary bent over the microscope, while Bulfinch examined the notebooks. '*Thieves!*'

Thorkel stood in the doorway leading to the mine yard, his eyes glaring behind the glasses. He was whitely livid with rage.

'So you would steal my discoveries. You have no right here! You are merely my employees whom I have discharged and instructed to leave!' He saw the notebook in Bulfinch's hand, and his voice rose to a scream of rage.

'My notes!'

Stockton and Baker seized him as he sprang at the biologist. Bulfinch smiled coldly.

'Restrain yourself, Dr Thorkel. Your actions are not reassuring.'

Thorkel relaxed, panting.

'I—you have no right here.'

'You are behaving irrationally. For your own good, and for the benefit of science, I must demand an explanation. To leave you here in the jungle would be nothing short of criminal. You are grossly overworked. You are not'—he hesitated—'not in a normal state mentally. There is no reason to be suspicious or to fear persecution.'

Thorkel sighed, removed his glasses, and rubbed his blind eyes with a weary gesture. 'I am sorry,' he murmured.

'Perhaps you are right, Doctor. I—I am experimenting with radioactivity.' He went to the mica-paned door and opened it, revealing a small closet, plated with lead. From the ceiling hung a projector, resembling the type used medically to treat cancer by radium rays.

'This is my condensor,' Thorkel said. 'You may examine it, Dr Bulfinch. I must trust you—I have shown this to no one else in the world.'

Bulfinch entered the closet. The others were at his heels, intently scrutinizing the projector which seemed the heart of the mystery.

Pedro paid no attention. He was opening, one by one, the boxes on the bench. And, abruptly, he paused, transfixed with astonishment. His lips formed the word, 'Pinto!'

A white mule was within the box. An albino mule, no more than eight inches high!

'Pedro!' Thorkel called sharply. The half-breed sprang up. His elbow overturned the box, which clattered to the floor.

The midget mule was flung out. Only Thorkel and Pedro saw the beast as it struggled up and raced across the floor.

The door was still ajar. The mannikin animal fled out into the night.

For a second Thorkel's eyes clashed with Pedro's.

'Come here,' the scientist said tonelessly. 'I want you to see this, too.'

The half-breed went toward Thorkel, his face blank with amazement. 'What—what has happened to—'

Thorkel smiled. He pointed to the closet where the others were still examining the projector. Pedro turned to look.

Thorkel moved with the swiftness of an uncoiled steel spring. He struck at Pedro. Caught unawares, the half-breed was hurled into the closet. The door slammed shut behind him.

Thorkel locked it with a swift movement. His hand closed on one of the switches nearby; he pulled it down. Instantly there was a low hum, which rose swiftly to a sibilant crackling buzz.

Green light blazed through the mica window.

From a shelf Thorkel took a heavy helmet and donned it. He leaned forward to peer through the mica pane.

'Thieves!' he whispered. 'I told you to go! I could not force you—but if you insist on staying, I must be sure that you will not interfere with my experiments or try to steal my secret. So you wished to help me, Dr Bulfinch? Well, you shall—but not quite as you expected!'

Thorkel's laughter rose above the crackling snarl of the condensor . . .

The infra-red lamp suspended from the ceiling sent down a rich, warm glow. Beneath it was a glass dish, containing a colorless liquid that was boiling gently, warmed by an electrode. From the dish steamed a whitish vapor which shrouded the floor, almost hiding the dim outlines nearby.

One of these figures writhed and sat up, tearing away the silken wrappings that bound it. The swart face of Pedro appeared. He sprang up, knee-deep in the white vapor, coughing and choking for breath.

Beside him another form stirred. Bill Stockton rose shakily, breathing in great gasps.

'Air—air's better up here . . . what the hell!' Discovering that he was naked save for the silk shroud, he adjusted it, looking rather like a Roman, with his harsh eagle face and keen eyes.

Mary and Baker were the next to appear. Then came the grim face of Dr Bulfinch. For a moment each was busy adjusting their makeshift garments.

'Where are we?' Pedro gasped. 'I cannot see—' He choked and coughed.

'Calm down,' Bulfinch said curtly. 'We won't be asphyxiated.' He sniffed and glanced at the light above. 'Ozone, ammonia, humidity, temperature—calculated to revive consciousness.'

'Where are we?' Mary asked. 'In the mine?'

They could not see beyond the small circle of light. Stockton gripped Pedro's arm.

'You know this place better than we do. Where are we? What's Thorkel done?'

Suddenly horror grew in Pedro's eyes as he remembered something. 'Pinto,' he gasped. 'He has made Pinto—*little*!'

'Nuts,' Stockton grunted. 'Let's grab hands and feel our way around. Come on!'

'He has made me little like my mule!' Pedro whispered.

Without warning the faint red glow of the lamp faded and died. It was almost utterly black. Stockton felt Mary's hand tighten in his own, and squeezed it reassuringly.

Light shafted in whitely. Instantly Stockton saw that they were in a cellar, at the foot of a flight of stairs that led up to an opening door. On the threshold stood Dr Thorkel, looking down at them. Satanas, the cat, crouched by the scientist's feet.

'He has made us little!' Pedro screamed.

And it was true! Thorkel was—a giant! A thirty-foot titan towered over them! The cellar door seemed as big as a two-story house; Satanas was a sabre-toothed tiger!

Bulfinch was chalk-white. He sprang back suddenly as Satanas spat down at the tiny group. Thorkel hastily bent down and picked up the cat. His voice was booming thunder.

'No, no—you must not frighten them,' he told the cat. Thorkel stepped down into the cellar, and the others shrank from this colossus. Mary's voice rose in a scream.

'Good,' said Thorkel. 'Vocal cords unimpaired, eh? You have no temperature? Dr Bulfinch, will you be good enough to take the pulse of your companions?'

Pedro broke and raced for the stairway. Thorkel nodded, smiling.

'Little creatures—their first instinct is to escape. Run if you like, then.'

And the wee folk fled . . .

Climbing those stairs was a feat. Each tread came up to their breasts. But, pushing, pulling, scrambling, the miniature humans swarmed toward the light. Soon they were gone from sight. Thorkel put down the cat and followed, shutting the cellar door. He turned to glance around the room. The little people had hidden themselves.

'Come out. You have nothing to fear,' he said smoothly.

Thorkel waited, and then sank down into a chair.

'Where is your scientific spirit, Dr Bulfinch?' He smiled. 'Did you not wish to join me in my experiments?' He mopped perspiration from his bald head and slid the chair away from the patch of sunlight that slanted in through the window fronting the mine yard.

Bulfinch's head appeared cautiously from behind one of Thorkel's discarded boots. He walked toward the giant.

'Come closer,' Thorkel urged.

Bulfinch obeyed, staring up at the other.

'What is the matter?' Thorkel said fearfully. 'Can you not speak?'

The biologist's voice was thin and high.

'Yes, I can speak. What have you done—and why?'

Thorkel leaned forward, his huge hand reaching toward the tiny figure on the floor. Bulfinch retreated in alarm.

'I only wish to weigh and measure you,' he said softly. He rose and settled back in his chair. 'Come out. I won't eat you. As you can see, I have reduced your size.'

His pale eyes, behind the thick glasses, watched intently as, emboldened, the others appeared one by one. Pedro had been hiding behind a chair leg; the others behind a stack of books on the floor. They advanced until they were in a group with Bulfinch.

'You should be proud,' Thorkel said. 'You are almost the first successful experiment—Pinto was the first, Pedro. Too bad you let him escape. Again I thank you, Mr Stockton, for identifying the iron crystals. They gave me the last clue.'

He blinked down at them. 'Till you came, I could reduce organic substances, but life could not be preserved in them. It is a matter of electronic compression of matter under ray bombardment. The radium in the mine gave me unimaginable power. Look.' He lifted a sponge from the table and squeezed it in his fist. 'That is it. Compression. But energy is required, rather than brute force—'

Baker spoke up suddenly. 'Did you do this to Mira?'

'The native girl—my housekeeper? Why, yes. But I failed—she was reduced in size, but she was dead. How do you know of her?' Thorkel did not wait for an answer. He rubbed his eyes wearily. 'I am very tired. It has taken days to reduce you, and I have not had one moment's sleep . . .' His voice trailed off wearily. Sleep smothered him.

Stockton was staring around.

'We've got to get out of here. Do you realize that this fiend intends to kill us all?'

Bulfinch looked a question. 'That scarcely—'

'He told us he murdered the native girl, didn't he? He's a cold-blooded devil.'

Instinctively they glanced at the door. The bar that locked it from the inside was thrice the height of Stockton's head.

Human beings—scarcely more than half a foot tall!

On the floor nearby a book stood on end—*Human Physiology*, by Granger. Stockton went to stand beside it. His head scarcely came to the top of the volume.

'Well?' he asked bitterly. 'Any suggestions?'

Bulfinch nodded. 'Yes. Books are handy things. If we can pile them up and reach the door-latch . . .'

It took time, but Thorkel did not awaken. A pencil, used as a lever, opened the door a crack. And then the little people were outside in the compound. Strange sight! A cactus patch not far away was taller than the tallest tree. The camp tables were fantastically high. A chicken was moving jerkily in its quest for food—and its bobbing comb rose higher than Stockton's head!

If it saw them, it made no hostile move. Slowly the tiny group moved forward, toward Bulfinch's tent. Each box and crate was a mountain to be skirted. The rough ground hurt their bare feet.

Pedro was glancing around nervously. Abruptly he cried out and pointed. Stockton whirled with the others, and he showed his panic.

Out of a crumbling hole in the mud hut's base Satanas, the cat, was crawling. The creature's eyes were intent on the little people. More formidable than a tiger, it wriggled free and bounded toward them, sharp fangs bared!

CHAPTER THREE: Death in the Jungle

Stockton seized Mary by the hand and dragged her toward the shelter of the cactus clump. The others were not slow in following. Baker paused to hurl a pebble at the cat, but the gesture was futile.

Snarling, Satanas came on. The cacti were too far away for safety. Hopelessness tore at Stockton as he realized that none of them could reach the clump. He could almost feel sharp fangs sinking into his flesh.

The cat spat viciously. There was an uproar of furious barks. As the little people miraculously found concealment amid the cactus spines, they turned to see Satanas fleeing from Paco, Pedro's dog.

'Whew!' Baker gasped. 'That was a close one.'

Bulfinch regarded him sombrely, tugging at his Vandyke. 'There will be more "close ones,"' he said with grim meaning. 'Every creature larger than a rat is apt to be a deadly menace.'

'What can we do?' Mary asked.

'First—food, weapons,' Stockton said. 'Then we'll deal with Thorkel and find some way out of this.'

The day dragged on, and Thorkel still slept. Satanas did not reappear. Mary engaged herself in making sandals, a difficult task at best, and worse when the knife is larger than you are.

As for Stockton, he managed to take the screw out of a pair of scissors, and one blade provided him with a serviceable weapon, about the size of a sword.

Thorkel's voice startled them when it came. He was leaning out the window, like a giant in the sky, regarding them.

'You are resourceful, my small friends,' his voice boomed out. 'But now come back. I must weigh and measure all of you.'

The group drew together. Thorkel laughed evilly at them.

'I won't harm you. Come, Dr Bulfinch,' he said silkily.

'I demand that you restore us to our normal size,' the biologist snapped.

'That is impossible,' the other said. 'At present, anyway. All my energies have been devoted to the problem of atomic shrinkage—compression. Perhaps, in time, I can find the antidote, the ray that will turn men to giants. But it will take months of research and experiment—perhaps years.'

'Do you mean we must remain like this—'

'I shall not harm you,' Thorkel smiled. 'Come—' He leaned forward. Bulfinch drew back, and, with an impatient grunt, Thorkel disappeared from the window. His feet thudded across the floor. Bulfinch hastily fled back to the others.

'The cactus,' he gasped, panting. 'Let's hide!'

But already Thorkel was emerging from the door. His figure loomed gigantic. A few quick strides, and he had cut off the retreat of his quarry. He crouched down, spreading his fingers wide.

Escape was impossible. Mary and Baker were gathered up in one titan hand. With the other Thorkel reached for the fleeing Bulfinch.

Pedro had secured a fork from somewhere, and held it like a spear. He thrust at the huge hand.

Chuckling, Thorkel brushed the weapon aside, knocking Pedro headlong. Contemptuously he stood up, still gripping Mary and Baker.

'Dr Bulfinch!' His voice was thunderous. 'Listen to me!'

The biologist was peering out from the depths of the cactus. 'Yes?'

'I wish to weigh and measure you. You are a scientist; your reactions will be more valuable than those of the others. I am conducting an experiment for Germany—my fatherland. If my reduction method proves successful, we will be able to reduce our armies to miniature size. Our men will be able to steal into enemy territory, sabotage industrial centers. And no one will suspect the destruction due to—men in miniature. You will not be harmed. I promise you that. Will you come out?'

Bulfinch shook his head stubbornly. His whole being revolted at the ruthless plan outlined by this sinister genius. A plan that might mean the death of thousands of innocent civilians.

'No? Then, perhaps, if I apply a little pressure—a very little—to these tiny people I hold so gently in my hand—'

The constricting fingers tightened. From Baker's lips came a grunt of pain. Mary's voice rose in a scream.

'Oh, damn!' Bulfinch snarled. 'All right, Thorkel. You win. Put them down.' He emerged from the cactus as the scientist gently deposited Baker and Mary on the ground. They were unharmed, but so giddy from the rapid descent that they could scarcely stand.

Calmly, Thorkel picked up Bulfinch's tiny figure. The biologist made no resistance. The others were left staring as Thorkel walked back to the mud house; then, swiftly, they fled into the cactus. There was silence.

'He won't hurt him,' Pedro said, without conviction.

Stockton stepped out from the protection of the cactus. 'I'll just make sure. Wait here.' He started toward the house, gripping his scissor-blade harder than was necessary.

It was minutes later when he reached the door, still slightly ajar. He peered through the crack, just in time to hear Bulfinch's cry and witness the murder of the biologist.

Thorkel was seated at his table. With one hand he gripped the tiny Bulfinch; with the other he pressed a wad of cotton down over his victim's face.

Then, swiftly, he dropped the limp body into a glass beaker. Stockton drew back, sick with horror, and his improvised sword made a noise against the door. Thorkel glanced down and saw the small watcher.

'So you would spy on me?' he asked quietly, and without haste picked up a butterfly net from the table. As he rose Stockton fled.

Thorkel got to the door just in time to see him disappear into the cactus. Nodding, he found a shovel and followed his quarry.

It took ten minutes to clear and break down the cactus bed. And then Thorkel realized that he was looking at the outlet of a tile drain pipe that extended to and under the compound wall. He straightened, staring nearsightedly across the barrier.

'You had better come back!' Thorkel shouted. 'You cannot live an hour in the jungle—and there is a storm approaching!'

Storm in the jungle—the greatest rain forest in the world. Bear, deer, and monkey fleeing from thunderbolt and unchained devils of the lightning. The screaming of parrots clinging to their wind-buffeted perches.

The black hell of night closed upon the jungle.

Through that madness fled the little people. And, by sheer luck, they found a cave in which they cowered through the eternal, dragging hours of shaking fury, helpless, hopeless beings in a world of gigantic menace . . .

It was dawn. Chilled, dispirited, and shivering, the little people emerged from their refuge. In the dawn light they examined each other.

'We look like hell,' Stockton said.

'I'm glad you include yourself,' Mary told him, trying to adjust her tangled hair. 'I wish I had a few pins.'

'They'd be as big as you are, about. What now?'

Baker had been talking to the half-breed. Now he turned to face the others.

'Pedro has an idea. If we can get to the river and find a boat, we can float downstream to civilization. There'll be help there.'

'That's an idea,' Stockton nodded. 'Which way is the water, Pedro?'

The half-breed pointed, and without delay they set out, plodding through the rain-wet jungle. Once a monkey, larger to them than a gorilla, swung down uncomfortably close, and once the inconceivable ferocity of a bear crossed their path, luckily without seeing them. They kept to a well-trodden path, but on all sides the monolithic trees stretched up, higher than skyscrapers. The weedy grass rose above their heads. It was a world of stark fantasy and lurking menace.

Once Stockton, lagging behind the others, saw Paco, the dog. He was frisking about an albino colt which was diligently cropping grass. For a second Stockton considered the idea of catching and riding the colt, but gave it up immediately. The beast was much too large. He shrugged and followed the rest of the band.

The river bank did not prove an insurmountable obstacle, though it took time to descend. They went upstream to a little cove, where Pedro, he said, had moored his canoe. Picking their way around a thick patch of weeds, they reached the craft. It was gigantic. Beached on the sand, it remained immovable no matter how they strained and pushed.

'Great idea,' Stockton grunted. 'It's like trying to move a steamship.'

'Well, even that can be done,' the girl told him. 'If you use rollers.'

'Isn't she smart?' Pedro said with naive admiration. 'We can cut bamboo—'

'Sure!' Baker joined in. 'We can rig up a lever and windlass—it'll take time, but that's all right.'

It took even more time than they had thought. With their crude tools, and the unexpected toughness of the plant-life to tiny hands, it took hours, and the morning dragged on with little accomplished.

Pedro lifted his head and dashed sweat from his dripping mustache. 'I hear—Paco, I think,' he said doubtfully.

'Never mind Paco,' Baker told him. 'Lend a hand with this windlass.'

'But Paco—he is a hunting dog. Dr Thorkel knows that. If he—'

'Time to rest,' Stockton decreed, and straightened, rubbing his aching back. Mary, who had been toiling with the rest, sank down with a groan. She tossed her red-gold hair back from her tired young face.

Stockton made a cup out of a tiny leaf and brought the girl water from the river. She drank it gratefully.

'No use to boil it,' the man explained. 'If there're any germs in the water, we can see 'em without a microscope.'

Pedro and Baker flung themselves down full length on the sand and lay panting. 'This is devil work,' the half-breed observed with conviction. 'If I live, I shall burn twenty candles before my patron saint.'

'If I live, I'll kill twenty bottles,' Baker said. 'But there's one guy I'd like to kill first.' His face darkened. He was remembering Mira, the native girl, whom Thorkel had murdered so casually. And poor Bulfinch.

'What about you, Bill?' Mary asked.

He glanced at her. 'I know what you mean. Well—I wouldn't even make a good beachcomber now. I might go native with the field mice.'

Abruptly Stockton turned to face her. 'No. I didn't mean that. This is pretty terrible, but it's shown me something. All this—' He flung out an arm toward the towering grasses in the background. 'Wonder and strangeness, which we never quite realize—until we're small. I—I was a good mineralogist once. I could be again. Remember those checks I tore up, Mary? I'm going to pay you back every cent they cost you. That's rather important to me now . . .' He frowned. 'If we come out of this alive—'

In the distance Paco barked again. Pedro stood up, shading his eyes with a calloused palm. 'It is Dr Thorkel,' he stated. 'He carries a specimen box, and Paco leads him.'

'Damn!' Stockton snapped. 'We've got to hide. Take to the water, to break the trail.'

'No,' Pedro said. 'There are alligators.' He nodded toward the tall patch of grass near them. 'We can hide in—' He stopped, and horror grew in his eyes.

Mary, following his glance, gave a little gasp and recoiled.

For something was coming out of the high grasses. Dragonlike and hideous it slid forward, cold eyes intent on the little people. The sunlight gleamed on rough, warty scales.

Only a lizard—but to Thorkel's victims it was like a triceratops, a dinosaur out of Earth's ferocious past!

Stockton barely had time to snatch up his scissor-blade sword before the reptile rushed. He was bowled over by that blind charge. Gasping, still clinging to his weapon, he scrambled to his feet.

Mary was backed up against a tall weed-stem, her eyes abrim with fear. Before her Pedro had planted his squat form.

He gripped a bit of wood, holding it like a cudgel—a matchstick in the hands of a mannikin!

The lizard came back, jaws agape, hissing. Baker had found a sharpened splinter of bamboo, and held it as a spear. He thrust, and the point glanced off the reptile's armored flank.

The barking of Paco was thunderously loud. A shadow fell on the group. Something seemed to swoop down out of the sky—and the vast face of Dr Thorkel stared at them as the man crouched down.

'So there you are!' he boomed. 'What is this? A lizard? Wait—'

In his left hand he gathered the struggling forms of Mary and Pedro. They struck vainly at the huge, imprisoning fingers. He reached toward Stockton.

Simultaneously the lizard rushed again. Stockton drove his blade at the gaping jaws; Baker thrust at the wattled throat. The creature gave back, writhed aside. Thorkel's hand reached out—

The reptile's jaws closed upon it! Thorkel screamed in pain as he jerked back, cursing with agonized fury. Mary and Pedro dropped unnoticed from the scientist's other hand.

Stockton fled toward them. 'The bushes! Quick!'

Habit made him say that. Actually, they darted into the concealing stems of the high grasses, thicker than a forest of bamboo. Behind them they heard Thorkel cursing; then he fell silent.

Paco barked.

'That damn dog of yours,' Baker growled. 'He's a hunter, all right.'

Thorkel's voice sounded. 'Come out! I know you're in the grass. Come out or I'll fire it.'

Stockton glanced at Mary's white face, and whispered an oath. Baker's thin lips were grim. Pedro rubbed his mustache.

'Paco—he will follow me,' the half-breed said. 'You stay here.'

And he was gone, racing through the grass forest.

There was a moment of silence. Then Stockton, galvanized into activity, crept forward, parting the fronds till he could see Thorkel. The scientist was holding a match-box in his fingers.

Blood dripped from one hand to the ground.

Paco's bark came from further away. Thorkel hesitated, looked around, and then extracted a match.

From downstream came Pedro's voice.

'Paco! *Fuera! Fuera!*'

Thorkel, lighting the match, looked up.

Abruptly he dropped it and snatched at the rifle he had laid down. He took steady aim.

The boom of the gun was deafening thunder.

Pedro screamed once. There was a faint splash from far away.

Sickness tugged at Stockton's stomach as he saw Thorkel go striding off. He went back to the others.

'Pedro's done for. That leaves three of us.'

'Damn Thorkel!' Baker ground out. Mary said nothing, but there was both pity and sorrow in her eyes. They heard Paco go racing past, to leap into the river and swim out.

Then the first coiling tendrils of smoke drifted through the grasses.

Instantly Stockton remembered the lit match that Thorkel had dropped. He seized Mary's hand and urged her forward.

'Come on, Steve,' he said urgently to Baker. 'He's trying to smoke us out. We can't stay here—'

'Come out!' roared the bellowing voice of Thorkel. 'Hear me?' His huge boots stamped through the grass patch.

And the fire spread, remorselessly, hungrily.

Mary was gasping with strain. 'I can't—go any further, Bill.'

'That's right,' Baker seconded. 'If we come out in the open, he'll see us. We're trapped.'

Stockton stared around. The flames were closing in upon them. Black smoke billowed up. Abruptly Stockton saw something that made his eyes widen.

The specimen case!

Thorkel's box, lying at the edge of the grasses!

Without a word Stockton raced toward it. He still had his improvised sword, and, leaping to a rock beside the box, he used it as a lever to pry the lid open. Instantly the others saw his intention.

Awkwardly, frantic with the need for haste, they clambered in. The lid had scarcely fallen before a jolt and a sense of swinging movement told them that Thorkel had remembered his property.

Through the small ventilators, covered with copper-wire mesh, daylight slanted in vaguely.

Would Thorkel open the case? they wondered.

CHAPTER FOUR: The Cyclops

It was night before Thorkel gave up the search. Wearily he pushed open the door of the mud house, put the shotgun on a chair, and dropped the specimen case on the table.

'They must be dead,' he groaned. 'But I must be sure. I must!'

He polished his spectacles, peering at them vaguely. His watery eyes blinked in puzzlement. Then he went to the door of the radium room and peered through the mica panel. Something he saw there made him turn to the mine-yard door. He flung it open, switched on a floodlight, and went out, leaving the door ajar.

As soon as he had left, the lid of the specimen case lifted. Three tiny people emerged. Fearfully they clambered out, crossed the plain of the table-top, and leaped down to the seat of Thorkel's chair. They gained the floor, and went toward the open door.

'He's busy with the windlass,' Mary whispered. 'Hurry!'

Stockton halted suddenly. 'Okay,' he said. 'But—I've stopped running. You two go on. I'm going to stay and—kill Thorkel, somehow.'

The others stared at him. 'But Bill!' Mary gasped. 'It's impossible! If we reach civilization—'

Stockton laughed bitterly.

'We've just been fooling ourselves all along. We can never reach civilization. If we launched a boat, we could never get ashore. We'd starve to death, or crack up in the rapids. We're imprisoned here, as surely as though we were in jail. We can't get away.'

'If we—' the girl began. Stockton cut her short.

'It's no use! We can't live long in the forest. Only luck has saved us so far. If we were savages—Indians, perhaps—but we're not. If we go out in the jungle again, it means death.'

'And if we stay here?' Baker asked.

Stockton's smile was grim. 'Thorkel will kill us. Unless we murder him first.'

'All right, suppose we manage to kill Thorkel,' Mary asked quietly. 'What then?'

'Then? We live.' Stockton nodded, a queer look in his eyes. 'I know. The projector only works one way. We can't regain our normal size, ever. Even if we were large enough to operate the machine, if we could rig up some windlass or lever, it wouldn't help. Thorkel is, I think, the only man in the world who could work out the formula for returning us to our normal size. There's not much chance of his doing that.'

Baker said slowly, 'If we kill Thorkel, we'll have to remain—like this—forever?'

'Yeah. And if we don't—he'll get us, sooner or later. Well?'

'It's a—a hard choice,' Mary whispered. 'But at least we'd be alive—'

Baker nodded, and pointed to where Thorkel's discarded gun lay across the chair.

It was aimed at the scientist's cot.

'By God!' Stockton grunted. 'That's it!'

Having come to a decision, the three acted quickly. They climbed the chair, and using books as props and the scissor-blade as a lever, adjusted the shotgun.

'Sight it at his pillow,' Stockton told Baker, who was looking down the gun barrel. 'Up a little . . . there! Right at his left ear!'

Mary was tying a piece of thread to the gun. 'Can you cock it, Bill?'

'Yeah.' He was straining with the lever. 'Okay.' But, despite Stockton's apparent assurance, he was feeling slightly sick. The choice was—horrible! To die at Thorkel's hands, or else to remain in this world of littleness forever . . .

'Thorkel's coming back!' There was panic in Mary's voice.

The three scurried to cover. Stockton managed to capture the thread's dangling end, and ran with it around a box, out of sight. Mary and Baker found shelter beside him.

The scientist's shadow fell across the threshold. He entered, yawning wearily.

Carelessly he scaled his hat on a corner and sat down on the cot, unlacing his boots.

Stockton's hand tightened on the thread. Would the titan notice the altered position of the shotgun?

Thorkel dropped his boots to the floor and started to lie down. Then, struck by a thought, he rose again and went to a cupboard, taking from it a dish of smoked meat and some cassava bread.

Placing this on the table, he drew up a chair and began to eat.

Apparently his eyes ached. Several times he polished his glasses, and presently discarded them entirely, substituting another pair which he took from a tray on the table. He ate slowly, nodding with weariness. And at last he removed the new pair of spectacles and slumped down, pillowing his head in his arms.

He slept.

'Oh, damn!' Baker said with heart-felt fury. 'We can't use the gun now. We couldn't prop it up at the right angle. It looks like the jungle, after all—unless maybe we can use a knife on him.'

Stockton looked speculatively at the scissor-blade. 'Wouldn't be sure enough. We've got to kill him, not disable him.'

'Disable him—that's it!' Mary said suddenly.

'Bill, he's blind without his glasses!'

The three stared at each other, new hope springing to life within them. 'That's it!' Stockton approved. 'We can hide them, and bargain with him, perhaps—'

'We must be quiet,' Mary warned.

But Thorkel slept heavily. He did not stir when the little people climbed up to the table, and, one by one, handed down the spectacles till they could be thrust out of sight through a hole in the floor.

'That's the last pair,' Mary said with satisfaction, peering down into the depths. 'He won't find them in a hurry.'

'The last but one,' Baker denied. 'Bill—' He stopped. Stockton was gone.

They saw him back on the table-top, tip-toeing toward the sleeping Thorkel. He skirted the specimen box and approached the spectacles, gripped in the scientist's huge hand.

Gingerly he attempted to disengage them. Thorkel stirred. He mumbled something, and his head lifted, slow with sleep.

Fear tightened Stockton's throat. On impulse he jerked the spectacles from Thorkel's hand and fled behind the specimen box.

Blinking, Thorkel felt around for the glasses. His pale eyes stared unseeingly.

There was a little thud. Stockton, crouching at the table-edge, saw the spectacles hit the floor, without breaking. He did not see Thorkel rise and fumble toward the specimen box.

Mary's voice was ice-shrill.

'Jump, Bill, jump!'

Hastily, Stockton slipped over the edge, hung by his hands, and dropped. The floor rushed up to meet him. He landed heavily, but sprang up and fled before Thorkel could see the movement.

The scientist said, a curious tremor in his voice, 'So you've come back. So you are here, eh?'

There was no answer. Thorkel stumbled to the back door, closed it, and put his back against it.

And, for the first time, Thorkel knew fear.

Thorkel tugged at his mustache. His voice shook when he spoke.

'You would dare attack me? Well, that is a mistake. You are shut up in this room. And I will find you—' He whirled at a fancied movement or sound, glaring blindly, swinging his bald head from side to side with a slow, jerky motion.

'I will find you!'

Stockton pulled Mary back farther into their place of concealment behind a crate. 'He's crazy with fear. Keep quiet!'

Thorkel began to stumble around the room, kicking aside apparatus, boxes, clothing.

He fell, and when he rose there was blood trickling from the corner of his mouth.

His hand closed on the shotgun. He snatched it up, and stood silent, waiting.

Without warning Thorkel flung up the gun and fired. The crashing echoes filled the room. Stockton peered out, saw that there was a gaping, splintered hole in the bottom of the back door.

Thorkel waited. Then a grim smile twisted his lips. He felt his way to the table and sought for the tray of extra glasses. His hand encountered nothing. The room was utterly still.

'Then—this is war?' Thorkel asked slowly. With a sudden furious motion he broke down the shotgun and gripped the barrel, holding it like a club.

He dropped to hands and knees and felt beneath the table. Slowly he advanced. In a moment, Stockton realized, he would find the glasses where they lay.

Stockton's sandaled feet made no sound as he raced forward. Before Thorkel could react, the geologist had sprung beneath his nose, snatched up the glasses, and smashed them against the table-leg.

Thorkel swung viciously with the gun-barrel.

Stockton, perforce, dropped the glasses and fled. The huge metal club missed him by inches. He vanished into the shadows.

Crouching in their hiding-places, the three little people stared, frozen, as the titan form of Thorkel rose above the table-edge. He was donning his glasses. One lens was splintered and useless.

Blood-stained, dirt-smeared, and terrible, the giant towered there. His voice rose in a shout of laughter.

'Now!' he roared. 'Now you can call me Cyclops!'

Swiftly he strode forward. With methodical haste he began to search the room, overturning boxes, flinging the cot aside to examine some cases beneath it. Stockton made a peremptory signal. Mary and Baker dashed out from their hiding-place between Thorkel's discarded boots. They followed Stockton swiftly toward the back door.

'Outside, quick!' he whispered. 'He can't see us. The cot's in the way.'

They clambered through the gaping hole the shotgun charge had made. It was not easy, and Mary's clothing caught on a sharp splinter.

The cloth ripped as Stockton jerked at it.

Footsteps thudded across the floor. The door was flung open. Thorkel switched on the floodlight.

His shadow momentarily hid the three as they raced forward. The mouth of the mine-shaft loomed up before them, a plank stretched across the pit.

'Down there!' Stockton gasped. 'It's our only chance.'

It was the only possible place of concealment. But Thorkel's one good eye did not miss the little people's movements as they scrambled over the brink and down the steep rock of the shaft-walls. Skirting the windlass, he fell to his hands and knees and crawled out upon the plank, steadying himself with one hand on the rope that ran down into black depths.

Stockton, clinging to a rock, realized that he still held his scissor-blade sword.

He lifted it in futile threat.

There was a splintering crack as Thorkel struck at his quarry. The gun-barrel clashed on rock. And, abruptly, the plank caved in and dropped.

Thorkel still gripped the windlass-rope with one hand, and that saved him. For a second he swung wildly, while the echoing crash of the falling wood and the gun-barrel echoed up from the depths. Then his grip became surer. Panting, he hung there briefly, his bald head gleaming with sweat.

He began to climb up the rope.

Stockton glanced around quickly. Mary was clinging to a sloping rock, her white face turned toward the giant.

Baker was looking at the mineralogist, and his gaunt gray features were twisted with hopeless fury.

Stockton made a quick gesture, pointed to his sword, and began to swarm back up to the surface.

Instantly Baker caught his meaning. If the rope to which Thorkel clung could be cut—

But it was thick, terribly thick, for a tiny man and a scissor-blade!

Thorkel pulled himself slowly upward. In a moment Baker saw, he would reach safety. The trader's lips drew back from his teeth in a mirthless grin; he abruptly rose and edged forward a few paces.

Then he sprang.

Out and down he went, and his clutching hands found Thorkel's collar. Before the scientist could understand what had happened, Baker was clawing and snarling like a terrier at his throat. Thorkel almost lost his grip.

Gasping with fear and rage, he shook his head violently, trying to knock his assailant free.

'You dirty killer!' Baker snarled.

He was tossed about madly, once almost crushed between Thorkel's chin and chest. And then, suddenly, Thorkel was falling . . .

With a whine and a whir the windlass ran out as the rope was severed. A long, quavering cry burst from Thorkel's throat as he dropped away into the darkness. Higher and higher it rose—and ended.

Stockton ran to the brink and peered over. Mary was clambering weakly up toward him. And, behind her, was Baker.

❖ ❖ ❖

Bill was standing beside an upright book, a curious expression on his face. He looked around vaguely.

'The machine—' he told Mary. 'Can you work it?'

Mary was poring over Thorkel's notebooks. She said despondently, 'It's no good, Bill. The device is only a condensor. It can't bring people back to normal size. We'll have to remain this size the rest of our lives. And now, we've got to get back to civilization, somehow—'

'As we are?' Baker's face fell. 'That's impossible.'

'Wait a minute,' Stockton interrupted. 'I've a hunch—do you remember when we first saw Thorkel, after he reduced us?'

'Yeah. So what?'

'He wasn't trying to kill us then. He just wanted to weigh and measure us. But after he examined Dr Bulfinch, he turned into a vicious killer. Why do you suppose that happened?'

'He probably intended to kill us all along. For trying to steal his secrets,' Baker suggested. 'He was probably afraid that we would warn the Allies of his plans.'

'Maybe. But he wasn't in any hurry at first. He knew he could dispose of us any time he wanted. Only after he examined Dr Bulfinch he—found out something that made it necessary to get rid of us in a hurry.'

Mary caught her breath. 'What?'

'I saw a white mule in the jungle a while ago. A colt. Paco was playing with it. At first I figured it might be Pinto's colt, but mules are sterile, of course. That meant two albino mules here—which isn't very probable—or else it was Pinto. Remember, Pedro said the dog used to play with the mule.'

'How big was the mule?' Baker asked abruptly.

'The size of a half-grown colt. Listen, Steve, when we first came out of the cellar I measured myself against that book—*Human Physiology*. It was just higher than my head. But now it only comes up to my chest!'

'We're growing!' Mary whispered. 'That's it.'

'Sure. That's what Thorkel found out when he examined Dr Bulfinch, and why he tried to kill us before we grew back to normal size. I think it's a progressively accelerative process. In two weeks, or perhaps ten days, we'll be back to normal.'

'It's logical,' the girl commented. 'Once the compressive force of radium power is removed, we expand—slowly but elastically. The electrons swing back to their normal orbits. The energy we absorbed under the ray will be liberated in quanta—'

'Ten days,' Baker murmured. 'And then we can go back down the river again!'

But it was a month before the three, once more normal in size, reached the Andean village that was their first destination. The sight of human beings, no longer gigantic, was warmly reassuring. Indians leaned against the huts, scratching lazily for fleas.

Peering down the archway along the street, a ragged Bill Stockton turned to grin at Mary.

'Looks good, eh?'

Baker was absorbed in thought. 'We've got to decide,' he said, scratching his stubbled cheek. 'One way, we get our pictures in the paper and tanks of free *pulque*. But it's just as likely we'll end up in a padded cell if we tell the truth. If we don't tell the truth—'

He paused, stiffening. A mangy cat had appeared from beyond the arch. Baker's muscles tensed; his breath burst out in an explosive '*Scat!*' as he sprang forward.

The cat vanished, shocked to the core.

Baker's chest inflated several inches. 'Well,' he said, with the quiet pride of achievement, 'did either of you see *that*?'

'No,' murmured Stockton, who was seizing the opportunity to kiss Mary. 'Go away. Quietly. And quickly.'

Baker shrugged and followed the cat, a predatory gleam in his eye.

The Diminishing Draft

Waldemar Kaempffert

Frivolous fingers play with Science's secrets in a perilous game of hide-and-seek

'Well, I've engaged an assistant,' I announced to my wife one day at luncheon.

'I am glad of that. You have been working much too hard. Who is he?'

'It isn't a "he,"' I replied as carelessly as I could. 'It's Jeanne Briand.'

'But why Jeanne Briand? What qualifications has she? What does she know of biochemistry?' she inquired, too searching, I thought, in that high-pitched, staccato voice of hers which latterly had grated on me.

'She's taken her master's degree,' I explained as best I could, 'and besides, she had a course in biology under Calhoun.'

The wife of a university professor may not be versed in the subject with which his name is identified, but she knows that academic standards are high. Knows that a vivacious, copper-haired, laughing-eyed girl who has dabbled in a few text-books and chased butterflies with a net is not ordinarily given an important post in a famous biochemical laboratory.

'I think you might have taken young Mitchel or some other post-graduate in your department.'

That was all we said. She suspected something. There was no question of it.

And so Jeanne was duly installed in my home laboratory. I made it very plain to her that she must keep regular hours, also that she must conduct herself as my assistant and not as the woman whom I loved and whom I hoped to wed.

❖ ❖ ❖

From the first I had my misgivings. It was Jeanne who conceived the idea of working in the laboratory with me—not I. She was as out of place among my instruments and reagent bottles as a wood nymph.

It is needless to dwell on the circumstances that swayed us, needless to recount here how difficult it was to part whenever we had passed an hour together, needless to picture the dreamy longing that hung over us both until our hands and lips touched again. That is a characteristic of every week-old love.

'Please let me help you in your work,' she pleaded over and over again. 'I want to be near you always. Let me do anything—anything. I can keep the instruments clean. I can write down your notes. It is unbearable to see you only like this, once in a long while. Let me work with you in the laboratory.'

'But you forget,' I reasoned, 'that the laboratory where I do most of my work is in my own house. And I am married. Some day we shall be together always. Think of the risks that we would run. We can't have a scandal. Sooner or later we would be discovered.'

I had intended to make a clean breast of the whole affair to my wife and free myself from my marital ties in the conventional way, even though it meant the end of my university career. But Jeanne could not and would not wait. A man of stronger will than mine would have yielded. The desire to have her ever near me, to see the winsome smile on her face, to sense her presence in the same room, moved me more than her arguments. In short, I yielded.

Scientifically speaking, she was all but useless in the laboratory. She had some talent for drawing, and so I employed her in making diagrams for my treatise on 'Experimental Evolution.'

She radiated femininity. She had an elfish way of interrupting me in my work. At the most critical stage in dissecting the head of an insect under the glass, she would come up and stroke my hair or kiss the nape of my neck. If I reproved her, she wept, which meant much kissing away of her tears and mollifying her with the endearments that all lovers automatically invent on the spur of the moment. And yet, she honestly tried to help me, simply because of her slavish devotion to me.

Although she needed constant supervision, her drawings were excellent. Indeed, they soon justified her presence in my laboratory in the eyes of the entire university.

It was about a fortnight after she became my nominal assistant that I assigned to her the task of making a series of sketches to demonstrate the effect of baroturpinol on parameba.

I may mention in passing that parameba is a microscopic animal—a

mere cell—found in stagnant ponds, and that in a dilute solution of baroturpinol the whole structure of the creature undergoes a remarkable
change. It was I who discovered the effect of baroturpinol on micro-
organisms of the parameba class. Immersed in baroturpinol the few cells
of which parameba is composed dwindle and dwindle under the microscope until finally the organism, still keeping its own shape, disappears.

I had completely misinterpreted this disappearance of microorgan-
isms under the action of baroturpinol. I thought that they merely disinte-
grated. It was Jeanne who taught me otherwise.

One day, while she was engaged in making the drawings which would
show the progressive disappearance of parameba, Jeanne exclaimed:

'They've come back again!'

'Who has?' I questioned, thinking that she was talking of people
whom we knew. Besides, I was engrossed in correcting the proofs of a
scientific paper.

'Why, the parameba. I can't understand it!'

A glance convinced me that she was right. In less than a minute I saw a
specimen literally grow under my eyes into a full-fledged parameba. I can
liken the proceeding only to the coming of an object toward one, with all
the attendant increase in size that the movement implies.

Perhaps I may make myself clearer if I say that the restoration of parameba, as I saw it then and many times after, was like a railway train traveling toward one from the distance. At first a far speck is visible; then the
outline of a locomotive engine can be distinguished; and at last a huge
machine and thundering cars threaten to crush one out of existence.

But that was not all. *Parameba came back alive!* Every biologist and
chemist supposed that baroturpinol was a deadly poison. At all events, I
had noticed that when any microorganism was brought into contact with
even a trace of baroturpinol, all activity ceased. Death seemed necessarily
to precede the process of shrinking. I could hardly believe my eyes when
I saw my resuscitated parameba moving about with that characteristic
tumbling motion by which it is so well known.

'What have you been doing?' I asked.

'Just what you told me to do.'

'Dear, dear Jeanne,' I said, taking her two hands in mine. 'Do you know
that you have made what may prove to be a very important discovery in
biology? Do you know that you may have upset the whole theory of life?'

She clapped her hands. But at the time the wonderful scientific significance of what she had seen was lost to her. She saw that I approved of her,
and she was happy.

But what did this astonishing revival of parameba mean? Over and over again I watched for the return of specimens under the microscope. Parameba would not return. I questioned Jeanne closely; I even watched her prepare a few slides herself, hoping that she had unconsciously departed from the routine that I had prescribed and had contaminated the baroturpinol in a way that would explain everything.

At last she remembered. She had touched the slide with a little glass rod in order to shift it on the stage of the instrument. The rod did not seem clean. She thought to improve matters by wiping it. A painstaking and conscientious laboratory worker would have used a piece of sterile cotton. Jeanne used her pocket handkerchief. It was clear enough that that little piece of linen was strangely linked with the accidental revivification of parameba.

My deduction was confirmed when I, too, experimented with the handkerchief. I deposited a single drop of stagnant water on a clean glass slide. Under the powerful lens I saw parameba tumbling about. Then I added a drop of baroturpinol (one gram of barturpinol to a cubic centimeter of distilled water is the proportion, as everyone knows), and at once all activity ceased. Apparently killed, the specimens of parameba began to shrink in that curious manner upon which I had already dilated. I took a glass rod and wiped it on Jeanne's handkerchief. First making sure that parameba had quite disappeared, I touched the little drop of moisture on the slide. My guess was right. It was Jeanne's handkerchief. Parameba came rushing back to life as startlingly as at first.

The handkerchief had been definitely linked with the phenomenon, but I was in the dark as much as ever. What mysterious properties had this little piece of fabric that it should thus divert the whole course of modern biochemistry?

'Tell me, Jeanne,' I said, 'did your handkerchief touch anything here—some solution?'

'No, I'm sure.'

'But you must have done something with it. Feel. It's a little damp.'

'I wiped my eyes with it,' she admitted reluctantly. 'I had been crying at something that you said.'

I did not stop to inquire what it was that I had said. A light dawned on me. Her tears had so uncannily brought back parameba to life! And tears—what are they, when stripped of all sentiment, but salt water?

A spectroscopic analysis of Jeanne's handkerchief convinced me that common salt had the property of bringing back parameba to life.

Dozens of experiments showed that almost any solution of salt would answer; the stronger it was the more quickly did life triumph over death.

✧ ✧ ✧

And now began an investigation which was a strange mixture of scientific research and love-making. To Jeanne it was like a play. She was very much bored when I would repeat tests perhaps twenty-five or fifty times simply to be sure of my results. But when we experimented with a new organism, she was all eagerness, all dancing eyes and clapping hands.

It was Jeanne who made the discovery in the first place, and Jeanne who developed its full possibilities. She had no well-considered plan of work: she simply allowed her impulses, her girlish whims to sway her.

'I want things to happen,' she would say, as I tried to explain to her how time-wasting was this unscientific, haphazard, blind plunging into a new and unexplored field. And yet, through her insatiable desire for excitement, her dramatic interest, we found out what really happened when higher organisms were subjected to the action of baroturpinol.

As for me, I confined myself entirely to simple-celled organisms, all so small that they cannot be seen with the naked eye. Here, I thought, was enough work to engage me for years. But that was too tame for Jeanne. She had the imagination and the daring that seem to accompany scientific ignorance.

I kept a little aquarium in one corner of the laboratory—a spawning glass jungle of fresh-water life. It was a never-ending source of entertainment for her. I have known her to sit for an hour at a time watching crayfish crawl lazily along on the bottom, or a school of tiny goldfish fighting for a crumb that she had mischievously tossed in.

One day—it was about two months after she came to me—she ran to me all radiant, holding a bowl at the bottom of which were two or three tiny golden flakes. They were so small that I had to hold the bowl against the window and view them by transmitted light.

'What have we here?' I asked, wondering what new fancy had seized her.

'Goldfish,' she said.

'Nonsense,' I retorted.

'Yes, they are,' she insisted. 'I took some Japanese goldfish from the aquarium and dropped them into baroturpinol, and they all shrank up like this.'

If the original discovery of parameba's disappearance and return had startled me, how shall I describe the stupefaction that this announcement called forth? I saw at once what I had only guessed at before. Parameba had shrunk beyond the limits of visibility under the microscope, which accounted for its utter disappearance. But the goldfish, being much larger, had shrunk until each became perhaps the size of a dot on the letter 'i.'

I gazed at the girl with increasing wonder. Never would it have occurred to me to leap at once from simple microscopic organisms to so high a form of life as a fish. On the other hand I must say that it was my academic timidity, if I may so call it: my systematic way of proceeding stepwise from one experiment to another, that had led to the original misconception of baroturpinol's effect.

To every physician and every biologist in the world, baroturpinol was simply a germicide. True, Tilden, who had discovered it, had noticed that it had a curious puckering effect on living tissue, for which reason it had been condemned as quite useless as a substitute for mercury bichloride, phenol, and similar agents, and had been adopted simply as a convenient and cheap hospital sterilizer. And now comes my Jeanne, my capricious, dancing, playful Jeanne, a mere trifler in science, and at once uncovers the hidden possibilities of a completely misunderstood compound, not because she is a biologist, but because she simply wants to be amused.

Obviously it was my business to find out whether, like the microscopic organisms that I had thus far examined, the baroturpinoled goldfish would be revivified by a solution of common salt. I decanted the liquid in the bowl, washed the inanimate, shimmering flakes in distilled water, and then filled the bowl with a solution of salt.

The drama of parameba's return to life was repeated on a more striking scale. Very slowly the dead creatures began to expand. Soon they assumed their normal shapes—not, I repeat, that they had lost them by shrinking, but simply that the curves of their bodies were developed. It was not until they had regained their full size that life itself returned.

To me the thing was as startling as if a man, who had been poisoned by prussic acid, and who had been pronounced dead, were to open his eyes, get up, and walk. I took some pains to explain all this to the intensely amused Jeanne, and I repeated the experiment with a particularly large goldfish which I abstracted from the aquarium. I made no impression whatever upon her. She promptly christened the fish 'Lazarus' when he came back to life, and adopted him as a pet.

This impulsiveness of hers, this reckless disregard of all system and plan, could this be a form of mental activity which I had been wrong in regarding rather lazily as showing only an average order of intellect? Some one has defined intuition as a swift deduction from present facts. If that be so—I am no psychologist—then we must reckon with intuition as well as with the slower and more deliberate methods of reasoning in scientific research.

If Jeanne was anything she was intuitive. I felt that I must credit her with powers that were denied me. After all it was she, and not I, who had stumbled upon the amazing action of baroturpinol. I had done little beyond repeating her fanciful experiments under rigorous scientific control. She showed me the stars, as it were: I merely counted them.

The possession of a common secret strengthened the tie between Jeanne and myself. It was as if we had found some beautiful, priceless gem which we had decided to keep for ourselves and never to show to the world. We lost all self-control. In the beginning we had maintained a semblance of formality. She kept regular laboratory hours, coming in the morning at nine and leaving at about five in the afternoon. It was always 'Professor Hollister' and 'Miss Briand' when we spoke to each other before others.

But in truth the hours that we spent together in the laboratory each day heightened our love for each other, made us more and more indispensable to each other. It became so difficult for us to leave each other out of our sight that we even went into the woods together for specimens to be experimented with in the laboratory. These specimens she could easily have gathered for me quite alone. The university students and the villagers began to talk about us.

It was my wife, of course, who imparted that information to me.

'You are making yourself ridiculous,' she announced.

'Indeed? How?'

'Everyone is talking about you.'

I pretended not to understand. An attempt of mine to divert her attention from a topic which it made me uneasy to discuss, failed ignominiously.

'Even the postmaster in the village comments on your conduct with Jeanne Briand. Everyone stopped talking when I came to the regular sewing-circle yesterday, and looked at me in a pitying sort of way. If you have no consideration for yourself, at least consider me.'

I got up and stalked out of the room. I was neither polite nor brave.

The time had come for action. I could not go on in this way. A scandal was inevitable, and the best that I could now do was to mitigate it in some way. Jeanne and I must separate until such time as I could free myself with the aid of the divorce courts. I must tell her.

She read in my face that something was wrong when I stepped into the laboratory late that afternoon.

'You are in trouble, dear,' she said. 'What is it? Tell me.'

And then I told her of the conversation with my wife, of the utter impossibility of concealing our true relations much longer.

'We must separate, Jeanne, if it's only for a little while—until I am free. And then we shall come back to each other again, and we will work together in the laboratory not as professor and assistant, but as man and wife.'

She burst into tears. Never before had I seen a human being in such distress. She was convulsed with anguish, so that her whole body shook. I took her in my arms and did my best to soothe her.

'It will only be for a little while,' I repeated over and over again. It was all that I could think of, all that I could say.

The sun had long since set, and the laboratory was soon quite dark. We sat together on the couch in the corner in close embrace, Jeanne's head on my shoulder.

'You must rest,' I said, and laid her on the couch and sat beside her.

She half-murmured, half-moaned something and let me do with her as I would.

How long she lay there I did not realize at the time. Hour after hour slipped by. At last it struck me that we could not stay thus all night—that I must take Jeanne home.

'Come,' I admonished her, 'we must go now. It is very late.'

I helped her to her feet, pressed a button, and turned on the electric light. She was as limp as a drooping flower, all numb and listless. I walked to the closet and took her hat from its peg.

As I did so I heard footsteps in the corridor leading to the laboratory. Who could this be?

Completely unnerved as I was, distracted by Jeanne's despair, I was incapable of thinking clearly. It was one in the morning by the laboratory clock. Jeanne never stayed in the laboratory later than six. No one must find her here now.

In my ordinary senses the fall of a footstep in the corridor would not have disturbed me. Now I acted automatically and with cowardly absurdity. I ran to the door and locked it instead of flinging it open wide.

There came a knock.

If some one had leveled a pistol at me and threatened to shoot me, I could not have been more alarmed. Jeanne, too, was frightened. We looked at each other questioningly, two helpless lovers.

'Let me in,' shrilled a voice outside. It was my wife's. From what she had told me earlier in the day, I inferred that she must have been watching Jeanne like a cat, and that she carefully noted when the girl came and went. Where to find her now she knew only too well.

Concealment was useless.

'What do you want?' I asked.

A flood of impassioned accusations followed, in which Jeanne was referred to as 'that woman,' with much incoherent repetition of the phrase 'wrecked home.' The situation was damning.

❖ ❖ ❖

Months ago I had decided that the divorce proceedings should be free from the usual scandal. But what a ghastly story this would make in the newspapers! I could read the suggestive headlines and the salaciously worded account of the manner in which my wife had trapped me—a university professor. The sensational newspapers in particular would rejoice in the opportunity of pilloring the supposedly academic scientist and of exposing him as if he were a libertine in cap and gown.

It was Jeanne who saved us. I stood like one paralyzed, not knowing what to do. It was the rustle of her skirt that brought me to my senses. I turned around just in time to see her raise a beaker of baroturpinol to her lips and pour it down.

I know that I cried out: for there was a sudden cessation of the clamor outside the door. I rushed to Jeanne's side. Good Heavens! What would the effect be?

Never had we experimented with baroturpinol on anything higher than a fish. She lost consciousness in my arms. I thought she was dead. She was pallid and stiff, as if *rigor mortis* had set in. Then came over her that change which I had observed under the microscope and in the test tube. Her form dwindled and dwindled in my arms as if it were slipping from me, until at last I held nothing but her limp clothes.

It was as if both her soul and her body had drifted away from the room. As if she had slipped out of her earthly fabric like a butterfly from its chrysalis. I dropped the bundle on the floor and began to grope within it. Somewhere within these folds I knew must be the shrunken body of my Jeanne.

At last I found it—a little white form. I slipped it into my pocket. The clothes and hat I stuffed into a chest.

My courage had returned now. I stepped to the door, unlocked it and flung it wide open. My wife entered, and with her a maid whom she evidently brought as a witness. Her lips were tightly drawn; her eyes were mere slits. If ever there was an infuriated woman bent on vengeance, it was she.

She looked about her. Under other circumstances her astonishment would have been comical. All this furtive watching, all these clamorous accusations—all for nothing? She darted to the closet in which Jeanne would hang her hat and coat and I my laboratory aprons, convinced that Jeanne was hidden there. She threw back the door with such violence that the knob indented the plaster wall.

'Where is she? What have you done with her?' she screamed.

'You see that you are mistaken; there is no one here.'

She saw that further inquiry would be useless. Outwitted but not deceived, she swept angrily out of the room. I locked the door after her.

I sat down at the laboratory table, took out of my pocket the thing that had once been my Jeanne, and placed it before me. My eyes were blurred with tears. So this was all that was left to me of Jeanne. This was the price of my weakness and my cowardice! She was dead now, and I felt as if I had been an accomplice in her suicide.

There comes an interval in every grief, an interval of calm, during which all mundane affairs seem trivial and even one's own misery becomes petty. It is as if one had passed out of a long, dark, narrow passageway into a vast open twilight beyond. In one of those intervals of calm I regained sufficient control of myself to examine the white remnant of Jeanne.

The thing that to my fevered touch had felt like a mere shapeless mass when I hastily thrust it into my pocket, revealed itself as a little statuette of wondrous beauty. It seemed carved out of ivory, this exquisite miniature, frozen Jeanne. What would not Cellini have given if he could have shaped a figure so beautiful?

Everything was white except the hair, her eyebrows, and the lashes of her closed eyes. The lips were delicately tinted like a budding rose, but they had not the rich color of pulsating life. As for her hair, it still lay in tiny coils about her head, a mass of twisted, coppery brown. Jeanne must have been in the act of falling when I caught her in my arms. One foot of the little figure was raised, and it seemed as if she were about to sink down on one knee.

A sculptor would have marveled at the mere material of which this rare work of art had been fashioned. It seemed like wax; yet it had nothing of the oiliness of wax to the touch. Could it be ivory? It was too exquisitely white.

And then the wonderful perfection of its detail! I was afraid to touch the lashes of the eyes, lest I should break them. And the little ears, how finely they were modeled! The little hands and feet, how scrupulously every curve and line and hollow had been preserved! And the dear body of her, how plastic for all its lifeless rigidity!

For the first time in my life I understood the ecstatic ravings of artists when they endeavored to reveal to others the beauty that is so evident to them. Beauty such as this left one inarticulate.

The face perplexed me—or rather its expression. Jeanne was all gaiety and animation. But this reduction of herself suggested nothing of that. How could it? Jeanne was motion personified, flitting hither and thither like a butterfly. These placid features, with no trace of the smile that lit up the dearest face in the world, were still and cold.

The aspect of this precious, pallid beauty, all that was left to me of Jeanne, overcame me. I know that I sobbed and I am not ashamed to own it. I vowed to myself that I would preserve this remnant of her, this visible evidence of her self-sacrifice, as a thing to be worshiped. I would enshrine it in some secret, fitting way: it would be my holy of holies.

Dawn was breaking. I washed my hot, fevered face and held a water soaked towel to my swollen eyes for a few minutes. Fresh air and a long walk would do me good, I thought. I wrapped the white figure tenderly in cotton, dropped it into my pocket, and then walked out into the open.

I must have wandered about in a stupor. For the life of me I cannot now tell where I went or how I returned. I know that the sun was well up in the heavens when I found myself in and went to my room. In the afternoon I had to give a lecture on Mendel's laws to the senior class in biology. I flung myself down on the bed, dressed as I was, hoping that I might snatch an hour's sleep, so that I might not appear too manifestly beside myself with grief.

I must have dozed for I was awakened by a knock at the door. It was the maid. I was wanted at the telephone.

'Say that I can't be disturbed,' I directed her.

'She says it's very important,' was the reply.

'Who does?'

'Miss Briand's landlady.'

My state of mind can be imagined when I say that I could not divine why Jeanne's landlady wished to speak to me on the telephone. I found out quickly enough when I answered.

Did I know where Miss Briand was? asked the voice over the telephone. She had not been at home all night, and it was now past noon. Was she at the laboratory yesterday? When did she leave? Should her disappearance be reported to the police?

I could tell from her voice that the woman was concerned more about herself than about Jeanne. She ran a respectable house, she insisted again and again. She did hope nothing had happened which would compromise her or her establishment. I reassured her as best I could and promised her that I would look into the matter of Jeanne's disappearance and communicate with her again.

Her reference to the police startled me. It brought me to my senses. It had not occurred to me before that a human being cannot step out of existence, as it were, unchallenged. Suppose the police were to descend on the laboratory and investigate!

What could I say? No one would believe me, of course, if I told the truth. About the experiments with parameba and how they had led step by step to Jeanne's undoing. Even if I summoned the best experts, even if they confirmed my discoveries, what biologist would be bold enough to administer baroturpinol to a human being and prove that even the highest forms of life yielded to the strange influence of that mysterious compound? And what human being, short of a madman could be found who would willingly sacrifice himself? Good Heavens!

And then there were Jeanne's clothes. They would surely be found in the chest.

I sank into a chair. My whole body was bathed in a perspiration of fright. Suppose that I were accused of murder? A divorce scandal was bad enough, but a murder, a murder—

Lecturing was out of the question. I telephoned to the university that illness would prevent me from attending and that the class was to be dismissed. I had to think this out; I must gain time. My case was clearly desperate.

All at once a ray of hope flashed upon me. Why not try salt? If parameba, a sea-urchin, a goldfish—and a fish is, after all, not so very low in the scale of evolution—can be restored to their natural proportions and to life, why not a human being? Yes, perhaps the salt solution would save me and bring back my Jeanne to me.

But what reason had I to suppose that because a few animals could be reduced and expanded at will, I might bring Jeanne back to life? Suppose that the little statuette should return to life, but to remain a mere miniature of Jeanne? That was too horrible!

Worse still, suppose that the figure should reassume the girl's natural shape, but that no spark of life would reanimate the body? What then? I should be worse off than ever. The white remnant of her that I carried with me could be hidden. The clothes in the chest, too, could be disposed of. No one could prove that Jeanne was really dead.

But a lifeless body—

I fled into the laboratory. If ever a man was on the verge of madness, it was I. Tormented by grief at the loss of Jeanne and stricken with terror at the prospect of arrest, I felt like a wild beast at bay.

I longed for some simple-minded, practical, unscientific friend to whom I could turn for counsel in my need. I knew the difference between a holothurian and a jellyfish, but in the cloistered university I had lost track of human hearts and problems. However, my problem was my problem; I alone could solve it.

It came to me very clearly at last that I owed it to Jeanne to make some effort at resuscitating all that was left of her. The resolution was more easily made than carried out. Where should I conduct this momentous experiment?

The laboratory naturally suggested itself first. I dismissed the thought almost at once. There was no vessel large enough to hold a human body, and suspicion might be aroused if I had one brought in. I might go to a hotel and engage a room and bath; the bathtub would surely serve the purpose.

But suppose that the little figure of Jeanne should swell and magnify, and suppose that life should not return. I would have to explain the presence of a corpse in my room—the corpse of a woman who had played a part in my life and for whom the police were searching. That would help neither Jeanne nor me. Better a thousand times that she should remain in my pocket than that!

Finally I came to the conclusion that I must go to some lonely place by the sea. Had we not discovered early in our investigations that any solution of salt, even seawater, performed the miracle of bringing back to life organisms which had been diminished by baroturpinol? Besides, would it not be easy to dispose of the corpse if life did not return?

I looked at my watch. It was just half past three. Glaston-by-the-Sea was three hours' distant by the railway. If I left this afternoon, by night all my doubts and fears would be dispelled.

I had not slept in twenty-four hours. Some rest I must have. My nerves were so unstrung that I could feel my eyelids quivering; I could hardly touch a book or an implement without dropping it.

So I went into my room, and bathed, and threw myself down on the bed to catch what little sleep I could.

Glaston-by-the-Sea is a fishing village comprising nothing more than a dozen houses. In front of it lies the ocean; in back tower cliffs of limestone. The sand stretches on either side of the village for miles and miles. Walk ten minutes away from the village and you might as well be in the Desert of Sahara for any signs of human life that you can see.

I knew the coast well; many a specimen had I collected among the rocks as the tide went out.

It was dark when I alighted from the train, four miles from Glaston. The full moon was rising in the east—a great round, yellow topaz that crept higher and higher in the sky. I had not counted on a bright night.

To carry out a hazardous experiment in the aspect of that cold, luminous disk seemed too public. It was so like a round, inscrutable face that looked down at me in benignant curiosity. Then it occurred to me how strangely fascinated Jeanne had always been by the full moon. How she had longed for the time when we might watch it rise together in some such lonely place as this, shut off from the strife and the clamor and the prying eyes of the world. I am not superstitious, but it did seem as if that great ball in the sky might be a good omen.

At about ten o'clock I reached the shore two miles above Glaston; for I had carefully avoided the village. It was flood tide. The sea was dappled with opalescent ripples. Now and then a swelling wave would roll up on the sands and the water would tumble reluctantly back again in a vast expanse of foam. Only the rhythmic wash of a smooth sea broke the silence of that moonlit solitude.

Jeanne's clothes and hat I had brought with me in a traveling-bag. I took them out and spread them on the beach just as I imagined she would have arranged them herself in her chamber.

Now that I thought of it, this idea of coming to Glaston and making an heroic attempt to bring Jeanne back to life seemed like a stroke of genius. What if the experiment did fail? What if the reduced image of herself did resume its normal shape, but without coming back to life? I could leave the corpse on the sands. It would seem as if she had died in some inexplicable way.

Here were her clothes all neatly arranged, testifying mutely in my behalf. There was no sign of violence.

One by one I took off my own clothes and laid them down beside Jeanne's. Very, very carefully I unwrapped the parcel in which I had carried her about. I feared that I might break off a strand of hair or nick a foot or hand.

Holding the figure in my outstretched hands as if it were a sacred image, I walked into the sea straight toward the moon, my face uplifted. This was more than a scientific experiment. Human life, human happiness, human love were at stake.

Now that I look back at the events of that unforgettable night, the whole proceeding must have seemed more like a religious ceremony than a frantic man's desperate effort to save the thing that he held most precious. Surely no worshiper who had ever entered an ancient Egyptian temple was more reverentially hopeful than I, nor more innocently expectant of a miracle that would sweep away all earthly doubts and reveal the hand of destiny itself pointing toward the light.

Slowly the water rose to my knees, to my waist, and at last to my breast. It lapped the frail figure in my hand. I clutched the thing lest it should slip from my grasp. How long I stood thus, shoulder-high in the waves, I do not know. Perhaps it was only five minutes, perhaps as long as a quarter of an hour.

I know that I was stricken with terror for a time; for the figure in my hands might have been made of stone for any change that I could feel.

Was I to fail? Was Jeanne hopelessly, irretrievably dead?

Then a moment came when the figure seemed to slip in my hands. I grasped it tighter lest I should lose it. Still it slipped—slipped as a fish slips in the hands. Now I realized what was happening. Jeanne was growing, literally growing in my crooked fingers! I almost swooned.

Even if the swelling miniature were not the most precious thing in the world to me, even if it did not mean happiness and life itself, I would have found it difficult to retain my self-control. Very, very slowly the figure grew to the size of a child. I had to hold it in my arms now; it was not only larger, but perceptibly heavier.

A doubt assailed me. Would it stop growing? I prayed that it might keep on.

Presently it grew so large that I could no longer hold it in my arms alone. I walked back a few steps and lowered the figure so that its feet touched the bottom. But I saw to it that it was completely immersed, fearful lest some monstrous effect might be produced if even a shoulder were dry and could not grow with the rest.

In half an hour, I should judge, what had been apparently an exquisite statuette, something that I could carry in my pocket, had become the full-sized form of my Jeanne. But it was still hard. There was no feeling of yielding flesh—nothing but the rigidity of so much clay.

For that I had been prepared by the observation that I had made in my laboratory. Life returned to a shrunken organism slowly, almost hesitantly.

At last I felt Jeanne soften in my arms. She was a thing of flesh now. Her form had become supple and flexible; I could feel it as so much tissue.

And then the miracle of miracles happened! Her bosom heaved; she sighed; her eyes opened. She moaned, and stared at me, utterly bewildered. Her mind could not orient itself at first. In a dim way she seemed to realize who I was.

I could feel her arms tighten about my neck, and so I carried her to the beach, in the most ecstatic and exalted state in which I have ever been.

I told my wife everything—everything of the initial experiments with parameba and the goldfish, everything except Jeanne's bold swallowing of the baroturpinol in a critical situation and of her subsequent miraculous reanimation. Jeanne meant all to me; and my wife had ceased to be, if I may say so, what she never was. I wanted a divorce, and I said so frankly.

'So this is to be the end?' she sobbed bitterly.

'I see no other way. To remain as we are, and to pretend that all is as it should be between us, would mean misery for both of us. It is better that we should part.'

'But what if I should refuse? Is it right that you should begin a new and happy life and that I, after all these years, should drift about aimlessly and wretchedly? This home is mine as much as yours. I made it what it is, and shall I give up everything for a woman whom I hate?'

There was much more in the same vein. I had not counted on this. It was partly bitter hatred of Jeanne that swayed her and partly wounded pride.

It had never occurred to me before that marriage means more to a woman than the building of a nest and the gratification of the mating instinct. In her scheme of existence the conventions or vanities of married life are enormously important. Her conjugal rights, the social status brought about by the mere act of marriage are to her what his patent of nobility is to a duke—something not to be relinquished without a struggle.

My wife refused point-blank to divorce me.

'But that is senseless,' I argued. 'If I stay here, our life will be a mere travesty; if I leave you and go my own way you will not be unhappier. What do you gain by refusing?'

'You can't marry a woman who has ruined my life, and whom I hate. By refusing to divorce you I destroy her. No decent man or woman will befriend her, knowing what she is to you.'

With that she flounced out of the room.

This turn of events I had not foreseen. I knew that divorce meant the end of my university career, and for that I was fully prepared. But to have the finger of scorn pointed at the woman I loved—

I am a social being. Companionship means much to me, and it meant as much to Jeanne. For a few months we might be sufficient to ourselves. Then would come a time when I would wish to spend an evening with congenial friends, and Jeanne with women who give teas and form organizations for the uplift of the poor and unenlightened.

What then? I could hardly venture to cross the thresholds of those temples of purity and virtue whither I would eventually be drawn, and on my arm a woman whose relations to me were regarded as scandalous.

And she—she would undoubtedly be rebuffed if she sought to enter the circle within which she now moved so freely.

You see that a scientist can be far more practical in his reasoning than the world supposes. After all, his whole training teaches him how to deal with facts.

I was to meet Jeanne that evening in a dense grove, near a little farmhouse about half a mile from the end of the trolley-line. Ever since her astonishing restoration we had arranged to see each other there three times a week. Her return to the laboratory was out of the question for the time being.

There she was at the appointed time and place, looking very demure in a neat white dress which she had made herself. She saw that I was troubled, and I told her at once the outcome of the afternoon's parley.

Either she would not or she could not see the situation in its true light. Was I not everything in her life? She was more than willing to forego ordinary social intercourse if she could only work and live with me. A thousand reasons she advanced to prove how unnecessary the outer world must be to us.

She was a born romanticist, living perpetually in a fairy castle on a mountain-top capped with silvery clouds. In that atmosphere there is no time; Jeanne lived only in the present. I could hope for no practical assistance from her. I must reason this problem out for myself.

So I changed the topic at the first opportunity, and we passed the rest of the evening in the usual lighthearted way.

During these meetings we talked chiefly of the romantic possibilities of baroturpinol.

'How simple and cheap it would be for us to travel,' she would ramble on. 'You could carry me in your pocket just as you did to Glaston; or I could pack you away in my handbag and take you with me. If I had a friend, I might even have myself sent to you by parcel-post. Salt water you can get everywhere.'

Of course I smiled at this, but I'm not so sure that Jeanne was not serious.

That was the last I ever saw of her.

Two days later I was to keep my tryst with Jeanne for the third time that week. I was in the grove at the appointed hour. She did not come. Was she detained? Or was she ill? I fretted and fumed, hoping that each figure that loomed up in the darkness (for the grove was near the road) might be Jeanne. At eleven o'clock I gave up all hope of seeing her that night.

My wife met me as I opened the door of my house.

'May I speak to you a moment?' she asked.

I hung up my hat and followed her into her own room. She took from her safe a little box and laid it on her dressing-table. Next she raised a window which opened on a paved court below. It was clear she was following a well-thought-out plan of action.

'I believe you wish to say something to me,' I said to relieve my suspense.

'Yes.' Nothing more.

She untied the box, concealed it from me as she did so. Presently she turned around, holding in her hand an envelope.

'Read this,' she said. 'It came yesterday.'

The envelope had been steamed open. It was addressed to me in Jeanne's handwriting.

'And so you open and read my letters?' I queried angrily.

'When I suspect that they concern me, I do,' she retorted coolly.

I reproduce it here. That letter and a lock of hair that she once gave me are all that I have of Jeanne.

Dearest Dick:

I have been thinking so much of that wonderful night on the beach at Glaston—the night when I was born again on the bosom of the sea, just as if I were another Aphrodite. How beautiful it was to awaken and find myself looking at you by the light of the moon! I want to live all that over again, to come back from oblivion and find myself clinging to you.

If I were to ask you, I know that you would never consent to my becoming a dead image of myself again. You would suspect my motive if I were to ask you for some baroturpinol. So I have bought what I need. If you will come to meet me in the grove beyond the farm at the usual time on Friday, you will find only a little white Jeanne in the midst of her clothes.

Put her in your pocket and take her with you to Glaston next Monday. The moon will then be full.

Jeanne

Was I frightened? I can hardly say. It was as if some one had struck me a blow. I was stunned.

Intuitively I sensed the diabolical thing that my wife had done. I had told her enough of my first experiments; the rest Jeanne's letter made sufficiently plain.

'When I read this,' she explained, all the while standing, 'I understood everything. I know now what happened in the laboratory that afternoon when I knocked at the door.

'Now, listen carefully to what I say. I have told you that I hate this woman, that I will not permit her to take from me what is rightfully mine. Late this afternoon I went to the place that she mentions in her letter. I did not know just when she was to meet you, and I didn't care. It was merely a matter of waiting. I hid myself behind some bushes and watched.

'A little while after sunset I saw her down the road. She came into the grove and sat down on the grass. Then she took off her hat and laid it beside her. She sat very quietly, looking down the road through the trees. At first I thought that she was afraid and that she would not take the solution at all. Then I realized why she did nothing. She was waiting for you.

'She was clever! She was not going to run the risk of leaving a heap of clothes in a grove an hour before you came, with the chance of arousing the curiosity of some boy who might wander into the grove. She would wait until she saw you far away. You would reach her just at the right moment. So it proved. I could see you myself fully a quarter of a mile away; it was still quite light. She never took her eyes off the road. I think she must have seen you before I did. She opened her handbag and took out a bottle before I caught my first glimpse of you.

'The next I knew, she had placed the bottle to her lips and drained it off. I turned away. I didn't want to see her shrivel up before my very eyes. A quarter of a minute, I thought, would be about long enough for her to shrink. So I counted fifteen and turned around. Where she had sat was only a heap of clothes.

'There was not a second to lose now. You were almost at the grove. I crawled out of the bushes and gathered up everything, clothes, hat, and all. Then I ran away from the place just as you were about to enter.'

All the while she had been handling the box. I knew what it contained, and my brain was feverishly busy devising and rejecting, over and over again, plans to get it away from her; by stealth if possible, by force if necessary. I should have leaped from my seat at once and seized her, but I sat still dazed, as if in a kind of hypnotic trance.

'And here is your Jeanne,' she almost screamed as she took out a white, sitting figure. 'You will never, never have her again. I take her so, and this—*this* is what I do to her!'

This time I did act. I leaped to my feet, knocked over the table that she had so ingeniously placed to obstruct me, and rushed at her.

But I was too late.

She was at the open window.

She raised her hand high above her head, posed there for a fraction of a second, the very incarnation of hate and vengeance. Then she dashed the white thing upon the stone pavement of the court below.

I heard it break into a hundred pieces as it struck.

Eight O'Clock in the Morning

Ray Faraday Nelson

At the end of the show the hypnotist told his subjects, 'Awake.'

Something unusual happened.

One of the subjects awoke all the way. This had never happened before. His name was George Nada and he blinked out at the sea of faces in the theatre, at first unaware of anything out of the ordinary. Then he noticed, spotted here and there in the crowd, the non-human faces, the faces of the Fascinators. They had been there all along, of course, but only George was really awake, so only George recognized them for what they were. He understood everything in a flash, including the fact that if he were to give any outward sign, the Fascinators would instantly command him to return to his former state, and he would obey.

He left the theatre, pushing out into the neon night, carefully avoiding giving any indication that he saw the green, reptilian flesh or the multiple yellow eyes of the rulers of earth. One of them asked him, 'Got a light buddy?' George gave him a light, then moved on.

At intervals along the street George saw the posters hanging with photographs of the Fascinators' multiple eyes and various commands printed under them, such as, 'Work eight hours, play eight hours, sleep eight hours,' and 'Marry and Reproduce.' A TV set in the window of a store caught George's eye, but he looked away in the nick of time. When he didn't look at the Fascinator in the screen, he could resist the command, 'Stay tuned to this station.'

George lived alone in a little sleeping room, and as soon as he got home, the first thing he did was to disconnect the TV set. In other rooms he could hear the TV sets of his neighbors, though. Most of the time the voices were human, but now and then he heard the arrogant, strangely bird-like croaks of the aliens. 'Obey the government,' said one croak. 'We

153

are the government,' said another. 'We are your friends, you'd do anything for a friend, wouldn't you?'

'Obey!'

'Work!'

Suddenly the phone rang.

George picked it up. It was one of the Fascinators.

'Hello,' it squawked. 'This is your control, Chief of Police Robinson. You are an old man, George Nada. Tomorrow morning at eight o'clock, your heart will stop. Please repeat.'

'I am an old man,' said George. 'Tomorrow morning at eight o'clock, my heart will stop.'

The control hung up.

'No, it won't,' whispered George. He wondered why they wanted him dead. Did they suspect that he was awake? Probably. Someone might have spotted him, noticed that he didn't respond the way the others did. If George were alive at one minute after eight tomorrow morning, then they would be sure.

'No use waiting here for the end,' he thought.

He went out again. The posters, the TV, the occasional commands from passing aliens did not seem to have absolute power over him, though he still felt strongly tempted to obey, to see these things the way his master wanted him to see them. He passed an alley and stopped. One of the aliens was alone there, leaning against the wall. George walked up to him.

'Move on,' grunted the thing, focusing his deadly eyes on George.

George felt his grasp on awareness waver. For a moment the reptilian head dissolved into the face of a lovable old drunk. Of course the drunk would be lovable. George picked up a brick and smashed it down on the old drunk's head with all his strength. For a moment the image blurred, then the blue-green blood oozed out of the face and the lizard fell, twitching and writhing. After a moment it was dead.

George dragged the body into the shadows and searched it. There was a tiny radio in its pocket and a curiously shaped knife and fork in another. The tiny radio said something in an incomprehensible language. George put it down beside the body, but kept the eating utensils.

'I can't possibly escape,' thought George. 'Why fight them?'

But maybe he could.

What if he could awaken others? That might be worth a try.

He walked twelve blocks to the apartment of his girl friend, Lil, and knocked on her door. She came to the door in her bathrobe.

'I want you to wake up,' he said.

'I'm awake,' she said. 'Come on in.'

He went in. The TV was playing. He turned it off.

'No,' he said. 'I mean really wake up.' She looked at him without comprehension, so he snapped his fingers and shouted, '*Wake up*! The masters command that you wake up!'

'Are you off your rocker, George?' she asked suspiciously. 'You sure are acting funny.' He slapped her face. 'Cut that out!' she cried. 'What the hell are you up to anyway?'

'Nothing,' said George, defeated. 'I was just kidding around.'

'Slapping my face wasn't just kidding around!' she cried.

There was a knock at the door.

George opened it.

It was one of the aliens.

'Can't you keep the noise down to a dull roar?' it said.

The eyes and reptilian flesh faded a little and George saw the flickering image of a fat middle-aged man in shirtsleeves. It was still a man when George slashed its throat with the eating knife, but it was an alien before it hit the floor. He dragged it into the apartment and kicked the door shut.

'What do you see there?' he asked Lil, pointing to the many-eyed snake thing on the floor.

'Mister…Mister Coney,' she whispered, her eyes wide with horror. 'You…just killed him, like it was nothing at all.'

'Don't scream,' warned George, advancing on her.

'I won't George. I swear I won't, only please, for the love of God, put down that knife.' She backed away until she had her shoulder blades pressed to the wall.

George saw that it was no use.

'I'm going to tie you up,' said George. 'First tell me which room Mister Coney lived in.'

'The first door on your left as you go toward the stairs,' she said. 'Georgie…Georgie. Don't torture me. If you're going to kill me, do it clean. Please, Georgie, please.'

He tied her up with bedsheets and gagged her, then searched the body of the Fascinator. There was another one of the little radios that talked a foreign language, another set of eating utensils, and nothing else.

George went next door.

When he knocked, one of the snake-things answered, 'Who is it?'

'Friend of Mister Coney. I wanna see him,' said George.

'He went out for a second, but he'll be right back.' The door opened a crack, and four yellow eyes peeped out. 'You wanna come in and wait?'

'Okay,' said George, not looking at the eyes.

'You alone here?' he asked, as it closed the door, its back to George.

'Yeah, why?'

He slit its throat from behind, then searched the apartment.

He found human bones and skulls, a half-eaten hand.

He found tanks with huge fat slugs floating in them.

'The children,' he thought, and killed them all.

There were guns too, of a sort he had never seen before. He discharged one by accident, but fortunately it was noiseless. It seemed to fire little poisoned darts.

He pocketed the gun and as many boxes of darts as he could and went back to Lil's place. When she saw him she writhed in helpless terror.

'Relax, honey,' he said, opening her purse, 'I just want to borrow your car keys.'

He took the keys and went downstairs to the street.

Her car was still parked in the same general area in which she always parked it. He recognized it by the dent in the right fender. He got in, started it, and began driving aimlessly. He drove for hours, thinking—desperately searching for some way out. He turned on the car radio to see if he could get some music, but there was nothing but news and it was all about him, George Nada, the homicidal maniac. The announcer was one of the masters, but he sounded a little scared. Why should he be? What could one man do?

George wasn't surprised when he saw the road block, and he turned off on a side street before he reached it. No little trip to the country for you, Georgie boy, he thought to himself.

They had just discovered what he had done back at Lil's place, so they would probably be looking for Lil's car. He parked it in an alley and took the subway. There were no aliens on the subway, for some reason. Maybe they were too good for such things, or maybe it was just because it was so late at night.

When one finally did get on, George got off.

He went up to the street and went into a bar. One of the Fascinators was on the TV, saying over and over again, 'We are your friends. We are your friends. We are your friends.' The stupid lizard sounded scared. Why? What could one man do against all of them?

George ordered a beer, then it suddenly struck him that the Fascinator on the TV no longer seemed to have any power over him. He looked at it again and thought, 'It has to believe it can master me to do it. The slightest hint of fear on its part and the power to hypnotize is lost.' They flashed George's picture on the TV screen and George retreated to the phone booth. He called his control, the Chief of Police.

'Hello, Robinson?' he asked.

'Speaking.'

'This is George Nada. I've figured out how to wake people up.'

'What? George, hang on. Where are you?' Robinson sounded almost hysterical.

He hung up and paid and left the bar. They would probably trace his call.

He caught another subway and went downtown.

It was dawn when he entered the building housing the biggest of the city's TV studios. He consulted the building directory and then went up in the elevator. The cop in front of the studio entrance recognized him. 'Why, you're Nada!' he gasped.

George didn't like to shoot him with the poison dart gun, but he had to.

He had to kill several more before he got into the studio itself, including all the engineers on duty. There were a lot of police sirens outside, excited shouts, and running footsteps on the stairs. The alien was sitting before the TV camera saying, 'We are your friends. We are your friends,' and didn't see George come in. When George shot him with the needle gun he simply stopped in mid-sentence and sat there, dead. George stood near him and said, imitating the alien croak, 'Wake up. Wake up. See us as we are and kill us!'

It was George's voice the city heard that morning, but it was the Fascinator's image, and the city did awake for the very first time and the war began.

George did not live to see the victory that finally came. He died of a heart attack at exactly eight o'clock.

Farewell to the Master

Harry Bates

CHAPTER ONE

From his perch high on the ladder above the museum floor, Cliff Sutherland studied carefully each line and shadow of the great robot, then turned and looked thoughtfully down at the rush of visitors come from all over the Solar System to see Gnut and the traveler for themselves and to hear once again their amazing, tragic story.

He himself had come to feel an almost proprietary interest in the exhibit, and with some reason. He had been the only freelance picture reporter on the Capitol grounds when the visitors from the Unknown had arrived, and had obtained the first professional shots of the ship. He had witnessed at close hand every event of the next mad few days. He had thereafter photographed many times the eight-foot robot, the ship, and the beautiful slain ambassador, Klaatu, and his imposing tomb out in the center of the Tidal Basin, and, such was the continuing news value of the event to the billions of persons throughout habitable space, he was there now once more to get still other shots and, if possible, a new 'angle.'

This time he was after a picture which showed Gnut as weird and menacing. The shots he had taken the day before had not given quite the effect he wanted, and he hoped to get it today; but the light was not yet right and he had to wait for the afternoon to wane a little.

The last of the crowd admitted in the present group hurried in, exclaiming at the great pure green curves of the mysterious time-space traveler, then completely forgetting the ship at sight of the awesome figure and great head of the giant Gnut. Hinged robots of crude manlike appearance were familiar enough, but never had Earthling eyes lain on one like this. For Gnut had almost exactly the shape of a man—a giant, but a man—with greenish metal for man's covering flesh, and greenish metal for man's bulging muscles. Except for a loin cloth, he was nude. He stood like the powerful god of the machine of some undreamed-of scientific civilization, on his face a look of sullen, brooding thought. Those who looked at him did not make jests or idle remarks, and those nearest him usually did not speak at all. His strange, internally illuminated red eyes were so set that every observer felt they were fixed on himself alone, and he engendered a feeling that he might at any moment step forward in anger and perform unimaginable deeds.

A slight rustling sound came from speakers hidden in the ceiling above, and at once the noises of the crowd lessened. The recorded lecture was about to be given. Cliff sighed. He knew the thing by heart; had even been present when the recording was made, and met the speaker, a young chap named Stillwell.

'Ladies and gentlemen,' began a clear and well-modulated voice—but Cliff was no longer attending. The shadows in the hollows of Gnut's face and figure were deeper; it was almost time for his shot. He picked up and examined the proofs of the pictures he had taken the day before and compared them critically with the subject.

As he looked a wrinkle came to his brow. He had not noticed it before, but now, suddenly, he had the feeling that since yesterday something about Gnut was changed. The pose before him was the identical one in the photographs, every detail on comparison seemed the same, but nevertheless the feeling persisted. He took up his viewing glass and more carefully compared subject and photographs, line by line. And then he saw that there *was* a difference.

With sudden excitement, Cliff snapped two pictures at different exposures. He knew he should wait a little and take others, but he was so sure he had stumbled on an important mystery that he had to get going, and quickly folding his accessory equipment he descended the ladder and made his way out. Twenty minutes later, consumed with curiosity, he was developing the new shots in his hotel bedroom.

What Cliff saw when he compared the negatives taken yesterday and today caused his scalp to tingle. Here was a slant indeed! And apparently no one but he knew! Still, what he had discovered, though it would have made the front page of every paper in the Solar System, was after all only a lead. The story, what really had happened, he knew no better than anyone else. It must be his job to find out.

And that meant he would have to secrete himself in the building and stay there all night. That very night; there was still time for him to get back before closing. He would take a small, very fast infrared camera that could see in the dark, and he would get the real picture and the story.

He snatched up the little camera, grabbed an aircab and hurried back to the museum. The place was filled with another section of the ever-present queue, and the lecture was just ending. He thanked Heaven that his arrangement with the museum permitted him to go in and out at will.

He had already decided what to do. First he made his way to the 'floating' guard and asked a single question, and anticipation broadened on his face as he heard the expected answer. The second thing was to find a spot where he would be safe from the eyes of the men who would close the floor for the night. There was only one possible place, the laboratory set up behind the ship. Boldly he showed his press credentials to the second guard, stationed at the partitioned passageway leading to it, stating that he had come to interview the scientists; and in a moment he was at the laboratory door.

He had been there a number of times and knew the room well. It was a large area roughly partitioned off for the work of the scientists engaged in breaking their way into the ship, and full of a confusion of massive and heavy objects—electric and hot-air ovens, carboys of chemicals, asbestos sheeting, compressors, basins, ladles, a microscope, and a great deal of smaller equipment common to a metallurgical laboratory. Three white-smocked men were deeply engrossed in an experiment at the far end. Cliff, waiting a good moment, slipped inside and hid himself under a table half buried with supplies. He felt reasonably safe from detection there. Very soon now the scientists would be going home for the night.

From beyond the ship he could hear another section of the waiting queue filing in—the last, he hoped, of the day. He settled himself as comfortably as he could. In a moment the lecture would begin. He had to smile when he thought of one thing the recording would say.

Then there it was again—the clear, trained voice of the chap Stillwell. The foot scrapings and whispers of the crowd died away, and Cliff could hear every word in spite of the great bulk of the ship lying interposed.

'Ladies and gentlemen,' began the familiar words, 'the Smithsonian Institution welcomes you to its new Interplanetary Wing and to the marvelous exhibits at this moment before you.'

A slight pause. 'All of you must know by now something of what happened here three months ago, if indeed you did not see it for yourself in the telescreen,' the voice went on. 'The few facts are briefly told. A little after 5:00 P.M. on September 16th, visitors to Washington thronged the grounds outside this building in their usual numbers and no doubt with their usual thoughts. The day was warm and fair. A stream of people was leaving the main entrance of the museum, just outside in the direction you are facing. This wing, of course, was not here at that time. Everyone was homeward bound, tired no doubt from hours on their feet, seeing the exhibits of the museum and visiting the many buildings on the grounds nearby. And then it happened.

'On the area just to your right, just as it is now, appeared the time-space traveler. It appeared in the blink of an eye. It did not come down from the sky; dozens of witnesses swear to that; it just appeared. One moment it was not here, the next it was. It appeared on the very spot it now rests on.

'The people nearest the ship were stricken with panic and ran back with cries and screams. Excitement spread out over Washington in a tidal wave. Radio, television, and newspapermen rushed here at once. Police formed a wide cordon around the ship, and army units appeared and trained guns and ray projectors on it. The direst calamity was feared.

'For it was recognized from the very beginning that this was no spaceship from anywhere in the Solar System. Every child knew that only two spaceships had ever been built on Earth, and none at all on any of the other planets and satellites; and of those two, one had been destroyed when it was pulled into the Sun, and the other had just been reported safely arrived on Mars. Then, the ones made here had a shell of a strong aluminum alloy, while this one, as you see, is of an unknown greenish metal.

'The ship appeared and just sat here. No one emerged, and there was no sign that it contained life of any kind. That, as much as any single thing, caused excitement to sky-rocket. Who, or what, was inside? Were the visitors hostile or friendly? Where did the ship come from? How did it arrive so suddenly right on this spot without dropping from the sky?

'For two days the ship rested here, just as you now see it, without motion or sign that it contained life. Long before the end of that time the scientists had explained that it was not so much a spaceship as a space-time traveler, because only such a ship could arrive as this one did—materialize. They pointed out that such a traveler, while theoretically understandable to us Earthmen, was far beyond attempt at our present state of knowledge, and that this one, activated by relativity principles, might well have come from the far corner of the Universe, from a distance which light itself would require millions of years to cross.

'When this opinion was disseminated, public tension grew until it was almost intolerable. Where had the traveler come from? Who were its occupants? Why had they come to Earth? Above all, why did they not show themselves? Were they perhaps preparing some terrible weapon of destruction?

'And where was the ship's entrance port? Men who dared go look reported that none could be found. No slightest break or crack marred the perfect smoothness of the ship's curving ovoid surface. And a delegation of high-ranking officials who visited the ship could not, by knocking, elicit from its occupants any sign that they had been heard.

'At last, after exactly two days, in full view of tens of thousands of persons assembled and standing well back, and under the muzzles of scores of the army's most powerful guns and ray projectors, an opening appeared in the wall of the ship, and a ramp slid down, and out stepped a man, godlike in appearance and human in form, closely followed by a giant robot. And when they touched the ground the ramp slid back and the entrance closed as before.

'It was immediately apparent to all the assembled thousands that the stranger was friendly. The first thing he did was to raise his right arm high in the universal gesture of peace; but it was not that which impressed those nearest so much as the expression on his face, which radiated kindness, wisdom, the purest nobility. In his delicately tinted robe he looked like a benign god.

'At once, waiting for this appearance, a large committee of high-ranking government officials and army officers advanced to greet the visitor. With graciousness and dignity the man pointed to himself, then to his robot companion, and said in perfect English with a peculiar accent, "I am Klaatu," or a name that sounded like that, "and this is Gnut." The names were not well understood at the time, but the sight-and-sound film of the television men caught them and they became known to everyone subsequently.

'And then occurred the thing which shall always be to the shame of the human race. From a treetop a hundred yards away came a wink of violet light and Klaatu fell. The assembled multitude stood for a moment stunned, not comprehending what had happened. Gnut, a little behind his master and to one side, slowly turned his body a little toward him, moved his head twice, and stood still, in exactly the position you now see him.

'Then followed pandemonium. The police pulled the slayer of Klaatu out of the tree. They found him mentally unbalanced; he kept crying that the devil had come to kill everyone on Earth. He was taken away, and Klaatu, although obviously dead, was rushed to the nearest hospital to see if anything could be done to revive him. Confused and frightened crowds milled about the Capitol grounds the rest of the afternoon and much of that night. The ship remained as silent and motionless as before. And Gnut, too, never moved from the position he had come to rest in.

'Gnut never moved again. He remained exactly as you see him all that night and for the ensuing days. When the mausoleum in the Tidal Basin was built, Klaatu's burial service took place where you are standing now, attended by the highest functionaries of all the great countries of the world. It was not only the most appropriate but the safest thing to do, for if there should be other living creatures in the traveler, as seemed possible at that time, they had to be impressed by the sincere sorrow of us Earthmen at what had happened. If Gnut was still alive, or perhaps I had better say functionable, there was no sign. He stood as you see him during the entire ceremony. He stood so while his master was floated out to the mausoleum and given to the centuries with the tragically short sight-and-sound record of his historic visit. And he stood so afterward, day after day, night after night, in fair weather and in rain, never moving or showing by any slightest sign that he was aware of what had gone on.

'After the interment, this wing was built out from the museum to cover the traveler and Gnut. Nothing else could very well have been done, it was learned, for both Gnut and the ship were far too heavy to be moved safely by any means at hand.

'You have heard about the efforts of our metallurgists since then to break into the ship, and of their complete failure. Behind the ship now, as you can see from either end, a partitioned workroom has been set up where the attempt still goes on. So far its wonderful greenish metal has proved inviolable. Not only are they unable to get in, but they cannot even find the exact place from which Klaatu and Gnut emerged. The chalk marks you see are the best approximation.

'Many people have feared that Gnut was only temporarily deranged, and that on return to function might be dangerous, so the scientists have completely destroyed all chance of that. The greenish metal of which he is made seemed to be the same as that of the ship and could no more be attacked, they found, nor could they find any way to penetrate to his internals; but they had other means. They sent electrical currents of tremendous voltages and amperages through him. They applied terrific heat to all parts of his metal shell. They immersed him for days in gases and acids and strongly corroding solutions, and they have bombarded him with every known kind of ray. You need have no fear of him now. He cannot possibly have retained the ability to function in any way.

'But—a word of caution. The officials of the government know that visitors will not show any disrespect in this building. It may be that the unknown and unthinkably powerful civilization from which Klaatu and Gnut came may send other emissaries to see what happened to them. Whether or not they do, not one of us must be found amiss in our attitude.

None of us could very well anticipate what happened, and we all are immeasurably sorry, but we are still in a sense responsible, and must do what we can to avoid possible retaliations.

'You will be allowed to remain five minutes longer, and then, when the gong sounds, you will please leave promptly. The robot attendants along the wall will answer any questions you may have.

'Look well, for before you stand stark symbols of the achievement, mystery, and frailty of the human race.'

The recorded voice ceased speaking. Cliff, carefully moving his cramped limbs, broke out in a wide smile. If they knew what he knew!

For his photographs told a slightly different story from that of the lecturer. In yesterday's a line of the figured floor showed clearly at the outer edge of the robot's near foot; in today's, *that line was covered*. Gnut had moved!

Or been moved, though this was very unlikely. Where was the derrick and other evidence of such activity? It could hardly have been done in one night, and all signs so quickly concealed. And why should it be done at all?

Still, to make sure, he had asked the guard. He could almost remember verbatim his answer:

'No, Gnut has neither moved nor been moved since the death of his master. A special point was made of keeping him in the position he assumed at Klaatu's death. The floor was built in under him, and the scientists who completed his derangement erected their apparatus around him, just as he stands. You need have no fears.'

Cliff smiled again. He did not have any fears.

Not yet.

Chapter Two

A moment later the big gong above the entrance doors rang the closing hour, and immediately following it a voice from the speakers called out, 'Five o'clock, ladies and gentlemen. Closing time, ladies and gentlemen.'

The three scientists, as if surprised it was so late, hurriedly washed their hands, changed to their street clothes and disappeared down the partitioned corridor, oblivious of the young picture man hidden under the table. The slide and scrape of the feet on the exhibition floor rapidly dwindled, until at last there were only the steps of the two guards walking from one point to another, making sure everything was all right for the night. For just a moment one of them glanced in the doorway of the laboratory, then he joined the other at the entrance. Then the great metal doors clanged to, and there was silence.

Cliff waited several minutes, then carefully poked his way out from under the table. As he straightened up, a faint tinkling crash sounded at the floor by his feet. Carefully stooping, he found the shattered remains of a thin glass pipette. He had knocked it off the table.

That caused him to realize something he had not thought of before: A Gnut who had moved might be a Gnut who could see and hear—and really be dangerous. He would have to be very careful.

He looked about him. The room was bounded at the ends by two fiber partitions which at the inner ends followed close under the curving bottom of the ship. The inner side of the room was the ship itself, and the outer was the southern wall of the wing. There were four large high windows. The only entrance was by way of the passage.

Without moving, from his knowledge of the building, he made his plan. The wing was connected with the western end of the museum by a doorway, never used, and extended westward toward the Washington Monument. The ship lay nearest the southern wall, and Gnut stood out in front of it, not far from the northeast corner and at the opposite end of the room from the entrance of the building and the passageway leading to the laboratory. By retracing his steps he would come out on the floor at the point farthest removed from the robot. This was just what he wanted, for on the other side of the entrance, on a low platform, stood a paneled table containing the lecture apparatus, and this table was the only object in the room which afforded a place for him to lie concealed while watching what might go on. The only other objects on the floor were the six manlike robot attendants in fixed stations along the northern wall, placed there to answer visitors' questions. He would have to gain the table.

He turned and began cautiously tiptoeing out of the laboratory and down the passageway. It was already dark there, for what light still entered the exhibition hall was shut off by the great bulk of the ship. He reached the end of the room without making a sound. Very carefully he edged forward and peered around the bottom of the ship at Gnut.

He had a momentary shock. The robot's eyes were right on him!—or so it seemed. Was that only the effect of the set of his eyes, he wondered, or was he already discovered? The position of Gnut's head did not seem to have changed, at any rate. Probably everything was all right, but he wished he did not have to cross that end of the room with the feeling that the robot's eyes were following him.

He drew back and sat down and waited. It would have to be totally dark before he essayed the trip to the table.

He waited a full hour, until the faint beams from the lamps on the grounds outside began to make the room seem to grow lighter; then he got up and peeped around the ship once more. The robot's eyes seemed to pierce right at him as before, only now, due no doubt to the darkness, the strange internal illumination seemed much brighter. This was a chilling thing. Did Gnut know he was there? What were the thoughts of the robot? What *could* be the thoughts of a man-made machine, even so wonderful a one as Gnut?

It was time for the cross, so Cliff slung his camera around on his back, went down on his hands and knees, and carefully moved to the edge of the entrance wall. There he fitted himself as closely as he could into the angle made by it with the floor and started inching ahead. Never pausing, not risking a glance at Gnut's unnerving red eyes, moving an inch at a time, he snaked along. He took ten minutes to cross the space of a hundred feet, and he was wet with perspiration when his fingers at last touched the one-foot rise of the platform on which the table stood. Still slowly, silently as a shadow, he made his way over the edge and melted behind the protection of the table. At last he was there.

He relaxed for a moment, then, anxious to know whether he had been seen, carefully turned and looked around the side of the table.

Gnut's eyes were now full on him! Or so it seemed. Against the general darkness, the robot loomed a mysterious and still darker shadow that, for all his being a hundred and fifty feet away, seemed to dominate the room. Cliff could not tell whether the position of his body was changed or not.

But if Gnut were looking at him, he at least did nothing else. Not by the slightest motion that Cliff could discern did he appear to move. His position was the one he had maintained these last three months, in the darkness, in the rain, and this last week in the museum.

Cliff made up his mind not to give away to fear. He became conscious of his own body. The cautious trip had taken something out of him—his knees and elbows burned and his trousers were no doubt ruined. But these were little things if what he hoped for came to pass. If Gnut so much as moved, and he could catch him with his infrared camera, he would have a story that would buy him fifty suits of clothes. And if on top of that he could learn the purpose of Gnut's moving—provided there was a purpose—that would be a story that would set the world on its ears.

He settled down to a period of waiting; there was no telling when Gnut would move, if indeed he would move that night. Cliff's eyes had long been adjusted to the dark and he could make out the larger objects well enough. From time to time he peered out at the robot—peered long and hard, till his outlines wavered and he seemed to move, and he had to blink and rest his eyes to be sure it was only his imagination.

Again the minute hand of his watch crept around the dial. The inactivity made Cliff careless, and for longer and longer periods he kept his head back out of sight behind the table. And so it was that when Gnut did move he was scared almost out of his wits. Dull and a little bored, he suddenly found the robot out on the floor, halfway in his direction.

But that was not the most frightening thing. It was that when he did see Gnut he did not catch him moving! He was stopped as still as a cat in the middle of stalking a mouse. His eyes were now much brighter, and there was no remaining doubt about their direction: he was looking right at Cliff!

Scarcely breathing, half hypnotized, Cliff looked back. His thoughts tumbled. What was the robot's intention? Why had he stopped so still? Was he being stalked? How could he move with such silence?

In the heavy darkness Gnut's eyes moved nearer. Slowly but in perfect rhythm the almost imperceptible sound of his footsteps beat on Cliff's ears. Cliff, usually resourceful enough, was this time caught flat-footed. Frozen with fear, utterly incapable of fleeing, he lay where he was while the metal monster with the fiery eyes came on.

For a moment Cliff all but fainted, and when he recovered, there was Gnut towering over him, legs almost within reach. He was bending slightly, burning his terrible eyes right into his own!

Too late to try to think of running now. Trembling like any cornered mouse, Cliff waited for the blow that would crush him. For an eternity, it seemed, Gnut scrutinized him without moving. For each second of that eternity Cliff expected annihilation, sudden, quick, complete. And then suddenly and unexpectedly it was over. Gnut's body straightened and he stepped back. He turned. And then, with the almost jerkless rhythm which only he among robots possessed, he started back toward the place from which he came.

Cliff could hardly believe he had been spared. Gnut could have crushed him like a worm—and he had only turned around and gone back. Why? It could not be supposed that a robot was capable of human considerations.

Gnut went straight to the other end of the traveler. At a certain place he stopped and made a curious succession of sounds. At once Cliff saw an opening, blacker than the gloom of the building, appear in the ship's side, and it was followed by a slight sliding sound as a ramp slid out and met the floor. Gnut walked up the ramp and, stooping a little, disappeared inside the ship.

Then, for the first time, Cliff remembered the picture he had come to get. Gnut had moved, but he had not caught him! But at least now, whatever opportunities there might be later, he could get the shot of the ramp connecting with the opened door; so he twisted his camera into position, set it for the proper exposure, and took a shot.

A long time passed and Gnut did not come out. What could he be doing inside? Cliff wondered. Some of his courage returned to him and he toyed with the idea of creeping forward and peeping through the port, but he found he had not the courage for that. Gnut had spared him, at least for the time, but there was no telling how far his tolerance would go.

An hour passed, then another, Gnut was doing something inside the ship, but what? Cliff could not imagine. If the robot had been a human being, he knew he would have sneaked a look, but, as it was, he was too much of an unknown quantity. Even the simplest of Earth's robots under certain circumstances were inexplicable things; what, then, of this one, come from an unknown and even unthinkable civilization, by far the most wonderful construction ever seen—what superhuman powers might he not possess? All that the scientists of Earth could do had not served to derange him. Acid, heat, rays, terrific crushing blows—he had withstood them all; even his finish had been unmarred. He might be able to see perfectly in the dark. And right where he was, he might be able to hear or in some way sense the least change in Cliff's position.

More time passed, and then, some time after two o'clock in the morning, a simple homely thing happened, but a thing so unexpected that for a moment it quite destroyed Cliff's equilibrium. Suddenly, through the dark and silent building, there was a faint whir of wings, soon followed by the piercing, sweet voice of a bird. A mocking bird. Somewhere in the gloom above his head. Clear and full throated were its notes; a dozen little songs it sang, one after the other without pause between— short insistent calls, twirrings, coaxings, cooings—the spring love song of perhaps the finest singer in the world. Then, as suddenly as it began, the voice was silent.

If an invading army had poured out of the traveler, Cliff would have been less surprised. The month was December; even in Florida the mocking birds had not yet begun their song. How had one gotten into that tight, gloomy museum? How and why was it singing there?

He waited, full of curiosity. Then suddenly he was aware of Gnut, standing just outside the port of the ship. He stood quite still, his glowing eyes turned squarely in Cliff's direction. For a moment the hush in the museum seemed to deepen; then it was broken by a soft thud on the floor near where Cliff was lying.

He wondered. The light in Gnut's eyes changed, and he started his almost jerkless walk in Cliff's direction. When only a little away, the robot stopped, bent over, and picked something from the floor. For some time he stood without motion and looked at a little object he held in his hand. Cliff knew, though he could not see, that it was the mocking bird. Its body, for he was sure that it had lost its song forever. Gnut then turned, and without a glance at Cliff, walked back to the ship and again went inside.

Hours passed while Cliff waited for some sequel to this surprising happening. Perhaps it was because of his curiosity that his fear of the robot began to lessen. Surely if the mechanism was unfriendly, if he intended him any harm, he would have finished him before, when he had such a perfect opportunity. Cliff began to nerve himself for a quick look inside the port. And a picture; he must remember the picture. He kept forgetting the very reason he was there.

It was in the deeper darkness of the false dawn when he got sufficient courage and made the start. He took off his shoes, and in his stockinged feet, his shoes tied together and slung over his shoulder, he moved stiffly but rapidly to a position behind the nearest of the six robot attendants stationed along the wall, then paused for some sign which might indicate that Gnut knew he had moved. Hearing none, he slipped along behind the next robot attendant and paused again. Bolder now, he made in one spurt all the distance to the farthest one, the sixth, fixed just opposite the port of the ship. There he met with a disappointment. No light that he could detect was visible within; there was only darkness and the all-permeating silence. Still, he had better get the picture. He raised his camera, focused it on the dark opening, and gave the film a comparatively long exposure. Then he stood there, at a loss what to do next.

As he paused, a peculiar series of muffled noises reached his ears, apparently from within the ship. Animal noises—first scrapings and pantings, punctuated by several sharp clicks, then deep, rough snarls, interrupted by more scrapings and pantings, as if a struggle of some kind were going on. Then suddenly, before Cliff could even decide to run back to the table, a low, wide, dark shape bounded out of the port and immediately turned and grew to the height of a man. A terrible fear swept over Cliff, even before he knew what the shape was.

In the next second Gnut appeared in the port and stepped unhesitatingly down the ramp toward the shape. As he advanced it backed slowly away for a few feet; but then it stood its ground, and thick arms rose from its sides and began a loud drumming on its chest, while from its throat came a deep roar of defiance. Only one creature in the world beat its chest and made a sound like that. The shape was a gorilla!

And a huge one!

Gnut kept advancing, and when close, charged forward and grappled with the beast. Cliff would not have guessed that Gnut could move so fast. In the darkness he could not see the details of what happened; all he knew was that the two great shapes, the titanic metal Gnut and the squat but terrifically strong gorilla, merged for a moment with silence on the robot's part and terrible, deep, indescribable roars on the other's; then the two separated, and it was as if the gorilla had been flung back and away.

The animal at once rose to its full height and roared deafeningly. Gnut advanced. They closed again, and the separation of before was repeated. The robot continued inexorably, and now the gorilla began to fall back down the building. Suddenly the beast darted at a manlike shape against the wall, and with one rapid side movement dashed the fifth robot attendant to the floor and decapitated it.

Tense with fear, Cliff crouched behind his own robot attendant. He thanked Heaven that Gnut was between him and the gorilla and was continuing his advance. The gorilla backed farther, darted suddenly at the next robot in the row, and with strength almost unbelievable picked it from its roots and hurled it at Gnut. With a sharp metallic clang, robot hit robot, and the one of Earth bounced off to one side and rolled to a stop.

Cliff cursed himself for it afterward, but again he completely forgot the picture. The gorilla kept falling back down the building, demolishing with terrific bursts of rage every robot attendant that he passed and throwing the pieces at the implacable Gnut. Soon they arrived opposite the table, and Cliff now thanked his stars he had come away. There followed a brief silence. Cliff could not make out what was going on, but he imagined that the gorilla had at last reached the corner of the wing and was trapped.

If he was, it was only for a moment. The silence was suddenly shattered by a terrific roar, and the thick, squat shape of the animal came bounding toward Cliff. He came all the way back and turned just between Cliff and the port of the ship. Cliff prayed frantically for Gnut to come back quickly, for there was now only the last remaining robot attendant between him and the madly dangerous brute. Out of the dimness Gnut did appear. The gorilla rose to its full height and again beat its chest and roared its challenge.

And then occurred a curious thing. It fell on all fours and slowly rolled over on its side, as if weak or hurt. Then panting, making frightening noises, it forced itself again to its feet and faced the oncoming Gnut. As it waited, its eye was caught by the last robot attendant and perhaps Cliff, shrunk close behind it. With a surge of terrible destructive rage, the gorilla waddled sideward toward Cliff, but this time, even through his panic, he saw that the animal moved with difficulty, again apparently sick or severely wounded. He jumped back just in time; the gorilla pulled out the last robot attendant and hurled it violently at Gnut, missing him narrowly.

That was its last effort. The weakness caught it again; it dropped heavily on one side, rocked back and forth a few times, and fell to twitching. Then it lay still and did not move again.

The first faint pale light of the dawn was seeping into the room. From the corner where he had taken refuge, Cliff watched closely the great robot. It seemed to him that he behaved very queerly. He stood over the dead gorilla, looking down at him with what in a human would be called sadness. Cliff saw this clearly; Gnut's heavy greenish features bore a thoughtful, grieving expression new to his experience. For some moments he stood so, then as might a father with his sick child, he leaned over, lifted the great animal in his metal arms, and carried it tenderly within the ship.

Cliff flew back to the table, suddenly fearful of yet other dangerous and inexplicable happenings. It struck him that he might be safer in the laboratory, and with trembling knees he made his way there and hid in one of the big ovens. He prayed for full daylight. His thoughts were chaos. Rapidly, one after another, his mind churned up the amazing events of the night, but all was mystery; it seemed there could be no rational explanation for them. That mocking bird. The gorilla. Gnut's sad expression and his tenderness. What could account for a fantastic melange like that!

Gradually full daylight did come. A long time passed. At last he began to believe he might yet get out of that place of mystery and danger alive. At 8:30 there were noises at the entrance, and the good sound of human voices came to his ears. He stepped out of the oven and tiptoed to the passageway.

The noises stopped suddenly and there was a frightened exclamation and then the sound of running feet, and then silence. Stealthily Cliff sneaked down the narrow way and peeped fearfully around the ship.

There Gnut was in his accustomed place, in the identical pose he had taken at the death of his master, brooding sullenly and alone over a space traveler once again closed tight and a room that was a shambles. The entrance doors stood open and, heart in his mouth, Cliff ran out.

A few minutes later, safe in his hotel room, completely done in, he sat down for a second and almost at once fell asleep. Later, still in his clothes and still asleep, he staggered over to the bed. He did not wake up till midafternoon.

Chapter Three

Cliff awoke slowly, at first not realizing that the images tumbling in his head were real memories and not a fantastic dream. It was recollection of the pictures which brought him to his feet. Hastily he set about developing the film in his camera.

Then in his hands was proof that the events of the night were real. Both shots turned out well. The first showed clearly the ramp leading up to the port as he had dimly discerned it from his position behind the table. The second, of the open port as snapped from in front, was a disappointment, for a blank wall just back of the opening cut off all view of the interior. That would account for the fact that no light had escaped from the ship while Gnut was inside. Assuming Gnut required light for whatever he did.

Cliff looked at the negatives and was ashamed of himself. What a rotten picture man he was to come back with two ridiculous shots like these! He had had a score of opportunities to get real ones—shots of Gnut in action—Gnut's fight with the gorilla—even Gnut holding the mocking bird—spine-chilling stuff!—and all he had brought back was two stills of a doorway. Oh, sure, they were valuable, but he was a Grade A ass.

And to top this brilliant performance, he had fallen asleep!

Well, he'd better get out on the street and find out what was doing.

Quickly he showered, shaved, and changed his clothes, and soon was entering a nearby restaurant patronized by other picture and newsmen. Sitting alone at the lunch bar, he spotted a friend and competitor.

'Well, what do *you* think?' asked his friend when he took the stool at his side.

'I don't think anything until I've had breakfast,' Cliff answered.

'Then haven't you heard?'

'Heard what?' fended Cliff, who knew very well what was coming.

'You're a fine picture man,' was the other's remark. 'When something really big happens, you are asleep in bed.' But then he told him what had been discovered that morning in the museum, and of the world-wide excitement at the news. Cliff did three things at once, successfully—gobbled a substantial breakfast, kept thanking his stars that nothing new had transpired, and showed continuous surprise. Still chewing, he got up and hurried over to the building.

Outside, balked at the door, was a large crowd of the curious, but Cliff had no trouble gaining admittance when he showed his press credentials. Gnut and the ship stood just as he had left them, but the floor had been cleaned up and the pieces of the demolished robot attendants were lined up in one place along the wall. Several other competitor friends of his were there.

'I was away; missed the whole thing,' he said to one of them—Gus. 'What's supposed to be the explanation for what happened?'

'Ask something easy,' was the answer. 'Nobody knows. It's thought maybe something came out of the ship, maybe another robot like Gnut. Say—where have you been?'

'Asleep.'

'Better catch up. Several billion bipeds are scared stiff. Revenge for the death of Klaatu. Earth about to be invaded.'

'But that's—'

'Oh, I know it's all crazy, but that's the story they're being fed; it sells news. But there's a new angle just turned up, very surprising. Come here.'

He led Cliff to the table where stood a knot of people looking with great interest at several objects guarded by a technician. Gus pointed to a long slide on which were mounted a number of short dark-brown hairs.

'Those hairs came off a large male gorilla,' Gus said with a certain hard-boiled casualness. 'Most of them were found among the sweepings of the floor this morning. The rest were found on the robot attendants.'

Cliff tried to look astounded. Gus pointed to a test tube partly filled with a light amber fluid.

'And that's blood, diluted—gorilla blood. It was found on Gnut's arms.'

'Good Heaven!' Cliff managed to exclaim. 'And there's no explanation?'

'Not even a theory. It's your big chance, wonder boy.'

Cliff broke away from Gus, unable to maintain his act any longer. He couldn't decide what to do about his story. The press services would bid heavily for it—with all his pictures—but that would take further action out of his hands. In the back of his mind he wanted to stay in the wing again that night, but—well, he simply was afraid. He'd had a pretty stiff dose, and he wanted very much to remain alive.

He walked over and looked a long time at Gnut. No one would ever have guessed that he had moved, or that there had rested on his greenish metal face a look of sadness. Those weird eyes! Cliff wondered if they were really looking at him, as they seemed, recognizing him as the bold intruder of last night. Of what unknown stuff were they made—those materials placed in his eye sockets by one branch of the race of man which all the science of his own could not even serve to disfunction? What was Gnut thinking? What could be the thoughts of a robot—a mechanism of metal poured out of man's clay crucibles? Was he angry at him? Cliff thought not. Gnut had had him at his mercy—and had walked away.

Dared he stay again?

Cliff thought perhaps he did.

He walked about the room, thinking it over. He felt sure Gnut would move again. A Mikton ray gun would protect him from another gorilla—or fifty of them. He did not yet have the real story. He had come back with two miserable architectural stills!

He might have known from the first that he would stay. At dusk that night, armed with his camera and a small Mikton gun, he lay once more under the table of supplies in the laboratory and heard the metal doors of the wing clang to for the night.

This time he would get the story—and the pictures.

If only no guard was posted inside!

Chapter Four

Cliff listened hard for a long time for any sound which might tell him that a guard had been left, but the silence within the wing remained unbroken. He was thankful for that—but not quite completely. The gathering darkness and the realization that he was now irrevocably committed made the thought of a companion not altogether unpleasant.

About an hour after it reached maximum darkness he took off his shoes, tied them together and slung them around his neck, down his back, and stole quietly down the passageway to where it opened into the exhibition area. All seemed as it had been the preceding night. Gnut looked an ominous, indistinct shadow at the far end of the room, his glowing red eyes again seemingly right on the spot from which Cliff peeped out. As on the previous night, but even more carefully, Cliff went down on his stomach in the angle of the wall and slowly snaked across to the low platform on which stood the table. Once in its shelter, he fixed his shoes so that they straddled one shoulder, and brought his camera and gun holster around, ready on his breast. This time, he told himself, he would get pictures.

He settled down to wait, keeping Gnut in full sight every minute. His vision reached maximum adjustment to the darkness. Eventually he began to feel lonely and a little afraid. Gnut's red-glowing eyes were getting on his nerves; he had to keep assuring himself that the robot would not harm him. He had little doubt but that he himself was being watched.

Hours slowly passed. From time to time he heard slight noises at the entrance, on the outside—a guard, perhaps, or maybe curious visitors.

At about nine o'clock he saw Gnut move. First his head alone; it turned so that the eyes burned stronger in the direction where Cliff lay. For a moment that was all; then the dark metal form stirred slightly and began moving forward—straight toward himself. Cliff had thought he would not be afraid—much—but now his heart stood still. What would happen this time?

With amazing silence, Gnut drew nearer, until he towered an ominous shadow over the spot where Cliff lay. For a long time his red eyes burned down on the prone man. Cliff trembled all over; this was worse than the first time. Without having planned it, he found himself speaking to the creature.

'You would not hurt me,' he pleaded. 'I was only curious to see what's going on. It's my job. Can you understand me? I would not harm or bother you. I . . . I couldn't if I wanted to! Please!'

The robot never moved, and Cliff could not guess whether his words had been understood or even heard. When he felt he could not bear the suspense any longer, Gnut reached out and took something from a drawer of the table, or perhaps he put something back in; then he stepped back, turned, and retraced his steps. Cliff was safe! Again the robot had spared him!

Beginning then, Cliff lost much of his fear. He felt sure now that this Gnut would do him no harm. Twice he had had him in his power, and each time he had only looked and quietly moved away. Cliff could not imagine what Gnut had done in the drawer of the table. He watched with the greatest curiosity to see what would happen next.

As on the night before, the robot went straight to the end of the ship and made the peculiar sequence of sounds that opened the port, and when the ramp slid out he went inside. After that Cliff was alone in the darkness for a very long time, probably two hours. Not a sound came from the ship.

Cliff knew he should sneak up to the port and peep inside, but he could not quite bring himself to do it. With his gun he could handle another gorilla, but if Gnut caught him it might be the end. Momentarily he expected something fantastic to happen—he knew not what; maybe the mocking bird's sweet song again, maybe a gorilla, maybe—anything. What did at last happen once more caught him with complete surprise.

He heard a sudden muffled sound, then words—human words—every one familiar.

'Gentlemen,' was the first, and then there was a very slight pause. 'The Smithsonian Institution welcomes you to its new Interplanetary Wing and to the marvelous exhibits at this moment before you.'

It was the recorded voice of Stillwell! But it was not coming through the speakers overhead, but much muted, from within the ship.

After a slight pause it went on:

'All of you must . . . must—' Here it stammered and came to a stop. Cliff's hair bristled. That stammering was not in the lecture!

For just a moment there was silence; then came a scream, a hoarse man's scream, muffled, from somewhere within the heart of the ship; and it was followed by muted gasps and cries, as of a man in great fright or distress.

Every nerve tight, Cliff watched the port. He heard a thudding noise within the ship, then out the door flew the shadow of what was surely a human being. Gasping and half stumbling, he ran straight down the room in Cliff's direction. When twenty feet away, the great shadow of Gnut followed him out of the port.

Cliff watched, breathless. The man—it was Stillwell, he saw now—came straight for the table behind which Cliff himself lay, as if to get behind it, but when only a few feet away, his knees buckled and he fell to the floor. Suddenly Gnut was standing over him, but Stillwell did not seem to be aware of it. He appeared very ill, but kept making spasmodic futile efforts to creep on to the protection of the table.

Gnut did not move, so Cliff was emboldened to speak.

'What's the matter, Stillwell?' he asked. 'Can I help? Don't be afraid. I'm Cliff Sutherland; you know, the picture man.'

Without showing the least surprise at finding Cliff there, and clutching at his presence like a drowning man would a straw, Stillwell gasped out:

'Help me! Gnut ... Gnut—' He seemed unable to go on.

'Gnut what?' asked Cliff. Very conscious of the fire-eyed robot looming above, and afraid even to move out to the man, Cliff added reassuringly: 'Gnut won't hurt you. I'm sure he won't. He doesn't hurt me. What's the matter? What can I do?'

With a sudden accession of energy, Stillwell rose on his elbows.

'Where am I?' he asked.

'In the Interplanetary Wing,' Cliff answered. 'Don't you know?'

Only Stillwell's hard breathing was heard for a moment. Then hoarsely, weakly, he asked:

'How did I get here?'

'I don't know,' said Cliff.

'I was making a lecture recording,' Stillwell said, 'when suddenly I found myself here ... or I mean in there—'

He broke off and showed a return of his terror.

'Then what?' asked Cliff gently.

'I was in that box—and there, above me, was Gnut, the robot. Gnut! But they made Gnut harmless! He's never moved!'

'Steady, now,' said Cliff. 'I don't think Gnut will hurt you.'

Stillwell fell back on the floor.

'I'm very weak,' he gasped. 'Something—Will you get a doctor?'

He was utterly unaware that towering above him, eyes boring down at him through the darkness, was the robot he feared so greatly.

As Cliff hesitated, at a loss what to do, the man's breath began coming in short gasps, as regular as the ticking of a clock. Cliff dared to move out to him, but no act on his part could have helped the man now. His gasps weakened and became spasmodic, then suddenly he was completely silent and still. Cliff felt for his heart, then looked up to the eyes in the shadow above.

'He is dead,' he whispered.

The robot seemed to understand, or at least to hear. He bent forward and regarded the still figure.

'What is it, Gnut?' Cliff asked the robot suddenly. 'What are you doing? Can I help you in any way? Somehow I don't believe you are unfriendly, and I don't believe you killed this man. But what happened? Can you understand me? Can you speak? What is it you're trying to do?'

Gnut made no sound or motion, but only looked at the still figure at his feet. In the robot's face, now so close, Cliff saw the look of sad contemplation.

Gnut stood so several minutes; then he bent lower, took the limp form carefully—even gently, Cliff thought—in his mighty arms, and carried him to the place along the wall where lay the dismembered pieces of the robot attendants. Carefully he laid him by their side. Then he went back into the ship.

Without fear now, Cliff stole along the wall of the room. He had gotten almost as far as the shattered figures on the floor when he suddenly stopped motionless. Gnut was emerging again.

He was bearing a shape that looked like another body, a larger one. He held it in one arm and placed it carefully by the body of Stillwell. In the hand of his other arm he held something that Cliff could not make out, and this he placed at the side of the body he had just put down. Then he went to the ship and returned once more with a shape which he laid gently by the others; and when this last trip was over he looked down at them all for a moment, then turned slowly back to the ship and stood motionless, as if in deep thought, by the ramp.

Cliff restrained his curiosity as long as he could, then slipped forward and bent over the objects Gnut had placed there. First in the row was the body of Stillwell, as he expected, and next was the great shapeless furry mass of a dead gorilla—the one of last night. By the gorilla lay the object the robot had carried in his free hand—the little body of the mocking bird. These last two had remained in the ship all night, and Gnut, for all his surprising gentleness in handling them, was only cleaning house. But there was a fourth body whose history he did not know. He moved closer and bent very low to look.

What he saw made him catch his breath. Impossible!—he thought; there was some confusion in his directions; he brought his face back, close to the first body. Then his blood ran cold. The first body was that of Stillwell, but the last in the row was Stillwell, too; there were two bodies of Stillwell, both exactly alike, both dead.

Cliff backed away with a cry, and then panic took him and he ran down the room away from Gnut and yelled and beat wildly on the door. There was a noise on the outside.

'Let me out!' he yelled in terror. 'Let me out! Let me out! Oh, hurry!'

A crack opened between the two doors and he forced his way through like a wild animal and ran far out on the lawn. A belated couple on a nearby path stared at him with amazement, and this brought some sense to his head and he slowed down and came to a stop. Back at the building, everything looked as usual, and in spite of his terror, Gnut was not chasing him.

He was still in his stockinged feet. Breathing heavily, he sat down on the wet grass and put on his shoes; then he stood and looked at the building, trying to pull himself together. What an incredible melange! The dead Stillwell, the dead gorilla, and the dead mocking bird—all dying before his eyes. And then that last frightening thing, the second dead Stillwell whom he had *not* seen die. And Gnut's strange gentleness, and the sad expression he had twice seen on his face.

As he looked, the grounds about the building came to life. Several people collected at the door of the wing, above sounded the siren of a police copter, then in the distance another, and from all sides people came running, a few at first, then more and more. The police planes landed on the lawn just outside the door of the wing, and he thought he could see the officers peeping inside. Then suddenly the lights of the wing flooded on. In control of himself now, Cliff went back.

He entered. He had left Gnut standing in thought at the side of the ramp, but now he was again in his old familiar pose in the usual place, as if he had never moved. The ship's door was closed, and the ramp gone. But the bodies, the four strangely assorted bodies, were still lying by the demolished robot attendants where he had left them in the dark.

He was startled by a cry behind his back. A uniformed museum guard was pointing at him.

'This is the man!' the guard shouted. 'When I opened the door this man forced his way out and ran like the devil!'

The police officers converged on Cliff.

'Who are you? What is all this?' one of them asked him roughly.

'I'm Cliff Sutherland, picture reporter,' Cliff answered calmly. 'And I was the one who was inside here and ran away, as the guard says.'

'What were you doing?' the officer asked, eyeing him. 'And where did these bodies come from?'

'Gentlemen, I'd tell you gladly—only business first,' Cliff answered. 'There's been some fantastic goings on in this room, and I saw them and have the story, but'—he smiled—'I must decline to answer without advice of counsel until I've sold my story to one of the news syndicates. You know how it is. If you'll allow me the use of the radio in your plane—just for a moment, gentlemen—you'll have the whole story right afterward—say in half an hour, when the television men broadcast it. Meanwhile, believe me, there's nothing for you to do, and there'll be no loss by the delay.'

The officer who had asked the questions blinked, and one of the others, quicker to react and certainly not a gentleman, stepped toward Cliff with clenched fists. Cliff disarmed him by handing him his press credentials. He glanced at them rapidly and put them in his pocket.

By now half a hundred people were there, and among them were two members of a syndicate crew whom he knew, arrived by copter. The police growled, but they let him whisper in their ear and then go out under escort to the crew's plane. There, by radio, in five minutes, Cliff made a deal which would bring him more money than he had ever before earned in a year. After that he turned over all his pictures and negatives to the crew and gave them the story, and they lost not one second in spinning back to their office with the flash.

More and more people arrived, and the police cleared the building. Ten minutes later a big crew of radio and television men forced their way in, sent there by the syndicate with which he had dealt. And then a few minutes later, under the glaring lights set up by the operators and standing close by the ship and not far from Gnut—he refused to stand underneath him—Cliff gave his story to the cameras and microphones, which in a fraction of a second shot it to every corner of the Solar System.

Immediately afterward the police took him to jail. On general principles and because they were pretty blooming mad.

Chapter Five

Cliff stayed in jail all that night—until eight o'clock the next morning, when the syndicate finally succeeded in digging up a lawyer and got him out. And then, when at last he was leaving, a Federal man caught him by the wrist.

'You're wanted for further questioning over at the Continental Bureau of Investigation,' the agent told him. Cliff went along willingly.

Fully thirty-five high-ranking Federal officials and 'big names' were waiting for him in an imposing conference room—one of the president's secretaries, the undersecretary of state, the underminister of defense, scientists, a colonel, executives, department heads, and ranking 'C' men. Old gray-mustached Sanders, chief of the CBI, was presiding.

They made him tell his story all over again, and then, in parts, all over once more—not because they did not believe him, but because they kept hoping to elicit some fact which would cast significant light on the mystery of Gnut's behavior and the happenings of the last three nights. Patiently Cliff racked his brains for every detail.

Chief Sanders asked most of the questions. After more than an hour, when Cliff thought they had finished, Sanders asked him several more, all involving his personal opinions of what had transpired.

'Do you think Gnut was deranged in any way by the acids, rays, heat, and so forth applied to him by the scientists?'

'I saw no evidence of it.'

'Do you think he can see?'

'I'm sure he can see, or else has other powers which are equivalent.'

'Do you think he can hear?'

'Yes, sir. That time when I whispered to him that Stillwell was dead, he bent lower, as if to see for himself. I would not be surprised if he also understood what I said.'

'At no time did he speak, except those sounds he made to open the ship?'

'Not one word, in English or any other language. Not one sound with his mouth.'

'In your opinion, has his strength been impaired in any way by our treatment?' asked one of the scientists.

'I have told you how easily he handled the gorilla. He attacked the animal and threw it back, after which it retreated all the way down the building, afraid of him.'

'How would you explain the fact that our autopsies disclosed no mortal wound, no cause of death, in any of the bodies—gorilla, mocking bird, or the two identical Stillwells?'—this from a medical officer.

'I can't.'

'You think Gnut is dangerous?'—from Sanders.

'Potentially very dangerous.'

'Yet you say you have the feeling he is not hostile.'

'To me, I meant. I do have that feeling, and I'm afraid that I can't give any good reason for it, except the way he spared me twice when he had me in his power. I think maybe the gentle way he handled the bodies had something to do with it, and maybe the sad, thoughtful look I twice caught on his face.'

'Would you risk staying in the building alone another night?'

'Not for anything.' There were smiles.

'Did you get any pictures of what happened last night?'

'No, sir.' Cliff, with an effort, held on to his composure, but he was swept by a wave of shame. A man hitherto silent rescued him by saying:

'A while ago you used the word "purposive" in connection with Gnut's actions. Can you explain that a little?'

'Yes, that was one of the things that struck me: Gnut never seems to waste a motion. He can move with surprising speed when he wants to; I saw that when he attacked the gorilla; but most other times he walks around as if methodically completing some simple task. And that reminds me of a peculiar thing: at times he gets into one position, any position, maybe half bent over, and stays there for minutes at a time. It's as if his scale of time values was eccentric, compared to ours; some things he does surprisingly fast, and others surprisingly slow. This might account for his long periods of immobility.'

'That's very interesting,' said one of the scientists. 'How would you account for the fact that he recently moves only at night?'

'I think he's doing something he wants no one to see, and the night is the only time he is alone.'

'But he went ahead even after finding you there.'

'I know. But I have no other explanation, unless he considered me harmless or unable to stop him—which was certainly the case.'

'Before you arrived, we were considering incasing him in a large block of glasstex. Do you think he would permit it?'

'I don't know. Probably he would; he stood for the acids and rays and heat. But it had better be done in the daytime; night seems to be the time he moves.'

'But he moved in the daytime when he emerged from the traveler with Klaatu.'

'I know.'

That seemed to be all they could think of to ask him. Sanders slapped his hand on the table.

'Well, I guess that's all Mr Sutherland,' he said. 'Thank you for your help, and let me congratulate you for a very foolish, stubborn, brave young man—young businessman.' He smiled very faintly. 'You are free to go now, but it may be that I'll have to call you back later. We'll see.'

'May I remain while you decide about that glasstex?' Cliff asked. 'As long as I'm here I'd like to have the tip.'

'The decision has already been made—the tip's yours. The pouring will be started at once.'

'Thank you, sir,' said Cliff—and calmly asked more: 'And will you be so kind as to authorize me to be present outside the building tonight? Just outside. I've a feeling something's going to happen.'

'You want still another scoop, I see,' said Sanders not unkindly, 'then you'll let the police wait while you transact your business.'

'Not again, sir. If anything happens, they'll get it at once.'

The chief hesitated. 'I don't know,' he said. 'I'll tell you what. All the news services will want men there, and we can't have that; but if you can arrange to represent them all yourself, it's a go. Nothing's going to happen, but your reports will help calm the hysterical ones. Let me know.'

Cliff thanked him and hurried out and phoned his syndicate the tip—free—then told them Sanders' proposal. Ten minutes later they called him back, said all was arranged, and told him to catch some sleep. They would cover the pouring. With light heart, Cliff hurried over to the museum. The place was surrounded by thousands of the curious, held far back by a strong cordon of police. For once he could not get through; he was recognized, and the police were still sore. But he did not care much; he suddenly felt very tired and needed that nap. He went back to his hotel, left a call, and went to bed.

He had been asleep only a few minutes when his phone rang. Eyes shut, he answered it. It was one of the boys at the syndicate, with peculiar news. Stillwell had just reported, very much alive—the real Stillwell. The two dead ones were some kind of copies; he couldn't imagine how to explain them. He had no brothers.

For a moment Cliff came fully awake, then he went back to bed. Nothing was fantastic any more.

Chapter Six

At four o'clock, much refreshed and with an infrared viewing magnifier slung over his shoulder, Cliff passed through the cordon and entered the door of the wing. He had been expected and there was no trouble. As his eyes fell on Gnut, an odd feeling went through him, and for some obscure reason he was almost sorry for the giant robot.

Gnut stood exactly as he had always stood, the right foot advanced a little, and the same brooding expression on his face; but now there was something more. He was solidly incased in a huge block of transparent glasstex. From the floor on which he stood to the top of his full eight feet, and from there on up for an equal distance, and for about eight feet to the left, right, back, and front, he was immured in a water-clear prison which confined every inch of his surface and would prevent the slightest twitch of even his amazing muscles.

It was absurd, no doubt, to feel sorry for a robot, a man-made mechanism, but Cliff had come to think of him as being really alive, as a human is alive. He showed purpose and will; he performed complicated and re-sourceful acts; his face had twice clearly shown the emotion of sadness, and several times what appeared to be deep thought; he had been ruth-less with the gorilla, and gentle with the mocking bird and the other two bodies, and he had twice refrained from crushing Cliff when there seemed every reason that he might. Cliff did not doubt for a minute that he was still alive, whatever that 'alive' might mean.

But outside were waiting the radio and television men; he had work to do. He turned and went to them and all got busy.

An hour later Cliff sat alone about fifteen feet above the ground in a big tree which, located just across the walk from the building, commanded through a window a clear view of the upper part of Gnut's body. Strapped to the limbs about him were three instruments—his infrared viewing mag-nifier, a radio mike, and an infrared television eye with sound pickup. The first, the viewing magnifier, would allow him to see in the dark with his own eyes, as if by daylight, a magnified image of the robot, and the others would pick up any sights and sounds, including his own remarks, and transmit them to the several broadcast studios which would fling them millions of miles in all directions through space. Never before had a pic-ture man had such an important assignment, probably—certainly not one who forgot to take pictures. But now that was forgotten, and Cliff was quite proud, and ready.

Far back in a great circle stood a multitude of the curious—and the fear-ful. Would the plastic glasstex hold Gnut? If it did not, would he come out thirsting for revenge? Would unimaginable beings come out of the traveler and release him, and perhaps exact revenge? Millions at their receivers were jittery; those in the distance hoped nothing awful would happen, yet they hoped something would, and they were prepared to run.

In carefully selected spots not far from Cliff on all sides were mobile ray batteries manned by army units, and in a hollow to the back of him, well to his right, there was stationed a huge tank with a large gun. Every weapon was trained on the door of the wing. A row of smaller, faster tanks stood ready fifty yards directly north. Their ray projectors were aimed at the door, but not their guns. The grounds about the building contained only one spot—the hollow where the great tank was—where, by close calculation, a shell directed at the doorway would not cause damage and loss of life to some part of the sprawling capital.

Dusk fell; out streamed the last of the army officers, politicians and other privileged ones; the great metal doors of the wing clanged to and were locked for the night. Soon Cliff was alone, except for the watchers at their weapons scattered around him.

Hours passed. The moon came out. From time to time Cliff reported to the studio crew that all was quiet. His unaided eyes could now see nothing of Gnut but the two faint red points of his eyes, but through the magnifier he stood out as clearly as if in daylight from an apparent distance of only ten feet. Except for his eyes, there was no evidence that he was anything but dead and unfunctionable metal.

Another hour passed. Now and again Cliff thumbed the levels of his tiny radio-television watch—only a few seconds at a time because of its limited battery. The air was full of Gnut and his own face and his own name, and once the tiny screen showed the tree in which he was then sitting and even, minutely, himself. Powerful infrared long-distance television pickups were even then focused on him from nearby points of vantage. It gave him a funny feeling.

Then, suddenly, Cliff saw something and quickly bent his eye to the viewing magnifier. Gnut's eyes were moving; at least the intensity of the light emanating from them varied. It was as if two tiny red flashlights were turned from side to side, their beams at each motion crossing Cliff's eyes.

Thrilling, Cliff signaled the studios, cut in his pickups, and described the phenomenon. Millions resonated to the excitement in his voice. Could Gnut conceivably break out of that terrible prison?

Minutes passed, the eye flashes continued, but Cliff could discern no movement or attempted movement of the robot's body. In brief snatches he described what he saw. Gnut was clearly alive; there could be no doubt he was straining against the transparent prison in which he had at last been locked fast; but unless he could crack it, no motion should show.

Cliff took his eye from the magnifier—and started. His unaided eye, looking at Gnut shrouded in darkness, saw an astonishing thing not yet visible through his instrument. A faint red glow was spreading over the robot's body. With trembling fingers he readjusted the lens of the television eye, but even as he did so the glow grew in intensity. It looked as if Gnut's body was being heated to incandescence!

He described it in excited fragments, for it took most of his attention to keep correcting the lens. Gnut passed from a figure of dull red to one brighter and brighter, clearly glowing now even through the magnifier. And then he moved! Unmistakably he moved!

He had within himself somehow the means to raise his own body temperature, and was exploiting the one limitation of the plastic in which he was locked. For glasstex, Cliff now remembered, was a thermoplastic material, one that set by cooling and conversely would soften again with heat. Gnut was melting his way out!

In three-word snatches, Cliff described this. The robot became cherry-red, the sharp edges of the icelike block rounded, and the whole structure began to sag. The process accelerated. The robot's body moved more widely. The plastic lowered to the crown of his head, then to his neck, then his waist, which was as far as Cliff could see. His body was free! And then, still cherry-red, he moved forward out of sight!

Cliff strained eyes and ears, but caught nothing but the distant roar of the watchers beyond the police lines and a few low, sharp commands from the batteries posted around him. They, too, had heard, and perhaps seen by telescreen, and were waiting.

Several minutes passed. There was a sharp, ringing crack; the great metal doors of the wing flew open, and out stepped the metal giant, glowing no longer. He stood stock-still, and his red eyes pierced from side to side through the darkness.

Voices out in the dark barked orders and in a twinkling Gnut was bathed in narrow crisscrossing rays of sizzling, colored light. Behind him the metal doors began to melt, but his great green body showed no change at all. Then the world seemed to come to an end; there was a deafening roar, everything before Cliff seemed to explode in smoke and chaos, his tree whipped to one side so that he was nearly thrown out. Pieces of debris rained down. The tank gun had spoken, and Gnut, he was sure, had been hit.

Cliff held on tight and peered into the haze. As it cleared he made out a stirring among the debris at the door, and then dimly but unmistakably he saw the great form of Gnut rise to his feet. He got up slowly, turned toward the tank, and suddenly darted toward it in a wide arc. The big gun swung in an attempt to cover him, but the robot side-stepped and then was upon it. As the crew scattered, he destroyed its breech with one blow of his fist, and then he turned and looked right at Cliff.

He moved toward him, and in a moment was under the tree. Cliff climbed higher. Gnut put his two arms around the tree and gave a lifting push, and the tree tore out at the roots and fell crashing to its side. Before Cliff could scramble away, the robot had lifted him in his metal hands.

Cliff thought his time had come, but strange things were yet in store for him that night. Gnut did not hurt him. He looked at him from arm's length for a moment, then lifted him to a sitting position on his shoulders, legs straddling his neck. Then, holding one ankle, he turned and without hesitation started down the path which led westward away from the building.

Cliff rode helpless. Out over the lawns he saw the muzzles of the scattered field pieces move as he moved, Gnut—and himself—their one focus. But they did not fire. Gnut, by placing him on his shoulders, had secured himself against that—Cliff hoped.

The robot bore straight toward the Tidal Basin. Most of the field pieces throbbed slowly after. Far back, Cliff saw a dark tide of confusion roll into the cleared area—the police lines had broken. Ahead, the ring thinned rapidly off to the sides; then, from all directions but the front, the tide rolled in until individual shouts and cries could be made out. It came to a stop about fifty yards off, and few people ventured nearer.

Gnut paid them no attention, and he no more noticed his burden than he might a fly. His neck and shoulders made Cliff a seat hard as steel, but with the difference that their underlying muscles with each movement flexed, just as would those of a human being. To Cliff, this metal musculature became a vivid wonder.

Straight as the flight of a bee, over paths, across lawns, and through thin rows of trees Gnut bore the young man, the roar of thousands of people following close. Above droned copters and darting planes, among them police cars with their nerve-shattering sirens. Just ahead lay the still waters of the Tidal Basin, and in its midst the simple marble tomb of the slain ambassador, Klaatu, gleaming black and cold in the light of the dozen searchlights always trained on it at night. Was this a rendezvous with the dead?

Without an instant's hesitation, Gnut strode down the bank and entered the water. It rose to his knees, then waist, until Cliff's feet were under. Straight through the dark waters for the tomb of Klaatu the robot made his inevitable way.

The dark square mass of gleaming marble rose higher as they neared it. Gnut's body began emerging from the water as the bottom shelved upward, until his dripping feet took the first of the rising pyramid of steps. In a moment they were at the top, on the narrow platform in the middle of which rested the simple oblong tomb.

Stark in the blinding searchlights, the giant robot walked once around it, then, bending, he braced himself and gave a mighty push against the top. The marble cracked; the thick cover slipped askew and broke with a loud noise on the far side. Gnut went to his knees and looked within, bringing Cliff well up over the edge.

Inside, in sharp shadow against the converging light beams, lay a transparent plastic coffin, thick walled and sealed against the centuries, and containing all that was mortal of Klaatu, unspoken visitor from the great Unknown. He lay as if asleep, on his face the look of godlike nobility that had caused some of the ignorant to believe him divine. He wore the robe he had arrived in. There were no faded flowers, no jewelry, no ornaments; they would have seemed profane. At the foot of the coffin lay the small sealed box, also of transparent plastic, which contained all of Earth's records of his visit—a description of the events attending his arrival, pictures of Gnut and the traveler, and the little roll of sight-and-sound film which had caught for all time his few brief motions and words.

Cliff sat very still, wishing he could see the face of the robot. Gnut, too, did not move from his position of reverent contemplation—not for a long time. There on the brilliantly lighted pyramid, under the eyes of a fearful, tumultuous multitude, Gnut paid final respect to his beautiful and adored master.

Suddenly, then, it was over. Gnut reached out and took the little box of records, rose to his feet, and started down the steps.

Back through the water, straight back to the building, across lawns and paths as before, he made his irresistible way. Before him the chaotic ring of people melted away, behind they followed as close as they dared, trampling each other in their efforts to keep him in sight. There are no television records of his return. Every pickup was damaged on the way to the tomb.

As they drew near the building, Cliff saw that the tank's projectile had made a hole twenty feet wide extending from the roof to the ground. The door still stood open, and Gnut, hardly varying his almost jerkless rhythm, made his way over the debris and went straight for the port end of the ship. Cliff wondered if he would be set free.

He was. The robot set him down and pointed toward the door; then, turning, he made the sounds that opened the ship. The ramp slid down and he entered.

Then Cliff did the mad, courageous thing which made him famous for a generation. Just as the ramp started sliding back in he skipped over it and himself entered the ship. The port closed.

Chapter Seven

It was pitch dark, and the silence was absolute. Cliff did not move. He felt that Gnut was close, just ahead, and it was so.

His hard metal hand took him by the waist, pulled him against his cold side, and carried him somewhere ahead. Hidden lamps suddenly bathed the surroundings with bluish light.

He set Cliff down and stood looking at him. The young man already regretted his rash action, but the robot, except for his always unfathomable eyes, did not seem angry. He pointed to a stool in one corner of the room.

Cliff quickly obeyed this time and sat meekly, for a while not even venturing to look around.

He saw he was in a small laboratory of some kind. Complicated metal and plastic apparatus lined the walls and filled several small tables; he could not recognize or guess the function of a single piece. Dominating the center of the room was a long metal table on whose top lay a large box, much like a coffin on the outside, connected by many wires to a complicated apparatus at the far end. From close above spread a cone of bright light from a many-tubed lamp.

One thing, half covered on a near-by table, did look familiar—and very much out of place. From where he sat it seemed to be a brief case—an ordinary Earthman's brief case. He wondered.

Gnut paid him no attention, but at once, with the narrow edge of a thick tool, sliced the lid off the little box of records. He lifted out the strip of sight-and-sound film and spent fully half an hour adjusting it within the apparatus at the end of the big table. Cliff watched, fascinated, wondering at the skill with which the robot used his tough metal fingers. This done, Gnut worked for a long time over some accessory apparatus on an adjoining table. Then he paused thoughtfully a moment and pushed inward a long rod.

A voice came out of the coffinlike box—the voice of the slain ambassador.

'I am Klaatu,' it said, 'and this is Gnut.'

From the recording!—flashed through Cliff's mind. The first and only words the ambassador had spoken. But, then, in the very next second he saw that it was not so. There was a man in the box! The man stirred and sat up, and Cliff saw the living face of Klaatu!

Klaatu appeared somewhat surprised and spoke quickly in an unknown tongue to Gnut—and Gnut, for the first time in Cliff's experience, spoke himself in answer. The robot's syllables tumbled out as if born of human emotion, and the expression on Klaatu's face changed from surprise to wonder. They talked for several minutes. Klaatu, apparently fatigued, then began to lie down, but stopped midway, for he saw Cliff. Gnut spoke again, at length. Klaatu beckoned Cliff with his hand, and he went to him.

'Gnut has told me everything,' he said in a low, gentle voice, then looked at Cliff for a moment in silence, on his face a faint, tired smile.

Cliff had a hundred questions to ask, but for a moment hardly dared open his mouth.

'But you,' he began at last—very respectfully, but with an escaping excitement—'you are not the Klaatu that was in the tomb?'

The man's smile faded and he shook his head.

'No.' He turned to the towering Gnut and said something in his own tongue, and at his words the metal features of the robot twisted as if with pain. Then he turned back to Cliff. 'I am dying,' he announced simply, as if repeating his words for the Earthman. Again to his face came the faint, tired smile.

Cliff's tongue was locked. He just stared, hoping for light. Klaatu seemed to read his mind.

'I see you don't understand,' he said. 'Although unlike us, Gnut has great powers. When the wing was built and the lectures began, there came to him a striking inspiration. Acting on it at once, in the night, he assembled this apparatus . . . and now he has made me again, from my voice, as recorded by your people. As you must know, a given body makes a characteristic sound. He constructed an apparatus which reversed the recording process, and from the given sound made the characteristic body.'

Cliff gasped. So that was it!

'But you needn't die!' Cliff exclaimed suddenly, eagerly. 'Your voice recording was taken when you stepped out of the ship, while you were well! You must let me take you to a hospital! Our doctors are very skillfull!'

Hardly perceptibly, Klaatu shook his head.

'You still don't understand,' he said slowly and more faintly. 'Your recording had imperfections. Perhaps very slight ones, but they doom the product. All of Gnut's experiments died in a few minutes, he tells me . . . and so must I.'

Suddenly, then, Cliff understood the origin of the 'experiments.' He remembered that on the day the wing was opened a Smithsonian official had lost a brief case containing film strips recording the speech of various world fauna. There, on that table, was a brief case! And the Stillwells must have been made from strips kept in the table drawer!

But his heart was heavy. He did not want this stranger to die. Slowly there dawned on him an important idea. He explained it with growing excitement.

'You say the recording was imperfect, and of course it was. But the cause of that lay in the use of an imperfect recording apparatus. So if Gnut, in his reversal of the process, had used exactly the same pieces of apparatus that your voice was recorded with, the imperfections could be studied, canceled out, and you'd live, and not die!'

As the last words left his lips, Gnut whipped around like a cat and gripped him tight. A truly human excitement was shining in the metal muscles of his face.

'Get me that apparatus!' he ordered—in clear and perfect English! He started pushing Cliff toward the door, but Klaatu raised his hand.

'There is no hurry,' Klaatu said gently; 'it is too late for me. What is your name, young man?'

Cliff told him.

'Stay with me to the end,' he asked. Klaatu closed his eyes and rested; then, smiling just a little, but not opening his eyes, he added: 'And don't be sad, for I shall now perhaps live again . . . and it will be due to you. There is no pain—' His voice was rapidly growing weaker. Cliff, for all the questions he had, could only look on, dumb. Again Klaatu seemed to be aware of his thoughts.

'I know,' he said feebly, 'I know. We have so much to ask each other. About your civilization . . . and Gnut's—'

'And yours,' said Cliff.

'And Gnut's,' said the gentle voice again. 'Perhaps . . . some day . . . perhaps I will be back—'

He lay without moving. He lay so for a long time, and at last Cliff knew that he was dead. Tears came to his eyes; in only these few minutes he had come to love this man. He looked at Gnut. The robot knew, too, that he was dead, but no tears filled his redlighted eyes; they were fixed on Cliff, and for once the young man knew what was in his mind.

'Gnut,' he announced earnestly, as if taking a sacred oath, 'I'll get the original apparatus. I'll get it. Every piece of it, the exact same things.'

Without a word, Gnut conducted him to the port. He made the sounds that unlocked it. As it opened, a noisy crowd of Earthmen outside trampled each other in a sudden scramble to get out of the building. The wing was lighted. Cliff stepped down the ramp.

The next two hours always in Cliff's memory had a dreamlike quality. It was as if that mysterious laboratory with the peacefully sleeping dead man was the real and central part of his life, and his scene with the noisy men with whom he talked a gross and barbaric interlude. He stood not far from the ramp. He told only part of his story. He was believed. He waited quietly while all the pressure which the highest officials in the land could exert was directed toward obtaining for him the apparatus the robot had demanded.

When it arrived, he carried it to the floor of the little vestibule behind the port. Gnut was there, as if waiting. In his arms he held the slender body of the second Klaatu. Tenderly he passed him out to Cliff, who took him without a word, as if all this had been arranged. It seemed to be the parting.

Of all the things Cliff had wanted to say to Klaatu, one remained imperatively present in his mind. Now, as the green metal robot stood framed in the great green ship, he seized his chance.

'Gnut,' he said earnestly, holding carefully the limp body in his arms, 'you must do one thing for me. Listen carefully. I want you to tell your master—the master yet to come—that what happened to the first Klaatu was an accident, for which all Earth is immeasurably sorry. Will you do that?'

'I have known it,' the robot answered gently.

'But will you promise to tell your master—just those words—as soon as he is arrived?'

'You misunderstand,' said Gnut, still gently, and quietly spoke four more words. As Cliff heard them a mist passed over his eyes and his body went numb.

As he recovered and his eyes came back to focus he saw the great ship disappear. It just suddenly was not there any more. He fell back a step or two. In his ears, like great bells, rang Gnut's last words. Never, never was he to disclose them till the day he came to die.

'You misunderstand,' the mighty robot had said. 'I am the master.'

The 4-Sided Triangle

William F. Temple

*You've often requested something from the old days. Here is a
classic reprinted from the November, 1939 Amazing Stories.
Whether it's a first or second reading for you, you'll enjoy this
unique solution to the eternal triangle.*

Three people were looking through a quartz window. The girl was
squashed uncomfortably between the two men, but at the moment neither she nor they cared. The object they were watching was too interesting.

The girl was Joan Leeton. Her hair was an indeterminate brown, and
owed its curls to tongs, not to nature. Her eyes were certainly brown, and
bright with unquenchable good humor. In repose her face was undistin-
guished, though far from plain; when she smiled, it was beautiful.

Her greatest attraction (and it was part of her attraction that she did not
realize it) lay in her character. She was soothingly sympathetic without becoming mushy, she was very level-headed (a rare thing in a woman) and
completely unselfish. She refused to lose her temper over anything, or take
offense, or enlarge upon the truth in her favor, and yet she was tolerant of
such lapses in others. She possessed a brain that was unusually able in its
dealings with science, and yet her tastes and pleasures were simple.

William Fredericks (called 'Will') had much in common with Joan, his
sympathy was a little more disinterested, his humor less spontaneous,
and he had certain prejudices. His tastes were reserved for what he considered the more worthy things. But he was calm and good-tempered,
and his steadiness of purpose was reassuring. He was black-haired, with
an expression of quiet content.

William Josephs (called 'Bill') was different. He was completely unstable. Fiery of hair, he was alternately fiery and depressed of spirit. Impul-

sive, generous, highly emotional about art and music, he was given to periods of gaiety and moods of black melancholia. He reached, at his best, heights of mental brilliance far beyond the other two, but long bouts of lethargy prevented him from making the best of them.

Nevertheless, his sense of humor was keen, and he was often amused at his own absurdly over-sensitive character; but he could not change it.

Both these men were deeply in love with Joan, and both tried hard to conceal it. If Joan had any preference, she concealed it just as ably although they were aware that she was fond of both of them.

The quartz window, through which the three were looking, was set in a tall metal container, and just a few feet away was another container, identical even to the thickness of the windowglass.

Overhead was a complex assemblage of apparatus: bulbous, silvered tubes, small electric motors that hummed in various unexpected places, makeshift screens of zinc, roughly soldered, coils upon coils of wire, and a network of slung cables that made the place look like a creeper-tangled tropical jungle. A large dynamo churned out a steady roar in the corner, and a pair of wide spark-gaps crackled continuously, filling the laboratory with a weird, jumping blue light as the day waned outside the windows and the dusk crept in.

An intruder in the laboratory might have looked through the window of the other container and seen, standing on a steel frame in a cubical chamber, an oil painting of 'Madame Croignette' by Boucher, delicately illuminated by concealed lights. He would not have known it, but the painting was standing in a vacuum.

If he had squeezed behind the trio at the other container and gazed through their window he would have seen an apparently identical sight: an oil painting of 'Madame Croignette' by Boucher, standing on a steel frame in a vacuum, delicately illuminated by concealed lights.

From which he would probably not gather much.

The catch was that the painting at which the three were gazing so intently was not quite the same as the one in the first container—not yet. There were minute differences in color and proportion.

But gradually these differences were righting themselves, for the whole of the second canvas was being built up atom by atom, molecule by molecule, into an exactly identical twin of the one which had felt the brush of Francois Boucher.

The marvelously intricate apparatus, using an adaption of a newly discovered magnetic principle, consumed only a moderate amount of power in arranging the lines of sympathetic fields of force which brought every proton into position and every electron into its respective balancing orbit. It was a machine which could divert the flow of great forces without the ability to tap their energy.

'Any minute now!' breathed Will.

Bill rubbed his breath off the glass impatiently.

'Don't do that!' he said, and promptly fogged the glass over again. Not ungently, he attempted to rub a clear patch with Joan's own pretty nose. She exploded into laughter, fogging the glass hopelessly, and in the temporary confusion of this they missed seeing the event they had been waiting days for—the completion of the duplicate painting to the ultimate atom.

The spark-gaps died with a final snap, a lamp sprang into being on the indicator panel, and the dynamo began to run whirringly down to a stop.

They cleaned the window, and there stood 'Madame Croignette' looking rather blankly out at them with wide brown eyes that exactly matched the sepia from Boucher's palette, and both beauty spots and every hair of her powdered wig in place to a millionth of a millimetre. It was identical.

Will turned a valve, and there was the hiss of air rushing into the chamber. He opened the window, and lifted the painting out gingerly, as if he half-expected it to crumble in his hands.

'Perfect—a beauty!' he murmured. He looked up at Joan with shining eyes. Bill caught that look, and unaccountably checked the impulsive whoop of joy he was on the point of letting loose. He coughed instead, and leaned over Joan's shoulder to inspect 'Madame Croignette' more closely.

'The gamble's come off,' went on Will. 'We've sunk every cent into this, but it won't be long before we have enough money to do anything we want to do—anything.'

'Anything—except to get Bill out of bed on Sunday mornings,' smiled Joan, and they laughed.

'No sensible millionaire would get out of bed any morning,' said Bill.

The steel and glass factory of Art Replicas, Limited, shone like a diamond up in the green hills of Surrey. In a financial sense, it had actually sprung from a diamond—the sale of a replica of the Koh-i-noor. That had been the one and only product of Precious Stones, Limited, an earlier company which was closed down by the government when they saw that it would destroy the world's diamond market.

A sister company, Radium Products, was going strong up in the north because its scientific necessity was recognized. But the hearts of the three company directors lay in Art Replicas, and there they spent their time.

Famous works of art from all over the world passed through the factory's portals, and gave birth to innumerable replicas of themselves for distribution and sale at quite reasonable prices.

Families of only moderate means found it pleasing to have a Constable or Turner in the dining room and a Rodin statuette in the hall. And this widely flung ownership of *objets d'art*, which were to all intents and purposes the genuine articles, strengthened interest in art enormously. When people had lived with these things for a little while, they began to perceive the beauty in them—for real beauty is not always obvious at a glance—and to become greedy for more knowledge of them and the men who originally conceived and shaped them.

So the three directors, Will, Bill, and Joan, put all their energy into satisfying the demands of the world for art, and conscious of their part in furthering civilization, were deeply content.

For a time.

Then Bill, the impatient and easily-bored, broke out one day in the middle of a Directors' Meeting.

'Oh, to hell with the Ming estimates!' he cried, sweeping a pile of orders from the table.

Joan and Will, recognizing the symptoms, exchanged wry glances of amusement.

'Look here,' went on Bill, 'I don't know what you two think, but I'm fed up! We've become nothing but dull business people now. It isn't our sort of life. Repetition, repetition! I'm going crazy! We're *research workers*, not darned piece-workers. For heaven's sake, let's start out in some new line.'

This little storm relieved him, and almost immediately he smiled too.

'But, really, aren't we?' he appealed.

'Yes,' responded Joan and Will in duet.

Well, what about it?'

Will coughed, and prepared himself.

'Joan and I were talking about that this morning, as a matter of fact,' he said. 'We were going to suggest that we sell the factory, and retire to our old laboratory and re-equip it.'

Bill picked up the ink-pot and emptied it solemnly over the Ming estimates. The ink made a shining lake in the center of the antique and valuable table.

'At last we're sane again,' he said. 'Now you know the line of investigation I want to open up. I'm perfectly convinced that the reason for our failure to create a living duplicate of any living creature was because the quotiety we assumed for the xy action—'

'Just a moment, Bill,' interrupted Will. 'Before we get on with that work, I—I mean, one of the reasons Joan and I wanted to retire was because—well—'

'What he's trying to say,' said Joan quietly, 'is that we plan to get married and settle down for a bit before we resume research work.'

Bill stared at them. He was aware that his cheeks were slowly reddening. He felt numb.

'Well!' he said. 'Well!' (He could think of nothing else. This was unbelievable! He must postpone consideration of it until he was alone, else his utter mortification would show.)

He put out his hand automatically, and they both clasped it.

'You know I wish you every possible happiness,' he said, rather huskily. His mind seemed empty. He tried to form some comment, but somehow he could not compose one sentence that made sense.

'I think we'll get on all right,' said Will, smiling at Joan. She smiled back at him, and unknowingly cut Bill to the heart.

With an effort, Bill pulled himself together and rang for wine to celebrate. He ordered some of the modern reconstruction of an exceedingly rare '94. He tried to be as merry as possible during their party.

The night was moonless and cloudless, and the myriads of glittering pale blue points of the Milky Way sprawled across the sky as if someone had cast a handful of brilliants upon a black velvet cloth. But they twinkled steadily, for strong air currents were in motion in the upper atmosphere.

The Surrey lane was dark and silent. The only signs of life were the occasional distant glares of automobile headlights passing on the main highway nearly a mile away, and the red dot of a burning cigarette in a gap between the hedgerows.

The cigarette was Bill's. He sat there on a gate staring up at the array in the heavens and wondering what to do with his life.

He felt completely at sea, purposeless, and unutterably depressed. He had thought the word 'heartache' was just a vague descriptive term. Now he knew what it meant. It was a solid physical feeling, an ache that tore him inside, unceasingly. He yearned to see Joan, to be with Joan, with his whole being. This longing would not let him rest. He could have cried out for a respite.

He tried to argue himself to a more rational viewpoint.

'I am a man of science,' he told himself. 'Why should I allow old Mother Nature to torture and badger me like this? I can see through all the tricks of that old twister. These feelings are purely chemical reactions, the secretion of the glands mixing with the blood-stream. My mind is surely strong enough to conquer that? Else I have a third-rate brain, not the scientific instrument I've prided myself on.'

He stared up at the stars glittering in their seeming calm stability, age-old and unchanging. But were they? They may look just the same when all mankind and its loves and hates had departed from this planet, and left it frozen and dark. But he knew that even as he watched, they were changing position at a frightful speed, receding from him at thousands of miles a second.

'Nature is a twister, full of illusions,' he repeated . . .

There started a train of thought, a merciful anesthetic in which he lost himself for some minutes.

Somewhere down in the deeps of his subconscious an idea which had, unknown to him, been evolving itself for weeks, was stirred, and emerged suddenly into the light. He started, dropped his cigarette, and left it on the ground.

He sat there stiffly on the gate and considered the idea.

It was wild—incredibly wild. But if he worked hard and long at it, there was a chance that it might come off. It would provide a reason for living, anyway, so long as there was any hope at all of success.

He jumped down from the gate and started walking quickly and excitedly along the lane back to the factory. His mind was already turning over possibilities, planning eagerly. In the promise of this new adventure, the heartache was temporarily submerged.

Six months passed.

Bill had retired to the old laboratory, and spent much of that time enlarging and re-equipping it. He added a rabbit pen, turned an adjacent patch of ground into burial-ground to dispose of those who died under his knife. This cemetery was like no cemetery in the world, for it was also full of dead things that had never died—because they had never lived.

His research got nowhere. He could build up, atom by atom, the exact physical counterpart of any living animal, but all such duplicates remained obstinately inanimate. They assumed an extraordinary life-like appearance, but it was frozen life. They were no more alive than wax-work images, even though they were as soft and pliable as the original animals in sleep.

Bill thought he had hit upon the trouble in a certain equation, but rechecking confirmed that the equation had been right in the first place. There was no flaw in either theory or practice as far as he could see.

Yet somehow he could not duplicate the force of life in action. Must he apply that force himself? How?

He applied various degrees of electrical impulses to the nerve-centers of the rabbits, tried rapid alternations of temperatures, miniature 'iron lungs,' vigorous massage—both external and internal—intravenous and spinal injections of everything from adrenalin to even more powerful stimulants which his agile mind concocted. And still the artificial rabbits remained limp bundles of fur.

Joan and Will returned from their honeymoon and settled down in a roomy, comfortable old house a few miles away. They sometimes dropped in to see how the research was going. Bill always seemed bright and cheerful enough when they came, and joked about his setbacks.

'I think I'll scour the world for the hottest thing in female bunnies and teach her to do a hula-hula on the lab bench,' he said. 'That ought to make some of these stiffs sit up!'

Joan said she was seriously thinking of starting an eating-house specializing in rabbit pie, if Bill could keep up the supply of dead rabbits. He replied that he'd already buried enough to feed an army.

Their conversation was generally pitched in this bantering key, save when they really got down to technicalities. But when they had gone, Bill would sit and brood, thinking constantly of Joan. And he could concentrate on nothing else for the rest of that day.

Finally, more or less by accident, he found the press-button which awoke life in the rabbits. He was experimenting with a blood solution he had prepared, thinking it might remain more constant than the natural rabbits' blood, which became thin and useless too quickly. He had constructed a little pump to force the natural blood from a rabbit's veins and fill them instead with his artificial solution.

The pump had not been going for more than a few seconds before the rabbit stirred weakly and opened its eyes. It twitched its nose, and lay quite still for a moment, save for one foot which continued to quiver.

Then suddenly it roused up and made a prodigious bound from the bench. The thin rubber tubes which tethered it by the neck parted in mid-air, and it fell awkwardly with a heavy thump on the floor. The blood continued to run from one of the broken tubes, but the pump which forced it out was the rabbit's own heart—beating at last.

The animal seemed to have used all its energy in that one powerful jump, and lay still on the floor and quietly expired.

Bill stood regarding it, his fingers still on the wheel of the pump. [1]

Then when he realized what it meant, he recaptured some of his old exuberance, and danced around the laboratory carrying a carboy of acid as though it were a Grecian urn.

Further experiments convinced him that he had set foot within the portals of Nature's most carefully guarded citadel. Admittedly he could not himself create anything original or unique in life. But he could create a living image of any living creature under the sun.

A hot summer afternoon, a cool green lawn shaded by elms and on it two white-clad figures, Joan and Will putting through their miniature nine-hole course. A bright-striped awning by the hedge, and below it, two comfortable canvas chairs and a little Moorish table with soft drinks. An ivy-covered wall of an old red-brick mansion showing between the trees. The indefinable smell of new-cut grass in the air. The gentle but triumphant laughter of Joan as Will foozled his shot.

That was the atmosphere Bill entered at the end of his duty tramp along the lane from the laboratory—it was his first outdoor excursion for weeks—and he could not help comparing it with the sort of world he had been living in: the benches and bottles and sinks, the eye-tiring field of microscope, the sheets of calculations under the glare of electric light in the dark hours of the night, the smell of blood and chemicals and rabbits.

And he realized completely that science itself wasn't the greatest thing in life. Personal happiness was. That was the goal of all men, whatever way they strove to reach it.

Joan caught sight of him standing on the edge of the lawn, and came hurrying across to greet him.

'Where have you been all this time?' she asked. 'We've been dying to hear how you've been getting on.'

'I've done it,' said Bill.

'Done it? Have you really?' Her voice mounted excitedly almost to a squeak. She grabbed him by the wrist and hauled him across to Will. 'He's done it!' she announced, and stood between them, watching both their faces eagerly.

Will took the news with his usual calmness, and smilingly gripped Bill's hand.

'Congratulations, old lad,' he said. 'Come and have a drink and tell us all about it.'

They squatted on the grass and helped themselves from the table. Will could see that Bill had been overworking himself badly. His face was drawn and tired, his eyelids red, and he was in the grip of a nervous tension which for the time held him dumb and uncertain of himself.

Joan noticed this, too, and checked the questions she was going to bombard upon him. Instead, she quietly withdrew to the house to prepare a pot of China tea which she knew always soothed Bill's migraine.

When she had gone, Bill, with an effort, shook some of the stupor from him, and looked across at Will. His gaze dropped, and he began to pluck idly at the grass.

'Will,' he began, presently, 'I—' He cleared his throat nervously, and started again in a none too steady voice. 'Listen, Will, I have something a bit difficult to say, and I'm not so good at expressing myself. In the first place, I have always been crazily in love with Joan.'

Will sat up, and looked at him curiously. But he let Bill go on.

'I never said anything because—well, because I was afraid I wouldn't make a success of marriage. Too unstable to settle down quietly with a decent girl like Joan. But I found I couldn't go on without her, and was going to propose—when you beat me to it. I've felt pretty miserable since, though this work has taken something of the edge off.'

Will regarded the other's pale face—and wondered.

'This work held out a real hope to me. And now I've accomplished the major part of it. I can make a living copy of any living creature. Now—do you see *why* I threw myself into this research? *I want to create a living, breathing twin of Joan, and marry her!*'

Will started slightly. Bill got up and paced restlessly up and down.

'I know I'm asking a hell of a lot. This affair reaches deeper than scientific curiosity. No feeling man can contemplate such a proposal without misgivings, for his wife and for himself. But honestly, Will, I cannot see any possible harm arising from it. Though, admittedly, the only good would be to make a selfish man happy. For heaven's sake, let me know what you think.'

Will sat contemplating, while the distracted Bill continued to pace.

Presently, he said: 'You are sure no physical harm could come to Joan in the course of the experiment?'

'Certain—completely certain,' said Bill.

'Then I personally have no objection. Anything but objection. I had no idea you felt that way, Bill, and it would make me, as well as Joan, very unhappy to know you had to go on like that.'

He caught sight of his wife approaching with a laden tray.

'Naturally, the decision rests with her,' he said. 'If she'd rather not, there's no more to it.'

'No, of course not,' agreed Bill.

But they both knew what her answer would be.

'Stop the car for a minute, Will,' said Joan suddenly, and her husband stepped on the foot-brake.

The car halted in the lane on the brow of the hill. Through a gap in the hedge the two occupants had a view of Bill's laboratory as it lay below in the cradle of the valley.

Joan pointed down. In the field behind the 'cemetery' two figures were strolling. Even at this distance, Bill's flaming hair marked his identity. His companion was a woman in a white summer frock. And it was on her that Joan's attention was fixed.

'She's alive now!' she whispered, and her voice trembled slightly.

Will nodded. He noticed her apprehension, and gripped her hand encouragingly. She managed a wry smile.

'It's not every day one goes to pay a visit to oneself,' she said. 'It was unnerving enough last week to see her lying on the other couch in the lab, dressed in my red frock—which *I* was wearing—so pale, and—Oh, it was like seeing myself dead!'

'She's not dead now, and Bill's bought her some different clothes, so cheer up,' said Will. 'I know it's a most queer situation, but the only possible way to look at it is from the scientific viewpoint. It's a unique scientific event. And it's made Bill happy into the bargain.'

He ruminated a minute.

'Wish he'd given us a hint as to how he works his resuscitation process, though,' he went on. 'Still, I suppose he's right to keep it secret. It's a discovery which could be appallingly abused. Think of dictators manufacturing loyal, stupid armies from one loyal, stupid soldier! Or industrialists manufacturing cheap labor! We should soon have a world of robots, all traces of individuality wiped out. No variety, nothing unique—life would not be worth living.'

'No,' replied Joan, mechanically, her thoughts still on that white-clad figure down there.

Will released the brake, and the car rolled down the hill toward the laboratory. The two in the field saw it coming, and walked back through the cemetery to meet it. They reached the road as the car drew up.

'Hello, there!' greeted Bill. 'You're late—we've had the kettle on the boil for half an hour. Doll² and I were getting anxious.'

He advanced into the road, and the woman in the white frock lingered hesitantly behind him. Joan tightened her lips and braced herself to face this unusual ordeal. She got out of the car, and while Will and Bill were grasping hands, she walked to meet her now living twin.

Apparently Doll had decided to face it in the same way, and they met with oddly identical expressions of smiling surface ease, with an undercurrent of curiosity and doubt. They both saw and understood each other's expression simultaneously, and bust out laughing. That helped a lot.

'It's not so bad, after all,' said Doll, and Joan checked herself from making the same instinctive remark.

'No, not nearly,' she agreed.

And it wasn't. For although Doll looked familiar to her, she could not seem to identify her with herself to any unusual extent. It was not that her apparel and hair-style were different, but that, somehow her face, figure, and voice seemed like those of another person.

She did not realize that hitherto she had only seen parts of herself in certain mirrors from certain angles, and the complete effect was something she had simply never witnessed.[3] Nor that she had not heard her own voice outside her own head, so to speak—never from a distance of some feet.

Nevertheless, throughout the meal she felt vaguely uneasy, though she tried to hide it, and kept up a fire of witty remarks. And her other self, too, smiled at her across the table and talked easily.

They compared themselves in detail, and found they were completely identical in every way, even to the tiny mole on their left forearm. Their tastes too, agreed. They took the same amount of sugar in their tea, and liked and disliked the same foodstuffs.

'I've got my eye on that pink iced cake,' laughed Doll. 'Have you?'

Joan admitted it. So they shared it.

'You'll never have any trouble over buying each other birthday or Christmas presents,' commented Will. 'How nice to know exactly what the other wants!'

Bill had a permanent grin on his face, and beamed all over the table all the time. For once he did not have a great deal to say. He seemed too happy for words, and kept losing the thread of the conversation to gaze upon Doll fondly.

'We're going to be married tomorrow!' he announced unexpectedly, and they protested their surprise at the lack of warning. But they promised to be there.

There followed an evening of various sorts of games, and the similar thought-processes of Joan and Doll led to much amusement, especially in the guessing games. And twice they played checkers and twice they drew.

It was a merry evening, and Bill was merriest of all. Yet when they came to say goodnight, Joan felt the return of the old uneasiness. As they left in the car, Joan caught a glimpse of Doll's face as she stood beside Bill at the gate. And she divined that under that air of gayety, Doll suffered the same uneasiness as she.

Doll and Bill were married in a distant registry office next day, using a fictitious name and birthplace for Doll to avoid any publicity—after all, no one would question her identity.

Winter came and went.

Doll and Bill seemed to have settled down quite happily, and the quartette remained as close friends as ever. Both Doll and Joan were smitten with the urge to take up flying as a hobby, and joined the local flying club. They each bought a single-seater, and went for long flights, cruising side by side.

Almost in self-protection from this neglect (they had no interest in flying) Bill and Will began to work again together, delving further into the mysteries of the atom. This time they were searching for the yet-to-be-discovered secret of tapping the potential energy which the atom held.

And almost at once they stumbled on a new lead.

Formerly they had been able to divert atomic energy without being able to transform it into useful power. It was as if they had constructed a number of artificial dams at various points in a turbulent river, which altered the course of the river without tapping any of its force—though that is a poor and misleading analogy.

But now they had conceived, and were building, an amazingly complex machine which, in the same unsatisfactory analogy, could be likened to a turbine-generator, tapping some of the power of that turbulent river.

The 'river' however, was very turbulent indeed, and needed skill and courage to harness. And there was a danger of the harness suddenly slipping.

Presently, the others became aware that Doll's health was gradually failing. She tried hard to keep up her usual air of brightness and cheerfulness, but she could not sleep, and became restless and nervous.

And Joan, who was her almost constant companion, suddenly realized what was worrying that mind which was so similar to hers. The realization was a genuine shock, which left her trembling, but she faced it.

'I think it would be a good thing for Doll and Bill to come and live here for a while, until Doll's better,' she said rather diffidently to Will one day.

'Yes, okay, if you think you can persuade them,' replied Will. He looked a little puzzled.

'We have far too many empty rooms here,' she said defensively. 'Anyway I can help Doll if I'm with her more.'

Doll seemed quite eager to come though a little dubious, but Bill thought it a great idea. They moved within the week.

At first, things did improve. Doll began to recover, and became more like her natural self. She was much less highly strung, and joined in the evening games with the other three with gusto. She studied Will's favorite game, backgammon, and began to enjoy beating him thoroughly and regularly.

And then Joan began to fail.

She became nervous, melancholy, and even morose. It seemed as though through helping Doll back to health, she had been infected with the same complaint.

Will was worried, and insisted on her being examined by a doctor.

The doctor told Will in private. 'There's nothing physically wrong. She's nursing some secret worry, and she'll get worse until this worry is eased. Persuade her to tell you what it is—she refuses to tell me.'

She also refused to tell Will, despite his pleadings.

And now Doll, who knew what the secret was, began to worry about Joan, and presently she relapsed into her previous nervous condition.

So it continued for a week, a miserable week for the two harassed and perplexed husbands, who did not know which way to turn. The following week, however, both women seemed to make an effort, and brightened up somewhat, and could even laugh at times.

The recovery continued, and Bill and Will deemed it safe to return to their daily work in the lab, completing the atom-harnessing machine.

One day Will happened to return to the house unexpectedly, and found the two women in each other's arms on a couch, crying their eyes out. He stood staring for a moment. They suddenly became aware of him, and parted, drying their eyes.

'What's up, Will? Why have you come back?' asked Joan, unsteadily, sniffing.

'Er—to get my slide-rule; I'd forgotten it,' he said. 'Bill wanted to trust his memory, but I think there's something wrong with his figures. I want to check up before we test the machine further. But—what's the matter with you two?'

'Oh, we're all right,' said Doll, strainedly and not very convincingly. She blew her nose, and endeavored to pull herself together. But almost immediately she was overtaken by another burst of weeping, and Joan put her arms around her comfortingly.

'Look here,' said Will, in a sudden and unusual exasperation, 'I've had about enough of this. You know that Bill and I are only too willing to deal with whatever you're worrying about. Yet the pair of you won't say a word—only cry and fret. How can we help if you won't tell us? Do you think we like to see you going on like this?'

'I'll tell you, Will,' said Joan, quietly.

❖ ❖ ❖

Doll emitted a muffled 'No!' but Joan ignored her, and went on: 'Don't you see that Bill has created another me in *every* detail? Every memory and every feeling? And because Doll thinks and feels exactly as I do, she's in love with you! She has been that way from the very beginning. All this time she's been trying to conquer it, to suppress it, and make Bill happy instead.'

Doll's shoulders shook with the intensity of her sobbing. Will laid his hands gently on them, consolingly. He could think of nothing whatever to say. He had not even dreamt of such a situation, obvious as it appeared now.

'Do you wonder the conflict got her down?' said Joan. 'Poor girl! I brought her here to be nearer to you, and that eased things for her.'

'But it didn't for you,' said Will, quietly, looking straight at her. 'I see now why you began to worry. Why didn't you tell me then, Joan?'

'How could I?'

He bit his lip, paced nervously over to the window, and stood with his back to the pair on the couch.

'What a position!' he thought. 'What can we do? Poor Bill!'

He wondered how he could break the sorry news to his best friend, and even as he wondered, the problem was solved for him.

From the window there was a view down the length of the wide, shallow valley, and a couple of miles away the white concrete laboratory could just be seen nestling at the foot of one of the farther slopes. There were fields all around it, and a long row of great sturdy oak trees started from its northern corner.

From this height and distance the whole place looked like a table-top model. Will stared moodily at that little white box where Bill was, and tried to clarify his chaotic thoughts.

And suddenly, incredibly, before his eyes the distant white box spurted up in a dusty cloud of chalk-powder, and ere a particle of it had neared its topmost height, the whole of that part of the valley was split across by a curtain of searing, glaring flame. The whole string of oak trees, tough and amazingly deep-rooted though they were, floated up through the air like feathers of windblown thistle-down before the blast of that mighty eruption.

The glaring flame vanished suddenly, like a light that had been turned out and left a thick, brown, heaving fog in its place, a cloud of earth that had been pulverized. Will caught a glimpse of the torn oak trees falling back into this brown, rolling cloud, and then the blast wave, which had traveled up the valley, smote the house.

The window was instantly shattered and blown in, and he went flying backwards in a shower of glass fragments. He hit the floor awkwardly and sprawled there, and only then did his laggard brain realize what had happened.

Bill's habitual impatience had at last been his undoing. He had refused to wait any longer for Will's return, and gone on with the test, trusting to his memory. And he had been wrong.

The harness had slipped.

A man sat on a hill with a wide and lovely view of the country, bright in summer sunshine, spread before him. The rich green squares of the fields, the white ribbons of the lanes, the yellow blocks of haystacks and gray spires of village churches, made up a pattern infinitely pleasing to the eye.

And the bees hummed drowsily, nearby sheep and cattle made the noises of their kind, and a neighboring thicket fairly rang with the unending chorus of a hundred birds.

But all this might as well have been set on another planet, for the man could neither see nor hear the happy environment. He was in hell.

It was a fortnight now since Bill had gone. When that grief had begun to wear off, it was succeeded by the most perplexing and unique problem that had ever beset a member of the human race.

Will had been left to live with two women who loved him equally violently. Neither could ever conquer or suppress that love, whatever they did. They knew that.

On the other hand, Will was a person who was only capable of loving one of the women. Monogamy is deeprooted in most normal people, and particularly so with Will. He had looked forward to traveling through life with one constant companion, and only one—Joan.

But now there were two Joans, identical in appearance, feeling, thought. Nevertheless, they were two separate people. And in between them he was a torn and anguished man, with his domestic life in shapeless ruins.

He could not ease his mental torture with work, for since Bill died so tragically, he could not settle down to anything in a laboratory.

It was no easier for Joan and Doll. Probably harder. To have one's own self as a rival—even a friendly, understanding rival—for a man's companionship and affection was almost unbearable.

This afternoon they had both gone to a flying club, to attempt to escape for a while the burden of worry, apparently. Though neither was in a fit condition to fly, for they were tottering on the brink of a nervous breakdown.

The club was near the hill where Will was sitting and striving to find some working solution to a unique human problem which seemed quite insoluble. So it was no coincidence that presently a humming in the sky caused him to lift dull eyes to see both the familiar monoplanes circling and curving across the blue spaces between the creamy, cumulus clouds.

He lay back on the grass watching them. He wondered which plane was which, but there was no means of telling, for they were similar models. And anyway, that would not tell him which was Joan and which was Doll, for they quite often used each other's planes, to keep the 'feel' of both. He wondered what they were thinking up there . . .

One of the planes straightened and flew away to the west, climbing as it went. Its rising drone became fainter. The other plane continued to bank and curve above.

Presently, Will closed his eyes and tried to doze in the warm sunlight. It was no use. In the darkness of his mind revolved the same old maddening images, doubts, and questions. It was as if he had become entangled in a nightmare from which he could not awake.

The engine of the plane overhead suddenly stopped. He opened his eyes, but could not locate it for a moment.

Then he saw it against the sun, and it was falling swiftly in a tailspin. It fell out of the direct glare of the sun, and he saw it in detail, revolving as it plunged so that the wings glinted like a flashing heliograph. He realized with a shock that it was but a few hundred feet from the ground.

He scrambled to his feet, in an awful agitation.

'Joan!' he cried, hoarsely. 'Joan!'

The machine continued its fall steadily and inevitably, spun down past his eye-level, and fell into the center of one of the green squares of the fields below.

He started running down the hill even as it landed. As the sound of the crash reached him, he saw a rose of fire blossom like magic in that green square, and from it a wavering growth of black, oily smoke mounted into the heavens. The tears started from his eyes, and ran freely.

When he reached the scene, the inferno was past its worst, and as the flames died he saw that nothing was left, only black, shapeless, scattered things, unrecognizable as once human or once machine.

There was a squeal of brakes from the road. An ambulance had arrived from the flying club. Two men jumped out, burst through the hedge. It did not take them more than a few seconds to realize that there was no hope.

'Quick, Mr Fredericks, jump in,' cried one of them, recognizing Will. 'We must go straight to the other one.'

The other one!

✧ ✧ ✧

Before he could question them, Will was hustled between them into the driving cabin of the ambulance. The vehicle was quickly reversed, and sped off in the opposite direction.

'Did—did the other plane—' began Will, and the words stuck in his throat.

The driver, with his eye on the road which was scudding under their wheels at sixty miles an hour, nodded grimly.

'Didn't you see, sir? They both crashed at exactly the same time, in the same way—tailspin. A shocking accident—terrible. I can't think how to express my sympathy, sir. I only pray that this one won't turn out so bad.'

It was as if the ability to feel had left Will. His thoughts slowed up almost to a standstill. He sat there numbed. He dare not try to think.

But, sluggishly, his thoughts went on. Joan and Doll had crashed at exactly the same time in exactly the same way. That was above coincidence. They must have both been thinking along the same lines again, and that meant they had crashed *deliberately!* They planned it!

He saw now the whole irony of it, and groaned.

Joan and Doll had each tried to solve the problem in their own way, and each had reached the same conclusion without being aware what the other was thinking. They saw that one of them would have to step out of the picture if Will was ever to be happy. They knew that one would have to step completely out, for life could no longer be tolerated by her if she had to lose Will.

And, characteristically, they had each made up their minds to be the self-sacrificing one.

Doll felt that she was an intruder, wrecking the lives of a happily married pair. It was no fault of hers: she had not asked to be created full of love for a man she could never have.

But she felt that she was leading an unnecessary existence, and every moment of it was hurting the man she loved. So she decided to relinquish the gift of life.

Joan's reasoning was that she had been partly responsible for bringing Doll into this world, unasked, and with exactly similar feelings and longings as herself. Ever since she had existed, those feelings had been ungratified, cruelly crushed and thwarted. It wasn't fair. Doll had as much right to happiness as she. Joan had enjoyed her period of happiness with Will. Now let Doll enjoy hers.

So it was that two planes, a mile apart, went spinning into crashes that were meant to appear accidental—and did, except to one man, the one who most of all was intended never to know the truth.

The driver was speaking again.

'It was a ghastly dilemma for us at the club. We saw 'em come down on opposite sides and both catch fire. We have only one fire engine, one ambulance. Had to send the engine to one, and rush this ambulance to the other. The engine couldn't have done any good at this end, as it happens. Hope it was in time where we're going!'

Will's dulled mind seemed to take this in quite detachedly. Who had been killed in the crash he saw? Joan or Doll? Joan or Doll?

Then suddenly it burst upon him that it was only the original Joan that he loved. That was the person whom he had known so long, around whom his affection had centered. The hair he had caressed, the lips he had pressed, the gay brown eyes which had smiled into his. He had never touched Doll in that way.

Doll seemed but a shadow of all that. She may have had memories of those happenings, but she never actually experienced them. They were only artificial memories. Yet they must have seemed real enough to her.

The ambulance arrived at the scene of the second crash.

The plane had flattened out a few feet from the ground, and not landed so disastrously as the other. It lay crumpled athwart a burned and blackened hedge. The fire engine had quenched the flames within a few minutes. And the pilot had been dragged clear, unconscious, badly knocked about and burned.

They got her into the ambulance, and rushed her to the hospital.

Will had been sitting by the bedside for three hours before the girl in the bed had opened her eyes.

Blank, brown eyes they were, which looked at him, then at the hospital ward, without the faintest change of expression.

'Joan!' he whispered, clasping her free arm—the other was in a splint. There was no response of any sort. She lay back gazing unseeingly at the ceiling. He licked his dry lips. It couldn't be Joan after all.

'Doll!' he tried. 'Do you feel all right?'

Still no response.

'I know that expression,' said the doctor, who was standing by. 'She's lost her memory.'

'For good, do you think?' asked Will, perturbed.

The doctor pursed his lips to indicate he didn't know.

'Good Lord! Is there no way of finding out whether she is my wife or my sister-in-law?'

'If you don't know, no one does, Mr Fredericks,' replied the doctor. 'We can't tell anything from her clothes, for they were burned in the crash, and destroyed before we realized their importance. We've often remarked their uncanny resemblance. Certainly you can tell them apart.'

'I can't!' answered Will, in anguish. 'There is no way.'

The next day, the patient had largely recovered her senses, and was able to sit up and talk. But a whole tract of her memory had been obliterated. She remembered nothing of her twin, and in fact nothing at all of the events after the duplication experiment.

Lying on the couch in the laboratory, preparing herself under the direction of Bill, was the last scene she remembered.

The hospital psychologist said that the shock of the crash had caused her to unconsciously repress a part of her life which she did not want to remember. She could not remember now if she wanted to. He said he might discover the truth from her eventually, but if he did, it would take months—maybe even years.

But naturally her memories of Will, and their marriage, were intact, and she loved him as strongly as ever.

Was she Joan or Doll?

Will spent a sleepless night, turning the matter over. Did it really matter? There was only one left now—why not assume she was Joan, and carry on? But he knew that as long as doubt and uncertainty existed, he would never be able to recover the old free life he had with Joan.

It seemed that he would have to surrender her to the psychologist, and that would bring to light all sorts of details which neither he, Joan, nor Bill had ever wished to be revealed.

But the next day something turned up which changed the face of things.

Searching the area of Bill's laboratory the police found the charred remains of personal letters, paid and receipted accounts and some experimental notebooks. They brought them to Will to interpret. With their consent he destroyed the personal papers.

In the most badly charred of the notebooks he found an account of Bill's attempt to infuse life into his replicas of living creatures.

The last pages were about the experiment of creating another Joan, and the last recognizable entry read:

'This clumsy business of pumping through pipes, in the manner of a blood transfusion, left a small scar at the base of Doll's neck, the only flaw in an otherwise perfect copy of Joan. I resented ...'

The rest was burned away, Will hurried to the hospital.

Wonderingly, the girl allowed him to examine her neck.

There was not the slightest sign of a scar anywhere on it.

'You are Joan,' he said, and embraced her as satisfactorily as her injuries would permit.

'I am Joan,' she repeated, kissing and hugging him back.

And at last they knew again the blessedness of peace of mind.

For once, Fate, which had used them so hardly, showed mercy, and they never knew that in the packet of Bill's receipted accounts, which Will had destroyed, was one from a famous plastic surgeon, which began:

'For removing operation scar from neck, and two days' nursing and attention.'

1 The only practical way of setting a stagnant circulation in motion. Pump the blood until the heart-pump works in sympathy.—Author.

2 'Doll' was the name he had chosen for Joan II, as he had told them on the 'phone in the morning when he had invited them to come to tea and meet her.—Author.

3 Joan discovered what many film stars discover when first seeing and hearing themselves on the screen: that one's own self appears almost as a stranger at the first detached view.—Author.

FP 1 Does Not Reply

Kurt Siodmak

Translated from the German by H. W. Farrell

Preface

In 1932 we did not have supersonic planes capable of crossing the Atlantic nonstop so the imaginative mind of Curt Slodmak (now ninety-five years old and still vital) proposed an artificial island in mid-Atlantic as a way station, a refueling station and overnight hotel for passengers. Never mind that time has passed by this concept, we still enjoy Jules Verne's *Around the World in 80 Days*, *20,000 Leagues Under the Sea* and sequel *The Mysterious Island*, and *A Trip to the Moon*, H.G. Wells' *War of the Worlds* and *The Shape of Things to Come*, Robert Heinlein's *The Roads Must Roll*, Aldous Huxley's *Brave New World*, Ray Bradbury's *Fahrenheit 451*, George Orwell's *1984*. Even though their prophecies did not exactly come true, the stories themselves are fascinating, and in this nostalgic vein I revive this sci-fi novel sixty-six years after its inception.

The American film version starred Conrad Veldt as the air ace Ellissen. Veldt is famous as the somnambulist in *The Cabinet of Dr Caligari*, Gwynplane in *The Man who Laughs*, the Nazi in *Casablanca*.

The German version starred Germany's most popular leading man of the day, Hans Albers, who appeared opposite Marlene Dietrich in *The Blue Angel*. In a secondary role was Peter Lorre, fresh from his triumph as the pitiable child-molester in *M*.

The French version starred Charles Boyer, who made Fritz Lang's fantasy *Liliom* around the same time, later the macabre *Gaslight* with Ingrid Bergman, and eventually followed his son's suicide with his own, a great loss to the silver screen.

The Spanish version—that's all that's known of it, that there was a Spanish version. Any information on this or any other foreign versions, appreciated.

Now, on to the saga of *Floating (aka Flying) Platform Number One*!

Forrest J. Ackerman

Chapter One: An Invisible Enemy?

In the captain's room high up in the control tower of the FP 1 the acting commander of that modern marvel sat alone at his desk. His head was propped wearily on his hands; his elbows were planted firmly on the desk in front of him.

Schmiedecke, temporarily in command of the FP 1, was a big powerfully built man. His shirt, open at the neck, disclosed a massive chest of which a professional strong man might well have been proud, but at that moment he felt there was not an ounce of strength left in him. He must keep awake, he must keep awake. The words throbbed through his aching head with monotonous, maddening insistence. Blindly, vacantly, he stared in front of him, seeing nothing. His eyes were red and bloodshot. He could not keep them open; the swollen eyelids kept closing automatically, damn 'em! Each time they did so he jerked back his head violently, drew in a deep breath in a desperate effort to drive away the overpowering desire to sleep. With a tremendous effort of will power he would open his eyes to their fullest extent, only to close them again a moment after—oh, blessed relief! God! what a fight it was! He must keep awake,—awake at all costs. So much depended on him. He had hardly dared close his eyes since he took over command of the FP 1.

To Schmiedecke had been intrusted the onerous task of taking Flying Platform Number 1, the great new floating airport, under tow to its destination—a point midway between the Azores and the Bermudas—where it was hoped to find a suitable and permanent anchorage. Schmiedecke had now reached Fayal in the Azores and at that moment the FP 1 was lying about a mile outside the harbor there. The constant strain of the long voyage, however, and the tremendous responsibility of the command were rapidly becoming too much for him.

The FP 1 was indeed a wonder, such as any sailor might be proud to have committed to his charge. It was an immense structure of steel and glass of truly gigantic proportions, a veritable floating island, displacing two hundred thousand tons. When safely anchored, it would provide a port of call, a convenient landing place for aircraft traveling between Europe and America. There they could refuel or refit or disembark passengers, for whose convenience a first-class luxury hotel had been constructed, overlooking the landing platform.

The upper portion of this remarkable leviathan consisted of a large steel platform, four hundred and fifty feet wide and over a quarter of a mile in length. On each side of the platform, which provided an ideal landing place, was a long range of buildings. On one side were the hangars, the repair shops, the storage tanks, and the dynamo houses where the electric power for the whole structure was generated. On the other side stood the hotel, with a magnificent glass façade looking out over the sea. It contained three hundred bedrooms with private baths, numerous public rooms, lounges, swimming baths,—in fact, all the most luxurious, up-to-date appointments of a modern first-class hotel. It had been specially designed to give its guests the illusion of being on *terra firma*.

The platform itself rested on immense buoys, extending one hundred and fifty feet below the water, passing through the restless upper waters of the sea, far down into the motionless depths. Thanks to this, these buoys, when filled with water as ballast, would anchor the FP 1 to one spot as firm and immovable as a rock. To make assurance of its complete stability doubly sure, however, when it was anchored, enormous steel dragnets were to be dropped from the buoys. Spreading out like the roots of a giant tree, the nets were intended to attach the FP 1 securely to the bed of the ocean. It would be in effect, if not in fact, an island.

The platform, when anchored, would be seventy-five feet above the surface of the sea and thus well out of reach of even the highest waves.

Nothing had been forgotten to perfect its working arrangements for the reception of aircraft. Four powerful cranes had been erected to facilitate the handling of all types of aircraft, particularly in the raising of seaplanes to the platform from the sea. A small electric railway was provided to haul the aircraft into the hangars. Automatic electric lifts and trapdoors gave means of access to the sea underneath the platform, where there was a small jetty and tunnel exit to the open sea for the use of the large motor boat which the FP 1 carried.

This marvellous floating airport—one of the greatest and most daring engineering feats of modern times—had been planned and designed by a young engineer, Bernard Droste, a protégé and ward of the famous shipbuilder Lennartz. The construction work had been carried out entirely at the Lennartz yards in Bremen. So important would be the revolution in air traffic which the establishment of an Atlantic airport would bring about, that a government loan had been promised Lennartz, the contract stipulating that the FP 1 should be anchored at its station between the Azores and the Bermudas, and an airplane have successfully landed on it, not later than a certain date.

This fateful day was the twenty-second of the present month of July, and it was the shortness of the time still left till then, and anxiety that he might not be up to time with the FP 1, that was robbing Schmiedecke, its acting commander, of his sleep.

Schmiedecke had been so nervous lest anything should go wrong that he had been afraid to allow himself to rest, with the result that he had hardly slept at all for the three weeks since the FP 1 started on its long tow.

In an effort to keep himself awake, Schmiedecke began to reckon up what sleep he had actually had in that time. There were one or two short snatches soon after the start. Then, on one occasion, he had fallen asleep from sheer exhaustion while he was sitting at the writing table, reading a radiogram from the Lennartz yards. He had simply collapsed under the table like a drunken man, and Sambach, damn the man! instead of waking him, had let him lie sprawling there for several hours, while the *Elbe* fought her way against that gale with the FP1 in tow and lost valuable time—they couldn't have made more than three knots an hour.

On another occasion at Fayal he had fallen sound asleep in a wine shop. He had gone in, intending only to sit down for a couple of minutes and have a drink. He must have slept a solid five hours there—and then the people had made him pay for five drinks! As if a sleeping man could drink—and beastly Malaga at that. Damned if he'd drink the sugary stuff, anyway. Damn it, it wasn't good enough; a man ought to be able for once to rest snugly in a decent bed with cool, white sheets and soft, feathery pillows, and have his sleep out...fall asleep comfortably, with darkness slowly growing on him...everything fading out—disappearing—dissolving...nobody able to get at him...to disturb him...no orders...no telegrams. Was that the wireless buzzing again? SOS...SOS...SOS...

'Mr Schmiedecke!'

The sound penetrated Schmiedecke's semiconsciousness. A groan escaped his lips. He flung out his arms. A glass clattered to the floor. The sharp sound of its fall made him open his eyes, their swollen lids lifting painfully. He opened his mouth and shut it with a snap, so that his teeth clicked together; then he was himself again.

'What's the matter?' he asked in a harsh, toneless voice. He cleared his throat, his chest seemed to creak, even his voice had gone to sleep—three weeks without sleep!

'Sambach, for God's sake, speak up!'

Sambach passed a shaking hand over his mouth.

'You ought to go to bed!' Schmiedecke snapped at him. 'I have the watch now. I—' He broke off, remembering that he had been almost asleep a moment before.

'The *Elbe* . . . Three boilers gone wrong . . .' said Sambach jerkily. 'Tubes broken . . . she can't go on . . . We'll be laid up for at least five days.'

'The *Elbe*?' queried Schmiedecke, striking his forehead; his brain began to function normally.

The two men stared at each other. Their faces seemed to grow more anxious as they looked into each other's eyes; then Schmiedecke turned away.

'Sabotage?' said Sambach in a low, questioning tone. He felt that he was not a coward. But what does being cowardly mean, after all? If a man has a wife and children at home, a boy of six, a tiny girl of three, he has got to . . .

'And,' continued Sambach, as unmoved as if he were reporting on the machinery, 'the staff of Engine Room One, who had shore leave yester-day, have all been taken to the hospital at Fayal, all five men, Junghaus, Meyring, Alster . . .'

Schmiedecke cut short the words with an impatient gesture. He leaned against the wall, his thoughts galloping furiously. Who was working against them? To whose interest was it that the FP 1 should not reach its place of anchorage? Lennartz had been nervous, for he had dispatched the FP 1 quietly, at night. Oh! why the devil hadn't Droste accompanied it?

Schmiedecke's glance turned to the window. Three dark streamers of smoke were hanging in the sky; they spread out like monstrous wings and sank down on the horizon, which was shimmering in the metallic glare of the sunlight. Three ocean-going tugs were towing a freight steamer towards harbor. The bow of the ship in tow was deep in the water, its stern high in the air, so that its propeller glittered in the sun. Three tugs! thought Schmiedecke with a sudden inspiration. He turned to Sambach in great excitement.

'Sambach, three tugs! We must have them! To hell with the *Elbe*! We needn't wait for the *Pillau*. Three ocean-going tugs! I'll go over to Fayal at once, speak to Droste by telephone and see if I can charter the tugs. Sam-bach, man, we'll be able to get this damn'd coffin to its place in time yet!'

He was the man of action once again. His face assumed its usual jolly look. His good-natured blue eyes twinkled at Sambach as if he were en-joying a good joke. Then he slammed the door behind him and hurried down the stairs.

Sambach, left alone, stared out of the window. The tugs were passing, like ants dragging behind them some animal they had captured. Sambach shrugged his shoulders. He felt convinced they were all drifting towards some fate that they could not avert, some fearful disaster—they, on the FP 1, were like a detachment of badly armed soldiers holding a forlorn hope against an invisible enemy with hopelessly superior weapons.

'We shall tow this coffin in time . . .' The words rang in his ears.

Coffin!

Coffin was the word Schmiedecke had used!

Chapter Two: Sabotage?

Bernard Droste, the young designer of the FP 1, slowly descended the staircase of the Lennartz mansion. He paused on the last step, nervously fingering his tie. He stared blankly after a servant who hurried past him with a laden tray towards the great glass door behind which a number of people could be seen moving to and fro. Lennartz, the famous ship-builder, was giving a small party, but Droste had made up his mind that he must see his chief. He was seriously perturbed at the news he had received by telephone from Schmiedecke a couple of hours ago from the Azores. A situation of the utmost gravity had arisen.

Lennartz will be upset when he hears Schmiedecke's information, he reflected. It seems a shame to have to disturb him when he has this party, but we must act quickly. I'm glad I made up my mind to see him at once. With luck, I can fix up the flight to the Azores and get away to-night. I can tell Lennartz about it quietly, say good-by to him and Gisela, and go straight from here to the airdrome just as quick as the car can take me.

Deep in thought he stood stroking his chin. Had it been a mistake on Schmiedecke's part to telephone? Perhaps it might have been safer if he had sent a telegram. Some one might have been listening on the line; but, again, were telegrams any more secret? Schmiedecke's news had disturbed him greatly. He went over his conversation with him again in his mind. Schmiedecke had said that the *Elbe* had broken down and that three nights running there had been mysterious attempts at sabotage on the FP 1. He had not dared to sleep at all and had asked if Droste could not possibly come out to the Azores. What the devil could the sabotage mean? Who was at the bottom of the trouble? Schmiedecke had evidently not been able to catch any one at it. Were any of the crew taking a hand in this dirty game? Droste thought it over. No! They were all thoroughly trustworthy men, Sambach, Künnecke, Hekker, the wireless operators, engineers, electricians, fitters and artificers. No, it was impossible that any of these men had anything to do with it. That left only the hotel staff, whom the hotel company had engaged, and they were all supposed to be efficient, reliable men. Well, the only redeeming feature of the news was that Schmiedecke had been able to charter those ocean-going tugs. That was a stroke of luck!

Droste pulled himself together. He would go and have it out with Lennartz. Just as he was about to open the door, Gisela Lennartz came out.

Gisela was looking radiant. Her black evening frock suited her fair beauty. She closed the door behind her and came towards him with a welcoming smile, which faded when she saw Droste's grave face. He did not seem to see her. Still wrapped in his thoughts, he gazed abstractedly at her, wondering absent-mindedly how her hair could be so fair. It shone like spun gold. Although they had been friends for so long, it seemed to him, in his curious frame of mind, as if he saw her properly for the first time.

'Whatever is the matter, Bernard!' exclaimed Gisela.

'Is your father in there?' asked Droste hastily, taking hold of the door handle.

'Wait a moment; you can't go about like that,' said Gisela, with some concern, and deftly she re-arranged his tie. 'Father is sitting with Hansly in a corner, smoking. Have you been introduced to Ellissen yet? I'm so glad I've got to know him. He came a few minutes ago. Pechtold is leading him about like a lion-tamer.' She laughed and kissed him, giving him a friendly pat on the shoulder as if he were her grown-up son, before he went into the room.

'So this is the farewell celebration,' Droste thought, as he opened the door. 'Here they are, all sitting round. As they couldn't have a public function, they had to have a party amongst themselves, even if official *cachet* was lacking. I wish the news hadn't leaked out. I begged Lennartz to keep quiet about the FP 1 having started. Pechtold must have let it out. I don't know what the old man sees in him. It's probably Pechtold who had gone and brought this Hansly here again. Hansly will soon get round the old man.'

Droste leaned against the wall and looked across at Lennartz, hoping to catch his eye, but the shipbuilder was deep in animated conversation with Hansly, and did not look up.

Pechtold approached. 'Ah! Good evening, Droste. I didn't expect to see you here.'

'Look here, I must speak to Lennartz at once.' Droste gripped his arm excitedly. 'I'd be awfully obliged if you would let him know. I don't want to disturb him where he is. You see, Hansly mustn't notice anything.'

'But what precisely is Hansly not to notice?' said Pechtold. He leaned forward expectantly, as if prepared to hear bad news.

'I've been speaking to Schmiedecke on the telephone. Sabotage has been attempted on the FP 1 again to-night.'

'On the flying platform?' Pechtold queried. 'That looks like dirty work. What are we going to do?'

In a few words Droste told him the conversation he had had with Schmiedecke on the telephone.

'I'm off to Fayal to-night,' ended Droste decidedly. 'I'm not going to wait a couple of days until your damn'd supply steamer has brought tools and spare parts and whatnot to the Azores. At the time I begged you to send everything with the FP 1. Now look what has happened!'

Pechtold appeared to be thinking hard.

'All the same, why shouldn't you wait a bit? There is no earthly use in setting off at random. Where are you going to get a steamer to do the towing? The *Elbe* is still under repair, and the *Pillau*, which is to take her place, can't arrive from the Bermudas in less than four days at the earliest.'

'That doesn't make the slightest difference to me,' said Droste excitedly. 'When we are once at sea, I can look after myself better than in a strange port. I'm going to start to-night. I've given Schmiedecke the necessary instructions. He is chartering three ocean-going tugs. I can't wait any longer. Time's short enough already.'

'Well, we seem to be in a devil of a pickle. I don't know what should be done. Perhaps it really is better for you to set off at once, Droste. You take a damn'd gloomy view of things though! It won't be so very dreadful if we do exceed the time limit. We are certain to get an extension of the contract put through, and there is always Hansly as well.'

Droste's face flushed with sudden anger. 'I suppose you're to get a percentage from Hansly, aren't you?' he sneered. A sudden mistrust of this tall, glib individual flashed across his mind. Pechtold had certainly been with the Lennartz shipyards for fifteen years, and Droste knew his value as a worker, but something underhanded was going on here. It struck him forcibly that Pechtold was purposely delaying matters. It seemed as if he had some interest in getting Hansly into this business. On the success or failure of the FP 1, the Lennartz shipyards were going to stand or fall. The recent history of the yards was not too successful. Orders had fallen off very much in the post-war years. Lennartz had gambled all on this one card. Sober, calculating business man though he was, he had always pursued the hitherto nebulous but irresistibly attractive vision of an established air route between Europe and America. His plan was, briefly, to anchor a huge floating airdrome in the ocean midway between the Azores and the Bermudas, on which airplanes could land and take on fuel. A big hotel on the floating platform would cater to the passengers. If this plan were carried out, New York could be reached by airplane in a very much shorter time than by any steamer.

Lennartz had strained his credit to the utmost and had accomplished the gigantic task in the face of the most bitter opposition of the shipping companies, who naturally saw in the project a serious menace to the transatlantic passenger trade. The German Government, however, had declared its readiness to support him in every possible way and had offered his company a substantial loan just as soon as the FP 1 had been successfully moored in its correct position and the first airplane had landed on the platform. A certain time limit, however, had been fixed; namely, the twenty-second of the present month; by which day the necessary conditions must have been carried out. Otherwise, the loan would not be forthcoming.

The work had been proceeding very slowly, thought Droste. Was Pechtold to blame for that? It was his business to see to the proper fitting out of the FP 1, but nevertheless the great leviathan had been sent off with only the most necessary tools and material, and with only a few weeks' provisions on board. Pechtold's instructions had been most specific. The platform must be as lightly loaded as possible, so that it could be more easily towed. And here was the man himself standing before him. Droste wondered what game he could be playing.

'So you think it would be better if I waited a little longer, Pechtold, and started, say, the day after to-morrow?' went on Droste. 'Who do you think is at the bottom of this sabotage business? The fact that the *Elbe* is not able to tow the FP 1 because she is lying at the Azores with her blasted boilers out of order seems to show that our enemies have got to work, all right. Can Hansly be behind it?' he added, forcing a smile.

Pechtold laughed loudly. 'I think you're letting your imagination run away with you, my dear chap. What proof can you possibly have that the *Elbe* was deliberately damaged?'

'What about Schmiedecke—'

'Schmiedecke!' broke in Pechtold contemptuously. 'Schmiedecke hasn't the brains. I've told you so often. How on earth you came to intrust Schmiedecke with such a difficult job beats me. However, start tonight, if you want to. I'll let the old man know. You can tell him yourself too, of course.'

Droste looked thoughtfully after Pechtold's retreating figure. No, he was not satisfied about him. After all, trouble was brewing, and the sooner he got to grips with it the better. Droste looked round the room. Funny, but he simply couldn't rid himself of the feeling that a fictitious gayety pervaded the gathering. Every one present appeared to be bright and cheerful, but the atmosphere was charged with a very definite feeling of suspense—as if some terrible tragedy was about to happen.

What would happen if the FP 1 did not arrive in time, if the contract with the government was broken and no extension of time granted? In that case, all their many months of labor and ceaseless endeavor would have proved in vain. The bankruptcy of the Lennartz shipyards would be an accomplished fact. The huge shipping combine controlled by Hansly would buy the FP 1 for a mere song. They might, of course, use it for airplanes carrying mails only, but they would take care that this menace to their passenger-carrying trade was removed for good. And so a step in the world's progress, the dream of bringing the people of two continents closer together, would be ended—perhaps for all time.

Droste saw Pechtold take Lennartz on one side and speak to him confidentially. Lennartz hastily excused himself to Hansly and came over to Droste.

'He has grown quite an old man,' thought Droste, a sudden wave of pity coming over him. 'His hair has been white ever since I knew him, but I can't think what's made him look so much older recently.'

'Do you really think it important to start for Fayal to-night, Droste?' asked Lennartz. He leaned against the wall, trying to give an appearance of carrying on a casual conversation with one of his guests, but there was ill-concealed anxiety in his eyes, and for the first time Droste noticed an unaccustomed weariness about him. Lennartz always addressed Droste by his surname, fond though he was of him. When he took the youthful Bernard, the son of one of his engineers who was killed in an accident, under his wing after his father's death, he called him by his surname from the very beginning, as he had done his father. Indeed, in course of time, the personalities of father and son had so merged in Lennartz's mind that he sometimes told Bernard jokingly that he had improved very much in the last thirty years, though he had been fairly efficient to begin with.

'My mind's made up, Herr Lennartz. I am starting in an hour. So much depends on it, you see,' said Droste. 'I've arranged with Schmiedecke to charter three tugs so that we can go to meet the *Pillau*. We gain three days by that, and nothing further can happen to us then!'

'Do you really think there is sabotage going on, Droste?'

'If there is, they haven't been able to do us any serious harm up till now, and I think once I am on the FP 1 there will be no further trouble.' He smiled grimly. 'What does Hansly really want of you now, after you have turned down his offer?'

'He assures me of his friendship, and his friendship is synonymous with his pocketbook. I must keep in with him, you see, because one can't leave too many doors open. All the same, I don't trust him!'

'Can one really trust any one!' said Droste bitterly, his eyes seeking out Pechtold. 'I only hope Pechtold doesn't leave me in the lurch.'

'Well, we must hope that everything will turn out all right,' said Lennartz, shaking Droste warmly by the hand. Droste sensed the affection of the old man for him, and the hope and confidence he placed in him. 'I won't disappoint him,' he thought, and smiled to hide his emotion.

'*Auf wiedersehen*, my boy; all my best wishes go with you.'

Lennartz turned away and Droste followed him with his eyes as he strode briskly across the room.

Chapter Three: Life Work in Danger

When Bernard Droste left the drawing-room shortly after his conversation with Lennartz, he felt that he had taken a final, irrevocable step, and that he was about to embark on a new and stirring adventure. It seemed to him as if he were leaving this familiar house for ever, that never again would its friendly lights greet him, never again would he see Gisela. His mind was clouded with a dark uncertainty. What would be the end of this great adventure of the FP 1? He closed the door behind him, crossed the brightly lit hall, and on a sudden impulse entered the library.

The room was paneled in dark oak, and at the window stood Gisela, her hair gleaming golden in the soft light. She was gazing out into the night, a dark, starless night, although on the far horizon was still a distant glow of light.

Droste closed the door gently behind him. How did Gisela know he would come? Was she waiting for him? He knew she must have been. Curious, he thought, how a sudden inspiration should bring them together again. He recollected many incidents of the same kind, when in response to some unspoken thought or wish, Gisela or he had done what the other wanted. It really seemed as if there was some truth in mental telepathy after all. That sort of thing had happened so often that there was really nothing in the least surprising in the fact that Gisela was here and apparently waiting for him.

No word of greeting escaped Gisela. A smile for a moment lit up her face. She really had nothing more to discuss with him. Vaguely she wondered whether she should wish him the usual conventional 'Best luck!' How empty and uninspired the phrase sounded.

'The car will be here in five minutes,' she said at last. 'Is there anything I can do for you?'

'Nothing, my dear,' replied Droste. 'I have got everything ready and as usual I travel light.'

He was trying to shake off the anxiety which had been pressing on him the whole day. These last few hours had seemed like an eternity. He tried to convince himself that there was nothing to worry about. He would soon be at the Azores and in a few days the FP 1 would be anchored safely and his great task completed. After that, he could brace himself to face fresh difficulties, because he anticipated that difficulties would arise in this business, which, after all, was like any other business. Robbed of its romance and the glamour of adventure, the great experiment of the FP 1 was essentially a commercial undertaking.

Droste had no fears for his own safety; in fact, no man could have more personal courage. To him his work meant more than his life—it was the threat to the FP 1 that worried him. He must really get to the bottom of the alarming series of incidents which he believed were being deliberately planned by some unknown enemy. Schmiedecke was not a man who in the normal course of things would be easily upset, and yet he had called him up on the telephone from the Azores. He would not have done that unless he anticipated serious trouble. Droste was entirely dominated by his work. He was like the dynamo of an engine which generates the driving power for the rest of the machinery. Urged on by the pace he himself set, the Lennartz shipyards had become a center of feverish activity, swallowing insatiably men and materials, building amid the din of clanging steel hammers, the ships of a new mercantile navy that would travel to and fro on the Seven Seas of the world.

Two long blasts of a Klaxon sounded in front of the window, and the powerful lights of a motor car lit up the drive.

'How I should like to be going with you,' said Gisela regretfully, 'but I couldn't leave Father, in any case.'

'I'll call you up at three o'clock every day, Gisela,' said Droste, smiling, 'on the short wave which the government is placing at our disposal. Then I can always let you know that everything is going on all right. It's only a few days now till the twenty-second, and you can tell the world that the FP 1 is going to be anchored by that date.'

He put out his hand to her. No lovers' farewells for him, just a friendly handshake.

The thought struck her that they had not spoken a word about themselves. She glanced inquiringly at Bernard's thin, drawn face. Did he never think of anything but work—work—work? Did it never enter his head that she was a woman and might expect something more; that a woman would not always let herself be set aside for machinery and business? In that last bitter moment, she realized that she knew nothing whatever of Droste's thoughts, nothing of his ways, that she was of no real significance in the world in which he lived, a world narrowly circumscribed by his work. Then, with a sudden insight, she understood and appreciated the wonderful qualities which her father saw in Bernard, and which made him depend upon him more and more, so that there was complete harmony in their relations, each trusting the other implicitly. Perhaps the only bond between Bernard and herself lay in the fact that she was Lennartz's daughter. Could she really be in love with Bernard in spite of this, she wondered? Still the words that might have made her feelings apparent would not come. She stammered out a few trite sentences.

'The car is waiting for you. To-morrow afternoon at three o'clock we will have a talk...and then...'

Droste pressed her hand. It did not seem to enter his head that she expected him to kiss her, or that he should say some kind, affectionate words, words that might have passed long ago between them. But even in that moment of farewell the vision of the FP 1—the fact that his life work and ambition was in danger—filled his mind and made him blind to everything else.

'At three o'clock in the afternoon, then, Gisela,' he said.

'At three o'clock! Just as if he were arranging a cocktail party with me,' thought Gisela bitterly, as she listened to his quick steps hurrying away. She went to the window for a last glimpse of him.

As the car drove away, she closed her eyes and did not see that he waved a last good-by to her.

Chapter Four: A Famous Airman

In Lennartz's drawing-room there was no sign of any tension, no hint of the drama that had been going on behind the scenes. A babble of conversation filled the room. The party had broken up into little groups chattering incessantly about every one and everything under the sun. A manservant came and went silently with a tray of glasses. Perhaps the general atmosphere of gayety had gone slightly to Axel Ellissen's head. It was certainly not the wine, for he was strictly temperate, as befitted a man of his calling, and he had not touched a drop of wine throughout the evening, contenting himself merely with innumerable cups of strong black coffee. The famous airman, however, was obviously enjoying himself. To a man of his type, used to periods of prolonged exile from civilization, it seemed good to be back, even for a little while, in the society which he affected to despise, but which nevertheless he enjoyed. His rugged, handsome face was wreathed in smiles as he talked to Thea Drews. Here was a woman who obviously interested him. She was so essentially feminine—and beautiful too. As she talked, she slowly waved an enormous fan of ostrich plumes. He gazed at her, fascinated. Curious how few women nowadays remembered the uses of a fan. Her voice fell on his ears like the sweetest music: 'Do you believe in mascots? I suppose most airmen carry them—danger breeds superstition—but then I'm never in danger, except sometimes from the glances of bold, bad eyes. I believe,' she exclaimed with mock melodrama, 'in the power of the evil eye!'

Ellissen smiled responsively.

'I shouldn't have thought you were a bit superstitious. I think the power of the evil eye belongs to dark eyes only, and mine, unfortunately, are light.'

He openly bestowed his favor on Thea Drews, into whose dark eyes he was gazing so intently. Evidently she had made an easy conquest, because he had not bothered about the other women who had thronged round him earlier in the evening, overwhelming him with gushing admiration.

'Well, I certainly believe in the power of your evil eye,' Thea retorted laughingly. She held her fan coquettishly in front of her and gazed at him mockingly over a screen of feathers. She continued her bantering conversation, her remarks becoming more daring as she observed the effect which dark eyes and provocative smiles were having on her companion. They had progressed swiftly in their sudden friendship, when some spirit of malice prompted her to question him about his recent polar expedition, which had ended disastrously for all his comrades, though it had brought him, the sole survivor, increased fame—or, rather, notoriety, for it had not by any means enhanced his personal reputation. It was a subject which he markedly disliked and avoided. Nevertheless she persisted.

'Tell me how you managed to survive while your companions . . .' she began again in a teasing tone.

'—were left in the lurch.' Ellissen finished the sentence calmly, controlling his anger as best he could.

He changed his tactics suddenly. 'I am staying at the European Hotel, if you want to see me again,' he said, looking insolently into her dark eyes. 'I really must ask you to excuse me now.' He rose, bowed stiffly, and moved off to join another group. 'That ought to choke her off,' he thought, pleased that he had had the courage to be rude to her. 'If it doesn't, she'll swallow anything.'

A few moments later, however, he turned round and cast a side glance at her. She had been following him with her eyes, which met his gaze calmly and boldly. She smiled.

Ellissen turned away abruptly, marvelling at the woman's persistence. She ought to have been a polar explorer, he thought ironically. Her skin is thick enough to withstand any amount of freezing.

He suddenly felt very lonely. 'I'll say good-by quietly and slip away,' he thought. Then a glimpse of his cheerless room at the European Hotel came into his mind. He frowned and stared fixedly at a dish of fruit which was standing in front of him. The sight of the warm colors of apricots and peaches made him shudder at the thought of his two lost, wasted years in the icy wastes of the Arctic. What would he not have given in those long gray days when the red sun had crept for a short time above the horizon and then sunk suddenly like a burnt-out candle, just to have gazed at the warm fruits of the South, symbol of the sun and returning life, which seemed so remote and beyond his reach.

He wandered into the entrance hall, his hands deep in his pockets, and examined in a disinterested manner the pictures on the walls,—pictures of beautiful women in old-time costumes, who smiled down at him, full of the joy of life. It was funny how little things could change one's whole outlook, make the whole world look different in a moment.

He found himself opposite the door of a room and looked in. The room seemed dark and empty. He could distinguish in one corner a low mirror, which reflected a narrow streak of light. He closed the door again, his curiosity satisfied, but was immediately seized with a strange desire to open the next door. He opened it gently, as if he were about to commit a theft. This room was dark also. He entered and stood listening attentively, conscious now of his childish curiosity. What a funny game for him to be playing.

Suddenly the room was flooded with dazzling light. Gisela Lennartz was standing at the window near the writing table, her hand on the switch of the light, gazing at him in astonishment.

'I beg your pardon,' said Ellissen, drawing back in confusion. He was about to leave, but stood rooted to the spot, knowing that he must explain his conduct. He looked so shamefaced, however, that Gisela burst out laughing.

'Do you make a habit of inspecting all the rooms in a house?' she asked. 'Or have you really lost your way?'

'To tell the truth, I was bored, just bored,' said Ellissen, promptly recovering his self-possession.

'And so you went into a strange room which you thought might or might not be occupied?'

'That is really my great trouble. You see, I can't do without people, and yet I can't stand being with a lot of people. So the best thing for me obviously is to sit in an empty room, knowing that there are plenty of people in the next room and that I can join them at any moment.'

He again tried to bow himself out and to put an end to an embarrassing situation.

'I'm afraid it is I who must apologize,' said Gisela. She pointed to a chair. It was a very definite invitation for him to sit down and talk.

'Of course, you couldn't possibly guess that there would be any one here.' She broke off in confusion. What could she talk to this man about? He had obviously run away from the other women, who had not given him a moment's peace all the evening.

'You see, there are too many people in the drawing-room for me,' said Ellissen frankly. 'I have lived for two years by myself. There were five of us to begin with, but one by one they died.' He shuddered. 'I have really forgotten what it is to talk easily and frankly with a fellow being. To go to parties and dances, even to meet people, is to me a torment. It is a terrible feeling to have. You simply cannot understand what it's like. I suppose I shall get over it some day, but at present it's rather awful.'

Gisela sympathized with him, and conversation began to flow more easily, for she certainly had a natural gift for putting people at their ease.

'I must seem very old-fashioned to you,' she said, after they had been talking for some time. More and more she was feeling drawn towards this lonely man, who had in his short life accomplished so much; and he was so different from the other men she knew.

'There are very few old-fashioned people left, unfortunately,' Ellissen replied. 'Things have changed a good deal during the two years in which I was marooned in the Arctic. People too seem different somehow, and I'm afraid I have no social graces.'

Gisela shook her head. 'I don't mean that. It is now considered quite the thing to appear to know everything and do everything. Young people think themselves cleverer than their elders. The distinctions between men and women are vanishing. Women insist on doing the same things as men in every possible way.'

'So I have observed, and it has got on my nerves very much,' said Ellissen ruefully, thinking of Thea Drews. He still felt rather embarrassed at the intimacy of their conversation, the emptiness of the room and the attractive seriousness of the girl.

'All young people to-day are inclined to be materialists,' went on Gisela, thinking of Bernard Droste. 'But I don't suppose there is as much truth in that as one would think. Perhaps there was a time after the war when one felt a compelling urge to revolt against Heaven knows what. And that is really the root of the trouble. We just don't realize what we are fighting against. We waste our energies and don't get anywhere. Our lives are wasted—wasted. Sometimes I feel that so strongly that I creep into a dark room all by myself and try to think it all out.'

Ellissen did not answer. He was not sure that he understood her. He had been lost in the ice and cut off from civilization for two years. What did he know about the world as it appeared to young people of the day, especially the women? He was certain, however, that the girl opposite him was cast in a very different mold from the gushing women he had encountered earlier in the evening, women who had tried their hardest to monopolize him—him, Ellissen, the great explorer. A feeling of revulsion swept over him, mingled to some extent with self-pity.

'We never find the person for whom we are seeking,' he remarked sententiously, conscious as he said it that he was not seeking any one in particular. He had not a single friend and would never have a friend. He was hated for his brutality and at the same time admired for his courage. 'I am in the world to look for adventure, and adventure I'm going to have,' was a frequent saying of his, and that was the aim to which he devoted his life. But he felt that he was growing old, and now for the first time in his life he was experiencing a new sensation in the presence of this girl—something that he had never known before. Why shouldn't he give up his present vagabond existence and try to adapt himself to the world as he found it? His career as an explorer was perhaps ended. On that last expedition his companions had died of starvation. He was the only one who had pulled through. Malicious rumors were in circulation, rumors that accused him of having left his comrades to die like rats in a trap. The newspapers were digging up some long-forgotten incidents from his earlier expeditions, twisting the facts so as to bring his conduct into as unfavorable a light as possible. There was even talk of forcing an inquiry into his leadership of the last expedition. Ellissen could afford to be contemptuous, for he knew his enemies could prove nothing—the Arctic wastes were wide and there had been no witnesses—but all this notoriety would not do his reputation any good in the long run.

He did not understand the world, and he did not want to understand it. He was conscious of something lacking in his life, and it suddenly seemed to him that perhaps this girl might bring him the happiness which he had always despised but without which, after all, life was not worth living. He toyed with the idea that had come to him. He was an impulsive man and he was apt to make rash decisions on which he staked everything, even although a moment's reflection would have proved them wrong.

'Do you know, I have actually declined the proposal of the Society for Arctic Exploration? Of course, you know all about that,' he said in a grave tone, as if this sentence ought to enlighten Gisela and make his thoughts clear to her. 'I could never again stand the utter loneliness of the Arctic, with the nearest human beings over a thousand miles away. I should like . . .'

He paused and thought absent-mindedly, 'What would I really like?'

'Why shouldn't you get a job in the shipyard? You would be useful to my father,' said Gisela. 'After all, you are a man of initiative and enterprise, and Father would value such qualities more than mere technical qualifications.'

Ellissen read into her simple suggestion a significance that Gisela had by no means intended. He certainly thought that he had succeeded in interesting her, and somehow the thought brought him a peculiar happiness.

'I think we ought to go back to the others now.' Gisela rose.

Ellissen walked behind her. She was very young and girlish, he decided, and then deep down in his heart his other self got the better of him. He had made himself ridiculous, opening his heart to a romantic young girl. He cursed himself for a fool as he silently followed Gisela into the drawing-room.

CHAPTER FIVE: SOS?

The telephone bell buzzed furiously in the control turret. Schmiedecke lifted the instrument impatiently. When the devil would Droste arrive to take over command? The worries and cares of his tremendous burden of responsibility were rapidly getting him down.

'Hello! Hello!' he shouted irritably. 'What's that?...You've caught another of 'em...Oh, the same one!...All right, I'll deal with him right now...Bring him up at once!'

A minute later a young man of rather dishevelled appearance stood before him, his arms held by two burly seamen. He had obviously not shaved for some days. His suit was stained and dirty. A battered hat perched insecurely on the back of his head at an angle which revealed a mass of curly, unbrushed hair, beneath which two eyes glared at him indignantly. From his neck was slung a camera which seemed to add to the incongruity of his appearance.

'You again!' Schmiedecke shouted at him. 'I've a dam' good mind to throw you overboard. I've had you sent away three times already and here you turn up again. I've told you I have strict orders not to allow any one to take photographs.'

'And I tell you I'm not taking photographs,' replied the young man boldly. 'I'm making a film, an exclusive record of one of the most epoch-making events—'

'Oh, stow all that!' broke in Schmiedecke angrily. 'I think I know how to deal with you.' He took a step forward and quickly took possession of the camera. 'I'm going to confiscate this,' he added, opening a drawer of his desk.

'You've no right to do that!' The young man was livid with rage. 'You can forbid me to take further photographs, but the law doesn't allow you to take away my property!'

'Doesn't it? Well, for the present, I'm in sole command here and I make my own laws,' replied Schmiedecke grimly. He examined the camera critically and then with his clumsy fingers he opened it and carefully took out the roll of film.

'Dammit, you'll pay for this! I'll lodge a complaint with the police. I'll charge you with theft. Come on, give me back that roll of film and I'll promise never—'

Without a word Schmiedecke handed him the camera.

'What about the roll?'

'You'll find that at the customs house—after we've left—'

He broke off suddenly. The distant hum of an airplane could be distinctly heard in the silence. Schmiedecke rushed to the window and leaned out, excitedly shouting orders which the pressman to his disappointment was unable to catch.

Immediately the powerful beams of a searchlight flashed out, flooding the landing platform with a glare of light and throwing the shadows of the masts into the control room.

Schmiedecke rushed out, followed by the two sailors. The pressman, whose presence they had in the excitement of the moment quite forgotten, ran to the window, determined, with true journalistic zeal, to find out what was happening. He was just in time to see an airplane swooping down on the landing platform. Good, he would take this episode, whatever it might mean. He seized the roll of film, which was still lying on the desk. In another moment he had pushed it into the camera and set the winding apparatus in motion as the airplane swooped past. Then, chuckling with delight, he put in a fresh spool, placed the exposed one in his pocket and dashed out, eagerly hoping to be in time for the landing of the plane.

All the searchlights that surrounded the landing platform were turned on. The glare was blinding as the powerful beams flooded the FP 1 from end to end with intense white brilliance, penetrated the darkness beyond and slowly swept the sky. The rays intersected, concentrated in a brilliant patch of light, and then traveled on, bathing the whole harbor in dazzling light, one moment picking a ship out of the darkness, the next throwing it back again.

The pressman stood still for a moment, astonished at the impressive spectacle. Concealing himself in the shadow of a large girder, he stared at the airplane which had just landed. After a few moments he slipped out again and, keeping his camera well-hidden, walked towards the little group which had gathered round the plane.

Schmiedecke was standing talking to the man who had just alighted from the plane. Just as the pressman was bringing out his camera, the newcomer swung round and discovered his presence. He was obviously annoyed and at once drew Schmiedecke's attention to him. Schmiedecke of course recognized him at once. He gave a sharp order, and in a moment the pressman was roughly seized and bundled into a lift which rapidly descended to a lower deck.

'That fellow ought to be chucked into the sea and left to drown,' cried Schmiedecke angrily. 'The devil only knows how he got on board the FP 1! I've had him turned off three times already, but he always appears again—from nowhere. Damn it! I'm seeing spooks everywhere. I'm so glad you're here, Bernard!' He placed a hand on Droste's shoulder.

'Just as glad as I am to be back on the FP 1,' replied Droste with conviction, gazing almost affectionately at the great flying platform which his genius had created. This wonder creation was his child, represented the labor and sacrifice of years given up to research, to planning and designing, overcoming a thousand difficulties. God! How he had slaved to bring this great idea of his to realization! And now at last here was the FP 1, a thing of beauty in spite of her immense and unwieldy bulk, floating proudly on the broad waters of the Atlantic.

'Tell me what has been happening,' said Droste. He looked round the platform and shouted, 'Turn the searchlights off!'

The great beams lingered in the night sky for a brief moment longer, then crept back into the gigantic eyes of the projectors. At last they were dimmed.

'I'm so glad you're here,' Schmiedecke repeated. The responsibility of the great undertaking had been too much for him. He was not by nature a leader, born to command. His brain functioned too slowly. He hated making decisions. He was happiest when there was work for his powerful hands to do. Broad-shouldered and rather clumsily built, he walked along in his shirt sleeves at Droste's side, looking almost a giant beside his slim, wiry companion.

They mounted the steps leading to the commander's room and sat down facing each other at the writing table.

'Damn that blasted photographer!' Schmiedecke exclaimed. 'He's taken back his roll of film again. I really can't help it, Droste; the fellow's as persistent as the devil—'

'That doesn't matter so much for the moment. Let's get down to business. What's been happening? You telephoned me quite an alarming report, didn't you? What's the trouble?'

'Alarming?' Schmiedecke echoed in astonishment. 'I only just said . . .' He broke off abruptly and flushed. 'God! I'm damned pleased to have you with me again, Droste,' he went on. 'Honestly, I've been at my wit's end. What to do, what to do! Every blasted thing going wrong. I couldn't face up to it myself. Listen now! The *Pillau* has left the Bermudas to-day. We've arranged to meet as near as possible on the thirtieth degree. We save a whole day by that. We can't wait here for the supply ship which Pechtold is sending out to us. Is it actually on the way?'

Droste nodded, drumming his fingers impatiently on the desk.

'Meanwhile, I've chartered three tugs,' Schmiedecke continued. 'We're going to leave in an hour. Luckily we've a calm sea for the moment and we can't miss the *Pillau*. We're in constant communication with her by wireless.

'What sort of tugs are they?' asked Droste. 'I couldn't see much in the darkness just now.'

'Owned by a Portuguese firm. They were lying in Fayal harbor as if they were waiting for us. Dam' good stroke of luck, I consider it. They towed a leaking English steamer into harbor a couple of days ago. I thought it would be all right, Droste,' ended Schmiedecke, doubt creeping into his voice as he looked at his commander's impassive face.

Droste merely nodded, making no comment.

Schmiedecke got up and walked about the little room. 'I couldn't control the business any longer,' he cried. 'I'm not really in favor of such a hurried departure. We certainly have a lot of tools and spare parts on board, but all for airplanes. Unfortunately we have only sufficient heavy oil to last us a couple of days. And no petrol has been loaded at all yet. I'm damned if I understand that fellow Pechtold. It worries me! I feel as if I've been deserted and thrown over by everybody, shut up in a box like this!'

'I'm sorry. The strain has obviously been too much for you,' said Droste, who had been listening to him attentively. 'Your mind's overwrought and your nerves are all to pieces. Possibly it's just your state of mind that made you telephone me.'

'No! Things keep on happening, I tell you. The *Elbe* towed us splendidly all the way. Then, just off Fayal, three of the boilers went wrong. Well, I'm not quite an idiot and I couldn't help wondering why her boilers should go wrong like they did. I examined them, of course, and in my opinion some of the tubes looked as if they had been sawed through— deliberately. There's something fishy about it.'

'Well, we must reckon on meeting with some accidents on an enterprise like this,' said Droste, frowning a trifle uneasily.

'Accidents, do you call them! Well, I think there's going to be a few more blasted accidents happening here with all that hotel staff—more than sixty waiters, they call themselves, lounging about the place. Yah! Waiters! Waiting for what? Pechtold could just as well have sent them later on. Have you seen them; have you had a look at their ugly faces? Why, you've only got to give them the once-over to see what a lot of blackguards they are. I've seen faces like theirs in prison—'

'Come, Schmiedecke!' laughed Droste. 'How long were you in prison?'

'Of course I haven't been in prison,' retorted Schmiedecke angrily. 'Don't try and be funny. When you've been in this blasted monkey house a couple of hours, you won't feel like joking. Damn it, Droste, you know what it's like when you just get a hunch about something. Well, I've got the feeling inside me that there's some dirty work going on—on the FP 1. Look!' his voice suddenly became confidential. 'What do you make of that?'

He handed Droste a broken piece of a key. 'That's been a skeleton key. I found it sticking in the lock of my cupboard.'

'And since when have you had anything worth stealing?'

'I have got all the plans and calculations locked up in there!'

'The calculations are no longer of any use to any one,' replied Droste, examining the skeleton key closely.

'What will we do if we're suddenly cast adrift on the way?'

Droste looked at him incredulously.

'I think you're going right off your head,' he answered. 'What you want, old man, is a good sleep. For God's sake, go and have it! Then you might be able to talk sense. Who in hell is going to make trouble on the FP 1? Why, the whole thing's—'

The sirens of the tugs suddenly sounded ominously through the night.

'Come on,' cried Droste. 'We're being taken in tow. Better get down.'

He got up and ran quickly down the narrow steps. Schmiedecke clattered after him. Perhaps, after all, the incidents that had so upset his peace of mind were what Droste had said—just accidents. The obvious self-confidence of his young commander inspired him with new courage.

They arrived at the fore end of the platform just at the moment when the hawsers lifted clear of the water and tightened. Dense smoke was belching out of the funnels of the tugs. The sea was quite calm. The gigantic FP 1 began to move slowly, almost imperceptibly, as if unwillingly following the little fire-spitting tugs, as they slowly forged their way through the night. The great tow had begun.

'Look at that! Those damned waiters are standing about everywhere,' cried Schmiedecke angrily. 'Not doing a blasted stroke! Instead of making themselves useful, they loaf about, dressed up to the nines in their evening togs, as if we were on a blasted pleasure cruise. Well, I suppose we're damned lucky not to have some women dumped on us as well. Hey, you!' he suddenly shouted across the crowd of men, who were on the long, overhanging balcony of the hotel. 'Send your boss over here to me! Any one would think they were passengers,' he added indignantly to Droste. 'They stand about the whole day, smoking and talking and laughing, and get the best food served up to them as well. I wish to God I could have a soft job like that for once in my life. Mark my words, though, when this damned box is anchored, and the first guests come to the hotel, nothing will be ready!'

He turned and found himself confronting a little fat man, who looked at him anxiously.

'Ah! Mr Damsky,' said Schmiedecke, 'I have now handed over the command to Mr Droste here, as you probably know. But none the less, I should like to ask you, don't you think it would be better if your staff behaved less like first-class passengers on a world cruise *de luxe*—lounging about the whole day long with their hands in their pockets!'

Damsky did not answer immediately. He stroked his round fat chin reflectively. 'Everything will be ready,' he said, bowing. 'There is only one question I should like to ask—I will, of course, see to it that the men behave in an orderly and seemly manner. How long, please, am I expected to make the stores last? I had made my arrangements on the assumption that we would take in provisions at the Azores. My company promised me definitely that provisions would come on the supply steamer, and now the steamer hasn't arrived.'

He bowed apologetically again and rubbed his hands in embarrassment.

'How long will the stores last out?' asked Droste anxiously.

Schmiedecke set his lips grimly, as if he saw fresh danger in what the hotel manager had said.

'I think, roughly speaking, for another eight days,' Damsky replied.

'The supply steamer will be here long before that,' Droste assured him. 'In the meantime, you needn't make the menu too luxurious.'

'I'll see at once that everything is in order,' said Damsky, and walked over to the waiters as if to set them to work at once.

'I suppose you'll say that the shortness of provisions is also the result of deliberate mismanagement?' Droste asked Schmiedecke, who only growled in answer.

'We'll meet the *Pillau* to-morrow, or at the latest the day after tomorrow. Then we can make double speed. The supply steamer is expecting us; it'll be at the anchoring place before us,' said Droste soothingly. 'Damn it, I should never have believed that a great burly fellow like you had so little nerve. Go and have a sleep! You need it! I'll wake you in good time. We'll relieve each other on watch.'

Droste clapped Schmiedecke on the shoulder, turned away and strode along the dark, echoing platform. The water gurgled gently as it lapped against the buoys.

We are making about six knots an hour, Droste calculated, and looked up at the brilliant stars, which shone brighter and clearer than in European skies. His glance traveled over the majestic front of the hotel, which looked as if it were made entirely of glass. In the windows, here and there, a tiny light flickered. The airplane hangars, their heavy doors closed, seemed dumpy and flat in comparison with the great mass of the hotel. The huge dark cranes stood ghostlike at the corners of the landing ground.

A feeling of pride, of indomitable power swept over Droste as he gazed around him. He felt he had at last reached the zenith of his life's desire, and thanked God that to him, while still a young man, had been granted the great boon of attaining the height of his ambition.

His labor and his brain had created this towering wonder in glass and steel. Every rivet in it was a part of his design. His imagination had conceived the sweep of the hangars, the grace of the pillars, the perfect stretch of the landing ground. In the race against competitors—he, the youngest, had won.

A slight wind had sprung up. The FP 1 moved slowly through the night, following the three little sea dragons which, belching fiery smoke, drew the mighty monster smoothly in their wake.

Droste descended the narrow steps to the engine room, and found a solitary man in it, busying himself with an oil can in his hand. Two Diesel engines, of five-thousand horse power each, were standing idle. In one corner a tiny engine was running, and a shining wheel was revolving so quickly that it seemed to be standing still.

Droste walked up to the man, who had pretended not to notice him.

'What is your name?' he asked.

'Girard,' replied the man, turning a swarthy, intelligent face to him.

'I don't recognize you,' said Droste, wondering where he had seen the man's face before.

'I'm from the *Elbe*.' The man put down the can and wiped his hands on some waste. 'I was transferred by Mr Schmiedecke. The five engineers are all down with dysentery at Fayal.' He picked up his can again.

Droste went out of the engine room, deep in thought. Dysentery! That was serious.

He mounted the endlessly long steps and opened the door of the room in which the wireless apparatus was installed.

'Well, Heinicke, how are you?' Droste greeted the wireless operator, who took off the head 'phones and welcomed him with a cheerful grin.

'Is there anything fresh?'

'We are going to run into a gale, Mr Droste, a strong, westerly one.'

Droste looked closely at the man's face. 'You're tired out, Heinicke; get some one to relieve you!'

'I can't, Mr Droste. Simmer was taken ill an hour ago—something wrong with his stomach.'

'All right. You go and have a sleep, and I'll remain here,' said Droste in a low voice. All the doubt and anxiety which had seized him once before, when starting his journey, had come over him again.

'Thank you very much, Mr Droste.' Heinicke staggered to his feet. 'I'm really very tired. I imagine I hear nothing but SOS calls, from sheer fatigue—'

'SOS?' queried Droste, putting on the head 'phones. He turned the switch, but there was no result.

Chapter Six: Presentiments

Pechtold walked rapidly along the wharves of the Lennartz shipyards, through which resounded the crashing blows of the mighty hammers; the staccato music of a thousand rivets being driven home into the giant plates added to the deafening din. With one bound he jumped over an iron girder in an undignified manner unusual to him, tore open the door of the general offices and took the stairs at a run, three at a time. He knocked at a green baize-covered door and without waiting for any reply strode quickly into the room.

Lennartz looked up in surprise.

'We haven't had a single word from the FP 1 for five hours,' said Pechtold. 'It's about time we did something about it. It looks as if something terrible has happened.'

'Are you trying to frighten me?' said Lennartz, looking at him sharply. 'It is very rash to jump at conclusions. There may have been some interference with the transmission. Probably the wireless operator has got into touch with them again. I do think you might have telephoned through to me, Pechtold, and not rushed over here like this. You don't seem to be able to control yourself these days. You get terribly excited about nothing at all.'

Pechtold plumped himself down heavily in a chair, drew out a silk pocket handkerchief, and mopped the perspiration from his brow before replying.

'I don't believe much in presentiments, Mr Lennartz, but if I may be so bold as to advise you again, I think you should play for safety. There is too much at stake. The government has only promised you the loan on condition that the FP 1 is anchored and the first airplane has landed by the twenty-second. We've got to allow for accidents, and if the anchoring is delayed beyond the contract time, the government will have an excellent opportunity for breaking the contract. They will certainly refuse us an extension.'

Lennartz gazed at Pechtold perplexedly. 'You mean to say that you have the nerve to come here and tell me that now! Only a few days ago you were still firmly convinced that the government would extend the contract time.'

Pechtold shrugged his shoulders.

'I'm doing everything I can. I spoke to Karleis, the chief adviser to the Ministry, again to-day. God knows what's going on there! I have a shrewd suspicion, however, that the government, being in a tight hole as regards money, will do their best to wriggle out of their promise. As you know, the country is really in a bad economic position, and if the government can save on the FP 1 contract, they certainly will do so.'

Lennartz reached for the telephone. Pechtold, however, stopped him.

'What's the good of speaking to the Ministry? You don't want to alarm them, and I saw the officials there less than an hour ago. For the moment, thank God, the danger is not acute.'

'Danger! You're constantly talking of danger!' Lennartz was getting excited now. 'What on earth do you want me to do? If the FP 1 is not at its station by the contract date, and the government refuses me the loan, you know as well as I do that we will have to sell the whole FP 1 and every other blasted thing to meet current obligations. What are you trying to get me to do?' he repeated.

Pechtold nodded approvingly. At last he was getting Lennartz to realize the urgency of the situation. He adjusted his eyeglasses and looked at Lennartz, his sly eyes narrowly contracting.

'It is my duty to point out to you every contingency that is likely to arise. Mind you, I don't say that the whole business is going to be an absolute fiasco, but I do think I must point out the possibility of failure. You have appointed me to a certain post, and I am trying to the best of my ability to carry out my duty satisfactorily. I am still of the opinion that Hansly should be . . .'

'Hansly!' cried Lennartz excitedly. 'What is there between you and Hansly!'

'Well, if you don't trust me, Mr Lennartz, I can of course resign.' Pechtold drew himself up to his full height and tried to look as dignified as possible. 'My advice, I assure you, is quite disinterested. I was thinking only of what is best from the firm's point of view.'

'Look here, Pechtold, don't be such a fool. I know you mean well, but I can't very well approach Hansly. I have refused his offer three times already!'

'Why can't you approach Hansly, Mr Lennartz? It is only a question of fresh negotiations. Hansly, I am sure, will prove amenable. Besides, in the course of time, it will be necessary for the airship lines and the ship companies to come to some agreement with each other for their common advantage. What seems quite beyond the bounds of practical politics to-day will in a few years' time be considered just as a matter of course. You mustn't forget, too, that Hansly has it in his power to keep the shipyards here as busy as he likes. I know, for instance, that we could get an order for a fifty thousand tonner from him if we handled him properly.'

'I'm not going to sell myself,' said Lennartz, walking to the window and gazing out over the shipyard, a busy scene of bustling activity from which he always derived a certain satisfaction.

'Would you like to see all these hundreds of workmen left unemployed—these half-built ships left to rust on the stocks?' asked Pechtold impressively, pointing with his long forefinger at the crowds of men down below. 'We must make our position secure. We can't justify staking everything on the one card. It's a crime . . .'

Lennartz swung round.

'Crime?'

Pechtold looked at him smilingly, then suddenly became embarrassed and commenced to polish his eyeglasses carefully.

'Yes, a crime, Mr Lennartz. I really believe it would be in your best interests to discuss the matter again with Hansly.'

Lennartz ran his hand through his white hair thoughtfully. He turned his gaze to the shipyard again. At last he turned on his heel.

'Tell Hansly that I should like to have a talk with him,' he said abruptly. 'But wait until tomorrow. If by then we still have had no word from the FP 1, send Hansly to me. Perhaps you're right, Pechtold; perhaps it's not my fate to see the realization of all my dreams and visions. Perhaps I have overestimated my power.'

'Very good, Mr Lennartz. To-morrow then.' Pechtold bowed and left the room. He paused at the door for an instant before closing it behind

240 SCIENCE-FICTION CLASSICS

him. For a moment he was on the point of turning back to say a cheery word to Lennartz, because he could see that the old man was beset with worries and might not resent a word or two of comfort from him. He hesitated, however, and then strode briskly away.

Chapter Seven: A Sinister Object

A dense bank of fog had fallen over the Atlantic. It had come down with the suddenness of a dropped curtain at the theater, blotting out everything from view. The great superstructures on the deck of the FP 1 were completely hidden in the all-enveloping grayness that settled on the landing platform in thick layers, swirled upwards in great eddies until it engulfed even the towering masts of the wireless. Through the fog glimmered dimly the lights of the tugs. The smoke from their funnels added to the funereal pall that lay on everything and rendered even the deck railings cold and clammy to the touch. Members of the crew clad in thick oilskins and sou'westers kept their feet with difficulty, as they groped their way blindly along the slippery decks.

'Why the blazes doesn't Droste have the searchlights turned on?' shouted Sambach, who was in command of the airplane hangars. The man at his side made no reply. He was Girard, the new enginer, a grim and taciturn fellow.

'Well, if he doesn't want to open his mouth, I won't force him to,' thought Sambach, disappearing through a doorway. Thank God he could breathe freely once more. That damned mist could no longer get at his throat.

Girard remained outside. He stood listening intently for any sound that might break the eerie stillness. Then he walked slowly to the end of the landing platform. Suddenly he stumbled against a man who was standing at the railing, staring out into the grayness.

'Dammit! What are you doing here?' Girard seized the man, who was swaying backwards and forwards. Then he saw it was Damsky.

'What are you doing, wandering about here?' Girard spoke roughly. 'You would be much better employed seeing that we get a decent feed. This is no weather for landlubbers to be about in!'

Damsky, who was still lurching about uncertainly, did not answer.

'What's the matter? Seasick?' asked Girard. He flashed the light of his torch on Damsky's face and stared into a pair of wide-open eyes that looked at him fixedly.

Girard pushed him away. 'What the devil's the matter with you, Damsky? Are you drunk or have you been taking drugs again? For God's sake, don't let the chief catch you like this. What the hell have you been taking? Morphia? Cocaine?'

He turned his torch on Damsky's face again.

'I ought really to report you,' he growled. 'It won't do! You can't go on taking drugs and going about in this condition. You'll just end up by getting fired. Come on!'

He shoved Damsky through a small doorway and propped him up against the wall.

'We're going to do a little business together,' he said sharply. 'I'm going to tell you something, and if you don't keep your mouth shut, I'll shut it for you. But if you keep quiet and are sensible, you can earn quite a pile of money through me.' He looked at him significantly and at the same time drew a wallet crammed with paper money out of his pocket.

Damsky gazed greedily at the notes.

'All good genuine dollar notes, Damsky. I've got lots of them and could get lots more. Would you like a few too?'

'What do you want me to do?'

Girard replaced the wallet in his pocket. 'You're in charge of the fire extinguishers on this floating steelworks, aren't you?' he asked.

Damsky nodded assent.

'Well, they couldn't have found a more stupid and unreliable man for the job. Fancy putting you in charge of all this new-fangled fire-extinguishing plant. It's supposed to put out any outbreak of fire by spraying carbonic acid, isn't it? Another of their queer ideas and, like all the others, no good. Now look here, Damsky; I'm going to give you a thousand dollars right now and in a few days, when we are on land again—' Girard smiled significantly—'there will be another thousand for you.' He drew out his bundle of notes again.

Damsky was all attention now. The blood rushed to his cheeks; his little eyes, round as marbles, seemed almost to start from their sockets.

'When we're on land again? I didn't think we were going to get back again very soon.'

Girard laughed. 'You wait! I bet we are all home again within a week. Now remember, there's two thousand dollars for you, if you do what I want.

'In the control room there are several cylinders of carbonic acid, connected in threes. Now in each case I have disconnected the middle cylinders. You are not to touch these. That's all I want of you. No interference. Understand?'

Damsky nodded.

Girard counted out ten hundred-dollar notes carefully and slipped them furtively into Damsky's hand. Then, unbuttoning his oilskins, he produced a gas mask, complete with goggles and a weird-looking metal snout. 'Put this in the wooden locker over the pressure gauge and don't let yourself be seen. Get me?'

'A gas mask,' stuttered Damsky, looking apprehensively at the sinister object.

'I thought you had been a soldier,' sneered Girard. 'The war, you know, taught even stupid men a hell of a lot of things they didn't know before. Now listen carefully to what I'm going to tell you. I may have to pump the contents of the middle cylinders through the spraying apparatus. You must be careful to see that the valve is always kept shut.'

'What the devil is the game?' cried Damsky. 'It looks to me like very dirty business.' He took the mask with some hesitation.

Girard's features hardened, his face twitched. A cruel, merciless light came into his eyes, as he gazed at the cowering Damsky.

'What I propose doing is no concern of yours—now. And in the meantime, till this business is over, you'll stop taking drugs. If I catch you at it—' He seized Damsky by the throat and shook him like a rat—'you'll go right overboard. Understand? Keep your mouth shut and you'll be all right! You'll do very well out of it. You'll get at least another thousand dollars.'

Almost reluctantly he released the wretched Damsky, who staggered back, half-choked.

'Now you can get out, and for God's sake, don't reel about like that.'

'It's all right. I don't think you'll have anything to grouse about,' muttered Damsky. He pulled himself together, shoved the notes into his pocket and, with a parting scowl at Girard, shuffled off.

Girard gazed after his retreating figure for a moment, then strode across the deck. Taking an electric torch from his pocket, he switched on the light, throwing its faint yellow gleams into the mist. Slowly he swung the torch in a circle several times. Three answering lights shone out of the mist. In the oppressive silence he could hear the engines of the tugs chug-chugging monotonously. Then the lights disappeared and there was a tremendous rattling of steel cables.

Girard stood listening; then, with a quick movement, he flung his torch in a high curve into the sea. Crouching low, he ran past the lighted front of the windows and disappeared through a little steel door which led to the engine room.

Chapter Eight: Mad Fantasies

Schmiedecke started out of his sleep with a cry. He had been dreaming again—a truly nerve-racking dream. He had fancied that he was sitting on a trapeze, high up under the dome of a circus, so high that the people below him looked like so many ants and their voices reached him only as a faint murmur. He was so terror-stricken that he could scarcely breathe. He felt the trapeze commence to sway slightly. Even in the middle of his nightmare he had apparently become bitterly conscious of the fact that he had not slept for three nights, realized even that he was dreaming; yet in spite of this the awful terror did not leave him. He could not wake. Mad fantasies scurried through his tired brain. Still the murmur of the people below reached his ears, grew in volume, became a mighty thunder, while the swaying of the trapeze became still more violent. At last he lost his grip and fell—down, down, down. He screamed in anguish and awoke.

Droste was standing before him, his face pale and drawn.

'We're drifting,' he cried, 'drifting—God knows where! We've broken loose. Do you understand!'

Schmiedecke stared at him, trying slowly, almost painfully, to collect his thoughts. He rubbed his eyes. 'Three days without sleep! Drifting?' he repeated. A strong wind was blowing outside the windows, the sound of which had been the murmur of the people in his dream. The walls of the room were swaying—the swinging of the trapeze.

'The tugs have cast off their hawsers without letting us know. We are no longer in tow.'

Schmiedecke sprang up and flung the window open. The wind rushed into his face. Using all his strength, he succeeded in closing it again and turned to face Droste. The man on whom so much responsibility had rested during that nerve-racking voyage was obviously distraught, almost at the end of his tether. With an effort he controlled himself.

'We must go after them, Droste. We've got a motor launch, at any rate. Order her to be manned immediately,' he said.

'But listen, listen, Schmiedecke. It was Hekker who brought me the news that we were drifting. Not another soul knows anything about it at present. The tugs abandoned us, that's certain—either because they were in danger, or because they've been bribed. Of course, if they cast off because of the gale, they will remain near us, at least till it gets light, and it's no earthly use sending a boat out to them. And in the other eventuality, it would be equally useless.' He smiled grimly. 'At the moment, there's no immediate danger, but I've just found out that the wireless isn't working. I've aroused Heinicke, and he is trying to find out what's wrong.'

'Is it the receiving apparatus?' asked Schmiedecke.

'No, the transmitter,' Droste answered quietly. 'We can still receive calls.'

A torrent of abuse escaped from Schmiedecke's lips. He swore wildly and continuously for at least a minute. It seemed to act as a relief to his over-burdened feelings and even to revive his energy. At last he became coherent again.

'What's to be done, Droste?'

'We can't do anything till it's daylight; then we'll get the wireless in working order again. There's nothing more to be done just now. Oh, one thing. The hotel staff mustn't find out at present; in the darkness, they won't be able to notice much. Of course, some of the crew must be told. Come along!'

Schmiedecke followed Droste resignedly. 'I told you so,' he muttered. 'You wouldn't believe me.'

'Any one can say "I told you so." It's easy to be wise after the event,' said Droste rather sharply.

As they reached the landing platform, the gale caught them and flung them against the wall of a hangar. The FP 1 was in darkness. Most of the population of the great leviathan were at that moment sound asleep. It would take more than a gale to shake universal confidence in the FP 1. There was nothing to worry about. What could happen on this gigantic floating airport, which was certainly stronger and safer than an Atlantic liner. Work would begin in a few days, so for the present surely they might sleep in peace.

'Why the devil don't you turn on the searchlights? Then perhaps you could spot the tugs,' shouted Schmiedecke. The sound of his voice was almost carried away by the gale.

'No, it wouldn't be any good, I'm afraid. The glare might wake every one up, and we mustn't risk a panic.'

They ascended the narrow staircase to the wireless room. A figure staggered towards them. It was Damsky.

'What are you doing here?' Droste spoke sharply.

Damsky braced himself up and almost let fall a small tray he was carrying.

'I—I brought the wireless operator some soup, because the rest of the cooks are asleep.'

Droste regretted his harshness. After all, it wasn't the man's duty to prepare food for the crew at night, far less take it to them. Obviously it was just pure good nature on Damsky's part.

'Go to bed now,' he said kindly. 'How long have you been about?'

'Forty—forty-eight hours,' stammered Damsky and disappeared.

'Maybe he sprinkled a little poison in the soup,' Schmiedecke commented sarcastically.

Droste laughed—a nervous, half-hysterical laugh, for he was becoming more and more conscious of the seriousness of the position.

'You're nothing but a silly idiot, Schmiedecke,' he said, 'ready to imagine all sorts of film crime business. Poison in the soup!' He laughed again, controlled himself with difficulty and entered the wireless room.

Heinicke was sitting at the transmitter. Every now and then his head nodded. Under his sunken eyes were dark circles. His face looked like a death's-head, the cheeks fallen in. The long slender fingers of his thin, delicate-looking hands rested on the key of the transmitter.

'I'm in touch with the shipyards,' said Heinicke. 'The defect has been remedied. I'm telegraphing our position. 35° 5' 23" longitude west, 33° 56' 2" lattitude north; 35° 5' 23", 33° 56' 2"...Have you got that?... FP 1 ... FP 1 ...

'I've got them now, all right,' he said excitedly, and they could see how relieved he was. 'What shall I telegraph?' He turned wearily to Droste.

'Let me sit down there,' was Droste's reply.

Heinicke readily gave him his place, and Droste was just about to seat himself at the operator's desk when suddenly the lamps of the wireless apparatus blazed up. For a moment they shone with the intensity of searchlights, flooding the room with dazzling brilliance, and then as suddenly they faded out. A spiral of blue smoke curled up from the woodwork of the switchboard and a pungent smell of burning rubber assailed their nostrils. Dazed and half-blinded, they staggered back. Quickly regaining his presence of mind, however, Heinicke stretched out his hand towards the lever of a switch. Droste pulled him back and put a cap which was lying on the table over his hand, so that he could draw back the lever in safety.

The switchboard was now burning fiercely. Heinicke picked up a hammer and smashed it with one blow. Seizing the bowl of soup which Damsky had just brought him, he poured it over the glowing wires, which hissed and spluttered like a nest of snakes that had been disturbed. With one stride, he sprang to the window and flung it open. The wind soon blew the smell of burning rubber out of the room and dispersed the clouds of smoke. Heinicke stooped over the switchboard and examined the burnt wires.

'High tension!' he muttered. 'The transmitter must have been brought into contact with a high-power current. A couple of thousand volts, at least!'

'That could only have come from the engine room,' Droste said decisively. Mentally he followed the course of the wires, trying to think of the possible connection with the power plant of the engine room.

'Who's on duty in the engine room?' he asked Schmiedecke, who was leaning against the wall, pale and still pretty well dazed.

'Some one certainly who can still keep on his legs,' answered Schmiedecke thoughtfully. 'Most of the others, confound them, are all laid up in sick bay. This neighborhood doesn't appear to be any too healthy for them.'

'Can you patch up the transmitter again?' asked Droste.

Heinicke shrugged his shoulders. 'I don't think so—even if I can, it will take a couple of days. I haven't enough spare parts. Only the barest necessities were given to me.'

'Jove!' thought Droste. 'Pechtold again! That must have been intentional! That man will have a lot to answer for.'

'Heinicke,' Droste laid his hand on the wireless operator's shoulder, 'everything depends on you now. We must get the apparatus in order again as soon as possible. That's absolutely essential. Everything depends on you—perhaps even our lives,' he added in a low tone.

CHAPTER NINE: A Sentence of Death

Droste and Schmiedecke rushed down to the engine room. As soon as they entered, they saw at once that something untoward had happened. The vast room seemed curiously empty. No movement or sound came from the mighty Diesel engines. The bright tiles used for the flooring reflected the light of innumerable lamps which flooded every corner with brilliant light. Droste was at once struck by the unaccustomed silence that brooded over the whole place. Not a soul was to be seen. Tense with excitement and expectation, he walked hurriedly round the room. Suddenly in a corner he noticed the half-recumbent figure of a man propped up against the wall. He took a closer grip of the revolver which he carried in his pocket, pressing the muzzle against the lining so that it would be instantly ready for use.

Schmiedecke followed him, ready to close with any antagonists. Obviously they must expect to meet with resistance at any moment, for this was nothing less than mutiny. Together they bent over the unconscious figure. Droste recognized him at once as Girard, the engineer from the *Elbe*. He touched the sleeping man lightly on the arm, but he did not move a muscle. Schmiedecke seized him by the shoulders and shook him.

Girard awoke as if from a deep sleep. His eyes blinked in the fierce glare of the electric light. Recognizing Droste, he got slowly to his feet. He still held a handful of oily waste, while a pair of nippers and some wire stuck out of his pockets.

'Why aren't you in your bed?' asked Droste, watching him closely.

'There was no one to relieve me,' growled Girard reluctantly. 'I can't get away. If there had been any chance, I would have been in bed, believe me!'

Schmiedecke distrusted the look on Girard's face.

'But you could have informed me, surely, that you must be relieved. How long have you been on duty?'

'Since we left the Azores, sir. Before that I was doing repairs on the *Elbe* without any time for rest. I had to patch up the boilers.'

Girard's eyes were almost shut again. It was only with an effort that he still held himself erect.

'Why the devil aren't the engines running?' asked Droste sharply. 'You could have left them running while you slept here. At any rate, you could have charged the accumulators.'

'The accumulators are all in order,' replied Girard sulkily. 'And I never leave the engines running while I am asleep.'

'Well, you can go to bed now. We'll take over.'

'Not exactly a pleasant customer!' remarked Droste, when Girard had gone. 'By the way, do you know what dysentery is?'

'Dysentery?' Schmiedecke replied. 'Of course, I've heard of it. But what's dysentery got to do with it?'

'All the men are down with it—and that blighter Girard knew what it was.' He was busy following the wires leading to the accumulators and testing the ampere gauges.

'Overcharged,' he said at last. 'Very highly overcharged!'

He then examined the portholes and found one that was not properly fastened. He put his head out for a moment and then closed and secured the window.

'You wait here a minute, Schmiedecke,' he cried, and ran swiftly up the spiral staircase, opened a hatchway and so got out on the roof of the engine room. The full force of the gale met him and pressed him against the iron ladder, but slowly and with difficulty he battled his way forward until he came to the foot of the aërial mast. He could hear the wires in the darkness above him vibrating like harp strings. He groped about until his hands touched a loose wire. Putting his left arm round the mast of the aërial to steady himself, he tried to draw the wire towards him. Slowly, inch by inch, the wire yielded. At last he managed to get the wire between his teeth, and crawling along on his stomach, so as to offer as little resistance to the gale as possible, he crept back over the slippery deck until he reached the trapdoor in the roof and slid down the ladder.

'I've got it!' he said to Schmiedecke in a satisfied tone.

He coiled up the wire quickly in a seaman-like fashion, and discovered that to one end a heavy ring was attached.

Schmiedecke weighed the ring in his hand.

'It seems to me that this was thrown over the aërial from the roof,' said Droste. 'The ring was meant to give it weight; then the wire was connected with the power current'—he pointed towards the accumulators—'and the wireless apparatus, which has no protection against such a strong current, was wrecked.'

'Whom do you suspect?' asked Schmiedecke. 'Girard?'

Droste shrugged his shoulders.

'It's no good deceiving ourselves. I'm sure that all this is part of a deliberately planned plot. These damned tugs lay conveniently in the harbor at Fayal so that we might be tempted to charter them. And of course it was all a put-up job. Once they got us out here, they would leave us in the lurch. As for the wireless apparatus . . . Damn it all, I keep on thinking of Pechtold . . . Heinicke must get the transmitter in order right away. I must warn Lennartz against Pechtold.'

'What will be the good of that?'

'What will be the good of that? Well, you're right; it can't improve things here, but don't you see what their game is. They simply want to delay us by all this rotten sabotage business until the contract time by which the FP 1 was to be anchored has expired. That's all they're trying to do. They don't want to endanger our lives. As a matter of fact, they couldn't do much to us. The FP 1 can't sink, unless her buoys are allowed to fill with water.'

'You still think you will keep within the time limit?' said Schmiedecke. 'When is the contract date?'

'The twenty-second of the month. And on that day, the offer of a loan from the government expires. We can all go home again on the twenty-third. That's all they want to do. You see, it's just a kindly thought on their part,' he added facetiously. 'They're trying to give us a couple of days' holiday here. Don't you find the Atlantic air terribly bracing?'

Schmiedecke, who always joked with difficulty, looked mystified. 'Do pull yourself together, Bernard,' he cried.

'And of course, by that time,' Droste continued, 'we'll all be in the soup.'

'Soup,' repeated Schmiedecke wonderingly.

'Yes, the FP 1, the shipyards, old Lennartz, you and me, and every mother's son of us.' He turned abruptly on his heel and left the engine room.

Schmiedecke gazed after Droste. The latter was walking on tiptoe and peering round him cautiously, as if a concealed enemy might spring out at him at any moment. Suddenly he half turned and flung back in his curious barking voice a parting shot at Schmiedecke.

'But if we're all bound for Davy Jones' locker, I'm going to make a fight for it. They haven't got us yet.'

He faced Schmiedecke with a look of triumph and determination on his face.

'Come on,' he shouted. 'Start the Diesel engines and open the sea-cocks. We must take in thirty thousand tons of water as ballast. How much have we got already?'

Schmiedecke glanced at the gauge above him.

'Only two thousand,' he shouted back, and his voice showed his alarm.

Fifteen thousand tons of water ballast had been taken in at the Azores, so that the FP 1 should offer sufficient resistance to rough weather. If the leviathan had not enough ballast and lay too high in the water, a heavy storm would certainly damage the huge buoys which served as anchors. It was plain that any one who wanted to endanger the FP 1 would realize that simple fact.

Who had poured out the thirteen thousand tons of water ballast? Was it Girard who had started the pumps? The questions raced through his mind—unanswerable.

Droste's stern voice rose above the gale.

'Two thousand! My God! Now you see what these devils are after. They want us to drift and be smashed to smithereens. Well, we'll beat 'em yet. Don't let any one but ourselves come into the engine room. The FP 1 can stand eighty thousand tons of water. If the shipyard has picked up Heinicke's wireless, they will send help and find us here. But if we are to drift, then God help us all!'

Schmiedecke was already calculating the amount of ballast that he must take in. He would stick to Droste and the FP 1 to the end, but he had an uncomfortable feeling, all the same, that his commander had pronounced sentence of death on them all.

Chapter Ten: An Impossible Demand and Every Conceivable Possibility

Darkness was falling as Gisela Lennartz drove her little car up to the offices of the shipyards. The smoke from the little steamers in the river hung heavy in the sweltering heat. The sky was reddened by the setting sun, and its gorgeous colors were reflected in duller tones on the oily surface of the harbor waters. A siren sounded the end of the day's work. The reverberating blows of the steam hammers ceased abruptly, and the deep buzzing sound of vibrating metal lingered for a moment in the air. Almost simultaneously the tread of hundreds of hurrying footsteps reëchoed through the yard. The quay was suddenly alive with men, who streamed homewards, a peaceful army which had just finished its daily battle for bread.

Gisela drove carefully over the uneven paving. She bent her head low over the steering wheel, hoping to avoid recognition, for at that moment she hated herself, her little car and the appearance of luxury and sheltered idleness which she must present to these workpeople. If they only knew my anxieties, they certainly wouldn't envy me, she thought.

She was going to fetch her father. It had been a rule for many years that her father should keep himself free for at least half an hour in the course of the day. His time between one and two o'clock belonged to her. In that interval, they were accustomed to lunch together, and his brief but welcome respite ended with the long-drawn screech of the two-o'clock siren from the yards. This rest in the middle of a strenuous working day was intended to conserve his energy and had certainly been of great benefit to Lennartz, who never spared himself. To-day, for the first time, her father had not come, although he had promised to keep this hour free, however great the pressure of work.

Pulling up at the entrance to the offices, Gisela jumped out of her car and rushed up the stairs to her father's private office.

Miss Helm was sitting in the outer room. Visitors had to get past her before they could see Lennartz. She was a prim, precise person whom one could not think of without her typewriter or her notebook. She had a long, aquiline nose on which a pair of spectacles was perilously perched. She certainly gave the impression of always working at high pressure, and her dominating manner was very successful in repelling unwelcome visitors.

As Gisela entered, Miss Helm looked up and stretched her thin lips in what she fondly imagined to be a smile of greeting.

'I'm sorry, Miss Lennartz, but the chief has an important conference on, and I'm afraid you cannot see him at present.'

How Gisela hated that word 'conference.' Everybody she wanted to see was always in conference. The word savored of anxieties and difficulties, and was enough to make any one feel hopelessly depressed. She smiled, however, as if she were in complete agreement with Miss Helm's opinion on this important point. But she was by no means ready to surrender even a tiny bit of her privileges, and she certainly was not going to let her father break a very good and pleasant habit. Today it might happen that he had something really important to discuss and was justified in neglecting her, but the same thing might well happen to-morrow and the next day, and she could foresee in that event the probability of her father considering that he need not take care of himself and coming to look on the regular midday luncheon as an unnecessary waste of time. No, he really must not be allowed to play ducks and drakes with his health in this manner. Looking after her father's health was Gisela's special care. It was more important than any conference, she had often told him, for if he fell ill, then what would happen to the conferences on which he staked so much.

Gisela opened the door of her father's room and entered, closing it quietly but resolutely behind her, for she knew that Miss Helm had jumped up from her chair in horror at this outrageous conduct, and followed her with the obvious intention of pulling her back.

She found her father engrossed in conversation with a man whom she knew by sight. Lennartz looked up, obviously surprised and displeased, but she was not going to let herself be frightened away.

'I ought to have fetched you hours ago,' she said, smiling. 'I'm sorry I'm late. Please forgive me.' She tactfully took all the blame on herself in order to appeal to his chivalry by pretending to be in the wrong.

The visitor stood up and bowed. It was Hansly, the Director of the United Shipowners' Company. He held out his hand to Gisela.

'It's my fault, I'm afraid, Miss Lennartz. I am sorry that I have detained your father. He waited for me and I, unfortunately, was two hours late. I was engaged in an important conference which was rather protracted.'

Gisela bit her lip as she heard the word conference for the second time within a few minutes. However, she nodded smilingly.

'I won't disturb you,' she said, quite self-possessed. 'When can I take you with me, Father?' At any rate, she was not going to let herself be turned out.

'Sit down for a minute, child. I'll be ready almost at once,' said Lennartz.

'Thank you, Father. I hope I'm not intruding,' said Gisela, and she sat down unobtrusively in a corner.

Her father shook his head absent-mindedly.

'You don't want me to remain here,' thought Gisela, looking at Hansly with a slight frown. 'But I shall certainly stay here until you've gone. That coward Pechtold has got Hansly here again. I know Father didn't want to negotiate with the shipowners. Surely he hasn't let himself be influenced by Pechtold. Father has got much older recently. Bernard ought to be here now,' and she remembered with a pang that she had received no news from the FP 1 for twenty-four hours.

'I'm sorry, Mr Lennartz,' said Hansly, resuming the discussion. 'I would try to meet you in every possible detail, and I'm sure we should soon come to some agreement, but there are these two main conditions which must be accepted if we are to come to terms. If I have to drop those, then it is useless to go further in the matter.'

'No, Mr Hansly, I should be sacrificing all my principles if I consented to your conditions. You stipulate that no passenger-carrying aircraft be allowed to land on the FP 1. That is an impossible demand. What is the good of my having undertaken this tremendous task if I am going to make such a sacrifice? After all, I built the FP 1 especially for transatlantic air traffic of all kinds. Mark that, Mr Hansly, *all* kinds.'

'But you would still be able to carry out the major portion of your plans if you agree to my conditions,' put in Hansly eagerly. 'We would allow you to accept mail traffic; and bear in mind that airplanes carrying mails would very possibly require only half the quantity of fuel, and of course could make use of the FP 1 to refuel. The element of safety would be doubled and letters and freight would reach New York in anything from forty-eight to sixty hours. That, Mr Lennartz, means a revolution in the economic intercourse of the world. It would bring two great nations—two continents—closer together. That is surely an ideal worth striving for. And, let me emphasize this again, the profit would be much greater. A passenger does not bring in nearly so much money as the same weight of letters and freight. Apart from all this, Mr Lennartz, you cannot expect me to help to create competition by air against the interests of my own shipping companies by agreeing to passenger air traffic using the FP 1. People would no longer travel on our ships, if they could fly safely from Berlin to New York in forty-eight hours. You will see, therefore, that it is quite impossible for me to do business with you unless you agree definitely that there shall be no passenger traffic.'

'If that is your last word, then all I can say is that I am sorry, Mr Hansly—'

'You should be sorry for yourself,' Hansly interrupted him. 'You will never get such an offer again in your life. Let me say once more that I would pay sixty per cent of the cost and guarantee sixty per cent of the share capital of the FP 1. All future orders for the construction of floating airports would go to your shipyards exclusively. In fact, we would be ready to guarantee orders for new construction to the extent of one hundred thousand tons yearly. You really cannot expect more. We only make one stipulation,—that you withdraw your claim to carry passengers. You're an idealist, not a business man, Mr Lennartz, if you refuse our offer.'

'Well, then, I'm an idealist!' said Lennartz gravely. 'I'm fighting for my ideal. I want to do something, however little, to help on the progress of the world.'

'Well, well, idealists generally come to a bad end!' Hansly slapped Lennartz heartily on the shoulder; 'but bear in mind that we have other ways of getting what we want. There is an airship company which is now going in for overseas air traffic and which is very closely connected with

us. I tell you, Lennartz, one day we'll eat you up! D' you hear? Eat you up—
so that there's nothing left of you. Why, man, can't you see, you'll be absolutely forced to shut up shop. You forget you haven't got the money
from the government yet, and the last installment from your bank is still
outstanding. What if the bank doesn't let you have it?'

Lennartz leaned forward and gazed at Hansly in astonishment. 'You're
surprisingly well informed, Mr Hansly. Where do you get your inside information, may I ask?'

Hansly bit his lip. Perhaps he had gone too far.

'Business men and diplomatists have their secrets, you know.'

'Well, I wish you luck in your project,' he said then, getting up. 'I will be
in the country some days yet and you can always get in touch with me. But
I warn you that my demands will probably increase. My future terms will
not be so favorable.'

Lennartz rose also.

'I'm sorry I cannot avail myself of your friendly offer,' he said ironically.
'It has been an honor to me to be allowed to discuss business with you.'
He bowed and held out his hand, which Hansly shook warmly.

'You've staked everything, Mr Lennartz, and you'll lose everything!'
said Hansly, smiling. From his tone they might have been discussing
nothing more serious than a friendly game of poker. 'I'm sure you will be
sorry for this one day.'

'I hope not,' replied Lennartz politely, and closed the door after Hansly,
who apparently had quite forgotten Gisela's presence.

As soon as he had gone, Lennartz's face suddenly became grave, almost haggard. Gisela sprang up and led him to his chair.

'I'm perfectly all right, my dear, only feeling a little tired and overworked,' said Lennartz, trying to smile, but he gratefully took the glass of
water which she handed him.

Gisela sat down opposite him and gazed at him anxiously. 'Are things
really going very badly with you, Father?' She restrained herself with difficulty from trying to comfort him in his obviously distressed state, for she
felt that she must appear to guess little or nothing of the shock which he
had received.

'I haven't had any news from Droste for twenty-four hours.' Lennartz
pulled himself together with an effort. 'I don't know what can be the trouble. The *Elbe* is lying at Fayal, and the *Pillau* has not reached the FP 1 yet. An
hour ago I had a message from the *Pillau* that she had lost touch with the
FP 1. There was no reply to her wireless messages and she feared the worst.'

He sprang up and paced the room restlessly, his hands clasped behind
his back.

'What can they mean by the worst?' he muttered. 'What can have happened? The FP 1 can't sink—of that I'm certain. Yet how can the wireless have failed? Surely Heinicke, who is our best technical engineer, could have repaired it within twenty-four hours.'

He sat down at his desk again. 'I'll talk to you frankly, Gisela. We'll discuss the whole matter and consider seriously what can be done.'

'Certainly, Father. I don't know much about it, but I would like to be of some help to you.'

'That's right, Gisela,' said Lennartz kindly. 'While there's life, there's hope! There is nothing so bad that some way of escape cannot be found. We must try to find a solution. We simply must get in touch with Droste again.'

'Why don't you ask the Portuguese Navy to help? They're bound to have seaplanes stationed at the Azores and they would surely help you. You could get in touch with them, at any rate, and give the direction the FP 1 must have taken and its probable position.'

Lennartz looked at his daughter thoughtfully. 'That won't do, Gisela. I— I can't do that!' He shook his head disconsolately. 'Even if I could bring myself to seek help from a foreign government, it would be no good. There's an agreement between Portugal and France which gives France the exclusive right to use the Azores as a landing place for overseas air traffic. It would certainly not be in the Portuguese interest to help a competitor like myself. Besides, that would make the matter public, and it mustn't leak out that something is wrong with the FP 1. If that happened, I shouldn't get the last installment of the loan from the bank. That would just add to my difficulties, and it's pretty certain that the government too would think twice about advancing money to subsidise a floating airport which doesn't keep afloat for a fortnight even,' he added bitterly.

'Oh, Father, you surely don't think that the FP 1—'

'I must take into account every conceivable possibility. It would be the end of everything if I had to make the matter public. As it is, I have tried to suppress all newspaper notices, all publicity about the FP 1 on purpose. No, that won't do, Gisela.'

He resumed his walk across the room.

'I'll call up Pechtold,' he said, reaching for the telephone. But Gisela gripped his arm impetuously.

'No, don't call him, please.'

Lennartz looked at her in surprise. Gisela bit her lip. She had no reason to give for her strange impulse. They remained silent for a few moments, thinking.

'Call up Ellissen,' said Gisela at last.

'What! Axel Ellissen?'

Gisela nodded emphatically. To her, the solution to their problem had been found.

'What can Ellissen do for us?' asked Lennartz. 'What makes you think of him?'

'Ellissen has an airplane of his own with him. You could rely on him to keep silent. I know I would trust him implicitly. He can fly to the Azores and search for the FP 1. He is the only available man who could undertake the flight immediately. He is quite accustomed to long ocean flights. Why, Father, he is just the man to help us! I'm sure he could!'

'I don't understand why you are so certain that he would undertake the flight. Why, you can scarcely know the man. Why should he risk his life to help me? You have no idea of his real character. I think he's one of the most selfish and unreliable men I have met—and an adventurer at that,' ended Lennartz. 'I don't want Ellissen's help.'

'But, Father, what can you have against him? Have we got so many friends ready and willing to help us that you can reject Axel Ellissen simply because you don't happen to like him? What is your objection to him?'

Lennartz turned to the window and stood with his hands clasped behind his back, staring down at the shipyard. 'Well, speaking frankly, I have nothing against him. I can't say exactly what my feelings about him really are. I just know that I don't like him.'

'Talk to him, anyhow,' pleaded Gisela. 'I'm sure he will help us.'

Reluctantly Lennartz took up the telephone.

'He is stopping at the European Hotel,' said Gisela. She remembered the name perfectly well—the European Hotel.

Lennartz rang up the hotel. The receiver shook a little in his hand. 'Is that the European Hotel? I would like to be put through to Mr Ellissen,' he said in a steady voice.

'Is that Ellissen? This is Lennartz speaking. I hope I'm not troubling you. I wanted to ask you a favor. I—I—Well, I had better go straight to the point. Perhaps it would have been better if I had come round to your hotel and seen you personally. As a matter of fact, the favor I want to ask is this. Will you place yourself at my disposal for a few days? You have an airplane available, I believe. And ready for flight, I presume?'

'What? ... You have no time? You're going away ... for three or four days ...'

Lennartz covered the mouthpiece of the telephone with his hand. His face was pale and drawn as he turned to Gisela. 'It's no good,' he said. 'He's going away.'

Frantically he spoke into the mouthpiece again, pleading, beseeching.

'I beg of you, Ellissen...You really can't...Ellissen, it's of the greatest importance to me. You are really my only hope...No, it's a matter... When?...In eight days...That's too late...No, thank you...I'll call up... Yes, I'll give you another call later.'

Lennartz hung up the receiver. 'He has no time to give me—I know Ellissen. It's impossible to make him change his mind. If he wants to go away, no one can stop him.' He looked at his daughter despairingly.

Gisela rose to her feet. She smiled at him, pulling on her gloves as if she were preparing to go.

'I'll speak to Ellissen, Father,' she said, cheerful decision in her voice.

'You won't be able to make him change his mind, Gisela. It's quite hopeless.' Lennartz shook his head testily. 'We must try something else.'

'No harm in trying, Father. I think Ellissen may perhaps be induced to change his mind. If you can't persuade him—perhaps a woman can.'

Chapter Eleven: Feminine Wiles

'Look here, I will not be disturbed again,' Ellissen's angry voice bellowed into the telephone. 'Under no circumstances will I speak to any one. If any one asks for me, say I have left.' He replaced the receiver abruptly and turned to his visitor.

'Asking favors, always favors—' There was a sneer in his voice. 'As if the sole purpose of my existence was to do people favors.'

'Oh, but I should like a favor from you too,' said his guest, as she leaned back against the cushions of the divan and languidly opened a cigarette case. 'Give me a light, my dear, and be nice to me.'

Thea Drews smiled at Ellissen. 'There must be a lot of things you don't understand. You always give me the impression that you resent women being a little more decided and determined than you are. You appear to regard it as a positive crime that we should say exactly what we want nowadays.'

'I was never in much doubt about that,' retorted Ellissen laughingly. He sat down beside her, took her hand and admired her long, slender fingers.

'I suppose this is your favorite occupation,' he said, gazing at her carefully manicured, scarlet-tinted finger nails.

'That's the weak point in our armor! We can no longer scratch a man's face for fear of breaking our nails! But tell me, Axel, aren't you the least bit surprised at my turning up here in your hotel—to say nothing of my cleverness in getting a room next to yours. I suppose I'm lucky not to have found some other woman here.'

Ellissen got up. Women were all like this. They forced themselves on him. Anything for a little entertainment in their dull and boring little lives; anything they wanted to do they did. He looked at Thea, who sat gazing up at him with her chin propped on her hands. There was no denying that she was attractive. Her eyebrows were curved into thin dark lines. The small mouth was enticingly red, full-lipped and luscious. Her hair was a deep copper color that contrasted strikingly and provocatively with her pale skin. She had stretched out her feet negligently. Her long, supple limbs showed through the soft black material of the clinging dress.

'You're a fool, Ellissen. Don't stare at me as if I were an exhibit in the museum. If you like me, be a little nicer to me. Come and sit by my side and don't run about like a cat on hot bricks. It would certainly have been nicer perhaps if we had met somewhere else. I hate hotel rooms—and love them at the same time. Just fancy how many people have sat here, how many pairs of happy lovers have met here secretly. Happiness and tragedy,' she cried, in mock melodramatic tones, 'have both reigned here! Methinks more tragedy than happiness!'

Ellissen put out his great hands and pulled her suddenly towards him. She lay quite still in his arms while he kissed her. Slowly her arms crept around his neck and she clung to him passionately.

Suddenly Ellissen tore himself away, and Thea sat back on the divan. Ellissen put his hands in his pockets and contemplated her. 'Do you collect lovers?' He looked at the beautiful face, taking in the curve of her mouth, the dark eyes which returned his gaze through half-closed lids. 'What do you really want from me?'

Thea began to laugh hysterically, in a manner which sent cold shivers down Ellissen's spine.

'Let's go away together,' said Thea at last. 'You certainly need a woman who would look after you. Won't you come away with me?' She got up, extinguished her cigarette carefully and slowly turned round till their eyes met. Impulsively she flung her arms round his neck and kissed him. For some moments they clung together in a passionate embrace. At last the spell was broken by the shrill clamor of the telephone bell.

Thea wrenched herself free. Ellissen snatched up the receiver.

'I've gone away,' he shouted angrily and threw the receiver down again. There was silence for a moment, and then the bell rang again. Ellissen swore as he picked up the infernal instrument again.

'What the devil's the matter! I've given orders that I am not to be disturbed...Who?' he asked. 'Oh, one moment!' He looked across the room, frowning thoughtfully. 'Say I'm coming down.' He hung up the receiver.

'You'll excuse me for a moment, won't you?' He was already at the door.

Thea ran after him. 'You'll come back at once, won't you? You're going away with me? Promise?'

'Of course,' he replied, disengaging himself from her embrace. 'Pack your things. We'll go to-day—anywhere you like!' He closed the door behind him and hurried down the stairs.

Gisela was waiting for him in the lounge.

She was standing near the entrance, looking pale and tired. As he greeted her, she put out her hand to him, slightly embarrassed.

'I'm so afraid I've intruded on you, Mr Ellissen, but I simply had to speak to you. You won't mind sparing me a few minutes of your time, will you?'

'The older I get, the less I seem to be able to get away from women,' thought Ellissen, mentally comparing Gisela with the woman whom he had just left and who even now was impatiently awaiting his return in his room.

'Let's go into the writing room for a minute and sit there.' He smiled in a friendly manner. 'There's generally no one in there.'

He followed her into the room. She was really most attractive. He felt again the strange fascination he had experienced a few days before in the Lennartz villa, as his eyes followed admiringly the exquisite lines of her young shoulders, the delicate, girlish curve of her throat. How beautiful she was, he thought, still a mere child, a defenceless girl who appealed to his protective instinct.

'This is an unexpected pleasure, Miss Lennartz,' he said. 'I didn't dream that I would see you again so soon.'

Gisela slowly took off her gloves. Her small hat was pressing on her forehead, so she removed it, smiling faintly at Ellissen. Under his cold, watchful eyes she felt rather ill at ease. 'He is certainly a wonderful man,' she thought. 'He knows exactly what he wants. He has strength and unlimited energy. Oh, if only I could persuade him to do this for me.' Mentally she contrasted the slender, slightly built Bernard with the big, broad-shouldered man who stood before her. She tried to put out of her mind the invidious comparison that she had conjured up involuntarily, but she could not succeed in doing so. The picture of Droste came before her persistently, the picture of a youth rather than a full-grown man such as Ellissen, with his strong, rugged features and powerful physique.

'My father tried to have a talk with you on the telephone. He had a certain proposition to make, but you told him that you couldn't give him the time he wanted. That wasn't very nice of you, was it?' She smiled charmingly.

Ellissen made a deprecating gesture. 'Yes, I told your father that I had lots of things to attend to at the moment and really wasn't available for other work. You cannot realize how many people have been wanting me to meet them and discuss various schemes by which they hope to utilize my services.'

He looked at her speculatively. He was rather puzzled as to how to deal with her. It seemed to him that the usual entreaties and feminine pleadings would soon follow if he pursued his usual tactics. 'What will she do?' he asked himself, and thought of the oceans of tears that he had seen women shed.

'Mr Ellissen, my father has set all his hopes on you. You are really the only person in the world who can help him.' Gisela lowered her eyes. 'We have had no news from—' She was going to say from Droste, but she hesitated and went on—'The FP 1 does not answer our wireless calls, and it is only a couple of days now till the time fixed by the government expires.'

'He can't possibly understand,' she thought. 'He knows nothing about the nature of the contract, and I can't possibly tell him Father's private business.'

Ellissen, however, did not inquire.

'Your father wants me to search for the FP 1?' he asked calmly, as if he understood the whole matter. 'Why doesn't he approach the government? They surely would do all they could to help him.'

'My father doesn't want it to get about that something may have happened to the FP 1. The bank would make difficulties about the next payment of the loan, and then all would be lost, and Hansly would get hold of everything.'

'I can't tell him any more,' she thought distractedly, and the chances of getting Ellissen to help her seemed suddenly further away than ever. All her efforts would be in vain against the stern inflexibility of this man.

Ellissen studied Gisela silently. The troubled, hopeless look in her eyes was irresistible. He took her hand, and she did not withdraw it.

'Well, it's got to be a business transaction, like any other,' he said slowly, his eyes, cold as the Arctic ice, looking at her intently. 'Have you any definite proposition to make to me?'

Gisela looked up hopefully. 'Perhaps he is a kind man after all,' she thought. 'Perhaps Father is doing him an injustice.'

'It's for you to say what sum you want—' she began.

Ellissen shook his head. 'I'll settle the financial side with your father. I—' His hold on her hand tightened. The question which hovered on his lips suddenly seemed to him coarse and unworthy. This girl with her soft eyes and trusting look imposed on him a peculiar feeling of restraint. At the same time he despised himself for allowing softer emotions to take possession of him in her presence. Of course she might be acting, as all women did, and if he treated her differently from other women, she would just laugh at him. On the other hand, perhaps he was entirely wrong.

'Well,' he continued, his eyes narrowing, 'I place myself at your disposal on one condition.' He was seized by a sudden overwhelming desire. The freshness of her youth attracted him irresistibly. Once before he had been seized with the same impulse—when he was sitting opposite her in the quiet study in her own home and saw for a moment a glimpse of a new and better future opening before him.

'What is the condition?' said Gisela in a low voice.

'That you accompany me on the flight!' he replied slowly and significantly, enjoying his momentary power over the girl. He noticed the sudden pallor of her cheeks. She had understood him. Her eyes gave the consent which her lips refused to speak.

'We'll start right away to-night,' said Ellissen. He bent and kissed her hand in token of their agreement. It felt cold and lifeless.

A sudden movement behind him startled him. He turned round swiftly. Thea was standing in the doorway, staring at them. With a well-simulated cry of surprise, she hastened toward Gisela, hands outstretched to greet her.

'You here!' she cried in delighted tones. 'Have you come to say good-by to our dear Axel Ellissen too?'

Gisela did not know what to say; she was overwhelmed with embarrassment.

'Mr Ellissen is just going away,' said Thea quickly. 'Just fancy, isn't it funny! He's going to Wiesbaden, and so am I. Am I not fortunate to have such a nice traveling companion? Have you got all your things packed, Axel?' She turned her dark eyes towards him, asking herself angrily why he could possibly want to waste his time with a stupid girl like Gisela Lennartz. It was annoying to think that he had hurried out of his room to speak to her.

'I have unfortunately had to alter my plans,' said Ellissen, deliberately trying to make his voice sound as casual as possible. 'I've just closed a contract with the Lennartz shipyards, and Miss Lennartz and I are leaving to-night at twelve.'

Thea drew back in undisguised amazement. What was the reason for this sudden change of front?

'Well, good-by for the present,' said Gisela, shaking Ellissen's hand, and with a slight bow towards Thea, she went quickly out of the room.

As soon as she was gone, Thea turned angrily towards Ellissen. 'Are you going away with that silly little goose? I'll never forgive you. You're going to throw me over! I know it!'

Ellissen took her hand and raised the beautifully manicured fingers to his lips.

'My dear lady,' he said laughingly. 'If all the hard things that women have wished me had happened, I should have been a dead man long ago.'

Chapter Twelve: A Nest of Rogues

'Sambach, Heinicke, Hekker, Künnecke—'

Droste was sitting at the small writing desk in the little room in the commander's turret. 'Who else is still to come?' He turned to Schmiedecke, who was standing at his side, staring out of the window into the mist. 'It isn't getting light yet, although it's six o'clock already.'

'This mist may be damned lucky for us,' answered Schmiedecke, without turning round. The whole orderly routine of his life had been shaken by recent incidents, and he was feeling absolutely miserable. How any one could plan the destruction of the FP 1 passed his comprehension.

The door opened and some more men entered. They ranged themselves round the room, silent and expectant. For a moment absolute silence reigned.

'Is everybody here now?' asked Droste, glancing rapidly at the faces around him. He breathed a sigh of relief. These were all men on whom he could rely implicitly. They had worked under his father before him and from them he had received guidance and instruction when as a young apprentice he had entered the Lennartz shipyards. He knew they trusted him, and out of their interest in their mutual work had grown a strong bond of respect and affection.

'I sent for you,' Droste began, choosing his words slowly and deliberately, 'because we find to our surprise that we have enemies, who are apparently doing their best to make things difficult for us. They have succeeded in putting us in rather a bad hole. The tugs have deserted us—they must have been bribed to leave us in the lurch—and we are drifting at the present moment.' He noticed signs of alarm on the countenances of the men around him.

'But don't get the wind up. Nothing can happen to us so long as you don't get panicky. There's no earthly reason for any alarm. As soon as this damned mist has lifted, we'll make signals of distress with the searchlights. That will attract some one's attention, all right,' he ended cheerily.

'But why don't we send out an SOS signal now?' cried a voice.

Droste looked grim. 'The transmitter has been wrecked—burnt completely out,' he answered.

At this news the men began to talk excitedly among themselves.

'Who wrecked the transmitter?' cried Künnecke, pushing himself in front of Droste's table.

Droste shrugged his shoulders. 'I can't tell you who actually did the damage, but I know it was done by a strong current conducted along a wire from the engine room to the aërial,' he explained.

'But who the devil was on duty in the engine room?'

'Girard,' put in Schmiedecke. 'Does any one know anything about Girard? We took him over from the *Elbe*.'

No one was able to give much information about Girard. He had made quite a favorable impression. He was inoffensive and kept to himself, and moreover appeared to be a good man at his job. On one occasion he had helped Heinicke in the construction of a new short-wave switch system, and he had also helped with some rather intricate work in connection with the fire-extinguishing installation. In fact, he had seemed to be able to turn his hand to anything and was certainly not shy of work of any kind. There was no apparent reason why he should play a double game.

'Well, we must be on the watch,' Droste resumed, 'and keep our ears open. After all, it will only be a couple of days at most. By that time, we are almost certain to have met some ship which will take us in tow. We can't sink. The FP 1 is absolutely seaworthy, whether it is being towed or not. It doesn't make much difference to our safety really whether we're drifting or anchored. But one thing we must do, and that is to try and keep order, and, above all, discipline. We've more than sixty men on board who are practically unoccupied at present, and as they haven't much to do, we must keep them from getting into any mischief. The best thing we can do is for all of us to get back to work straight away. We'll all stand by each other. Meantime, let's keep our courage up; that's the great thing.'

Droste's remarks had the desired effect. The excitement of the men had already subsided. They appeared to be quite keen to do whatever he wished.

'Schmiedecke will give you all revolvers before you go,' continued Droste. 'I'm not taking any chances, you understand. If we are armed, we'll be ready for anything that may happen. It's only a precaution, but we don't know the hotel staff as we do each other, and we must take the necessary steps to protect ourselves, if they prove troublesome. And now, Schmiedecke, let's bring out the artillery!'

Droste's bearing was reassuringly cool and confident.

Schmiedecke opened the door of the writing table in which several re-volvers were kept.

'We're damnably short of tools and spare parts,' muttered Sambach to Droste. 'The FP 1 shouldn't have started with so little in the way of proper equipment. I had the feeling all along that something would happen through that. We've got nothing but aircraft tools and spare propellers and engine parts. What the devil's the good of that stuff to us now? Why,' he laughed bitterly, 'we've not even got enough lifeboats to take us off.'

'Cut that kind of talk,' retorted Droste sharply. 'We've no need of lifeboats yet. In any case, what would have been the use of lugging boats with us! We've got the big motor launch, and that'll hold every one if necessary. Getting scared, I suppose, for your own wretched life!' he added sneeringly. 'Well, if that's the case, for God's sake don't go about trying to frighten other people. Why, man, any old woman would have more guts than you.'

'I didn't mean you to take it like that,' Sambach growled apologetically, pocketing the revolver which Schmiedecke handed him. 'Of course, you know I'm not afraid,' he added. 'After all, nothing much could happen to us.'

'We might run short of food,' said Droste frankly. 'We really are damned short of provisions, as a matter of fact. Oh, if any of you see the fat Damsky, send him to me. And keep the hotel gentry quiet, if they notice that the FP 1 isn't traveling. But treat 'em gently. Don't come to blows with 'em.'

The men trooped out, laughing. They had already forgotten their fears. There was work to be done, and that was the best possible tonic they could have. True, the danger that threatened them meant extra duty and more work, but they were accustomed to jobs that placed sudden demands on their powers of endurance, and they did not mind that in the least. But if any man forgot the seriousness of his position, there was always the revolver in his pocket to remind him of the new turn of events.

Sambach was half ashamed of the protest he had made to Droste. He felt that perhaps some explanation was due to his comrades.

'It's all very fine for you to laugh,' he said, in rather aggrieved tones to Künnecke, 'but I'm the father of a family, and there are always hungry mouths to feed. What will happen at home if I'm drowned here, like a rat in a trap? It's different with you; you're a bachelor, and nobody'll cry about you.'

'Oh, stow that drivel! Father of a family!—Hungry mouths!—That's the sort of sob-stuff you always come out with the moment things get a bit hot. And you're damn' well wrong too. There would be a lot of crying and cackling over me. I started a hen roost myself a couple of weeks ago,' replied Künnecke.

'Gawd, I don't know what's wrong with me. I seem to have gone all to pieces. Do you really think there's no danger? Mind you, I don't like Droste giving us these popguns. What do we want 'em for, if there's nothing in the wind?'

'I think it was damn' decent of Droste to show us he had complete faith in us. It all goes to show that he knows us and knows that we'll stick by him. He doesn't trust that waiter crowd, that's evident. You can't rely on a lot of Dagoes. Of course, I don't know what'll happen—and mind you, I'm not saying anything will happen, but in any case it's much better to be prepared. Now, at any rate, we'll be able to defend ourselves.'

'There you go! Even you are beginning to talk about danger too. I wish to God I had stayed at home. I was damn' lucky to come through the war alive, and now I seem to have run into this. If there's going to be any shooting, Künnecke, I'll go stark, staring mad.'

Künnecke placed a hand on his shoulder. 'There won't be any shooting. You can bet your life, but if there is, just you go to your cabin and get into your bunk while it's going on. I'll let you know when the row's blown over. Hullo, there goes the fat boss of the kitchen! Hi! Damsky! You're to go to the chief at once. Hurry up! He's waiting to see you.'

Damsky jumped like a frightened rabbit when he heard Künnecke calling to him. He nodded his head and scuttled away in a great hurry. They gazed at each other in speechless amazement at the strange effect of Künnecke's words. Then both burst out laughing and walked on.

Immediately after the men had left the commander's room, Droste confided his plans to Schmiedecke.

'Thank God, I can trust these fellows. Now I can see my way more clearly and feel more confident. We've got the two Diesel engines, at any rate. One isn't quite in working order yet, but the other is sufficiently powerful to give all the current that's needed. The truth of the matter is, Schmiedecke, time was getting short and old Lennartz hadn't always the necessary cash. He had taken on something that often seemed more than he could handle. If the government could have advanced the promised loan a month earlier, we should have been in a very different position. And then that idiot Pechtold—either he is really an idiot, in which case I don't understand the old man working with him for so long, or else he's a scoundrel, and it's more incomprehensible than ever how he has contrived to bluff every one for so long.

'Well, that's that,' added Droste resignedly. 'Now we'll get the motor launch out. It has a three hundred horse-power engine and enough petrol to do us. We'll link up the hawsers and see if it can tow this damned box. It might work all right.'

Schmiedecke shook his head doubtfully. 'Three hundred horse power? I should say it was absolutely impossible. How far do you think you'll get with it?'

'If the FP 1 can only be made to tack, that'll be some good. I can turn the FP 1 to the wind, so that it won't get its force broadside on; then I'll be able to decide in what direction we are drifting. By the way, Schmiedecke,' he added, as a sudden thought struck him, 'have you opened the flooding valves yet? With more than thirty thousand tons of ballast, we'll be fairly stationary against the current, and our best anchor, of course, is the depth of our draught.'

Schmiedecke nodded. 'At the moment we are taking in a thousand tons an hour.'

'Who is in the engine room now?' asked Droste, remembering that Girard had never been relieved.

'Girard came back almost immediately, and I handed over to him again just for the time being. There's no one else there,' replied Schmiedecke.

'Do you think Girard had anything to do with what's been happening?'

Schmiedecke shrugged his shoulders. 'Do I think? What the devil's the use of thinking it? Maybe he has, but I've not got sufficient proof. We've not a single clue really as to who it can be, and God knows how we're going to find out... Well, I only wanted to stand by while you saw the men. I'll go back to the engine room now and relieve Girard. He can go to bed and I'll keep my eyes skinned. I've got the feeling now I mistrust everybody on board. Did you notice how that Damsky fellow was creeping and crawling about?'

'Damsky?' Droste broke off abruptly, for at that moment he saw Damsky himself standing in the doorway, staring at Schmiedecke with startled eyes. It was impossible for him not to have heard the last words. Droste cleared his throat. It was all very embarrassing, but he must make the best of the situation.

'Sit down, Damsky,' he said with a friendly gesture, and paused, while Damsky, looking very ill at ease, slowly seated himself. 'Tell me how you really got into this nest of rogues,' he began facetiously. It was a shrewd shot that might get home.

'Nest of rogues?' repeated Damsky. 'What do you mean?' and there was a tremor in his voice.

Droste laughed. 'I was only joking,' he said. 'What are you so frightened about?' He had not seriously entertained any suspicions of Damsky, but the man's attitude certainly did not help to establish confidence. 'The managing director of the hotel gave you your job, and he must have known what he was about. I'm not doubting that. Tell me, where were you before you joined the FP 1?'

'I was head chef, sir, at the Negresco at Nice, and I only took on this job at the urgent request of the company.'

'Hm!' said Droste. 'All the hotel staff are under you, aren't they?'

'Yes, I'm in charge of the hotel and stores.'

'Well,' remarked Droste coldly, extinguishing his cigarette. 'There's something important I want to tell you. We've suffered a slight mishap. The tugs that were towing us have cast off, in order not to endanger themselves. I want you particularly to see that your people don't get panicky. At the moment, we're drifting. There's nothing dangerous about that in itself, but I don't feel sure how the rest of your staff may take it, when they get to know about it. Of course, you must tell them and explain to them that there is no danger. Take it from me that I hold you responsible for their behavior. They must be kept quiet. Strict discipline must be maintained, I hope you understand me—?' He looked straight at Damsky, whose face had gone the color of chalk. In fact, with his large, fat, white face, stumpy nose and protruding eyes, he bore a ridiculous resemblance to a frightened bulldog.

After a moment Damsky pulled himself together. He got up and bowed stiffly. 'Of course, of course, Commander,' he said, breathing heavily. 'I'll see to it that all is quiet. I will keep order. You may rely on me absolutely!'

'Good,' said Droste curtly. He began to dislike Damsky more and more. He wished he had seen what sort of people were being sent on board the FP 1, but it was no use worrying about that now. There was nothing to be done but to concentrate on getting out of the mess as best he could with the means at his disposal.

'You may go,' said Droste. 'Remember, I rely on you!'

'I am very grateful to you for your confidence in me!' Damsky bowed again. 'I will see at once that everything is in order. Everything in its place. Everything in order!' He went out, still muttering something about 'in order.'

'What do you think of this "in order" lunatic?' Droste said, turning to Schmiedecke, but Schmiedecke smiled grimly and left the room without replying.

CHAPTER THIRTEEN: The Sea Waits

Droste listened. The sound of footsteps had died away. It was getting lighter in the room, and the lights were beginning to burn yellow. The mist was lifting at last. Slowly it dissolved in patches, and then suddenly there was daylight. Droste looked out over the glittering waters of the Atlantic, which reflected the first rays of the sun from an almost motionless surface. He shivered slightly. These long nights without sleep had made him a bit shaky. He flung back his shoulders and drew in a deep breath. A new day was before him. Would it mean a renewed attack by the unknown enemy? Heaven alone knew what further misfortune was in store for them. Schmiedecke was lucky, he thought. His mind was at rest, for he had safely transferred his responsibilities to his commander's shoulders. Droste allowed his thoughts to wander. That inexplicable twist that so often occurs in day-dreaming made him think suddenly of Gisela, and he realized with something approaching dismay that he had not thought of her at all since he had come on board the FP 1. He was disappointed and annoyed with himself. Could he love her so little, had the events of last night been so stunning and overwhelming that they could drive her right out of his thoughts?

A wave of remorse, of love and longing for Gisela swept over him. He remembered with shame how he had taken advantage of her good nature and her patience in not wishing to interfere in any way with his work, and had really shamefully neglected her when it suited him. How could he have been such a fool, such an utter idiot, as to put her quite out of his mind for the sake of his work? After all, that was not the most important thing in life. Or was it? Now that he could call to mind his behavior in the last few weeks, he realized bitterly that he had not shown very much love for her. Had she then been so completely satisfied with their friendship that she had not noticed the absence of great and overwhelming passion? What was she doing now? Was she thinking of him at all, wondered Droste, and there was an ache in his heart, a sudden sense of loss, of something he had missed in his life. Standing here on the FP 1, which represented his great dream come true, the dream for which he had sacrificed so much, even love, his thoughts went out to her across the wide waste of waters, and it seemed to him as if she responded. He felt her presence near him, soothing and comforting him. A feeling of deep peace stole over him. He realized the strength of his love and where his true happiness lay. At that moment, he vowed that his whole future would be devoted to Gisela and to her alone. It was a memorable moment in his life, a moment in which he tried for the first time to survey his achievements, with all that they had cost him. Supposing he were to perish with the FP 1. His life work would disappear with him, everything undone, everything forgotten. If he died now, had Gisela's life been enriched one little bit by him? What happiness had he ever given her?

Something very like a groan escaped Droste, and his lips moved in a prayer that his life might not end just yet. With all his soul he prayed for just one hour, a couple of minutes even, in which he might speak to Gisela again. He longed for the sight of her eyes, her mouth, the sound of her voice, and the touch of her hands. He craved for the love which he had never yet learned to know. 'Let me live, let me live!' he cried distractedly, 'and I will beg Gisela to forgive me all my shortcomings. I must see her again. I can't die, I can't die!' His eyes swept the wide waters of the Atlantic to the far horizon. 'It's horrible the way the sea waits for us all,' he muttered to himself. 'Perhaps in a short time it will have claimed us. Who knows; we may throw ourselves into it in despair, or its waves may destroy the whole of the FP 1 underneath our very feet. God! I don't want to die yet. I want to live—for Gisela!'

With an effort he pulled himself together, ashamed of his weakness, and leaving the commander's room, he descended to the platform. A warm wind fanned his face gently, the sea was calm, the horizon stretched wide and empty. Fresh strength came to him; he felt his new-found love surging through him, renewing his courage and energy, and making him feel unconquered and unconquerable.

He hurried to the end of the landing platform, where he saw Sambach and called to him. Duty was uppermost in his thoughts again. There were lives which must be protected, the lives of men who had loved ones to mourn for them if they perished.

'Sambach,' he said, 'take a man and see to the motor launch. The sea is absolutely calm now and we should take the chance to try to tow the FP 1. Take Hekker or Künnecke. You get on best with them.'

He crossed to the impressive entrance to the hotel. A man in resplendent uniform was standing near, busy with a noisy vacuum cleaner. He did not even look round as Droste entered.

'Good morning,' said Droste.

He was rewarded only with a hostile look. The man stopped work, left the cleaner lying where it was, and disappeared hastily up the stairs. Droste looked after him, wondering whether the man had been spying or keeping watch on his movements. He decided that he must speak to Damsky about it and ascended the wide staircase. His footsteps made no sound on the thick carpet which covered the stairs. A bronze balustrade curved gracefully upwards. The walls were bare, with the exception of two enormous pictures representing Commerce and Industry. The sight of these magnificent panels annoyed Droste. 'Couldn't they have thought of something better than hanging those expensive things on the walls?' he muttered, recalled disgustedly the amount of money which Lennartz had paid for these decorations. At the top of the stairs he hesitated, trying to remember the plan of this absurd building. 'On the left the ballroom, on the right the card room, on the first floor the drawing-rooms and lounges,' he recited to himself. Looking at the luxury around him, he smiled in amusement at the thought of the famous Munich professor who had designed the building, the bearded old man who did not look at all as if he had any taste for luxury of this kind.

Droste opened the door of the card room. To his surprise, he saw a number of men lounging about, dressed in immaculate evening dress, so immaculate, in fact, that they gave the impression of being too exclusive to mix with inferior beings. Some were lolling at their ease in luxurious chairs, while others were looking idly out of the window. They looked round when he entered, as if they positively resented his intrusion.

'Just a lot of damned waiters,' muttered Droste. 'They think they're social ornaments, with their new evening suits and the manners that they have picked up at the Negresco and the Ritz—a nice lot to deal with.'

'Good morning,' he said, bowing ironically towards them. He was shaking with internal laughter. With difficulty he refrained from laughing aloud. The ludicrousness of the situation struck him forcibly.

The men made no reply.

'Gentlemen,' proceeded Droste, 'you astonish me, lounging about like this. Is there so little to do? Hasn't Mr Damsky given you any orders yet? Or am I perhaps mistaken? Perhaps you were engaged merely to travel first class! The crew are all at work. Why aren't you? What are you doing, loafing about in here?'

To his annoyance none of the men took the slightest notice of him. He waited a moment, his gorge rising.

'We're waiting to be drowned!' answered one of them at last.

Droste looked at the speaker. He saw a hard-bitten, vicious face.

'That's just damned insolence and nothing more,' said Droste angrily. At that moment, he would have given anything if he could have driven his fist into the man's sneering face. As if at a pre-conceived signal, the men suddenly got up and surrounded him threateningly.

'Now, look here, it's no good you trying to humbug us,' said the man who had previously spoken. 'We know very well what's going on. For you can take it from me we've had a good look round this blasted coffin. Where are the boats? Do you take us for a lot of silly landlubbers? Do you think we don't know what danger we're in? Why, we could lie here a year without a ship coming near us. What we want of you is to put us on land as quickly as possible.'

Droste smiled contemptuously. 'I can see you fancy yourselves. You're very pleased with your own cleverness, aren't you? Since you found out that we were no longer being towed, you've been spending your time discussing how you're going to get out of it. I should like to know what the hell you think is going to happen, if you don't wait till the supply ship reaches us.'

'Supply ship!' jeered the man. He edged slowly nearer to Droste. 'You can't kid us with any faked-up yarn of a supply ship. We're on a coffin ship—d' you hear?—a coffin ship! The wireless won't work, and if we can't get off this damned ship soon, we're all dead 'uns. That's about the size of it, I figure. I'm not blind. I was in the wireless room a little while ago, and I know what's happened to the radio. Mark my words, we're going to get off this blasted FP 1, and we know how we're going to do it.'

'Indeed,' said Droste. He was rapidly thinking who could have let this fellow into the wireless room. Old Heinicke would have to get a rap over the knuckles for that.

'There's a big motor launch slung under the platform and there's enough petrol in it to take all of us sixty men to land. You've damn' well got to have that boat ready for us.'

Droste was in a tight corner and he knew it. It occurred to him that he might fire through the window and some one would be certain to come, but this gang might set about him at any moment, and he could not hold out against that number for more than a couple of minutes. It was doubtful whether help would arrive in time.

'I don't know who has been putting all this rot into your heads,' he said abruptly. 'There's no danger at all at present. For the moment the weather is settled, the sea is quite calm, and nothing can happen. You were engaged for services on board the FP 1. What we do with the FP 1 is our affair. You do your duty, we'll do ours.'

He turned away and tried to break through the barrier which the men formed around him.

'You stop here,' roared the spokesman threateningly, and Droste saw that he was holding a revolver in his hand.

Droste coolly took his own weapon out of his pocket. 'You see, I'm quite prepared for this kind of joke,' he cried. If necessary, he would put a swift end to all this nonsense. His only chance was to be quicker than any of the others.

His opponent refused to give way. 'You don't move from this spot until you have given the order that the motor boat is to be got ready for us. We've thought it all out carefully. The sea's calm, and we've got a good chance, and we're damn' well going. So now you know!'

Droste smiled. He felt perfectly calm. He had a curious conviction that nothing would happen to him, whatever he might do.

'Can't be done,' he said, shaking his head. 'I want the boat myself. I'm going to make an attempt to tow the FP 1 with it.'

His statement was answered by a round of solid cursing. 'You won't let us take the boat? Then we'll bloody well force you to!'

Droste laughed in spite of his rage. 'You blasted idiots! What good will it do you if you do me in? You'll want some one to take charge of the boat, and none of my men would raise a finger to help you. As a matter of fact, the boat has already been launched, and we're now trying to fix up the hawsers. You're even bigger fools than I thought you were, if you are counting on the support of any of my men. I can tell you one thing. I . . .'

He did not finish his sentence, but ducked rapidly to dodge a dangerous blow which he saw coming just in time. Without a moment's hesitation, he threw himself at his opponents, hitting out vigorously with his left hand. At the same time raising his right which held the revolver, he fired the contents of its magazine through the window of the room.

The men scattered in all directions.

Droste leaped to the door. To open and slam it behind him was the work of a moment. He dashed down the stairs, stumbling over that wretched vacuum cleaner at the foot. The force of his fall sent him flying towards the entrance door, where he picked himself up at once and looked behind him. There was no one following, so he opened the door and went out quietly.

His men were rushing up from all sides, as he came out.

Droste waved them away, saying coolly, 'No, there's nothing the matter! Get back to work!'

His men stopped doubtfully and glanced up at the windows of the hotel. They looked at their commander and slowly and reluctantly they went back to their posts.

Droste put his hands in his pockets and lounged past the front of the hotel again. 'If these fellows want a shot at me,' he thought, 'they've got a good chance now. And they needn't fancy they've put the wind up me.' But everything remained quiet.

He went towards the end of the huge platform.

A lift was just coming up. It pushed open a trapdoor automatically and appeared above the platform. Sambach stepped out of it.

'Everything is ready, Mr Droste,' he said, avoiding his commander's eye.

'What the devil's the matter with you, Sambach? Have you caught the infection from these hotel fellows?' asked Droste. He related his adventure in a few words and concluded, 'We must see to it that everybody who is not absolutely reliable is disarmed at once.'

Sambach looked distinctly uncomfortable. 'Then I ought to give up my revolver too,' he said at last, and he did not attempt to disguise the reluctance in his voice.

Completely taken aback, Droste stared at his pale face. 'Look here, Sambach, don't be so silly. We've got the most beautiful clear weather here. It's just as if we were at home on the Alster. We're perfectly all right. What on earth's the matter with you?'

'I don't know. Somehow this patch of good weather only seems to make everything appear more horrible.'

'Good God, man, what're you talking about?'

'Well, I should like to be safe home again,' said Sambach dejectedly. 'I can't help feeling all these waiter fellows are right in wanting to get out of here as soon as possible.'

'Don't talk nonsense, Sambach.' Droste's voice was earnest, but kind. 'If you really feel like that about it, you're perfectly free to go with them. I'm disappointed, though. I should never have dreamed that you of all people would have lost your nerve like this.'

Sambach shook his head. 'Of course, you know I won't go. I couldn't leave the FP 1 without you, but it's a terrible position, all the same.'

He listened to Droste's orders regarding the towing with the same air of resignation, then saluted and disappeared in the lift again.

A moment later Droste heard the regular stroke of the motor-boat engines. He turned and walked back to the hotel. Mounting the stairs, he pushed open the door of the card room, but the waiters had disappeared. He made a careful inspection of the corridors to find out whether any of them were lurking about, for he thought it would be wise to keep an eye on these fellows, who were out to make trouble and would render his position even more difficult if they could.

Entering the kitchens, he saw Damsky standing at an enormous cooking stove.

'Hullo, Damsky,' cried Droste. 'How many days will the stores last?' It had occurred to him that it would be a good idea to get Damsky to spread the news that the motor launch was at the disposal of those who wished to leave the FP 1.

Damsky's head emerged from a cloud of steam. He appeared to be somewhat more at ease than when Droste had last seen him. He made his usual rather obsequious bow.

'We've got provisions for about five days—not more. I have just found out that many of the cases which should contain provisions have only straw and sand in them. Others are empty, just empty,' he repeated. 'I have very little meat left, and I can't keep that much longer.'

Droste took this latest blow of fortune without moving a muscle. The position was now much more serious than he had suspected.

'Put provisions for two days in the motor boat immediately,' he said sharply, 'and tell your staff they can leave the FP 1 at once if they wish. I don't want them. And I think you had better take their revolvers away too, or they will be shooting each other before long.'

'Provisions? Revolvers? Boats?' Damsky, completely bewildered, repeated the words blankly.

The man's crass stupidity and complete lack of understanding was the last straw of annoyance. For once, Droste was in danger of completely losing his self-control.

'I'm sick of the whole lot of you and tired of the sight of your blasted faces round me. Your cowardly lot of skulkers have been threatening me, Damsky. It's rank mutiny. D'you get that? Well, I'm giving them a chance. I'm going to give them the opportunity of getting out of it. That's what they asked for, and that's what they'll get. But later on, when we're in communication with land again, I'll take damned good care to see that the whole affair is reported to the Board of Marine.' And in a towering rage Droste flung himself out of the kitchen.

He walked back again to the end of the landing platform, got into a lift, and let himself down. The lift stopped at the dark, dimly lit passage leading to the boat-landing stage at sea level. He went along a small gangway towards the light. High above his head rose the steel supports of the huge platform. Almost at his feet lapped the strangely calm waters of the Atlantic. He could see the huge buoys stretching deep down into the green water. He noticed that the water was now rippling slightly against the massive pillars on which the platform rested, and realized to his delight that the FP 1 was moving forward slowly. Gazing ahead, he could just see the motor launch, which was attempting to tow the FP 1. He shouted through his hollowed hands, Sambach heard him and turned the launch and came slowly to the landing stage. Künnecke sprang out and made it fast.

'It would do all right, Droste,' said Sambach. 'We can turn the FP 1 in this calm sea, but we can't tow it.'

'Well, it doesn't matter now,' answered Droste drily, 'I've arranged to hire out the boat. Would you like to go with it, Sambach?'

Sambach looked blankly at Droste and shook his head. 'Nothing doing,' he said. 'I reckon I'll stay with you.'

The noise of hurrying footsteps made them swing round. Coming down the narrow ladders in a sort of procession was a crowd of waiters, each carrying a kit bag in his hand. They were obviously eager to take the first opportunity of getting away. Droste looked at them in disgust. Damsky had evidently lost no time in spreading the news.

'These damned swine oughtn't to be allowed to take luggage with them. There isn't enough room in the boat for all that stuff,' growled Künnecke. The villainous-looking individual who had assumed charge of the waiters stepped up to Künnecke.

'Would you mind telling me if the boat would move faster if we did not have so much luggage?'

'Damn' clever idea of yours,' sneered Künnecke. 'Of course, you swine, you'd get home twice as quickly with only one man aboard as you would with sixty.'

The man glared at him in reply and, muttering curses, got into the boat. In the meantime, his companions had lined up on the narrow gangway.

Suddenly the engine of the launch broke into a roar. The boat shot forward into the dark tunnel underneath the platform, heading for the open sea. The men who had been left behind on the gangway shouted with rage and astonishment. Curses and imprecations rent the air. The sound of the engine echoed back dully, getting fainter and fainter.

'The dirty swine's gone off without us,' screamed the man standing nearest Droste, and ran with outstretched arms along the narrow gangway, yelling like a madman.

The next minute a terrific crash like a mighty hammer striking on iron resounded through the darkness of the tunnel,—like some weird and terrifying knell of doom. For a moment the motor boat stood out sharply silhouetted against the sky, as it emerged into the open, then it stopped, shivered and staggered, as if it had been hurled out of its course by a terrific blow. Again there was the crash of iron on iron. A column of water rose, and the boat disappeared in a whirlpool. Every one rushed to the end of the platform, hustling each other on the narrow gangway and shouting, but the boat was no longer to be seen.

Droste had remained standing where he was, taking no notice of the tumult raging round him.

'The blighter was trying to bolt for it, and he's run the boat against one of the buoys,' he heard Künnecke say at his side.

'There goes the first of us,' Sambach answered. 'You see, none of us can escape our fate.'

Chapter Fourteen: Of Ice and Sun

Gisela closed the door of the shabby little room in the hotel at Fayal and looked around with mixed feelings. She examined the dingy wall paper with its curled-up edges. Then, seating herself on the solitary wooden chair beside the ramshackle table, she gazed out of the window. The end of another day, she thought dismally. It had been a long, wild flight to the Azores. Ellissen, usually foolhardy, had for once been cautious and made the flight in fairly easy stages, with short landings of only one hour at a time—an hour in Paris, a short time at Saragossa and Cadiz. Now here she was sitting in Fayal and staring at the rotting wall paper of the musty hotel room. The mist which they had encountered throughout their journey had, of course, been the main reason for Ellissen's caution. It had lain thickly over the fair fields of France, shrouded the mountains of the Pyrenees, had even risen out of the Mediterranean to greet them, and now it almost hid from view this dirty backyard of a little Portuguese hotel in the Azores.

Gisela tried valiantly to keep her spirits up; she was, at any rate, two thousand miles nearer her goal. Thank heaven the mystery would soon be solved. Ellissen was bound to find the FP 1, and everything would come right. Bernard would be safe. She repeated the name softly to herself. 'Bernard . . . Bernard . . . Bernard.' Strange that her heart should remain so unresponsive. No longer did she experience the slightest thrill or expectancy at the thought of Bernard.

She felt more than a little frightened, and the realization of her nervous state seemed to increase her uneasiness. Her thoughts turned to Ellissen. Ellissen, yes, she was afraid of him. She fastened her leather coat up to her chin and went towards the door.

She stopped at the sound of heavy footsteps approaching. Quickly she turned the key in the lock. The handle moved under the grip of a firm hand.

'One moment, I'm changing,' Gisela called out and hurried about the room.

'Will you come down, please, when you're ready,' Ellissen's deep voice answered, and she listened with bated breath to the footsteps receding slowly along the corridor.

Gisela called herself a silly fool for letting her nerves get the better of her. After all, there was nothing to be afraid of. When she had recovered her self-possession, she went downstairs and found Ellissen in the little barroom in lively conversation with the landlord. The latter resembled the proverbial hairdresser rather than mine host of an inn. Over his forehead hung a greasy lock of hair, and his little black mustache was absurdly waxed.

'That's not Madeira, you scamp. You needn't think you're going to swindle me,' cried Ellissen, in a sort of broken English that the landlord appeared to understand. 'You change the labels on the casks? Yes? I know something about wine; don't you try it on again!' He threatened him with his fist, but evidently he was pretending to be angrier than he was, for he sank back in his chair, laughing to himself.

The landlord bowed obsequiously. 'Certainly, Señor,' he said resignedly, quickly changing two of the labels on the huge casks which formed an appropriately decorative background to his portly frame. He filled a glass and with a complacent smile pushed it over to Ellissen. This foreigner was not so simple as he had thought.

Ellissen sipped his drink, nodded his satisfaction, and went over to Gisela with the glass in his hand.

'Did you see what that scoundrel was doing?' he laughed. 'He thought he was going to fool us by exchanging the labels of the dearest and the cheapest of his Madeiras. Good Madeira is rare and he evidently thought we would order the best and drink the worst without knowing the difference. Well, let's sit down, Gisela, and make ourselves comfortable.' He motioned her to a chair.

Gisela forced a rather uneasy smile. So he was beginning to be familiar, calling her Gisela. She noticed he was wearing exactly the same leather jacket as he had worn during their flight, and wondered why he had not taken it off. He seemed to be quite gay, without a care in the world; he did not even look sleepy, although he had not closed his eyes for two days.

'Why haven't you changed?' he asked, pointing to her leather costume. 'You said you were doing so.'

'Why haven't you changed?' she asked in return.

'For the perfectly good reason that I am starting on the flight to-night,' said Ellissen, and laughed at her astonished face. 'I must go to-night,' he added. 'We've not got much time to lose. The mist generally disperses when the moon rises and I should easily be able to pick out the search-lights of the FP 1, so perhaps the job will be over and done with by to-morrow.' And he laughed gayly.

'You mean to say that you are starting again tonight?' she asked.

Ellissen felt that he had impressed her. It pleased his vanity, and he called to the landlord to bring more wine.

'You really ought to take better care of yourself,' Gisela continued. 'You're taking too much out of yourself.'

Ellissen nodded his head ironically. 'That advice should have been given me when I was making my way alone through the ice fields of the Arctic, with a sack of frozen meat over my shoulder! I'm used to hardships, you know.' He drank some wine in silence for a moment, as if he had been suddenly reminded of something unpleasant.

'I hope this confounded mist will soon lift. It's been with us all the way from Germany,' he said, with a searching glance at the gray, opaque wall in front of the window.

'It won't to-night, Señor.' The landlord at the bar appeared to understand and speak any language.

'You think it won't? Well, you may be right. Besides, we've jolly well earned a rest.'

Putting down her glass, Gisela rose and held out her hand to say good night.

'Hello, what's the matter? Do you want to go to bed already? I'm going to finish this wine first.'

'Honestly, I'm tired,' she said wearily. 'After the strain of these last few days.'

Ellissen was quite concerned. 'Of course, Gisela, you ought to have been in bed long ago,' he said, taking her hand; 'but no, I hate being alone.' He gazed up at her pleadingly. His big strong face took on a soft, almost wistful expression, looking ridiculously like that of a schoolboy begging for some special favor.

Gisela reluctantly sat down again. Ellissen put a glass of wine in front of her, which, however, she did not touch.

'Please.' He pointed to the glass. 'Don't leave me to drink alone.' He raised his own glass. '*Bon voyage* to both of us,' he cried merrily.

Gisela smiled and drank. She felt the rich golden wine flowing down her throat, sending a warm glow through her and giving her a wonderful feeling of calm contentment.

Ellissen filled up her glass, which she had only half emptied.

'A superstition of mine,' he said, laughing apologetically. 'I simply can't bear to see a glass standing half empty. It's unlucky, you know. A glass must be full or empty. No half measures for me.' He quaffed his wine in deep gulps. His face relaxed in a smile. Gisela saw to her surprise that his usually stern features softened. A smile flickered round the corners of his mouth, his eyes grew almost tender.

'You know, I like this place.' Ellissen laid a hand on her arm. It was an unintentional contact, but Gisela did not draw her arm away. 'I wouldn't mind having a house here, not far from the sea, somewhere in these islands, or perhaps farther south, where there is at least no cold. I can't bear any more cold.' He shivered, as a momentary vision of the dreary Arctic wastes crossed his mind.

'Believe me, I know what cold means. It feels as if every inch of your flesh were being slowly cut into strips with a knife. You can't protect yourself from it. It's like breathing liquid air, with the wind rushing down your throat like icy water, and the sky looking as if it were cut out of a hard, dark block of ice. You're scarcely able to move your limbs, your finger joints stiffen, and you long to lie down on the ground and let the snow cover you, mountains of snow under which you think you might get warm. No, I'll never go back to the Arctic. At least, dammit, I don't know.' He stared in front of him, slowly sipping his wine and for the moment apparently quite oblivious of Gisela.

'You know, you just cease to be human up there in the ice,' he went on quietly. 'You have different feelings, different ideas of right and wrong.

You're an animal, nothing more than a frightened animal. And your miserable spark of life becomes so valuable, so precious a thing to you, that there ceases to be such a thing as comradeship or pity, only the urge of self-preservation, stronger than anything, stronger than all reason, all claims of humanity. All you want is to live and have a little sun—feel the sun just once again!

'And then, if you're lucky, you get away, and when you've got out of the ice and are back once again where the sun is really warm—God! it's all like a dream. Here you're civilized, obedient to laws. You don't understand your former actions. You're hated and execrated now. It's enough to make you cut your throat. Everything is different when you get back to civilization. And it's all the result of the damned ice and the damned sun.

'You can never be happy any more when you've been in that cold hell. Everything is turned to dust and ashes. There's no object in life and you live for yourself alone. You're an outcast of society, and you despise your fellow men but can't live without them. That's hell!

'You haven't even the courage to make an end of it all, because for that kind of courage you need a conviction that something better will be gained, and it's damned difficult to believe that.

'Even death has become a matter of indifference to me. It promises no release. What are human beings really like? I'm afraid I just don't understand other men, and all they see in me is a man who has murdered his comrades, and all women do is to rush after me. I don't like them, but I amuse myself with them. I feel sort of cut off from the rest of mankind. I have lost all desire, all hope—

'All hope and all desire,' he repeated dramatically, and for the first time he raised his eyes and looked intently at Gisela. She gazed back, fascinated, at those extraordinary eyes, at his broad shoulders, his straight body, his powerful arms, and with a flash of insight she understood him at this moment as certainly no one had ever understood him before.

'And yet I still have one longing, the longing not to feel myself an outcast, but a good citizen, a decent man in the opinion of decent people. I sometimes wish that, Gisela, but the feeling doesn't last long. I only have it for a second or two at long, long intervals. Then I end by laughing at myself and my wish. What good would it be if I were different? Would I stand higher in the opinion of my fellow men? I don't care a fig for their opinion, but I have, all the same, a tremendous longing to be like them.'

He fell into silence and sipped some more wine. Gisela looked at him with compassion in her eyes, wondering if he was waiting for her to answer him, and knowing that she could not discuss—could not talk to him, although she recognized now that a lonely, groping fellow creature was appealing to her.

Complete darkness had fallen. The landlord had lighted a yellow oil lamp, which threw a flickering light on the table at which the two were sitting.

Gisela rose to her feet. The leather costume which she wore suddenly felt like armor. She had a longing to be swimming in a wide, sunlit sea. She stretched herself, gazing down at the man sitting before her with his head bent, so motionless that he might have been asleep. Impulsively she stooped and kissed him tenderly. It was just a sisterly kiss on the forehead, such as she had given to Bernard Droste, when on a certain memorable occasion he had come to her full of plans, seeking inspiration from her to carry them out. She was quite indifferent to the presence of the landlord, who was standing at the bar, gazing appreciatively at the scene.

Ellissen did not stir as she kissed him, not a sign escaped him to show that he was conscious of her caress, and the soft touch of her lips. Without a word she went out of the smoky little barroom, slowly ascended the rickety wooden staircase to her bedroom. She was unable to fall asleep for a long time. Late in the night she thought she heard Ellissen making his way along the passage, a trifle unsteadily, so it seemed, or was that uncharitable. Then the door of his room banged. She stared up at the dingy ceiling of her room and waited for the first ray of daylight, as if waiting for release from a dark dungeon.

Chapter Fifteen: A Floating Coffin

On the FP 1 a few determined men were holding out against what seemed to be terrible odds.

'If these blackguards attack the engine room, we're as good as done for,' Schmiedecke said angrily. 'You're captain here, Droste, and you know you've just got to say the word. Why the devil don't you let us fire on these fellows? I can't understand what you're waiting for. Do you want them to destroy the whole FP 1 first?'

Droste took no notice of Schmiedecke. He was standing quietly waiting in the commander's turret, grimly looking down at the men who had collected at the entrance door of the hotel, shouting to one another and gesticulating. He turned round, went up to a switchboard and pressed the lever which controlled the current for the searchlights. With one rapid movement he turned them all on. Giant beams of light leaped into the sky. The FP 1 seemed to float under great arc lights of immense power, the rays of which penetrated the glass buildings, gilded the towering dark masts, and were reflected on the smooth surface of the landing platform.

There was an ominous silence for a moment, then the uproar broke out afresh.

'We're lucky; they can't see us up here. We're quite in darkness. But damn the mist! I can't even tell those madmen down there that we're trying to call for help by signalling with the searchlights. We must wait till they get a bit quieter.'

Droste stared down at the seething crowd below him.

'Look! There's Girard,' whispered Schmiedecke, gripping his arm excitedly.

Raised on some vantage point, a man was standing, waving his arms and shouting to the surrounding crowd. It was Girard. His sharp, swarthy face glowed with passion. This was his hour. He looked like an actor who rather fancied himself in front of an admiring audience. The man had all the stereotyped gestures of a demagogue.

'Let me have a shot at him, Captain,' demanded Schmiedecke furiously. 'That's a bit too thick! He's trying to incite the crew to mutiny!'

Schmiedecke forced the window open, but Droste pulled him back.

'Don't do anything for the moment. Let the blackguard shout. We want to hear what he's saying first!'

A current of fresh air blew through the room. Schmiedecke turned round quickly, grasping his revolver. Damsky was standing at the door. His face was puffy and had a greenish tinge. His thick lips protruded. He looked like a man who had just escaped death and was absolutely beside himself with terror.

'What in hell's the matter?' Droste shouted.

'Girard,' gasped Damsky. 'Girard!'—he made an aimless gesture downwards towards the platform.

'What the devil's the matter with you? Out with it, man!'

'He's stirring up the men—telling them to rush the stores—they think they're going to starve—'

'Go on, get out of here, and take damned good care that you keep the stores safe. That's your job. Don't waste time coming bleating to us. Dammit, man, we've got eyes and can see for ourselves what's happening.'

Damsky remained standing at the door, however, all the muscles of his face twitching.

'Girard told me that I am to—that I am not to—' He suddenly stopped and did not know how to go on, for what was he to do? Was he to betray Girard? Then Girard would throw him overboard. But it was all Girard's fault that they were all going to die like rats in a trap.

'Oh, go to the devil, you stuttering idiot.'

Damsky's lower jaw dropped. 'It's all Girard's fault,' he muttered, as he turned away hopelessly and crept down the stairs. Suddenly he quickened his pace and broke into a run. A few moments later they saw him darting past the excited crowd of men and dashing into the engine room.

'He's going stark, staring cracked,' said Droste, shaking his head. 'I'm damned if I understand the kind of people they've dumped on us here. Well, boys—I'm going down now to try to get the men back to work. There! Look at that! Our people are joining that crowd of ruffians now.'

The engineers and artificers could be seen mingling with the excited group surrounding Girard.

'Stay here,' shouted Droste, 'and keep that revolver in your pocket. If we once start shooting, it will be all up with us.'

He hurried down the steps. Schmiedecke did not hesitate a moment about following him. Nothing could make him desert Droste. He had a fatherly affection for that clever young man and was certainly going to stand by him in the terrible danger which had suddenly come on him like a bolt from the blue and shattered the dream of a lifetime. Without a moment's thought, he rushed after him and overtook him on the landing platform. They could hear Girard's strident tones ringing out above the confused murmur of angry voices. He was gesticulating wildly and shouting at the top of his voice.

'They've enticed us on board this coffin,' he shouted, indicating with a contemptuous gesture the towering structures of the FP 1. 'But the blighters only brought a few days' food, so that we've got to starve. That's enterprise for you! Risking our lives for a pack of brainless idiots like that. Why, men, there are no boats. Even the smallest cockleshell of a ship has its proper number of boats that you can get into before the sharks get you. Well, boys, we needn't put up with it, and we won't. Have we sold our lives? No! We've only sold our labor!' Suddenly he caught sight of Droste and pointed derisively at him. 'And that young milksop over there! A blasted half-baked fledgling was put in command over us! No wonder there isn't sufficient food on board! Well, we'll take no more of his orders. We'll do what we can to get safely back to land, even if this floating coffin has to sink for it. We've had enough of Droste! I'm in command here now, and we'll have a different state of affairs, I can promise. Come on, lads; we'll make sure of our food, at any rate. Otherwise, it'll all be gone before we get there.'

His speech was punctuated by cries of approval from his audience. The men started to move away in the direction of the storehouses, but suddenly Droste sprang in amongst them, clearing a way for himself with his fists. In a twinkling of an eye, he had reached Girard and sent him spinning.

'Look here, men, will you listen to me for one minute. That's all I ask you. Do you think it's going to do you any good, behaving like this? We're only waiting for the mist to lift; then we'll be able to make signals with our searchlights. Look at 'em, boys,' and he raised his hand dramatically aloft. 'They can be seen for a hundred miles.'

Shouts that drowned his words were the only reply.

'If you plunder the stores,' shouted Droste, trying to make his voice heard above the uproar, 'there'll be absolutely nothing to eat, and in a few days you'll really starve. You've got to be reasonable. God knows you're not children. If you go on as you are doing, then so much the worse for you. Let me tell you that if you attempt to touch the stores, I'll take the strongest possible measures.'

'The dirty dog's threatening us,' screamed one of the men. 'Knock his blasted block off!' A score of fists were shaken in Droste's face, but he remained calm.

Künnecke and Sambach were standing next to Schmiedecke, and Droste, throwing a quick look round, saw Heinicke as well, standing beside two trusted workers from the Lennartz shipyards. Yes, these men would stand by him all right.

He again endeavored to address the men. 'Be reasonable,' he shouted. 'What do you really want? You know, it's your own fault. I've done everything I could. Why, didn't I even place the motor launch at your disposal, and wasn't it your own leader who let you down and tried to bolt in it himself? A nice fellow to put your trust in. I tell you again, there's no danger at the present moment if you behave reasonably, but if you don't, we shall all go under, and God help us!'

The tumult increased. 'He's only trying to make fools of us. The blighter wants to keep all the food for himself!' The men surged forward again, streaming in an irresistible wave towards the storerooms. They were going to make sure of the provisions while they had the chance.

'Any man who enters that door will be shot,' shouted Droste.

No one was listening to him, however. They were all scurrying along the landing platform, pushing each other and yelling, an angry, ugly, jostling mob.

Droste ran after them. He gave a sigh of relief as he saw that the doors of the great storerooms were shut. The maddened crowd thundered with their fists on the iron panels. Suddenly a shot rang out.

The doors flew open. Schmiedecke was standing in the narrow entrance with Künnecke and Hekker. All three held a revolver in each hand,

and at that dramatic moment the lighting current failed. The searchlights dimmed and the lights in the windows slowly faded. Thinner and fainter they grew, until they disappeared into the misty darkness.

Schmiedecke fortunately had the presence of mind to slam the doors shut again. Droste raced towards the engine house. He was so struck with horror at this new blow that his blood froze within him. What the devil could be wrong with the Diesel engines? The current had not been switched off. Some mysterious hand was surely at work. He rushed forward wildly, colliding against men in the darkness, cursing and swearing, until at last he came to the door of the engine room and tore it open. The inner door was barred. He flung himself against it with all his strength. It was so dark that he could not see his hand before his eyes, but he could hear men breathing near him.

'Open this damn' door,' shouted voices behind him. The whole crew seemed to have followed him.

'Get a crowbar—a crowbar, d'you hear,' gurgled a choking voice.

Droste was pressing against the door, but a heavy weight seemed to be crushing him. He gasped for breath. His ears sang. He could get no air. In a desperate struggle to breathe, he tore his collar open, and then sank down into the utter darkness of unconsciousness.

Chapter Sixteen: Terrible Uncertainty

The rays of the morning sun shone brightly over Fayal, turning the placid waters of the harbor into a lake of molten gold. It was not yet ten o'clock, but a shimmering heat haze hung low over the ground. The air was tremulous in the hot sun and already most of the inhabitants had sought the shelter of their shuttered houses, or lay listlessly in the shadows of archways. Not for them the fierce struggle for existence that is waged ceaselessly in less fortunate climes. Life in these happy isles was a much less serious business. The narrow cobbled streets of the little town were quite deserted. A solitary dog trotted past the hotel, paused a moment to nose about some garbage and finding by good luck an old bone, stretched its emaciated body contentedly in the friendly shadow of the wall.

Gisela, from the window of her room, gazed vacantly at it—the only living thing in sight. She awaited the return of Axel Ellissen impatiently. He had been gone a matter of four hours, and according to his own estimate, he should be back again in another four hours. He had decided that the FP 1 could only be found by a systematic search, assuming, of course, that it could not be farther than a thousand miles from Fayal. It was probable that it was much nearer, judging from the position which it had given in its last radio message. If the surrounding seas could be thoroughly searched in arcs of a circle radiating from its last known position, the FP 1 must be found—that is to say, if it had not already gone to the bottom. Before leaving, Ellissen had explained his plans to Gisela and had quite calmly and indifferently discussed the possible doom that might by this time have overtaken the crew of the FP 1. She had been struck by the change in him, for once again he was the intrepid airman, keen on his work and prepared to discuss with her enthusiastically the details of his plans.

'People are all too soft,' he had remarked. 'They attach too much importance to death. The main thing in life is not just being alive, but being active, doing something. If the FP 1 has already sunk—well, the spirit of progress has claimed many victims throughout the ages, and it must be always so.' So calmly had he spoken of the possibility of disaster that Gisela was prepared for the worst. Even the thought of Bernard Droste having met his death out there on his dream ship no longer distressed her. For the first time she was able to view death with a clear understanding as a necessary risk that any one who cared for science and the progress of humanity must incur.

And now she was waiting for Ellissen's return, not with anxiety, for Ellissen's courageous philosophy had to some extent banished any fear from her mind, although she was not sure within herself how long this new tranquillity would last.

She started as she suddenly heard her name called. A little boy approached her, and not without difficulty he made her understand that she was wanted on the telephone. She got up at once and followed the barefooted messenger, who hurried on before her down the narrow street and across the little square, on which the noonday sun beat down pitilessly.

'Here, miss!' said the boy, pointing to a dingy door above which hung a post-office sign.

She entered the small, stuffy room. Seated at a wooden table, was a black curly-haired Portuguese with magnificent mustachios. In front of him was a plate containing some sort of cooked vegetable which he appeared to be relishing immensely. He directed her with a nod to a corner, where she saw another man in a tattered uniform. He had an antiquated telephone receiver in his hand and he beckoned to her with an air of importance. It was not every day that the little post office had a long-distance call.

'Fayal, Azores. Fayal,' the man was saying excitedly into the mouthpiece. 'Is that Madrid? What? . . . Fayal speaking! Germany—Yes. Bremen? Is that Bremen? Fayal speaking!'

Gisela's hand shook as she took the receiver from the man.

'Speak clearly, madam,' said the official, pursing up his lips to show Gisela how it should be done. 'The connection is none too good. It's via Madrid.'

Gisela hesitated nervously, experiencing an overwhelming desire to hang up the receiver and rush out of the room. Fighting back the impulse, she listened attentively, and at last heard an indistinct voice. 'Madrid, Madrid speaking.' The line buzzed as if a thousand people were talking at the same time. 'Paris, Hullo-o-oh, Paris!' A penetrating feminine voice, followed by the murmur of a deep baritone repeating in a very comforting German voice, 'Bremen speaking. Is that Paris?' Madrid intervened, then the line crackled, and a deep sustained buzzing commenced.

'Father,' called Gisela. 'Father.' The men in the post-office room went on talking, without troubling to lower their voices. 'Father,' called Gisela again. The buzzing died away and she heard her father's voice quite clearly.

'Hullo, Gisela. Can you hear me?'

Gisela could not answer for a moment. Her excitement and emotion were too great. Then her words came in a rush. 'Is that you, Father? Ellissen has left already and is hoping to find the FP 1,' she said into the mouthpiece as clearly as she could. 'Don't worry, Father; it'll come all right.'

'Come all right,' echoed the voice at the other end of the long, long line. 'I'm meeting with more difficulties—payment—the bank, I'm afraid, is going to let me down. It's most important that Ellissen should hurry.'

'Yes, Father, I understand. You must hope for the best and be brave. So much depends on Ellissen, and I'm sure he won't fail us now.'

'Yes—' said the voice, fading into the distance, and Paris was on the line again. A buzzing sound again intervened. 'Madrid! Hullo, Madrid,' called Paris.

'Hullo!'

'Exchange, Exchange,' cried Gisela, pressing down the switch repeatedly, just as she did at home when she got a wrong number. 'Exchange, are you there?'

Madrid was on the line again, talking with Paris. The line clicked and ticked and coughed and spluttered. Hundreds of voices seemed to be murmuring.

'Exchange!' called Gisela desperately. Then the comforting German voice sounded again. 'One moment, miss,' said a man's voice, clear and reassuring. Far away, three thousand miles away, but none the less comforting. 'Just one moment, miss.' Ah, her father's voice again!

'Gisela. Thank goodness, I've got through to you again. If Ellissen can get any news to us within the next four days, everything will be all right.

D' you understand? I can hold out for another four days. After that, the contract date will be up and I'm pretty well certain that there's not the slightest chance of getting an extension—'

'I'm cutting you off,' said Paris.

'Is that Fayal?' asked Madrid.

'It'll be all right, Father. Ellissen will do it all right. Good-by, Father,' Gisela called over the line.

'Madrid, Madrid,' called Paris. The instrument rang shrilly, the sound throbbing through Gisela's head. The man in the ancient uniform snatched the receiver out of Gisela's hand and began to talk quickly into the mouthpiece, gesticulating at the same time.

Gisela took a step backwards and pressed her hands to her ears. It all seemed so strange, that aggravatingly short conversation with her father far away in Bremen.

'You found the connection good? Yes?' the official inquired politely, and nodded, beaming with satisfaction. 'A splendid connection with Bremen.'

'Yes, thank you!' said Gisela, smiling as in duty bound. 'Very good.' She politely refrained from telling him that the next time some one was making a long-distance call, he might refrain from speaking during the conversation. Somehow she hoped that she would never have occasion to use that most aggravating instrument again. It had been dreadful, almost torture. Why couldn't Ellissen have taken her with him to look for the FP 1? She felt so helpless here without him. No one could stand this waiting—this terrible uncertainty.

She walked slowly back to the little hotel in the blazing sunshine, thinking of Ellissen. What was he doing? One or two fishermen lounging in the shadow gazed wonderingly at her distraught face, but she kept on her way, not looking to the right or to the left.

CHAPTER SEVENTEEN: The Devil's Work

Darkness had already fallen when Ellissen at last entered the barroom of the little hotel. Gisela had heard the welcome sound of his propeller half an hour before, but she had remained in her room in spite of its almost unbearable sultriness, for she had not sufficient will power left to try to learn Ellissen's news sooner and thus put an end to the almost maddening uncertainty.

As she heard Ellissen's booming voice greeting the landlord downstairs, she felt a momentary annoyance that the deep and masculine voice was so unemotional, so unsympathetic. In any case she had waited so long for his return that now the crucial moment had come, her courage failed her. She listened. Ellissen was still in the barroom. Her annoyance increased. She sprang up and hurried downstairs. Ellissen was standing at the bar, a glass in his hand. He turned round slowly as she came in, nodded to her smilingly, and then turned to the landlord again. As he set down his glass, his hand shook violently. Wonderingly he examined his trembling fingers, then stuck them in his pocket, as if he wanted deliberately to conceal them.

'What's the matter? Are you hurt?' cried Gisela, looking at him with frightened eyes.

'This has never happened to me before,' Ellissen said, in a tone of genuine surprise. 'So you noticed that my hand was shaking, Gisela. I'm getting old, you know. I shouldn't feel like that at my time of life. Why, in another year, a flight of a couple of hours will be too big a job for me.' He smiled, but Gisela could see that the smile was forced.

'I'll go and sleep for three hours now. Then it will be daylight and I'll start again. I suppose you thought I'd bring you news already. Don't try and deny it, you little optimist! You think it's only a matter of one, two, three, and the thing's done. One has got to learn to wait, to be patient. Even a woman has to do that sometimes,' he added a little mockingly, looking at her anxious face. 'Come on, be cheerful,' he went on reassuringly. 'As long as Axel Ellissen hopes, there's hope!'

'Oh, I haven't given up hope,' said Gisela, forcing a smile. 'Of course, I didn't expect you would find the FP 1 right off, at your very first attempt. I—I wanted to ask you—Oh, it's so terrible to wait here—I simply can't stay here in this hotel and count the hours while you—Oh, do let me go with you! Please take me with you to-morrow.'

Ellissen raised his eyebrows. This was a very different Gisela from the frightened little girl that he had said good-by to that morning. He shook his head.

'You don't know what you're asking,' he said at last. 'It's quite on the cards we might not return, and I can assure you it's more unpleasant than waiting here. I should have thought you were comparatively free from feminine caprices. Some women are never happy unless they have a grievance.'

'You misunderstand me,' said Gisela. 'It's not hysteria. Waiting here is worse than death. You must take me with you, Mr Ellissen. I can't go through another day in this wretched place, waiting and wondering what's happening. I would much rather be doing something—sharing danger with you, I mean.' She stopped suddenly, ashamed of having said so much.

Ellissen looked at her with penetrating eyes. 'We'll start in three hours then,' he said quickly. 'At sunrise. Get my mechanic to explain to you anything that's necessary.' He nodded curtly and went out of the room.

Gisela waited a few moments, her heart beating wildly at the thrill which Ellissen's consent had given her. Thank heaven, at any rate tomorrow would be different, and she would be taking her share in the great adventure, instead of hanging about this wretched hotel, almost beside herself with anguish and anxiety. She slipped quietly out of the house, half afraid that he might return to alter his decision.

Ellissen's airplane was parked in a large field near the town. Gisela knew she could find it without much difficulty, and she set out at a rapid pace down the deserted main street. Soon she was climbing the steep incline that led from the town to the open country. Not a sound broke the stillness of the night except the distant surge of the breakers. Far below lay the harbor with its many twinkling lights, and beyond that stretched the illuminated waters of the Atlantic, holding somewhere in its vast expanse the secret of the FP 1.

She trudged on determinedly, impelled by an impulse that she could not explain, but which urged her to reach the airplane as soon as possible. Come what may, she would make certain that the airplane would not leave without her! Ellissen would have no opportunity to go back on his promise.

At a bend of the road, she suddenly glimpsed the red and green signal lamps of the airplane and could just make out its graceful lines as it rested—birdlike even in repose—in the great flat meadow which Ellissen had selected as an ideal landing ground. She guessed that Thornten, Ellissen's mechanic, was still at work, testing lights and engine, and indeed every stay and wire of the plane on which so much depended. A good man, Thornten, she said to herself,—queer in his manner and difficult to get on with, but trustworthy.

As she approached, Thornten climbed out of the cockpit and threw the beams of an electric torch in her direction.

'Who's there?' he called out challengingly. 'Good God, it's Miss Lennartz. What on earth's brought you out here at this time of night? Nothing wrong, I hope.'

'No, everything's all right, Thornten,' said Gisela. 'But I've news for you that may surprise you. I've had a talk to-night with Mr Ellissen, and he has promised to take me with him tomorrow—and you—well, I'm afraid you will have to stay behind.'

Thornten stared at her blankly. She was quite calm and collected and yet her voice thrilled with pleasure as she made her startling announcement.

'Well, I'm damned! That's the limit! Taking women with him. Reckon he must be going clean off his head. I always said he would. I know that type.'

'But Thornten—' Gisela couldn't refrain from smiling. 'You can't have anything against me?'

'Against you? Good Lord, no, miss!' Thornten shook his head. 'It's not that, but I've always said Mr Ellissen is determined to break his neck some day. I've told him that to his face more than once, but he only laughed at me. And now he's going to take you with him! Well, I think it's a mistake, you mark my words. Women on this here *terra firma* are all right, but women and airplanes just don't match. Oh, yes, I know you've flown from Germany, but this flight to-morrow is different. I daresay you know when you go up, but God only knows when you'll come down.'

'If Mr Ellissen is going to break his neck, as you say, then you can thank your stars you needn't be there as well.'

'I'm not thanking any stars, miss,' Thornten replied testily. 'All I says is I've been with him a good many years now and I thought he had given up risking his neck for other people, but I see he hasn't and of course I admire him for it. In any case, I could still have stood it for these few days more and seen this job through. However, if he doesn't want me—if he thinks that you can do it better—then he's welcome—' He began to gather his tools together in silence.

'Tell him that the plane's OK. The petrol tank's filled and if he wants anything he can send me a postcard. And he might remember to give me an honorable mention in his will. He won't leave me anything, of course!' he concluded maliciously, and moved away.

'Thornten!' called Gisela.

The mechanic, however, did not look round, but disappeared into the darkness, still grumbling to himself. It was impossible to tell to what extent he meant his remarks to be taken seriously. He was naturally grumpy without being intentionally rude. He got on very well with Ellissen as a rule, and often they argued with each other in their abrupt gruff manner, but Ellissen seemed to understand and like his eccentric mechanic.

More than a little nonplussed, Gisela waited a few moments. Not a sound broke the stillness. Thornten had utterly vanished. Well, why should she care what a half-witted mechanic thought. He was a bit queer in the head, that was all. She got into the airplane, balancing herself precariously as she clambered into the cockpit. She fastened the safety strap round herself, as if the flight was about to begin, and leaning back in the narrow seat looked up at the sky.

It was a starry night. Somehow the sky seemed brighter and nearer than it did at home. Wonderingly her eyes gazed at the stars, hundreds and thousands of stars, little worlds, some of them perhaps inhabited by strange forms of life. Could they be people like ourselves? She smiled at her whimsical fancy. But after all, was it not a colossal conceit to think that our little earth, a mere dot among the billions of stars that made up the universe, was the only one that had a moving, teeming life on its surface, beings who breathed, who could feel, think, love and hate?

Perhaps there is some one just like myself up there, thought Gisela. Some one on one of those stars millions of miles away staring into the sky just as I am, thinking the same thoughts, having similar troubles and similar hopes. Or perhaps there are two—Gisela smiled to herself—a couple like Bernard and me—who have said farewell to each other just as we have—farewell which may be for ever—and like us they cannot find words to express their feelings. Work comes between them—life work— so much to do, so little done. There is no time for mere words. Nothing happens once only, thought Gisela. Everything has a beginning and ultimately must find an ending. Our hopes and fears, all our little emotions, pass and are forgotten—and the world goes on. We make too little of our joys and too much of our sorrows, and the result is we always seem to be starving for a little happiness and surfeited with troubles.

She closed her eyes. She still saw the stars through her closed eyelids. A cool, fresh breeze blowing off the sea surged and sang in the wings of the plane. Gisela lost herself in her dreams and with a faint smile on her lips she slipped into a calm sleep.

'Thornten!' a powerful voice boomed out. She awoke and saw Ellissen standing by the airplane. He greeted her with a nod. 'Have you seen Thornten?' he called out, as if she were a hundred yards away. He did not give the slightest sign of surprise at seeing her in the plane.

It was daylight. Had she been asleep? For how long? It was surely only a minute since Thornten had limped off in the darkness.

'Thornten said everything was ready.' Gisela sat upright and looked down at Ellissen. 'He said he had done everything that was necessary and the plane was perfect. Then he went off to bed. Shall I fetch him?'

'Don't bother. I don't want him. So you have been sleeping in the plane? I suppose you thought I might regret my decision?'

Gisela nodded. That was just what she had thought.

'Well, let's be off. Our course is to the southwest!' cried Ellissen, getting into the plane. 'As the plane has a starter, I suppose Thornten thinks himself quite superfluous.'

He placed a long thin canvas bag carefully in the cockpit.

'Is that a rifle?' asked Gisela, surprised.

Ellissen nodded his head grimly. 'Yes, I've got into the habit of taking

FP 1 Does Not Reply

one with me on my flights. You never know what may happen. Supposing we had to come down on a desert island,' he added, with a laugh. 'It
might be useful to us. If we didn't want to starve, we would have to shoot
birds. By Jove, I should like to play Robinson Crusoe with you as a companion.' Ellissen laughed. He had slept well, and he seemed to Gisela as if
he had not a care in the whole wide world. Never had he seemed so full of
youthful spirits.

'All clear!' he shouted. The propeller started with a terrific roar and settled down to a deep, steady hum.

Gisela in reply put her hand on his shoulder, for her words were
drowned by the noise. The airplane taxied along the meadow, then rose
smoothly into the air. Fayal shrank under their feet, and the sea stretched
wide below—a limitless expanse of blue water, shining and dancing in
the light of the morning sun.

Some brown-sailed fishing boats lay in the harbor. A couple of small
steamers ploughed their way through the water, looking like flies struggling on a pond. The plane shot steeply upwards, the horizon sank away,
the earth seemed to contract. The coasts of the Azores faded in the dim
distance. They were alone in the cloudless sky. The propeller hummed.
The engine spluttered like the rattle of a machine gun, but Gisela was
quite unconscious of the noise. She stared intently in front of her, her eyes
fixed on Ellissen's broad back, her mind intent on this great adventure,
and all that it might mean to her. The plane obeyed the least touch of its
pilot's hand. It climbed higher and higher, until it seemed to be floating
over the sun, which had shot into the heavens to join in the race.

Gisela looked at her watch. They had been flying for nearly two hours
now. Not a trace of land, not a ship was to be seen. It seemed to her almost
as if they were standing still in their flight, that some giant power held
them fixed to the one spot, and the propeller was revolving impotently in
the soft, warm air.

Suddenly, however, the plane seemed to lose its even balance for a
moment. It swayed violently and then descended sheer towards the sea,
but Ellissen regained complete control over it without any difficulty.

'There's a leak in the reserve tank,' he shouted through the speaking
tube. 'I can't tell exactly, but the petrol supply must be getting low. We
must get back.'

He lifted the plane again in great spiral loops and turned its head towards land. Gisela trembled with excitement and anxiety. Her lips
moved in prayer. She was listening anxiously to a voice within her. She
believed that if she could only listen to the promptings of this inner

voice and understand what it told her, it would help her to find Bernard. She held her breath. Every stroke of the propeller increased the agony of mind she was enduring.

'Ellissen,' she called suddenly into the speaking tube, 'don't go back!'

Ellissen turned his head. 'What's the matter?' he shouted above the noise of the propeller.

'Don't go back; please don't go back. We are quite near,' Gisela cried again. She could not explain to him what prompted her. She put all her strength into her voice. He must listen to her, he must obey her.

'It can't be done, I tell you,' Ellissen shouted back. 'If we get a wind against us, we won't be able to make land, and we'll both be drowned! D'you hear me?'

'Please,' Gisela called again.

'To-morrow,' answered Ellissen, 'we'll fly over this same stretch again.'

Gisela hung tightly to the straps that held her in her seat. She sought feverishly for words to persuade him, to convince him that she was right. She pressed her lips together, concentrating all her will power.

With an exclamation of annoyance, Ellissen turned his head. 'You realize we may lose our lives through this?' he shouted into the speaking tube. Then he swung the plane round.

They flew in silence. Gisela felt with tremendous relief that the speed of the airplane had increased. It seemed to rush through space and she knew now that it was going towards its goal. She stared at a point on the far horizon and with trembling hands clutched her glasses, then put them down again, excitedly thinking she could see better without them. She raised them, however, again to her eyes. Yes, yes, she was sure!

'There,' cried Gisela, her voice cracking with emotion. 'There's the FP 1.'

Ellissen grasped his glasses.

'Exactly to the east,' Gisela continued, with her mouth to the speaking tube. Could it be that she had seen nothing? She had spoken automatically, without grasping the meaning of what she was saying. No, she was convinced it was the truth.

It might be a steamer, Ellissen decided, looking intently through his binoculars. He had discovered a long black object which lay like a streak on the water.

'It may be the FP 1, after all,' he went on, his voice growing excited. 'My God, I believe you're right! I see no smoke and no funnels.'

Gisela was sitting bolt upright in her seat, every muscle in her body rigid. She heard that still small voice within her again. Its promptings had never failed her. She knew now with certainty that it was the FP 1 and that it would only be a matter of a few minutes now until the wheels of the airplane touched its platform.

The great bulk of the FP 1 loomed larger. Already they could distinguish its massive pillars running deep into the sea, and the long flat buildings of the hotel and the power houses, with the high masts of the aërial standing out sharply. Nearer and nearer they came. It was rushing to meet them. Now they were above it, and the plane, after making a complete circle, descended rapidly, so that the landing platform seemed to be rising to meet them. Suddenly, however, Ellissen turned the nose of the plane upwards again.

'I don't see a soul,' he shouted. Again he swooped and flew along the platform from end to end. 'Not a soul,' he repeated. 'All very mysterious. The lookout surely is bound to have seen us.'

'They have all left,' thought Gisela, her heart sinking. 'They've abandoned the FP 1.'

'Hold tight,' called Ellissen. The plane approached the FP 1 again in a steep downward curve. Gisela clung to her seat. The giant masts and turrets of the deck structure seemed to rush past her, then the wheels of the plane touched the landing platform. Ellissen had judged the distance to a nicety, and the plane ran along for a short distance and came to a standstill.

Ellissen stood up and looked round him.

Not a soul to be seen anywhere.

Cupping his hands to his mouth, he sent out a long penetrating 'Hello-o-o!'

A shot rang out and a bullet whizzed past his head.

'Take cover,' roared Ellissen, pushing Gisela back into her seat.

A loud report sounded almost in her ear. She opened her eyes. Ellissen was standing up, holding his rifle ready to fire again. Then he dropped back into his seat and looked across at the hotel buildings. From the roof came a clattering noise, then a pane of glass shattered with a sharp crack, and a body crashed to the floor of the platform.

Ellissen looked all round. Still no one to be seen. He raised his rifle again. Noticing Gisela's startled expression, however, he turned to her.

'Don't stir,' he said between his clenched teeth. 'There's been the devil's work here.'

Chapter Eighteen: All Poisoned?

Ellissen jumped out of the airplane and stood prepared for any attack, rifle in hand.

The sun shone pitilessly down, and the dazzlingly white buildings of the FP 1 shimmered in the heat haze. An air of absolute peace and calm hung over the deserted landing platform. Ellissen looked up grimly at Gisela, who was still seated in the airplane. He seemed about to say something to her, but suddenly turned away and walked unconcernedly to the middle of the platform. He stood here apparently listening for something, but nothing stirred.

Gisela climbed out of the airplane and crouched below the fusilage. Ellissen glanced round, anxious for her safety, but turned away again as he saw that she was in a safe position, sheltered by the wheels. In a few moments he came back to her.

'You had better come with me,' he said briskly, motioning with his head for her to follow him. 'Walk behind me and watch the other building over there for any trouble.'

She did as she was told and followed close behind him in the shelter of his broad back.

'I think that must have been the only man about,' said Ellissen. 'It can't be a trap. They've had plenty of opportunity to shoot us if they wanted to!'

They had just reached the shattered window of the hotel when he seized Gisela's arm in so strong a grip that she involuntarily winced. He stopped suddenly and pointed to the huddled figure of a man which lay amongst the broken pieces of glass. She gave a little cry of horror.

'Don't be frightened,' he said coolly. 'That blighter can't do us any harm. There's no more danger to be feared from him.' As he pushed the broken glass on one side with his foot, Gisela clutched his arm.

'My God! Look at that!' she gasped. Ellissen himself was so startled at the sight before them that he blurted out an oath.

The head of the body which was lying at their feet had a gray snout like some repulsive animal, weird, round, glassy eyes which goggled up at them horribly.

'It's a gas mask,' said Elissen, after a second glance, in a tone of relief. He sniffed the air carefully to see whether he could detect the presence of gas.

'Don't look at him. He's not a very pleasant sight,' he said to Gisela, as he stooped over the dead man. But Gisela was now perfectly calm and collected. All feeling seemed dead in her. She was prepared for any horrors.

Ellissen pulled the gas mask off the dead man and revealed a fat face, blue and distorted, with thick swollen lips. He turned the body over, face downwards. Then he rolled it on to its back again.

'He must have been suffocated,' he said. 'I didn't shoot him. There's no sign of a bullet hole, and these scratches are the result of his fall.' He stared at Gisela doubtfully. He was thoroughly surprised and perturbed, and his mind was working feverishly, seeking some explanation of the mystery.

'He must have been wearing this gas mask for some time,' he continued. 'He would have been dead, even if he had not fallen. I believe he must have had a stroke. It looks like it. But why on earth did he keep on the gas mask?'

Ellissen stroked his chin in a puzzled manner, brooding over the incident.

'Let's go on,' said Gisela.

'Very well, then, but look out for the smell of gas,' said Ellissen. 'The best plan will be for one of us to enter the rooms alone and the other to wait until called. I'll take the mask with me. It might be useful.' He stooped down and took the gas mask from the body.

'You go in front,' he said to Gisela gruffly. 'That's the only way we can manage. You wouldn't care to put on the mask if I collapsed, and besides, you wouldn't have the strength to carry me out if I did. I could certainly put on the mask if necessary,' he added rather hesitatingly, examining the mask closely and noting with a grimace that there was a sticky streak of moisture over the mouth-piece.

Gisela stepped into a dark room. The switches were to the left of the entrance in all the rooms, she thought, recalling with startling clearness the plan of the hotel that she had seen. Her fingers groped along the wall in the darkness, found the switch and turned it on, but no light resulted. With an exclamation of annoyance, she felt her way to the farther side of the room, till her hands touched a small wheel, which she turned slowly. The shutters of a window opened, and the room was suddenly flooded with daylight.

'Mr Ellissen,' she called. 'Everything is all right in here.'

Ellissen entered and looked round the room carefully; then he nodded. 'Nobody here. Let's go on,' he grunted.

Gisela opened the door leading into the vestibule. It was very useful having the plan of the hotel in her head. She remembered it clearly—vestibule, ballroom on the left—card room on the right.

Ellissen stood in the doorway beside her, sniffing the air suspiciously. There seemed no trace of gas. 'I don't smell anything here,' he said irritably, the uncertainty and strain of the position evidently beginning to tell on him.

Gisela opened the shutters and let in the light. 'Be careful,' called Ellissen loudly, as his eyes made out a dim figure of a man crouched on the floor. He went over to the recumbent figure and turned him over on his back. The face was distorted in agony.

Ellissen felt the heart. 'He's still alive,' he said. He gently raised one of the man's eyelids and added, 'It looks as if he has been drugged. He must have had an overdose. Open the door, please.'

Gisela dashed to the door of the hotel and flung it open. Ellissen carried the man out into the fresh air and laid him down in the shadow of a deck awning.

'He'll come round, all right—at least, it's to be hoped so. There's nothing more we can do for him just now, so we'd better get on. Let's go.'

They went together into the card room and opened the shutters there. A terrible spectacle confronted their horrified eyes. A ghostly company of card players were sitting at the tables, cards still in their hands, a little heap of paper money lying before each of them. Their distorted faces were bowed on their chests, as if they had all fallen asleep in the midst of a game.

'Poor devils! We must open the windows as wide as possible,' said Ellissen, 'and get in fresh air.'

Gisela helped him to open the shutters of all the windows, and leaving the card room, they went up the staircase together.

'I can't make out what has happened,' confessed Ellissen. 'It beats me absolutely. I'm anxious to see whether these fellows will recover. I wonder if they have been poisoned.'

'Do you think they could all have been poisoned?' asked Gisela, in a cold, toneless voice. Her feelings were still completely numb from the shock, and she did not as yet appreciate the full horror of the situation.

'It certainly looks like it,' answered Ellissen. His mind was still searching for some explanation. Here was a mystery indeed, if ever there was one. How was it possible to send every one to sleep at the same moment? With gas? It must have been with gas, otherwise what was the explanation of the gas mask on the dead man?

Suddenly Gisela's nerves got the better of her. She could stand it no longer. Bernard was here, Bernard was among those sleepers—perhaps would never wake again. Somewhere he was lying unconscious, in need of her.

'Bernard,' she screamed at the top of her voice. She was about to dash away, with some vague idea of looking for him in her confused mind, but Ellissen stopped her.

'None of that,' he cried sternly, seizing her angrily by the arm. 'You must stay with me. We don't know what's wrong yet. Do you want to look for some one specially?' he added. 'If you are only patient, we'll find all aboard in time. At present, you must remember that one life is just as important as another.'

'I'm sorry; I forgot myself,' Gisela said with downcast eyes.

One by one all the rooms of the hotel were inspected. In one they found a man lying in bed unconscious, in another a man sprawling on a sofa, with the butt of a cigar in his mouth. In practically every room unconscious men were sitting and lying about everywhere, cramped and contorted. Many had their hands clutching their throats, as though they had awakened for a moment, semi-conscious, gasping for air. In one spot a number were lying one on top of the other like a pile of carelessly heaped soiled linen. All had the same ghastly expression of horror about their twisted mouths, the same distorted faces and tightly clenched fists.

Gisela walked bravely past all these silent figures, clinging tightly to Ellissen.

In the kitchen the cooks, dressed in white, lay around their cooking stoves. In one corner crouched the huddled-up figure of a boy with a blue apron round him, and a shoe which he had been cleaning still in his hand. He was snoring heavily; a queer rattling noise came from his throat. His face, like those of the others, was horribly distorted. Ellissen was forcibly reminded of a gallery of waxworks he had visited in his youth, where the wax figures had a clockwork contrivance inside them which made their chests move realistically as if they were actually breathing.

At last they completed their tour of inspection of the rooms.

'How many men were there on the FP 1?' asked Ellissen.

'There were sixty on the hotel staff alone—perhaps more. They were to get everything ready for the arrival of guests. That's why they were on board. And there were twenty or thirty engineers, and—'

'Who else?' asked Ellissen sharply.

'Bernard,' said Gisela in a low voice.

'Who the devil is Bernard?'

'Bernard Droste,' explained Gisela. 'The commander.'

Ellissen grunted. At last the search of the long main corridor of the hotel was completed.

'That seems to account for pretty well all of the hotel staff,' said Ellissen, as they walked through the kitchen. 'I think they'll come round all right. It's like the old fairy tale of the "Sleeping Beauty".' He smiled quite cheerfully, as if he had made the welcome discovery that it had all been a fairy tale specially staged for his amusement. 'Exactly like the "Sleeping Beauty",' he repeated, and laughed. 'Quite a satisfying explanation of the mystery!'

Death and all the dreadful sights they had seen had evidently made no impression on him, thought Gisela. She could not understand the complete change in his mood.

'Even the head chef was there all right, and I'll bet when he wakes up, that kitchen boy will get a box on the ears!' went on Ellissen in the same ridiculous strain.

'I don't think your jokes are very well timed,' said Gisela, smiling in spite of herself.

'I'm only saying these things to keep our minds off more serious matters. After all, we must keep our spirits up,' said Ellissen, growing serious again. 'But let's go on. It's funny we don't notice any odor of gas about.'

Gisela's unnatural calm broke. Once again she imagined a voice within her, calling, calling, calling. She knew it must be Bernard, and led by some blind instinct, she hurried off to seek for him, hastening her steps as she heard Ellissen shouting after her. Breathless, she came to a door, flung it open, and ran up a narrow staircase as fast as she could.

Her heart was throbbing wildly. The stairs seemed endless. She came at last to a door which she knew led into the commander's room in the turret. She flung it open and saw Droste sitting at his desk, the telephone receiver in his hand, his head bowed on one arm.

With a cry of anguish, Gisela rushed up to him, clasped his head to her breast, and put ear to his mouth. Thank God, he was still breathing, though almost imperceptibly.

'Bernard,' she cried, looking into his face. A groan behind her made her start. She looked round and saw the body of a big, burly man, who had obviously slipped from a chair that stood near him. He lay where he had fallen, staring with unseeing eyes at the ceiling.

'Schmiedecke!' she cried in astonishment. Even he, faithful old Schmiedecke, had not been able to protect Bernard, for whom, she was sure, he would have given his life.

'For God's sake, come quickly, Mr Ellissen,' cried Gisela, still holding Bernard's head in her hands.

Ellissen appeared in the doorway and stood watching her dumbfounded. He came over to her and, drawing back Droste's head, looked grimly at his unconscious face.

'Well, we must try to bring him round,' he said, after a pause. Her belief in Ellissen's powers gave her renewed hope. He was so self-confident he could even joke in the presence of death. She felt sure that he would be able to bring Bernard back to life.

He at once set to work, raising Droste's arms up and pressing them down against his chest. Minutes passed slowly before a deep sigh came from Droste's lips.

'That's good,' Ellissen said, without looking up. 'Straighten his legs.'

Droste groaned again. Gradually a little color came back into his face. At last he opened his eyes slowly and stared vacantly at Gisela.

'Thank God, his consciousness is returning. But his mind is still a blank,' Ellissen cried, continuing to work his arms up and down. Manfully he labored for some time, and then, with perspiration running down his face, he ceased his exertions. 'He'll soon come round now,' he announced.

Gisela bent low over Droste and whispered 'Bernard' in his ear.

'It would be much better for him if you left him alone,' remarked Ellissen abruptly, and he rose to his feet. He went over to the helpless Schmiedecke and turned him on his back.

Droste's senses appeared to be returning. His lips moved.

'Ellissen,' he gasped, struggling for breath, then he turned his head. 'Gisela!' He made an effort to get to his feet, but sank back with a groan.

'You must rest—rest—rest. Can you hear me? Don't you understand,' said Gisela, looking furtively across the room at Ellissen, who was now practising artificial respiration on Schmiedecke. She thought she detected a frown on his face. Apparently he took no further interest in Droste, once he had performed the necessary task of restoring animation to his seemingly lifeless body.

'Gisela.' The whisper came again from Droste, who was struggling to get to his feet. He passed his hand over his face with a vacant look.

'Let him sit down on a chair and come and help me over here. That would be far more sensible,' barked Ellissen, glaring at her. Then he bent again over Schmiedecke. 'By Jove, this fellow has a perfectly marvellous chest—marvellous!'

Chapter Nineteen: An Inexplicable Offer

Miss Helm, Lennartz's secretary, held the cablegram doubtfully and anxiously to her short-sighted eyes. She turned to the telephone switchboard and began to press the knobs, calling up the various sections of the ship-yards in search of her employer. She met with no success until eventually she tried the wireless room.

'Some one is looking for you, Mr Lennartz,' said the wireless operator, after answering Miss Helm's call. He handed over the receiver to Lennartz, who was sitting beside him, put the head 'phones over his ears again and slowly turned the synchronizer.

'Please inquire what they are wanting, Emmerich,' replied Lennartz, but as the young man went to take the receiver from him, he altered his mind, as though ashamed of his momentary weakness, and began to speak into the 'phone himself.

'A message from the Azores,' said Miss Helm's voice, 'signed Thornten.'

'Oh, yes, Thornten; Ellissen's mechanic,' answered Lennartz. 'Is it bad news?'

There was a pause before Miss Helm answered, then she read the telegram: '"Ellissen overdue ten hours. Wire instructions."'

Lennartz received the news in silence. Why had Thornten cabled and not Gisela? He wished he could find an answer to that question.

'Thank you very much, Miss Helm,' he said, after a moment. 'Don't mention this to any one, please.'

Miss Helm rang off. She was depressed at the news, but she felt rather aggrieved. What could Mr Lennartz think of her, telling her not to mention it, as if she were likely to do so. It was most unnecessary of him. She adjusted her eyeglasses carefully, a habit she had when agitated, and suddenly looking up, saw Pechtold in front of her desk, just leaning over to pick up the telegram.

She was, however, quicker than Pechtold and removed it out of reach. An old feud existed between them, and she disliked him wholeheartedly.

'What's that?' asked Pechtold overbearingly. 'Is it news?'

She bent over her machine and shook her head without making any answer. He knew that he could not make Miss Helm speak once she had made up her mind not to, so he went away.

He went towards the wireless room, wondering what was happening behind the scenes.

'Shall I keep on trying, Mr Lennartz?' asked Emmerich. He was a slight, almost delicate-looking young fellow, a protégé of Droste's, who had known him from his schooldays and had given him his present position. Emmerich could be thoroughly trusted. He was one of the many men holding positions in the yards on whom Droste knew he could absolutely rely without any fear of being let down or disappointed in any way.

It's no good his trying any more, thought Lennartz. He has been sitting here for two days, trying in vain to get the FP 1. Now Ellissen is also missing. Why wasn't that cablegram signed by Gisela, he asked himself again distractedly.

'You'll never get the FP 1,' said Lennartz aloud. Emmerich sat up and his face flushed with emotion.

'I'll get them, all right,' he said. 'For the moment the FP 1 isn't calling, but I'll catch the first signal, if I stay here till I drop!'

'I'll send some one to relieve you,' said Lennartz kindly.

Emmerich shook his head. 'There's no question of that, Mr Lennartz. Mr

Droste knows that I am on duty here—and as long as I'm here, there's a good chance of our finding them,' he answered firmly, with a touch of pride in his voice.

The door opened and Pechtold appeared.

'I've been looking for you the whole morning, Mr Lennartz. An official from the bank sent word that he would call about midday. I arranged with him for one o'clock. I must apologize for having made the appointment without consulting you.'

'Who is it?' asked Lennartz sharply.

'Arnhem, one of the directors.'

'Arnhem from the bank! By Jove, I knew they'd make difficulties.'

Lennartz stood up, determination showing in every muscle of his face. This was going to be a fight to the finish, and he was ready for it, but the question why Gisela had not signed the telegram tormented him.

'I don't think there's anything in it,' replied Pechtold with indifference. 'Probably one of the usual routine calls that banks are so fond of, and they want to lend weight and importance to it by sending a big noise.

'By the way, what news have you of the FP 1? Have you got into touch with them yet, Emmerich?'

Emmerich made no reply. He had the same dislike for Pechtold as Miss Helm had.

'We're not in touch yet,' said Lennartz hastily. 'I should like a talk with you, Pechtold. Will you come to my room?'

They went to his private office and Lennartz sank heavily into the big chair at his desk. 'Ellissen is overdue!' he said with some hesitation.

Pechtold started. 'Ellissen! You have had news then. How long is he overdue?' He thought of the cablegram he had seen in Miss Helm's hand. Hansly must be informed at once. Ellissen missing now! Things were certainly going badly for Lennartz.

'Who sent the cablegram?' asked Pechtold cautiously. 'Your daughter? Is she coming back? Will she report Ellissen's disappearance to the authorities out there?'

'I'm in considerable doubt as to what should be done. You know, we must be careful with the Portuguese. They have that agreement with France, stipulating that only French airships may land in the Azores for the purposes of overseas air traffic. Besides, you may be sure that by the time they had jogged their officials to take action—you know how slowly they move—there would be nothing left to find.'

They sat looking at each other in silence for a time.

'It was Thornten who cabled,' said Lennartz at last, keeping his eyes fixed on a picture of the launch of a steamer that hung on the opposite wall.

'Was Ellissen flying alone?' asked Pechtold. 'Or who could have been flying with him?' He stopped, inwardly aghast at the thought that occurred to him. Even if he was a man who stuck at nothing to gain his end, still he had not wanted the girl involved; he had not meant her life to be endangered, or anything to happen to her. Could she have accompanied Ellissen in his flight? She was not a person who could bear to be idle or who was afraid to take risks. Why the devil did Lennartz sit there so apathetically? Hadn't the same thought struck him, that his daughter might have gone with Ellissen and Thornten had remained behind? But whatever Lennartz's thought, he showed no trace of agitation.

'Miss Helm,' called Lennartz.

The secretary appeared in the doorway.

'Cable "Urgently request news of Gisela Lennartz. Will try to arrange other matter from here." Address the cable to Thornten.'

Lennartz nodded, and Miss Helm closed the door. She took her eyeglasses off again and began to polish them. That was the third time that day that they had got dim. She wiped her eyes. Tears prevented her from reading the lines which she had just taken down.

'What more can one do?' asked Lennartz.

Pechtold shrugged his shoulders. Was the old shipbuilder really so cold-blooded, or was he exercising marvellous self-control? It seemed quite clear that his daughter must have accompanied Ellissen in the airplane from the Azores. He surely ought to show some sentiment, some sign of emotion.

Pechtold felt consumed with rage and hate as he gazed at the impassive face before him. What was going on behind that mask? He felt there might be an element of surprise behind Lennartz's reserve. The only safe course was to ruin him absolutely, not to let him compromise with Hansly; get him completely in his power. Then, by God, when I change places with him, he thought, I'll treat him as condescendingly as he's treating me.

'I should like to persuade myself that Arnhem is only coming here as a matter of form,' he said. 'One never knows with banks. They begin to make difficulties when the whole matter appears settled.'

'What do you mean by that?' asked Lennartz sharply. Pechtold was startled. He ought not to have said a thing like that. It might make Lennartz suspicious.

'That's merely my purely private opinion, of course,' he said, pretending to be aggrieved at Lennartz's abruptness. 'Now for the other matter—the supply ship. I'll have to send a message to her captain. Shall he bring her back if he doesn't meet the FP 1 at the anchoring place? I'll give him instructions—'

'You'll do nothing of the kind. You will give no instructions, please,' interrupted Lennartz sharply, rising to his feet. 'The steamer is to wait till the FP 1 arrives. She's not to move from the spot.'

'Even if—' began Pechtold, trying to offer an objection.

'Even if she lies there for months!' Lennartz sat down again and began to write, without taking any further notice of Pechtold, who waited for a moment, then bowed and went to the door. That will cost you something, Lennartz, he thought, as he left the room.

As soon as Pechtold had gone, Miss Helm knocked gently and entered. She looked thoroughly upset. Even her usual prim appearance was slightly dishevelled.

Lennartz looked up. 'What is it, Miss Helm?' he asked kindly, laying aside his pen.

'I—I wanted to ask—I beg your pardon, Mr Lennartz—but the cablegram to Thornten—it can't be possible that our Miss Gisela is with Mr Ellissen in the airplane.' She took out a small handkerchief and blew her nose violently, which seemed to soothe her feelings.

'We must try and be brave, Miss Helm,' replied Lennartz, smiling gravely. 'We must wait and not lose our heads. It can't be so bad as it seems. I'm sure that everything will come right in the end.'

Miss Helm blew her nose again vigorously and drew a long breath, because she always got hiccups when she cried. Then she said in her usual calm voice:

'I beg your pardon, Mr Lennartz. I forgot to tell you that Mr Arnhem is waiting. I asked him to wait because Pechtold was with you.'

'Oh,' said Lennartz, leaning back in his armchair. 'Show him in.'

Miss Helm went out, her handkerchief pressed to her mouth. A moment later she ushered Arnhem into the room. The banker shook hands with Lennartz and seated himself comfortably in an armchair, accepting the cigar which Lennartz offered him. He was slightly distressed at the prospect of the coming interview. He was a fat, good-natured little man, who had known Lennartz for many years, and it was going to be deucedly awkward.

While Arnhem was settling himself and lighting his cigar, Lennartz's mind was working rapidly. He knew he would require all his cleverness and astuteness at this interview, for the fate of his shipyards depended on the good will of the bank.

Arnhem contemplated his cigar thoughtfully. 'The last installment of the loan we are advancing you is due on the nineteenth,' he remarked, as a sort of opening move.

Lennartz nodded.

'The bank has sent me,' continued Arnhem; 'I'm only a minor official, of course, and they always send me when they have something unpleasant to communicate. I hope you won't feel a grudge against me for my mission, Mr Lennartz!' He made a deprecating gesture, then took a long pull at his cigar and slowly emitted a stream of smoke into the air, as if trying to gain time.

'Are you going to make difficulties?' asked Lennartz coldly.

'*I* am not,' said Arnhem sympathetically. 'Please don't attribute the bank's actions to me.'

'You know, Mr Arnhem, I have to pay my employees and workmen punctually. I made an agreement with your bank and you undertook to place at my disposal the sums I wanted on fixed dates. My workmen can't be asked to wait for their wages. I must pay them.'

Arnhem sighed. 'You look too far ahead, Mr Lennartz. You are too pessimistic. I only want to prepare you for our requiring some further guarantee, that otherwise possibly—'

'I know what your "possibly" means,' retorted Lennartz excitedly. 'Your "possibly" means an already accomplished fact. I will sue you and force you to pay. The agreement is binding, and I'll hold your bank responsible for any loss that I sustain!'

'Mr Lennartz, don't talk of going to law. Litigation is a long and costly business and it's no good to any one except the lawyers. You need money at once and if you take action against us, it will be all the longer, even if you succeed, before you can get the money.'

Lennartz grunted. 'Well, what do you want me to do?'

Arnhem fidgeted with his cigar. 'We have learned,' he said, 'that you are no longer in touch with the FP 1, and that you have commissioned Ellissen, the well-known aviator, to look for it. In other words—'

'Your intelligence service works very well. You know almost more than I do!' Lennartz interrupted ironically.

'Well, in other words, the valuable consideration for our credit to you is not available at the moment.' He laughed as if he had made a good joke. 'And the government won't pay a penny for a thing that is not delivered. There are only a very few days now until the twenty-second.'

'I understand that perfectly well,' said Lennartz calmly. 'But what have you come to suggest that I should do?'

'Well, I believe you've had an offer from Hansly,' Arnhem went on. 'Now if we had Hansly's endorsement, we would place any sum at your disposal!'

Lennartz shook his head.

'You forget that we had to raise the money ourselves first.' Arnhem leaned back in his chair, crossed his legs, and narrowed his eyes, as if he

were making some intricate calculation. 'Our principal, of course, re-
quires the same guarantees from us as we require from you.'

'Then Hansly is your principal, I suppose?' queried Lennartz ironically.
Dammit, he saw now the web that had been woven round him.

Arnhem shrugged his shoulders. 'I'm not empowered to give you any
information on that point,' he answered in a low tone.

'I understand it now,' said Lennartz icily. 'I have borrowed money and
it was Hansly's money. Now Hansly is trying to squeeze me. He wants to
force me to come to terms with him. There are other things which have
happened that I am sure can be put down to Hansly's account also. But,
by God! I'll show him that I know it too, some day!'

'If you have any opportunity to do so,' suggested Arnhem. 'As things
are at the moment, Mr Lennartz, it's a bad business, a very bad business.'
He flung out his hands in a gesture of hopelessness. 'If I could, I would
lend you the money myself as a private transaction.'

Lennartz bowed slightly. 'I can only thank you for the good will you
express.'

Arnhem rose to his feet and picked up his hat. 'I am, unfortunately, not
one of the chief directors,' he said. 'My powers may be limited, but my
hands aren't completely tied, and if the nineteenth comes and you want
money, I might know somebody who would let you have it.'

'At one hundred per cent interest?' queried Lennartz bitterly.

Arnhem turned red. 'You misjudge me.' He laughed awkwardly. 'I can't
blame you for it. I should probably have said the same myself in your position. But if you have news by the nineteenth, if you're sure that the FP 1
will be anchored on the twenty-second—I know you wouldn't mislead
me, we have known each other too long—' He held out his hand, and
added in a whisper, I'll ask nine and one-half per cent, not one hundred.'

'Thank you. I don't understand your making such an offer,' said
Lennartz, hope reviving in him.

'But I understand myself thoroughly,' remarked Arnhem quietly. 'I
must tell you honestly I'm not doing it for your sake only, by any means.
Our business transactions sometimes are'—he made a gesture of disgust—'I have wanted for years to carry through a good, honest, old-
fashioned business transaction once again, for my own pleasure.' He
pressed Lennartz's hand and took his departure.

Chapter Twenty: Death May Be Near

'Droste,' Schmiedecke spoke anxiously, 'you're still looking paler than
any of us. Why don't you go and lie down for a couple of hours? Every-

thing is pretty well in order now, and every one's been got out into the fresh air. That damned stuff doesn't seem to have had any after effects.' He made a wry face at the thought of the gas. His face, however, was still pale and his skin had a greenish tinge.

Droste leaned against the wall of the engine room. 'God, I'd like to know what did happen,' he said distractedly. 'The door of the engine house was barred and bolted, and Girard was in there, gassed like everybody else. The Diesel engines aren't running. I must go down at once and see about them.' He turned to go, but his legs gave way and he collapsed. Schmiedecke hurried towards him and picked him up, panting as he did so, for the weight was almost too much for him in his weak state. He tried to drag him to a couch, but his strength gave out and he cried for help.

Gisela rushed in. 'Is it Bernard?' she cried. 'Oh, let me help you, Schmiedecke. No, you mustn't try to carry him yourself. I'll take his feet. Be sensible. What good will it do us if you collapse too. Here we are. Bring him in here.'

They laid Droste on the bed in his own room. In a few moments he came to and stared at Schmiedecke and Gisela in a dazed sort of way. He struggled to get up.

'I thought you had more sense,' Gisela rebuked him. 'It's very foolish of you, when you are so sick, to try to go about and do things.' She gently pushed him back on to the pillows. 'Stay with him and see that he keeps to his bed,' she said to Schmiedecke, and hurried from the room.

'I'm damned if I'm going to lie here like a sick dog,' said Droste, as soon as she was gone.

'That's right, you say what you like, but I'm jolly well going to see that you take things easy. Now do be sensible,' begged Schmiedecke. 'I'll take off your boots, at any rate, whether you like it or not. Lie down for an hour, at least, and then I'll lie down and you can relieve me. There's nothing to be lost by your closing your eyes for a couple of minutes.'

Droste lay back. 'Very well,' he said, 'you're all too strong for me. But remember about the Diesel engines. Why aren't they running? The flooding valves are still open, Schmiedecke. Dammit, man, we must have taken in more than thirty thousand tons of water long ago. If we don't shut them soon, we'll go to the bottom, and how the devil are we going to close them without the engines.'

'Be quiet!' Schmiedecke spoke gruffly. 'A couple of hours don't matter yet. When you're on your legs again properly, we'll soon find a way out. The accumulators are charged. There will be sufficient power in them to close the valves.'

'Oh, yes, the accumulators,' said Droste. 'That's a relief. They'll do the trick, all right.'

Gisela came in with a bottle of whisky and a couple of glasses. 'There's nothing left in the stores,' she said excitedly, as she poured out some whisky for the two men. 'I've just been down there, and the storeroom looks like a grocer's shop that has just been looted. Why don't you lie down too, Schmiedecke? You look just about done in,' she added.

Schmiedecke passed his hand over his face, at the same time winking at Gisela. 'I'll do that later. I'm going to take the watch until Droste relieves me.'

'That's very good of you, Schmiedecke. If you feel fit enough,' said Gisela, nodding to Schmiedecke, to show him that she understood. 'You take the watch, then, and Bernard will relieve you in a couple of hours.'

The sound of Schmiedecke's heavy footsteps receded in the distance. Gisela and Droste were alone together. She looked with concern at his haggard face, as he lay staring up at the ceiling of the room.

'Won't you try to sleep, Bernard?' she asked in a low tone. 'You really ought to try and doze off. It would be the best possible thing for you just now.' She drew the blind as she spoke.

Droste made a feeble motion with his hand. 'Leave the blind, Gisela. I like to have light. I'm very glad to see you sitting near me. I don't want to sleep.' He still breathed heavily through his open mouth.

Gently she laid her hand on his forehead, and he closed his eyes. She sat like this for a long time, studying his pale, drawn face. Just as she thought he had at last fallen asleep, his lips moved.

'Gisela,' he whispered, without opening his eyes. 'Do you know, I'm a very lucky man. I begged and prayed that you might sit beside me just once and lay your hand on my forehead, and I've got my prayer. Now I feel everything will come right.'

'Don't talk; please don't talk. Try to sleep,' said Gisela reprovingly, but there was happiness in her voice.

'I have treated you very badly—no, you needn't shake your head—I have neglected you and devoted all my time to my work. I didn't know—' He paused and sought for words. 'Happiness doesn't lie in work alone, Gisela, but I didn't realize that.'

He has broken through his reserve at last, she thought. I never really understood how reticent he was where he or his work was concerned. I ought to have helped him more.

'Gisela, d' you understand? I feel such a criminal,' he went on. 'I feel as if I had wished you to be here and that's what has brought you into this danger. For you know we are in danger. We may all be drowned.'

Suddenly a thought struck him. 'Ellissen's plane has some petrol left. You must fly black with him. Promise me to go at once. I can't bear you to stay any longer on the FP 1. We don't know what's going to happen, and you mustn't remain in this danger.'

'Very well, Bernard,' Gisela answered quietly. There was no need for him to know yet that there was very little petrol left in the plane, certainly not enough for such a long flight. At least, she was with him now, and fate was indeed kind to prevent her leaving him.

'I have always loved you dearly, Gisela. You know that. Only I couldn't just express it. I'm so stiff and awkward, not much good at talking and saying things, but now I feel I can speak of my love for you. Tell me, Gisela, have you never guessed it? Have I always appeared to you cold and unkind?' he asked excitedly.

'I have always known that you loved me, Bernard.'

Droste sighed, relieved.

'It's strange. I'm glad now that everything has turned out as it has, for I can see all this had to happen to bring about my happiness. What an egotist I am! I've never had time,' he laughed, contemptuous of himself; 'time has always seemed to fly. I was always working, and I never had enough time to do everything I thought I had to do. Now I can see that that idea of there being so much to be done and so much haste needed is all nonsense. It's wrong to live that way, you know. We might just as well take things easy and remember we are human beings with our own lives to live to the best possible advantage. Rushing about doing things, working for other people, makes us overlook the most important things in life. We pass them by without seeing them. Don't you think a man is happier, Gisela, if he lives quietly for himself and those he loves, even if he dies without having done anything in particular? That to me is the best life. Don't you think that to be human we ought to take time to get to know ourselves? Don't you think so, Gisela?' He sat up and looked at her with feverish, excited eyes.

'Yes, I do. We certainly have a duty to ourselves as well as to other people,' Gisela answered soothingly, and she gently drew him down on to the pillows again. She took his hot face between her hands and kissed him tenderly. Droste put his arm around her shoulders. This was the fulfillment of his dream. Now he had not lived in vain, even if death were near. Love, which he had so blindly, so scornfully ignored, had come into his life at last. She was content to rest there, feeling the comforting protection of his arms; but uneasily conscious of some one's gaze, she turned around and saw the tall figure of Ellissen framed in the doorway. He stared at her as she raised her head. His hands were pressed against the doorposts, and the muscles of his arms stiffened so that he seemed almost to press them apart. His face looked pale, and yet absolutely impassive. She could not tell what terrible thoughts were passing through his mind.

'Mr Ellissen,' she cried, breaking the tension. 'Will you pull down the blind, please. The sun is rather strong in here.'

Ellissen looked at her blankly, then he turned away abruptly as though he had not heard her request. He slammed the door behind him, and the sound of his retreating footsteps fell heavily on the silence.

She looked at Droste, but he appeared to have at last fallen asleep.

Chapter Twenty-One: Imminent Danger

There was a sound of quick footsteps running up the stairs, and Sambach burst excitedly into the room.

'Mr—Mr Droste,' he stammered, dropping into a chair. 'What's to be done? Those swine have raided the stores, cleared out everything. They started the moment they had come round from the gas. I tried to stop them, but it was no good. I can hardly keep on my legs myself.'

Droste sprang up. 'Stay here, Gisela.' He was feverishly flushed, but otherwise seemed to Gisela to be rested and refreshed. 'Where the devil's Schmiedecke got to? Isn't it time he was coming off his watch?' he said to Sambach, pulling on his boots as he spoke.

'You must take care of yourself, Bernard,' put in Gisela.

He looked at her tenderly for a moment. 'I'm quite all right again. Come along! We must find Ellissen too. Where can he be?'

They dashed out and a moment after Gisela saw them running across the platform towards the storeroom.

'Ellissen! Ellissen!' shouted Droste as he ran. He suddenly caught sight of Ellissen standing in front of his airplane with his rifle in his hand, keeping at bay an angry crowd of men who swarmed in front of the plane.

'Now listen, you men. I've still eight shots in the magazine,' shouted Ellissen, 'and the first man that comes a step nearer will get a bullet through him. Have a little sense. There's hardly any petrol left in the tanks of my plane, so I can't get away myself.'

'Lies! A pack of dirty lies, that's all,' cried a voice, high-pitched with excitement. 'He wanted to get the woman on board again and clear out and leave us in the lurch, the dirty dog. Come on, we'll stop that!'

The speaker felt his shoulder roughly gripped. He looked round and saw Droste beside him in the middle of the crowd.

'Do you think you can pilot an airplane, you fool?' asked Droste threateningly. 'If any one has a right to get away in the plane it certainly isn't you.

What have you got there? You damned swine, you've been raiding the stores.' He snatched a package from the man's hands, out of which some tins of preserved food fell.

'You're a pack of silly idiots,' shouted Droste, beside himself with anger. 'You seem determined not to give yourselves a chance. Do you think it will do you any good stealing food like this? When it gets short, you'll only be fighting among yourselves. Now listen to me. I'm still commander here, and I'm damn' well going to see that my orders are obeyed. Hand back all the stuff you've taken from the storehouse. Everything has got to be properly rationed. As far as I'm concerned, you can appoint a couple of men to see that the stuff is replaced. And mark this, none of you can have the plane. It's here to fetch help for us all.'

He turned his back contemptuously on the men, who slowly scattered, muttering to themselves. Droste found himself alone with Ellissen. He turned to him and said in a low voice, 'Is it true, Ellissen, that you haven't any petrol?'

'Well, you couldn't get far with what I've got. The most you could do would be to try to find a ship. There certainly isn't enough to get to the Azores,' Ellissen answered, in a surly voice. He walked away, deliberately ignoring Droste's presence. The commander stared at Ellissen's retreating figure in astonishment.

'So that's that,' he said to himself. 'Well, dammit,' and he turned on his heel and went towards the engine rooms.

Schmiedecke was standing by the Diesel engines, a large screwdriver in his hand, while Girard appeared to be testing the switchboard.

'Look here, Girard,' called Droste. 'Go to your room at once. You're not to come near the engines again until I have spoken to you.'

Girard threw a side glance full of venom at Droste and left the room without a word.

'Well, have you found what's wrong?' asked Droste.

Schmiedecke nodded and came slowly down the ladder from which he had been examining the Diesel engines.

'Of course, it's just as I thought,' grunted Schmiedecke. 'Just plain blank sabotage. As plain as a pikestaff. No attempt to hide it. Look what I've just found here. The discharge valves of the fuel suppliers have been removed,—taken out of both engines.'

'The discharge valves,' cried Droste, startled. 'Haven't we spare ones?'

Schmiedecke looked at his commander almost pityingly. 'You can bet your bottom dollar they have gone too! God! It's enough to make a man swear for a week! Look at these enormous engines. Beauties, aren't they?

And all lying useless now. I can do nothing with them. Just because a few miserable little valves are missing!'

Droste walked up and down the engine room. He halted suddenly. 'Schmiedecke,' he said, in a tense voice, 'we're slowly but surely taking in water. We must have taken in over forty thousand tons already.'

'Sure,' answered Schmiedecke, unconcerned. 'We take in a thousand tons an hour. It was at your orders, anyhow, that I opened the flooding valves in the first place.'

'Well, dammit, man, switch on the accumulators and close them. It's very lucky the accumulators are fully charged. The rogues we are up against aren't so clever as they think they are. We'll do them down yet.'

Striding across to the switchboard, Schmiedecke pressed three levers, one after the other, at the same time watching the dials of the gauges which were above the levers.

'Droste!' he cried. 'Droste!' His voice rose to a hoarse shout. He was working one of the levers wildly up and down. He let it go, tapped the ampere gauge and pointed to the dial with a trembling hand. The hand of the indicator was lying askew across the bottom of the glass front. It had obviously been broken off and replaced to appear as if in order.

Droste hurriedly tested all the gauges in turn, giving a rap on each dial. In every case the indicator promptly fell down.

They stood and stared at each other with blanched faces.

'Some damned scoundrel has broken off the indicators and then managed to make it appear as if the current were on and the accumulators fully charged,' said Droste.

'He wasn't such a fool as you thought. He seems to have anticipated everything. Droste, I'm afraid there's no hope now. We'll have to drown.' Schmiedecke seated himself on the floor and hid his face in his hands.

'Are you rounding on me too?' asked Droste bitterly.

Schmiedecke looked up and shook his head. 'No, it was just a little too much all at once,' he groaned. 'You can't blame me—'

'We must think what is to be done.' Droste sat down beside Schmiedecke. 'I don't see that the matter is so hopeless, but it will be hopeless, if that hotel crowd finds out.'

'Well, you can't keep the news to yourself, so it won't be long before every one knows about it.'

Droste got up, closed and bolted the heavy iron doors. 'Now look here, old man, just follow what I'm going to say and contradict me if you like. Well, the first cheerful thing is this, and don't forget it. We can take in eighty thousand, possibly even ninety thousand, tons of water before the

FP 1 goes down. We have therefore forty to fifty hours before us. Something will turn up in that time.'

'What the hell do you think *is* going to turn up?' asked Schmiedecke.

'We're going to get the valves put right,' replied Droste determinedly. He certainly looked as if he had every confidence in their sudden and magical reappearance. 'Damsky is dead,' he continued. 'He was suffocated in his gas mask. Now it stands to reason that if Damsky was wearing a gas mask, he had something to do with the gas. It was he who gassed us all, for he was the only one who escaped it. And how do you think he managed to gas us all at one go like that? Well, for the moment the answer is immaterial. The important thing is, who was behind him? Damsky had no technical knowledge of machinery. I know that; he hadn't a scrap. You may say he was only pretending so, but I say he wasn't. Damsky was a stupid man and no one would have intrusted him with such a job. Only a technical engineer could carry it out.'

'Girard?' queried Schmiedecke.

'Yes,' hissed Droste. 'You took him over from the *Elbe*. I've looked through his papers. He seems to have been originally engaged in Hamburg. Before that he had been in a chemical works. Why did the *Elbe* sign him on? So that you might take him over. The whole affair was obviously prearranged. Girard went ashore with the engineers at Fayal. They all sat and had drinks together, and then the engineers were taken ill.'

Schmiedecke stared at Droste in amazement. 'How the hell do you know that?'

'He invited Heinicke too, but Heinicke didn't go. What can be Girard's object? It's not to sink the FP 1. To whose interest could it be to actually sink the FP 1—to send her to the bottom of the ocean? Why, nobody's. And that's the saving of us all.'

'You're mad,' replied Schmiedecke, thoroughly perplexed.

'Think a little. If the FP 1 disappears, a new flying platform will be built. If not by us, certainly by somebody else. It's too good an idea, although I say it myself, to be lost. That's one comfort, at any rate. Yes, old man, you can count on that. In any event, we're going to have a flying platform. The time is ripe for it. Our enemies realized that too. Now whoever owns the first flying platform has a tremendous advantage. It is therefore to our enemies' interest to get hold of the FP 1 and not to sink her. I think that's quite clear. You see, they have only got to get us into financial difficulties and buy us up, and they can do that simply by preventing the FP 1 being anchored by the twenty-second. There are only a few days left. So what is their plan of action? They destroy the wireless apparatus, create trouble for us among the people on board, and render the Diesel engines useless.

We can't signal either by wireless or by means of our searchlights. When the twenty-second is past, mark my words, the valves will turn up again and everything will be all right. And the FP 1 will be intact. But Schmie-decke, they will have ruined us, as no money will be forthcoming from the government. That is their quite simple, very clever little plan.'

Droste got up.

'Come on, let's look for the valves. They must be on board. The black-guard who's at the bottom of all this sabotage can't be anxious to drown himself along with us. It's very decidedly not part of his plan to let the FP 1 go down.'

'But he won't give up the valves before the twenty-second. And sup-posing your theory is wrong and it was Damsky who took the valves; and supposing he threw them into the sea? What then—?'

'Then there is only one thing left for us to do,' Droste replied. 'Pray that we may have a quick end. But we have a chance still, and I'm not going to miss any possibility. You must take all the men whom you can trust and search the FP 1 systematically from end to end. If the valves are still on board, we are bound to find them that way. In the meantime, I'll interview Girard.'

As Droste left the engine room he was hailed by Ellissen, who came across the platform with great strides to meet him. He had slung his rifle over his shoulders, giving the faintly absurd effect of a big-game hunter.

'What are you going to do now, Droste? Are we going to wait patiently until we're starved?'

'It won't come to that,' retorted Droste, who had begun to conceive an intense dislike for this cold, stern-featured man. 'We'll be drowned before then,' he added grimly.

'What? Won't the FP 1 hold together?' said Ellissen, stamping his foot on the steel plates of the deck, as if to reassure himself of its strength and solidity.

'The sea cocks are open and the water's pouring in. We can't close them because the engines aren't running and there's no other way of doing the trick.'

'But surely you have hand pumps?' queried Ellissen, frowning and gnawing his lower lip thoughtfully.

'You can't pump out forty thousand tons of water with hand pumps. It would be useless to scare the men unnecessarily by trying. But if you want to be of some help, perhaps you wouldn't mind coming along with me while I speak to Girard. I'm damned certain he knows more about the origin of these incidents than any one else.'

Together they went along to Girard's room. He was lying on his bed when they entered and raised himself casually as they came in, waiting for Droste to speak.

'Girard,' began Droste, 'you may as well drop all pretence now. I suppose you're pretty well satisfied with the result of your scheming. I wonder if you have any intention of letting us all drown.'

'I don't know what you're talking about,' said Girard, rising to his feet. He walked slowly to a chair, sat down and began to put on his shoes in a manner of studied indifference.

'You know perfectly well what I mean. I'll tell you, all the same. We're gradually sinking, and it's only a matter of a few hours before the sharks get us.'

Girard looked up dubiously. 'Sinking? How the devil do you make that out?' he asked.

'The flooding valves are open and the engines have been rendered useless. The accumulators aren't charged. There's no possibility at all of closing the valves.'

'What a pity,' said Girard casually. 'I suppose my precious life will be cut short too.'

'I'll see to that now,' roared Ellissen, suddenly catching him by the scruff of his neck and dragging him to his feet.

Girard's fist, however, shot out at almost the same moment, and Ellissen staggered back.

Droste threw himself between them. 'Fighting won't settle the matter,' he shouted. 'Look here, Girard, you've got to tell us where you've hidden the valves. You can't let us drown.'

'Let me get at him! I'll get it out of him,' shouted Ellissen, wild with rage. 'Let me get hold of the skunk and I'll soon squeeze the truth out of him.'

'I tell you I haven't got the valves,' cried Girard. 'I know nothing about them. Why should you settle on me if things go wrong? I don't know what *I've* done.'

'Let's talk the matter out quietly.' Droste seated himself and motioned to Ellissen to follow his example. 'Now look here, Girard, I know positively that all these recent incidents, the deliberate destruction of the valves, interference with the Diesel engines, are due to sabotage, and you are certainly the one that gives me most grounds for suspicion. I've a very strong suspicion, for instance, that you only invited the engineers on shore at Fayal so that you might be able to tamper with their drinks and make them all ill enough to be sent to the hospital.'

'All very well thought out,' interjected Girard, with a sneer.

'You aren't an engineer. You were employed in a chemical works before this. No doubt your education has been superior to that of the other engineers. It's no damn' good your pretending, Girard; I know all about you. You've held very different posts from this.'

'I work where I like, Mr Droste. I didn't force your firm to engage me. I was engaged by them without my making any effort to get the job.'

'That I can't tell now, and it makes no difference. Why won't you confess that you have hidden the valves? Think, is it worth it? Destroying so many lives for the sake of a few paltry dollars. Dammit, man, we only need another few thousand tons of water on board and down we go. There's not a minute to lose. We must begin to pump now. It will soon be too late to be any good. Remember, there are men on board who have wives and families at home to think of. And now there's a woman, too. Have you no heart, man!'

Girard rose hastily and threw a glance out of the window. The surface of the sea was already nearer and the horizon appeared to be higher. The FP 1 was visibly deeper in the water. A shade of uneasiness passed over his countenance, then it hardened again.

'You're talking nonsense, Mr Droste,' he began hesitatingly. Then, speaking more rapidly and decisively, he continued, 'I have nothing to do with the matter. Do you think it was I who gassed every one? You yourself found me lying unconscious in the engine room. How could I have taken the valves away when I was lying there dead to the world? I was unconscious for longer than you were. It could only have been Damsky. Damsky went mad and it must have been he who took the valves after he had gassed us all. The engine house has a trapdoor through which you can get out. Damsky got in through that, took the valves and closed the trapdoor again. That's how it came about that the door was bolted when you found me.'

'You seem damned sure how it all happened,' Ellissen snarled. 'And how did Damsky manage to gas everybody at once?'

Girard looked at him with genuine astonishment in his eyes. 'Don't you really know?' he said. 'That's very simple. If you come with me, I'll soon show you.' He led the way to a small room, followed by Droste and Ellissen.

'The fire-extinguishing installation is in here,' he explained. 'There are the carbonic acid cylinders, each three of them connected by a forked tubing. By means of this valve here, any one of the three can be specially connected with the main network of tubes, and the carbonic acid then flows through them into all the rooms, because, as you know, there are outlets at regular intervals throughout all the rooms, so that it is a simple matter to let the gas filter into every room, and in fact throughout the whole flying platform. The system is of your own construction, Mr Droste,' he bowed ironically. 'Hasn't it struck you that cylinders could also be attached which might hold something more powerful than mere carbonic acid—a poison gas, for instance?' He ran his finger round the neck of one of the cylinders, and a fine green powder came off on to it. 'Does that look like carbonic acid?' he said mockingly.

Droste looked at him in horrified amazement.

'Do you want to make out that Damsky smuggled cylinders of poison gas in here and then gassed us all?' asked Droste, watching Girard's face sharply.

'That's how it was done,' replied Girard, without a tremor. 'I helped with the fitting here. I assembled the cylinders myself after we left Fayal. Damsky gave me the order to put one of these smaller cylinders between every two of the large ones, and the small ones contained the poison gas. But after all, the gas doesn't appear to have been very poisonous. Perhaps we should say just a temporary anæsthetic.'

'You weren't surprised to get such an order from Damsky?'

'Every one on board has two sets of duties. You know that as well as I do. Damsky was in charge of food and supplies and at the same time looked after the fire-extinguishing installation. Is there anything more you would like to know?' he added insolently, turning to go.

'Perhaps you wouldn't mind suggesting to us where the valves are,' sneered Ellissen. 'Why don't you help Schmiedecke to look for them? You've the best chance of finding them.'

They let Girard go. He did not stop to look round.

'That's a nice sort of fellow.' Droste looked after him, exasperated. 'It means nothing to him that we are all in imminent danger of drowning.'

'I think I've got his measure,' said Ellissen thoughtfully. 'Yes, I understand him all right—but you wait a bit. I'll get his weak spot yet. The low-down, snivelling, yellow cur!'

Chapter Twenty-Two: A Half-Veiled Threat

Night had fallen. There was a ring around the moon and the stars were hidden by a thin mist. All was quiet on the FP 1. The only sounds to be heard were the footsteps of the sentries whom Droste had posted over the quarters of the hotel employees as soon as darkness had fallen. He was determined if possible to prevent any further disturbance there.

Some of the men were still about, but the greater number had already gone to bed, where they were lying tossing restlessly, oppressed by fear of the fate hanging over them. The darkness in which the FP 1 within and without was wrapped, owing to the failure of the engines, added to the macabre horror of the situation.

'D'you hear that?' exclaimed one of the younger waiters nervously. 'God! It's like prison. There! D'you hear the footsteps going up and down? He's posted sentries over us.'

'Oh, turn over and go to sleep, for God's sake,' answered the voice of an older man from the bunk above him. 'You may not get another chance. Tomorrow you may be drifting about face upwards, half-eaten by sharks.'

'Shut up!' retorted the other resentfully. 'Hold your jaw, can't you? You'll be the first to squeal when this blasted box begins to sink.'

'Don't you worry about them out there. Let 'em wave their revolvers in our faces if they like. I've got enough food for a few days, but it won't be much good to me. Haven't you noticed that this rat-trap is slowly settling down? Dammit, you could work it out to a nicety! Just how long it'll be before the water is up to our chins.'

'That's a lie,' cried the young man in a choking voice. 'That's a bloody lie!' His voice rose to a scream. 'The FP 1 isn't sinking, blast you! It can't sink!'

'Go on, stuff your pillow into your mouth, if you want to howl,' retorted the jeering voice above him. 'You'd better make up your mind we're damn' well going down. I have. I've been at sea for thirty years and I've escaped twice before. But blast you all, I know I'm booked now for Davy Jones', all right. This is a coffin ship we're on, a coffin ship, d'you hear me? I smelt it the moment I got aboard. "Paul," I said to myself, said I, "there's something wrong here. You ain't ever going to set foot on dry land again."'

'Then why the hell did you come on board? Why didn't you keep out of it?'

The other was silent for a moment or two. 'It shows how young you are, sonny, to ask a thing like that,' he said at last. 'It ain't no good trying to escape death when you're once booked. The richest man can't dodge it. It'll have you whatever you do! If you stayed on land, you might get a chimneypot on your head or be run over by a motor car—Fate would have you just the same. You look at the older men on board, my lad, men old enough to be your father. Are they worrying, I ask you? No, they knows it's all up. Some men die young and some die old; that's the only difference, and I'm blowed if I know which have the best of it really. Will you have a drop of whisky?'

The young man made no reply. It was his first sea voyage and he couldn't face the thought that it was going to be his last.

'Come on, have a pull at the bottle,' said the voice from the upper bunk good-naturedly. 'Hurry up and take it.'

A choking sob was his only answer.

'All right, don't if you don't want it. What are you doing now? Praying, I bet. That's right, pray away, my lad. Only the very old or the very young pray, so you might pray for me too. I ain't old enough to pray for myself.'

He looked out into the night and his voice became serious. 'Mind you, I'm not saying that things aren't looking pretty bad for us,' he remarked thoughtfully. 'There's not a light to be seen, so the engines can't be running. The blasted power has gone west. They were going to signal with the searchlights to-night if they could. Yes, sonny, we're done for, all right. I could have sworn that from the start. A blasted coffin ship!' He lay down in his bunk again and stared into the darkness.

'There's one thing I never could get over,' he murmured. 'This is such a rotten half-and-half sort of life. When we are at sea, we want to be ashore; and when we're ashore for a few days, we want to be at sea again. We never get any blasted fun out of life. Now if I had my life over again, I should like to be the captain of a sailing ship. Not a blinking steward, a half-baked landlubber.'

He took a long, gurgling pull at his whisky bottle.

'My God! Keep quiet,' he whispered suddenly. 'There's a woman out there in front of the window! D'you see?' He leaned out of the small window in great excitement, just in time to see the figures of a man and a woman disappearing into the darkness.

It was Gisela and Ellissen, engaged in earnest conversation. Ellissen, as he walked along by her side, was trying to suit his stride to her light tread.

'I'm getting foolish in my old age,' said Ellissen. 'I never seem to be able to say what I want when talking to you. D'you remember that time at the Azores? I said all sorts of foolish things. When I try and talk with you, I always seem to say the wrong things. I've got to know where I am with you. I'm not going on like this.'

Gisela with some alarm wondered what he was going to say next. Of course, it was her own fault. She ought never to have come out here with him in the darkness, just because he had asked her. Then she felt ashamed of her nervousness. After all, this man had begged her to try and understand him; he was only asking her now to let him talk to her. It would be quite wrong to refuse. Why should she repulse him when he had done her nothing but kindness? He had risked his life for her. It was through her that he was now on the doomed FP 1. It was for her sake that he had run into this danger.

Ellissen took her by the arm. 'Tell me,' he said abruptly, 'what is there between you and Bernard Droste?'

'What is there between us?' she asked, astonished, slowly freeing herself. What right had he to ask her such a question? 'I've known Droste since I was a child. We were brought up together.'

'Are you going to marry him?'

'Perhaps,' answered Gisela in a low voice. 'If—if we get away from here alive.' She stopped and leaned over the railings, staring down into the dark waters.

'So that's it! I understand. D'you think I'm going to let myself be played with?' asked Ellissen. And there was a half-veiled threat in his voice. 'You needn't think I'm a silly boy whom you can do as you like with. Dammit all, there have been too many women in my life for one to make a fool of me now!'

'You have no right to say that, Mr Ellissen. I never had any thought of making a fool of you.'

'Then what do you think I made this flight for? Do you think it was for your father's sake, or for the glory of finding this damned derelict? I suppose you want to pretend I took you with me to help me! We made an agreement, you know, even if I was decent enough not to put it into words. And now this Droste fellow turns up.'

Gisela was at a loss what to say. She ought to leave him without further ado, she thought; ought never to speak to him again. What right had he to think of her and speak to her in such a way? She recalled the scene in the hotel lounge, the favor she had asked him, and the look in his eyes when he made his condition, and her tacit consent. He had said it was a business transaction, but he had sent the other woman away on her account and he had spoken of reciprocity.

She could not disguise her distress. Her lips were quivering.

'Why don't you answer me?' Ellissen demanded ruthlessly. 'You know what our agreement was. You belong to me and you may as well get accustomed to the idea. I've never confided in any one as I have in you, and when we were flying together and you begged me to keep on, when I wanted to turn back, I felt then that you were the one woman in the world for me. I want some one to feel about me as you feel about Droste. You were thinking of him all the time on our flight, weren't you?'

'Yes,' she murmured, so low that Ellissen had to bend his head to catch the sound.

'There, you own up to it! I knew it too, and I'm going to make you carry out your agreement with me.'

'You're wrong, quite wrong, I say. I never promised you anything.' Gisela turned at bay, ready to fight for all that was dear to her. The stars were coming out, the moon was shining now, and she could see Ellissen towering above her. 'I won't try to excuse myself. I did persuade you to go on this flight; but then I knew you loved danger, and you were the only man who could help me. I did no wrong in not telling you about Droste. I never thought you were reckoning what you could gain by helping me. It's rotten to think that you have done this for just what you can get out of it. If there have been so many women in your life, what can I matter to you? Why worry me, when we are all so near death. Do you want to try at such a time to hold me to *your* interpretation of an agreement that I made because there was no other way of helping my father and my friend?'

'Such is my intention,' replied Ellissen in an unmoved voice.

'Is that chivalrous, or even manly?' she asked reproachfully.

Ellissen was silent. She could hear him breathing heavily, and saw how he gripped the railing with his powerful hands, struggling with strong emotion.

'You're not going to get out of it as easily as all that,' he muttered, after a pause. 'He or I, we'll take an equal chance. There's the plane. Some one must try and find a ship before we reckon the game is completely up. Droste and I will draw lots which of us is to fly the plane. If no ship is found, then it's certain death for those on the FP 1 as well as whoever is in the airplane.'

'And supposing the valves are found in the meantime and we on the FP 1 are saved?' Gisela parried.

'One of us two, Droste or I, must make the flight to-morrow. There isn't room for us both on the FP 1. If Droste wins the draw, you won't see me again, even if I should find a ship. But if I win and remain here—' He broke off his sentence with a startled exclamation, as the rays of an electric torch fell on them.

'Gisela!' It was Droste's astonished voice which they heard. 'I've been looking for you everywhere. Who is—?'

'She will come in a moment,' interrupted Ellissen.

The light vanished and Droste turned and went away.

Ellissen and Gisela, he thought. He was profoundly disturbed. I'm too late after all. All my good resolutions are useless. I have lost her. I might have known it. I must have been blind not to see it. Why should Ellissen have risked his life? Why did she make such a dangerous flight with him? She must have trusted him because she loved him.

He recalled how Gisela had kissed him when he was weak and helpless and all he had tried to say to her then. Could lost time be made up for by words? Could she have understood him? Her kisses, after all, had been those of a mother soothing a sick child, not those of a woman for the man she loves. It is my own fault, he thought despairingly. I had my opportunity for years and did not take it. And now, when some one else comes along, I regret it. Her father's wish that we should marry doesn't after all give me any right. It's ridiculous of me to think that settled it. But dammit, I love her all the same, and I'll fight for her. Ellissen shan't have her. By God, no! I'll speak to him. Perhaps I'm mistaken about it, he thought, with a rush of hope.

Hurrying along the platform, searching in his mind for some way to solve the difficulty, he came on Ellissen's airplane standing there in the darkness, and a sudden inspiration came to him. He got into the cockpit and examined the petrol gauge with the aid of his electric torch. There was enough fuel for a flight of about eight hundred miles, he estimated; perhaps not quite so far. That was the solution! Either he or Ellissen could make a flight in search of a ship. One of them had got to leave the FP 1. The one who made the flight would disappear for good, whether he was successful in finding a ship or not. The other would remain where he was, with a chance of life and Gisela.

Quite himself again, now that he had seen the way out, Droste went into the messroom, where he found Schmiedecke sitting at the table. He looked very harassed, and as Droste came in, burst out eagerly, 'I've got it at last! I know what was wrong with Damsky.—I've nearly gone off my head trying to think it all out,' he continued, 'but now I've got it. Damsky was mad!'

'But we know that,' retorted Droste.

Schmiedecke nodded his head excitedly. 'You remember he was always talking about getting everything in order? He had got that on the brain. So after he had gassed us all, he must have gone round, dragging us all into the places where he thought we all ought to be, for everything to be shipshape and in order on the FP 1. Don't you see it? He dragged some of the men into the kitchen, some into their bunks, some into the card room, putting cards in their hands, and he dragged you and me into the commander's turret—'

'And Girard back into the engine room. He must originally have been lying wherever he had hidden the valves!' exclaimed Droste, seeing the truth in a flash.

Schmiedecke's jaw dropped. He stared helplessly at Droste. 'Well, I'm damned!' he managed to get out at last. 'If Damsky hadn't had that cranky idea about order—a place for everything and everything in its place, we wouldn't be so near drowning now. Well, he made a damned thorough job of it, I must say. God! I always thought the man was a hard worker!'

CHAPTER TWENTY-THREE: The Valves!

It was unnecessary cruelty to go on forcing the men to wait in utter idleness for the inevitable end, shut up with nothing to do but watch the surface of the sea coming threateningly nearer. Droste had realized this and decided that he must give them something to do to occupy their minds. He could not go on keeping them in check by force alone. That could only end in murder being done.

Accordingly he had withdrawn the sentries, summoned together all on board and told them the seriousness of the position without reserve, keeping nothing back except Girard's share in the matter. He then explained his plans, namely, that some of them should search the FP 1 systematically from end to end for the missing valves, while others got to work at the hand pumps in the meantime, although these pumps would not have any appreciable effect in stemming the inrush of the water. He divided them into three parties, one to man the pumps, the other two to search the FP 1, beginning at opposite ends. The airplane, he assured them, would set off at midday to look for help.

The men dispersed cheerfully enough. After their nerve-racking spell of inactivity, the prospect of work was a relief—and if there was work to be done, all hope could not be gone. Those told off to man the pumps fought for first turn at the job; they were glad of a chance of using their muscles again, and though they knew it wasn't much use, still it might give a little longer time for a ship to appear or for the valves to be found.

There was a spirit of fresh hope and confidence in the air. The stores found their way mysteriously back to the storeroom. The men swarmed about busily, almost cheerful now that they had work to do.

Gisela had gone to Droste's room to try and busy herself in doing something for him. A big cupboard stood in one corner of the room. The bed was in disorder. Droste had been sleeping in it for several nights past, fully dressed even to his boots. She stripped the bed of its coverings and dusted and tidied the room with care, trying to express her affection for him by these little services.

She had not been able to talk to him since her scene the night before with Ellissen. She had looked for him immediately afterwards to tell him all about it, but he was already in bed and asleep when she found him. He lay there so limp, so obviously tired and exhausted, that she decided to wait till the next morning and had retired, closing the door again gently without waking him.

She realized clearly that either Ellissen or Droste would have to undertake the flight in search of help. This chance could certainly not be neglected. They were the only men on the FP 1 who could pilot an airplane, so it must be one of them. Ellissen might well claim that it was Droste's duty to go. He could put forward the danger he had already run to find the FP 1 as a reason why he himself should not go. If he did, Droste would never dispute the matter with him. Was it not, after all, generous and self-sacrificing of Ellissen to offer to draw lots with Droste?

If Droste loses, I will go with him on the flight, she resolved, and the thought calmed her. The decision seemed to restore her peace of mind. Would it be cowardly of her to accompany Droste to death? Is it cowardice to sacrifice one's life to make death easy for the man one loves? she asked herself.

She opened the heavy cupboard and was stooping to get out fresh linen for the bed when she heard a slight noise and the door opened cautiously. She turned round quickly, stifling a cry.

Girard was standing behind her. His whole attitude told her that he had been about to spring on her and overpower her if she had not looked around just in time.

Gisela recoiled before his threatening look.

'I beg your pardon,' said Girard politely, concealing whatever intention he might have had, and putting his hands in his pockets. 'Mr Droste has sent me to fetch something.' He made a movement towards the cupboard. Gisela moved to one side to let him pass. He went to the cupboard and took a black leather case out of a large trunk.

'Have you opened this case?' he asked quietly.

Gisela shook her head, astonished at the question and his manner.

He turned away at once and left the room without saying anything further. Suddenly a tremendous doubt assailed her. What a fool she was! Bernard had sent him! That sounded most unlikely. She hurried to the door.

'Hand over that case,' she heard Ellissen's voice demand sharply. Then she heard a sound of blows being struck, and muttered curses, of heavy breathing as the two men struggled in a close embrace.

She looked out and saw that Ellissen had seized Girard, who was fighting desperately to get free. It was a terrific struggle and evidently Girard could not hope to hold out long against the big, powerful airman. First one and then the other had the advantage. Ellissen was fighting hard to get the leather case out of Girard's grip, but the latter suddenly threw it away from him as hard as he could. It slid along the smooth floor of the corridor and struck against the wall, flying open as it did so.

'The valves!' gasped Ellissen, as he saw it open. Shaking himself free of Girard's grasp, he gave him a terrific blow that sent him senseless to the ground.

Gisela gazed breathlessly at Ellissen.

The valves!

Ellissen stared down at the unconscious man lying at his feet; then, with a grim smile, he picked up the leather case and, taking Girard by the head and shoulders, dragged him to the door of one of the rooms, which he opened.

'Mr Ellissen!' Gisela tried to call, but no sound came. She pressed her hands to her mouth and listened, her head strained forward. She could hear no sound from the room into which Ellissen had disappeared with Girard.

She went back into Droste's room and sat down on the unmade bed, trying to collect her thoughts.

The valves! Ellissen had found the valves! Then everything was all right now, thank God! Droste would not need to make any flight. She would tell Ellissen—yes, that was the problem—what would she tell Ellissen?

In imagination she already heard the steady throbbing of the Diesel engines and saw the bright rays of the searchlights flitting over the sky. She listened again, but no sound came from the other room. What was happening? Why didn't Ellissen hurry along the corridor and tell every one that the valves had been found? Why was he wilfully leaving every one in suspense and fear? Why had he dragged Girard into the room? Could he have killed him by that terrific blow? She could find no answer to the riddle of Ellissen's behavior.

Suddenly she heard voices coming along the passage. She pulled herself together, smoothed back her hair, got up hurriedly and opened the door to see who it was.

Schmiedecke was just outside with some of the men. 'The search has commenced,' he said to her, trying to bring a note of confidence into his voice.

She was about to tell him that Ellissen had already found the valves, when the door of the other room opened at last and Ellissen appeared with Girard beside him. The latter was rather battered, but had recovered sufficiently to mop his face energetically with a handkerchief.

'That you, Schmiedecke?' called Ellissen. 'I've turned everything upside down in this room already. The valves aren't there. Girard's searched and I watched him do it properly. What's going to happen if the things don't turn up?' he laughed quite cheerily.

No one replied to the sally.

'Have you looked in Droste's room?' Schmiedecke asked Gisela.

The girl shook her head absently, opened the door wide and stood staring blankly after Ellissen, as he went along the passage with Girard at his side.

Chapter Twenty-Four: Tricked!

Ellissen and Droste met in the engine house a few minutes later. 'I was looking for you,' said Droste.

'And I was wanting to see you,' laughed Ellissen.

The two men stood face to face and scanned each other closely.

This man has courage at any rate, thought Droste. The nearer we're getting to death, the more cheerful he seems to be. He could not forbear to say something of this to Ellissen.

'Do you always get so cheerful,' he asked him, half ironically, 'when the prospects of life get beautifully less every minute?' Ellissen seemed to him a complete anachronism. The fellow ought to have lived a few hundred years earlier, when men went about in armor and were always fighting and risking their lives just for the fun of the thing.

'It's this hot weather that makes me so cheerful,' Ellissen laughed. 'I'm not so lively when it's cold, I can assure you. Let's sit down and have a chat, Droste, if you've got something to say to me. You can stay,' to Girard. 'We may want you. By the way, Droste, it might interest you to know that I've taken Girard into my service, and I'm not going to let him out of my sight. Girard,' he cried, 'acknowledge that you deliberately got us into this damnable mess. Now, be honest, Girard,' he added tauntingly.

Girard's face darkened, but he did not dare to show resentment.

'Sit down,' Ellissen went on, waving his hand condescendingly to him. 'When do we start?' he said, turning to Droste.

'Do you want us to make the flight together?' asked Droste coldly. He did not relish very much the prospect of dying in the company of this sneering, hard-faced adventurer.

'No, it's quite enough if one of us gets killed,' replied Ellissen, in a friendly tone. 'The FP 1 is big, but it isn't big enough to hold us both. I take it, my young friend, that you understand what I mean?'

'I'm not your young friend,' replied Droste quietly. 'I am the commander of the FP 1. But I quite agree with you that there's not room for both of us here.'

'Spoken like a man!' Ellissen drew out his pipe and tobacco pouch and threw the latter across to Droste. Droste ignored the proffered pouch, but took out from his pocket a blackened, well-used pipe, polished it affectionately on his sleeve, filled it from his own pouch, lit up and threw the match away negligently.

Ellissen, who had silently waited to see whether Droste would offer him a light, now took out his own matches and also filled and lit his pipe.

'We seem to understand each other admirably,' he remarked approvingly. 'It's a pity. I should have liked you to sample some of my tobacco.'

Droste looked at him questioningly.

'I'm a man of sentiment. I should have had fewer pangs of conscience later on, if you had,' explained Ellissen in quite friendly tones, and he sucked vigorously at his pipe. 'Well, what is it to be? If the one who makes the flight finds a ship, is he to disappear for good, as far as the other is concerned?'

Droste nodded assent.

'You're just my sort,' said Ellissen heartily, slapping him on the shoulder. 'No need to waste a word. We understand each other without talking.'

'Well, if you think so, why the devil don't you keep your mouth shut? I wish you would.' Droste got up and knocked out his pipe.

'No sentimental farewells allowed. We'll take our medicine like men.' Ellissen took out his match box again. 'Will you draw first?'

He took two matches and broke the head off one. Holding them in his hand so that only two ends were visible, he offered them to Droste.

Droste looked him straight in the eye and put out his hand.

Ellissen's eyes dropped. He bit his lip. 'Dammit, I'm not going to hold these things. Here you; you take them,' he said, handing them to Girard.

Droste had observed these signs of agitation. 'Never forget to be human, Ellissen. Gisela herself is essentially human,' he said quietly.

'Will you draw and have done with it!' Ellissen shouted at him, his face deathly white. 'I'll take the left.'

'That leaves me the right then—the shorter loses,' said Droste.

Girard opened his right hand and Droste took the match. It was the one without a head. He stared at the bit of wood. Fate was against him. He was not destined to remain with Gisela.

'That's well over,' laughed Ellissen, relieved. 'Yes, thank God, that's over,' he repeated with a sigh. 'Thanks, my worthy friend,' he said, winking at Girard, who kept his eyes averted.

'I'll start at once. You can go to Gisela and talk to her till I'm well away,' said Droste in a strangled voice. 'I hope to be ready in a few minutes.'

'Droste!' cried Ellissen. But the young commander did not look around. He hastily walked out of the room.

'Hell, that was touch and go, but an old Arctic explorer was bound to be lucky,' said Ellissen, sitting down again.

'With the help of the devil and of me,' completed Girard, opening his other hand. The match in that hand also had no head.

Chapter Twenty-Five: 'Beast!'

Gisela was just about to leave Droste's room in search of him when she encountered Ellissen at the door. She had waited until Schmiedecke's search of the room was finished, then she had made the bed and closed the cupboard. The realization of danger had slowly grown upon her until it now completely obsessed her mind. She felt she ought to see Bernard at once and tell him that Ellissen had got hold of the valves, which Girard had hidden just as they thought. She could not understand how Ellissen could remain silent when he knew where the valves were and could have set all their minds at rest with a word.

Gisela felt completely bewildered, at a loss to understand herself or Ellissen or anything. What did it all mean? Was Ellissen playing a double game? What could his reason possibly be?

She remembered his reputation. How it was said that in moments of danger he changed into a selfish wild beast, who cared nothing for the lives of others, a man to whom murder was nothing. She remembered also how strangely he had talked that night at Fayal in the barroom of the little hotel.

Suddenly she guessed—more, she knew—why he was acting like this. After the fight with Girard, when he had knocked him down, he must have pledged him to complete secrecy about the valves and, in fact, made him become his accomplice. He was probably unaware that she had seen the incident and knew that Girard had the valves, but of this she was not quite certain.

Now, when she wanted to leave the room to find Droste, here was Ellissen standing in the doorway. His attitude reminded her of the former occasion on which she had seen him in similar circumstances, when he was watching her talking to Droste in this very room.

'You must stay here,' he said gruffly, stopping her as she advanced towards the door.

'No, let me pass,' she exclaimed angrily. But he held her back as easily as if she were a child, and pressed her into a chair.

'So you were going to look for Droste?' he queried. 'Well, I've just come from him. He doesn't want to be disturbed for a moment.' He sat down opposite her, looking like a giant on the little chair, and leaned towards her.

Gisela looked at him sharply. Was he lying, or had Bernard really sent him?

'You remember our talk last night?' he asked, fixing her with his light, almost colorless eyes. 'That was the turning point of my fate. I have waited all my life for such a turning point and now it has come.' His face was quite expressionless as he went on. 'I asked you, Gisela. I told you there was only one solution. Droste or I must go. And you were silent and did not contradict me. Well, we've had it out together. Droste and I have tried our luck—'

'And Bernard has lost!' cried Gisela despairingly, and tried to rush from the room. Ellissen pushed her back.

'You sit here,' he said excitedly. 'Bernard Droste has ceased to exist, as far as you are concerned. We have drawn lots, and he has lost.'

Gisela stared at him blankly; then she went deathly pale. She sat down and closed her eyes in an effort to master her emotion. So this was the true Ellissen unmasked. He had gambled, drawn lots for life or death with Bernard, and Bernard was the loser.

It was no fair game either, for if Ellissen had lost, the valves would suddenly have been found, and the flight would have become unnecessary. Now Bernard had lost, and Ellissen would be rid of him. And then, after he had gone to certain death, the valves would be found. And through a merciful providence, which the malicious hand of Ellissen was guiding, they would all be safe and Bernard gone to his doom. Gisela trembled with suppressed rage and agony of mind.

'The loser must not come back—must never reappear, even if he survives—will probably really be lost in any case? I suppose that was part of your damnable arrangement?' she asked in a low tone, clasping her hands together.

Ellissen nodded..

'What a thoroughgoing blackguard he is,' she thought. 'People are right after all when they haven't a good word to say for him.'

He had spoken of the stronger of the two winning. Was he to prove the stronger in this case?

'I'm glad you're beginning to be sensible,' said Ellissen, laying his heavy hand on Gisela's shoulder. She closed her eyes and did not move.

'It is fate, Gisela. Just fate. If I had lost, he would have been sitting here and I should be going instead, quietly without any good-by, just as he is.'

He hasn't gone yet, thank God! thought Gisela. She could hear the irregular whirring of the airplane engines, as they endeavored to start it up. Ellissen is going to keep me here, I know, so that I can't go to Bernard. Well, I must try. Perhaps Ellissen may not be the stronger of us two, after all.

'He's going without saying good-by,' she said quietly. 'That's very hard.'

'But very brave and manly.' Ellissen smiled, secretly relieved at the quiet way she seemed to be taking it. 'You can be proud of him.

'Oh, Gisela, can't you see—' he began. His head was very near hers now. 'Gisela, I've got what I wanted. I can speak now quite freely. No one stands between us. Once these dangers are over, we will go away to some distant country where no one knows us, where there are mountains, and the hot sun is always shining. That is what I have been looking forward to all my life. But I never thought at one time that some day the wish would be fulfilled. Gisela, you will come, won't you?' He stood up and tried to draw her to him. Suddenly the mighty roar of airplane engines penetrated into the little room, and she heard the more ominous sound of the strokes of the propeller. Her heart beat wildly within her.

'Gisela!' Ellissen's face was just above her.

'You beast!' she cried, looking him full in the face with burning scorn.

Ellissen turned pale. He looked as if he had been stabbed to the heart.

'Beast!' she repeated, straining away from him without taking her contemptuous eyes from his face.

Hatred and contempt filled her, but as she looked at him, she could see that he had read her thoughts and knew that she had seen through him. Suddenly he began to tremble, big, strong, unscrupulous man though he was, and seemed to wither into a miserable creature who had brought about his own destruction. Pity began to stir in her. Ellissen tried to speak. He held out both hands appealingly and slowly lowered them again. It was absolutely hopeless, he saw. She knows all, he thought, clenching his fists in despair. All his treachery, the false game he had played with Droste, all his meanness had been revealed to her. He had hoped she would love him and that through the purifying flame of her love he would become a new man. Now his hopes were shattered through his own rottenness. What did he care about life if this girl spurned him?

The sounds of the engine had ceased again.

If she speaks, thought Ellissen, if she says a word, or shows just how much she hates me, I don't know what I may do. I'll—He dared not think about it. He slowly lifted his eyes and looked at Gisela. Her face softened. Pity had conquered. She saw in him only a poor, miserable creature who knew no better than to stoop to treachery and crime to attain his own ends, and yet had sufficient good left in him to despise himself. Was there any way by which the good which must be in him could be reached?

Gisela held out her hand. His face twitched. He gazed on the proffered hand, touched it lightly, almost reverently, turned abruptly away and walked out of the room.

He hurried down the stairs and out on to the platform, and rushed towards the plane. Schmiedecke was about to start the propeller again. 'Droste!' he shouted as he ran, 'Droste!' Pushing his way through the mechanics who were standing around, he again shouted to Droste, who was already seated in the cockpit, ready to take off.

'Gisela wants you for a moment,' cried Ellissen.

Droste shook his head and made a sign to Schmiedecke to start.

'For God's sake, don't be a damned idiot,' cried Ellissen wildly. 'You must listen to me. Gisela wants to speak to you. It's a matter of life and death to her. Go and see her at once!'

The commander looked at him in astonishment. With a grim smile playing round his lips, he climbed out of the airplane. 'I shall be back in a couple of minutes,' he said, walking away, the men making room for him to pass.

Ellissen waited until Droste had gone, then he swung himself into the seat which Droste had just vacated. 'Start it up,' he shouted to Schmiedecke, who was staring at him, speechless with surprise. 'Start it up! Can't you hear me?'

At that moment he felt a hand on his arm and, looking round, saw Girard standing beside him. There was a sneering grin on his face.

'It may suit you to go alone, my friend,' he said threateningly, 'but I'm going too. I must get away from here. When the FP 1 is found, Droste will have me arrested and I shall land in jail. I don't exactly like the idea of that, so I'm going along with you.'

'No, Girard, I'm damned if you are,' exclaimed Ellissen. 'I don't think there's much chance that I'll find a ship. Stand aside. D'you hear me? Stand aside, if you value your life.'

'My life,' answered Girard, 'is at the moment not as valuable as yours. It may not be worth much, all things considered. I'd rather go with you.' He made a sudden spring and got into the vacant seat behind Ellissen. 'You can't bluff me, Ellissen. Nothing's going to happen to you. You're not the sort to let yourself be downed.'

'Dammit, man, get out of this plane,' Ellissen warned him impatiently. Schmiedecke had started the propeller.

'I'm going to stay where I am,' said Girard grimly, and he rammed the muzzle of a revolver into Ellissen's back. 'We sink or swim together!'

'Schmiedecke!' Ellissen waved to him excitedly. 'For God's sake, remember the valves! They are in Room 45, in a black leather case. Contact!'

'Contact!' answered the dazed Schmiedecke. The plane shot along the landing platform and slowly mounted in the air; then it came around in a wide circle and swooped down again as it crossed the FP 1. The men standing on the platform raised a cheer as the plane passed low over their heads. For a moment Schmiedecke caught a glimpse of Ellissen. It seemed to him that he was laughing and shouting. Then the plane rose steeply again and, heading to the southwest, swiftly disappeared from sight.

Chapter Twenty-Six: The Whole Truth

In the early hours of July 18th, a beautiful clear night, with the stars of the Southern Cross shining brilliantly from a cloudless sky, the look-out man of the steamer *Pillau*, which was cruising at about latitude 30°, suddenly observed mysterious lights on the port bow. Shining through the darkness a considerable distance away they appeared to be signalling—short-short-short, long-long-long, short-short-short—over and over again. With a nerve-racking persistence, the SOS signal flashed through the night in all directions in long points of light which looked like giant fingers appealing for help.

Captain Schneider, the captain of the *Pillau*, immediately turned out all hands and ordered full speed ahead in the direction from which the searchlight signals were flashing. In after years he was in the habit of boasting that he had given the old tub's boiler all the steam they could stand and knocked sixteen knots out of her, a fine performance for an eighteen-year-old tramp, which had been planned to do twelve when she was first built. He also got in touch at once by wireless with his sister ship, the supply steamer, *Tangiers II*, which was then some twenty miles due north, and in response she also clapped on full steam and hurried to the rescue.

Captain Schneider was firmly convinced that the signals must proceed from the missing FP 1, and when, in the rays of the rising sun, they were no longer visible, he kept on the course which he had laid in the direction of the signals with unabated hope.

At about eight o'clock the *Pillau* came in sight of the FP 1, lying very low in the water. It was indeed only the continuance of the unusual calm that had saved the FP 1 from disaster or damage, even after the valves had been found. Though the engines had been running at high pressure, they had not been able to reduce by any appreciable amount the dangerous quantity of water that had already been taken in. As the morning wore on, the sun became hotter and hotter. Even under the awnings of the captain's deck the heat was almost unbearable. By half-past eleven the *Pillau* had come within hailing distance of the FP 1, and in a few minutes Captain Schneider was being rowed over to it.

To his surprise, he was received by those on board with rousing cheers, as if he were some foreign potentate on a visit of inspection. Everything was apparently in exceptionally good order, except for the remarkable lowness of the platform in the water. But one other thing caused him some surprise. It was Droste's first order to him, for he came under a superior officer's command as long as the *Pillau* and the FP 1 were in company. Droste told him to have a substantial meal prepared for the men of the FP 1 immediately, even although the supply ship, the *Tangiers II*, would not reach them for another hour and a half.

Droste's pleasure and relief at the sight of the *Pillau* had been unalloyed. According to his calculations, they were not far from the exact position originally arranged for anchoring, namely 30° 17' 23" W longitude, and 32° 1' 34" N latitude. They therefore should reach the actual spot in one day, if the *Tangiers II* helped the *Pillau* to tow the FP 1. Thank God, success was in sight at last! Spurred by the approaching realization of his long-cherished dream, he did not spare himself. He worked like a Trojan, not taking a minute's rest, and superintended personally the securing of the hawsers between the FP 1 and the two ships that were to tow her to success. As soon as the hawsers were fixed, he triumphantly ordered them to get under weigh at once, without waiting to transfer any stores.

Cheers once again sounded from the FP 1 as the hawsers at last tightened and the great floating platform began to move slowly in the wake of the steamers. It was a remarkable thing that no one on board spoke of the incidents which had occurred during the time it was drifting. The men of the FP 1, though they worked side by side with the *Pillau's* crew, told them nothing. It seemed to be tacitly understood that the past should be buried, if Droste would allow it, and this Droste seemed ready to do.

A general atmosphere of good will prevailed. Captain Schneider was much struck by the zeal and willingness of the men of the FP 1. The energy and cheerfulness with which they carried out their allotted duties inspired even the efficient and remarkably well-disciplined crew of the *Pillau* to emulation.

After work was over, the evening hours were devoted to various forms of sport and entertainment on deck. Captain Schneider was not sorry, on the whole, when he had towed the FP 1 to the anchoring place, and turned homewards after the anchorage of the floating platform had been successfully completed. He had noticed that dissatisfaction was springing up among his crew, who were jealous of the free-and-easy entertainments they saw in full swing every evening. It was only some months later, when Captain Schneider returned to the FP 1 as Marine Superintendent of the airport, that he learned the whole truth of the FP 1's eventful voyage, and then many things that he had seen and heard and wondered at became clear to him.

Twenty-Seven: The Floating Airport Functions!

The news, the great news for which they had been waiting and longing and praying, had reached the Lennartz shipyards at last. Emmerich, the wireless operator, who could hardly keep awake at his post, for the prolonged nervous strain and lack of sleep had almost proved too much for him, tore downstairs to his employer's office at racing speed. He could still hear the crackling of the wireless signals sounding maddeningly in his ears. Laughing excitedly to himself, he waved a piece of paper in his hands as he rushed through Miss Helm's room without taking any notice of her and plunged into Lennartz's sanctuary, so quickly that the startled girl had no time to say a word to stop him. And now he stood in front of Lennartz himself, struggling for breath, and almost in a state of collapse.

'What's the matter, Emmerich? Sit down for a moment and get your breath,' said Lennartz in a weary voice, raising his head at the noise of Emmerich's excited entry. His face was worn with anxiety and overwork, his eyes were rimmed with dark shadows, his mouth, with its closely compressed lips, showed the tremendous will power that had kept him at his desk through many long weary hours, while he kept hoping against hope for news. Now that the news had come he could scarcely realize it.

'I've got him,' gasped Emmerich, hugging the paper to his heart. 'They're safe,' he went on happily, 'and everything is all right.' He laid his message on the table in front of Lennartz, who stared at it blankly, unable to decipher it.

'Read it out to me, Emmerich. You have taken it down in shorthand,' he said, passing his hand over his forehead, an action which seemed to remove some invisible veil, for his face cleared, and his eyes brightened.

'Certainly, sir. Radiogram from FP 1 "All well on board. *Pillau* and *Tangiers II* have reached us. In tow again. Hope to reach anchorage this morning. Gisela safe on board",' recited Emmerich, without looking at the paper, for the words had burnt themselves into his brain. 'Addressed to Emmerich, wireless operator, personally! And it says something else as well, Mr Lennartz. It continues,' Emmerich passed his hand over his mouth—'"Difficulties caused by Pechtold's actions. Recommend caution." That's what it says.' Emmerich pointed to the paper with his long, thin forefinger. 'And addressed to me personally. That shows how important it was that I should remain on duty. Mr Droste knew that he could always count on my being at my post.'

Lennartz rubbed his eyes and leaned back in his chair. His face had gone gray. He stared at the paper, following with his finger the shorthand signs which he could not read.

'All well on board,' he muttered. 'Gisela—Droste!' He drew a deep breath. 'Well, anything else, Emmerich? Thank you very much, my boy. You've done very well indeed.' He looked up at Emmerich, surprised at receiving no answer, and saw that he had fallen sound asleep, his head on his arm, his thin, fair, boyish face still smiling.

Lennartz went over to him and placed his hand gently on his shoulder.

'Personally—to Emmerich—wireless operator,' murmured Emmerich, without opening his eyes.

Miss Helm had by this time come into the room and was standing respectfully at the door, quivering with outraged propriety at Emmerich's slight to her employer's dignity.

'He must be mad,' began Miss Helm indignantly, when for the first time she saw the sleeping Emmerich.

Lennartz put his finger to his lips and then stooped and picked up the small, slight, boyish figure. He carried him into the little private room leading out of his office and laid him on the sofa.

'Cover him up and let him sleep it out,' he said to the astonished Miss Helm.

She opened a cupboard without a word and took out a soft, warm rug. 'With your best traveling rug?' she asked, in a tone of faint protest, and seemed very surprised when Lennartz nodded assent.

He returned to his office and had just sat down at his desk when the telephone at his elbow rang sharply.

'This is the Ministry of Finance—Karleis, adviser to the Ministry speaking. I am calling you up personally, Mr Lennartz, as I want to have a word with you. I've unfortunately been away for a few days, otherwise you would have heard from me sooner. I'm quite ready—I thought I should like to tell you—to agree to an extension of the contract, even if the flying platform should be anchored a few days later than originally agreed. A part of the sum promised will be at your disposal on the twenty-second, in any case. We are at the moment very interested in your project. Since the Azores agreement between France and Portugal has been ratified, we are more than ever anxious to support any attempt to render airships independent of the Azores as a port of call.

'And now there's a little secret that I would like to tell you. Of course, I'm speaking in confidence. Proposals for the creation of various floating airports similar to the FP 1 have already been put forward, and I am sure that these will be sanctioned. You may rest assured we will not forget you and your shipyards, Mr Lennartz, when the orders are placed. And now let me wish you luck.'

'It's really very kind of you,' said Lennartz. 'And now would you be good enough to tell me one thing?' He cleared his throat nervously, fearing the confirmation of Pechtold's treachery. 'Has my manager Pechtold applied to you recently for an extension of the contract? I am, as a matter of fact, a little afraid of not being quite ready on the appointed date.'

'Pechtold? Pechtold?' repeated Karleis. 'Oh, yes, I remember! The gentleman with the beard. No, I have never heard anything from him since you introduced him to me as your manager.'

'Not even had a telephone call from him, Mr Karleis?'

'No, I am quite certain. I've never spoken to him since that meeting.'

Lennartz slowly put down the receiver. This was proof indeed of Pechtold's treachery. The old shipbuilder trembled with rage. He sat perfectly still, staring in front of him for some minutes before he could regain control of himself. He rang for Miss Helm and told her to send for Pechtold.

Half an hour later, Pechtold was sitting facing him. Lennartz studied him carefully, as if he were a stranger whom he had never seen before. Dammit, he mused, the man has no chin. Of course, he wears that beard because he has got no chin. There must be some secret understanding between all chinless people to grow beards. I'm going to kick him out, but that isn't enough punishment. It wouldn't do to let him off like that.

Pechtold nervously fingered his beard. 'I should like to talk to you frankly again, Mr Lennartz,' he said cautiously.

'I've been waiting for you to do so for months. It would have made the position very much clearer,' answered Lennartz icily. He casually picked up a glistening steel letter-opener which lay on his desk.

Pechtold quailed beneath Lennartz's steady gaze. 'I find, Mr Lennartz, that I should not be doing justice to myself by continuing my work in these yards. The twenty-second will be here in three days, and the FP 1 is not yet found. I regard the prospects as so black that I have completely lost confidence, and I feel my work would suffer in consequence.'

Lennartz nodded and smiled. 'You are anticipating my wishes,' he said heartily.

Pechtold looked at him keenly. So the old fox wants to keep up appearances to the end, he thought. His courage will soon ebb.

'I've been astonished at the composure with which you have received the news of the disappearance of your daughter and Ellissen the airman,' Pechtold went on, preparing for his great stroke. 'It can unhappily no longer be concealed from the public, for the first news of the mishap is in this morning's paper.' He drew a newspaper from his pocket.

Lennartz waved it away. 'We will contradict the news,' he replied indifferently. But Pechtold noticed that he seemed to take a firmer grip of the letter-opener. His whole manner seemed to him unnatural. After all, it was not unknown for apparently sane people to be seized by a sudden mad impulse and run amok.

'I regret I must tender my resignation, Mr Lennartz,' said Pechtold bluntly, determined to end the conversation and get away as quickly as he could.

'No regrets, Pechtold, no regrets! To tell the truth, it's a pleasure to me.'

Pechtold looked anxiously towards the door, convinced now that the strain had been too much for Lennartz's mind. He was obviously no longer the cool, calm business man whose keen brain and organizing ability had helped to launch the FP 1.

'You're clever,' continued Lennartz, in the same unmoved tone. 'You've been able to conceal for years the fact that you are a villain of the deepest dye. That in itself is a remarkable performance. Your resignation does not quite end our connection, however. There are one or two matters I want cleared up—matters in which you have played a double game, if I'm not very much mistaken.'

The roar of the dying lion, thought Pechtold. That wouldn't frighten him. Lennartz had certainly got wind of something. What could it be? Not anything he could prove. Well, if he played his cards well, there was nothing to stop him from being head of these yards.

'Get out,' Lennartz suddenly shouted at him.

Pechtold looked at his distorted face, absolutely livid with rage, and backed hastily towards the door. Luckily the old shipbuilder did not attempt to follow him. 'Remember me to Hansly,' he called after his disappearing figure. By this time Pechtold had reached the door and wrenched it open, still obsessed with the idea that he was dealing with a madman. 'God! I certainly will remember him to Hansly!' he muttered viciously to himself.

He walked rapidly down the corridor, stepped into a telephone box and, taking up the receiver, asked to be put on to the Northern Hotel.

After a moment he heard Hansly's voice.

'Is that Hansly?' said Pechtold hurriedly. 'I must see you immediately. I can't say much here. I'm speaking from the yards. But I want to speak to you at once. I—'

'At the moment I have very little time,' broke in Hansly coolly. 'I don't see how I can manage it. As a matter of fact, I have arranged to go off by the midday train to Berlin.'

'To Berlin? Everything is going on well. Why don't you stay here?' cried Pechtold. 'The FP 1 is missing and won't turn up again and we'll get the Lennartz shipyards for a song. Old Lennartz is only waiting for an offer.'

'Can't you call me up later when I'm in Berlin?' asked Hansly.

'Listen, can't you!'

'I'm sorry, old man, I'm just rushing off to lunch.'

'Lunch, damn you! What's the good of talking about your lunch?' cried Pechtold indignantly. 'The FP 1 has—'

'Has just been safely anchored,' said Hansly, completing the sentence for him. 'I say, Pechtold, you really should invest a little more money in the affair and buy yourself a midday paper. You're very much behind the times.'

'Hansly!' shrieked Pechtold, working the telephone switch frantically, but Hansly had rung off. Pechtold slammed down the receiver. He tugged reflectively at his beard for a moment, then, gazing furtively about him, he crept to the door and hurried quietly down the stairs.

In the entrance hall two men were waiting for him.

'Mr Pechtold?' queried one, raising his hat politely.

Pechtold looked at him, and then his eyes slowly traveled round the room. No escape. He nodded blankly and apathetically. The game was up. He walked towards the door. On the front steps he gazed round once more at the great chimney of the power house which was belching forth a cloud of dark smoke, a triumphant sign of prosperity. Shrugging his shoulders, he stepped quickly into the waiting motor car, followed closely by the two men. A word to the driver and the car moved away.

By the morning of the twentieth the anchoring of the FP 1 was completed, and its wireless flashed the news to the world that the first airport was now open. Within a few hours airplanes from both sides of the Atlantic were winging their way towards it, prominent newspapers of both continents having offered large money prizes to the first plane to land on it.

Chapter Twenty Eight: Grande Hotel Finale

All the searchlights of the FP 1, the world's first floating airport, were sweeping the night sky, flashing out a radiant welcome to the guests who were flying from Europe and America to be present at the dinner party which was to usher in the festivities in honor of the successful anchoring of the great airport. Giant rays formed triumphal arches of light in the sky, through which the beams of other searchlights picked out the planes of the guests as they approached, and guided them until they safely landed on the platform.

The great hotel itself was ablaze with light. Not only was every room illuminated, but the outline of the vast building was festooned with thousands of colored lamps. From the control turret glowed a brilliant red signal light which threw a soft rosy glow on the slender grace of the lighthouse tower which crowned the roof of the hotel. From its summit a green revolving light sent out its proud message of success over the ocean.

Dinner had been in progress for some time and the usual boring speech-making was about to begin when Howard Pringle, editor of a world-famous news agency, smilingly suggested to his charming partner that they might escape into the fresh air for a few moments. She readily agreed. Choosing a favorable moment, he signed to her and they unostentatiously slipped out of the overcrowded dining room.

Pringle stepped out into the open air with a sigh of relief, breathing in the cool sea breeze thankfully. Having paid this brief tribute to the excellence of the Atlantic air, he took out a cigar and lit it with keen anticipation.

'It's lovely out here, Miss Müller,' he said, taking the arm of the tall, slender, beautifully dressed woman by his side. 'It's one of the pleasures I most enjoy—to step out of a smoky, crowded room into the cool, fresh night air.'

'Really, you don't seem to value this vaunted pleasure very highly,' laughed the girl at his side, glancing mischievously at his cigar.

'My dear Miss Müller, how unkind of you to laugh at me!'

He threw the cigar over the railing of the platform. The tiny spark disappeared into the blackness and was extinguished far below on one of the buoys. Pringle looked after it regretfully, then he looked up at the sky, where streaks of dawn on the distant horizon were beginning to mark the passing of the night.

'Men are, always will be, incurably romantic,' he said thoughtfully. 'Here we are—you and I—standing on the most up-to-date structure of modern times, in the middle of the Atlantic, hundreds and hundreds of miles from the nearest land, admiring the night and the stars and the wide sea, as calmly and as safely as if our feet were firmly planted on mother earth.'

'I never knew that you were so romantic. Quite poetical, I assure you!' laughed Miss Müller.

Pringle nodded ruefully.

'I've managed pretty well to conceal the fact till now,' he answered. 'To be romantic has its drawbacks, you know. Everything in this world is unhappily so obvious, so cut and dried, no surprise about it.'

He listened, as the sound of cheering came from the dining room.

'Do you hear that? Guess what it is! The engagement of our young genius, Bernard Droste, to Gisela Lennartz, daughter of the famous builder of the FP 1, is being announced. There's young love and the happy ending for you, just as it happens in a thousand films.'

'She's a pretty girl!'

'Have you ever seen an ugly girl as the heroine of a happy ending?' Pringle demanded. 'Of course you haven't. Real life is just as writers of romance depict it. There's nothing original or imaginative about life. It all works out to the logically happy ending.'

'It's a lucky thing, then, that there are still writers—and other men too—who see romance in everything,' replied Miss Müller, with a touch of mockery in her voice.

Pringle stopped in front of a large broken window and wrinkled up his face thoughtfully.

'Now you're joking,' he said with a sigh, as he contemplated the glass-less window frame.

Miss Müller looked at him in surprise. His tone had suddenly become serious.

Pringle turned to her and with a slight wave of his hand indicated the window. 'Look! a broken window-pane—temporarily boarded up—an accident—a mere trifle—only a matter of broken glass. But look how the floor is scratched here, as if some one had been dragged along. And see! There's a hole—a bullet hole, I wager!' He raised his hand in a melodramatic gesture. 'One of our writers of romance ought to see this. Jove! What a plot he could make out of it. Even I could write the most wonderful, the most sensational story around this broken window. A broken window! A broken promise! Hopes once soaring high only to be dashed. One man's dream fulfilled, and another's shattered. A broken window—a broken heart—who knows?'

The Veldt

Ray Bradbury

'George, I wish you'd look at the nursery.'

'What's wrong with it?'

'I don't know.'

'Well, then.'

'I just want you to look at it, is all, or call a psychologist in to look at it.'

'What would a psychologist want with a nursery?'

'You know very well what he'd want.' His wife paused in the middle of the kitchen and watched the stove busy humming to itself, making supper for four.

'It's just that the nursery is different now than it was.'

'All right, let's have a look.'

They walked down the hall of their soundproofed, Happy-life Home, which had cost them thirty thousand dollars installed, this house which clothed and fed and rocked them to sleep and played and sang and was good to them. Their approach sensitized a switch somewhere and the nursery light flicked on when they came within ten feet of it. Similarly, behind them, in the halls, lights went on and off as they left them behind, with a soft automaticity.

'Well,' said George Hadley.

They stood on the thatched floor of the nursery. It was forty feet across by forty feet long and thirty feet high; it had cost half again as much as the rest of the house. 'But nothing's too good for our children,' George had said.

The nursery was silent. It was empty as a jungle glade at hot high noon. The walls were blank and two dimensional. Now, as George and Lydia Hadley stood in the center of the room, the walls began to purr and recede into crystalline distance, it seemed, and presently an African veldt appeared, in three dimensions; on all sides, in colors reproduced to the final pebble and bit of straw. The ceiling above them became a deep sky with a hot yellow sun.

George Hadley felt the perspiration start on his brow.

'Let's get out of the sun,' he said. 'This is a little too real. But I don't see anything wrong.'

'Wait a moment, you'll see,' said his wife.

Now the hidden odorophonics were beginning to blow a wind of odor at the two people in the middle of the baked veldtland. The hot straw smell of lion grass, the cool green smell of the hidden water hole, the great rusty smell of animals, the smell of dust like a red paprika in the hot air. And now the sounds: the thump of distant antelope feet on grassy sod, the papery rustling of vultures. A shadow passed through the sky. The shadow flickered on George Hadley's upturned, sweating face.

'Filthy creatures,' he heard his wife say.

'The vultures.'

'You see, there are the lions, far over, that way. Now they're on their way to the water hole. They've just been eating,' said Lydia. 'I don't know what.'

'Some animal.' George Hadley put his hand up to shield off the burning light from his squinted eyes. 'A zebra or a baby giraffe, maybe.'

'Are you sure?' His wife sounded peculiarly tense.

'No, it's a little late to be sure,' he said, amused. 'Nothing over there I can see but cleaned bone, and the vultures dropping for what's left.'

'Did you hear that scream?' she asked.

'No.'

'About a minute ago?'

'Sorry, no.'

The lions were coming. And again George Hadley was filled with admiration for the mechanical genius who had conceived this room. A miracle of efficiency selling for an absurdly low price. Every home should have one. Oh, occasionally they frightened you with their clinical accuracy, they startled you, gave you a twinge, but most of the time what fun for everyone, not only your own son and daughter, but for yourself when you felt like a quick jaunt to a foreign land, a quick change of scenery. Well, here it was!

And here were the lions now, fifteen feet away, so real, so feverishly and startlingly real that you could feel the prickling fur on your hand, and your mouth was stuffed with the dusty upholstery smell of their heated pelts, and the yellow of them was in your eyes like the yellow of an exquisite French tapestry, the yellows of lions and summer grass, and the sound of the matted lion lungs exhaling on the silent noontide, and the smell of meat from the panting, dripping mouths.

The lions stood looking at George and Lydia Hadley with terrible green-yellow eyes.

'Watch out!' screamed Lydia.

The lions came running at them.

Lydia bolted and ran. Instinctively, George sprang after her. Outside, in the hall, with the door slammed, he was laughing and she was crying, and they both stood appalled at the other's reaction.

'George!'

'Lydia! Oh, my dear poor sweet Lydia!'

'They almost got us!'

'Walls, Lydia, remember; crystal walls, that's all they are. Oh, they look real, I must admit—Africa in your parlor—but it's all dimensional super-ractionary, supersensitive color film and mental tape film behind glass screens. It's all odorophonics and sonics, Lydia. Here's my handkerchief.'

'I'm afraid.' She came to him and put her body against him and cried steadily. 'Did you see? Did you *feel*? It's too real.'

'Now, Lydia . . .'

'You've got to tell Wendy and Peter not to read any more on Africa.'

'Of course—of course.' He patted her.

'Promise?'

'Sure.'

'And lock the nursery for a few days until I get my nerves settled.'

'You know how difficult Peter is about that. When I punished him a month ago by locking the nursery for even a few hours—the tantrum he threw! And Wendy too. They live for the nursery.'

'It's got to be locked, that's all there is to it.'

'All right.' Reluctantly he locked the huge door. 'You've been working too hard. You need a rest.'

'I don't know—I don't know,' she said, blowing her nose, sitting down in a chair that immediately began to rock and comfort her. 'Maybe I don't have enough to do. Maybe I have time to think too much. Why don't we shut the whole house off for a few days and take a vacation?'

'You mean you want to fry my eggs for me?'

'Yes.' She nodded.

'And darn my socks?'

'Yes.' A frantic, watery-eyed nodding.

'And sweep the house?'

'Yes, yes—oh, yes!'

'But I thought that's why we bought this house, so we wouldn't have to do anything?'

'That's just it. I feel like I don't belong here. The house is wife and mother now and nursemaid. Can I compete with an African veldt? Can I give a bath and scrub the children as efficiently or quickly as the automatic scrub bath can? I can not. And it isn't just me. It's you. You've been awfully nervous lately.'

'I suppose I have been smoking too much.'

'You look as if you didn't know what to do with yourself in this house, either. You smoke a little more every morning and drink a little more every afternoon and need a little more sedative every night. You're beginning to feel unnecessary too.'

'Am I?' He paused and tried to feel into himself to see what was really there.

'Oh, George!' She looked beyond him, at the nursery door. 'Those lions can't get out of there, can they?'

He looked at the door and saw it tremble as if something had jumped against it from the other side.

'Of course not,' he said.

At dinner they ate alone, for Wendy and Peter were at a special plastic carnival across town and had televised home to say they'd be late, to go ahead eating. So George Hadley, bemused, sat watching the dining-room table produce warm dishes of food from its mechanical interior.

'We forgot the ketchup,' he said.

'Sorry,' said a small voice within the table, and ketchup appeared.

As for the nursery, thought George Hadley, it won't hurt for the children to be locked out of it awhile. Too much of anything isn't good for anyone. And it was clearly indicated that the children had been spending a little too much time on Africa. That sun. He could feel it on his neck, still, like a hot paw. And the *lions*. And the smell of blood. Remarkable how the nursery caught the telepathic emanations of the children's minds and created life to fill their every desire. The children thought lions, and there were lions. The children thought zebras, and there were zebras. Sun—sun. Giraffes—giraffes. Death and death.

That *last*. He chewed tastelessly on the meat that the table had cut for him. Death thoughts. They were awfully young, Wendy and Peter, for death thoughts. Or, no, you were never too young, really. Long before you knew what death was you were wishing it on someone else. When you were two years old you were shooting people with cap pistols.

But this—the long, hot African veldt—the awful death in the jaws of a lion. And repeated again and again.

'Where are you going?'

He didn't answer Lydia. Preoccupied, he let the lights glow softly on ahead of him, extinguish behind him as he padded to the nursery door. He listened against it. Far away, a lion roared.

He unlocked the door and opened it. Just before he stepped inside, he heard a faraway scream. And then another roar from the lions, which subsided quickly.

He stepped into Africa. How many times in the last year had he opened this door and found Wonderland, Alice, the Mock Turtle, or Aladdin and his Magical Lamp, or Jack Pumpkinhead of Oz, or Dr Doolittle, or the cow jumping over a very real-appearing moon—all the delightful contraptions of a make-believe world. How often had he seen Pegasus flying in the sky ceiling, or seen fountains of red fireworks, or heard angel voices singing. But now, this yellow hot Africa, this bake oven with murder in the heat. Perhaps Lydia was right. Perhaps they needed a little vacation from the fantasy which was growing a bit too real for ten-year-old children. It was all right to exercise one's mind with gymnastic fantasies, but when the lively child mind settled on *one* pattern . . .? It seemed that, at a distance, for the past month, he had heard lions roaring, and smelled their strong odor seeping as far away as his study door. But, being busy, he had paid it no attention.

George Hadley stood on the African grassland alone. The lions looked up from their feeding, watching him. The only flaw to the illusion was the open door through which he could see his wife, far down the dark hall, like a framed picture, eating her dinner abstractedly.

'Go away,' he said to the lions.

They did not go.

He knew the principle of the room exactly. You sent out your thoughts. Whatever you thought would appear.

'Let's have Aladdin and his lamp,' he snapped.

The veldtland remained; the lions remained.

'Come on, room! I demand Aladdin!' he said.

Nothing happened. The lions mumbled in their baked pelts.

'Aladdin!'

He went back to dinner. 'The fool room's out of order,' he said. 'It won't respond.'

'Or—'

'Or what?'

'Or it *can't* respond,' said Lydia, 'because the children have thought about Africa and lions and killing so many days that the room's in a rut.'

'Could be.'

'Or Peter's set it to remain that way.'

'Set it?'

'He may have got into the machinery and fixed something.'

'Peter doesn't know machinery.'

'He's a wise one for ten. That IQ of his—'

'Nevertheless—'

'Hello, Mom. Hello, Dad.'

The Hadleys turned. Wendy and Peter were coming in the front door, cheeks like peppermint candy, eyes like bright blue agate marbles, a smell of ozone on their jumpers from their trip in the helicopter.

'You're just in time for supper,' said both parents.

'We're full of strawberry ice cream and hot dogs,' said the children, holding hands. 'But we'll sit and watch.'

'Yes, come tell us about the nursery,' said George Hadley.

The brother and sister blinked at him and then at each other. 'Nursery?'

'All about Africa and everything,' said the father with false joviality.

'I don't understand,' said Peter.

'Your mother and I were just traveling through Africa with rod and reel; Tom Swift and his Electric Lion,' said George Hadley.

'There's no Africa in the nursery,' said Peter simply.

'Oh, come now, Peter. We know better.'

'I don't remember any Africa,' said Peter to Wendy. 'Do you?'

'No.'

'Run see and come tell.'

She obeyed.

'Wendy, come back here!' said George Hadley, but she was gone. The house lights followed her like a flock of fireflies. Too late, he realized he had forgotten to lock the nursery door after his last inspection.

'Wendy'll look and come tell us,' said Peter.

'She doesn't have to tell me. I've seen it.'

'I'm sure you're mistaken, Father.'

'I'm not, Peter. Come along now.'

But Wendy was back. 'It's not Africa,' she said breathlessly.

'We'll see about this,' said George Hadley, and they all walked down the hall together and opened the nursery door.

There was a green, lovely forest, a lovely river, a purple mountain, high voices singing, and Rima, lovely and mysterious, lurking in the trees with colorful flights of butterflies, like animated bouquets, lingering in her long hair. The African veldtland was gone. The lions were gone. Only Rima was here now, singing a song so beautiful that it brought tears to your eyes.

George Hadley looked in at the changed scene. 'Go to bed,' he said to the children.

They opened their mouths.

'You heard me,' he said.

They went off to the air closet, where a wind sucked them like brown leaves up the flue to their slumber rooms.

George Hadley walked through the singing glade and picked up something that lay in the corner near where the lions had been. He walked slowly back to his wife.

'What is that?' she asked.

'An old wallet of mine,' he said.

He showed it to her. The smell of hot grass was on it and the smell of a lion. There were drops of saliva on it, it had been chewed, and there were blood smears on both sides.

He closed the nursery door and locked it, tight.

In the middle of the night he was still awake and he knew his wife was awake. 'Do you think Wendy changed it?' she said at last, in the dark room.

'Of course.'

'Made it from a veldt into a forest and put Rima there instead of lions?'

'Yes.'

'Why?'

'I don't know. But it's staying locked until I find out.'

'How did your wallet get there?'

'I don't know anything,' he said, 'except that I'm beginning to be sorry we bought that room for the children. If children are neurotic at all, a room like that—'

'It's supposed to help them work off their neuroses in a healthful way.'

'I'm starting to wonder.' He stared at the ceiling.

'We've given the children everything they ever wanted. Is this our reward—secrecy, disobedience?'

'Who was it said, "Children are carpets, they should be stepped on occasionally"? We've never lifted a hand. They're insufferable—let's admit it. They come and go when they like; they treat us as if we were offspring. They're spoiled and we're spoiled.'

'They've been acting funny ever since you forbade them to take the rocket to New York a few months ago.'

'They're not old enough to do that alone, I explained.'

'Nevertheless, I've noticed they've been decidedly cool toward us since.'

'I think I'll have David McClean come tomorrow morning to have a look at Africa.'

'But it's not Africa now, it's Green Mansions country and Rima.'

'I have a feeling it'll be Africa again before then.'

A moment later they heard the screams.

Two screams. Two people screaming from downstairs. And then a roar of lions.

'Wendy and Peter aren't in their rooms,' said his wife.

He lay in his bed with his beating heart. 'No,' he said. 'They've broken into the nursery.'

'Those screams—they sound familiar.'

'Do they?'

'Yes, awfully.'

And although their beds tried very hard, the two adults couldn't be rocked to sleep for another hour. A smell of cats was in the night air.

'Father?' said Peter.

'Yes.'

Peter looked at his shoes. He never looked at his father any more, nor at his mother. 'You aren't going to lock up the nursery for good, are you?'

'That all depends.'

'On what?' snapped Peter.

'On you and your sister. If you intersperse this Africa with a little variety—oh, Sweden perhaps, or Denmark or China—'

'I thought we were free to play as we wished.'

'You are, within reasonable bounds.'

'What's wrong with Africa, Father?'

'Oh, so now you admit you have been conjuring up Africa, do you?'

'I wouldn't want the nursery locked up,' said Peter coldly. 'Ever.'

'Matter of fact, we're thinking of turning the whole house off for about a month. Live sort of a carefree one-for-all existence.'

'That sounds dreadful! Would I have to tie my own shoes instead of letting the shoe tier do it? And brush my own teeth and comb my hair and give myself a bath?'

'It would be fun for a change, don't you think?'

'No, it would be horrid. I didn't like it when you took out the picture painter last month.'

'That's because I wanted you to learn to paint all by yourself, son.'

'I don't want to do anything but look and listen and smell; what else is there to do?'

'All right, go play in Africa.'

'Will you shut off the house sometime soon?'

'We're considering it.'

'I don't think you'd better consider it any more, Father.'

'I won't have any threats from my son!'

'Very well.' And Peter strolled off to the nursery.

'Am I on time?' said David McClean.

'Breakfast?' asked George Hadley.

'Thanks, had some. What's the trouble?'

'David, you're a psychologist.'

'I should hope so.'

'Well, then, have a look at our nursery. You saw it a year ago when you dropped by; did you notice anything peculiar about it then?'

'Can't say I did; the usual violences, a tendency toward a slight paranoia here or there, usual in children because they feel persecuted by parents constantly, but, oh, really nothing.'

They walked down the hall. 'I locked the nursery up,' explained the father, 'and the children broke back into it during the night. I let them stay so they could form the patterns for you to see.'

There was a terrible screaming from the nursery.

'There it is,' said George Hadley. 'See what you make of it.'

They walked in on the children without rapping.

The screams had faded. The lions were feeding.

'Run outside a moment, children,' said George Hadley. 'No, don't change the mental combination. Leave the walls as they are. Get!'

With the children gone, the two men stood studying the lions clustered at a distance, eating with great relish whatever it was they had caught.

'I wish I knew what it was,' said George Hadley. 'Sometimes I can almost see. Do you think if I brought high-powered binoculars here and—'

David McClean laughed dryly. 'Hardly.' He turned to study all four walls. 'How long has this been going on?'

'A little over a month.'

'It certainly doesn't *feel* good.'

'I want facts, not feelings.'

'My dear George, a psychologist never saw a fact in his life. He only hears about feelings; vague things. This doesn't feel good, I tell you. Trust my hunches and my instincts. I have a nose for something bad. This is very bad. My advice to you is to have the whole damn room torn down and your children brought to me every day during the next year for treatment.'

'Is it that bad?'

'I'm afraid so. One of the original uses of these nurseries was so that we could study the patterns left on the walls by the child's mind, study at our leisure, and help the child. In this case, however, the room has become a channel toward—destructive thoughts, instead of a release away from them.'

'Didn't you sense this before?'

'I sensed only that you had spoiled your children more than most. And now you're letting them down in some way. What way?'

'I wouldn't let them go to New York.'

'What else?'

'I've taken a few machines from the house and threatened them, a month ago, with closing up the nursery unless they did their homework. I did close it for a few days to show I meant business.'

'Ah, ha!'

'Does that mean anything?'

'Everything. Where before they had a Santa Claus now they have a Scrooge. Children prefer Santas. You've let this room and this house replace you and your wife in your children's affections. This room is their mother and father, far more important in their lives than their real parents. And now you come along and want to shut it off. No wonder there's hatred here. You can feel it coming out of the sky. Feel that sun. George, you'll have to change your life. Like too many others, you've built it around creature comforts. Why, you'd starve tomorrow if something went wrong in your kitchen. You wouldn't know how to tap an egg. Nevertheless, turn everything off. Start new. It'll take time. But we'll make good children out of bad in a year, wait and see.'

'But won't the shock be too much for the children, shutting the room up abruptly, for good?'

'I don't want them going any deeper into this, that's all.'

The lions were finished with their red feast.

The lions were standing on the edge of the clearing watching the two men.

'Now *I'm* feeling persecuted,' said McClean. 'Let's get out of here. I never have cared for these damned rooms. Make me nervous.'

'The lions look real, don't they?' said George Hadley. 'I don't suppose there's any way—'

'What?'

'—that they could *become* real?'

'Not that I know.'

'Some flaw in the machinery, a tampering or something?'

'No.'

They went to the door.

'I don't imagine the room will like being turned off,' said the father. 'Nothing ever likes to die—even a room.'

'I wonder if it hates me for wanting to switch it off?'

'Paranoia is thick around here today,' said David McClean. 'You can follow it like a spoor. Hello.' He bent and picked up a bloody scarf. 'This yours?'

'No.' George Hadley's face was rigid. 'It belongs to Lydia.'

They went to the fuse box together and threw the switch that killed the nursery.

The two children were in hysterics. They screamed and pranced and threw things. They yelled and sobbed and swore and jumped at the furniture.

'You can't do that to the nursery, you can't!'

'Now, children.'

The children flung themselves onto a couch, weeping.

'George,' said Lydia Hadley, 'turn on the nursery, just for a few moments. You can't be so abrupt.'

'No.'

'You can't be so cruel.'

'Lydia, it's off, and it stays off. And the whole damn house dies as of here and now. The more I see of the mess we've put ourselves in, the more it sickens me. We've been contemplating our mechanical, electronic navels for too long. My God, how we need a breath of honest air!'

And he marched about the house turning off the voice clocks, the stoves, the heaters, the shoe shiners, the shoe lacers, the body scrubbers and swabbers and massagers, and every other machine he could put his hand to.

The house was full of dead bodies, it seemed. It felt like a mechanical cemetery. So silent. None of the humming hidden energy of machines waiting to function at the tap of a button.

'Don't let them do it!' wailed Peter at the ceiling, as if he was talking to the house, the nursery. 'Don't let Father kill everything.' He turned to his father. 'Oh, I hate you!'

'Insults won't get you anywhere.'

'I wish you were dead!'

'We were, for a long while. Now we're going to really start living. Instead of being handled and massaged, we're going to *live*.'

Wendy was still crying and Peter joined her again. 'Just a moment, just one moment, just another moment of nursery,' they wailed.

'Oh, George,' said the wife, 'it can't hurt.'

'All right—all right, if they'll only just shut up. One minute, mind you, and then off forever.'

'Daddy, Daddy, Daddy!' sang the children, smiling with wet faces.

'And then we're going on a vacation. David McClean is coming back in half an hour to help us move out and get to the airport. I'm going to dress. You turn the nursery on for a minute, Lydia, just a minute, mind you.'

And the three of them went babbling off while he let himself be vacuumed upstairs through the air flue and set about dressing himself. A minute later Lydia appeared.

'I'll be glad when we get away,' she sighed.

'Did you leave them in the nursery?'

'I wanted to dress too. Oh, that horrid Africa. What can they see in it?'

'Well, in five minutes we'll be on our way to Iowa. Lord, how did we ever get in this house? What prompted us to buy a nightmare?'

'Pride, money, foolishness.'

'I think we'd better get downstairs before those kids get engrossed with those damned beasts again.'

Just then they heard the children calling, 'Daddy, Mommy, come quick—quick!'

They went downstairs in the air flue and ran down the hall. The children were nowhere in sight. 'Wendy? Peter!'

They ran into the nursery. The veldtland was empty save for the lions waiting, looking at them. 'Peter, Wendy?'

The door slammed.

'Wendy, Peter!'

George Hadley and his wife whirled and ran back to the door.

'Open the door!' cried George Hadley, trying the knob. 'Why, they've locked it from the outside! Peter!' He beat at the door. 'Open up!'

He heard Peter's voice outside, against the door.

'Don't let them switch off the nursery and the house,' he was saying.

Mr and Mrs George Hadley beat at the door. 'Now, don't be ridiculous, children. It's time to go. Mr McClean'll be here in a minute and . . .'

And then they heard the sounds.

The lions on three sides of them, in the yellow veldt grass, padding through the dry straw, rumbling and roaring in their throats.

The lions.

Mr Hadley looked at his wife and they turned and looked back at the beasts edging slowly forward, crouching, tails stiff.

Mr and Mrs Hadley screamed.

And suddenly they realized why those other screams had sounded familiar.

❖ ❖ ❖

'Well, here I am,' said David McClean in the nursery doorway. 'Oh, hello.' He stared at the two children seated in the center of the open glade eating a little picnic lunch. Beyond them was the water hole and the yellow veldtland; above was the hot sun. He began to perspire. 'Where are your father and mother?'

The children looked up and smiled. 'Oh, they'll be here directly.'

'Good, we must get going.' At a distance Mr McClean saw the lions fighting and clawing and then quieting down to feed in silence under the shady trees.

He squinted at the lions with his hand up to his eyes.

Now the lions were done feeding. They moved to the water hole to drink.

A shadow flickered over Mr McClean's hot face. Many shadows flickered. The vultures were dropping down the blazing sky.

'A cup of tea?' asked Wendy in the silence.

The Racer

Ib Melchior

Willie felt the familiar intoxicating excitement. His mouth was dry; his heart beat faster, all his senses seemed more aware than ever. It was a few minutes before 0800 hours—his time to start.

This was the day. From all the Long Island Starting Fields the Racers were taking off at 15-minute intervals. The sputter and roar of cars warming up were everywhere. The smell of oil and fuel fumes permeated the air. The hubbub of the great crowd was a steady din. This was the biggest race of the year—New York to Los Angeles—100,000 bucks to the winner! Willie was determined to better his winning record of last year: 33 hours, 27 minutes, 12 seconds in Time. And although it was becoming increasingly difficult he'd do his damnedest to better his Score too!

He took a last walk of inspection around his car. Sleek, lowslung, dark brown, the practically indestructible plastiglass top looking deceptively fragile, like a soap bubble. Not bad for an old-fashioned diesel job. He kicked the solid plastirubber tires in the time-honored fashion of all drivers. Hank was giving a last-minute shine to the needle-sharp durasteel horns protruding from the front fenders. Willie's car wasn't nicknamed 'The Bull' without reason. The front of the car was built like a streamlined bull's head complete with bloodshot, evil-looking eyes, iron ring through flaring nostrils—and the horns. Although most of the racing cars were built to look like tigers, or sharks, or eagles, there *were* a few bulls—but Willie's horns were unequalled.

'Car 79 ready for Start in five minutes,' the loudspeaker blared. 'Car 79. Willie Connors, driver. Hank Morowski, mechanic. Ready your car for Start in five minutes.'

Willie and Hank took their places in 'The Bull.' At a touch by Willie on the starter the powerful diesel engine began a low purr. They drove slowly to the starting line.

'Last Check!' said Willie.

'Right,' came Hank's answer.

'Oil and Fuel?'

'40 hours.'

'Cooling Fluid?'

'Sealed.'

'No-Sleeps?'

'Check.'

'Energene Tabs?'

'Check.'

'Thermo Drink?'

'Check.'

The Starter held the checkered flag high over his head. The crowds packing the grandstands were on their feet. Hushed. Waiting.

'Here we go!' whispered Willie.

The flag fell. A tremendous cry rose from the crowd. But Willie hardly heard it. Accelerating furiously he pushed his car to its top speed of 190 miles an hour within seconds—shooting like a bullet along the straight-away toward Manhattan. He was elated; exhilarated. He was a Racer. And full of tricks!

Willie shot through the Tunnel directly to Jersey.

'Well?' grumbled Hank. 'Can you tell me now?'

'Toledo,' said Willie. 'Toledo, Ohio. On the Thruway. We should make it in under three hours.'

He felt a slight annoyance with Hank. There was no reason for the man to be touchy. He knew a driver didn't tell *anyone* the racing route he'd selected. News like that had a habit of getting around. It could cost a Racer his Score.

'There's not much chance of anything coming up until after we hit Toledo,' Willie said, 'but keep your eyes peeled. You never know.'

Hank merely grunted.

It was exactly 1048 hours when 'The Bull' streaked into the deserted streets of Toledo.

'OK—what now?' asked Hank.

'Grand Rapids, Michigan,' said Willie laconically.

'Grand Rapids! But that's—that's an easy 300 miles detour!'

'I know.'

'Are you crazy? It'll cost us a couple of hours.'

'So Grand Rapids is all the way up between the Lakes. So who'll be expecting us up there?'

'Oh! Oh, yeah, I see,' said Hank.

'The *Time* isn't everything, my friend. Whoever said the shortest distance between two points is a straight line? The *Score* counts too. And here's where we pick up *our* Score!'

The first Tragi-Acc never even knew the Racer had arrived. 'The Bull' struck him squarely, threw him up in the air and let him slide off its plasti-glass back, leaving a red smear behind and somewhat to the left of Willie—all in a split second . . .

Near Calvin College an imprudent coed found herself too far from cover when the Racer suddenly came streaking down the campus. Frantically she sprinted for safety, but she didn't have a chance with a driver like Willie behind the wheel. The razor sharp horn on the right fender sliced through her spine so cleanly that the jar wasn't even felt inside the car.

Leaving town the Racer was in luck again. An elderly woman had left the sanctuary of her stone-walled garden to rescue a straying cat. She was so easy to hit that Willie felt a little cheated.

At 1232 hours they were on the speedway headed for Kansas City.

Hank looked in awe at Willie. 'Three!' he murmured dreamily, 'a Score of three already. And all of them Kills—for sure. You *really* know how to drive!'

Hank settled back contentedly as if he could already feel his 25,000 dollar cut in his pocket. He began to whistle '*The Racers Are Roaring*' off key.

Even after his good Score it annoyed Willie. And for some reason he kept remembering the belatedly pleading look in the old woman's eyes as he struck her. Funny *that* should stay with him . . .

He estimated they'd hit Kansas City at around 1815 hours, CST. Hank turned on the radio. Peoria, Illinois, was warning its citizens of the approach of a Racer. All spectators should watch from safety places. Willie grinned. That would be him. Well—he wasn't looking for any Score in Peoria.

Dayton, Ohio, told of a Racer having made a Tragic Accident Score of one, and Fort Wayne, Indiana, was crowing over the fact that three Racers had passed through without scoring once. From what he heard it seemed to Willie he had a comfortable lead, both in Time and Score.

They were receiving Kansas City now. An oily-voiced announcer was filling in the time between Racing Scores with what appeared to be a brief history of Racing.

'. . . and the most popular spectator sports of the latter half of the 20th Century were such mildly exciting pursuits as boxing and wrestling. Of course the spectators enjoyed seeing the combatants trying to maim each other, and there was always the chance of the hoped-for fatal accident.

'Motor Racing, however, gave a much greater opportunity for the Tragic Accidents so exciting to the spectator. One of the most famed old speedways, Indianapolis, where many drivers and spectators alike ended as bloody Tragi-Accs, is today the nation's racing shrine. Motor Racing was already then held all over the world, sometimes with Scores reaching the hundred mark, and long-distance races were popular.

'The modern Race makes it possible for the entire population to . . .'

'Willie switched off the radio. Why did they always have to stress the *Score? Time* was important too. The *speed*—and the *endurance*. That was part of an Ace Racer as well as his scoring ability. He took an Energene Tab. They were entering Kansas City.

The check point officials told Willie that there were three Racers with better Time than he, and one had tied his Score. 'The Bull' stayed just long enough in the check point pit for Hank to make a quick engine inspection—then they took off again. It was 1818 hours, CST, when they left the city limits behind. They'd been driving over nine hours.

About 50 miles along the Thruway to Denver, just after passing through a little town called Lawrence, Willie suddenly slowed down. Hank, who'd been dozing, sat up in alarm.

'What's the matter?' he cried. 'What's wrong?'

'Nothing's wrong,' Willie said irritably. 'Relax. You seem to be good at that.'

'But why are you slowing down?'

'You heard the check point record. Our Score's already been tied. We've got to better it,' Willie answered grimly.

The plastirubber tires screeched on the concrete speedway as Willie turned down an exit leading to a Class II road.

'Why down here?' asked Hank. 'You can only go about 80 MPH.'

A large lumi-sign appeared on the side of the road ahead—

LONE STAR
11 Miles

it announced.

Willie pointed. 'That's why,' he said curtly.

In a few minutes Lone Star came into view. It was a small village. Willie was traveling as fast as he could on the secondary road. He plowed through a flock of chickens, hurtled over a little mongrel dog, which crawled yelping towards the safety of a house and the waiting arms of a little girl, and managed to graze the leg of a husky youth who vaulted a high wooden fence—then they were through Lone Star.

Hank activated the little dashboard screen which gave them a rear view. 'That's not going to do much for our Score,' he remarked sourly.

'Oh, shut up!' Willie exploded, surprising both himself and Hank.

What was the *matter* with him? He couldn't be getting tired already. He swallowed a No-Sleep. That'd help.

Hank was quiet as they sped through Topeka and took the Thruway to Oklahoma City, but out of the corner of his eyes he was looking speculatively at Willie, hunched over the wheel.

It was getting dusk. Willie switched on his powerful headbeams. They had a faint reddish tint because of the coloring of 'The Bull's eyes. They had just whizzed through a little burg named Perry, when there was a series of sharp cracks. Willie started.

'There they go again!' chortled Hank. 'Those dumb hinterland hicks will never learn they can't hurt us with their fly-poppers.' He knocked the plastiglass dome affectionately. 'Takes atomic pellets to get through this baby.'

Of course! He *must* be on edge to be taken by surprise like that. He'd run into the Anti-Racers before. Just a handful of malcontents. The Racing Commission had already declared them illegal. Still—at every race they took pot shots at the Racers; a sort of pathetic defiance. Why should anyone want to do away with Racing?

They were entering the outskirts of Oklahoma City. Willie killed his headbeams. No need to advertise.

Suddenly Hank grabbed his arm. Wordlessly he pointed. There— garish and gaudy—gleamed the neon sign of a theater . . .

Willie slowed to a crawl. He pulled over to the curb and the dark car melted into the shadows. He glanced at the clock. 2203 hours. Perhaps . . .

Down the street a man cautiously stuck his head out from the theater entrance. Warily he emerged completely, looking up and down the street carefully. He did not see 'The Bull.' Presently he ventured out into the center of the roadway. He stood still listening for a moment. Then he turned and beckoned towards the theater. Immediately a small group of people emerged at a run.

Now!

The acceleration slammed the Racers back in their seats. 'The Bull' shot forward and bore down on the little knot of petrified people with appalling speed.

This time there was no mistaking the hits. A quick succession of pars had Willie calling upon all his driving skill to keep from losing control. Hank pressed the Clean-Spray button to wash the blood off the front of the dome. He sat with eyes glued to the rear view screen.

'Man, oh man,' he murmured. 'What a record! What a Score!' He turned to Willie. 'Please,' he said, 'please stop. Let's get out. I know it's against regulations, but I've just gotta see how we did. It won't take long. We can afford a couple of minutes' Time now!'

Suddenly Willie felt he had to get out too. This was the biggest Tragi-Acc he'd ever had. He had a vague feeling there was something he wanted to do. He brought the car to a stop. They stepped out.

Within seconds the deserted street was swarming with people. Now the Racers were out of their car they felt safe. And curious. A few of them pressed forward to take a look at Willie. Naturally he was recognized. His photo had been seen in one way or another by everyone.

Willie was gratified by this obvious adulation. He looked about him. There were many people in the street now. But—but they were not all fawning and beaming upon him. Willie frowned. Most of them looked grim—even hostile. Why? What was wrong? Wasn't he one of their greatest Racers? And hadn't he just made a record Score? Given them a Tragi-Acc they wouldn't soon forget? What was the matter with those hicks?

Suddenly the crowd parted. Slowly a young girl walked up to Willie. She was beautiful—even with the terrible anger burning on her face. In her arms she held the still body of a child. She looked straight at Willie with loathing in her eyes. Her voice was low but steady when she said:

'*Butcher*!'

Someone in the crowd called: 'Careful, Muriel!' but she paid no heed. Turning from him she walked on through the crowd, parting for her.

Willie was stunned.

'Come on, let's get out of here,' Hank said anxiously.

Willie didn't answer. He was looking back through the crowd to the scene of his Tragi-Acc. Never before had he stopped. Never before had he been this close. He could hear the moaning and sobbing of the Maims over the low murmur of the crowd. It made him uneasy. Back there they worked hurriedly to get the Tragi-Accs off the street. *There were so many of them* ... Butcher ...?

All at once he was conscious of Hank pulling at him.

'Let's get roaring! Let's go!'

Quickly he turned and entered the car. Almost at once the street was empty. He turned on his headbeams and started up. Faster—and faster. The street was dead—empty ...

No! There! Someone! Holding a ...

It was butcher—no, *Muriel*. She stood rooted to the spot in the middle of the street holding the child in her arms. In the glaring headlights her face was white, her eyes terrible, burning, dark . . .garish and gaudy— gleamed the neon sign of a theater . . .

Willie and passed . . .

They'd lost 13 minutes. Now they were on their way to El Paso, Texas. The nagging headache Willie'd suffered the whole week of planning before the race had returned. He reached for a No-Sleep, hesitated a second, then took another.

Hank glanced at him, worriedly. 'Easy, boy!'

Willie didn't answer.

'That Anti-Racer get under your skin?' Hank suggested. 'Don't let it bother you.'

'Butcher,' she'd said. 'Butcher!'

Willie was staring through the plastiglass dome at the racing pool of light from the headbeams. 'The Bull' was tearing along the Thruway at almost 180 MPH.

What was that? There—in the light? It was a face—terrible, dark eyes— getting larger—larger—*Muriel*! It was butcher—no, Muriel! No—it was a Racer—a Racing Car with Muriel's face, shrieking down upon him— closer—closer . . .

He threw his arms in front of his face. Dimly he heard Hank shout 'Willie!' He felt the car lurch. Automatically he tightened his grip on the wheel. They had careened close to the shoulder of the speedway. Willie sat up. Ahead of him the road was clear—and empty.

It was still dark when they hit El Paso. The radio told them their Oklahoma Score. Five and eight. Five Kills—eight Maims! Hank was delighted. They were close to setting a record. He'd already begun to spend his $25,000.

Willie was uneasy. His headache was worse. His hands were clammy. He kept hearing Muriel's voice saying: 'Butcher'—'Butcher'—'Butcher!' . . .

But he was *not* a butcher. He was a Racer! He'd show them. He'd win this race.

El Paso was a disappointment. Not a soul in sight. Phoenix next.

The clock said 0658 hours, MST, when they roared into Phoenix. The streets were clear. Willie had to slow down to take a corner. As he sped into the new street he saw her. She was running to cross the roadway. Hank whooped.

'Go, Willie! Go!'

The girl looked up an instant in terror.

Her face!

It was the old woman with the cat! No!—it was Muriel. Muriel with the big, dark eyes . . .

In the last split second Willie touched the power steering. 'The Bull' responded immediately, and shot past the girl as she scampered to safety.

'What the hell is the matter with you?' Hank roared at Willie. 'You could've scored! Are you out of your head?'

'We don't need her. We'll win without her. I—I—'

Yes, why hadn't he scored? It wasn't Muriel. Muriel was back in butcher—in—Oklahoma City. Damn this headache!

'Maybe so,' said Hank angrily. 'But I wanna be sure. And what about the bonus for setting a record? Ten thousand apiece. And we're close.' He looked slyly at Willie. 'Or—maybe you've lost your nerve. Wonder what the Commission will say to that?'

'I've got plenty of nerve,' Willie snapped.

'Prove it!' said Hank quickly. He pointed to the dashboard map slowly tracing their progress. 'There. See that village? With the screwy name? *Wikieup*! Off the Thruway. Let's see you score there!'

Willie said nothing. He hadn't lost his nerve, he knew that. He was the best of the Racers. No one could drive like he could; constant top speed, and the stamina it took, the split-second timing, the unerring judgment—

'Well?'

'All right,' Willie agreed.

They hadn't even reached Wikieup when they spotted the farmer. He didn't have a chance. 'The Bull' came charging down upon him. But in the last moment the car veered slightly. One of the horns ripped the man's hip open. In the rear view screen Willie saw him get up and hobble off the road.

'You could've made it a Kill,' Hank growled accusingly. 'Why didn't you?'

'Bad road,' Willie said. 'The wheel slipped on a stone.'

That's what must have happened, he thought. He didn't consciously veer away from the man. He was a good Racer. He couldn't help a bad road.

Needles was left behind at 1045 hours, PST. No one had been out. Hank turned on the radio to a Needles station:

'. . . has just left the city going West. No other Racer is reported within twenty minutes of the city. We repeat: A Racer has just left . . .'

Hank clicked it off. 'Hear that?' he said excitedly. 'Twenty minutes. They don't expect anyone for twenty minutes!' He took hold of Willie's arm. 'Turn around! Here's where we can get ourselves that Record Score. Turn around, Willie!'

'We don't need it.'

'I do! *I want that bonus*!'

Willie made no answer.

'Listen to me, you two-bit Racer!' Hank's tone was menacing. 'You or nobody else is going to cheat me out of that bonus. You've been acting mighty peculiar. More like an Anti-Racer! Ever since you stopped at that Tragi-Acc back there. Yeah! That girl—that Anti-Racer who called you a—a butcher. Listen! You get that Record Score, or I'll report you to the Commission for having snooped around a Tragi-Acc. You'll never race again!'

Never race again! Willie's brain was whirling. But he *was* a Racer. Not a butcher. A *Racer*. Record Score? Yes—that's what he had to do. Set a record. Be the best damned Racer of them all.

Without a word he turned the car. In minutes they were back at the Needles suburbs. That building. A school house. And there—marching orderly in two rows with their teacher, a class, a whole class of children . . .

'The Bull' came charging down the street. Only a couple of hundred feet now to that Record Score . . .

But what was that—it was . . . they were *Muriel*—they were all Muriel. Terrible, dark eyes. No!—they were children—the child in Muriel's arms. *They were all the child in Muriel's arms*! Were they already moaning and screaming? Butcher! *Butcher*! No! He couldn't butcher them—he was a *Racer*—not a *butcher*. *Not a butcher*! Deliberately he swung the car to the empty side of the street.

Suddenly he felt Hank's hands up on the wheel. 'You—dirty—lousy—Anti-Racer!' the mechanic snarled as he struggled for the wheel.

The car lurched. The two men fought savagely for control. They were only yards from the fleeing children.

With a violent wrench Willie turned the wheel sharply. The car was going 165 miles an hour when it struck the school house and crashed through the wall into the empty building.

The voices came to Willie through thick wads of cotton—and they kept fading in and out.

'. . . *dead instantaneously. But the Racer is still* . . .'

It sounded like the voice of Muriel. Muriel . . .

'. . . *keeps calling for* . . .'

Willie tried to open his eyes. Everything was milky white. Why was there so much fog? A face was bending over him. Muriel? No—it was not Muriel. He lost consciousness again.

When he opened his eyes once more he knew he was not alone. He turned his head. A girl was sitting at his bedside. Muriel . . .

It *was* Muriel.

He tried to sit up.

'It's you! But—but, how . . . ?'

The girl put her hand on his arm.

'The radio. They said you kept calling for "Muriel." I knew. Never mind that now.'

She looked steadily at him. Her eyes were not terrible—not burning—only dark, and puzzled.

'Why did you call for *me*?' she asked earnestly.

Willie struggled to sit up.

'I wanted to tell you,' he said, 'to tell you—I—I am not a butcher!'

The girl looked at him for a long moment. Then she leaned down and whispered to him:

'*Nor a Racer!*'

The Thought-Monster

Amelia Reynolds Long

The first of the series of outrages was the case of Welton Grimm. Grimm was a retired farmer with a little place about three miles from town, who apparently had not an enemy in the world; yet one morning he was discovered dead in a patch of woods near his home with a look of horror on his face that made the flesh creep on those who found him. There were no marks of violence upon the body; only that expression of horrified revulsion at unspeakable things. Two doctors, a coroner, and a jury puzzled over it, and at last gave out the statement that he had been the victim of a heart attack—which nobody believed.

For a while the case was discussed, as all such things are in small towns. Then, just as it was about to drop into oblivion, the second blow fell: another man, a stranger this time, was found dead under identical circumstances in the same spot. Before the town could digest this, two half-grown boys were added to the list of victims, and the very next night a woman was found dead under similar conditions about a mile distant.

The police scoured the countryside for the culprit—for it was now admitted that the deaths were the result of foul play—but to no avail. They could find nothing: there seemed to be nothing to find. But when again the Terror struck, this time claiming for its victim the mayor himself, the townspeople decided that something drastic must be done at once; and they sent to New York for a detective.

He came—a keen-witted, intelligent man named Gibson, with a long list of brilliant exploits behind him. After going over the case with the chief of police, he pointed out a fact that was so obvious it was a wonder we had not seen it ourselves.

'Those people have died of fright,' he said. 'There is someone, probably an escaped lunatic, hiding in the woods who is so hideous that the very sight of him frightens the beholder to death. Since all the deaths occurred within a mile of each other, you will find him hiding somewhere within that comparatively small area.'

'But we searched the woods,' objected the chief. 'We searched them thoroughly. There wasn't the sign of a thing.'

'Did you ever search at night?' asked Gibson.

'Well, no,' the chief admitted.

'Whatever your Terror is,' went on the detective, 'he is too clever to come out in daylight. But at night he is sure of himself; so that is when we must lie in wait for him.'

Everyone saw the sense of this plan, but few were willing to try it. At last, however, Gibson collected some half-dozen men, and they stationed themselves, armed to the teeth, throughout the patch of woods to wait for the thing. They had a series of prearranged whistle signals by which they could communicate with one another should occasion arise.

The night passed quietly; but in the morning it was found that the outrages had taken a new turn: Gibson had completely disappeared! The woods were searched for him and a pond was drained for his body, but without result. Then, about a week later, he wandered into town—a mouthing, gibbering idiot!

The morale of the people began to break under this new horror. And to add to their consternation, the grave of the mayor was opened the night before Gibson's return, and his body dragged half out of the coffin. A great mass meeting, for the purpose of taking counsel against the Terror, was now called. The hall was jammed to capacity, for all came who could come.

One of the town councilmen was addressing the assembly. He was in the most earnest part of his address when suddenly he stopped. No one had been conscious of any of the doors opening, yet we all knew that another presence had entered the room! There was an apprehensive shuffling of feet and craning of necks as uneasiness among the crowd grew. The speaker took a sip of water, and tried to go on, but without success. And then it was as if a thin veil began to form between us and the electric chandelier overhead.

With that, hysteria broke loose. There was a stampede for the exits, in which three people were trampled to death. Later, the body of the speaker was found upon the platform. The face was twisted into a mask of overwhelming horror.

The people were stunned. They crept into their churches to pray. And, as if in answer to their prayers, came Michael Cummings, psychic investigator.

✧ ✧ ✧

Cummings first presented himself before the town council. 'I have been reading about your trouble down here,' he said, 'and I would like to try my hand at solving the mystery.'

He was welcomed with open arms.

He did not consider the possibility of an escaped lunatic in the neighborhood, as Gibson had done. 'No madman could be responsible for all this,' he said when someone mentioned the subject. 'It takes more than the sight of a poor, deranged mind to kill a strong man. I believe that there is a supernatural force at work; possibly one of the little-understood elementals that are sometimes aroused or liberated by a disturbance of the laws of nature. I shall go out to the woods around dusk this evening and look the ground over.'

'But, man,' gasped the town treasurer, 'that's suicide! No man comes out of there alive who enters after nightfall.'

'There is little danger until after night has actually fallen,' smiled Cummings. 'Besides, even should I meet the Terror, I am armed against it in a way that none of the others were.'

He went, but learned nothing. The next morning a farmer, who lived about half a mile away, was found dead in his barn.

That afternoon Cummings called upon Dr Bradley, who was the coroner. 'I am going to make a strange request, Doctor,' he began. 'I am going to ask that you permit me to photograph the eyes of this poor man.'

The doctor, greatly mystified, gave his consent.

'In a case of violent death,' Cummings explained as he set up his apparatus, 'an image of the last thing seen is usually photographed upon the retina of the eye. I want to see whether a carefully developed enlargement won't show us that image.'

At Bradley's interested request, he promised to let him know the results of the experiment. Two or three hours later, therefore, he returned to the doctor's office.

'I have drawn a blank,' he confessed. 'The eye shows absolutely nothing.'

'Your theory didn't work, then?' asked Bradley sympathetically.

'No,' Cummings answered. 'And yet I don't see how it could have failed in a case of this kind. There is one alternative: perhaps there was nothing for the dying man to see.'

'But,' objected the doctor, 'I thought it was what he saw that killed him.'

'Fear,' said Cummings, 'can enter a man's soul through other senses than sight. Anyway, I shall work on that hypothesis for a while, and see where it leads me.' Abruptly he changed the subject. 'Who lives in that rambling old place half a mile out from town?' he asked.

'A scientist named Walgate,' answered the doctor. 'I'll admit,' he went on quickly, 'that the location of his house and his being something of a recluse make it look as if he might be concerned with the mystery, but we have proof that he isn't. For one thing, he was here in town in the company of the most reputable people the nights that the first three outrages took place.'

'Could he have any sort of creature concealed about the place on which he might be experimenting?' asked Cummings.

'No,' answered Bradley. 'He isn't that kind of a scientist. Psychology in its most abstract form is his line. In fact, I was around to see him myself, thinking he might possibly have something like that.'

'I wonder,' said Cummings, 'if you would mind going again.'

The next day they called upon Dr Walgate. They found a courteous, scholarly man plainly as much concerned over the mysterious deaths as they were.

'Doctor,' asked Cummings presently, 'have you ever considered the possibility of the Terror's being nothing physical at all, but a kind of psychical entity?'

The doctor shot him a keen, swift glance. 'Yes,' he said. 'I have considered that.'

'And you have come to the conclusion—?'

'It is difficult to come to a conclusion in matters like this unless one has some definite point to start from.'

To Bradley's surprise, Cummings did not follow up this very evident lead, but soon brought the visit to a close. 'Why didn't you press the psychical entity opening?' he asked a little reproachfully as they walked back to town. 'It was plain that Walgate either suspects or knows something in that direction.'

'Suspects, may even know, but can not prove,' corrected Cummings. 'But he is the type of man who will not speak until he *can* prove. Meanwhile to attempt to force his confidence would defeat our own purpose.'

At Cummings' suggestion, the people in the outlying districts kept violet-shaded lights burning outside their houses after nightfall.

'The thing which we are fighting,' he said, 'is supernatural, and our best weapon against it is the violet ray, which is highly inimical, and sometimes even fatal, to it.'

'Look here,' said Bradley, 'aren't you introducing a little too much legerdemain into this? I can accept a primitive natural force run amuck, but when you begin to fight it with colored lights, I grow skeptical. Is this an attempt to give the people a mental sedative?'

Cummings only smiled, and the people went on burning their lights. The outrages ceased.

'It looks as if you had razed the ghost after all,' admitted Bradley when a month had passed unmarred by any fresh tragedy.

But Cummings shook his head. 'No,' he said, 'I have only staved him off temporarily. As soon as we should cease to use the lights, he would return. More, he may even grow strong enough to resist them. I think that in a day or two I shall visit Walgate. Perhaps I can induce him to talk.'

But that time never came. That night a car drove into town with a dead man in the driver's seat, his hands gripped to the wheel in convulsions. In the tonneau sat two more corpses whose faces, like that of the driver, were contorted with stark terror. Only the ruler-like straightness of the road and the vise-like grip of those dead hands upon the wheel had kept the car from overturning. It was like a challenge from the Terror to the town.

For the first time, Cummings was discouraged. 'We can protect ourselves,' he said, 'but we can not protect those who come here from the outside. Something must be done at once, and yet there is nothing that can be done. The situation is even more appalling than the tragedies themselves.'

And then, in the gray of early morning something *was* done.

Cummings and Bradley were sitting in the doctor's office when the telephone rang. Bradley answered it.

'Is that Dr Bradley?' The voice at the other end was hoarse and strained. 'This is Dr Walgate. I want you and Mr Cummings to come up to my house in half an hour. Walk straight in without ringing, and go into the living-room. There you will find a manuscript lying on the table. I want you to read it. But do not come until half an hour from now.'

'But why—what—?' stuttered Bradley in his excitement.

'Do as I tell you,' interrupted Walgate's voice. 'That is all.' A metallic click told that he had hung up.

'What do you make of it?' asked Bradley when he had repeated the message to Cummings. 'Is it a trap?'

'No, it is not,' answered Cummings promptly, 'it is not a trap. Walgate is no fool, and he accordingly will not take us for any. We had better do as he tells us.'

'Including waiting the specified half-hour before going out?'

'Yes. We don't know what he intends to do. An attempt to improve upon his directions might ruin his plans.'

Watches in hand, they sat counting off the minutes. At last Cummings rose. 'We can start now,' he said. 'Come.'

They drove out to Walgate's house, and entered as he had directed.

Bradley noticed that in the near-by woods no birds sang, and that in the house itself an unearthly stillness brooded. He experienced an unnerving intuition of new horrors about to be laid bare.

They proceeded into the living-room, and Cummings pressed the electric light button, for the daylight was still dim and uncertain. Placed conspicuously on the table was a small bundle of manuscript.

'We may as well read these now,' said Bradley. 'There's no use stopping to look for Walgate; he undoubtedly used that half-hour to make his getaway.'

Cummings picked up the manuscript and began to glance through it. 'It seems to be part of a diary,' he said. 'It is made up of entries beginning about a year ago. It looks—' He broke off to read several sentences under his breath. 'I think I had better read this aloud from the beginning,' he said.

He began to read:

'*Aug. 4.* Have been studying the material existence of thought. A fascinating subject. If thoughts have material existence, why could not the thought essence be concentrated to—Off on that wild theory again! I am too old for this nonsense.

'*Aug. 7.* I wonder if many of the so-called psychic phenomena, such as table-tipping and the like, are not in some way connected with the materiality of thought. I am tempted to try a few simple experiments.

'*Aug. 11.* I have been wasting time on these silly experiments. I must return to my respectable psychological studies.

'*Aug. 13.* Success! Today I moved a small object by the power of thought alone! Since this can be done, what will not be possible once the power is properly developed?

'*Aug. 25.* I have complete mental control! And now my old theory returns. Shall I consider it seriously? It seems too silly even to write down here; and yet—

'*Aug. 27.* I shall do it! I shall create a mental being by the concentrated power of pure thought! I am making arrangements with an architect to build in my house a room lined with lead, since lead is least conductive to thought waves, and so will not permit the precious thought essence to escape.

'*Sept. 16.* The room is finished. I have been spending five hours a day in it, concentrating upon my thought creature.

'*Oct. 18.* Today I thought I detected a kind of gathering tension in the atmosphere, but probably it was my imagination. It is too early to look for results.

'*Nov. 24.* The strain of my experiment is beginning to take my strength.

'*Dec. 12.* I fainted today in the lead room.

'*Dec. 29.* Have been forced to give up my experiment temporarily because of my health. Have locked the lead room in order that the thought essence may be preserved until I can return to complete my work.

'*Jan. 5.* Am recovering rapidly.

'*Jan. 18.* All my work has gone for nothing, and through the carelessness of a servant! Mrs Jensen, in a fervor of house-cleaning, unlocked and left open the door of the lead room! If I am to go on with my experiment, I must begin again at the beginning, for all the precious thought-essence has escaped. And just when success was so near! I have discharged Mrs Jensen. I shall keep no more servants.

'*May 1.* We have had a sad accident here. Welton Grimm, a neighbor of mine, was found dead this morning on the road which runs by the patch of woods between his farm and my house. A pity. Grimm was barely past the prime of life. Dr Bradley says it was heart failure.

'*May 15.* A strange coincidence; a stranger who was stopping in town was found dead in almost the same place that they found poor Grimm. Oddly enough, the cause of death was the same, too. Some of our more superstitious citizens are alarmed.

'*May 17.* Something is wrong here. Two boys, who, fired by the talk of their elders, had gone exploring after dark in the region where the deaths occurred, were found dead there early this morning. Someone is responsible for these tragedies; coincidence does not go so far.

'*May 18.* Another! A woman this time. On the face of each of the victims is a look of acutest terror. What can it mean?

'*May 20.* Had a most peculiar experience today. I was sitting in my study at dusk. Suddenly I felt that I was not alone; that there was another intelligence in the room with me. I looked up. There was no one there. I switched on the lights, and the illusion vanished. Am I becoming the victim of nerves?

'*May 25.* Another victim; this time our mayor. What is this Terror that is stalking among us? The people have sent to New York for a detective.

'*June 1.* I am being haunted. Three times this week I have felt distinctly that someone was following me, but when I turned to look, there was no one. Dr Bradley called. Discussed series of tragedies.

'*June 2.* I am not alone in the house. Something is living here with me. I enter a room, and know that it has just been occupied by another; I go down a dark hall, and feel something lurking in the shadows. Yet I search, and find nothing. Only brilliant lights can hold the thing at bay.

'*June 3.* Gibson, the New York detective, has disappeared. Is he, too, a victim of the Terror?

'A thought has come to me: Is there any connection between the Terror and the Thing that occupies my house with me?

'*June 5*. I have solved the mystery of the Terror, and the solution is more awful than was the mystery itself. I had gone into the lead room for some books that were stored there. Presently I became aware that something was in the room with me. This time I did not look up, but stood perfectly still, waiting and listening. And then the air was filled with something that had being, yet was not made of matter. Great, waving tentacles were groping for my mind, trying to suck it into themselves! With a scream, I rushed from the room. The experiment which I began last fall had succeeded without my knowing it, and I have let a thought-monster loose upon the community!

'*June 7*. Even a thought-monster can not live without food. On what does this demon subsist? Can it be that—

'*June 9*. Last night I committed an atrocious crime against society, but it had to be. I entered the cemetery, and opened the grave of the mayor. One glance at his blackening face showed me that he had died an imbecile. My suspicions were right; the thought-monster is a mental vampire, feeding upon the minds of its victims!

'*June 10*. Gibson has returned, but his mind is gone. The intelligence that was James Gibson has been swallowed up in the maw of my detestable invention! I am responsible for his state, and for the deaths of those other poor wretches; but what can I do? If I tell the people the nature of this force that is terrorizing the community, they will not believe me. What ordinary man could accept a creature created entirely of thought?

'*June 12*. The Thing is growing bolder. Last night it entered the town hall, where nearly a thousand people were assembled, and caused a panic. Three people were killed, not including one of our councilmen, who fell a victim to the Thing. I am four more times a murderer! Can not heaven show me a way to put an end to this?

'*June 14*. Michael Cummings, a psychical investigator, is here to run down the Terror. Will he succeed? I doubt it.

'*June 16*. Another man has died.

'*June 18*. Cummings and Dr Bradley were here today. Do they suspect me of being concerned with this series of deaths? They are right; and yet how far from the truth! No human mind could ever conceive the awfulness of that. I was tempted to tell Cummings my whole story, but held back. What proof could I offer him? How convince him that I was not mad? Even the relief of confession is denied me, for I would not be believed.

'*June 30*. Cummings is checkmating the Terror by means of the violet ray. Cummings' work is only temporary, but it has given me an idea. The violet ray, sufficiently intensified, can destroy a psychic force. I shall have the lead room fitted with violet lights; then lure the Thing there and destroy it.

'*July 3*. Have begun work wiring the lead room. I must do the work myself, since I dare not bring an electrician here for fear of the Terror. So far it has not tried to attack me.

'*July 10*. I have completed my task. But the Thing suspects something, and will not go near the room. I can feel its tentacles groping for my mind, trying to read my thoughts. I think it would attack me if it dared, but for some reason it fears me; perhaps because I am its creator.

'*July 22*. The Thing is becoming desperate through lack of food. I can feel that it is planning some bold move. Is it marking me for its next victim?

'*July 24*. This is the last entry I shall ever make in this diary, and it is addressed to you, Dr Bradley and Mr Cummings. Tonight I was in town when the death-car arrived. I knew then that the thought-monster must be destroyed at once.

'Nature always meets a vital emergency, and so she met this one. As I looked upon those four poor beings whose minds had gone to feed the thing I had created and whose lives had flickered out in the horror of what was happening to them, I saw clearly the one way to stop the havoc for which I was responsible.

'When I telephoned you, I bade you wait half an hour before coming here in order that I might arrive ahead of you and put the first part of my plan into execution; for I feared that should I take you into my confidence beforehand, one of you, through distorted humanitarian motives, might attempt to stop my going through with my design.

'This, then, is my plan. I shall go into the lead room with all mental guards down. The Thing has been particularly inimical to me lately, and, finding me in that state, will follow me in. Then I will close the door on both of us. I do not think that the Thing will suspect; a hungry beast is seldom wary of traps. When the door is safely closed, I will turn on the violet lamps. By the time you arrive and reach the end of these papers, those lamps will have done the work for which they were designed.

'You will find the lead room at the end of the hall on the first floor. Open the door carefully (it is not locked), and, if you receive the faintest intimation of an Intelligence beyond, slam it shut again and wait for the lights to complete their task. Mr Cummings had better attend to this. If you receive no such intimation, you will know that the monster is dead and that the curse so unintentionally laid upon you all is lifted forever. In your charity, do what to you seems best with the other thing you will find there; the thing that will have been

'JULIAN WALGATE.'

✧ ✧ ✧

As Cummings read the last sentence, Bradley made a dash for the door. 'Not so fast,' Cummings called after him. 'Where are you going? '

'Going!' Bradley paused momentarily in the hall. 'To that lead room, of course. The man is killing himself! Don't you see it?'

Deliberately Cummings placed the diary on the table. 'If any harm was to come to Walgate,' he said, 'the damage is already done. If not, a few minutes more in there can do him no harm, while our too hurried and careless entry may undo the work for which he was ready to pay, the highest price in man's power.'

He passed the doctor and led the way down the hall, stopping before the last door. Slowly he turned the knob, and pushed the door open a few inches. A bar of vivid purple light fell across his face.

'Is it all right? ' Bradley whispered, close behind him.

'I think so.' Cummings opened the door a bit further. In the room beyond was an atmosphere of snapped tension; of climax that had passed.

They stepped across the threshold. And then they became aware that the room still held a living occupant. From the far corner, his clothing wrinkled and torn, his hair and trim Vandyke beard in disarray, there shambled toward them a helpless, mindless idiot!

The Twonky

Lewis Padgett

The skilled—but very!—workman was a bit confused, and, in his daze, made something a little out of—time. Quite a little something, too. It looked like a standard radio, but unlike most of those complex gadgets, this one would wash the dishes!

The turnover at Mideastern Radio was so great that Mickey Lloyd couldn't keep track of his men. It wasn't only the draft; employees kept quitting and going elsewhere, at a higher salary. So when the big-headed little man in overalls wandered vaguely out of a storeroom, Lloyd took one look at the brown dungaree suit—company provided—and said mildly, 'The whistle blew half an hour ago. Hop to work.'

'Work-k-k?' The man seemed to have trouble with the word.

Drunk? Lloyd, in his capacity as foreman, couldn't permit that. He flipped away his cigarette, walked forward, and sniffed. No, it wasn't liquor. He peered at the badge on the man's overalls.

'Two-oh-four, m-mm. Are you new here?'

'New. Huh?' The man rubbed a rising bump on his forehead. He was an odd-looking little chap, bald as a vacuum tube, with a pinched, pallid face and tiny eyes that held dazed wonder.

'Come on, Joe. Wake up!' Lloyd was beginning to sound impatient. 'You work here, don't you?'

'Joe,' said the man thoughtfully. 'Work. Yes, I work. I make them.' His words ran together oddly, as though he had a cleft palate.

With another glance at the badge, Lloyd gripped Joe's arm and ran him through the assembly room. 'Here's your place. Hop to it. Know what to do?'

The other drew his scrawny body erect. 'I am—expert,' he remarked. 'Make them better than Ponthwank.'

'OK,' Lloyd said. 'Make 'em, then.' And he went away.

The man called Joe hesitated, nursing the bruise on his head. The overalls caught his attention, and he examined them wonderingly. Where—oh, yes. They had been hanging in the room from which he had first emerged. His own garments had, naturally, dissipated during the trip—what trip?

Amnesia, the thought. He had fallen from the ... the something ... when it slowed down and stopped. How odd this huge, machine-filled barn looked! It struck no chord of remembrance.

Amnesia, that was it. He was a worker. He made things. As for the unfamiliarity of his surroundings, that meant nothing. He was still dazed. The clouds would lift from his mind presently. They were beginning to do that already.

Work. Joe scuttled around the room, trying to goad his faulty memory. Men in overalls were doing things. Simple, obvious things. But how childish—how elemental! Perhaps this was a kindergarten.

After a while Joe went out into a stock room and examined some finished models of combination radio-phonographs. So that was it. Awkward and clumsy, but it wasn't his place to say so. No. His job was to make Twonkies.

Twonkies? The name jolted his memory again. Of course he knew how to make Twonkies. He'd made them all his life—had been specially trained for the job. Now they were using a different model of Twonky, but what the hell! Child's play for a clever workman.

Joe went back into the shop and found a vacant bench. He began to build a Twonky. Occasionally he slipped off and stole the material he needed. Once, when he couldn't locate any tungsten, he hastily built a small gadget and made it.

His bench was in a distant corner, badly lighted, though it seemed quite bright to Joe's eyes. Nobody noticed the console that was swiftly growing to completion there. Joe worked very, very fast. He ignored the noon whistle, and, at quitting time, his task was finished. It could, perhaps, stand another coat of paint—it lacked the Shimmertone of a standard Twonky. But none of the others had Shimmertone. Joe sighed, crawled under the bench, looked in vain for a relaxopad, and went to sleep on the floor.

A few hours later he woke up. The factory was empty. Odd! Maybe the working hours had changed. Maybe—Joe's mind felt funny. Sleep had cleared away the mists of amnesia, if such it had been, but he still felt dazed.

Muttering under his breath, he sent the Twonky into the stock room and compared it with the others. Superficially it was identical with a console radio-phonograph combination of the latest model. Following the pattern of the others, Joe had camouflaged and disguised the various organs and reactors.

He went back into the shop. Then the last of the mists cleared from his mind. Joe's shoulders jerked convulsively.

'Great Snell!' he gasped. 'So that was it! I ran into a temporal snag!'

With a startled glance around, he fled to the storeroom from which he had first emerged. The overalls he took off and returned to their hook. After that, Joe went over to a corner, felt around in the air, nodded with satisfaction, and seated himself on nothing, three feet above the floor. Then Joe vanished.

'Time,' said Kerry Westerfield, 'is curved. Eventually it gets back to the same place where it started. That's duplication.' He put his feet up on a conveniently outjutting rock of the chimney and stretched luxuriously. From the kitchen Martha made clinking noises with bottles and glasses.

'Yesterday at this time I had a Martini,' Kerry said. 'The time curve indicates that I should have another one now. Are you listening, angel?'

'I'm pouring,' said the angel distantly.

'You get my point, then. Here's another. Time describes a spiral instead of a circle. If you call the first cycle *a*, the second one's *a plus 1*—see? Which means a double Martini tonight.'

'I know where that would end,' Martha remarked, coming into the spacious, oak-raftered living room. She was a small, dark-haired woman with a singularly pretty face and a figure to match. Her tiny gingham apron looked slightly absurd in combination with slacks and silk blouse. 'And they don't make infinity-proof gin. Here's your Martini.' She did things with the shaker and manipulated glasses.

'Stir slowly,' Kerry cautioned. 'Never shake. Ah—that's it.' He accepted the drink and eyed it appreciatively. Black hair, sprinkled with gray, gleamed in the lamplight as he sipped the Martini. 'Good. Very good.'

Martha drank slowly and eyed her husband. A nice guy, Kerry Westerfield. He was forty-odd, pleasantly ugly, with a wide mouth and an occasional sardonic gleam in his gray eyes, as he contemplated life. They had been married for twelve years, and liked it.

From outside, the late faint glow of sunset came through the windows, picking out the console cabinet that stood against the wall by the door. Kerry peered at it with appreciation.

'A pretty penny,' he remarked. 'Still—'

'What? Oh. The men had a tough time getting it up the stairs. Why don't you try it, Kerry?'

'Didn't you?'

'The old one was complicated enough,' Martha said, in a baffled manner. 'Gadgets. They confuse me. I was brought up on an Edison. You wound it up with a crank, and strange noises came out of a horn. That I could understand. But now—you push a button, and extraordinary things happen. Electric eyes, tone selections, records that get played on both sides, to the accompaniment of weird groaning and clicking from inside the console—probably you understand those things. I don't even want to. Whenever I play a Crosby record in a superdooper like that, Bing seems embarrassed.'

Kerry ate his olive. 'I'm going to play some Debussy.' He nodded toward a table. 'There's a new Crosby record for you. The latest.'

Martha wriggled happily. 'Can I, maybe, huh?'

'Uh-huh.'

'But you'll have to show me how.'

'Simple enough,' said Kerry, beaming at the console. 'Those babies are pretty good, you know. They do everything but think.'

'I wish it'd wash the dishes,' Martha remarked. She set down her glass, got up, and vanished into the kitchen.

Kerry snapped on a lamp nearby and went over to examine the new radio, Mideastern's latest model, with all the new improvements. It had been expensive—but what the hell? He could afford it. And the old one had been pretty well shot.

It was not, he saw, plugged in. Nor were there any wires in evidence—not even a ground. Something new, perhaps. Built-in antenna *and* ground. Kerry crouched down, looked for a socket, and plugged the cord into it.

That done, he opened the doors and eyed the dials with every appearance of satisfaction. A beam of bluish light shot out and hit him in the eyes. From the depths of the console a faint thoughtful clicking proceeded. Abruptly it stopped. Kerry blinked, fiddled with dials and switches, and bit at a fingernail.

The radio said, in a distant voice, 'Psychology pattern checked and recorded.'

'Eh?' Kerry twirled a dial. 'Wonder what that was? Amateur station—no, they're off the air. Hm-m-m.' He shrugged and went over to a chair beside the shelves of albums. His gaze ran swiftly over the titles and composers' names. Where was the 'Swan of Tuolema'? There it was, next to 'Finlandia,' for no apparent reason. Kerry took down the album and opened it in his lap. With his free hand he extracted a cigarette from his pocket, put it between his lips, and fumbled for the matches on the table beside him. The first match he lit went out.

He tossed it into the fireplace and was about to reach for another when a faint noise caught his attention. The radio was walking across the room toward him. A whiplike tendril flicked out from somewhere, picked up a match, scratched it beneath the table top—as Kerry had done—and held the flame to the man's cigarette.

Automatic reflexes took over. Kerry sucked in his breath, and exploded in smoky, racking coughs. He bent double, gasping and momentarily blind.

When he could see again, the radio was back in its accustomed place.

Kerry caught his lower lip between his teeth. 'Martha,' he called.

'Soup's on,' her voice said.

Kerry didn't answer. He stood up, went over to the radio, and looked at it hesitantly. The electric cord had been pulled out of its socket. Kerry gingerly replaced it.

He crouched to examine the console's legs. They looked like finely finished wood. His exploratory hand told him nothing. Wood—hard and brittle.

How in hell—

'Dinner!' Martha called.

Kerry threw his cigarette into the fireplace and slowly walked out of the room. His wife, setting a gravy boat in place, stared at him.

'How many Martinis did you have?'

'Just one,' Kerry said in a vague way. 'I must have dozed off for a minute. Yeah. I must have.'

'Well, fall to,' Martha commanded. 'This is the last chance you'll have to make a pig of yourself on my dumplings, for a week, anyway.'

Kerry absently felt for his wallet, took out an envelope, and tossed it toward his wife. 'Here's your ticket, angel. Don't lose it.'

'Oh? I rate a compartment!' Martha thrust the pasteboard back into its envelope and gurgled happily. 'You're a pal. Sure you can get along without me?'

'Huh? Hm-m-m—I think so.' Kerry salted his avocado. He shook himself and seemed to come out of a slight daze. 'Sure, I'll be all right. You trot off to Denver and help Carol have her baby. It's all in the family.'

'We-ell, my only sister—' Martha grinned. 'You know how she and Bill are. Quite nuts. They'll need a steadying hand just now.'

There was no reply. Kerry was brooding over a forkful of avocado. He muttered something about the Venerable Bede.

'What about him?'

'Lecture tomorrow. Every term we bog down on the Bede, for some strange reason. Ah, well.'

'Got your lecture ready?'

Kerry nodded. 'Sure. For eight years he had taught at the University, and he certainly should know the schedule by this time!

Later, over coffee and cigarettes, Martha glanced at her wrist watch. 'Nearly train time. I'd better finish packing. The dishes—'

'I'll do 'em.' Kerry wandered after his wife into the bedroom and made motions of futile helpfulness. After a while, he carried the bags down to the car. Martha joined him, and they headed for the depot.

The train was on time. Half an hour after it had pulled out, Kerry drove the car back into the garage, let himself into the house and yawned mightily. He was tired. Well, the dishes, and then beer and a book in bed.

With a puzzled look at the radio, he entered the kitchen and did things with water and soap chips. The hall phone rang. Kerry wiped his hands on a dish towel and answered it.

It was Mike Fitzgerald, who taught psychology at the University.

'Hiya, Fitz.'

'Hiya. Martha gone?'

'Yeah. I just drove her to the train.'

'Feel like talking, then? I've got some pretty good Scotch. Why not run over and gab a while?'

'Like to,' Kerry said, yawning again, 'but I'm dead. Tomorrow's a big day. Rain check?'

'Sure. I just finished correcting papers, and felt the need of sharpening my mind. What's the matter?'

'Nothing. Wait a minute.' Kerry put down the phone and looked over his shoulder, scowling. Noises were coming from the kitchen. What the hell!

He went along the hall and stopped in the doorway, motionless and staring. The radio was washing the dishes.

After a while he returned to the phone. Fitzgerald said, 'Something?'

'My new radio,' Kerry told him carefully. 'It's washing the dishes.'

Fitz didn't answer for a moment. His laugh was a bit hesitant. 'Oh?'

'I'll call you back,' Kerry said, and hung up. He stood motionless for a while, chewing his lip. Then he walked back to the kitchen and paused to watch.

The radio's back was toward him. Several limber tentacles were manipulating the dishes, expertly sousing them in hot, soapy water, scrubbing them with the little mop, dipping them into the rinse water, and then stacking them neatly in the metal rack. Those whip-lashes were the only sign of unusual activity. The legs were apparently solid.

'Hey!' Kerry said.

There was no response.

He sidled around till he could examine the radio more closely. The tentacles emerged from a slot under one of the dials. The electric cord was dangling. No juice, then. But what—

Kerry stepped back and fumbled out a cigarette. Instantly the radio turned, took a match from its container on the stove, and walked forward. Kerry blinked, studying the legs. They couldn't be wood. They were bending as the . . . the thing moved, elastic as rubber. The radio had a peculiar sidling motion unlike anything else on earth.

It lit Kerry's cigarette and went back to the sink, where it resumed the dishwashing.

Kerry phoned Fitzgerald again. 'I wasn't kidding. I'm having hallucinations or something. That damned radio just lit a cigarette for me.'

'Wait a minute—' Fitzgerald's voice sounded undecided. 'This is a gag—eh?'

'No. And I don't think it's a hallucination, either. It's up your alley. Can you run over and test my knee-jerks?'

'All right,' Fitz said. 'Give me ten minutes. Have a drink ready.'

He hung up, and Kerry, laying the phone back into its cradle, turned to see the radio walking out of the kitchen toward the living room. Its square, boxlike contour was subtly horrifying, like some bizarre sort of hobgoblin. Kerry shivered.

He followed the radio, to find it in its former place, motionless and impassive. He opened the doors, examining the turntable, the phonograph arm, and the other buttons and gadgets. There was nothing apparently unusual. Again he touched the legs. They were not wood, after all. Some plastic, which seemed quite hard. Or—maybe they were wood, after all. It was difficult to make certain, without damaging the finish. Kerry felt a natural reluctance to use a knife on his new console.

He tried the radio, getting local stations without trouble. The tone was good—unusually good, he thought. The phonograph—

He picked up Halvorsen's 'Entrance of the Boyards' at random and slipped it into place, closing the lid. No sound emerged. Investigation proved that the needle was moving rhythmically along the groove, but without audible result. Well?

Kerry removed the record as the doorbell rang. It was Fitzgerald, a gangling, saturnine man with a leathery, wrinkled face and a tousled mop of dull-gray hair. He extended a large, bony hand.

'Where's my drink?'

"Lo, Fitz. Come in the kitchen. I'll mix. Highball.'

'Highball.'

'OK' Kerry led the way. 'Don't drink it just yet, though. I want to show you my new combination.'

'The one that washes dishes?' Fitzgerald asked. 'What else does it do?'

Kerry gave the other a glass. 'It won't play records.'

'Oh, well. A minor matter, if it'll do the housework. Let's take a look at it.' Fitzgerald went into the living room, selected 'Afternoon of a Faun,' and approached the radio. 'It isn't plugged in.'

'That doesn't matter a bit,' Kerry said wildly.

'Batteries?' Fitzgerald slipped the record in place and adjusted the switches. 'Ten inch—there. Now we'll see.' He beamed triumphantly at Kerry. 'Well? It's playing now.'

It was.

Kerry said, 'Try that Halvorsen piece. Here.' He handed the disk to Fitzgerald, who pushed the reject switch and watched the lever arm lift.

But this time the phonograph refused to play. It didn't like 'Entrance of the Boyards.'

'That's funny,' Fitzgerald grunted. 'Probably the trouble's with the record. Let's try another.'

There was no trouble with 'Daphnis and Chloe.' But the radio silently rejected the composer's 'Bolero.'

Kerry sat down and pointed to a nearby chair. 'That doesn't prove anything. Come over here and watch. Don't drink anything yet. You, uh, you feel perfectly normal?'

'Sure. Well?'

Kerry took out a cigarette. The console walked across the room, picking up a match book on the way, and politely held the flame. Then it went back to its place against the wall.

Fitzgerald didn't say anything. After a while he took a cigarette from his pocket and waited. Nothing happened.

'So?' Kerry asked.

'A robot. That's the only possible answer. Where in the name of Petrarch did you get it?'

'You don't seem much surprised.'

'I am, though. But I've seen robots before—Westinghouse tried it, you know. Only this—' Fitzgerald tapped his teeth with a nail. 'Who made it?'

'How the devil should I know?' Kerry demanded. 'The radio people, I suppose.'

Fitzgerald narrowed his eyes. 'Wait a minute. I don't quite understand—'

'There's nothing to understand. I bought this combination a few days ago. Turned in the old one. It was delivered this afternoon, and—' Kerry explained what had happened.

'You mean you didn't know it was a robot?'

'Exactly. I bought it as a radio. And … and … the damn thing seems almost alive to me.'

'Nope.' Fitzgerald shook his head, rose, and inspected the console carefully. 'It's a new kind of robot. At least—' He hesitated. 'What else is there to think? I suggest you get in touch with the Mideastern people tomorrow and check up.'

'Let's open the cabinet and look inside,' Kerry suggested.

Fitzgerald was willing, but the experiment proved impossible. The presumably wooden panels weren't screwed into place, and there was no apparent way of opening the console. Kerry found a screwdriver and applied it, gingerly at first, then with a sort of repressed fury. He could neither pry free a panel or even scratch the dark, smooth finish of the cabinet.

'Damn!' he said finally. 'Well, your guess is as good as mine. It's a robot. Only I didn't know they could make 'em like this. And why in a radio?'

'Don't ask me,' Fitzgerald shrugged. 'Check up tomorrow. That's the first step. Naturally I'm pretty baffled. If a new sort of specialized robot has been invented, why put it in a console? And what makes those legs move? There aren't any casters.'

'I've been wondering about that, too.'

'When it moves, the legs look—rubbery. But they're not. They're hard as … as hardwood. Or plastic.'

'I'm afraid of the thing,' Kerry said.

'Want to stay at my place tonight?'

'N-no. No. I guess not. The—robot—can't hurt me.'

'I don't think it wants to. It's been helping you, hasn't it?'

'Yeah,' Kerry said, and went off to mix another drink.

The rest of the conversation was inconclusive. Fitzgerald, several hours later, went home rather worried. He wasn't as casual as he had pretended, for the sake of Kerry's nerves. The impingement of something so entirely unexpected on normal life was subtly frightening. And yet, as he had said, the robot didn't seem menacing—

❖ ❖ ❖

Kerry went to bed, with a new detective mystery. The radio followed him into the bedroom and gently took the book out of his hand. Kerry instinctively snatched for it.

'Hey!' he said. 'What the devil—'

The radio went back into the living room. Kerry followed, in time to see the book replaced on the shelf. After a bit Kerry retreated, locking his door, and slept uneasily till dawn.

In dressing gown and slippers, he stumbled out to stare at the console. It was back in its former place, looking as though it had never moved. Kerry, rather white around the gills, made breakfast.

He was allowed only one cup of coffee. The radio appeared, reprovingly took the second cup from his hand, and emptied it into the sink.

That was quite enough for Kerry Westerfield. He found his hat and topcoat and almost ran out of the house. He had a horrid feeling that the radio might follow him, but it didn't, luckily for his sanity. He was beginning to be worried.

During the morning he found time to telephone Mideastern. The salesman knew nothing. It was a standard model combination—the latest. If it wasn't giving satisfaction, of course, he'd be glad to—

'It's OK,' Kerry said. 'But who made the thing? That's what I want to find out.'

'One moment, sir.' There was a delay. 'It came from Mr Lloyd's department. One of our foremen.'

'Let me speak to him, please.'

But Lloyd wasn't very helpful. After much thought, he remembered that the combination had been placed in the stock room without a serial number. It had been added later.

'But who *made* it?'

'I just don't know. I can find out for you, I guess. Suppose I ring you back.'

'Don't forget,' Kerry said, and went back to his class. The lecture on the Venerable Bede wasn't too successful.

At lunch he saw Fitzgerald, who seemed relieved when Kerry came over to his table. 'Find out any more about your pet robot?' the psychology professor demanded.

No one else was within hearing. With a sigh Kerry sat down and lit a cigarette. 'Not a thing. It's a pleasure to be able to do this myself.' He drew smoke into his lungs. 'I phoned the company.'

'And?'

'They don't know anything. Except that it didn't have a serial number.'

'That may be significant,' Fitzgerald said.

Kerry told the other about the incidents of the book and the coffee, and Fitzgerald squinted thoughtfully at his milk. 'I've given you some psych tests. Too much stimulation isn't good for you.'

'A detective yarn!'

'Carrying it a bit to extremes, I'll admit. But I can understand *why* the robot acted that way—though I dunno how it managed it.' He hesitated. 'Without intelligence, that is.'

'Intelligence?' Kerry licked his lips. 'I'm not so sure that it's just a machine. And I'm not crazy.'

'No, you're not. But you say the robot was in the front room. How could it tell what you were reading?'

'Short of X-ray vision and superfast scanning and assimilative powers, I can't imagine. Perhaps it doesn't want me to read anything.'

'You've said something,' Fitzgerald grunted. 'Know much about theoretical—machines—of that type?'

'Robots?'

'Purely theoretical. Your brain's a colloid, you know. Compact, complicated—but slow. Suppose you work out a gadget with a multimillion radioatom unit embedded in an insulating material—the result is a brain, Kerry. A brain with a tremendous number of units interacting at light-velocity speeds. A radio tube adjusts current flow when it's operating at forty million separate signals a second. And—theoretically—a radio-atomic brain of the type I've mentioned could include perception, recognition, consideration, reaction and adjustment in a hundred-thousandth of a second.'

'Theory.'

'I've thought so. But I'd like to find out where your radio came from.'

A page came over. 'Telephone call for Mr Westerfield.'

Kerry excused himself and left. When he returned, there was a puzzled frown knitting his dark brows. Fitzgerald looked at him inquiringly.

'Guy named Lloyd, at the Mideastern plant. I was talking to him about the radio.'

'Any luck?'

Kerry shook his head. 'No. Well, not much. He didn't know who had built the thing.'

'But it was built in the plant?'

'Yes. About two weeks ago—but there's no record of who worked on it. Lloyd seemed to think that was very, very funny. If a radio's built in the plant, they *know* who put it together.'

'So?'

'So nothing. I asked him how to open the cabinet, and he said it was easy. Just unscrew the panel in the back.'

'There aren't any screws,' Fitzgerald said.

'I know.'

They looked at one another.

Fitzgerald said, 'I'd give fifty bucks to find out whether that robot was really built only two weeks ago.'

'Why?'

'Because a radioatomic brain would need training. Even in such matters as the lighting of a cigarette.'

'It saw me light one.'

'And followed the example. The dish-washing—hm-m-m. Induction, I suppose. If that gadget has been trained, it's a robot. If it hasn't—' Fitzgerald stopped.

Kerry blinked. 'Yes?'

'I don't know what the devil it is. It bears the same relation to a robot that we bear to *eohippus*. One thing I do know, Kerry; it's very probable that no scientist today has the knowledge it would take to make a...a thing like that.'

'You're arguing in circles,' Kerry said. 'It was made.'

'Uh-huh. But how—when—and by whom? That's what's got me worried.'

'Well, I've a class in five minutes. Why not come over tonight?'

'Can't. I'm lecturing at the Hall. I'll phone you after, though.'

With a nod Kerry went out, trying to dismiss the matter from his mind. He succeeded pretty well. But dining alone in a restaurant that night, he began to feel a general unwillingness to go home. A hobgoblin was waiting for him.

'Brandy,' he told the waiter. 'Make it double.'

Two hours later a taxi let Kerry out at his door. He was remarkably drunk. Things swam before his eyes. He walked unsteadily toward the porch, mounted the steps with exaggerated care, and let himself into the house.

He switched on a lamp.

The radio came forward to meet him. Tentacles, thin, but strong as metal, coiled gently around his body, holding him motionless. A pang of violent fear struck through Kerry. He struggled desperately and tried to yell, but his throat was dry.

From the radio panel a beam of yellow light shot out, blinding the man. It swung down, aimed at his chest. Abruptly a queer taste was perceptible under Kerry's tongue.

After a minute or so, the ray clicked out, the tentacles flashed back out of sight, and the console returned to its corner. Kerry staggered weakly to a chair and relaxed, gulping.

He was sober. Which was quite impossible. Fourteen brandies infiltrate a definite amount of alcohol into the system. One can't wave a magic wand and instantly reach a state of sobriety. Yet that was exactly what had happened.

The—robot—was trying to be helpful. Only Kerry would have preferred to remain drunk.

He got up gingerly and sidled past the radio to the bookshelf. One eye on the combination, he took down the detective novel he had tried to read on the preceding night. As he had expected, the radio took it from his hand and replaced it on shelf. Kerry, remembering Fitzgerald's words glanced at his watch. Reaction time, four seconds.

He took down a Chaucer and waited, but the radio didn't stir. However, when Kerry found a history volume, it was gently removed from his fingers. Reaction time, six seconds.

Kerry located a history twice as thick.

Reaction time, ten seconds.

Uh-huh. So the robot did read the books. That meant X-ray vision and superswift reactions. Jumping Jehoshaphat!

Kerry tested more books, wondering what the criterion was. 'Alice in Wonderland' was snatched from his hand; Millay's poems were not. He made a list, with two columns, for future reference.

The robot, then, was not merely a servant. It was a censor. But what was the standard of comparison?

After a while he remembered his lecture tomorrow, and thumbed through his notes. Several points needed verification. Rather hesitantly he located the necessary reference book—and the robot took it away from him.

'Wait a minute,' Kerry said. 'I *need* that.' He tried to pull the volume out of the tentacle's grasp, without success. The console paid no attention. It calmly replaced the book on its shelf.

Kerry stood biting his lip. This was a bit too much. The damned robot was a monitor. He sidled toward the book, snatched it, and was out in the hall before the radio could move.

The thing was coming after him. He could hear the soft padding of its . . . its feet. Kerry scurried into the bedroom and locked the door. He waited, heart thumping, as the knob was tried gently.

A wire-thin cilia crept through the crack of the door and fumbled with the key. Kerry suddenly jumped forward and shoved the auxiliary bolt into position. But that didn't help, either. The robot's precision tools—the specialized antenna—slid it back; and then the console opened the door, walked into the room, and came toward Kerry.

He felt a touch of panic. With a little gasp he threw the book at the thing, and it caught it deftly. Apparently that was all that was wanted, for the radio turned and went out, rocking awkwardly on its rubbery legs, carrying the forbidden volume. Kerry cursed quietly.

The phone rang. It was Fitzgerald.

'Well? How'd you make out?'

'Have you got a copy of Cassen's "Social Literature of the Ages"?'

'I don't think so—no. Why?'

'I'll get it in the University library tomorrow, then.' Kerry explained what had happened. Fitzgerald whistled softly.

'Interfering, is it? Hm-m-m. I wonder—'

'I'm afraid of the thing.'

'I don't think it means you any harm. You say it sobered you up?'

'Yeah. With a light ray. That isn't very logical.'

'It might be. The vibrationary equivalent of thiamin chloride.'

'Light?'

'There's vitamin content in sunlight, you know. That isn't the important point. It's censoring your reading—and apparently it reads the books, with superfast reactions. That gadget, whatever it is, isn't merely a robot.'

'You're telling me,' Kerry said grimly. 'It's a Hitler.'

Fitzgerald didn't laugh. Rather soberly, he suggested, 'Suppose you spend the night at my place?'

'No,' Kerry said, his voice stubborn. 'No so-and-so radio's going to chase me out of my house. I'll take an ax to the thing first.'

'We-ell—you know what you're doing, I suppose. Phone me if…if anything happens.'

'OK,' Kerry said, and hung up. He went into the living room and eyed the radio coldly. What the devil was it—and what was it trying to do? Certainly it wasn't merely a robot. Equally certainly, it wasn't alive, in the sense that a colloid brain is alive.

Lips thinned, he went over and fiddled with the dials and switches. A swing band's throbbing, erratic tempo came from the console. He tried the short-wave band—nothing unusual there. So?

So nothing. There was no answer.

After a while he went to bed.

At luncheon the next day he brought Cassen's 'Social Literature' to show Fitzgerald.

'What about it?'

'Look here.' Kerry flipped the pages and indicated a passage. 'Does this mean anything to you?'

Fitzgerald read it. 'Yeah. The point seems to be that individualism is necessary for the production of literature. Right?'

Kerry looked at him. 'I don't know.'

'Eh?'

'My mind goes funny.'

Fitzgerald rumpled his gray hair, narrowing his eyes and watching the other man intently. 'Come again. I don't quite—'

With angry patience, Kerry said, 'This morning I went into the library and looked up this reference. I read it all right. But it didn't mean anything to me. Just words. Know how it is when you're fagged out and have been reading a lot? You'll run into a sentence with a lot of subjunctive clauses, and it doesn't percolate. Well, it was like that.'

'Read it now,' Fitzgerald said quietly, thrusting the book across the table.

Kerry obeyed, looking up with a wry smile. 'No good.'

'Read it aloud. I'll go over it with you, step by step.'

But that didn't help. Kerry seemed utterly unable to assimilate the sense of the passage.

'Semantic block, maybe,' Fitzgerald said, scratching his ear. 'Is this the first time it's happened?'

'Yes...no. I don't know.'

'Got any classes this afternoon? Good. Let's run over to your place.'

Kerry thrust away his plate. 'All right. I'm not hungry. Whenever you're ready—'

Half an hour later they were looking at the radio. It seemed quite harmless. Fitzgerald wasted some time trying to pry a panel off, but finally gave it up as a bad job. He found pencil and paper, seated himself opposite Kerry, and began to ask questions.

At one point he paused. 'You didn't mention that before.'

'Forgot it, I guess.'

Fitzgerald tapped his teeth with the pencil. 'Hm-m-m. The first time the radio acted up—'

'It hit me in the eye with a blue light—'

'Not that. I mean—what it said.'

Kerry blinked. 'What *it* said?' He hesitated. 'Psychology pattern checked and noted,' or something like that. I thought I'd tuned in on some station and got part of a quiz program or something. You mean—'

'Were the words easy to understand? Good English?'

'No, now that I remember it,' Kerry scowled. 'They were slurred quite a lot. Vowels stressed.'

'Uh-huh. Well, let's get on.' They tried a word-association test.

Finally Fitzgerald leaned back, frowning. 'I want to check this stuff with the last tests I gave you a few months ago. It looks funny to me—damned funny. I'd feel a lot better if I knew exactly what memory was. We've done considerable work on memonics—artificial memory. Still, it may not be that at all.'

'Eh?'

'That—machine. Either it's got an artificial memory, has been highly trained, or else it's adjusted to a different *milieu* and culture. It has affected you—quite a lot.'

Kerry licked dry lips. 'How?'

'Implanted blocks in your mind. I haven't correlated them yet. When I do, we may be able to figure out some sort of answer. No, that thing isn't a robot. It's a lot more than that.'

Kerry took out a cigarette; the console walked across the room and lit it for him. The two men watched with a faint shrinking horror.

'You'd better stay with me tonight,' Fitzgerald suggested.

'No,' Kerry said. He shivered.

The next day Fitzgerald looked for Kerry at lunch, but the younger man did not appear. He telephoned the house, and Martha answered the call.

'Hello! When did you get back?'

'Hello, Fitz. About an hour ago. My sister went ahead and had her baby without me—so I came back.' She stopped, and Fitzgerald was alarmed at her tone.

'Where's Kerry?'

'He's here. Can you come over, Fitz? I'm worried.'

'What's the matter with him?'

'I . . . I don't know. Come right away.'

'OK,' Fitzgerald said, and hung up, biting his lips. He was worried. When, a short while later, he rang the Westerfield bell, he discovered that his nerves were badly out of control. But sight of Martha reassured him.

He followed her into the living room. Fitzgerald's glance went at once to the console, which was unchanged; and then to Kerry, seated motionless by a window. Kerry's face had a blank, dazed look. His pupils were dilated, and he seemed to recognize Fitzgerald only slowly.

'Hello, Fitz,' he said.

'How do you feel?'

Martha broke in. 'Fitz, what's wrong? Is he sick? Shall I call the doctor?'

Fitzgerald sat down. 'Have you noticed anything funny about that radio?'

'No. Why?'

'Then listen.' He told the whole story, watching incredulity struggle with reluctant belief on Martha's face. Presently she said, 'I can't quite—'

'If Kerry takes out a cigarette, the thing will light it for him. Want to see how it works?'

'N-no. Yes. I suppose so.' Martha's eyes were wide.

Fitzgerald gave Kerry a cigarette. The expected happened.

Martha didn't say a word. When the console had returned to its place, she shivered and went over to Kerry. He looked at her vaguely.

'He needs a doctor, Fitz.'

'Yes.' Fitzgerald didn't mention that a doctor might be quite useless.

'What is that thing?'

'It's more than a robot. And it's been readjusting Kerry. I told you what's happened. When I checked Kerry's psychology patterns, I found that they'd altered. He's lost most of his initiative.'

'Nobody on earth could have made that—'

Fitzgerald scowled. 'I thought of that. It seems to be the product of a well-developed culture, quite different from ours. Martian, perhaps. It's such a specialized thing that it naturally fits into a complicated culture. But I *do not* understand why it looks exactly like a Mideastern console radio.'

Martha touched Kerry's hand. 'Camouflage?'

'But why? You were one of my best pupils in psych, Martha. Look at this logically. Imagine a civilization where a gadget like that has its place. Use inductive reasoning.'

'I'm trying to. I can't think very well. Fitz, I'm worried about Kerry.'

'I'm all right,' Kerry said.

Fitzgerald put his fingertips together. 'It isn't a radio so much as a monitor. In this other civilization, perhaps every man has one, or maybe only a few—the ones who need it. It keeps them in line.'

'By destroying initiative?'

Fitzgerald made a helpless gesture. 'I don't know! It worked that way in Kerry's case. In others—I don't know.'

Martha stood up. 'I don't think we should talk any more. Kerry needs a doctor. After that we can decide upon that.' She pointed to the console.

Fitzgerald said, 'It'd be rather a shame to wreck it, but—' His look was significant.

The console moved. It came out from its corner with a sidling, rocking gait and walked toward Fitzgerald. As he sprang up, the whiplike tenacles flashed out and seized him. A pale ray shone into the man's eyes.

Almost instantly it vanished; the tentacles withdrew, and the radio returned to its place. Fitzgerald stood motionless. Martha was on her feet, one hand at her mouth.

'Fitz!' Her voice shook.

He hesitated. 'Yes? What's the matter?'

'Are you hurt? What did it do to you?'

Fitzgerald frowned a little. 'Eh? Hurt? I don't—'

'The radio. What did it do?'

He looked toward the console. 'Something wrong with it? Afraid I'm not much of a repair man, Martha.'

'Fitz.' She came forward and gripped his arm. 'Listen to me.' Quick words spilled from her mouth. The radio. Kerry. Their discussion—

Fitzgerald looked at her blankly, as though he didn't quite understand. 'I guess I'm stupid today. I can't quite understand what you're talking about.'

'The radio—you know! You said it changed Kerry—' Martha paused, staring at the man.

Fitzgerald was definitely puzzled. Martha was acting strangely. Queer! He'd always considered her a pretty level-headed girl. But now she was talking nonsense. At least, he couldn't figure out the meaning of her words—there was no sense to them.

And why was she talking about the radio? Wasn't it satisfactory? Kerry had said it was a good buy, with a fine tone and the latest gadgets in it. Fitzgerald wondered, for a fleeting second, if Martha had gone crazy.

In any case, he was late for his class. He said so. Martha didn't try to stop him when he went out. She was pale as chalk.

Kerry took out a cigarette. The radio walked over and held a match.

'*Kerry!*'

'Yes, Martha?' His voice was dead.

She stared at the . . . the radio. Mars? Another world—another civilization? What was it? What did it want? *What was it trying to do?*

Martha let herself out of the house and went to the garage. When she returned, a small hatchet was gripped tightly in her hand.

Kerry watched. He saw Martha walk over to the radio and lift the hatchet. Then a beam of light shot out, and Martha vanished. A little dust floated up in the afternoon sunlight.

'Destruction of life-form threatening attack,' the radio said, slurring the words together.

Kerry's brain turned over. He felt sick, dazed and horribly empty. Martha—

His mind—churned. Instinct and emotion fought with something that smothered them. Abruptly the dams crumbled, and the blocks were gone, the barriers down. Kerry cried out hoarsely, inarticulately, and sprang to his feet.

'*Martha!*' he yelled.

She was gone. Kerry looked around. Where—

What had happened? He couldn't remember.

He sat down in the chair again, rubbing his forehead. His free hand brought up a cigarette, an automatic reaction that brought instant response. The radio walked forward and held a lighted match ready.

Kerry made a choking, sick sound and flung himself out of the chair. He remembered now. He picked up the hatchet and sprang toward the console, teeth bared in a mirthless rictus.

Again the light beam flashed out.

Kerry vanished. The hatchet thudded onto the carpet.

The radio walked back to its place and stood motionless once more. A faint clicking proceeded from its radioatomic brain.

'Subject basically unsuitable,' it said, after a moment. 'Elimination has been necessary.' *Click!* 'Preparation for next subject completed.'

Click.

'We'll take it,' the boy said.

'You won't be making a mistake,' smiled the rental agent. 'It's quiet, isolated, and the price is quite reasonable.'

'Not so very,' the girl put in. 'But it *is* just what we've been looking for.'

The agent shrugged. 'Of course an unfurnished place would run less. But—'

'We haven't been married long enough to get any furniture,' the boy grinned. He put an arm around his wife. 'Like it, hon?'

'Hm-m-m. Who lived here before?'

The agent scratched his cheek. 'Let's see. Some people named Westerfield, I think. It was given to me for listing just about a week ago. Nice place. If I didn't own my own house, I'd jump at it myself.'

'Nice radio,' the boy said. 'Late model, isn't it?' He went over to examine the console.

'Come along,' the girl urged. 'Let's look at the kitchen again.'

'OK, hon.'

They went out of the room. From the hall came the sound of the agent's smooth voice, growing fainter. Warm afternoon sunlight slanted through the windows.

For a moment there was silence. Then—

Click!

Who Goes There?

John W. Campbell, Jr

Chapter One

The Place stank. A queer, mingled stench that only the ice-buried cabins of an Antarctic camp know, compounded of reeking human sweat, and the heavy, fish-oil stench of melted seal blubber. An overtone of liniment combated the musty smell of sweat-and-snow-drenched furs. The acrid odor of burnt cooking fat, and the animal, not-unpleasant smell of dogs, diluted by time, hung in the air.

Lingering odors of machine oil contrasted sharply with the taint of harness dressing and leather. Yet, somehow, through all that reek of human beings and their associates—dogs, machines and cooking—came another taint. It was a queer, neck-ruffling thing, a faintest suggestion of an odor alien among the smells of industry and life. And it was a lifesmell. But it came from the thing that lay bound with cord and tarpaulin on the table, dripping slowly, methodically onto the heavy planks, dank and gaunt under the unshielded glare of the electric light.

Blair, the little bald-pated biologist of the expedition, twitched nervously at the wrappings, exposing clear, dark ice beneath and then pulling the tarpaulin back into place restlessly. His little bird-like motions of suppressed eagerness danced his shadow across the fringe of dingy gray underwear hanging from the low ceiling, the equatorial fringe of stiff, graying hair around his naked skull a comical halo about the shadow's head.

Commander Garry brushed aside the lax legs of a suit of underwear, and stepped toward the table. Slowly his eyes traced around the rings of men sardined into the Administration Building. His tall, stiff body straightened finally, and he nodded. 'Thirty-seven. All here.' His voice was low, yet carried the clear authority of the commander by nature, as well as by title.

'You know the outline of the story back of that find of the Secondary Pole Expedition. I have been conferring with Second-in-Command McReady, and Norris, as well as Blair and Dr Copper. There is a difference of opinion, and because it involves the entire group, it is only just that the entire Expedition personnel act on it.

'I am going to ask McReady to give you the details of the story, because each of you has been too busy with his own work to follow closely the endeavors of the others. McReady?'

Moving from the smoke-blued background, McReady was a figure from some forgotten myth, a looming, bronze statue that held life, and walked. Six-feet-four inches he stood as he halted beside the table, and, with a characteristic glance upward to assure himself of room under the low ceiling beams, straightened. His rough, clashingly orange windproof jacket he still had on, yet on his huge frame it did not seem misplaced. Even here, four feet beneath the drift-wind that droned across the Antarctic waste above the ceiling, the cold of the frozen continent leaked in, and gave meaning to the harshness of the man. And he was bronze—his great red-bronze beard, the heavy hair that matched it. The gnarled, corded hands gripping, relaxing, gripping and relaxing on the table planks were bronze. Even the deep-sunken eyes beneath heavy brows were bronzed.

Age-resisting endurance of the metal spoke in the cragged heavy outlines of his face, and the mellow tones of the heavy voice. 'Norris and Blair agree on one thing; that animal we found was not—terrestrial in origin. Norris fears there may be danger in that; Blair says there is none.

'But I'll go back to how, and why, we found it. To all that was known before we came here, it appeared that this point was exactly over the South Magnetic Pole of Earth. The compass does point straight down here, as you all know. The more delicate instruments of the physicists, instruments especially designed for this expedition and its study of the magnetic pole, detected a secondary effect, a secondary, less powerful magnetic influence about 80 miles southwest of here.

'The Secondary Magnetic Expedition went out to investigate it. There is no need for details. We found it, but it was not the huge meteorite or magnetic mountain Norris had expected to find. Iron ore is magnetic, of course; iron more so—and certain special steels even more magnetic. From the surface indications, the secondary pole we found was small, so small that the magnetic effect it had was preposterous. No magnetic material conceivable could have that effect. Soundings through the ice indicated it was within one hundred feet of the glacier surface.

'I think you should know the structure of the place. There is a broad plateau, a level sweep that runs more than 150 miles due south from the

Secondary station, Van Wall says. He didn't have time or fuel to fly farther, but it was running smoothly due south then. Right there, where that buried thing was, there is an ice-drowned mountain ridge, a granite wall of unshakable strength that has dammed back the ice creeping from the south.

'And four hundred miles due south is the South Polar Plateau. You have asked me at various times why it gets warmer here when the wind rises, and most of you know. As a meteorologist I'd have staked my word that no wind could blow at -70 degrees—that no more than a 5-mile wind could blow at -50—without causing warming due to friction with ground, snow and ice, and the air itself.

'We camped there on the lip of that ice-drowned mountain range for twelve days. We dug our camp into the blue ice that formed the surface, and escaped most of it. But for twelve consecutive days the wind blew at 45 miles an hour. It went as high as 48, and fell to 41 at times. The temperature was -63 degrees. It rose to -60 and fell to -68. It was meteorologically impossible, and it went on uninterruptedly for twelve days and twelve nights.

'Somewhere to the south, the frozen air of South Polar Plateau slides down from that 18,000-foot bowl, down a mountain pass, over a glacier, and starts north. There must be a funneling mountain chain that directs it, and sweeps it away for four hundred miles to hit that bald plateau where we found the secondary pole, and 350 miles farther north reaches the Antarctic Ocean.

'It's been frozen there since Antarctica froze twenty million years ago. There never has been a thaw there.

'Twenty million years ago Antarctica was beginning to freeze. We've investigated, thought and built speculations. What we believe happened was about like this.

'Something came down out of space, a ship. We saw it there in the blue ice, a thing like a submarine without a conning tower or directive vanes, 280 feet long and 45 feet in diameter at its thickest.

'Eh, Van Wall? Space? Yes, but I'll explain that better later.' McReady's steady voice went on.

'It came down from space, driven and lifted by forces men haven't discovered yet, and somehow—perhaps something went wrong then— it tangled with Earth's magnetic field. It came south here, out of control probably, circling the magnetic pole. That's a savage country there, but when Antarctica was still freezing it must have been a thousand times more savage. There must have been blizzard snow, as well as drift, new snow falling as the continent glaciated. The swirl there must have been particularly bad, the wind hurling a solid blanket of white over the lip of that now-buried mountain.

'The ship struck solid granite head-on, and cracked up. Not every one of the passengers in it was killed, but the ship must have been ruined, her driving mechanism locked. It tangled with Earth's field, Norris believes. No thing made by intelligent beings can tangle with the dead immensity of a planet's natural forces and survive.

'One of its passengers stepped out. The wind we saw there never fell below 41, and the temperature never rose above -60. Then—the wind must have been stronger. And there was drift falling in a solid sheet. The *thing* was lost completely in ten paces.' He paused for a moment, the deep, steady voice giving way to the drone of wind overhead, and the uneasy, malicious gurgling in the pipe of the galley stove.

Drift—a drift-wind was sweeping by overhead. Right now the snow picked up by the mumbling wind fled in level, blinding lines across the face of the buried camp. If a man stepped out of the tunnels that connected each of the camp buildings beneath the surface, he'd be lost in ten paces. Out there, the slim, black finger of the radio mast lifted 300 feet into the air, and at its peak was the clear night sky. A sky of thin, whining wind rushing steadily from beyond to another beyond under the licking, curling mantle of the aurora. And off north, the horizon flamed with queer, angry colors of the midnight twilight. That was spring 300 feet above Antarctica.

At the surface—it was white death. Death of a needle-fingered cold driven before the wind, sucking heat from any warm thing. Cold—and white mist of endless, everlasting drift, the fine, fine particles of licking snow that obscured all things.

Kinner, the little, scar-faced cook, winced. Five days ago he had stepped out to the surface to reach a cache of frozen beef. He had reached it, started back—and the drift-wind leapt out of the south. Cold, white death that streamed across the ground blinded him in twenty seconds. He stumbled on wildly in circles. It was half an hour before rope-guided men from below found him in the impenetrable murk.

It was easy for man—or *thing*—to get lost in ten paces.

'And the drift-wind then was probably more impenetrable than we know.' McReady's voice snapped Kinner's mind back. Back to welcome, dank warmth of the Ad Building. 'The passenger of the ship wasn't prepared either, it appears. It froze within ten feet of the ship.

'We dug down to find the ship, and our tunnel happened to find the frozen—animal. Barclay's ice-ax struck its skull.

'When we saw what it was, Barclay went back to the tractor, started the fire up and when the steam pressure built, sent a call for Blair and Dr Copper. Barclay himself was sick then. Stayed sick for three days, as a matter of fact.

'When Blair and Copper came, we cut out the animal in a block of ice, as you see, wrapped it and loaded it on the tractor for return here. We wanted to get into that ship.

'We reached the side and found the metal was something we didn't know. Our beryllium-bronze, non-magnetic tools wouldn't touch it. Barclay had some tool-steel on the tractor, and that wouldn't scratch it either. We made reasonable tests—even tried some acid from the batteries with no results.

'They must have had a passivating process to make magnesium metal resist acid that way, and the alloy must have been at least 95 per cent magnesium. But we had no way of guessing that, so when we spotted the barely opened lock door, we cut around it. There was clear, hard ice inside the lock, where we couldn't reach it. Through the little crack we could look in and see that only metal and tools were in there, so we decided to loosen the ice with a bomb.

'We had decanite bombs and thermite. Thermite is the ice-softener; decanite might have shattered valuable things, where the thermite's heat would just loosen the ice. Dr Copper, Norris and I placed a 25-pound thermite bomb, wired it, and took the connector up the tunnel to the surface, where Blair had the steam tractor waiting. A hundred yards the other side of that granite wall we set off the thermite bomb.

'The magnesium metal of the ship caught, of course. The glow of the bomb flared and died, then it began to flare again. We ran back to the tractor, and gradually the glare built up. From where we were we could see the whole ice-field illuminated from beneath with an unbearable light; the ship's shadow was a great, dark cone reaching off toward the north, where the twilight was just about gone. For a moment it lasted, and we counted three other shadow-things that might have been other—passengers—frozen there. Then the ice was crashing down and against the ship.

'That's why I told you about that place. The wind sweeping down from the Pole was at our backs. Steam and hydrogen flame were torn away in white ice-fog; the flaming heat under the ice there was yanked away toward the Antarctic Ocean before it touched us. Otherwise we wouldn't have come back, even with the shelter of that granite ridge that stopped the light.

'Somehow in the blinding inferno we could see great hunched things, black bulks glowing, even so. They shed even the furious incandescence of the magnesium for a time. Those must have been the engines, we knew. Secrets going in blazing glory—secrets that might have given Man the planets. Mysterious things that could lift and hurl that ship—and had soaked in the force of the Earth's magnetic field. I saw Norris' mouth move, and ducked. I couldn't hear him.

'Insulation—something—gave way. All Earth's field they'd soaked up twenty million years before broke loose. The aurora in the sky above licked down, and the whole plateau there was bathed in cold fire that blanketed vision. The ice-ax in my hand got red hot, and hissed on the ice. Metal buttons on my clothes burned into me. And a flash of electric blue seared upward from beyond the granite wall.

'Then the walls of ice crashed down on it. For an instant it squealed the way dry-ice does when it's pressed between metal.

'We were blind and groping in the dark for hours while our eyes recovered. We found every coil within a mile was fused rubbish, the dynamo and every radio set, the earphones and speakers. If we hadn't had the steam tractor, we wouldn't have gotten over to the Secondary Camp.

'Van Wall flew in from Big Magnet at sun-up, as you know. We came home as soon as possible. That is the history of—that.' McReady's great bronze beard gestured toward the thing on the table.

Chapter Two

Blair stirred uneasily, his little, bony fingers wriggling under the harsh light. Little brown freckles on his knuckles slid back and forth as the tendons under the skin twitched. He pulled aside a bit of the tarpaulin and looked impatiently at the dark ice-bound thing inside.

McReady's big body straightened somewhat. He'd ridden the rocking, jarring steam tractor forty miles that day, pushing on to Big Magnet here. Even his calm will had been pressed by the anxiety to mix again with humans. It was lone and quiet out there in Secondary Camp, where a wolf-wind howled down from the Pole. Wolf-wind howling in his sleep—winds droning and the evil, unspeakable face of that monster leering up as he'd first seen it through clear, blue ice, with a bronze ice-ax buried in its skull.

The giant meteorologist spoke again. 'The problem is this. Blair wants to examine the thing. Thaw it out and make micro slides of its tissues and so forth. Norris doesn't believe that is safe, and Blair does. Dr Copper agrees pretty much with Blair. Norris is a physicist, of course, not a biologist. But he makes a point I think we should all hear. Blair has described the microscopic life-forms biologists find living, even in this cold and inhospitable place. They freeze every winter, and thaw every summer—for three months—and live.

'The point Norris makes is—they thaw, and live again. There must have been microscopic life associated with this creature. There is with every living thing we know. And Norris is afraid that we may release a plague— some germ disease unknown to Earth—if we thaw those microscopic things that have been frozen there for twenty million years.

'Blair admits that such micro-life might retain the power of living. Such unorganized things as individual cells can retain life for unknown periods, when solidly frozen. The beast itself is as dead as those frozen mammoths they find in Siberia. Organized, highly developed life-forms can't stand that treatment.

'But micro-life could. Norris suggests that we may release some disease-form that man, never having met it before, will be utterly defenseless against.

'Blair's answer is that there may be such still-living germs, but that Norris has the case reversed. They are utterly non-immune to man. Our life-chemistry probably—'

'Probably!' The little biologist's head lifted in a quick, birdlike motion. The halo of gray hair about his bald head ruffled as though angry. 'Heh. One look—'

'I know,' McReady acknowledged. 'The thing is not Earthly. It does not seem likely that it can have a life-chemistry sufficiently like ours to make cross-infection remotely possible. I would say that there is no danger.'

McReady looked toward Dr Copper. The physician shook his head slowly. 'None whatever,' he asserted confidently. 'Man cannot infect or be infected by germs that live in such comparatively close relatives as the snakes. And they are, I assure you,' his clean-shaven face grimaced uneasily, '*much* nearer to us than—*that*.'

Vance Norris moved angrily. He was comparatively short in this gathering of big men, some five-feet-eight, and his stocky, powerful build tended to make him seem shorter. His black hair was crisp and hard, like short, steel wires, and his eyes were the gray of fractured steel. If McReady was a man of bronze, Norris was all steel. His movements, his thoughts, his whole bearing had the quick, hard impulse of steel spring. His nerves were steel-hard, quick-acting—swift-corroding.

He was decided on his point now, and he lashed out in its defense with a characteristic quick, clipped flow of words. 'Different chemistry be damned. That thing may be dead—or, by God, it may not—but I don't like it. Damn it, Blair, let them see the monstrosity you are petting over there. Let them see the foul thing and decide for themselves whether they want that thing thawed out in this camp.

'Thawed out, by the way. That's got to be thawed out in one of the

402 SCIENCE-FICTION CLASSICS

shacks tonight, if it is thawed out. Somebody—who's watchman tonight? Magnetic—oh, Connant. Cosmic rays tonight. Well, you get to sit up with that twenty-million-year-old mummy of his.

'Unwrap it, Blair. How the hell can they tell what they are buying if they can't see it? It may have a different chemistry. I don't know what else it has, but I know it has something I don't want. If you can judge by the look on its face—it isn't human so maybe you can't—it was annoyed when it froze. Annoyed, in fact, is just about as close an approximation of the way it felt as crazy, mad, insane hatred. Neither one touches the subject.

'How the hell can these birds tell what they are voting on? They haven't seen those three red eyes, and that blue hair like crawling worms. Crawling—damn, it's crawling there in the ice right now!

'Nothing Earth ever spawned had the unutterable sublimation of devastating wrath that thing let loose in its face when it looked around this frozen desolation twenty million years ago. Mad? It was mad clear through—searing, blistering mad!

'Hell, I've had bad dreams ever since I looked at those three red eyes. Nightmares. Dreaming the thing thawed out and came to life—that it wasn't dead, or even wholly unconscious all those twenty million years, but just slowed, waiting—waiting. You'll dream, too, while that damned thing that Earth wouldn't own is dripping, dripping in the Cosmos House tonight.

'And, Connant,' Norris whipped toward the cosmic ray specialist, 'won't you have fun sitting up all night in the quiet. Wind whining above— and that thing dripping—' He stopped for a moment, and looked around.

'I know. That's not science. But this is, it's psychology. You'll have nightmares for a year to come. Every night since I looked at that thing I've had 'em. That's why I hate it—sure I do—and don't want it around. Put it back where it came from and let it freeze for another twenty million years. I had some swell nightmares—that it wasn't made like we are—which is obvious—but of a different kind of flesh that it can really control. That it can change its shape, and look like a man—and wait to kill and eat—

'That's not a logical argument. I know it isn't. The thing isn't Earth-logic anyway.

'Maybe it has an alien body-chemistry, and maybe its bugs do have a different body-chemistry. A germ might not stand that, but, Blair and Copper, how about a virus? That's just an enzyme molecule, you've said. That wouldn't need anything but a protein molecule of any body to work on.

'And how are you so sure that, of the million varieties of microscopic life it may have, *none* of them are dangerous? How about diseases like hydrophobia—rabies—that attack any warm-blooded creature, whatever its body-chemistry may be? And parrot fever? Have you a body like a parrot, Blair? And plain rot—gangrene—necrosis, do you want? *That* isn't choosy about body-chemistry!'

Blair looked up from his puttering long enough to meet Norris' angry, gray eyes for an instant. 'So far the only thing you have said this thing gave off that was catching was dreams. I'll go so far as to admit that.' An impish, slightly malignant grin crossed the little man's seamed face. 'I had some, too. So. It's dream-infectious. No doubt an exceedingly dangerous malady.

'So far as your other things go, you have a badly mistaken idea about viruses. In the first place, nobody has shown that the enzyme-molecule theory, and that alone, explains them. And in the second place, when you catch tobacco mosaic or wheat rust, let me know. A wheat plant is a lot nearer your body-chemistry than this other-world creature is.

'And your rabies is limited, strictly limited. You can't get it from, nor give it to, a wheat plant or a fish—which is a collateral descendant of a common ancestor of yours. Which this, Norris, is not.' Blair nodded pleasantly toward the tarpaulined bulk on the table.

'Well, thaw the damned thing in a tub of formalin if you must thaw it. I've suggested that—'

'And I've said there would be no sense in it. You can't compromise. Why did you and Commander Garry come down here to study magnetism? Why weren't you content to stay at home? There's magnetic force enough in New York. I could no more study the life this thing once had from a formalin-pickled sample than you could get the information you wanted back in New York. And—if this one is so treated, *never in all time to come can there be a duplicate!* The race it came from must have passed away in the twenty million years it lay frozen, so that even if it came from Mars then, we'd never find its like. And—the ship is gone.

'There's only one way to do this—and that is the best possible way. It must be thawed slowly, carefully, and not in formalin.'

Commander Garry stood forward again, and Norris stepped back muttering angrily. 'I think Blair is right, gentlemen. What do you say?'

Connant grunted. 'It sounds right to us, I think—only perhaps he ought to stand watch over it while it's thawing.' He grinned ruefully, brushing a stray lock of ripe-cherry hair back from his forehead. 'Swell idea, in fact—if he sits up with his jolly little corpse.'

Garry smiled slightly. A general chuckle of agreement rippled over the group. 'I should think any ghost it may have had would have starved to death if it hung around here that long, Connant,' Garry suggested. 'And you look capable of taking care of it. "Ironman" Connant ought to be able to take out any opposing players, still.'

Connant shook himself uneasily. 'I'm not worrying about ghosts. Let's see that thing. I—'

Eagerly Blair was stripping back the ropes. A single throw of the tarpaulin revealed the thing. The ice had melted somewhat in the heat of the room, and it was clear and blue as thick, good glass. It shone wet and sleek under the harsh light of the unshielded globe above.

The room stiffened abruptly. It was face up there on the plain, greasy planks of the table. The broken half of the bronze ice-ax was still buried in the queer skull. Three mad, hate-filled eyes blazed up with a living fire, bright as fresh-spilled blood, from a face ringed with a writhing, loathsome nest of worms, blue, mobile worms that crawled where hair should grow—

Van Wall, six feet and 200 pounds of ice-nerved pilot, gave a queer, strangled gasp and butted, stumbled his way out to the corridor. Half the company broke for the doors. The others stumbled away from the table.

McReady stood at one end of the table watching them, his great body planted solid on his powerful legs. Norris from the opposite end glowered at the thing with smouldering hate. Outside the door, Garry was talking with half a dozen of the men at once.

Blair had a tack hammer. The ice that cased the thing *schluffed* crisply under its steel claw as it peeled from the thing it had cased for twenty thousand thousand years—

Chapter Three

'I know you don't like the thing, Connant, but it just has to be thawed out right. You say leave it as it is till we get back to civilization. All right, I'll admit your argument that we could do a better and more complete job there is sound. But—how are we going to get this across the Line? We have to take this through one temperate zone, the equatorial zone, and half way through the other temperate zone before we get it to New York. You don't want to sit with it one night, but you suggest, then, that I hang its corpse in the freezer with the beef?' Blair looked up from his cautious chipping, his bald, freckled skull nodding triumphantly.

Kinner, the stocky, scar-faced cook, saved Connant the trouble of answering. 'Hey, you listen, mister. You put that thing in the box with the meat, and by all the gods there ever were, I'll put you in to keep it company. You birds have brought everything movable in this camp in onto my mess tables here already, and I had to stand for that. But you go putting things like that in my meat box or even my meat cache here, and you cook your own damn grub.'

'But, Kinner, this is the only table in Big Magnet that's big enough to work on,' Blair objected. 'Everybody's explained that.'

'Yeah, and everybody's brought everything in here. Clark brings his dogs every time there's a fight and sews them up on that table. Ralsen brings in his sledges. Hell, the only thing you haven't had on that table is the Boeing. And you'd 'a' had that in if you coulda figured a way to get it through the tunnels.'

Commander Garry chuckled and grinned at Van Wall, the huge Chief Pilot. Van Wall's great blond beard twitched suspiciously as he nodded gravely to Kinner. 'You're right, Kinner. The aviation department is the only one that treats you right.'

'It does get crowded, Kinner,' Garry acknowledged. 'But I'm afraid we all find it that way at times. Not much privacy in an Antarctic camp.'

'Privacy? What the hell's that? You know, the thing that really made me weep, was when I saw Barclay marchin' through here chantin' "The last lumber in the camp! The last lumber in the camp!" and carryin' it out to build that house on his tractor. Damn it, I missed that moon cut in the door he carried out more'n I missed the sun when it set. That wasn't just the last lumber Barclay was walkin' off with. He was carryin' off the last bit of privacy in this blasted place.'

A grin rode even on Connant's heavy face as Kinner's perennial good-natured grouch came up again. But it died away quickly as his dark, deep-set eyes turned again to the red-eyed thing Blair was chipping from its cocoon of ice. A big hand ruffed his shoulder-length hair, and tugged at a twisted lock that fell behind his ear in a familiar gesture. 'I know that cosmic ray shack's going to be too crowded if I have to sit up with that thing,' he growled. 'Why can't you go on chipping the ice away from around it— you can do that without anybody butting in, I assure you—and then hang the thing up over the power-plant boiler? That's warm enough. It'll thaw out a chicken, even a whole side of beef, in a few hours.'

'I know,' Blair protested, dropping the tack hammer to gesture more effectively with his bony, freckled fingers, his small body tense with eagerness, 'but this is too important to take any chances. There never was a find like this; there never can be again. It's the only chance men will ever have, and it has to be done exactly right.

'Look, you know how the fish we caught down near the Ross Sea would freeze almost as soon as we got them on deck, and come to life again if we thawed them gently? Low forms of life aren't killed by quick freezing and slow thawing. We have—'

'Hey, for the love of Heaven—you mean that damned thing will come to life!' Connant yelled. 'You get the damned thing—Let me at it! That's going to be in so many pieces—'

'NO! *No*, you fool—' Blair jumped in front of Connant to protect his precious find. 'No. Just *low* forms of life. For Pete's sake let me finish. You can't thaw higher forms of life and have them come to. Wait a moment now—hold it! A fish can come to after freezing because it's so low a form of life that the individual cells of its body can revive, and that alone is enough to re-establish life. Any higher forms thawed out that way are dead. Though the individual cells revive, they die because there must be organization and cooperative effort to live. That cooperation cannot be re-established. There is a sort of potential life in any uninjured, quick-frozen animal. But it can't—can't under any circumstances—become active life in higher animals. The higher animals are too complex, too delicate. This is an intelligent creature as high in its evolution as we are in ours. Perhaps higher. It is as dead as a frozen man would be.'

'How do you know?' demanded Connant, hefting the ice-ax he had seized a moment before.

Commander Garry laid a restraining hand on his heavy shoulder. 'Wait a minute, Connant. I want to get this straight. I agree that there is going to be no thawing of this thing if there is the remotest chance of its revival. I quite agree it is much too unpleasant to have alive, but I had no idea there was the remotest possibility.'

Dr Copper pulled his pipe from between his teeth and heaved his stocky, dark body from the bunk he had been sitting in. 'Blair's being technical. That's dead. As dead as the mammoths they find frozen in Siberia. Potential life is like atomic energy—there, but nobody can get it out, and it certainly won't release itself except in rare cases, as rare as radium in the chemical analogy. We have all sorts of proof that things don't live after being frozen—not even fish, generally speaking—and no proof that higher animal life can under any circumstances. What's the point, Blair?'

The little biologist shook himself. The little ruff of hair standing out around his bald pate waved in righteous anger. 'The point is,' he said in an injured tone, 'that the individual cells might show the characteristics they had in life, if it is properly thawed. A man's muscle cells live many hours after he has died. Just because they live, and a few things like hair and fingernail cells still live, you wouldn't accuse a corpse of being a Zombie, or something.

'Now if I thaw this right, I may have a chance to determine what sort of world it's native to. We don't, and can't know by any other means, whether it came from Earth or Mars or Venus or from beyond the stars.

'And just because it looks unlike men, you don't have to accuse it of being evil, or vicious or something. Maybe that expression on its face is its equivalent to a resignation to fate. White is the color of mourning to the Chinese. If men can have different customs, why can't a so-different race have different understandings of facial expressions?'

Connant laughed softly, mirthlessly. 'Peaceful resignation! If that is the best it could do in the way of resignation, I should exceedingly dislike seeing it when it was looking mad. That face was never designed to express peace. It just didn't have any philosophical thoughts like peace in its make-up.

'I know it's your pet—but be sane about it. That thing grew up on evil, adolesced slowly roasting alive the local equivalent of kittens, and amused itself through maturity on new and ingenious torture.'

'You haven't the slightest right to say that,' snapped Blair. 'How do you know the first thing about the meaning of a facial expression inherently inhuman? It may well have no human equivalent whatever. That is just a different development of Nature, another example of Nature's wonderful adaptability. Growing on another, perhaps harsher world, it has different form and features. But it is just as much a legitimate child of Nature as you are. You are displaying the childish human weakness of hating the different. On its own world it would probably class you as a fish-belly, white monstrosity with an insufficient number of eyes and a fungoid body pale and bloated with gas.

'Just because its nature is different, you haven't any right to say it's necessarily evil.'

Norris burst out a single, explosive, 'Haw!' He looked down at the thing. 'May be that things from other worlds don't *have* to be evil just because they're different. But that thing *was!* Child of Nature, eh? Well, it was a hell of an evil Nature.'

'Aw, will you mugs cut crabbing at each other and get the damned thing off my table?' Kinner growled. 'And put a canvas over it. It looks indecent.'

'Kinner's gone modest,' jeered Connant.

Kinner slanted his eyes up to the big physicist. The scarred cheek twisted to join the line of his tight lips in a twisted grin. 'All right, big boy, and what were you grousing about a minute ago? We can set the thing in a chair next to you tonight, if you want.'

'I'm not afraid of its face,' Connant snapped. 'I don't like keeping a wake over its corpse particularly, but I'm going to do it.'

Kinner's grin spread. 'Uh-huh.' He went off to the galley stove and shook down ashes vigorously, drowning the brittle chipping of the ice as Blair fell to work again.

CHAPTER FOUR

'*Cluck*,' reported the cosmic ray counter, '*cluck-brrrp-cluck.*' Connant started and dropped his pencil.

'Damnation.' The physicist looked toward the far corner, back at the Geiger counter on the table near that corner, and crawled under the desk at which he had been working to retrieve the pencil. He sat down at his work again, trying to make his writing more even. It tended to have jerks and quavers in it, in time with the abrupt proud-hen noises of the Geiger counter. The muted whoosh of the pressure lamp he was using for illumination, the mingled gargles and bugle calls of a dozen men sleeping down the corridor in Paradise House formed the background sounds for the irregular, clucking noises of the counter, the occasional rustle of falling coal in the copper-bellied stove. And a soft, steady *drip-drip-drip* from the thing in the corner.

Connant jerked a pack of cigarettes from his pocket, snapped it so that a cigarette protruded and jabbed the cylinder into his mouth. The lighter failed to function, and he pawed angrily through the pile of papers in search of a match. He scratched the wheel of the lighter several times, dropped it with a curse and got up to pluck a hot coal from the stove with the coal tongs.

The lighter functioned instantly when he tried it on returning to the desk. The counter ripped out a series of clucking guffaws as a burst of cosmic rays struck through to it. Connant turned to glower at it, and tried to concentrate on the interpretation of data collected during the past week. The weekly summary—

He gave up and yielded to curiosity, or nervousness. He lifted the pressure lamp from the desk and carried it over to the table in the corner. Then he returned to the stove and picked up the coal tongs. The beast had been thawing for nearly eighteen hours now. He poked at it with an unconscious caution; the flesh was no longer hard as armor plate, but had assumed a rubbery texture. It looked like wet, blue rubber glistening under droplets of water like little round jewels in the glare of the gasoline pressure lantern. Connant felt an unreasoning desire to pour the contents of the lamp's reservoir over the thing in its box and drop the cigarette into it. The three red eyes glared up at him sightlessly, the ruby eyeballs reflecting murky, smoky rays of light.

He realized vaguely that he had been looking at them for a very long time, even vaguely understood that they were no longer sightless. But it did not seem of importance, of no more importance than the labored, slow motion of the tentacular things that sprouted from the base of the scrawny, slowly pulsing neck.

Connant picked up the pressure lamp and returned to his chair. He sat down, staring at the pages of mathematics before him. The clucking of the counter was strangely less disturbing, the rustle of the coals in the stove no longer distracting.

The creak of the floorboards behind him didn't interrupt his thoughts as he went about his weekly report in an automatic manner, filling in columns of data and making brief, summarizing notes.

The creak of the floorboards sounded nearer.

Chapter Five

Blair came up from the nightmare-haunted depths of sleep abruptly. Connant's face floated vaguely above him; for a moment it seemed a continuance of the wild horror of the dream. But Connant's face was angry, and a little frightened. 'Blair—Blair you damned log, wake up.'

'Uh-eh?' The little biologist rubbed his eyes, his bony, freckled fingers crooked to a mutilated child-fist. From surrounding bunks other faces lifted to stare down at them.

Connant straightened up. 'Get up—and get a lift on. Your damned animal's escaped.'

'Escaped—what!' Chief Pilot Van Wall's bull voice roared out with a volume that shook the walls. Down the communication tunnels other voices yelled suddenly. The dozen inhabitants of Paradise House tumbled in abruptly, Barclay, stocky and bulbous in long woolen underwear, carrying a fire extinguisher.

'What the hell's the matter?' Barclay demanded.

'Your damned beast got loose. I fell asleep about twenty minutes ago, and when I woke up, the thing was gone. Hey, Doc, the hell you say those things can't come to life. Blair's blasted potential life developed a hell of a lot of potential and walked out on us.'

Copper stared blankly. 'It wasn't—Earthly,' he sighed suddenly. 'I—I guess Earthly laws don't apply.'

'Well, it applied for leave of absence and took it. We've got to find it and capture it somehow.' Connant swore bitterly, his deep-set black eyes sullen and angry. 'It's a wonder the hellish creature didn't eat me in my sleep.'

Blair stared back, his pale eyes suddenly fear-struck. 'Maybe it di—er—uh—we'll have to find it.'

'You find it. It's your pet. I've had all I want to do with it, sitting there for seven hours with the counter clucking every few seconds, and you birds in here singing night-music. It's a wonder I got to sleep. I'm going through to the Ad Building.'

Commander Garry ducked through the doorway, pulling his belt tight. 'You won't have to. Van's roar sounded like the Boeing taking off down wind. So it wasn't dead?'

'I didn't carry it off in my arms, I assure you,' Connant snapped. 'The last I saw, that split skull was oozing green goo, like a squashed caterpillar. Doc just said our laws don't work—it's unearthly. Well, it's an unearthly monster, with an unearthly disposition, judging by the face, wandering around with a split skull and brains oozing out.'

Norris and McReady appeared in the doorway, a doorway filling with other shivering men. 'Has anybody seen it coming over here?' Norris asked innocently. 'About four feet tall—three red eyes—brains oozing— Hey, has anybody checked to make sure this isn't a cracked idea of humor? If it is, I think we'll unite in tying Blair's pet around Connant's neck like the Ancient Mariner's albatross.'

'It's no humor,' Connant shivered. 'Lord, I wish it were. I'd rather wear—' He stopped. A wild, weird howl shrieked through the corridors. The men stiffened abruptly, and half turned.

'I think it's been located,' Connant finished. His dark eyes shifted with a queer unease. He darted back to his bunk in Paradise House, to return almost immediately with a heavy .45 revolver and an ice-ax. He hefted both gently as he started for the corridor toward Dogtown. 'It blundered down the wrong corridor—and landed among the huskies. Listen—the dogs have broken their chains—'

The half-terrorized howl of the dog pack changed to a wild hunting melee. The voices of the dogs thundered in the narrow corridors, and through them came a low rippling snarl of distilled hate. A shrill of pain, a dozen snarling yelps.

Connant broke for the door. Close behind him, McReady, then Barclay and Commander Garry came. Other men broke for the Ad Building, and weapons—the sledge house. Pomroy, in charge of Big Magnet's five cows, started down the corridor in the opposite direction—he had a six-foot-handled, long-tined pitchfork in mind.

Barclay slid to a halt, as McReady's giant bulk turned abruptly away from the tunnel leading to Dogtown, and vanished off at an angle. Uncertainly, the mechanician wavered a moment, the fire extinguisher in his hands, hesitating from one side to the other. Then he was racing after Connant's broad back. Whatever McReady had in mind, he could be trusted to make it work.

Connant stopped at the bend in the corridor. His breath hissed suddenly through his throat. 'Great God—' The revolver exploded thunderously; three numbing, palpable waves of sound crashed through the confined corridors. Two more. The revolver dropped to the hard-packed snow of the trail, and Barclay saw the ice-ax shift into defensive position. Connant's powerful body blocked his vision, but beyond he heard something mewing, and, insanely, chuckling. The dogs were quieter; there was a deadly seriousness in their low snarls. Taloned feet scratched at hard-packed snow, broken chains were clinking and tangling.

Connant shifted abruptly, and Barclay could see what lay beyond. For a second he stood frozen, then his breath went out in a gusty curse. The Thing launched itself at Connant, the powerful arms of the man swung the ice-ax flatside first at what might have been a hand. It scrunched horribly, and the tattered flesh, ripped by a half-dozen savage huskies, leapt to its feet again. The red eyes blazed with an unearthly hatred, an unearthly, unkillable vitality.

Barclay turned the fire extinguisher on it; the blinding, blistering stream of chemical spray confused it, baffled it, together with the savage attacks of the huskies, not for long afraid of anything that did, or could live, held it at bay.

McReady wedged men out of his way and drove down the narrow corridor packed with men unable to reach the scene. There was a sure fore-planned drive to McReady's attack. One of the giant blow-torches used in warming the plane's engines was in his bronzed hands. It roared gustily as he turned the corner and opened the valve. The mad mewing hissed louder. The dogs scrambled back from the three-foot lance of blue-hot flame.

'Bar, get a power cable, run it in somehow. And a handle. We can electrocute this—monster, if I don't incinerate it.' McReady spoke with an authority of planned action. Barclay turned down the long corridor to the power plant, but already before him Norris and Van Wall were racing down.

Barclay found the cable in the electrical cache in the tunnel wall. In a half minute he was hacking at it, walking back. Van Wall's voice rang out in a warning shout of 'Power!' as the emergency gasoline-powered dynamo thudded into action. Half a dozen other men were down there now; the coal kindling were going into the firebox of the steam power plant. Norris, cursing in a low, deadly monotone, was working with quick, sure fingers on the other end of Barclay's cable, splicing in a contactor in one of the power leads.

The dogs had fallen back when Barclay reached the corridor bend, fallen back before a furious monstrosity that glared from baleful red eyes, mewing in trapped hatred. The dogs were a semi-circle of red-dipped muzzles with a fringe of glistening white teeth, whining with a vicious eagerness that near matched the fury of the red eyes. McReady stood confidently alert at the corridor bend, the gustily muttering torch held loose and ready for action in his hands. He stepped aside without moving his eyes from the beast as Barclay came up. There was a slight, tight smile on his lean, bronzed face.

Norris' voice called down the corridor, and Barclay stepped forward. The cable was taped to the long handle of a snow-shovel, the two conductors split, and held 18 inches apart by a scrap of lumber lashed at right angles across the far end of the handle. Bare copper conductors, charged with 220 volts, glinted in the light of pressure lamps. The Thing mewed and halted and dodged. McReady advanced to Barclay's side. The dogs beyond sensed the plan with the almost-telepathic intelligence of trained huskies. Their whimpering grew shriller, softer, their mincing steps carried them nearer. Abruptly a huge, night-black Alaskan leapt onto the trapped thing. It turned squalling, saber-clawed feet slashing.

Barclay leapt forward and jabbed. A weird, shrill scream rose and choked out. The smell of burnt flesh in the corridor intensified; greasy smoke curled up. The echoing pound of the gas-electric dynamo down the corridor became a slogging thud.

The red eyes clouded over in a stiffening, jerking travesty of a face. Armlike, leglike members quivered and jerked. The dogs leapt forward, and Barclay yanked back his shovel-handled weapon. The thing on the snow did not move as gleaming teeth ripped it open.

Chapter Six

Garry looked about the crowded room. Thirty-two men, some tensed nervously standing against the wall, some uneasily relaxed, some sitting, most perforce standing, as intimate as sardines. Thirty-two, plus the five engaged in sewing up wounded dogs, made thirty-seven, the total personnel.

Garry started speaking. 'All right, I guess we're here. Some of you—three or four at most—saw what happened. All of you have seen that thing on the table, and can get a general idea. Anyone hasn't, I'll lift—' His hand strayed to the tarpaulin bulking over the thing on the table. There was an acrid odor of singed flesh seeping out of it. The men stirred restlessly, hasty denials.

'It looks rather as though Charnauk isn't going to lead any more teams,' Garry went on. 'Blair wants to get at this thing, and make some more detailed examination. We want to know what happened, and make sure right now that this is permanently, totally dead. Right?'

Connant grinned. 'Anybody that doesn't agree can sit up with it tonight.'

'All right then, Blair, what can you say about it? What was it?' Garry turned to the little biologist.

'I wonder if we ever saw its natural form.' Blair looked at the covered mass. 'It may have been imitating the beings that built that ship—but I don't think it was. I think that was its true form. Those of us who were up near the bend saw the thing in action; the thing on the table is the result. When it got loose, apparently, it started looking around. It saw Antarctica still frozen as it was ages ago when the creature first saw it—and froze. From my observations while it was thawing out, and the bits of tissue I cut and hardened then, I think it was native to a hotter planet than Earth. It couldn't, in its natural form, stand the temperature. There is no life-form on Earth that can live in Antarctica during the winter, but the best compromise is the dog. It found the dogs, and somehow got near enough to Charnauk to get him. The others smelled it—heard it—I don't know—anyway they went wild, and broke chains, and attacked it before it was finished. The thing we found was part Charnauk, queerly only half-dead, part Charnauk half-digested by the jellylike protoplasm of that creature, and part the remains of the thing we originally found, sort of melted down to the basic protoplasm.

'When the dogs attacked it, it turned into the best fighting thing it could think of. Some other-world beast apparently.'

'Turned,' snapped Garry. 'How?'

'Every living thing is made up of jelly—protoplasm and minute, submicroscopic things called nuclei, which control the bulk, the protoplasm. This thing was just a modification of that same worldwide plan of Nature; cells made up of protoplasm, controlled by infinitely tinier nuclei. You physicists might compare it—an individual cell of any living thing—with an atom; the bulk of the atom, the space-filling part, is made up of the electron orbits, but the character of the thing is determined by the atomic nucleus.

'This isn't wildly beyond what we already know. It's just a modification we haven't seen before. It's as natural, as logical, as any other manifestation of life. It obeys exactly the same laws. The cells are made of protoplasm, their character determined by the nucleus.

'Only in this creature, the cell-nuclei can control those cells at *will*. It digested Charnauk, and as it digested, studied every cell of his tissue, and shaped its own cells to imitate them exactly. Parts of it—parts that had time to finish changing—are dog-cells. But they don't have dog-cell nuclei.' Blair lifted a fraction of the tarpaulin. A torn dog's leg with stiff gray fur protruded. 'That, for instance, isn't dog at all; it's imitation. Some parts I'm uncertain about; the nucleus was hiding itself, covering up with dog-cell imitation nucleus. In time, not even a microscope would have shown the difference.'

'Suppose,' asked Norris bitterly, 'it had had lots of time?'

'Then it would have been a dog. The other dogs would have accepted it. We would have accepted it. I don't think anything would have distinguished it, not microscope, nor X-ray, nor any other means. This is a member of a supremely intelligent race, a race that has learned the deepest secrets of biology, and turned them to its use.'

'What was it planning to do?' Barclay looked at the humped tarpaulin.

Blair grinned unpleasantly. The wavering halo of thin hair round his bald pate wavered in the stir of air. 'Take over the world, I imagine.'

'Take over the world! Just it, all by itself?' Connant gasped. 'Set itself up as a lone dictator?'

'No,' Blair shook his head. The scalpel he had been fumbling in his bony fingers dropped; he bent to pick it up, so that his face was hidden as he spoke. 'It would become the population of the world.'

'Become—populate the world? Does it reproduce asexually?'

Blair shook his head and gulped. 'It's—it doesn't have to. It weighed 85 pounds. Charnauk weighed about 90. It would have become Charnauk, and had 85 pounds left, to become—oh, Jack for instance, or Chinook. It can imitate anything—that is, become anything. If it had reached the Antarctic Sea, it would have become a seal, maybe two seals. They might have attacked a killer whale, and become either killers, or a herd of seals. Or maybe it would have caught an albatross, or a skua gull, and flown to South America.'

Norris cursed softly. 'And every time it digested something, and imitated it—'

'It would have had its original bulk left, to start again,' Blair finished. 'Nothing would kill it. It has no natural enemies, because it becomes whatever it wants to. If a killer whale attacked it, it would become a killer whale. If it was an albatross, and an eagle attacked it, it would become an eagle. Lord, it might become a female eagle. Go back—build a nest and lay eggs!'

'Are you sure that thing from hell is dead?' Dr Copper asked softly.

'Yes, thank Heaven,' the little biologist gasped. 'After they drove the dogs off, I stood there poking Bar's electrocution thing into it for five minutes. It's dead and—cooked.'

'Then we can only give thanks that this is Antarctica, where there is not one, single, solitary, living thing for it to imitate, except these animals in camp.'

'Us,' Blair giggled. 'It can imitate us. Dogs can't make four hundred miles to the sea; there's no food. There aren't any skua gulls to imitate at this season. There aren't any penguins this far inland. There's nothing that can reach the sea from this point—except us. We've got brains. We can do it. Don't you see—*it's got to imitate us - it's got to be one of us — that's the only way it can fly an airplane - fly a plane for two hours, and rule - be - all Earth's inhabitants*. A world for the taking—*if it imitates us!*

'It didn't know yet. It hadn't had a chance to learn. It was rushed—hurried—took the thing nearest its own size. Look—I'm Pandora! I opened the box! And the only hope that can come out is—that nothing can come out. You didn't see me. I did it. I fixed it. I smashed every magneto. Not a plane can fly. Nothing can fly.' Blair giggled and lay down on the floor crying.

Chief Pilot Van Wall made a dive for the door. His feet were fading echoes in the corridors as Dr Copper bent unhurriedly over the little man on the floor. From his office at the end of the room he brought something, and injected a solution into Blair's arm. 'He might come out of it when he wakes up,' he sighed, rising. McReady helped him lift the biologist onto a near-by bunk. 'It all depends on whether we can convince him that thing is dead.'

Van Wall ducked into the shack brushing his heavy blond beard absently. 'I didn't think a biologist would do a thing like that up thoroughly. He missed the spares in the second cache. It's all right. I smashed them.'

Commander Garry nodded. 'I was wondering about the radio.'

Dr Copper snorted. 'You don't think it can leak out on a radio wave, do you? You'd have five rescue attempts in the next three months if you stop the broadcasts. The thing to do is talk loud and not make a sound. Now I wonder—'

McReady looked speculatively at the doctor. 'It might be like an infectious disease. Everything that drank any of its blood—'

Copper shook his head. 'Blair missed something. Imitate it may, but it has, to a certain extent, its own body-chemistry, its own metabolism. If it didn't, it would become a dog—and be a dog and nothing more. It has to be an imitation dog. Therefore you can detect it by serum tests. And its chemistry, since it comes from another world, must be so wholly, radically different that a few cells, such as gained by drops of blood, would be treated as disease germs by the dog, or human body.'

'Blood—would one of those imitations bleed?' Norris demanded.

'Surely. Nothing mystic about blood. Muscle is about 90 per cent water; blood differs only in having a couple per cent more water, and less connective tissue. They'd bleed all right,' Copper assured him.

Blair sat up in his bunk suddenly. 'Connant—where's Connant?'

416 SCIENCE-FICTION CLASSICS

The physicist moved over toward the little biologist. 'Here I am. What do you want?'

'Are you?' giggled Blair. He lapsed back into the bunk contorted with silent laughter.

Connant looked at him blankly. 'Huh? Am I what?'

'*Are* you there?' Blair burst into gales of laughter. '*Are* you Connant? The beast wanted to be a *man*—not a dog—'

Chapter Seven

Dr Copper rose wearily from the bunk, and washed the hypodermic carefully. The little tinkles it made seemed loud in the packed room, now that Blair's gurgling laughter had finally quieted. Copper looked toward Garry and shook his head slowly. 'Hopeless, I'm afraid. I don't think we can ever convince him the thing is dead now.'

Norris laughed uncertainly. 'I'm not sure you can convince me. Oh, damn you, McReady.'

'McReady?' Commander Garry turned to look from Norris to McReady curiously.

'The nightmares,' Norris explained. 'He had a theory about the nightmares we had at the Secondary Station after finding that thing.'

'And that was?' Garry looked at McReady levelly.

Norris answered for him, jerkily, uneasily. 'That the creature wasn't dead, had a sort of enormously slowed existence, an existence that permitted it, none the less, to be vaguely aware of the passing of time, of our coming, after endless years. I had a dream it could imitate things.'

'Well,' Copper grunted, 'it can.'

'Don't be an ass,' Norris snapped. 'That's not what's bothering me. In the dream it could read minds, read thoughts and ideas and mannerisms.'

'What's so bad about that? It seems to be worrying you more than the thought of the joy we're going to have with a mad man in an Antarctic camp.' Copper nodded toward Blair's sleeping form.

McReady shook his great head slowly. 'You know that Connant is Connant, because he not merely looks like Connant—which we're beginning to believe that beast might be able to do—but he thinks like Connant, talks like Connant, moves himself around as Connant does. That takes more than merely a body that looks like him; that takes Connant's own mind, and thoughts and mannerisms. Therefore, though you know that the thing might make itself *look* like Connant, you aren't much bothered, because you know it has a mind from another world, a totally unhuman mind, that couldn't possibly react and think and talk like a man we know, and do it so well as to fool us for a moment. The idea of the creature imitating one of us is fascinating, but unreal because it is too completely unhuman to deceive us. It doesn't have a human mind.'

'As I said before,' Norris repeated, looking steadily at McReady, 'you can say the damnedest things at the damnedest times. Will you be so good as to finish that thought—one way or the other?'

Kinner, the scar-faced expedition cook, had been standing near Connant. Suddenly he moved down the length of the crowded room toward his familiar galley. He shook the ashes from the galley stove noisily.

'It would do it no good,' said Dr Copper, softly as though thinking out loud, 'to merely look like something it was trying to imitate; it would have to understand its feelings, its reaction. It *is* unhuman; it has powers of imitation beyond any conception of man. A good actor, by training himself, can imitate another man, another man's mannerisms, well enough to fool most people. Of course no actor could imitate so perfectly as to deceive men who had been living with the imitated one in the complete lack of privacy of an Antarctic camp. That would take a super-human skill.'

'Oh, you've got the bug too?' Norris cursed softly.

Connant, standing alone at one end of the room, looked about him wildly, his face white. A gentle eddying of the men had crowded them slowly down toward the other end of the room, so that he stood quite alone. 'My God, will you two Jeremiahs shut up?' Connant's voice shook. 'What am I? Some kind of a microscopic specimen you're dissecting? Some unpleasant worm you're discussing in the third person?'

McReady looked up at him; his slowly twisting hands stopped for a moment. 'Having a lovely time. Wish you were here. Signed: Everybody.

'Connant, if you think you're having a hell of a time, just move over on the other end for a while. You've got one thing we haven't; you know what the answer is. I'll tell you this, right now you're the most feared and respected man in Big Magnet.'

'Lord, I wish you could see your eyes,' Connant gasped. 'Stop staring, will you! What the hell are you going to do?'

'Have you any suggestions, Dr Copper?' Commander Garry asked steadily. 'The present situation is impossible.'

'Oh, is it?' Connant snapped. 'Come over here and look at that crowd. By Heaven, they look exactly like that gang of huskies around the corridor bend. Benning, will you stop hefting that damned ice-ax?'

The coppery blade rang on the floor as the aviation mechanic nervously dropped it. He bent over and picked it up instantly, hefting it slowly, turning it in his hands, his brown eyes moving jerkily about the room.

Copper sat down on the bunk beside Blair. The wood creaked noisily in the room. Far down a corridor, a dog yelped in pain, and the dog-drivers' tense voices floated softly back. 'Microscopic examination,' said the doctor thoughtfully, 'would be useless, as Blair pointed out. Considerable time has passed. However, serum tests would be definitive.'

'Serum tests? What do you mean exactly?' Commander Garry asked.

'If I had a rabbit that had been injected with human blood—a poison to rabbits, of course, as is the blood of any animal save that of another rabbit—and the injections continued in increasing doses for some time, the rabbit would be human-immune. If a small quantity of its blood were drawn off, allowed to separate in a test-tube, and to the clear serum, a bit of human blood were added, there would be a visible reaction, proving the blood was human. If cow, or dog blood were added—or any protein material other than that one thing, human blood—no reaction would take place. That would prove definitely.'

'Can you suggest where I might catch a rabbit for you, Doc?' Norris asked. 'That is, nearer than Australia; we don't want to waste time going that far.'

'I know there aren't any rabbits in Antarctica,' Copper nodded, 'but that is simply the usual animal. Any animal except man will do. A dog for instance. But it will take several days, and due to the greater size of the animal, considerable blood. Two of us will have to contribute.'

'Would I do?' Garry asked.

'That will make two,' Copper nodded. 'I'll get to work on it right away.'

'What about Connant in the meantime?' Kinner demanded. 'I'm going out that door and head off for the Ross Sea before I cook for him.'

'He may be human—' Copper started.

Connant burst out in a flood of curses. 'Human! *May* be human, you damned saw-bones! What in hell do you think I am?'

'A monster,' Copper snapped sharply. 'Now shut up and listen.' Connant's face drained of color and he sat down heavily as the indictment was put in words. 'Until we know—you know as well as we do that we have reason to question the fact, and only you know how that question is to be answered—we may reasonably be expected to lock you up. If you are—unhuman—you're a lot more dangerous than poor Blair there, and I'm going to see that he's locked up thoroughly. I expect that his next stage will be a violent desire to kill you, all the dogs, and probably all of us. When he wakes, he will be convinced we're all unhuman, and nothing on the planet will ever change his conviction. It would be kinder to let him die, but we can't do that, of course. He's going in one shack, and you can stay in Cosmos House with your cosmic ray apparatus. Which is about what you'd do anyway. I've got to fix up a couple of dogs.'

Connant nodded bitterly. 'I'm human. Hurry that test. Your eyes—Lord, I wish you could see your eyes staring—'

Commander Garry watched anxiously as Clark, the dog-handler, held the big brown Alaskan husky, while Copper began the injection treatment. The dog was not anxious to cooperate; the needle was painful, and already he'd experienced considerable needle work that morning. Five stitches held closed a slash that ran from his shoulder across the ribs half way down his body. One long fang was broken off short; the missing part was to be found half-buried in the shoulder bone of the monstrous thing on the table in the Ad Building.

'How long will that take?' Garry asked, pressing his arm gently. It was sore from the prick of the needle Dr Copper had used to withdraw blood.

Copper shrugged. 'I don't know, to be frank. I know the general method, I've used it on rabbits. But I haven't experimented with dogs. They're big, clumsy animals to work with; naturally rabbits are preferable, and serve ordinarily. In civilized places you can buy a stock of human-immune rabbits from suppliers, and not many investigators take the trouble to prepare their own.'

'What do they want with them back there?' Clark asked.

'Criminology is one large field. A says he didn't murder B, but that the blood on his shirt came from killing a chicken. The State makes a test, then it's up to A to explain how it is the blood reacts on human-immune rabbits, but not on chicken-immunes.'

'What are we going to do with Blair in the meantime?' Garry asked wearily. 'It's all right to let him sleep where he is for a while, but when he wakes up—'

'Barclay and Benning are fitting some bolts on the door of Cosmos House,' Copper replied grimly. 'Connant's acting like a gentleman. I think perhaps the way the other men look at him makes him rather want privacy. Lord knows, heretofore we've all of us individually prayed for a little privacy.'

Clark laughed bitterly. 'Not anymore, thank you. The more the merrier.'

'Blair,' Copper went on, 'will also have to have privacy—and locks. He's going to have a pretty definite plan in mind when he wakes up. Ever hear the old story of how to stop hoof-and-mouth disease in cattle?

'If there isn't any hoof-and-mouth disease, there won't be any hoof-and-mouth disease,' Copper explained. 'You get rid of it by killing every animal that exhibits it, and every animal that's been near the diseased animal. Blair's a biologist, and knows that story. He's afraid of this thing we loosed. The answer is probably pretty clear in his mind now. Kill everybody and everything in this camp before a skua gull or a wandering albatross coming in with the spring chances out this way and—catches the disease.'

Clark's lips curled in a twisted grin. 'Sounds logical to me. If things get too bad—maybe we'd better let Blair get loose. It would save us committing suicide. We might also make something of a vow that if things get bad, we see that that does happen.'

Copper laughed softly. 'The last man alive in Big Magnet—wouldn't be a man,' he pointed out. 'Somebody's got to kill those—creatures that don't desire to kill themselves, you know. We don't have enough thermite to do it all at once, and the decanite explosive wouldn't help much. I have an idea that even small pieces of one of those beings would be self-sufficient.'

'If,' said Garry thoughtfully, 'they can modify their protoplasm at will, won't they simply modify themselves to birds and fly away? They can read all about birds, and imitate their structure without even meeting them. Or imitate, perhaps, birds of their home planet.'

Copper shook his head, and helped Clark to free the dog. 'Man studied birds for centuries, trying to learn how to make a machine to fly like them. He never did do the trick; his final success came when he broke away entirely and tried new methods. Knowing the general idea, and knowing the detailed structure of wing and bone and nerve-tissue is something far, far different. And as for otherworld birds, perhaps, in fact very probably, the atmospheric conditions here are so vastly different that their birds couldn't fly. Perhaps, even, the being came from a planet like Mars with such a thin atmosphere that there were no birds.'

Barclay came into the building, trailing a length of airplane control cable. 'It's finished, Doc. Cosmos House can't be opened from the inside. Now where do we put Blair?'

Copper looked toward Garry. 'There wasn't any biology building. I don't know where we can isolate him.'

'How about East Cache?' Garry said after a moment's thought. 'Will Blair be able to look after himself—or need attention?'

'He'll be capable enough. We'll be the ones to watch out,' Copper assured him grimly. 'Take a stove, a couple of bags of coal, necessary supplies and a few tools to fix it up. Nobody's been out there since last fall, have they?'

Garry shook his head. 'If he gets noisy—I thought that might be a good idea.'

Barclay hefted the tools he was carrying and looked up at Garry. 'If the muttering he's doing now is any sign, he's going to sing away the night hours. And we won't like his song.'

'What's he saying?' Copper asked.

Barclay shook his head. 'I didn't care to listen much. You can if you want to. But I gathered that the blasted idiot had all the dreams McReady had, and a few more. He slept beside the thing when we stopped on the trail coming in from Secondary Magnetic, remember. He dreamt the thing was alive, and dreamt more details. And—damn his soul—knew it wasn't all dream, or had reason to. He knew it had telepathic powers that were stirring vaguely, and that it could not only read minds, but project thoughts. They weren't dreams, you see. They were stray thoughts that thing was broadcasting, the way Blair's broadcasting his thoughts now— a sort of telepathic muttering in its sleep. That's why he knew so much about its powers. I guess you and I, Doc, weren't so sensitive—if you want to believe in telepathy.'

'I have to,' Copper sighed. 'Dr Rhine of Duke University has shown that it exists, shown that some are much more sensitive than others.'

'Well, if you want to learn a lot of details, go listen in on Blair's broadcast. He's driven most of the boys out of the Ad Building; Kinner's rattling pans like coal going down a chute. When he can't rattle a pan, he shakes ashes.

'By the way, Commander, what are we going to do this spring, now the planes are out of it?'

Garry sighed. 'I'm afraid our expedition is going to be a loss. We cannot divide our strength now.'

'It won't be a loss—if we continue to live, and come out of this,' Copper promised him. 'The find we've made, if we can get it under control, is important enough. The cosmic ray data, magnetic work, and atmospheric work won't be greatly hindered.'

Garry laughed mirthlessly. 'I was just thinking of the radio broadcasts. Telling half the world about the wonderful results of our exploration flights, trying to fool men like Byrd and Ellsworth back home there that we're doing something.'

Copper nodded gravely. 'They'll know something's wrong. But men like that have judgment enough to know we wouldn't do tricks without some sort of reason, and will wait for our return to judge us. I think it comes to this: men who know enough to recognize our deception will wait for our return. Men who haven't discretion and faith enough to wait will not have the experience to detect any fraud. We know enough of the conditions here to put through a good bluff.'

'Just so they don't send "rescue" expeditions,' Garry prayed. 'When— if—we're ever ready to come out, we'll have to send word to Captain Forsythe to bring a stock of magnetos with him when he comes down. But—never mind that.'

'You mean if we don't come out?' asked Barclay. 'I was wondering if a nice running account of an eruption or an earthquake via radio—with a swell windup by using a stick of decanite under the microphone—would help. Nothing, of course, will entirely keep people out. One of those swell, melodramatic "last-man-alive-scenes" might make 'em go easy though.'

Garry smiled with genuine humor. 'Is everybody in camp trying to figure that out too?'

Copper laughed. 'What do you think, Garry? We're confident we can win out. But not too easy about it, I guess.'

Clark grinned up from the dog he was petting into calmness. 'Confident, did you say, Doc?'

CHAPTER EIGHT

Blair moved restlessly around the small shack. His eyes jerked and quivered in vague, fleeting glances at the four men with him; Barclay, six feet tall and weighing over 190 pounds; McReady, a bronze giant of a man; Dr Copper, short, squatly powerful; and Benning, five-feet-ten of wiry strength.

Blair was huddled up against the far wall of the East Cache cabin, his gear piled in the middle of the floor beside the heating stove, forming an island between him and the four men. His bony hands clenched and fluttered, terrified. His pale eyes wavered uneasily as his bald, freckled head darted about in birdlike motion.

'I don't want anybody coming here. I'll cook my own food,' he snapped nervously. 'Kinner may be human now, but I don't believe it. I'm going to get out of here, but I'm not going to eat any food you send me. I want cans. Sealed cans.'

'OK, Blair, we'll bring 'em tonight,' Barclay promised. 'You've got coal, and the fire's started. I'll make a last—' Barclay started forward.

Blair instantly scurried to the farthest corner. 'Get out! Keep away from me, you monster!' the little biologist shrieked, and tried to claw his way through the wall of the shack. 'Keep away from me—keep away—I won't be absorbed—I won't be—'

Barclay relaxed and moved back. Dr Copper shook his head. 'Leave him alone, Bar. It's easier for him to fix the thing himself. We'll have to fix the door, I think—'

The four men let themselves out. Efficiently, Benning and Barclay fell to work. There were no locks in Antarctica; there wasn't enough privacy to make them needed. But powerful screws had been driven in each side of the door frame, and the spare aviation control cable, immensely strong, woven steel wire, was rapidly caught between them and drawn taut. Barclay went to work with a drill and a keyhole saw. Presently he had a trap cut in the door through which goods could be passed without unlashing the entrance. Three powerful hinges from a stock-crate, two hasps and a pair of three-inch cotter-pins made it proof against opening from the other side.

Blair moved about restlessly inside. He was dragging something over to the door with panting gasps and muttering, frantic curses. Barclay opened the hatch and glanced in, Dr Copper peering over his shoulder. Blair had moved the heavy bunk against the door. It could not be opened without his cooperation now.

'Don't know but what the poor man's right at that,' McReady sighed. 'If he gets loose, it is his avowed intention to kill each and all of us as quickly as possible, which is something we don't agree with. But we've something on our side of that door that is worse than a homicidal maniac. If one or the other has to get loose, I think I'll come up and undo those lashings here.'

Barclay grinned. 'You let me know, and I'll show you how to get these off fast. Let's go back.'

The sun was painting the northern horizon in multi-colored rainbows still, though it was two hours below the horizon. The field of drift swept off to the north, sparkling under its flaming colors in a million reflected glories. Low mounds of rounded white on the northern horizon showed the Magnet Range was barely awash above the sweeping drift. Little eddies of wind-lifted snow swirled away from their skis as they set out toward the main encampment two miles away. The spidery finger of the broadcast radiator lifted a gaunt black needle against the white of the Antarctic continent. The snow under their skis was like fine sand, hard and gritty.

'Spring,' said Benning bitterly, 'is come. Ain't we got fun! I've been looking forward to getting away from this blasted hole in the ice.'

'I wouldn't try it now, if I were you.' Barclay grunted. 'Guys that set out from here in the next few days are going to be marvelously unpopular.'

'How is your dog getting along, Dr Copper?' McReady asked. 'Any results yet?'

'In thirty hours? I wish there were. I gave him an injection of my blood today. But I imagine another five days will be needed. I don't know certainly enough to stop sooner.'

'I've been wondering—if Connant were—changed, would he have warned us so soon after the animal escaped? Wouldn't he have waited long enough for it to have a real chance to fix itself? Until we woke up naturally?' McReady asked slowly.

'The thing is selfish. You didn't think it looked as though it were possessed of a store of the higher justices, did you?' Dr Copper pointed out. 'Every part of it is all of it, every part of it is all for itself, I imagine. If Connant were changed, to save his skin, he'd have to—but Connant's feelings aren't changed; they're imitated perfectly, or they're his own. Naturally, the imitation, imitating perfectly Connant's feelings, would do exactly what Connant would do.'

'Say, couldn't Norris or Van give Connant some kind of a test? If the thing is brighter than men, it might know more physics than Connant should, and they'd catch it out,' Barclay suggested.

Copper shook his head wearily. 'Not if it reads minds. You can't plan a trap for it. Van suggested that last night. He hoped it would answer some of the questions of physics he'd like to know answers to.'

'This expedition-of-four idea is going to make life happy.' Benning looked at his companions. 'Each of us with an eye on the others to make sure he doesn't do something—peculiar. Man, aren't we going to be a trusting bunch! Each man eyeing his neighbors with the grandest exhibition of faith and trust—I'm beginning to know what Connant meant by "I wish you could see your eyes." Every now and then we all have it, I guess. One of you looks around with a sort of "I-wonder-if-the-other-*three*-are look." Incidentally, I'm not excepting myself.'

'So far as we know, the animal is dead, with a slight question as to Connant. No other is suspected,' McReady stated slowly. 'The "always-four" order is merely a precautionary measure.'

'I'm waiting for Garry to make it four-in-a-bunk,' Barclay sighed. 'I thought I didn't have any privacy before, but since that order—'

None watched more tensely than Connant. A little sterile glass test-tube, half-filled with straw-colored fluid. One—two—three—four—five drops of the clear solution Dr Copper had prepared from the drops of blood from Connant's arm. The tube was shaken carefully, then set in a beaker of clear, warm water. The thermometer read blood heat, a little thermostat clicked noisily, and the electric hotplate began to glow as the lights flickered slightly.

Then—little white flecks of precipitation were forming, snowing down in the clear straw-colored fluid. 'Lord,' said Connant. He dropped heavily into a bunk, crying like a baby. 'Six days—' Connant sobbed, 'six days in there—wondering if that damned test would lie—'

Garry moved over silently, and slipped his arm across the physicist's back.

'It couldn't lie,' Dr Copper said. 'The dog was human-immune—and the serum reacted.'

'He's—all right?' Norris gasped. 'Then—the animal is dead—dead forever?'

'He is human,' Copper spoke definitely, 'and the animal is dead.'

Kinner burst out laughing, laughing hysterically. McReady turned toward him and slapped his face with a methodical one-two, one-two action. The cook laughed, gulped, cried a moment and sat up rubbing his cheeks, mumbling his thanks vaguely. 'I was scared. Lord, I was scared—'

Norris laughed brittlely. 'You think we weren't, you ape? You think maybe Connant wasn't?'

The Ad Building stirred with a sudden rejuvenation. Voices laughed, the men clustering around Connant spoke with unnecessarily loud voices, jittery, nervous voices relievedly friendly again. Somebody called out a suggestion, and a dozen started for their skis. Blair. Blair might recover—Dr Copper fussed with his test-tubes in nervous relief, trying solutions. The party of relief for Blair's shack started out the door, skis clapping noisily. Down the corridor, the dogs set up a quick yelping howl as the air of excited relief reached them.

Dr Copper fussed with his tubes. McReady noticed him first, sitting on the edge of the bunk, with two precipitin-whitened test-tubes of straw-colored fluid, his face whiter than the stuff in the tubes, silent tears slipping down from horror-widened eyes.

McReady felt a cold knife of fear pierce through his heart and freeze in his breast. Dr Copper looked up.

'Garry,' he called hoarsely. 'Garry, for God's sake, come here.'

Commander Garry walked toward him sharply. Silence clapped down on the Ad Building. Connant looked up, rose stiffly from his seat.

'Garry—tissue from the monster—precipitates too. It proves nothing. Nothing but—but the dog was monster-immune too. That one of the two contributing blood—one of us two, you and I, Garry—*one of us is a monster.*'

CHAPTER NINE

'Bar, call back those men before they tell Blair,' McReady said quietly. Barclay went to the door; faintly his shouts came back to the tensely silent men in the room. Then he was back.

'They're coming,' he said. 'I didn't tell them why. Just that Dr Copper said not to go.'

'McReady,' Garry sighed, 'you're in command now. May God help you. I cannot.'

The bronzed giant nodded slowly, his deep eyes on Commander Garry.

'I may be the one,' Garry added. 'I know I'm not, but I cannot prove it to you in any way. Dr Copper's test has broken down. The fact that he showed it was useless, when it was to the advantage of the monster to have that uselessness not known, would seem to prove he was human.'

Copper rocked back and forth slowly on the bunk. 'I know I'm human. I can't prove it either. One of us two is a liar, for that test cannot lie, and it says one of us is. I gave proof that the test was wrong, which seems to prove I'm human, and now Garry has given that argument which proves me human—which he, as the monster, should not do. Round and round and round and round and—'

Dr Copper's head, then his neck and shoulders began circling slowly in time to the words. Suddenly he was lying back on the bunk, roaring with laughter. 'It doesn't have to prove one of us is a monster! It doesn't have to prove that at all! Ho-ho. If we're *all* monsters it works the same! We're all monsters—all of us—Connant and Garry and I—and all of you.'

'McReady,' Van Wall, the blond-bearded Chief Pilot, called softly, 'you were on the way to an MD when you took up meteorology, weren't you? Can you make some kind of test?'

McReady went over to Copper slowly, took the hypodermic from his hand, and washed it carefully in 95 per cent alcohol. Garry sat on the bunk-edge with wooden face, watching Copper and McReady expressionlessly. 'What Copper said is possible,' McReady sighed. 'Van, will you help here? Thanks.' The filled needle jabbed into Copper's thigh. The man's laughter did not stop, but slowly faded into sobs, then sound sleep as the morphia took hold.

McReady turned again. The men who had started for Blair stood at the far end of the room, skis dripping snow, their faces as white as their skis. Connant had a lighted cigarette in each hand; one he was puffing absently, and staring at the floor. The heat of the one in his left hand attracted him and he stared at it, and the one in the other hand, stupidly for a moment. He dropped one and crushed it under his heel slowly.

'Dr Copper,' McReady repeated, 'could be right. I know I'm human—but of course can't prove it. I'll repeat the test for my own information. Any of you others who wish to may do the same.'

Two minutes later, McReady held a test-tube with white precipitin settling slowly from straw-colored serum. 'It reacts to human blood too, so they aren't both monsters.'

'I didn't think they were,' Van Wall sighed. 'That wouldn't suit the monster either; we could have destroyed them if we knew. Why hasn't the monster destroyed us, do you suppose? It seems to be loose.'

McReady snorted. Then laughed softly. 'Elementary, my dear Watson. The monster wants to have life-forms available. It cannot animate a dead body, apparently. It is just waiting—waiting until the best opportunities come. We who remain human, it is holding in reserve.'

Kinner shuddered violently. 'Hey. Hey, Mac. Mac, would I know if I was a monster? Would I know if the monster had already got me? Oh Lord, I may be a monster already.'

'You'd know,' McReady answered.

'But we wouldn't,' Norris laughed shortly, half-hysterically.

McReady looked at the vial of serum remaining. 'There's one thing this damned stuff is good for, at that,' he said thoughtfully. 'Clark, will you and Van help me? The rest of the gang better stick together here. Keep an eye on each other,' he said bitterly. 'See that you don't get into mischief, shall we say?'

McReady started down the tunnel toward Dogtown, with Clark and Van Wall behind him. 'You need more serum?' Clark asked.

McReady shook his head. 'Tests. There's four cows and a bull, and nearly seventy dogs down there. This stuff reacts only to human blood and—monsters.'

McReady came back to the Ad Building and went silently to the wash stand. Clark and Van Wall joined him a moment later. Clark's lips had developed a tic, jerking into sudden, unexpected sneers.

'What did you do?' Connant exploded suddenly. 'More immunizing?'

Clark snickered, and stopped with a hiccough. 'Immunizing. Haw! Immune all right.'

'That monster,' said Van Wall steadily, 'is quite logical. Our immune dog was quite all right, and we drew a little more serum for the tests. But we won't make any more.'

'Can't—can't you use one man's blood on another dog—' Norris began.

'There aren't,' said McReady softly, 'any more dogs. Nor cattle, I might add.'

'No more dogs?' Benning sat down slowly.

'They're very nasty when they start changing,' Van Wall said precisely, 'but slow. That electrocution iron you made up, Barclay, is very fast. There is only one dog left—our immune. The monster left that for us, so we could play with our little test. The rest—' He shrugged and dried his hands.

'The cattle—' gulped Kinner.

'Also. Reacted very nicely. They look funny as hell when they start melting. The beast hasn't any quick escape, when it's tied in dog chains, or halters, and it had to be to imitate.'

Kinner stood up slowly. His eyes darted around the room, and came to rest horribly quivering on a tin bucket in the galley. Slowly, step by step, he retreated toward the door, his mouth opening and closing silently, like a fish out of water.

'The milk—' he gasped. 'I milked 'em an hour ago—' His voice broke into a scream as he dived through the door. He was out on the ice cap without windproof or heavy clothing.

Van Wall looked after him for a moment thoughtfully. 'He's probably hopelessly mad,' he said at length, 'but he might be a monster escaping. He hasn't skis. Take a blow-torch—in case.'

The physical motion of the chase helped them; something that needed doing. Three of the other men were quietly being sick. Norris was lying flat on his back, his face greenish, looking steadily at the bottom of the bunk above him.

'Mac, how long have the—cows been not—cows—'

McReady shrugged his shoulders hopelessly. He went over to the milk bucket, and with his little tube of serum went to work on it. The milk clouded it, making certainty difficult. Finally he dropped the test-tube in the stand and shook his head. 'It tests negatively. Which means either they were cows then, or that, being perfect imitations, they gave perfectly good milk.'

Copper stirred restlessly in his sleep and gave a gurgling cross between a snore and a laugh. Silent eyes fastened on him. 'Would morphia—a monster—' somebody started to ask.

'Lord knows,' McReady shrugged. 'It affects every Earthly animal I know of.'

Connant suddenly raised his head. 'Mac! The dogs must have swallowed pieces of the monster, and the pieces destroyed them! The dogs were where the monster resided. I was locked up. Doesn't that prove—'

Van Wall shook his head. 'Sorry. Proves nothing about what you are, only proves what you didn't do.'

'It doesn't do that,' McReady sighed. 'We are helpless. Because we don't know enough, and so jittery we don't think straight. Locked up! Ever watch a white corpuscle of the blood go through the wall of a blood vessel? No? It sticks out a pseudopod. And there it is—on the far side of the wall.'

'Oh,' said Van Wall unhappily. 'The cattle tried to melt down, didn't they? They could have melted down—become just a thread of stuff and leaked under a door to re-collect on the other side. Ropes—no—no, that wouldn't do it. They couldn't live in a sealed tank or—'

'If,' said McReady, 'you shoot it through the heart, and it doesn't die, it's a monster. That's the best test I can think of, offhand.'

'No dogs,' said Garry quietly, 'and no cattle. It has to imitate men now.

And locking up doesn't do any good. Your test might work, Mac, but I'm afraid it would be hard on the men.'

Chapter Ten

Clark looked up from the galley stove as Van Wall, Barclay, McReady and Benning came in, brushing the drift from their clothes. The other men jammed into the Ad Building continued studiously to do as they were doing, playing chess, poker, reading. Ralsen was fixing a sledge on the table; Van and Norris had their heads together over magnetic data, while Harvey read tables in a low voice.

Dr Copper snored softly on the bunk. Garry was working with Dutton over a sheaf of radio messages on the corner of Dutton's bunk and a small fraction of the radio table. Connant was using most of the table for cosmic ray sheets.

Quite plainly through the corridor, despite two closed doors, they could hear Kinner's voice. Clark banged a kettle onto the galley stove and beckoned McReady silently. The meteorologist went over to him.

'I don't mind the cooking so damn much,' Clark said nervously, 'but isn't there some way to stop that bird? We all agreed that it would be safe to move him into Cosmos House.'

'Kinner?' McReady nodded toward the door. 'I'm afraid not. I can dope him, I suppose, but we don't have an unlimited supply of morphia, and he's not in danger of losing his mind. Just hysterical.'

'Well, we're in danger of losing ours. You've been out for an hour and a half. That's been going on steadily ever since, and it was going for two hours before. There's a limit, you know.'

Garry wandered over slowly, apologetically. For an instant, McReady caught the feral spark of fear—horror—in Clark's eyes, and knew at the same instant it was in his own. Garry—Garry or Copper—was certainly a monster.

'If you could stop that, I think it would be a sound policy, Mac,' Garry spoke quietly. 'There are—tensions enough in this room. We agreed that it would be safe for Kinner in there, because everyone else in camp is under constant eyeing.' Garry shivered slightly. 'And try, try in God's name, to find some test that will work.'

McReady sighed. 'Watched or unwatched, everyone's tense. Blair's jammed the trap so it won't open now. Says he's got food enough, and keeps screaming "Go away, go away—you're monsters. I won't be absorbed. I won't. I'll tell men when they come. Go away." So—we went away.'

'There's no other test?' Garry pleaded.

McReady shrugged his shoulders. 'Copper was perfectly right. The serum test could be absolutely definitive if it hadn't been—contaminated. But that's the only dog left, and he's fixed now.'

'Chemicals? Chemical tests?'

McReady shook his head. 'Our chemistry isn't that good. I tried the microscope, you know.'

Garry nodded. 'Monster-dog and real dog were identical. But—you've got to go on. What are we going to do after dinner?'

Van Wall had joined them quietly. 'Rotation sleeping. Half the crowd asleep; half awake. I wonder how many of us are monsters? All the dogs were. We thought we were safe, but somehow it got Copper—or you.' Van Wall's eyes flashed uneasily. 'It may have gotten every one of you—all of you but myself may be wondering, looking. No, that's not possible. You'd just spring then. I'd be helpless. We humans must somehow have the greater numbers now. But—' he stopped.

McReady laughed shortly. 'You're doing what Norris complained of in me. Leaving it hanging. "But if one more is changed—that may shift the balance of power." It doesn't fight. I don't think it ever fights, It must be a peaceable thing, in its own—inimitable—way. It never had to, because it always gained its end—otherwise.'

Van Wall's mouth twisted in a sickly grin. 'You're suggesting then, that perhaps it already *has* the greater numbers, but is just waiting—waiting, all of them—all of you, for all I know—waiting till I, the last human, drop my wariness in sleep. Mac, did you notice their eyes, all looking at us?'

Garry sighed. 'You haven't been sitting here for four straight hours, while all their eyes silently weighed the information that one of us two, Copper or I, is a monster certainly—perhaps both of us.'

Clark repeated his request. 'Will you stop that bird's noise? He's driving me nuts. Make him tone down, anyway.'

'Still praying?' McReady asked.

'Still praying,' Clark groaned. 'He hasn't stopped for a second. I don't mind his praying if it relieves him, but he yells, he sings psalms and hymns and shouts prayers. He thinks God can't hear well way down here.'

'Maybe He can't,' Barclay grunted. 'Or He'd have done something about this thing loosed from hell.'

'Somebody's going to try that test you mentioned, if you don't stop him,' Clark stated grimly. 'I think a cleaver in the head would be as positive a test as a bullet in the heart.'

'Go ahead with the food. I'll see what I can do. There may be something in the cabinets.' McReady moved wearily toward the corner Copper had used as his dispensary. Three tall cabinets of rough boards, two locked, were the repositories of the camp's medical supplies. Twelve years ago McReady had graduated, had started for an internship, and been diverted to meteorology. Copper was a picked man, a man who knew his profession thoroughly and modernly. More than half the drugs available were totally unfamiliar to McReady; many of the others he had forgotten. There was no huge medical library here, no series of journals available to learn the things he had forgotten, the elementary, simple things to Copper, things that did not merit inclusion in the small library he had been forced to content himself with. Books are heavy, and every ounce of supplies had been freighted in by air.

McReady picked a barbiturate hopefully. Barclay and Van Wall went with him. One man never went anywhere alone in Big Magnet.

Ralsen had his sledge put away, and the physicists had moved off the table, the poker game broken up when they got back. Clark was putting out the food. The click of spoons and the muffled sounds of eating were the only sign of life in the room. There were no words spoken as the three returned; simply all eyes focused on them questioningly, while the jaws moved methodically.

McReady stiffened suddenly. Kinner was screeching out a hymn in a hoarse, cracked voice. He looked wearily at Van Wall with a twisted grin and shook his head. 'Hu-uh.'

Van Wall cursed bitterly, and sat down at the table. 'We'll just plumb have to take that till his voice wears out. He can't yell like that forever.'

'He's got a brass throat and a cast-iron larynx,' Norris declared savagely. 'Then we could be hopeful, and suggest he's one of our friends. In that case he could go on renewing his throat till doomsday.'

Silence clamped down. For twenty minutes they ate without a word. Then Connant jumped up with an angry violence. 'You sit as still as a bunch of graven images. You don't say a word, but oh, Lord, what expressive eyes you've got. They roll around like a bunch of glass marbles spilling down a table. They wink and blink and stare—and whisper things. Can you guys look somewhere else for a change, please?

'Listen, Mac, you're in charge here. Let's run movies for the rest of the night. We've been saving those reels to make 'em last. Last for what? Who is it's going to see those last reels, eh? Let's see 'em while we can, and look at something other than each other.'

'Sound idea, Connant. I, for one, am quite willing to change this in any way I can.'

'Turn the sound up loud, Dutton. Maybe you can drown out the hymns,' Clark suggested.

'But don't,' Norris said softly, 'don't turn off the lights altogether.'

'The lights will be out.' McReady shook his head. 'We'll show all the cartoon movies we have. You won't mind seeing the old cartoons, will you?'

'Goody, goody—a moom pitcher show. I'm just in the mood.' McReady turned to look at the speaker, a lean, lanky New Englander, by the name of Caldwell. Caldwell was stuffing his pipe slowly, a sour eye cocked up to McReady.

The bronze giant was forced to laugh. 'OK, Bart, you win. Maybe we aren't quite in the mood for Popeye and trick ducks, but it's something.'

'Let's play Classifications,' Caldwell suggested slowly. 'Or maybe you call it Guggenheim. You draw lines on a piece of paper, and put down classes of things—like animals, you know. One for "H" and one for "U" and so on. Like "Human" and "Unknown" for instance. I think that would be a hell of a lot better game. Classification, I sort of figure is what we need right now a lot more than movies. Maybe somebody's got a pencil that he can draw lines with, draw lines between the "U" animals and the "H" animals for instance.'

'McReady's trying to find that kind of a pencil,' Van Wall answered quietly, 'but we've got three kinds of animals here, you know. One that begins with "M." We don't want any more.'

'Mad ones, you mean. Uh-huh. Clark, I'll help you with those pans so we can get our little peep-show going.' Caldwell got up slowly.

Dutton and Barclay and Benning, in charge of the projector and sound mechanism arrangements, went about their job silently, while the Ad Building was cleared and the dishes and pans disposed of. McReady drifted over toward Van Wall slowly, and leaned back in the bunk beside him. 'I've been wondering, Van,' he said with a wry grin, 'whether or not to report my ideas in advance. I forgot the "U animals" as Caldwell named it, could read minds. I've a vague idea of something that might work. It's too vague to bother with though. Go ahead with your show, while I try to figure out the logic of the thing. I'll take this bunk.'

Van Wall glanced up, and nodded. The movie screen would be practically on a line with his bunk, hence making the pictures least distracting here, because least intelligible. 'Perhaps you should tell us what you have in mind. As it is, only the unknowns know what you plan. You might be— unknown before you got it into operation.'

'Won't take long, if I get it figured out right. But I don't want any more all-but-the-test-dog-monsters things. We better move Copper into this bunk directly above me. He won't be watching the screen either.'

McReady nodded toward Copper's gently snoring bulk. Garry helped them lift and move the doctor.

McReady leaned back against the bunk, and sank into a trance, almost, of concentration, trying to calculate chances, operations, methods. He was scarcely aware as the others distributed themselves silently, and the screen lit up. Vaguely Kinner's hectic, shouted prayers and his rasping hymn-singing annoyed him till the sound accompaniment started. The lights were turned out, but the large, light-colored areas of the screen reflected enough light for ready visibility. It made men's eyes sparkle as they moved restlessly. Kinner was still praying, shouting, his voice a raucous accompaniment to the mechanical sound. Dutton stepped up the amplification.

So long had the voice been going on, that only vaguely at first was McReady aware that something seemed missing. Lying as he was, just across the narrow room from the corridor leading to Cosmos House, Kinner's voice had reached him fairly clearly, despite the sound accompaniment of the pictures. It struck him abruptly that it had stopped.

'Dutton, cut that sound,' McReady called as he sat up abruptly. The pictures flickered a moment, soundless and strangely futile in the sudden, deep silence. The rising wind on the surface above bubbled melancholy tears of sound down the stove pipes. 'Kinner's stopped,' McReady said softly.

'For God's sake start that sound then, he may have stopped to listen,' Norris snapped.

McReady rose and went down the corridor. Barclay and Van Wall left their places at the far end of the room to follow him. The flickers bulged and twisted on the back of Barclay's gray underwear as he crossed the still-functioning beam of the projector. Dutton snapped on the lights, and the pictures vanished.

Norris stood at the door as McReady had asked. Garry sat down quietly in the bunk nearest the door, forcing Clark to make room for him. Most of the others had stayed exactly where they were. Only Connant walked slowly up and down the room, in steady, unvarying rhythm.

'If you're going to do that, Connant,' Clark spat, 'we can get along without you altogether, whether you're human or not. Will you stop that damned rhythm?'

'Sorry.' The physicist sat down in a bunk, and watched his toes thoughtfully. It was almost five minutes, five ages while the wind made the only sound, before McReady appeared at the door.

'We,' he announced, 'haven't got enough grief here already. Somebody's tried to help us out. Kinner has a knife in his throat, which was why he stopped singing, probably. We've got monsters, madmen and murderers. Any more "M's" you can think of, Caldwell? If there are, we'll probably have 'em before long.'

CHAPTER ELEVEN

'Is Blair loose?' someone asked.

'Blair is not loose. Or he flew in. If there's any doubt about where our gentle helper came from—this may clear it up.' Van Wall held a foot-long, thin-bladed knife in a cloth. The wooden handle was half-burnt, charred with the peculiar pattern of the top of the galley stove.

Clark stared at it. 'I did that this afternoon. I forgot the damn thing and left it on the stove.'

Van Wall nodded. 'I smelled it, if you remember. I knew the knife came from the galley.'

'I wonder,' said Benning, looking around at the party warily, 'how many more monsters have we? If somebody could slip out of his place, go back of the screen to the galley and then down to the Cosmos House and back—he did come back, didn't he? Yes—everybody's here. Well, if one of the gang could do all that—'

'Maybe a monster did it,' Garry suggested quietly. 'There's that possibility.'

'The monster, as you pointed out today, has only men left to imitate. Would he decrease his—supply, shall we say?' Van Wall pointed out. 'No, we just have a plain, ordinary louse, a murderer to deal with. Ordinarily we'd call him an "inhuman murderer" I suppose, but we have to distinguish now. We have inhuman murderers, and now we have human murderers. Or one at least.'

'There's one less human,' Norris said softly. 'Maybe the monsters have the balance of power now.'

'Never mind that,' McReady sighed and turned to Barclay. 'Bar, will you get your electric gadget? I'm going to make certain—'

Barclay turned down the corridor to get the pronged electrocuter, while McReady and Van Wall went back toward Cosmos House. Barclay followed them in some thirty seconds.

The corridor to Cosmos House twisted, as did nearly all corridors in Big Magnet, and Norris stood at the entrance again. But they heard, rather muffled, McReady's sudden shout. There was a savage scurry of blows, dull *ch-thunk*, *shluff* sounds. 'Bar—Bar—' And a curious, savage mewing scream, silenced before even quick-moving Norris had reached the bend.

Kinner—or what had been Kinner—lay on the floor, cut half in two by the great knife McReady had had. The meteorologist stood against the wall, the knife dripping red in his hand. Van Wall was stirring vaguely on the floor, moaning, his hand half-consciously rubbing at his jaw. Barclay, an unutterably savage gleam in his eyes, was methodically leaning on the pronged weapon in his hand, jabbing—jabbing, jabbing.

Kinner's arms had developed a queer, scaly fur, and the flesh had twisted. The fingers had shortened, the hand rounded, the fingernails become three-inch long things of dull red horn, keened to steel-hard razor-sharp talons.

McReady raised his head, looked at the knife in his hand and dropped it. 'Well, whoever did it can speak up now. He was an inhuman murderer at that—in that he murdered an inhuman. I swear by all that's holy, Kinner was a lifeless corpse on the floor here when we arrived. But when It found we were going to jab it with the power—It changed.'

Norris stared unsteadily. 'Oh, Lord, those things can act. Ye gods—sitting in here for hours, mouthing prayers to a God it hated! Shouting hymns in a cracked voice—hymns about a Church it never knew. Driving us mad with its ceaseless howling—

'Well. Speak up, whoever did it. You didn't know it, but you did the camp a favor. And I want to know how in blazes you got out of that room without anyone seeing you. It might help in guarding ourselves.'

'His screaming—his singing. Even the sound projector couldn't drown it.' Clark shivered. 'It was a monster.'

'Oh,' said Van Wall in sudden comprehension. 'You were sitting right next to the door, weren't you! And almost behind the projection screen already.'

Clark nodded dumbly. 'He—it's quiet now. It's a dead—Mac, your test's no damn good. It was dead anyway, monster or man, it was dead.'

McReady chuckled softly. 'Boys, meet Clark, the only one we know is human! Meet Clark, the one who proves he's human by trying to commit murder—and failing. Will the rest of you please refrain from trying to prove you're human for a while? I think we may have another test.'

'A test!' Connant snapped joyfully, then his face sagged in disappointment. 'I suppose it's another either-way-you-want-it.'

'No,' said McReady steadily. 'Look sharp and be careful. Come into the Ad Building. Barclay, bring your electrocuter. And somebody—Dutton—stand with Barclay to make sure he does it. Watch every neighbor, for by the Hell these monsters came from, I've got something, and they know it. They're going to get dangerous!'

The group tensed abruptly. An air of crushing menace entered into every man's body, sharply they looked at each other. More keenly than ever before—*is that man next to me an inhuman monster?*

'What is it?' Garry asked, as they stood again in the main room. 'How long will it take?'

'I don't know, exactly,' said McReady, his voice brittle with angry determination. 'But I *know* it will work, and no two ways about it. It depends on a basic quality of the *monsters*, not on us. "*Kinner*" just convinced me.' He stood heavy and solid in bronzed immobility, completely sure of himself again at last.

'This,' said Barclay, hefting the wooden-handled weapon, tipped with its two sharp-pointed, charged conductors, 'is going to be rather necessary, I take it. Is the power plant assured?'

Dutton nodded sharply. 'The automatic stoker bin is full. The gas power plant is on stand-by. Van Wall and I set it for the movie operation and—we've checked it over rather carefully several times, you know. Anything those wires touch, dies,' he assured them grimly. '*I* know that.'

Dr Copper stirred vaguely in his bunk, rubbed his eyes with fumbling hand. He sat up slowly, blinked his eyes blurred with sleep and drugs, widened with an unutterable horror of drug-ridden nightmares. 'Garry,' he mumbled, 'Garry—listen. Selfish—from hell they came, and hellish shellfish—I mean self—Do I? What do I mean?' He sank back in his bunk, and snored softly.

McReady looked at him thoughtfully. 'We'll know presently,' he nodded slowly. 'But selfish is what you mean all right. You may have thought of that, half-sleeping, dreaming there. I didn't stop to think what dreams you might be having. But that's all right. Selfish is the word. They must be, you see.' He turned to the men in the cabin, tense, silent men staring with wolfish eyes each at his neighbor. 'Selfish, and as Dr Copper said *every part is a whole*. Every piece is self-sufficient, an animal in itself.

'That, and one other thing, tell the story. There's nothing mysterious about blood; it's just as normal a body tissue as a piece of muscle, or a piece of liver. But it hasn't so much connective tissue, though it has millions, billions of life-cells.'

McReady's great bronze beard ruffled in a grim smile. 'This is satisfying, in a way. I'm pretty sure we humans still outnumber you—others. Others standing here. And we have what you, your other-world race, evidently doesn't. Not an imitated, but a bred-in-the-bone instinct, a driving, unquenchable fire that's genuine. We'll fight, fight with a ferocity you may attempt to imitate, but you'll never equal! We're human. We're real. You're imitations, false to the core of your every cell.

'All right. It's a showdown now. You know. You, with your mind reading. You've lifted the idea from my brain. You can't do a thing about it.

'Standing here—

'Let it pass. Blood is tissue. They have to bleed, if they don't bleed when cut, then, by Heaven, they're phony! Phony from hell! If they bleed—then that blood, separated from them, is an individual—*a newly formed individual in its own right, just as they, split, all of them, from one original, are individuals!*

'Get it, Van? See the answer, Bar?'

Van Wall laughed very softly. 'The blood—the blood will not obey. It's a new individual, with all the desire to protect its own life that the original—the main mass from which it was split—has. The *blood* will live—and try to crawl away from a hot needle, say!'

McReady picked up the scalpel from the table. From the cabinet, he took a rack of test-tubes, a tiny alcohol lamp, and a length of platinum wire set in a little glass rod. A smile of grim satisfaction rode his lips. For a moment he glanced up at those around him. Barclay and Dutton moved toward him slowly, the wooden-handled electric instrument alert.

'Dutton,' said McReady, 'suppose you stand over by the splice there where you've connected that in. Just make sure nothing pulls it loose.'

Dutton moved away. 'Now, Van, suppose you be first on this.'

White-faced, Van Wall stepped forward. With a delicate precision, McReady cut a vein in the base of his thumb. Van Wall winced slightly, then held steady as a half inch of bright blood collected in the tube. McReady put the tube in the rack, gave Van Wall a bit of alum and indicated the iodine bottle.

Van Wall stood motionlessly watching. McReady heated the platinum wire in the alcohol lamp flame, then dipped it into the tube. It hissed softly. Five times he repeated the test. 'Human, I'd say.' McReady sighed, and straightened. 'As yet, my theory hasn't been actually proven—but I have hopes. I have hopes.

'Don't, by the way, get too interested in this. We have with us some unwelcome ones, no doubt. Van, will you relieve Barclay at the switch? Thanks. OK, Barclay, and may I say I hope you stay with us? You're a damned good guy.'

Barclay grinned uncertainly; winced under the keen edge of the scalpel. Presently, smiling widely, he retrieved his long-handled weapon.

'Mr Samuel Dutt—*Bar*!'

The tensity was released in that second. Whatever of hell the monsters may have had within them, the men in that instant matched it. Barclay had no chance to move his weapon as a score of men poured down on that thing that had seemed Dutton. It mewed, and spat, and tried to grow fangs—and was a hundred broken, torn pieces. Without knives, or any weapon save the brute-given strength of a staff of picked men, the thing was crushed, rent.

Slowly they picked themselves up, their eyes smouldering, very quiet in their emotions. A curious wrinkling of their lips betrayed a species of nervousness.

Barclay went over with the electric weapon. Things smouldered and stank. The caustic acid Van Wall dropped on each spilled drop of blood gave off tickling, cough-provoking fumes.

McReady grinned, his deep-set eyes alight and dancing. 'Maybe,' he said softly, 'I underrated man's abilities when I said nothing human could have the ferocity in the eyes of that thing we found. I wish we could have the opportunity to treat in a more befitting manner these things. Something with boiling oil, or melted lead in it, or maybe slow roasting in the power boiler. When I think what a man Dutton was—

'Never mind. My theory is confirmed by—by one who knew? Well, Van Wall and Barclay are proven. I think, then, that I'll try to show you what I already know. That I too am human.' McReady swished the scalpel in absolute alcohol, burned it off the metal blade, and cut the base of his thumb expertly.

Twenty seconds later he looked up from the desk at the waiting men. There were more grins out there now, friendly grins, yet withal, something else in the eyes.

'Connant,' McReady laughed softly, 'was right. The huskies watching that thing in the corridor bend had nothing on you. Wonder why we think only the wolf blood has the right to ferocity? Maybe on spontaneous viciousness a wolf takes tops, but after these seven days—abandon all hope, ye wolves who enter here!

'Maybe we can save time. Connant, would you step for—'

Again Barclay was too slow. There were more grins, less tensity still, when Barclay and Van Wall finished their work.

Garry spoke in a low, bitter voice. 'Connant was one of the finest men we had here—and five minutes ago I'd have sworn he was a man. Those damnable things are more than imitation.' Garry shuddered and sat back in his bunk.

And thirty seconds later, Garry's blood shrank from the hot platinum wire, and struggled to escape the tube, struggled as frantically as a suddenly feral, red-eyed, dissolving imitation of Garry struggled to dodge the snake-tongue weapon Barclay advanced at him, white-faced and sweating. The Thing in the test-tube screamed with a tiny, tinny voice as McReady dropped it into the glowing coal of the galley stove.

Chapter Twelve

'The last of it?' Dr Copper looked down from his bunk with bloodshot, saddened eyes. 'Fourteen of them—'

McReady nodded shortly. 'In some ways—if only we could have permanently prevented their spreading—I'd like to have even the imitations back. Commander Garry—Connant—Dutton—Clark—'

'Where are they taking those things?' Copper nodded to the stretcher Barclay and Norris were carrying out.

'Outside. Outside on the ice, where they've got fifteen smashed crates, half a ton of coal, and presently will add ten gallons of kerosene. We've dumped acid on every spilled drop, every torn fragment. We're going to incinerate those.'

'Sounds like a good plan.' Copper nodded wearily. 'I wonder, you haven't said whether Blair—'

McReady started. 'We forgot him! We had so much else! I wonder—do you suppose we can cure him now?'

'If—' began Dr Copper, and stopped meaningly.

McReady started a second time. 'Even a madman. It imitated Kinner and his praying hysteria—' McReady turned toward Van Wall at the long table. 'Van, we've got to make an expedition to Blair's shack.'

Van looked up sharply, the frown of worry faded for an instant in surprised remembrance. Then he rose, nodded. 'Barclay better go along. He applied the lashings, and may figure how to get in without frightening Blair too much.'

Three quarters of an hour, through -37° cold, they hiked while the aurora curtain bellied overhead. The twilight was nearly twelve hours long, flaming in the north on snow like white, crystalline sand under their skis. A 5-mile wind piled it in drift lines pointing off to the northwest. Three quarters of an hour to reach the snow-buried shack. No smoke came from the little shack, and the men hastened.

'Blair!' Barclay roared into the wind when he was still a hundred yards away. 'Blair!'

'Shut up,' said McReady softly. 'And hurry. He may be trying a long hike. If we have to go after him—no planes, the tractors disabled—'

'Would a monster have the stamina a man has?'

'A broken leg wouldn't stop it for more than a minute,' McReady pointed out.

Barclay gasped suddenly and pointed aloft. Dim in the twilit sky, a winged thing circled in curves of indescribable grace and ease. Great white wings tipped gently, and the bird swept over them in silent curiosity. 'Albatross—' Barclay said softly. 'First of the season, and wandering way inland for some reason. If a monster's loose—'

Norris bent down on the ice, and tore hurriedly at his heavy, windproof clothing. He straightened, his coat flapping open, a grim blue-metaled weapon in his hand. It roared a challenge to the white silence of Antarctica.

The thing in the air screamed hoarsely. Its great wings worked frantically as a dozen feathers floated down from its tail. Norris fired again. The bird was moving swiftly now, but in an almost straight line of retreat. It screamed again, more feathers dropped and with beating wings it soared behind a ridge of pressure ice, to vanish.

Norris hurried after the others. 'It won't come back,' he panted.

Barclay cautioned him to silence, pointing. A curiously, fiercely blue light beat out from the cracks of the shack's door. A very low, soft humming sounded inside, a low, soft humming and a clink and clank of tools, the very sounds somehow bearing a message of frantic haste.

McReady's face paled. 'Lord help us if that thing has—' He grabbed Barclay's shoulder, and made snipping motions with his fingers, pointing toward the lacing of control-cables that held the door.

Barclay drew the wire-cutters from his pocket, and kneeled soundlessly at the door. The snap and twang of cut wires made an unbearable racket in the utter quiet of the Antarctic hush. There was only that strange, sweetly soft hum from within the shack, and the queerly, hectically clipped clicking and rattling of tools to drown their noises.

McReady peered through a crack in the door. His breath sucked in huskily and his great fingers clamped cruelly on Barclay's shoulder. The meteorologist backed down. 'It isn't,' he explained very softly, 'Blair. It's kneeling on something on the bunk—something that keeps lifting. Whatever it's working on is a thing like a knapsack—and it lifts.'

'All at once,' Barclay said grimly. 'No. Norris, hang back, and get that iron of yours out. It may have—weapons.'

Together, Barclay's powerful body and McReady's giant strength struck the door. Inside, the bunk jammed against the door screeched madly and crackled into kindling. The door flung down from broken hinges, the patched lumber of the doorpost dropping inward.

Like a blue-rubber ball, a Thing bounced up. One of its four tentacle-like arms looped out like a striking snake. In a seven-tentacled hand a six-inch pencil of winking, shining metal glinted and swung upward to face them. Its line-thin lips twitched back from snake-fangs in a grin of hate, red eyes blazing.

Norris' revolver thundered in the confined space. The hate-washed face twitched in agony, the looping tentacle snatched back. The silvery thing in its hand a smashed ruin of metal, the seven-tentacled hand became a mass of mangled flesh oozing greenish-yellow ichor. The revolver thundered three times more. Dark holes drilled each of the three eyes before Norris hurled the empty weapon against its face.

The Thing screamed in feral hate, a lashing tentacle wiping at blinded eyes. For a moment it crawled on the floor, savage tentacles lashing out, the body twitching. Then it staggered up again, blinded eyes working, boiling hideously, the crushed flesh sloughing away in sodden gobbets.

Barclay lurched to his feet and dove forward with an ice-ax. The flat of the weighty thing crushed against the side of the head. Again the unkillable monster went down. The tentacles lashed out, and suddenly Barclay fell to his feet in the grip of a living, livid rope. The Thing dissolved as he held it, a white-hot band that ate into the flesh of his hands like living fire. Frantically he tore the stuff from him, held his hands where they could not be reached. The blind Thing felt and ripped at the tough, heavy, windproof cloth, seeking flesh—flesh it could convert—

The huge blow-torch McReady had brought coughed solemnly. Abruptly it rumbled disapproval throatily. Then it laughed gurglingly, and thrust out a blue-white, three-foot tongue. The Thing on the floor shrieked, flailed out blindly with tentacles that writhed and withered in the bubbling wrath of the blow-torch. It crawled and turned on the floor, it shrieked and hobbled madly, but always McReady held the blow-torch on the face, the dead eyes burning and bubbling uselessly. Frantically the Thing crawled and howled.

A tentacle sprouted a savage talon—and crisped in the flame. Steadily McReady moved with a planned, grim campaign. Helpless, maddened, the Thing retreated from the grunting torch, the caressing, licking tongue. For a moment it rebelled, squalling in inhuman hatred at the torch of icy snow. Then it fell back before the charring breath of the torch, the stench of its flesh bathing it. Hopelessly it retreated—on and on across the Antarctic snow. The bitter wind swept over it twisting the torch-tongue; vainly it flopped, a trail of oily, stinking smoke bubbling away from it—

McReady walked back toward the shack silently. Barclay met him at the door. 'No more?' the giant meteorologist asked grimly.

Barclay shook his head. 'No more. It didn't split?'

'It had other things to think about,' McReady assured him. 'When I left it, it was a glowing coal. What was it doing?'

Norris laughed shortly. 'Wise boys, we are. Smash magnetos, so planes won't work. Rip the boiler tubing out of the tractors. And leave that Thing alone for a week in this shack. Alone and undisturbed.'

McReady looked in at the shack more carefully. The air, despite the ripped door, was hot and humid. On a table at the far end of the room rested a thing of coiled wires and small magnets, glass tubing and radio tubes. At the center a block of rough stone rested. From the center of the block came the light that flooded the place, the fiercely blue light bluer than the glare of an electric arc, and from it came the sweetly soft hum. Off to one side was another mechanism of crystal glass, blown with an incredible neatness and delicacy, metal plates and a queer, shimmery sphere of insubstantiality.

'What is that?' McReady moved nearer.

Norris grunted. 'Leave it for investigation. But I can guess pretty well. That's atomic power. That stuff to the left—that's a neat little thing for doing what men have been trying to do with 100-ton cyclotrons and so forth. It separates neutrons from heavy water, which he was getting from the surrounding ice.'

'Where did he get all—Oh. Of course. A monster couldn't be locked in—or out. He's been through the apparatus caches.' McReady stared at the apparatus. 'Lord, what minds that race must have—'

'The shimmery sphere—I think it's a sphere of pure force. Neutrons can pass through any matter, and he wanted a supply reservoir of neutrons. Just project neutrons against silica—calcium—beryllium—almost anything, and the atomic energy is released. That thing is the atomic generator.'

McReady plucked a thermometer from his coat. 'It's 120° in here, despite the open door. Our clothes have kept the heat out to an extent, but I'm sweating now.'

Norris nodded. 'The light's cold. I found that. But it gives off heat to warm the place through that coil. He had all the power in the world. He could keep it warm and pleasant, as his race thought of warmth and pleasantness. Did you notice the light, the color of it?'

McReady nodded. 'Beyond the stars is the answer. From beyond the stars. From a hotter planet that circled a brighter, bluer sun they came.'

McReady glanced out the door toward the blasted, smoke-stained trail that flopped and wandered blindly off across the drift. 'There won't be any more coming, I guess. Sheer accident it landed here, and that was twenty million years ago. What did it do all that for?' He nodded toward the apparatus.

Barclay laughed softly. 'Did you notice what it was working on when we came? Look.' He pointed toward the ceiling of the shack.

Like a knapsack made of flattened coffee-tins, with dangling cloth straps and leather belts, the mechanism clung to the ceiling. A tiny, glaring heart of supernal flame burned in it, yet burned through the ceiling's wood without scorching it. Barclay walked over to it, grasped two of the dangling straps in his hands, and pulled it down with an effort. He strapped it about his body. A slight jump carried him in a weirdly slow arc across the room.

'Anti-gravity,' said McReady softly.

'Anti-gravity,' Norris nodded. 'Yes, we had 'em stopped, with no planes, and no birds. The birds hadn't come—but they had coffee-tins and radio parts, and glass and the machine shop at night. And a week—a whole week—all to itself. America in a single jump—with anti-gravity powered by the atomic energy of matter.

'We had 'em stopped. Another half hour—it was just tightening these straps on the device so it could wear it—and we'd have stayed in Antarctica, and shot down any moving thing that came from the rest of the world.'

'The albatross—' McReady said softly. 'Do you suppose—'

'With this thing almost finished? With that death weapon it held in its hand?

'No, by the grace of God, who evidently does hear very well, even down here, and the margin of half an hour, we keep our world, and the planets of the system too. Anti-gravity, you know, and atomic power. Because *They* came from another sun, a star beyond the stars. *They* came from a world with a bluer sun.'

Acknowledgements

About the Anthologist

Forrest J. Ackerman saw his first fantastic film—the lost *One Glorious Day*—in 1922. Ten years later he published the first known list of what he would eventually come to call "imagi-movies." He has edited over two hundred issued of imagi-movie magazines, including the seminal *Famous Monsters of Filmland*, *Monster World*, *Spacemen & Women,* and *Forrest J. Ackerman's Filmonsterzine*.

Among his numerous honors, Ackerman has won six Hugos—beginning with the first Hugo awarded—as well as two Golden Saturns from the Academy of Science Fiction, Fantasy & Horror Films. He has been responsible for a score of books, including *Reel Future, Sci-Fi Monsters, This Island Earth*, and *Ackermanthology*.

He was married for forty-one years to Wendayne "Rocket to the Rue Morgue" Ackerman, who lost her life in 1990 as the aftermath of the Ackermans' being mugged in Naples, Italy, and he dedicates this collection to her memory.

Other Science Fiction Titles
from TV Books

The Twilight Zone Complete Stories
  ISBN: 1-57500-111-X   US: $22.95

The Guardians Trilogy
Book I: The Krilov Continuum
  ISBN: 1-57500-033-4   US: $9.95
Book II: Berserker
  ISBN: 1-57500-048-2   US: $9.95
Book III: Black Dog
  ISBN: 1-57500-091-1   US: $9.95

The Invasion: Earth Companion
  ISBN: 1-57500-031-8   US: $16.95
Invasion: Earth: The Last Echo
  ISBN: 1-57500-032-6   US: $9.95